D.J. O'NE

EXIT: NO EXIT

back
street
books

Copyright Information

Exit: No Exit by D.J. O'Neill.
Copyright 2021 D.J. O'Neill
ISBN 9798720050214
Published by D.J. O'Neill in 2021
All Rights Reserved

D.J. O'Neill has asserted his right under the Copyright, Designs and Patents Act, 1988, to be identified as author of this work. All Rights Reserved. This book may not be reproduced in whole or in part, by mimeograph, photocopy, or any other means, electronic or physical, without express written permission of the author.

For further information, contact the author at:
dermotjohnoneil@yahoo.co.uk

Formatting by John Haines

Set in TNR & Garamond typefont

About the Author

Dermot O'Neill was born in Liverpool of Welsh and Irish parents. Having graduated from Aberystwyth University he worked variously as a baker, builder, painter and decorator, countryside ranger, and tree feller until finally finding employment with the Customs and Excise in London. He escaped from full time work some three months later.

Dermot lives in Wales where he currently works as a dry stone waller.

He is a keen fly fisherman and travels often to New Zealand in pursuit of a 10lb brown trout.

About this Book

An angry young comedian who hates laughter. A struggling artist who wants to be a successful artist. A successful artist who seeks failure. A businessman with the Midas touch. An anarchist who sets out to destroy money. Millionaires whose only want is to become billionaires. 7 billion people. The ever encroaching city. And Midascorp, the corporation that threatens to overshadow it all. The fight for the future is on, but with the onset of climate change and a financial meltdown to reckon with, time is running short.

'Every child is special. So where do all the ordinary people come from?'

The film, Code 46.

'A state which dwarfs its men in order that they may be more docile instruments in its hands even for beneficial purposes will find that with small men no great thing can really be accomplished. . . .'

John Stuart Mill, on Liberty

'This happy breed of men, this little world. . . . This blessed plot, this earth, this realm. . . . This. . . .

Shakespeare, King Richard ii

1

Ed.
The Blowthrough

Ed left home with exceptionally high hopes of his new job, it promised him a fresh start though the work itself was a disappointment. It grew terrible in him, after a time, that strange feeling. You were supposed to lie at interviews if you wanted a job, but Ed didn't. He knew exactly what he wanted from life, and it wasn't work. It wasn't money either.

It was a hot summer's day, the sun was blasting through the windows off the sea, when the back door burst open. Ed came striding in to the kitchen, swung his backpack off his shoulder and let it drop to the floor. He went straight to the sink, turned on the tap and threw a handful of cold water over his hot face. He took a long and refreshing drink out of his cupped hands. 'I'm back!' he shouted over his shoulder in to the house, the water dripping off his tanned face.

Ed's mum entered the kitchen, followed by his father and then his gran. Crowding the doorway they stared at Ed in disbelief.

'You're back?' said Ed's mum.

'And forth,' grinned Ed.

'Holiday?' she asked, though she sounded doubtful.

'Isn't every day?' answered Ed.

His mother groaned. His father exploded:

'Four days you've been gone, just four days, that's all! So what was it this time?'

'The smell,' said Ed, holding out an arm, offering a sleeve for inspection.

The rank stink of the fish factory was still on Ed's clothes. 'Well go on, smell it,' he said.

Grimacing, his father pushed Ed's arm away. 'There's always something with you, isn't there? With labouring it was dust. You even complained about the heat at the bakery.'

'It was the middle of summer,' said Ed, 'I almost died in there.'

'You'd have got used to it. But no, not you. You can't stick at anything.'

So far this year Ed has been a builder's labourer, a deckhand, a shelf stacker, an apprentice roofer, a tablehand at a bakery, a farm labourer, a painter and decorator, and a gardener. This inability to hold down a job was a constant source of conflict between Ed and his dad. For Ed's dad it was enough to have a job, any job, and to stick with that. He worked in a factory that made tools. He had worked in that factory all his life. It was a matter of pride to him. His responsibilities to his house, his job and his family had reigned him in. But Ed did not wish to be tamed, he knew that much.

'You had a damned good job at the factory. A job for life! And what did you do?'

'It was the noise,' protested Ed. 'I couldn't hear myself think.'

'Think? You didn't have to think! It wasn't that kind of job.'

'It wasn't any kind of job.'

'You don't want to work, do you? You're going to run out of jobs, the way you're going, and then what will you do? You won't have a future.'

'This is the 80s, Dad. That is the future – you read the papers.'

Sighing, Ed's parents shook their heads. They knew exactly how Ed should live his life. Settle down, they tell him. Get a job. Buy yourself a house. But for God's sake do something with your life.

'All your friends have settled and got jobs,' said Ed's mum.

'You should be starting out on a career by now,' said Ed's dad.

Career: To move erratically from job to job and from place to place. Ed grinned at the thought.

'You can wipe that smile off your face right now,' said his dad. 'And don't think you're going to hang around here all summer fishing for trout and climbing mountains like you did last year. You're going to work. Fishing and climbing mountains,' he snorted, 'that's all you think about.'

After fishing, climbing mountains gave Ed his sense of purpose. He travelled the country climbing mountains. Snowdon, Scafell Pike, Ben Nevis, Caher, Carauntuahill.... He had climbed them all. It was like he was collecting them.

Ed's dad shook his head. 'I just don't understand you.'

Ed's mother sighed. 'I don't know where he gets it from, I really don't,' she said.

Ed's father was Irish, his mother Welsh. Ed had been born in Liverpool. They lived in Wales. Mountains surrounded them. You could see the sea.'

'So what are you going to do now?' asked Ed's dad. Ed shrugged.

'You don't know, and why would you? You've no qualifications, no skills. You know what you are, don't you? You can tell just by looking at you.'

Ed's hair was long and had been bleached blonde by the sun. He was unshaven. His jeans were patched and patched again. His faded red T-shirt was holed and was frayed at the collar. His leather boots scuffed. And he was lean, you could count his ribs, but his bronzed skin bulged with hard muscle.

'A tramp, that's what you look like. It's what you'll become. You don't know what you want, do you?'

Ed shrugged. He knew what he didn't want.

He crossed to the window where he stood staring out across the town. It was a small town, a half town, fringing as it did the shore of a crescent bay. Cheerfully coloured houses leant at all angles. There were flowers in the gardens that had been planted in bouquets. The place depressed Ed. There was nothing here. People had always gone from here, young people, the best. Those with hopes and ambition, those with dreams to pursue. Ed was a dreamer.

'He's miles away, just look at him, even when he's here he's somewhere else.' And, making a gesture with his hands as though pushing Ed away, Ed's dad skirted the table and sat down.

Ed continued to stare out of the window. Bright sunlight shone off the sea. A boat sat balanced on the horizon. A jet marked the sky with white vapour.

Once, when Ed had been apprenticed to a plasterer, he had been taught that in order for the plaster to remain pliable it had to be kept in a state of constant motion. The tradesman that Ed worked for had shuffled the plaster between his trowel and the hawk with such speed and skill that the flowing mass appeared to float idly beside him in the air. That way it remained pliable and could be shaped. Life has since taught Ed that lesson about many things.

Ed turned from the window. 'I'm going to travel,' he said.

'Travel?' his father laughed. 'So, it's travel now, is it?'

'I want to see the world, to be out there doing, discovering new things!'

'The world's been discovered.'

'Not by me it hasn't.'

Travel. The word was a symbol to Ed. It meant freedom, adventure, new things. Newness. It was like finding a crack in the ready-made world and then squeezing through, discovering on the other side an endless scroll of living and opportunity, like flying beyond restriction in to some larger space.

Ed's dad shook his head. "Travel. You've been travelling around in circles all your life.'

'Well I'm not staying around here to end up like you lot.'

'Why you ungrateful. . . .' Ed's dad was up out of his chair and around the table in seconds.

Ed ducked, avoiding the blow, and snatching up his pack he made for the door. His father ran after him.

'Careful of the step!' warned Ed's gran.

Ed cleared the step. But his father, treading in the hollow, felt his foot slide out from under him on the smoothly worn slate. He slipped a second time, off his other foot, threw his arms out for balance and grabbed the wall. He stood gripping the stonework until he had regained his composure, cursing Ed, for, with all his comings and goings, the hollowed out step had to be his fault. One day, perhaps, he will look upon that step and will think fondly of Ed. It might be the only impression that Ed will ever make.

Ten times in as many weeks Ed has left this house and he has always left in the same manner. He was a strange sight, head down, fists clenched, muttering to himself beneath his breath as he stormed off down the lane and in to town. He did not know exactly where he was going, but the lane was steep and its gradient chose the immediate route for him.

A stream cascaded amongst the houses and raced with the sound of shattered glass, its impatient water slowed eventually by the slow and oily harbour. The sun shone round and brilliant from a clear blue sky. Ed's back was warm and moist beneath his pack and there was a spring to his step that had not been there before.

As usual, Ed's family stood and watched his progress from the rear of the house. His father shook his head. 'He'll be back,' he complained. Ed's mother wrung her hands. 'But will he settle?'

'Travel,' said Ed's gran, 'gets a man nowhere, he'll see.'

2

Andy, Jigsaw. Poggett.
The Lost Generation

It was ten o'clock in the morning and Andy had been sent by his mother to wake his father. There was a cup of cold tea on the bedside table. Andy put a fresh cup of tea beside the first cup.

'Come on, Dad, wake up. It's ten o'clock. You'll be late for the dole.' It had got to him, thought Andy. But if you let it get to you then you're not ever going to get up in the morning and say, 'Hey, it's a bright new day!' Andy crossed to the window and threw open the curtains. It was a grey and dismal day, pouring with rain.

Andy's dad groaned, pulled the covers over his head and went back to sleep. There was a sound like bricks being delivered down the staircase. Andy hurtled down the hallway, grabbed his coat off the hook and pulled open the front door. He stepped out in to the street, in to the cold and wet, letting the door slam behind him.

Facing him, a waste ground strewn with old bricks, beyond that, rows and rows of terraced houses, some of them derelict, their windows and doors boarded or bricked up. At the bottom of the road ran the river, fringed with abandoned docks, gutted and roofless warehouses, skeletal cranes, mounds of scrap, rusted silos, a single ship. The air rang to the bang and scrape of awkward heavy metal being shifted. Seagulls, then a sheet of newspaper flew past, followed by a crisp packet.

Turning up the collar of his combat jacket, Andy hurried off to sign on. Passing the shops he met Mr Truitt, his friend Jigsaw's dad. He was emerging from the bookies, smoking.

'A'right Andy lad, how's things?'

'A'right Mister Truitt.' Andy eyed the cigarette. 'Erm, A couldn't nick a ciggie off yeh, could I?'

'Sure, Andy. Here.'

Mister Truitt reached in to his jacket and pulled out a packet of 10 Capstan Full Strengths. He tapped out a cigarette and handed it to Andy. Andy broke the cigarette in half, pocketing one half and gripping the other between his lips. Turning his back to the wind Mister Truitt bent and he struck a match, offering his cupped hand to Andy. Two puffs of smoke tore off in to the air.

The coarse, strong smoke seared Andy's throat and lungs, making him cough.

'Christ, Mister Truitt, get cancer before it gets you, eh?' Tangy shreds of tobacco stuck to Andy's lips. He spat the shreds off.

Mr Truitt grinned. 'You sorted yourself out at the dole yet, Andy'?'

'No.' Andy's face hardened. 'Just off ter see 'em now, like.'

'How long's it been now?'

'Too long. Almost five weeks.'

Five whole weeks without money, living off his parents, scrounging a quid here and there off his friends, sponging the odd drink.

Andy blew smoke in to the air. The wind tore it away.

'So how's yer Dad, Andy?'

Andy shrugged. 'Could be worse. Least one of us's still earning.'

Mister Truitt laughed, he coughed laughing. 'You should be a comic, Andy, that's what our Jimmy says.' He took a drag on his cigarette. 'Did he tell yeh that I offered him a job?'

'A job? He's workin? Your Jigsaw?'

'Are you joking? Turned me down, said he wanted something better for himself.'

Andy smiled. 'Well he doesn't want to be a plumber, Mister Truitt, does he like. A mean, fair do's, but he's got 'A' levels, ain' he. He went to Bootle Tech like. Not like us.'

'Bits of paper, Andy, that's all they are. And what good are they? Except maybe to write on for some job you won't get. But plumbing now, that's a trade. People need plumbers, Andy.'

'Your Jigsaw's got big plans though, ain' he? A mean, you know Jigsaw.'

'Plans? Schemes more like. Delusions of grandeur, is what they are. A big house in Blundellsands? How the hell does he think he's goin to get that sittin on his arse?'

Andy shrugged. 'It's not Jigsaw's fault though, is it? A mean, it's not like it was in your day. There are no proper jobs.'

'Andy, son, there were no jobs where I came from in my day either, do you understand that? Do you see what I'm saying, Andy?'

Andy shrugged.

'Too much education, it's given him ideas. And that queer posh accent of his, what's all that about? 'Mister Truitt stared at Andy. 'He isn't, you know, is he?'

'Wha?'

'You know. Queer.'

'Queer? Jigsaw? Nar. A mean, he doesn't hang around with no women like, but yeh don't see me with no women neither, do yeh, eh? An' I'm not queer, Am just broke. They're not interested in yeh if yer broke, Mister Truitt.'

Andy took a last drag on his cigarette before it burnt his fingertips. He checked out the butt then threw it away.

'Mr Truitt?' he asked.

'Andy?'

'That job yeh offered Jigsaw, any chance of givin' it ter me, like?'

'Ah, now, Andy, I'm terribly sorry, son, but I haven't really got the work, you know. I was just wantin' to give the lad a chance at something, something real, you know, to get him off his arse an maybe start him in the trade, like. A man can go anywhere if he has a trade. It'd get him away from this place anyways. Youse should be thinking about that yourself, you know.'

'Just thought I'd ask, is all,' Andy shrugged.

'No harm in asking, Andy. Well, I'd best get back to work. Look after yerself, yeah? Oh, an Andy?'

'Wha'?'

'Here. 'Mister Truitt threw him the pack of cigarettes. Andy beamed. 'Aw, cheers! Ta, Mr Truitt.'

Andy entered the run-down Social Security offices. He approached the counter at his signing on point: K to 0.

'Ah, Mister O'Shea,' said the clerk, a dark, good looking girl with a husky voice. Andy had once thought of asking her out, but he never had. He didn't know why. No, he knew exactly why.

Andy flipped her his UB40.

'And what have you been doing to find work?' she was obliged to ask Andy that. It was part of the new social contract that was being imposed.

'Nuthin',' said Andy. 'I mean, I've got a job, haven' I? It's a job to find work. A full time job.'

The girl grinned. She liked Andy.

'You have been looking for work?'

'Course I av. Been down the job centre, loads.'

'Have you tried security. There are plenty of jobs in security.'

'Hey, my old man werked in security after he got made redundant from the docks. It's fucken shite. The pay's shite. The hours are shite. Thee only keep yis long's thee need yeh. Where's the security in that?'

The girl grinned. 'Maybe Job Club could help.'

She meant it as a suggestion, but to Andy it was a threat.

Job club? Like a fishing club, is it? Nah, more like a proper club, to beat the unemployed with, thought Andy, but he said nothing.

The girl passed Andy a form to sign. Andy picked up the pen he was offered and he signed the form. He slid the form back across the counter then picked up and pocketed his UB40. He kept the pen. He stood there, waiting.

'A still haven't been paid, y' know. A still aven 'ad no Giro, an it's bin almost five weeks now. How am I supposed to manage on nothing, eh?'

'I'm sorry, Andy, really, but, as I already explained, it takes six weeks for the department to process a new claim.'

'But it's not a new claim, is it, eh? It was youse lot that signed me off, by error, not me. I would never have signed me off. I've never had no job, me. It was youse, not doing your jobs properly.'

'I'm sorry,' The girl shrugged,' but they're the rules.'

Later, at the job centre, Andy stood scanning the boards, looking at the 20 or so jobs on offer: Security. Security. Security. Part time labourer wanted. Security, flexible employment opportunities. Dishwasher wanted. Part time shelf stacker wanted.

Removing a card from the board he wrote on the back of it: *Thousands of jobs in Jeopardy: Liverpool Man Secures Arabian Deal*. Then he pinned it back on the board and stood back to admire his handiwork.

Jigsaw wasn't in. His mother didn't know where he was. 'Gone out,' she told Andy. He headed off to see his grandad.

The numerous tall high rises of Rapunzel Heights dominated the bare hillside. To Andy, it looked like the planners had gathered together all the great works on architecture, books by Wren, Carbousier, Norman Foster and had simply stood them on end.

The bottom floor flats were boarded up, the boards scrawled with graffiti. The lifts were not working and the unlit stairwells stank of piss. They echoed to Andy's footfalls.

Andy knocked on the door. No answer.

Andy crossed flagged over squares, past snapped off trees and attempts at green grass that had been churned to mud. Litter swirled angrily about the squares and was swept high in to the sky like children's kites. The swirling filthy gale held Andy in place, wrapping him in newspaper, sweet wrappers, greasy chip papers, polythene bags. He snapped out a curse, and the fierce wind whipped it away.

The open parkland, the wind-blown squares, this wasn't space, this was emptiness.

Andy spent the afternoon wandering around deserted docks, empty warehouses, abandoned quays. He sat on an iron capstan with a view of the river. 'I see no ships,' he said, scanning the empty horizon, 'only hardships.'

Andy left the docks, following the canal. He climbed the railings by the Strand and he wandered through the shopping centre with its empty concrete plazas and corridors of shops.

Coming down the escalator, he met Micka, a mate of his who played centre forward for the pub league football team in which Andy played centre half.

'Aright, Andy, mate,' grinned Micka, pleased to see him, 'how's it going, lar?'

'Aright. Yourself?'

'Keepin outta trouble, ain't been caught anyhow. Ain't seen you around much, eh.'

'I ain't been round.'

'Wassup?'

'Skint, aren't I.' He told Micka the story.

'The bastards! Thee signed yeh off?'

'Got me mixed up with someone else, didn't thee. Some fucker with the same surname. An a fucken job, bastard!'

'Cunts. Still, think of all the money you'll have when it comes through.'

'I was thinking of retiring on it,' said Andy. 'Be able to, time I get it.'

Micka laughed. 'You playing this Sundee, then?'

'Course I am,' he said. 'Against that crowd from The One Inn, innit?'

'We should hammer them, easy,' said Micka, 'theer fucken shite.'

'One Inn.' Andy laughed. 'We got four in last time we played 'em.' Andy had scored one goal and had set up two of the others. Micka had scored three. Andy was turning in to the best centre half, if not the best player in the league, some people reckoned. He had certainly become a much more aggressive player than last season.

'The way yew been playin', dominating the midfield, will fucken get twenty in.'

The two stood talking football for a time. Then Micka saw a girl that he knew coming out of Dolcis. 'Got a go,' he told Andy. 'See yeh Sundee, yeah. Oh, an And?'

Micka retraced his steps. He held out his hand to Andy. 'The three nicker? Fer the ground, and the ref, like?'

'Give it yeh Sundee, Micka, yeah?'

There was a busker in the concourse, playing guitar and singing Bob Dylan numbers. Andy headed over to him and made like he was interested in the music, which he found depressing. There was a good scattering of coins in the case, he noticed. But he didn't have the bottle for it.

It was four o'clock and Andy was hungry. He entered a supermarket, intending to swipe some chocolate and a can of Coke. The moment he entered the store he was shadowed by a security guard. The guard followed him around until he exited the store.

A dog came hurrying along the pavement, carrying a partially inflated football in its mouth. Andy called it over. The dog dropped the ball at Andy's feet, it stared at the ball, then it barked at Andy.

Chased by the dog, Andy dribbled the ball down Stanley Road, round passers-by, crisp packets, styrofoam cartons, a flattened Coke can. He nutmegged a shopper. He provided himself with a running commentary: 'It's two-all now in the dying moments of extra time in this the world cup final. But here come England. It's O'Shea. . . he swerved around a pedestrian. 'It's just O'Shea and the goalie now. Andy shoots,' he said. 'It's there!' he shouted, 'It's a goal!' as the ball, curling in flight, disappeared between the gate posts of an old house. The dog ran to retrieve the ball.

That goal made Andy feel good. He realised that he needed a good kick-around and so he headed off to the school playing fields. But the playing fields were empty. Then he noticed the recently erected sign:

NO TRESPASSING. NO BALL GAMES.
NO DOGS. NO GOLF EITHER.
By order. Maximum fine 100 pounds.

'Bastards!' Andy picked a stone off the road and he hurled it at the sign. It missed, landing on the pitch. The dog shot through the railings and ran to fetch it.

There was a shout. 'Oi! You! You with the dog!' A groundsman came running out of the school and made straight for Andy.

Andy legged it, followed by the dog.

Andy stopped at the Queen's Arms, his local, on his way home. But there wasn't anyone he knew in there.

Back outside, on the waste ground, Andy reclaimed the football off the dog. He tossed it in the air, bent and caught it on his neck. Standing, Andy shrugged the ball in to the air, catching it, then holding it, on his foot.

With the dog running around him barking, contesting possession, Andy began to kick the ball in the air from foot to foot until he'd reached 100, then he flicked the ball on to his right knee, then his left, hit it first off his right shoulder and then his left, headed the ball, passed it from his left shoulder to his right, and then off both of his knees again. Andy called it the fountain and he was just about to repeat the manoeuvre when he noticed that there was someone stood watching him.

An oldish man in a flat cap and overcoat with a ruddy and weather-beaten face, rheumy eyes, and a nose patterned with blood vessels.

'You look like you could keep that up for ever. How long can you keep it up?' he asked Andy.

Andy caught the ball on his foot then held it there. 'How long you got?' he grinned and, folding his arms, he leant against the pub wall, still holding the ball on his foot.

'How do you do that?'

'Easy, y' just pretend yer feet are yer hands, like.'

The man laughed. 'Do you play for a team?' he asked.

'Sunday league pubs. Playin this Sunday.' Andy told him where.

'I'll see if I can make it,' said the man. 'I'd like to see you play.' The man walked off, crossing the road when he saw the two youths, one of them hooded and walking with a swagger, come toward him.

It was Jigsaw and Pogget.

They nodded to Andy, aggressive uplifts of the head, like they were pointing their chins at him.

Pogget wore a hoodie, a brand new shell suit, in blue with white stripes, and new sneakers. Jigsaw wore a suit jacket of tan wool flecked with yellow, a black turtle necked sweater, black jeans and black suede boots. There was a book in his jacket pocket, not a novel, but a treatise on economics.

'Called round to see youse earlier,' said Andy. 'Only you weren' in.'

'I went the library, to read the papers.'

'You took him to the library?' said Andy, frowning, indicating Pogget.

'They have the *Sport* too.'

Pogget was stood looking at the dog which was stood looking at the two new arrivals.

'Oos is the dog?' asked Pogget, reaching down to pat it.

'Dunno,' shrugged Andy, 'just some dog.' He addressed the dog, 'Fuck off dog.' The dog angled its head at Andy.

'Nice dog,' said Pogget, warming to the dog and letting it lick his face. The dog wagged its tail, setting its whole rear end in motion.

'Chirpy fucker, isn't he?' said Jigsaw.

'Well, yeah, is alright fer dogs, innit,' said Pogget.

Jigsaw frowned at him.

'Thee get fed don't thee, an thee don't ave ter werk fer it or nuthin. An if thee want, y' know, anuther dog lyke, all thee av ter do is go the park or trot off down sum jigger, lyke.'

'Fuck'nell, Pogget,' said Andy, 'thee av ter sniff arse too, y' know, ave yeh considered that?'

Grimacing, Pogget pushed the dog forcibly away from him before wiping his face.

'We going in for a drink then?' said Jigsaw.

Andy patted his pockets. 'You got any money, cos I aint.'

'Wharra bout the dog?' said Pogget.

Andy kicked the ball down the road. The dog ran after it and the three friends entered the pub.

White light streamed in from outside through the uncurtained windows. The pub was empty except for a group of three girls who were sat drinking in the lounge. They looked all done up for a night on the town. The girls looked over at the three friends as they approached the bar.

'Three social security sunrises, please,' Jigsaw told the barman. The girls turned away, resuming their conversation, heads together, giggling.

The barman pushed himself upright off the bar, fetched down three pint glasses, lined them along the counter, poured orange squash in to the glasses and then filled them with tap water. 'Youse want anything in them drinks?' he asked.

'No thanks,' said Jigsaw.

'Just our lips,' said Andy.

'Har bloody har,' said the barman with a scowl. 'That'll be 15p, thank you.' The three friends chose a table from where they could sit and study the girls. They sat facing them, staring. The girls ignored them.

Andy pulled the pack of 10 Capstan Full Strength out of his pocket. He lit up a cigarette, took a pull. He offered one to Jigsaw, then Pogget. They sat smoking, throwing glances at the girls.

The girls stood, knocking back their drinks, and left the pub.

The three friends sat and stared disconsolately in to their barely touched sunrises.

Andy said, 'There must be some good looking women somewhere that would like us.'

'It's not us personally they object to,' said Jigsaw, 'it's our economic circumstances.'

'Is cuz we aven gorrany money,' said Pogget. 'Fact, av got minus money, me, A owe a undred quid now, with tha last fine.'

'Fucken hell, Pogget, a hundred quid? How y' ever gonna repay that?' asked Andy.

Pogget shrugged. 'Dunno. Av ter think a sumthin, won't I?'

'You might have to get yourself a job,' said Jigsaw.

The three friends crossed themselves as a protection against work. It was a theatrical gesture, though there was a degree of precaution in it.

Andy took a long pull on his cigarette, but it had lost its power. He worked the ember off in to the ashtray and replaced what remained of it in the pack. He pocketed the pack. Jigsaw drew breath to say something but breathed out instead.

Pogget found a tiny hole in his imitation leather seat cover where the stitches had come undone in one seam and he began to work at it with his finger, enlarging the tear and pulling out a lump of foam. He pushed it back in and the foam leapt out again. He left it there on the floor.

'I 'eard there's a job goan down a tha new Tescos,' said Pogget.

'Yeah, an' I heard there's a Loch Ness monster,' said Andy. 'Yeh shouldn't believe everything that y' hear.' He picked up his glass and he considered taking a drink from it, but did not.

'Stacking shelves for fuck all an hour, you call that a job,' said Jigsaw.

They would rather not work. So long as they weren't trapped in some shitty job then everything could still seem possible for them.

'We can't stay on the dole forever though, can we?' said Andy.

'Why not? 'said Pogget.

'It would be too fucken depressin',' said Andy.

'In any case, ' said Jigsaw, 'being unemployed will be impossible soon.'

'It's impossible now,' said Andy.

'Yer talking bollocks yew are,' said Pogget. 'Yer can't help but be on the dole round ere, yeh just are. It's what happens ter yeh after yeh leave skewel.'

'They got him off it easily enough,' said Jigsaw.

'That was a mistake,' said Andy, 'An am back on it now, aren't I. Almost.'

'Yeah, how thee gonna gerrus off the dole, eh?' said Pogget, 'When there arn enough jobs.'

'There won't ever be enough jobs,' said Jigsaw, 'and that suits them fine. They need people to be unemployed.'

'You wha?'

Jigsaw had been unable to understand it, not at first. All those millions unemployed, all that industry abandoned. How could a country be managed so badly? It wasn't. A place wasn't turned inside out and upside down without benefiting someone. Bit by bit they were changing everything, taking things apart and then putting them back together but in a different way.

'They've smashed the unions,' said Jigsaw, 'and now they're going to smash us. They want people to be unemployed. It keeps wages down. But they've got all the unemployed that they need now. From now on it will be our fault that we're unemployed. People will be forced in to work, any work, and for less pay. We'll be conned and threatened and squeezed and squeezed until it'll be easier to be in work.'

'Bastards!' said Andy.

'But we'll av jobs then, won't we?' said Pogget.

'If that's what you want then, fine,' said Jigsaw. 'But it won't be unemployment that will blight your life, it will be work. Endless, unfulfilling, unproductive work. Their work, not yours, and for next to nothing. But it doesn't have to be like that.' There was a gleam in Jigsaw's eye.

'No,' said Andy. 'Forget it. Am not interested, aright? I am not getting involved, not after last time.'

'But you haven't heard what it is yet.'

'I don't need to, do I? A told yeh, Am having nothing more ter do with yer get rich quick schemes.'

Autographed Liverpool and Everton strips and footballs, all forged. Signed copies of books by internationally renowned authors, the books bought in some charity shop and the signatures forged. Pieces of the holy cross, the wood prised from railway sleepers. His call boy service, another farce. Jigsaw was forever coming up with ways of making money.

'So things didn't work out quite as I'd hoped. But this time it will be different.'

'Go on,' said Pogget.

'Drugs,' said Jigsaw, grinning.

'Drugs!' Andy blanched. The barman looked over.

'Keep your voice down,' warned Jigsaw. 'We don't want everyone to know. We haven't got any yet.'

'For-get it,' said Andy. 'No fucken way.'

'I'm not suggesting that we take them,' said Jigsaw. 'Look, this could be our one big chance to get ourselves out of here. Our only chance.'

Andy's laugh was full of scorn. 'And where do we get the money to buy the drugs? Haven't thought about that, have yeh, eh? No, thought not.'

'Well at least I'm trying. Unlike you two. You two will never get out of here. You two will have nothing.'

The three friends sat and stared in to their barely touched sunrises.

It was Saturday. Andy grabbed his coat, took his football from under the stairs, his dad's flat cap from off the coat-hanger, and headed in to town.

He chose a pitch on the pedestrianised section of Bold Street. He was a little apprehensive at first but his nerves soon left him once he started doing tricks. He attracted quite a crowd. His dad's hat, placed before him on the ground, began to fill with coins. But the first police patrol that came along moved Andy on. No licence.

Andy, Pogget and Jigsaw each received letters threatening them with Job club. They would from now on have to attend Job Club every morning at 9.30am, starting next week. They were informed that if they did not attend without a sufficiently good reason then their benefit would be stopped. At job club they would be taught how to write job applications, use the telephone and practice their interview technique.

The job club was held in the vestry of a disused church. A register was taken at the start of the session, just like at school. There were twenty people present, each of them resentful and bored. Shafts of bright sunlight streamed in through tall arched windows. It was a beautiful day, outdoors.

The supervisor, a tall man in a worn suit, the tie pulled loose and his collar open, addressed the room.

'Right then,' he said breezily, rubbing his hands together, 'let's get ourselves a job. Now—'

There was the slam of the door as someone came in to the room.

'You're late,' the supervisor told Andy.

'For what?' asked Andy.

The supervisor demanded his name, checking it off the register. Andy took the vacant place between Jigsaw and Pogget.

'Okay.' The supervisor looked out at the twenty uninterested faces, some of which were becoming increasingly hostile. 'I want you to forget all that fairy tale bullshit about what you want to do and concentrate on what's actually out there.'

Andy and Jigsaw exchanged glances.

'So, everyone got a pen and paper?'

Reluctantly, pens were lifted to the air before being thrown, some slammed, back on to the desks. An air of increasing hostility permeated the room.

'And a copy of the yellow pages?'

His query was met with nods and grunts.

'Then let's get to it.'

Clenching his teeth, breathing heavily through his nose, Andy reached for his yellow pages, snatching it toward him, gripping the thin yellow paper in his hand and, carelessly, noisily, he turned the pages: *security, office cleaning, fast food, warehousing. . . .*

Everyone was expected to be something: a shelf stacker, a security guard, a labourer, road sweeper, waiter, dishwasher, a clerk. . . It wouldn't matter what job you chose. It wouldn't matter to them, and it wouldn't matter to the job. When you wanted work and could not find the work that you wanted that was when it crushed you. When work was no better than the dole, but harder, and more hopeless, it could destroy you completely.

After, outside, on the steps of job club, in the space and the fresh air, the empty afternoon ahead felt like the best kind of freedom. People came streaming out of the building. Everyone just wanted to get away from the place, just like at work.

The supervisor hurried down the steps and in to the street, got in to his car and sped off.

Andy looked around for something to kick. He grabbed and pulled the railings. He felt that he was being boxed in, that the opportunities available to him were narrowing, that there were fewer and fewer outlets for his energies. There was so much to be had, so much that was possible, and everything was impossible. The anger built in him. 'Fucken work,' he said. 'They hold it up to yeh like it's some kind a holy fucken grail, when all's it is is some poxy job like. Those fucken bastards, they expect us to live without hope!'

People get tired of trying. They end up wanting to kick things. Andy had tried enough. He felt the need to snap trees, to steal and to torch cars, to beat the shite out of someone. He kicked the railings.

'Fuken 'ell,' said Pogget, lighting up. 'Is worse'n fucken skewel in there.'

'Well we are just going to have to put up with it,' said Jigsaw.

'Well Am not puttin up with it,' said Andy, 'thee've already stopped my dole.' He still hadn't been paid. 'Fuck it!' he said, and he kicked the railings again.

'Come on,' said Jigsaw, edging away, pulling Andy with him by his sleeve. A police car had appeared at the top of the street. The three friends hurried away in the opposite direction.

The dole was a safety net, it stopped people taking to the streets. It took away the hunger. It took away the urgency, and the rage. It took away the fight. It kept those without hope, if not hopeful, then subdued. It kept them passively unoccupied. The dole protected people on both sides of the system. It protected the system. They forget that, the bosses and the owners and the deities. When everything is up and running they think that everything should be run for them.

It was two o'clock in the afternoon and Andy was in bed, dreaming that he was Spike Milligan.

He was still in bed at three, playing football for Liverpool. He tried to motivate himself. Get up will you and make it happen. No good lying there in wait, in never fucking happen land. The thing would happen to someone else.

Out on the street, walking and looking, hoping he'd discover an opportunity. Or be discovered. He would be plucked from obscurity and have sudden fame. Or a woman, maybe, who liked him for who he was. Walking to be rid of himself. To pass the time. Passing by. Another day gone. That someone owed him.

Andy got up late, and he went to bed late. Going to bed was boring, he fell asleep. He dreamt that he was in a fight. But his punches were powerless.

Andy woke up scared. He went to bed scared. What if it was going to be like this all his life?

'Andy, wake up!' It was his mother, shaking him by the shoulder. 'You'll be late for the dole, son.'

She put a fresh mug of tea down on the bedside table.

The dole offices had been refurbished. Andy barely recognised the place. Inside smelt of fresh paint. The paint was grey: dark grey floor, pale grey ceilings, grey walls. Even the furniture was grey.

Was this some kind of sick joke?

In place of the old wooden counter there was a dark grey plastic counter. The old alphabetic divisions had been replaced. *Point 1, Point 2, Point 3, Point 4.* The new signs hung at intervals above the counter. No one seemed to know where they were supposed to sign on. There was confusion everywhere.

Strange how soon things return to normal, thought Andy.

He placed his UB40 on the counter, sliding it under the plastic window, pushing it toward the clerk.

'Wrong signing point, sorry,' she told Andy. 'This is Point 2. F's to J's? You're an O, O'Shea, you want Point 3.'

There was a long queue at point 3.

Andy sighed. He picked up his card but remained staring at the girl. 'Point 1, Point 2, Point 3. So what do you call Enquiries now? Pointless?'

The girl shot out a laugh. Soon everyone in the office was laughing. The clerks, the unemployed, everyone. Laughter filled the crowded office.

'Sod it!' said Andy. 'Sod the whole fucken lot of yis!' He slammed his fist hard down on the counter.

The laughter stopped. It was replaced by the chatter of keyboards and the slow shuffle of feet.

Andy came in through the front door, slamming it behind him, walked down the hall, climbed the stairs to his room, slammed shut the door and got straight in to the bed. He pulled the covers over his head because he was crying. He was nothing, a nobody, and he always would be. He was just one of the unemployed. Even if he got a job, he would still be nobody.

'Go on,' he urged, 'laugh your way out of this, you always do.' But he could think of nothing to laugh at.

'I av fucken well ad it up ter 'ere,' Andy told his father at breakfast the next morning.

'Andy! Language,' scolded his mother. 'I don't know why can't you speak properly, like your friend James.'

Andy formed his mouth in to a perfect circle. 'Sorry, I have fucking well had it up to here,' he said, in a posh accent.

His mother reddened, his father choked on his tea. Andy got up from the table and went upstairs. He came down with his holdall.

His mother draped a scarf around his shoulders, and wrapped it once around his neck. She rested her hands on his chest for a long moment. Then she patted his chest. She held his face in her hands and she kissed him on the forehead.

Andy pulled himself away. He felt his eyes smart.

His father shook him by the hand. 'Look after yourself, son. And don't worry, it'll be all right one day, you'll see.'

'I know. It's just the other three hundred and sixty four days every year that worry me.'

'That's the spirit, son.'

There was a knock on the door.

Jigsaw and Pogget were stood waiting for him in the street. Pogget held a plastic carrier bag, Jigsaw a small suitcase.

'So, where will youse go?' asked Andy's father.

Jigsaw and Pogget shrugged. Andy shrugged. 'Dunno. Perhaps everywhere. Who knows?'

Andy stepped from the warm shelter of the house, out in to the grey and puddled street. He looked up the street, then he started to walk.

3

Clemence.
As I Walked out one Midsummer Day and in to a Lamp-post

Clemence Tartt had no immediate plans for the future. He had just that summer graduated from Cambridge University with a double first in Applied Mathematics and Economics, and had not intended to apply for any jobs. Instead, he had planned to do nothing for a time. He needed time to think in order to make the right decision about his future. He had spent three long years studying and he had a lot on his mind. But Clemence's parents, both professionals, one a corporate lawyer, the other a doctor - a paediatrician at Liverpool's Alder Hey hospital - had high hopes for Clemence, so they had him apply for a position in the City with a leading investment bank.

It was six o'clock in the morning when Clemence's alarm went off. At ten past six his father called up from the foot of the stairs, but there was no answer. He hurried up the stairs.

'Clemence!' he shouted, hammering on the bedroom door. 'Get up. Now! Or you'll be late for the interview.'

Clemence woke. The interview! He sat bolt upright in bed. He was dreading the interview. Maybe he was being unduly pessimistic but there was no doubt in his mind that he would get the job.

Clemence felt his spirits sink.

Cursing, he disentangled himself from his sheets, got reluctantly out of bed and shuffled to where his suit hung on its coat hanger from the wardrobe door with all the appearance of a hanged man.

The thin cotton shirt felt cold on his skin, the woollen trousers itchy and uncomfortable. The lumpish knot of his tie felt strange and tight against his throat. His jacket was tight about his shoulders and pulled at his elbows when he lifted his arms. Clemence shrugged his shoulders and pulled down his sleeves, only to have them creep back up again, exposing his wrists. He was too tall, his arms too long, his wrists bony. He felt uncomfortable in the suit, not because it did not fit him particularly well but because it made him feel different, not himself. That suit felt too much like a uniform.

He glanced over to the midden heap of clothes on the bedroom chair. He was going to miss those comfortable baggy cords, loose fitting multicoloured jumpers, and his old combat jacket with the CND sign stitched to the lapel.

Clemence picked up his comb. He bent to the mirror on his bedroom wall and was pulling it with some difficulty through his longish, tangled hair when his father shouted up the stairs to him.

'Clemence! Get a move on there!'

'Coming Dad,' he cried, and, crossing the room to the door, he pulled at the handle which came off in his hand. 'Five minutes, okay,' he shouted.

Clemence was accident prone. When he was younger the people at the hospital who treated his injuries assured Clemence's parents that it was his rapid growth that was the source of the problem and that he would eventually grow out of his clumsiness. Clemence grew to be a gangly youth of over six feet tall, capable of rendering himself semi-conscious on the tallest of doorframes. He had encounters with light shades, was clipped on the head by low branches, road signs and the signs of shops. He was forever walking in to things. He trod on people's toes, including his own. It were as though he were unsure of where he ended and where everything else began. The house was destroyed with him. Relatives and friends alike dreaded his visits, calling him the polterguest. He was, as someone once said, the clumsiest thing on all fours.

Clemence entered the breakfast room some ten minutes later. His father folded and put aside his Times, his mother her Telegraph, and, when Clemence pulled a chair out from under the table to sit down, they both lifted their tea cups off the table and in to the air, out of harms way. Clemence sat down at the table without incident. His mother got up from the table and, using a tea towel, she fetched him a plate full of bacon, sausage and eggs from where she had been keeping it warm under the grill.

'Mind the plate now, it's hot,' she said, setting it down in front of him.

But Clemence couldn't face breakfast, he was too anxious about the interview. He reached out, pushing away the plate, burning his fingertips.

'Clemence!' chided his mother.

'I'll just have some toast,' he said, sucking his burnt fingertips. Then, reaching for the toast, he knocked over the sauce bottle. His mother righted the bottle.

'Nervous, eh?' said his father.

Clemence answered with a shrug.

'Isn't it exciting,' said his mother. 'Just think, you'll be working in London.' She winked at Clemence's father, his father nodded. 'I think that we should all go up to London,' she said, 'all three of us, this weekend, and start looking for a flat.' A glance of pure pleasure passed between his parents.

'A flat?' Clemence frowned.

'It'll be our little present to you, for doing so well,' said his father.

'But I haven't got the job yet,' said Clemence.

'Oh Clemence,' said his mother, 'of course you'll get the job.'

'You've got exactly what they are looking for,' his father assured him. 'They've probably already made up their mind to take you on. They want to see you is all.'

'He's just nervous,' said his mother.

'I'm not nervous,' said Clemence.

'I'd best be off,' said his father, glancing at the clock. He stood up from the table and out of his chair, and, lifting his jacket off the chair he swung it on, taking one last sip of tea before picking up his case and his neatly folded copy of the *Times*.

His mother stood. 'We'll meet later at the Adelphi, to celebrate. I've booked us a table for eight thirty.'

Clemence opened his mouth to protest.

'You'll have plenty of time, Clemence,' said his father. 'And good luck with the interview,' he said as he left the room.

'He doesn't need luck, do you, Clemence,' said his mother. 'Oh, and Clemence?' she said.

'Yes?'

'Your comb, dear. It's still in your hair.'

The interview was held in the City, at Partington House, the headquarters of Lemmon Brothers, Investment Bankers. Clemence was met at reception by a young and pretty secretary who escorted him via the elevator up to the fifth floor and then through a vast office-scape, the whole floor crammed with desks of computer screens. Arriving at the interview room the girl knocked on the solid black door. Telling Clemence to wait she let herself in, the heavy black door closing slowly then clicking shut behind her.

Clemence had a headache. The stuffy, over heated building, the neon lighting, the smell of carpet, and his increasing anxiety made him feel ill.

The door opened and the secretary ushered Clemence in to the room, then she left the room.

Directly in front of him, seated behind a huge, and highly polished conference table, on which rested a single thin folder and a solitary desk diary, sat two men.

Robert Nichols, head of Futures, and William Rand, of Acquisitions, introduced themselves. They were well-fed men in their mid-thirties. They motioned for Clemence to sit down.

'You have a rather impressive C.V.,' said Nicholls, reaching for and tapping the file. 'A double first, no less. Two years as editor of the University magazine. An article in the *Economist* on. . . . ' He reached for the the file.

'Stone age economics and the Irish potato famine?' said Clemence.

Rand smiled. 'I think you'll find we are somewhat more up to date here,' he said.

The men took it in turns to ask Clemence about himself. They asked him about his interests. They told him about Lemmon Brothers and its operations.

'The City is changing,' said Nicholls, 'and everything will have to change with it. Lemmon Brothers are spearheading that change.'

'What we're looking for,' Rand told him, staring him in the eye, 'is aggressive go getters, the very best. If you get the job, we'll expect the full 110% from you.'

Rand asked Clemence what he knew about money.

'It can't buy happiness?' Clemence said.

The two looked blankly at Clemence, then at each other, before bursting out laughing.

'Oh, very good,' said Rand. 'We must remember that one.' And, repeating the phrase, they burst out laughing again.

Clemence spent the next twenty minutes telling Nicholls and Rand everything that he knew about money. He was well aware of the role of capital in the modern economy. He talked about creating money. He understood that those who owned money and who dealt in money could not make money like those who made things to sell and to trade could make money. They did not work as others worked, the rabbit farmers of money maintained their wealth by unlocking money, by making money work. There was a prodigious amount of wealth tied up in industry and in property that was worth billions to anyone shrewd enough and hard-nosed enough to be able to release it. And there were ways of conjuring up money. Clemence talked of relaxing the rules on credit, of the need to increase debt. He described the business of making money to Nicholls and Rand as they both knew and understood it. 'Future money, now,' he concluded.

The men were impressed at his understanding.

Rand looked to Nicholls. Nicholls nodded. They stared at Clemence. 'So, when can you start?' asked Nicholls.

'Start?' Clemence looked stunned.

'When would you like to start?' asked Rand.

'I've got the job?'

Smiling, the two men nodded.

Nicholls and Rand reached over the desk to offer Clemence their congratulations. Clemence shook the proffered hands.

'July, I suppose,' said Clemence, after some thought. It was now the 15th of June.

'July?' Both Rand and Nicholls looked surprised. Disappointed. 'When in July, exactly?' asked Rand, frowning.

'The thirty-first,' said Clemence, without the least hesitation. 'There are some things I have to do first,' he explained.

Rand reached for his desk diary, he opened it and was just about to make the entry on the appropriate page when Clemence stopped him.

'Oh no,' said Clemence, 'not this July.'

The dining room of the Adelphi Hotel.

Clemence was sat diagonally across from his parents, looking contrite. On the table between them, cooling in a silver ice bucket, leant a magnum of champagne. Clemence's father, yelling: 'YOU DID WHAT?'

'Oh, Clemence, why?' said his mother, throwing her hands to her face.

'Because all my life I've only ever done what you told me to. Go to college, you said. So I went to college. I wanted to study literature or the classics, maybe even music. Do accountancy or economics, you said. So I did. I've done what you wanted. I've followed your advice.'

'It was sound advice.'

'Given for your benefit.'

'So you could have the best future possible.'

'But did you ever for one moment consider what I wanted, really wanted. For myself.'

'You never told us what you wanted.'
'I daren't. You would never have approved.'
'So what do you want?'

Clemence came down the stairs carrying his violin case, a full backpack hanging off one shoulder. He walked in to the living room and his parents followed him. They followed him in to the kitchen, where he eventually found his combat jacket draped over a chair.

'Clemence,' said his father, 'just listen to me for a minute. Will you please listen to what I'm saying.'

'You are not talking me out of this, my mind is made up.'

'But where will you go? You don't even know where you're going.'

Clemence shrugged. 'Spain, maybe, like Laurie Lee. Or perhaps Greece, overland through the Balkans, like Patrick Lee Fermor. I'll just hitch around, see where I end up.'

'Clemence, just because your friends do these things doesn't mean that you have to go off and do them too,' said his mother. 'Will you think about this?'

'I have thought about it.'

'Well it seems like a half-baked idea to me,' said his father.

'It's not half-baked, it's fully baked,' said Clemence.

'But what on earth will you do for money? Have you considered that?'

'I'll busk. I can get a job anytime, didn't I already prove that? If things get too difficult, if it all comes to nothing then I'll get a job.'

'What kind of a job?'

'Casual jobs. Fruit picking, dishwashing, that kind of thing.'

His father shook his head.

His mother seemed very disappointed in him. 'Oh, Clemence. All that hard work, all those years of education wasted, how can you throw all that away like this?'

'I'm not throwing it all away. And education is never wasted, otherwise it would not be education.'

His parents offered to buy him an around the world plane ticket. They thought that if they could nip what they called "this idiocy" in the bud, if they could give him his freedom, but with a definite starting date and a finishing date, then they could contain him, get him back on course.

Clemence refused. That was not the kind of travelling that he wanted to do.

His father made him out a cheque for £3,000. Clemence handed it back. With that kind of money he would not have to busk or find work, instead he would take the easy way out always whenever he was in difficulty. He had always had it easy, but he wanted to live life on the edge for a change, have worthwhile experiences, things that he could later write about.

His father tucked the cheque in to Clemence's breast pocket. 'Take it Clemence, please, for your mother's sake. She will only worry about you.'

Clemence shouldered his pack, picked up his violin case, said good-bye to his parents and left the house, his footsteps crunching on the long gravel drive. Passing the open iron gates, that let out on to Chestnut Avenue, a loose strap on his backpack caught on the ironwork, checking Clemence, and, for one moment, it looked like he had changed his mind.

4

Natasha.
A Lust for Life

Mention the name Natasha to people of her day and they don't think artist, capital A, a completely different image springs to mind: Party animal. Drunk. Naked in the fountain at Trafalgar Square. Dancing barefoot through museums. Talking through films. Laughter in waiting rooms. Cheerful at funerals. Dressed in yellow. Wild when drunk. Money to burn. . . .

The two girls came running down the street laughing and screeching. It was a Saturday afternoon and Natasha was out on the town with her best friend, Sadie Sommers. They had met up for dinner several hours earlier at a favourite restaurant in Soho and they were now very drunk.

Sadie, a buxom redhead, lost a shoe. Retracing her steps she bent to pick it up, flung a hand to her face and clasped her mouth. She hurried to a nearby rubbish bin and threw up.

Natasha, tall, thin and long haired, came running back for her. 'Fucking hell, Sade, you alright?'

'No,' said Sadie, lifting her head temporarily out of the stinking metal bin only to plunge it back in again.

It was a bright summer's day and the streets were crowded. Several passers by looked on in disgust. A man in a smart blue blazer stopped to tell the girls that they were a bloody disgrace.

'Do you know who my father is?' asked an indignant Natasha.

'No?' said the man.

'Good. Then fuck off, you old fart.'

Sadie's face was ugly and tear stained. 'I shouldn't have had that second bottle of red,' she said, brushing her hair off her face and smearing her freckled cheeks with mascara. 'I should have stuck to the vodka.' She plunged her head back toward the bin and threw up, missing the bin this time.

'Come on,' said Natasha, 'let's get you cleaned up. Then I'll buy you another dress.'

Half an hour later, the girls came bursting through the doors of a busy pub.

'Two vodkas and orange,' shouted Natasha, jostling for space and waving a crisp fifty in the air. 'Doubles,' she added, laughing.

'Each,' shouted Sadie with a shriek. 'And forget the orange,' she laughed. Gulping her drinks Natasha pushed a way through the jostling crowd. She put some money in the jukebox. Cindy Lauper, *Girls Just Want To Have Fun*, began blasting out.

Loud music. Flashing lights. Natasha and Sadie danced. Standing off, then writhing close, pressing their bodies against each other then leaping apart. Twisting and throwing back their heads, the sweat flew from their wet hair.

Exhausted, Sadie stopped dancing, hauled herself across the dance floor to a table and sat down. Natasha came and dropped down beside her.

'I'm flagging, Nat.'

The music changed. It got louder, livelier. The Bangles, *Walk Like An Egyptian*, blasted out.

A party from the City piled in. Alpha males, collars and ties, gathered around magnums of champagne, laughing.

'Come on,' said Natasha, and, jumping to her feet, she took hold of Sadie's hands and hauled her upright.

In the toilets, locked in a cubicle together, Sadie took another snort of powder off Natasha's car key. Natasha glanced at her watch. It was 8:30pm.

'Shit! Sade. The exhibition!'

The girls came flying in through the gallery doors.

As she hurtled past him, the gallery owner, Henry Marsden, long silver hair tied back in a ponytail, jacket sleeves rolled up on his forearms, grabbed Sadie by the elbow and he swung her to a stop.

'You're late,' he growled.

'Well I'm here now.' And, undoing the buttons on her coat, she wrestled herself out of it and swung it at Henry Marsden so that it wrapped itself around him before dropping to the floor.

'My God,' he said, eyes wide and staring, 'you could have dressed a little - more.'

Sadie was well stacked and bra-less, and her skimpy dress tight. She put a curve in her back and she pushed herself out. Her nipples, like two detonation caps, strained at the thin material. She wobbled sideways on her heels.

'You're drunk,' said Henry Marsden.

'And you're a preten. . . .'

Natasha dragged Sadie, laughing, in to the exhibition.

Big Naked Women Partying, Big Naked Women Shopping, Big Naked Women Running, Big Naked Women Dancing, Bathing, Eating, Drunk, Asleep. . . . The canvases were huge, like their subjects.

Several other artists were being exhibited but it was Sadie's Big Naked Women paintings that everyone had come to see. And Sadie herself, of course. She was soon surrounded by admirers.

Natasha stood on the edge of the crowd sipping from a glass of white wine. Then she made a circuit of the walls, coming finally to the painting, *Sea and Sky*, by Enzo. She didn't recognise the name.

A small card carried an explanation of the work, its author, Henry Marsden:

Sea and Sky, by Enzo. The pictorial vocabulary of soft edged rectangles and muted colours comes across with an utterly personal conviction. In this work one can physically sense the trajectory of the artist's tentative intuitions and reflective uncertainties as they build to compositional resolutions of the most exquisite precariousness.

The artist had painted two rectangles one above the other, one blue, the other not so blue and they had been turned in to language.

Sadie eventually broke free of her admirers and came over to join Natasha.

'Where are the drinks? I need a top up.'

Natasha pointed with her glass. 'Who's that?' she asked.

He was tall and had long dark wavy hair and was dressed untidily in a black leather jacket, a black turtle necked sweater and faded black jeans. He looked like he had slept in his clothes. But it was the odd and different sized shoes which he was wearing that astonished Natasha. She didn't know that he had different sized feet, that he stole his shoes from the racks outside of shoe shops where the single shoe, considered to be inviolate, is vulnerable to such attack.

'A nobody, is who,' said Sadie.

'Ah, you mean another artist.'

'If you can call his work art.'

'Oh, he's coming over.'

'Natasha. Baggie.' Sadie held out her hand. 'Toilets. Now!'

But Natasha wanted to stay and get to know this strange looking character in the motorbike boot and wellington with the huge dark eyes.

'Here,' said Sadie, and she thrust her near empty wine glass against Natasha's chest and let go of it. 'Look after that. I'm going to the bog for a re-boost.'

Natasha did not know who Enzo was but Enzo knew who Natasha was. He had seen pictures of her in the magazines. Shots of her stepping from taxi cabs, of her staggering drunk out of nightclubs.

'She's something, isn't she, your friend?' he said.

'Yes, that's Sadie Sommers,' said Natasha. 'She painted those pictures.'

'I know.' He didn't sound too enthusiastic.

'You don't like her work?' Natasha frowned. 'Why not?'

'Isn't it obvious?' he said, to which Natasha shrugged.

'They're just pictures, pictures of fat ladies, that's all.'

'Well that's what they're supposed to be,' frowned Natasha. 'At least you can tell what her pictures are, not like that work.' She pointed to the canvas, *Sea and Sky*. 'What is that supposed to be?'

'What do you think it is?'

'Well, the sea and the sky. Obviously. But that interpretation relies entirely on the title. It could be anything. Infinity, maybe?'

'Precisely, it could be anything. It makes you think. Whereas those pictures of fat ladies they are just pictures of fat ladies. But great art ought to tell you something. Sadie's pictures are like. . . well, like that pot over there.' Enzo pointed with his glass toward a Greek urn that was stood on a shoulder high column. They began to walk over to it.

The pot's creator, a sandy haired man with a foppish fringe and wearing a blue shirt and corduroys, thinking that his work was being appreciated came over and introduced himself. He insisted on explaining the ideas and inspiration behind his work.

Sadie appeared, fully charged and ready for action. Instead she found Natasha and Enzo discussing some sort of pot thing with this dweeb type person.

'What the fuck is this?' she asked. She wanted to see some action, not stand about discussing pottery.

'This,' said Natasha, grinning, the laughter building up in her, 'is a geek's urn.'

Sadie shrieked, she doubled over laughing, lost her balance and, throwing back her arms, knocked the pot off its stand.

The pot exploded in to pieces on the floor. The sound echoed around the gallery.

Henry Marsden burst through the crowd. He grabbed both girls by their wrists and he hauled them toward the exit. Natasha went willingly. Sadie fought. 'Let me go! Let me go! She shouted. This is my exhibition. I'm the artist, for fucksakes!'

Henry Marsden pushed the girls out through the doors and in to the street, first Sadie, and then Natasha, followed by their coats and bags.

'One is supposed to exhibit one's paintings,' he said, 'not oneself!' And he shut the doors on the girls.

Natasha let out a long, howling laugh, lunged forwards, bent double and vomited in to the gutter.

Enzo offered to hail the girls a taxi and to take them home. To his place. Tonight had been his first ever exhibition and his friends were throwing a party in celebration.

Sadie was reluctant - she wanted to be feted by her more recent peers, not hang out with a bunch of would be artists. But there was a party going on inside her that was bursting to get out. Natasha readily agreed. She had taken a fancy to Enzo, especially now that she knew he was a struggling artist.

Natasha was attracted to quirky, off centre people, to anyone living on the edge in any way. She avoided successful people, she preferred struggling people, anyone that was trying for something they might not get and who knew it but who were trying for it anyway. Anyone with sufficient enough talent, anyone crazy enough or desperate enough to think that they had a chance, or astute enough to know that it was their only chance. People with the guts to stick two fingers up to the world and to go their own way, even if that was all that they were doing. It was enough. Being with them meant that Natasha was sticking two fingers up to the world too. And, though Sadie might no longer meet the requirement, being the success that she was, she still stuck two fingers up to the world. She was still The Sade. Maybe more so.

The party was in a squat in Hoxton, an old shop that was now being run as an artists colony. Everyone at the party seemed to be either a painter, a sculptor, a writer, a poet or a musician, or were certainly trying to be, or they were at college studying such things. A loud roar went up when Enzo entered. There was applause. People congratulated him, offered him drinks.

When it was known that Sadie Sommers had arrived she became the centre of attention.

She attracted a large crowd, though there were some that avoided her, those who were resentful of her success. Success meant money, and money would be why some would be forced to stop trying and would fail, and why others would become successful and remain artists.

Natasha had met some of these people before. They were friends of Sadie's, from her art school days. They were forever bumping in to them on the street, at parties and in pubs, and Natasha had always thought them the most interesting people she had ever met. They drank and did drugs, talked about drinking and doing drugs, about art, writing, music, and what it was, and what the world was and how as artists they were going to change that. Art was the medium through which they saw and understood the world and they believed that if they could somehow change art then it must follow that the world must change too.

Natasha was not interested in changing the world, all she was interested in was having a good time. She did not want to talk about art, she did not know how to. She had not been educated in art and such talk intimidated her and, though Natasha listened in apparent earnest, she would rather party. Feeling increasingly marginalised, she soon grew bored.

Natasha was beautiful, but Sadie was proving to be more fun. The party soon began to rage around her.

Eventually, the talking stopped. There was just music and dancing, drinking and smoking and pairing off.

Natasha had to fight off the attentions of several drunk and inarticulate and fumbling men. She wanted to go home, but she was too drunk, too tired to even try. She took her drink - a full bottle of cheap wine - and a monster bag of chip sticks, and she locked herself in the bathroom with a rug and several cushions where, listening to the party as it crashed and rumbled on around her, she fell asleep in the bath. But when someone in need of the toilet broke down the door she was forced to leave the house in search of a taxi.

It was late the next morning when Natasha awoke in the Mews house, alone. No Sadie. She wasn't in the spare bedroom and nor when Natasha checked in the lounge neither was she on the couch. As a precaution, Natasha checked the doorstep. She had no recollection of the night before. The last thing she remembered was being ejected from the gallery. Ordinarily, she would have then rung Sadie on her mobile, but they hadn't brought their mobiles out with them since they had been travelling light, for shopping purposes. Mobile phones, sneered Natasha, you needed a mobile home to carry them in. They were like bricks.

Natasha rang Sadie on the house phone. No answer. Probably in bed still, crashed out, she reasoned.

After several strong coffees Natasha felt steady enough to drive home. She locked up the Mews House, got in to her Ferrari and left Chelsea for

Greatscapes.

*

The Plane-Smith family had lived and farmed at Greatscapes in Norfolk ever since the Conquest. The present house dated from the mid-18th century, when the parkland now surrounding it had been laid out by the great English landscape gardener, Capability Brown, though some of the out buildings surrounding the house dated back to the middle ages.

A cloud of white dust lifted off the gravelled drive as the Ferrari tore toward the house, a huge block like mansion of porticoes and tall windows at the summit of a cascade of stone steps. The car slewed to a halt in front of the house. But instead of going in to the house Natasha hurried around the back, through a gate in the high stone wall there, crossed the kitchen garden and disappeared in to an outbuilding.

Her parents wouldn't allow her to have her studio in the house.

There was every piece of equipment in that studio that it was necessary to have to make just about anything, art wise: a pottery wheel and kiln, a huge easel, the best and most expensive oils, a vast collection of the best brushes, the best canvas.

Wherever you looked, there were pictures, landscapes for the most part, in oils, hung on the walls and propped against the walls and against her workbench, the stepladder, against the sink...

Natasha needed to create things. She could not explain her need, except as an urge. It was the same urge that told her to get drunk, or to have sex, to sing, to dance, to wear yellow, to like sunflowers, the bright sun.

Natasha placed herself before the easel on which stood her most recent canvas. The picture was a landscape, the view from the window to the rear. Looking at the picture was like looking out of the window itself, it was so lifelike, except that the picture was unfinished.

Natasha could paint. She had real ability, an eye for detail. Her paintings were like photographs. But looking at her work she understood now that her pictures said nothing, they were just pictures, when they ought to say something. Enzo is right, she admitted to herself. To be an artist, a great artist, that is, required something much more. The accomplishment lay elsewhere.

Natasha replaced the canvas with a blank one. But she could think of nothing to paint. No other way of presenting the thing. And it was much too nice a day to spend indoors, painting.

It was shortly after six in the evening and Natasha was at home having dinner with her parents, her father seated at one end of the long, highly polished dining table, her mother at the other, with Natasha in the middle on one side.

There was silence in the room, save for the sound of cutlery working on best china.

Through the tall windows, a view of well-tended parkland. Bright light streaming in, making the floor shine. The wooden floor polished to a brilliant if treacherous gloss. The sideboard, the silver dinner service, everything laid out just as it should, everything in its time-honoured place, as it was throughout the house.

Cleanliness and order. But there is a duty to be performed to such things: they have to be kept that way. It had created something other than a house. Maybe, thought Natasha, that was why she was so attracted to disorder, to untidiness. It did not get in the way of anything. This house was always in the way, of everything.

'Your mother and I,' said Natasha's father, breaking the silence, 'We've been thinking about this idea of yours, of attending art school?'

'This year, yes,' said Natasha keenly.

'Yes, well, I'm afraid it's not really what we want for you.'

'You hated school, if you remember,' said her mother.

'I didn't hate it, there were just better things going on elsewhere.'

'Best we forget the idea,' said her father.

'But I want to paint.'

'There are lots of other things you could be doing,' said her mother.

Her father agreed. 'Look, if you really are interested in art then why don't I fix you up with a position with one of the big auction houses. They are always on the lookout for someone with your connections. I'll ring Sotheby's tomorrow, speak to Charles about it.'

Her parents might sound reasonable but there was never any question of Natasha getting her own way. Maybe if they sounded reasonable then their refusal would also appear reasonable.

'I don't want a job in art.'

'Quite,' said her mother, 'You don't need to do anything.'

Natasha felt she would explode, but she controlled herself. 'I want to paint and to learn how to do it properly.'

'But your paintings are wonderful, dear,' said Lady Plane-Smith.

'And what exactly do you need to know? That Van Gogh only ever sold one painting?'

'What's the point of knowing that?'

'It's what they'll teach you in art school. Not everyone makes it financially as a painter, not even the successful ones,' he said, smiling at his own wit. 'No.'

'No? No what?'

'You are not going to art school.' His voice hardened, grew louder: 'We are not having you associating with the kind of persons that frequent such places.'

'What do you mean, kind of persons? You make a lot of money from artists. They painted the pictures in your collection, in case you'd forgotten.'

'And I make a lot of money from factory workers too, I dare say, but I don't wish to associate with them. Artists? Drop outs and drug abusers.' Sir Geoffrey's anger began to show. He snatched up the newspaper lying beside him on the table. The *Daily Mail*. He shook it at Natasha. It was already open on the relevant page.

Nigel Dempster's supercilious, self-satisfied face stared out at her from the Diary page.

Speechless, Natasha gaped at the article.

'Getting drunk and making a spectacle of yourself, being evicted from galleries.' Her father's voice was full of disgust. 'And now the whole world knows about it! Well it is not going to happen again. You are going to stop this! We've had enough.'

'And I've had enough of this,' said Natasha, standing.

'Sit down! From now on, you're grounded.'

'Grounded?' Natasha sat.

'Keys, Natasha.' Sir Geoffrey held out his hand. 'I want the keys to the Mews house. And the Ferrari.'

'The car's mine.' It had been her parent's 18th birthday present to her.

'We've tolerated your behaviour for too long,' said her father, a finger hammering on the newspaper. 'I'm cutting off your allowance.'

Natasha reached in to her jeans pocket, pulled out her keys, removed her car key from the key-ring, banged the keys down on the table and fled the room, slamming the door behind her. Then the front door slammed, then the door of her Ferrari. The engine roared in to life and the car sped off down the drive.

Natasha sold her Ferrari and she moved in to a squat in a run-down building in Hoxton which she shared with a group of other would be artists.

They were for the most part indigent and idle - they partied, they drank too much, they took drugs. They were exactly the kind of people that her parents had wished to protect her from. Not one of them worked. They lived life in contradiction of every known law of economics and survival, and yet they thrived. It was this loose bohemian lifestyle in which they lived, allowing of everything, that core of rebelliousness which was the very ethos and life blood of their being, the fact that they were pushing at the boundaries wherever they found them, that made them the most lively, the most vital and entertaining, the most necessary people in Natasha's eyes. She enjoyed the energy that being with them generated. Convinced that their futures lay elsewhere, they had created for themselves a breathing space from an increasingly more frantic and threatening world, something that many would later come to see as their greatest achievement. Impoverished and essentially alone, but with everything ahead of them. These were people that no one wanted to be. Everyone wanted to have done the thing, not to do it. There was a difference.

For Natasha, though, doing it was the whole point. The house, the car, money . . . you could be given those. But if you wanted to be an artist then you had to do that for yourself. She threw herself in to the life.

Natasha partied, drank, took drugs. But she also visited the galleries, she attended openings and exhibitions. She applied for art school. And she painted, painted, painted.

She immersed herself in art. She painted in the styles of the greats: Picasso, Degas, Cèzanne and particularly Van Gogh. She thought that if she copied enough artists and perfected their styles then she would become that kind of artist, their genius somehow transferring itself to her.

It was easy to think that you were learning when maybe all that you were doing was doing things differently.

One day, Natasha showed Enzo her work. He came round to her flat especially.

Yellow landscapes, yellow flowers, whirling yellow suns.

'They're very good,' he said.

'But?'

'There's already been Van Gogh,' Natasha. 'You should paint what you feel, not copy others.'

She really did want to be able to paint like Van Gogh. Finding your own inimitable style, that was the thing, and Natasha was finding that difficult.

'Do you even know who Van Gogh was, Natasha?'

'Well of course I do.'

'He was a failure, he thought he was.'

'Everyone keeps telling me that. So?'

'He felt that he had failed to paint what it was that he wanted to paint, what he felt he must, what he felt inside, do you understand? But he always fell short of his vision, and the frustration of that drove him insane.'

'But just look at what that created.'

Enzo nodded his agreement. 'Have you any more pictures?' he asked.

'No,' she said. Because they were all the same.

'What you need, Natasha, is to paint passionately, like you live your life.'

The thing struck Enzo then. Or maybe he had always known it. But it seemed to surprise him, it was so obvious.

You would need to live life first before you could paint life. You had to immerse yourself in the world before you could hope to show what the world was.

'Forget painting for now, Nat, get out there and live instead. Live sensuously, live dangerously, live sensationally. But for God's sake live. See and do everything! Fill yourself so full of life that it threatens to explode from you in a painting. Maybe then you can create great art. Life, Natasha, it's the blood and guts of the artist.'

It explained why some artists create nothing, but it seemed to galvanise Enzo. He stubbed out his cigarette, knocked back his drink, and hurried off. It was not the last time that Natasha met him, but it was one of the few times on which she saw him over the next few years. Rumour informed her of his progress, that he had shut himself away, spurning all contact, to work on his masterpieces.

Great works of art may well be inspired, but they are no sudden thing. They might leap from the brush and be accomplished in days, even hours, but that is an illusion. Such works require great wellsprings, huge upsurges of feeling and of knowledge before they can be given birth. The great and accomplished thing only looks simple because it appears complete.

Output, that was when the artist created work.

Input, that was the time the artist spent preparing, when she plugged herself in to life, storing up the raw material, the necessary information, all the feelings and experiences, all the essential energies that drive art. It was the time the artist needed to recharge the physical and creative batteries that fed art. Not a deliberate thing perhaps, but an osmosis.

It would come one day, Natasha was certain. It would burst out of her, one great painting after another, in an unstoppable stream.

Artists can spend several years on input, waiting for genius to strike.

Natasha partied. She drank. She went to raves. She was accepted at art school, and was thrown out for non-attendance at the end of her first year. It was a crazy time. Ever day Natasha discovered some new thing, yet another possibility. She was in the company of the most extraordinary people, people with ideas. When the money from the sale of her Ferrari ran out she took a pitch on the Bayswater Road and sold caricatures at £5 a time. She felt an excitement, a fantastic sense that incredible things were about to happen for her. She would paint great pictures, she was sure, but for now it was enough to hang out and to be as crazy and as free and as fun loving and as experimental as everyone else.

It is virtually impossible for the talented, the beautiful, and the imaginative not to mess up. What a time they are having. They never once consider the consequences of their behaviour, so assured are they of rescue by that benign and golden force, their latent talent.

It was over two years since Natasha had moved to London and she was now working in an art gallery in Shoreditch. She drove a beaten up Hillman estate and had left the Hoxton squat, finding it too squalid, and was now living in a flat on her own in a house in Dalton. She had just received notice that the rent on her flat was to be increased and she was thinking of moving to a smaller, cheaper flat in Shoreditch, near to her work.

She packed her clothes in to black bin bags and she filled several boxes with her books. Then there were the hundreds of empty wine bottles from all her parties to get rid of. Finally, there was just that one last room to empty.

Many people have a room in their homes which they keep for a specific purpose and then fill up with junk, with things of no immediate use but which they still want to keep and which they then forget about.

There were rolls of carpet, an unwanted desk, a lamp-stand, a vacuum cleaner with a broken fan belt, several large suitcases, stacks of boxes, a backpack, chairs, a large portfolio case. An easel with a canvas on it.

Natasha went and she stood before her easel. But there was no painting there. How could there be? Just a blank canvas covered in dust: abandoned in the way that childhood discards things in its wake.

Natasha felt tired and empty and full of regret. Her spirits sank. She was overcome with weariness. It was depressing.

She stood contemplating the work she had yet to do. When she could have done it all by now.

People often wish that time had done for them what they should have done for themselves. When what they really have to do is to start again. The past was the present once.

Natasha picked up a paint brush. She stood poised in front of the empty canvas. She tapped the end of the brush against her teeth.

But nothing occurred to her. No divine intervention came to her aid, as she had hoped it would. Not today then.

*

Natasha left her job at the gallery.

Emboldened by a fresh sense of purpose, but devoid of urgency, she packed all of the materials that she would need, bundled them in to her car and proceeded to Wales.

She was without any kind of plan, yet she was unconcerned. She felt protected somehow, confident that everything would turn out well for her. Unprepared, and ignorant of virtually everything, and thus able to gain the full benefit of her education, she threw herself wholeheartedly and without regret to the mercy of events.

5

Collision Course

Pogget checked the petrol gauge, Jigsaw the tax disc. The inside of the car smelt of petrol. There were crisp packets, bust cassette tapes and empty drinks cans in the footwells. A pair of dice hung down from the rear-view mirror. Jigsaw ripped them off.

Pogget sat gunning the engine. The engine sounded rough but everything came together at high revs. He fought the stick in to first gear and let out the clutch. The engine stalled.

'Fucksakes,' said Andy, 'move it, will yeh, before someone see us.' He turned to look out the back window.

'Look, let's just forget this,' said Jigsaw. 'Let's go and nick us a better car.'

'Yeh an the fucken filth'll' take one look at us goin' by and give chase. Looker wha' append us tha' time A got tha' tidy BM fer us ter go up the Lakes in. First plod we drove past fucken cum after us didn'e, an we aden' even left the Pewel. Adter dump the car 'n leggit cross the railway lines teh gerra way. We were lucky to gerraway. But who's gonna stop us in this arl piece a shit, eh?' Pogget reached back under the steering column of the rusted old Escort.

'We won't get nicked fer takin an drivin away,' said Andy, 'we'll get done fer fucken parkin. Fucken gerrit started, will yeh. Come on.'

'What d'yer think am trying ter do,' said Pogget, twisting as he sat upright in his seat, 'tie up me fucken shoes?'

'Well get on wir it then,' snarled Andy, 'or we'll be going away alright. Fer a fucken stretch.'

Pogget reached back under the steering column, letting out a cry of triumph as the engine roared in to life.

'So, youse decided where we're goin' yet?' he asked, settling himself upright in his seat, gripping the steering wheel.

Andy wanted to go to Scotland, to look for work on the oil rigs. There were plenty of jobs he'd been told, and the money was good. Jigsaw was sceptical. What chance did they have, really, of getting a good job on the rigs? They had no skills. They'd be cleaners or dishwashers, skivvies, wherever they went. Jigsaw wanted them to go to London, that was where the real money was, he said. And wherever there was money being made there was going to be money making scams. Pogget wasn't fussed either way. Wherever they fetched up he intended going on the rob. He just wanted to get out of Liverpool to avoid the court summons for not paying his fines.

'London,' said Jigsaw, 'like we agreed.'

'We didn't agree,' said Andy, 'we tossed a coin. An when it cum up heads for Scotland yer made us do best out a three.'

'And London won. I just think London is our best bet. It's a rational decision based on the facts. London, Pogget.'

Andy did not want to go to London. Neither did he want to leave Liverpool, but he didn't want to stay there either. There was nothing for them in Liverpool. But what was waiting for them in London? They knew no one in London. People lived on the streets in London. They had no plan, no idea whatsoever of what they would do once they got there. There were supposed to be jobs down South. But they didn't want jobs, they wanted money. They were just getting out, escaping. Even Jigsaw was a little apprehensive about going there now that the moment had come. London was only four hours away.

Pogget let out the clutch and the engine bit. He was just about to drive away when Andy shouted out a warning: 'Police!'

The patrol car glided by and continued on to the junction with Stanley Road. They watched it turn the corner and disappear.

'What did A tell yeh,' said Pogget, patting the steering wheel. 'Sound thinkin, eh?' and he eased the car out in to the road.

Andy sat staring out of the window at the passing streets. Now that he was leaving, the city looked different to him. The once familiar streets appeared strangely unfamiliar, like he no longer belonged here.

It was one of those cold, sunny days in early spring when the shadows of clouds raced along the ground, a day of high white clouds and blue sky. Some people were dressed against the cold in hats and coats, others were in shirt sleeves. They were a hard looking people, thin and pale with gaunt faces.

Pogget wound down his window. 'Fucken no-marks!' he shouted, giving them the vees.

They were coming to the end of Stanley Road where it joined up with Scotland Road. The lights were in their favour but were about to change. Pogget put his foot down, but instead of taking a left for the East Lancs, the quickest way to the M6, he took a right.

'You're going the wrong way, Pogget!' said Jigsaw.

'Am not.'

'You goin' the tunnel way?' frowned Andy.

'It's longer, Pogget,' said Jigsaw. 'And you have to pay a pound,'

'A quid? ter get owra Liverpool? Bargain,' said Andy.

'A just thought like, why doan we go ter Wales?' said Pogget.

'Wales?' said Andy and Jigsaw.

'Why not?' said Pogget.

'Because, Pogget,' said Jigsaw, 'it's just countryside, there's nothing there. You want to be a farmer or a coal miner, do you?'

'It's the sheep he's after,' said Andy, 'Hey, A fancy ewe!'

'What A meen is why doan we go ter Lundun through Wales? Av a bit of an olidee first like. Yeh?'

'Why not?' shrugged Andy, nodding.

The three friends laughed. They seemed relieved. The moving between places and being in neither of them offered them something of a breathing space. Nothing would matter for a time. Even if they could not escape, it felt possible so long as they were moving. This knowledge that you were no longer trapped in the one place, or in the one life, but that you were going somewhere, somewhere new and different and unknown, kept some people on the move all their lives.

Andy sat forwards, pushing his head between the front seats. 'An yeh never know, it might be alright in Wales.'

Reluctantly, Jigsaw agreed.

For now, it was enough to be leaving Liverpool. And maybe it was better to be going to a place than to actually get there and be in the place and then have nowhere else to go. They would drive and drive, and maybe somewhere along the way things would be different for them.

'Wayels here we cum,' said Pogget and, pulling hard on the steering wheel, he swapped lanes, sweeping the car between two buses and then down the curving, high walled approach road to the tunnel.

Clemence took the taxi in to town from his home in Chestnut Avenue, Crosby, and there he caught the train to Chester, he took a taxi to the outskirts and then he began to hitch. His first lift took him to Mold. He still wasn't sure of his destination, but that no longer mattered. He had resolved his dilemma by deciding to go to wherever whoever picked him up was going. What did it matter where he went, so long as he was on the move and had adventures.

Pogget swept past the hitchhiker then pulled in at the side of the road. He kept his foot on the accelerator, keeping up the engine revs to stop it from stalling.

'What do yeh wanna pick up a hitchhiker for?' objected Andy. 'Just lookerim, the gangly twat, is aright fer youse two but there'll be hardly no room in the back here if he gets in, not with that backpack.'

Pogget said nothing, he sat there grinning, gripping the steering wheel, staring in to the rear view mirror.

'Wait till he gets here,' said Jigsaw, 'Then drive off. Here he comes.'

Clemence came running awkwardly toward the car clutching his violin case in both hands and with his pack bouncing on his back.

As he reached the car, Pogget let out the clutch, but the car stalled. Clemence put his violin case on the roof, struggled out of his pack, pulled open the rear passenger door and forced his pack in to the car, hitting Andy in the face with it. He was reaching for his violin case when the engine roared in to life and the car sped away from him up the road, leaving him balanced, with his back bowed and clutching his violin case as though he were making an offering of it.

'So what we got?' said Jigsaw, twisting in his seat.

Andy opened the pack. He pulled out a set of waterproofs, a down sleeping bag, a pair of corduroy trousers, a thick woolen jumper, several checked shirts, a white shirt, two T-shirts, a small gas stove, a tin mug, a vango tent, a carry mat and finally a pair of huge leather walking boots stuffed with balled up woollen socks and several pairs of white Y fronts. Andy held up the Y fronts before throwing them at Jigsaw. Jigsaw flung them out the window.

'That it?' frowned Jigsaw.

There was a zipped pocket on the top flap. Andy unzipped it and pulled out a tin plate, a knife and fork, several maps of Europe and some unused notebooks and threw them to one side. He upended the pack and gave it a shake. Something fell out in to the footwell.

'What is it?' asked Jigsaw, twisting in his seat. 'What you got?'

Pogget glanced in the mirror before he twisted around too.

Andy was holding a wedge of money, he was fanning the notes out, like a hand of cards.

'Jesus! There's fucken three hundred nicker here,' he said, grinning.

'YES!' shouted Pogget, 'Nice one! An yew said don't stop for no hitchhikers. Knob-ed.'

Pogget switched on the radio. Suzie and the Banshees were playing. He turned up the volume and began patting out the beat on the steering wheel, he wiggled the steering wheel. An oncoming car blazed its headlights and blasted its horn as it swerved past, missing them by inches. Pogget gave it the vees.

When Ed heard the car approach he turned and, sticking out his thumb, he stood looking at the car. The car passed him and drove on, disappearing around the bend. Just for a moment, when its brake lights had come on, Ed had thought that it might be stopping for him, but it was just slowing for the bend. Ed carried on walking. The soles of Ed's feet were sore and his legs ached and he had the beginnings of a headache from the weight of the pack digging in to his shoulders.

Pogget parked up in the first place that he found where the verge was wide enough to take the car.

'Same as last time,' said Jigsaw, 'okay? The minute he slings his pack in you hit the road.'

'He didn't look like he'd have that much,' said Andy. 'Looked like a tramp to me.'

'Yeh, well he woan av nuthin in a minit,' laughed Pogget.

The moment that Ed came around the bend in the road and saw the car parked up on the verge with its engine still running he hurried toward it.

Bending down, looking in to the car through the open window, he saw three rough looking characters with shaved heads and pinched, mean faces staring out at him.

'You want a lift?' asked Jigsaw.

'Sure,' said Ed. He pulled open the back door, swung his pack off his shoulder and, holding it tight against his chest, and with one deft and practised movement, he ducked in to the car and sat down, pushing to one side and in to the footwell the heaped up clothes, the tent, sleeping bag and boots, that had been piled up on the seat. He pulled the door shut behind him.

Pogget and Jigsaw exchanged glances. They looked in the mirror at Andy for some indication of what to do. Andy shrugged. Pogget gunned the engine and the car pulled out in to the road.

*

Natasha drove her battered Hillman Imp estate out of Aberystwyth and parked just over the crest of the steep hill on the narrow verge and as tight as possible to the hedge. She got out of the Hillman and she opened the rear doors. She removed an adjustable easel, a stretchered canvas and then her leather satchel, containing her paints and brushes and her numerous sketchbooks. She locked the car and she lifted her easel over the gate and then she climbed the gate. She made her way through the long grass to the centre of the field and, after choosing a suitable spot, she set up her equipment.

'So where y' headed?' asked Andy.
  'Aber,' said Ed.
  'Aber?'
  'Aberystwyth. It's on the coast. You going that way?' He sounded hopeful.
  'Nah,' said Pogget, 'Goan nowhere, really, sort of on olidee like.'
  'If you need to stop for anything anywhere?' asked Jigsaw. He was looking for a way to separate Ed from his pack.
  'I'm fine,' said Ed, 'I've already got everything I need, in here.' And he patted his pack.
  'Been travelling?' asked Andy. 'A mean, abroad, like?'
  Ed was tanned a deep bronze and his long blonde hair was bleached almost white by years in the sun.
  'Where did you go?' asked Jigsaw.
  'All over. Australia, Asia, India, Nepal, America, South America, the South Pacific.' Ed told them about his travels.
  'Wha' yew doin back ere?' asked Pogget, 'Yew soft or sumthin?' Ed didn't answer.
  'So what's it like, this Aber?' asked Andy, 'What's there?'
  'Just Aber,' said Ed, remembering.
  'Wharabowt pubs?' asked Pogget, 'An the wimmin, wharra the wimin lyke?'
  'The place is full of pubs. As for women.' Ed smiled, remembering. He told them about Meredith Hughes and YoYo Jo.
  'YoYo? I like the sound of her,' said Jigsaw.
  'What about work?' asked Andy. 'Is there any work?'
  'Plenty,' said Ed, 'You could have a different job each week if you wanted.'
  'So, what do you do?' Andy asked.
  'A different job each week.' Ed laughed, and Andy and Jigsaw and Pogget found themselves laughing too.

*

When Clemence had his pack stolen his very first thought was to return home. He had no tent, no change of clothes, and no money, save for the little in his wallet - ten pounds. But he still had his violin. So why go home, except to replace those lost things. Clemence finally got a lift in an old landrover pulling a stock trailer full of sheep. The cab stank of sheep, of sheep shit, wet sheepdog, and hay and silage, and of the farmer and his unwashed clothes. There was the reek of cooked mutton about him too. He was an old and weather-beaten man. He was returning to Wales from market in Wrexham, he told Clemence. Clemence asked him about farming. It was all grants and bureaucracy, the farmer complained. That was how it was going. As for the big supermarkets, he wasn't prepared to talk about them - he didn't have such language. He was chapel, he said, and he laughed. Clemence asked him what he would do if ever they stopped paying out the grants. The farmer didn't know. He supposed he'd have go back to farming, and he burst out laughing again. They drove up in to the mountains.

Natasha built up her composition in three tiers: first the sea, then the land - the beach and hills and mountains - then the racing sky. She painted slowly, taking great pains. Skylarks hovered in the air above her. Wood-pigeons called from the nearby trees. The sun was warm on her face. The day vibrated with life and light and movement.

The shifting nature of the sea and the sky, and the changing colours of the mountains all caused her difficulty. There was an energy at work in the landscape which she failed to capture. The sky, the sea, even the solid land, with the grass and the trees blowing in the wind, and with cloud shadows racing over it all possessed movement. But the harder that Natasha tried to capture that movement then the more detailed her work became and the more rigid she made it. Natasha picked up her palette knife and she scraped off the paint and she began again.

It was a glorious day on the coast, but inland, on the moors and in the mountains, it threatened rain. Thick dark clouds began to gather about the peaks.

The farmer stopped the landrover on a deserted moor at the junction of two roads. The right fork would take him eventually to his farm, the left would take Clemence to the nearest town, some ten miles away.

Clemence climbed awkwardly from the landrover out in to the cold and mist. He slammed shut the door and looked on as the red tail lights of the landrover disappeared in to the mist.

There was silence, just the wind, and the occasional sound of a sheep. Clemence was soon wet from the mist. The wind blew holes in the mist. The bleak moorland hadn't looked so vast or so threatening from the landrover but now it seemed to stretch away in every direction. There were peat hags and small black ponds and tiny black lakes everywhere. The wind blew the rank grass silver then green. A number of grazing sheep stopped what they were doing to stare at Clemence.

Clemence stood waiting in the road, but no cars came. Not in either direction.

He began to walk, but the further he walked the more doubtful he became of his direction. Then he remembered his map.

Clemence angled the map, trying to make it fit the geography, which it did not. According to the map he was nowhere to be found. He was, he presumed, at the intersection of the four creases where there was a hole in the map. Then the wind caught the map, snatching it from him. Clemence chased after it.

It began to rain, heavily. There were woods up ahead at the side of the road and Clemence ran to take shelter in them. They were dark pine woods but further down the slope they turned to oak. It was very quiet in the woods. At first the going was easy. Then the ground steepened and became more difficult. Clemence slithered down steepening slopes of mossed over boulders and precipitous and mossy crags. The slippery moss covered stones and the roots of trees tripped Clemence. He rolled down the bank, banging his head on a rock before landing heavily on his back on a track beside a stream.

'I caught my first ever trout in that river,' said Ed.

They had just crossed over a mountain pass and were now driving out of cloud in to bright sunshine, down a narrow and winding road beside a fast running river.

Ed told them the story of his first fish. Ed talked about fishing in such a way that by the time he had finished they all wanted to go fishing. They stopped the car in a lay-by and the four of them slid down the steep bank to the river where the river spilt over moss covered rocks in to a deep, amber pool. The four of them sat down in the sun on a grassy bank and they took off their boots and trainers and then they peeled off their socks.

Ed took Andy upstream to look for trout.

Jigsaw sat in the sun on the warm ground beneath an oak tree. Pogget began climbing the tree. He hung from his arms from a branch and he edged out along the branch and began to bounce up and down on it. The branch snapped, dumping him on the ground. Pogget threw the broken limb in to the river where the current swept it downstream, before jamming between some rocks.

Ed and Andy returned with a fish, a one pound brown trout that Ed had caught with his hands.

Pogget went to get some wood and light a fire. Ed prepared the fish, slitting it open along its belly using a Swiss Army knife. The knife had a little saw that could be used to cut timber, as well as a screwdriver, a bottle and can opener, and an awl for punching holes in things, removing stones, or scraping dirt from beneath a fingernail. Pogget admired the knife. He liked the weight of it in his hand. Ed gutted the fish, tearing out the glistening, stinking insides with his bloodied hands before throwing them in the river. He removed the blood sack along its spine using his thumb then he rinsed the fish in the fast stream. Pogget built up a small fire and when it had been burning long enough Ed made a bed of hot coals on which he then placed the fish.

The soft white flesh tasted sweet. Ed garnished his with sorrel. The leaf tasted sharp and tangy. 'Like vinegar,' said Andy. Pogget declined, saying that salad was for puffs. Jigsaw shook his head when Ed offered him some, he wasn't going to eat anything that grew so close to the ground.

The sun dipped behind the trees. It grew cool by the river in the shade. Above the cold river flowed a cold stream of air that sucked every bit of coldness it could find down toward the river. The cold moving air chilled the friends. Without the sun, the water became dark and impenetrable, and the mossy rocks, the cold black water and the deep clefted earth were all changed. It became damp and dark in the little valley. Ed put out the cooking fire, throwing the burning sticks in to the river. Jigsaw and Andy scooped handfuls of water from the stream and they poured it on the glowing embers, extinguishing them with a hiss in a plume of steam. Ed covered the extinguished fire with gravel.

Pogget hurried off up the slope toward the car, followed by Jigsaw and then Andy. Pogget was first in to the car. He reached beneath the steering column and he started the engine.

First Andy, then Jigsaw jumped in.

'Hang on,' said Andy. 'Where's Ed?'

Andy got out of the car, he cupped his hands around his mouth and he shouted in to the valley: 'Ed! ED!'

Pogget grew impatient. He sounded the horn.

Ed remained by the river. He was looking for his knife, which he had mislaid. A snapped off branch, jammed in the stream between some rocks, caught his eye. The torn and yellow-white scar on the mossy tree annoyed Ed almost as much as the loss of his knife.

Everyone has something inside them that makes them tick, that makes them forget themselves entirely.
　One minute Natasha was lost in her work, and the next. A car came sweeping around the corner, its roof catching the sun. The sun flashed suddenly in to existence, dazzling Natasha. She saw a car speed by that seemed out of control. The four occupants of the car saw a tall, slim, dark haired girl stood before an easel in the centre of a green field. Her face was dark and tanned and very beautiful.
　'Kop an eye full a tha,' said Pogget.
　'Keep your eye on the road. THE ROAD, POGGET!' shouted Jigsaw as the car mounted the verge, hit the Hillman, and then bounced back in to the road.
　Ed, Andy, Jigsaw and Pogget were pressed back in their seats as the road, which was steep, pointed them skyward. They crested the hill, and saw the sea stretched out before them. Which was when the car plummeted. It seemed to fall out of the sky in to the town below - grey roofs shining in the sun, streets, gable ends, a ruined castle, half a pier, churches, chapels, a cluttered harbour, pubs, a curving promenade, the university . . . the tumbled scree slope of a town lay spread out beneath them in an untidy heap. Ed felt his stomach churn. Aber. After all those years of travelling he was home.

Home: Concentric circles of familiar places radiating ever outward from a more familiar centre. House, street, town, country. Home. Your point of reference. Where you operate from. That draws you in. A place to come and to go from. To be contacted at. That you made: that made you. The place where you keep your things, like the things you made, the records of your achievements, your catalogue of memories: your letters, your photographs, the odd souvenir. Where you keep yourself. Homing in. Home coming. Welcome home. Home.
　It was the instant when one world ended and another began.
　Ed halted for a moment upon the back step. He took a deep breath, steeled himself then stepped inside.
　'You're back!' said Ed's mother.
　'Didn't I tell you that travelling would get him nowhere,' said Ed's gran.
　Even his father seemed pleased to see him. 'Welcome back,' he said and he

shook his hand.

Everyone began laughing and talking at the same time. They made a great fuss of Ed. His mother fed him biscuits and cups of tea, then she sat him down to a huge fry up. In came the neighbours, followed by Ed's friends. The kitchen was crowded. Beer appeared: bottles, cans. There was loud laughter. A neighbour sang a sea shanty. Ed's friends burst in to song. Ed opened up his pack, and one by one he showed off his souvenirs. He told stories of his travels.

'So tell me,' said Ed's father, 'Now that you're back, what exactly do you intend doing with yourself?'

Everyone fell quiet. They knew exactly what was coming.

'What do you mean, do with myself? I've only just got back.'

Ed's friends and neighbours began to creep off, taking the gaiety and the laughter and the singing with them.

'You don't know?' Ed's father threw his hands to the air.

'I've only just got back from going around the world.'

'It's time you started living in the real world.'

The real world. Everyone threatened you with the real world. But what was that? It was the world of work, and home ownership, the world that Ed's father inhabited. There was no place in it for any other world, that raw outside where there were other people, and other places, and other, different ways of knowing things.

Suddenly, to Ed, the world seemed somewhere from long ago.

Ed's mother went upstairs to prepare his room but when she came down there was just Ed's father and gran sat in the kitchen.

'Now where's he gone?' she asked.

Clemence sat upright on the wet ground and he reached behind him and he checked his head where he had bashed it on a rock when he had fallen. Next thing he was up on his feet searching frantically for his violin. He found it undamaged in some bushes. Retrieving it he cut himself on some briars.

It was dark in the woods by the stream. Clemence did not want to risk the climb back up to the road on the slippery rocks so he opted to follow the track beside the stream. After a short distance he emerged in to a clearing and there, silhouetted against the sky, was the dark outline of a house, a one storied cottage. Clemence hurried toward it only to discover that it was derelict.

Natasha surveyed the damage to her car. There was a huge dent in the bodywork that was scraped with white paint and the wing mirror was destroyed. The driver's door was so buckled that it proved difficult to open and when finally she did get it open it would not close properly.

Instead of going north, as she had planned, Natasha drove the car back in to town where she reported the incident at the police station. 'Yes,' she told the desk sergeant, 'that's right, a white Ford Escort with four youths driving it.' No, she didn't have the registration.

She then drove the car to the garage to have it repaired. The mechanic told her that the work would cost close to £100 and could take up to two weeks.

'We're going to have to replace that door and do some welding to the chassis,' he informed her.

Natasha had no choice but to remain in town. She took a room at The Castle, a public house not far from the sea-front. After dropping off her gear Natasha grabbed a sketchbook from her satchel and she went for a walk along the prom. Strolling by the sea, she soon forgot her troubles. A person could step out of that town any time they wanted.

After having dropped Ed off in town Andy, Jigsaw and Pogget drove to the beach, parking up on the promenade by the ruined castle. They got out of the car and inspected the damage to the wing. Then they crossed the promenade to the railings where they stood looking at the sea.

Sweeping hillsides ended suddenly in steep cliffs. The town, too, seemed to be a remnant of something: the tall sea-front buildings, appearing to mimic the cliffs in their relationship to the sea. The sea was flat calm and blue and full of light and it slid lazily up and down the shore. Everywhere seemed bathed in a clear and bluish light. Further down the coast they saw other, smaller towns.

'It's like the edge of the world,' said Andy.

'A different werld,' said Pogget.

'Fucken hope so,' said Andy.

Andy went in to town for chips, leaving Jigsaw and Pogget to collect driftwood for a fire. He came back twenty minutes later with three portions of chips and a carrier bag full of beer and a box of matches.

They ate their chips on the beach then they lit the fire. They sat around the fire drinking and looking out to sea.

'We need to sort out where we're going to stay tonight,' said Jigsaw.

'We've got the tent,' said Andy, 'we can camp here.'

Jigsaw objected. 'We can't put that up on the beach, it's all stones.'

'Am sleepin on the beach,' said Pogget, 'is not gonna rain, an it's free, innit.'

He began to burrow in to the stones, shaping them to his body. 'Is a'right, is like a bean bag,' he said.

Jigsaw found the stones hard and uncomfortable and the idea ridiculous. He suggested that since they were now flush with money they should get a room for the night in one of the sea-front hotels.

Ed climbed the path above the cliffs from where he sat looking out across the town and out to sea. There was a distant view of mountains on the horizon.

Ed had travelled as far as you could get, and he had kept on travelling, and it had led him home. It seemed to surprise Ed, that having travelled around the world he should end up right back where he had started.

Home, it happened to you every time, no matter where you went. It could even catch you unawares, as, slowly, a place closed in on you. Even the strangest places become familiar, they become home after a time. Ed had been a stranger in Wales too, once, he remembered. Home, either you came back to it or you made it elsewhere. You couldn't escape it.

The sun touched the sea and the sea flared. The sky turned gradually toward darkness. The air chilled. Andy, Jigsaw and Pogget edged a little closer to the fire. The glow illuminating their faces.

The stones beneath them became a little more uncomfortable.

'Let's go in to town,' said Andy and he lifted his can and finished off the last of his beer.

'We might ger off with sum birds,' said Pogget. 'Stay wi' them fer the night.'

The lure of the town was very strong. Music boomed out through the open doors of pubs. There was laughter and singing in the streets. The streets were crowded with people. A gang of girls in short skirts and high heels ran noisily out of one pub, crossed the street, and ran howling in to another pub. Andy, Jigsaw and Pogget followed after them.

The morning dawned bright and clear.

Clemence woke with a start. Something, an insect, was crawling across his face. Jumping to his feet he ran out of the cottage, brushing wood lice, centipedes, damp moss, flakes of wood and leaf mould from his clothes.

Birdsong. And huge oaks clutching mossy boulders in their roots. And bluebells everywhere. Primroses carpeting the riverbank. And bright sunlight winking at him through the trees, flashing off the swiftly flowing stream.

Clemence took a drink from the stream and then he washed the blood from the wound on his head and from his matted hair. Then he returned to the cottage. He checked the walls, and found them to be sound. He took out his pen knife, unclasped it and he poked it in to a beam. The knife folded shut on the iron like wood, catching his fingers. The great frames, the purlins and the rafters were all solid oak. Many of the roof slates were loose and there were holes in the roof where some were missing, but it would be no problem to replace them, he reckoned.

Ed woke. His eyebrows lifted on his forehead, then his eyes flashed open. He sat upright in bed, listening and alert, but he heard nothing. Just a distant rumble like the sea. He sat thinking for a time. A few seconds. He got quickly out of bed, crossed to the window and pulled back the curtains.
　Aber.
　Ed felt his spirits sink.
　Ed had been in paradise for a time: coral atolls, turquoise seas, swaying palms. . . and now he was not. He was right back where he had started. And it was like something had gone wrong.

Bright sunlight blazed off the water, waking Andy. He woke Jigsaw and Pogget. Pogget was in the sleeping bag. Andy was on the carry-mat, wrapped in the tent like it was a bivvy bag. Jigsaw lay on his back in a hollow on the hard stones.
　The three friends smelt of woodsmoke and beer. They had splitting hangovers, their bodies ached from the hard stones and they were cold and hungry, making them morose and irritable with each other.
　'Let's go,' said Andy.
　They had a piss at the foot of the promenade wall. Then, after gathering up their gear, they dragged themselves off the beach and on to the prom and traipsed back to where they had left the car.
　'Where's the car?' said Pogget.
　'I don't believe this,' said Andy. 'Some fucker's nicked our car.'

6

Terminus

And then there was the sea. Being by the sea made Aber special. It was not an empty sea. Blue headlands filled the horizon north and south. There was the occasional fishing boat. Schools of porpoise and dolphins. There is always something to look at on the sea, even when it is empty. There were days, summer evenings particularly, when the sea was so calm and full of light that everyone stopped what they were doing and went to look at it. Even those that lived in the town who saw the sea every day felt the need to make pilgrimages to it. People are attracted to edges.

It was a beautiful day in late June. The sun blazed. People took off their clothes and they lay on the beaches in the hot sun. The beach was crowded with people.
    A group of four girls stepped off the prom on to the beach and stood there for a time looking for the best site. They chose a place to sit not too far from where Jigsaw and Pogget were sitting. Jigsaw looked up from his newspaper. Pogget, who had been hammering a small stone against a bigger stone, stopped hammering and stared at the girls as they spread towels on to the shingle, stripped down to their bikinis and sat down. 'Waw! Cud do wit sum a tha,' he said.
    Jigsaw cast him a disapproving look before returning his attention to his newspaper, the Times. It was not long before he was eyeing the girls over it. An involuntary groan, full of pain, of longing, escaped from Jigsaw. He had to cough to disguise it.
    Andy came out of the sea. He pulled off his snorkelling gear, placing the

mask on top of his pile of clothes to protect the glass from the stones and picked up his towel - it had dried and stiffened in the sun and it felt abrasive and it smelt - and he roughed up his hair with it. Andy was tanned and he was muscular and when he towelled down his back his stomach muscles bulged. Work was making Andy strong.

'They're looking over at us,' said Jigsaw, lowering his paper.

One of the girls had glanced over, nudging the girls either side of her, but by the time Andy looked over the girls had turned away.

Andy studied the girls. The curve of their hips, the way the girls sat, the way they moved. They had perfect girl shapes. Long hair, long, lithe limbs, flat stomachs, narrow waists. He was looking for faults. Jigsaw had once told him that you could find fault with most girls, some small part of them that lets them down. If they are beautiful in every other way but one then that might eat away at their confidence, giving you your chance at them. But these girls were perfect.

'Luk at them. Luk at her,' said Pogget.

'I'm looking,' said Andy.

'Is Mee-shell Feefer,' said Pogget, staring.

'You've no chance there.' Andy sighed. 'That's Meredith Hughes.' She had once been pointed out to him in a pub. 'The last bloke she was with was a doctor up the hospital, had an house an a flash BMW an everything, but she still dumped him though, didn't she?'

'Well maybe she'd like a bit of rough fer a change,' said Pogget.

'What, you still got those warts on yer cock, av yeh?'

'There's this bloke in town's got a jade bead on his, had it purin there special. Thas juz like a wart, innit?' Pogget indicated on a bent finger exactly where the bead was.

Andy, Jigsaw and Pogget sat and they looked at those girls. They wanted those girls. They looked at them so hard that the girls no longer looked back. The girls sat and they moved in certain ways. They were thinking of those boys and how they looked to them. The boys were groaning at the unfairness of it all, thinking that they were never going to have those girls.

Pogget thrust a fist down in to his shorts, thumb uppermost, like a hitch hiker, and he leant backward to show off the result. 'Hey, girls!' he shouted, 'wanna cum over ear an vote. Am havin an election.' He began to laugh.

'Jesus, Pogget, desist, will yer,' said Andy.

The girls got up and moved further down the beach.

'Now look what you done.' Andy reached out and he slapped Pogget on the back of the head.

'We've got no chance with him around,' said Jigsaw, shaking his head in a show of disapproval. He turned to Andy. 'Are you voting then?' he asked.

It was election day, or something. The poll booths were open anyway. Some countries get turned upside down during an election. They go crazy. They think that everything will change for them.

'Voting? Me?, ' Andy grew angry. 'I wouldn't vote, not for any of them, I wouldn't, not to vote them in. But I'd vote to get them out. Politicians,' he spat, 'gobshites.'

'Politics, it's all lies and falsehoods,' said Jigsaw. 'All's it is is about getting elected, then, once they're in, it's just bullshit games between lawyers and moneymakers. Democracy is tyranny. Because for all those people who vote and who get what they want, there are all those others who vote and who get what they do not want, and they are forced to accept it. And democracy neuters their protests.'

'Did you hear the news?' Andy grinned, 'What that slag Thatcher said: 'I am not standing for another election.' Andy did her accent perfectly. 'I think we've had far too many as it is."

'You made that up,' said Jigsaw, disappointed, 'I was just about to break in to my champagne money.'

The day slowed. Bright sun shone off flat water. It grew hotter. The lazy sea slid up and down the shore. The three friends lay on their backs in the hot sun and they dozed.

It was soon four o'clock.

Andy climbed to his feet. He was on the night shift at the bakery. 12 hours, from 6pm to 6am. And it was a good hours walk out to the industrial estate.

'You know I could get youse two a job if you wanted.'

'You'd get us a job?' said Jigsaw. 'You'd do that, to us, to your best mates.'

'There's always jobs going at the bakery.'

'Well of course there are.'

It was hot, uncomfortable work and Andy often complained of it. His forearms were still criss-crossed with scars from the burns he had received when he had first started.

Andy's job was to stand at the end of a large track-oven and to knock the bread out of the tins as they emerged and then stack the tins and their lids in the racks that were waiting in line behind him. It was hard, fast work and its pace was dictated by the machine. The job required a certain kind of worker. It produced a certain kind of person too, eventually, if they could stick it. People left the bakery all the time, but those who remained and who stuck it out were like people everywhere who do heavy, difficult work. They may hate it, but it made them feel good to know that they had what it took. Not everyone did. Andy was good at the work, not least because he was glad to be working. For the first time in his life he was earning money, almost £100 a week.

'That job treats you like a machine,' said Jigsaw. 'You don't operate that machine, it operates you. That machine just works you harder. When are you going to realise that there are badly paid jobs and there are better paid jobs but there are no good jobs. No thank you, Andy. It is not for me, work.'

'Yeah,' said Pogget, 'Yeh can stick yer job, we don't need no fucken job, do we?'

Pogget always seemed to have money. Jigsaw was flush too, despite being on the dole, having somehow managed to acquire close to a thousand pounds. His champagne money, he called it.

'We're doing very well for ourselves, thank you,' said Jigsaw.

'We dough wan' no work,' said Pogget. 'Dough, gerrit, haha!'

'You could come in with us, you know,' offered Jigsaw.

Andy snorted. 'Oh, an' how long is that little scam o' yours goin' ter last, do yeh think? One year. It's a fucken con, business enterprise. Yer a fucken con artist you.'

Andy picked up his towel and his snorkelling gear and he left the beach, making his way back to his room at The Boars Head, a small pub and guest house on a back street running parallel with the promenade, and just visible though a gap in the buildings, where he got ready for work.

For a time, the dole had offered anyone that had wanted it the chance of hassle free unemployment. There were so many people unemployed that it had been easy to avoid the shite and the low paid work, any work, simply by holding out for what you wanted. For what you said you wanted. That had provided a breathing space and was a great springboard for all kinds of talent, allowing anyone who needed it the time which they required to concentrate on their passions. People could get on and do otherwise unlikely things. Now, though, it had become necessary to put everyone back to use. Remaining unemployed had become increasingly more difficult. The whole grabbing ethos of the era insisted on activity. There were insufficient alternatives, less ways to escape work and increasingly fewer places to escape to. There was every discouragement to be idle now. People were being pressured in to work, in to any work, low paid work, and there was plenty of it. The trick now was to find a use before use was made of you. But maybe the lucky, the clever, the street wise and the talented could escape their new use. Jigsaw certainly thought so.

*

It was eight o'clock in the evening and Jigsaw was seated in his chair, in the bay window of the large room that he shared with Andy and Pogget, looking out at the sea. The sun was lowering toward the horizon, filling the sea with yellow light, turning the sky golden. The sun shining off the buildings made them golden. Sunlight glowed warmly off Jigsaw's tanned skin. He felt strangely, almost lazily, content.

Pogget was lying on his bed, smoking, reading the *Sport* - looking at it anyway – and listening to David Bowie on his walkman whilst toying with a Swiss Army knife, the one that he had stolen from Ed. He pulled out the spike contraption, tested its point for sharpness, and began cleaning under his nails with it. He had the music on loud. The music sounded tinny to Jigsaw. Pogget began to sing, loudly, tonelessly.

As the sun continued its descent toward the sea a chill breeze began to blow in through the window. Jigsaw got up from his chair, closed the window and went to the bathroom to prepare himself.

There was a gig on at the Kings Hall where a local band was playing that he was interested in. He was hoping to convince them to let him be their manager.

Jigsaw knew that bands when they are starting out don't have managers, they don't have much of anything. All the band has is their music, and their idea of themselves, and a certain faith in that. But what they have most of is hope, and that hope makes them vulnerable. A good manager can offer a band everything. A new band will suffer knock backs all the time. But a good manager will keep them motivated. He will keep offering them everything, for a percentage.

Jigsaw had signed up for the Business Enterprise scheme, as a band manager. He had talked up a good business plan, he had everyone convinced. He even dressed the part. All he needed now was the band.

And if Jigsaw could convince them at Business Enterprise that he was going to manage successful bands then they also had to accept that Pogget could become a roadie and provide security for the band.

It was a con, and everyone was in on it. It was just another way that they had of massaging the unemployment figures.

Jigsaw dressed himself, with careful and solemn ceremony, completely in black: black jeans, black turtle necked sweater, black jacket, the sleeves rolled up his forearms, black socks, black shoes. He was growing his hair long. Smoothing it with his hands, he tried again to pull it behind his head in an attempt to make a pony tail, but it was not yet long enough. He combed it back instead. Lastly, he flipped on some reflective shades, but then he took them off again, hooking them in to the breast pocket of his jacket. His outfit now complete, he stood admiring himself in the mirror. Perfect. He really did look the part.

People had to be made to think that you were successful if you were going to become successful, reckoned Jigsaw. If you looked like what you were supposed to be then that made it easier for you. Believing that you were successful people would be fooled in to thinking that they would have a chance at it themselves. That way you could use them.

Some places are full of hopeful, talented and ambitious people, all wanting to go places but who have nowhere to go, who feel that they have been nowhere, much, and done nothing, yet. Places like that can be full of trapped energies looking for release. Sometimes that makes those places the place to be. Sometimes.

Loud music, flashing lights. The band were hopeless, too loud. But people seemed to be enjoying themselves. They were jumping up and down, pogoing to the music, drinking, smoking, eyeing each other up, falling down drunk, getting back up again, pairing off. Someone, yet another student out celebrating the end of term, sidled up to Jigsaw. He had to shout in to Jigsaw's ear, the music was so loud. The student slipped some notes to Jigsaw and Jigsaw slipped him something in return. They touched fists and then parted.

Students. They leave home to study and then they discover all those other things. Sex, drink, drugs, they were the real education. Everything else you can get from a book.

Hanging around the pubs, going to gigs and to parties in the hills in search of a band to manage, Jigsaw had come across the drug scene. Financed by Business Enterprise, through their generous expenses scheme, he had set himself up as a supplier. He travelled to Fishguard, Cardiff and Swansea to buy grass, resin and ecstasy, as much as he could afford, and then he sold it on at the gigs and parties he frequented.

It was late when he eventually returned home. Pogget was out, and would doubtless not be back until the early hours, and Andy was working at the bakery. Jigsaw bent down and reached under his bed, he lifted a square out of the carpet, that he had previously cut out with a Stanley knife, and he prised up the short length of loose floorboard that he had sawn out using a junior hacksaw blade. He slipped all his unsold product in to the hole, along with a roll of money, then he replaced the board and, over that, the carpet. When he went to bed he fell quickly asleep, smiling.

Ed woke with the light. He got out of bed, crossed to the window and pulled back the curtains.

He looked out across the rooftops on to a shimmering blue sea and cloudless sky. It was the same kind of day as yesterday, and the day before that. And the same town.

He had been home almost a month now and he had still not found work. He knew that he needed to do something, but he did not know what. He needed a job, because without a job to identify you, and without money, and the things it could buy, what were you really?

But what about experiences, wondered Ed, what about knowledge, what about ability? Yes, but memory faded, circumstances changed, knowledge became redundant, and ability too. But it was different with things. Things could be clung to. Things you could keep, cherish. Things were proof. They concealed a whole world of inadequacies. Things were achievements in themselves.

Ed, though, thought that he knew the nature of things much too well to be caught in their wanting. Wanting things would begin to take possession of him, harnessing him to their acquisition, trapping him in a job, a single place. Ed did not want to be trapped, he knew that much.

Ed lay on his stomach on the warm ground in the hot sun and he reached down in to the cold water and he felt beneath the bank where the bank was undercut and shaded and cool. Trout sought out such places in bright weather when the rivers ran clear and were low. They lay in the stream on the gravel in the dark and they mouthed the water and swayed gently in the stream on the amber current.

Ed moved his hand toward a fish, the fish lifted in the stream and swam slowly out of reach.

The closeness of the fish, the need to keep hidden, and to contain himself, created a tension in Ed. Sliding forward on his chest he worked his way along the bank, then he parted the dry grass and eased his hand back in to the water. The fish darted out from under the bank and shot upstream.

Ed cursed as he stood, brushing the grass from himself, and he blew out his breathe, filling his cheeks as something more than air emptied from him.
Ed retrieved his haversack and he put it on, then he picked up his rod and he resumed fishing. He was soon absorbed in fishing and in the river.

Fishing separated Ed from the world, it became a much different place, a much younger - an ancient, more vital and necessary place. For all its clamour, the world ceased to exist. There was just fishing, and the river, and Ed's increasing understanding of it. If Ed no longer believed in the world then he could still believe in fishing, and in the river. Something about the need to hunt, the urge to seek a thing and, in order to do so, to understand it and to do so fully, and then to conquer it, even if only to prove that understanding or simply to exercise it, explained the world to Ed. Ed felt deeply connected to something when he picked up his rod and began to stalk the river in search of fish, and it was not just to fishing. He was connecting with himself, perhaps, and with the river, certainly. The river emerges from a place so ancient that it can not be changed, and it remains as a connection to that place. There was something more than fish to be discovered in a river. Some part of Ed needed the symbol of the river and the meaning which the river gave to him just as much as he needed to fish the river. He could have bought that fish in a shop, but that was not fishing, it was not fishing's purpose. There was something more to fishing than catching fish. Ed could barely begin to explain it, least of all to himself, but he did not have to. Fishing was necessary to him. Besides, he had always fished, as far back as he could remember. There were things so primeval, that were embedded so deep in the psyche that even now they remained strong and alive in some people. Ed could believe in fishing, just as he believed in climbing mountains.

What Ed was after, what he wanted – it was a long time ambition of his – was to catch a 10lb wild brown trout. There were some people who told Ed that there was no such thing as a 10lb wild brown trout. How could there be, when the rivers had been ruined by pollution and exhausted through overfishing. But Ed knew that such fish must exist somewhere. They had to. There are certain quantities that stand out as benchmarks that, when you cross them, become achievements, they mark you out. Ed put all his aimlessness and wandering and hope and want in to catching such a fish.

Ed kept low as he walked and he walked slowly, he studied the water ahead, trying to spot fish, just as he studied the water itself, the flows and eddies that told him where the fish were most likely to be.

Ed saw no fish, the bright sun shining off the surface of the water made it impenetrable. Flashes of bright light exploded off the water, dazzling Ed. But under the trees the river flowed green and clear and shaded. Damselflies touched its surface here and there. Swallows scythed and dipped.

It was midday and the surrounding hay fields blazed yellow in the hot sun. Ed found a pebbly beach on a bend in the river that was overhung by a tree. He rested his rod against the tree, took off his pack and collected up some driftwood. After building up a small fire he filled his billycan with water and then he sat down with his back against the tree to wait for it to boil.

*

Natasha walked barefoot through the long grass, the hem of her yellow dress flicking left and right as she walked. Halfway across the field she began to get the distinct feeling she was being watched. She stopped, turning, and, shading her eyes, looked toward the river. The bright sky and the blaze of light reflecting off the water dazzled Natasha. She saw only the river and the silhouettes of trees.

Ed, looking at her through the long grass, had ducked quickly out of sight when she had stopped and turned in his direction. It had been instinct that had caused him to remain concealed and now it was guilt that kept him hidden. Ed feared that Natasha might think that he had been spying on her, and he did not want her to know that he had.

Ed had seen Natasha before, several times, but always at a distance, always when he was occupied in other things. He had first seen her the day that that they had crashed in to her car. Ed had wanted to stop but Pogget only laughed and Andy had to explain that the car was stolen. The next time Ed saw her, a few weeks later, she was driving the car through town, the damaged door now replaced with one of a different colour, making the car distinct. On another occasion, whilst out walking on the cliffs, he had seen her sketching on the beach far below, but by the time he had scrambled down she was already gone.

Hurriedly, Ed extinguished the remains of his fire, grabbed up his gear, his fishing rod and his bag, and hurried after her. He saw her disappear in to the trees where the valley narrowed, the river flowing through a gorge. He hurried towards the trees, where there was a long, deep pool with a rapids at its head. Passing the pool, he looked down in to the water, and was stopped dead by what he saw.

There was a huge dark shape suspended in the water. The fish moved sideways now and then, languidly picking off the food being brought to it on the current.

Ed crouched low and he retreated a few feet and he stared at the fish for a long time. His heart beat fast and his breathing had become shallow. Sweat dripped off his forehead in to his eyes and when he lifted his hands to wipe it off he noticed that they were shaking.

The sun beat down upon Ed. It grew hot in his hair.

Keeping low, Ed backed off in to the field and he made his way downstream some fifteen yards where, regaining the river, he slid down the undercut bank on to a thin strip of beach. Bent over, using the bank as cover, Ed moved carefully along the beach to within ten yards of the fish. He crouched down on his haunches. Bright sunlight glared off the water, obscuring the fish. Ed lifted himself up, slowly, cautiously raising his head and he brought the shadow of a tree forwards on the water until he could see the fish. Ed crept forward a little, as far as he dare, until he had a good view of the fish, then he knelt upon his knees on the hard round stones at the water's edge. He did not feel the hard stones and sharp gravel press in to his knees, so focused was he on his quarry. For a long time, Ed watched the movements of the fish. He might only get the one try at it and there were things that he needed to observe and to understand first.

Ed looked to the sun. The sun was to his right. Ed would need to cast his leader in front of and to the left of the fish so that the shadow of it would not fall across the fish, alarming the fish.

The water was swift and the fish was feeding midwater and in midstream. Ed removed the dry fly that he had been fishing and he tied on a smallish hare and copper - a fly tied with hare's fur and weighted with copper to make it sink. Ed forgot his nervousness; he no longer heard the river, nor the sound of birdsong. He was focused entirely on the river and on fishing.

Ed stripped some line off his reel and he dropped it on to the water, allowing it to drift downstream, until the stream had tugged it straight. When Ed had sufficient line out on the water he raised the rod and, with a flick, he lifted, almost peeled the line effortlessly off the water, then, as it lifted, he punched the rod forward and immediately changed the aim of the rod across the stream. The line curved, in a wide but tight description of the movement that Ed had made with the rod tip, before firing out in a tight arc across the river toward the opposite bank, the arc unfurling fast from its centre in to a straightening line. Ed was getting aloft the line he estimated he would need to reach the fish.

There was artistry in Ed's casting, a power and grace that sent the line curving silently through the air as though without effort. It was like he was drawing in the air a tight loop, which he then miraculously erased, and began to draw elsewhere.

The weighted nymph landed with a barely audible 'plip' on to the gliding surface of the stream. Behind it, the line descended weightlessly on the surface, and the river began to bring it back.

Ed retrieved the approaching line, pulling it in with his left hand at the same pace as that of the river, all the time keeping the line straight to maintain contact with the fly.

The fish hung in the stream, and then it lifted. It came up sideways, there was a flash as it turned. Gripping the line, Ed raised his rod.

Everything tightened, it went solid, as though Ed had hooked the river itself. It was the full weight of the fish hanging motionless in the water. Ed pulled on the fish.

The reel screamed as the fish ran, stripping line from the reel. Ed let it run, he lowered the rod, and he held it sideways and he applied a gentle pressure to the drum of the reel with the palm of his free hand in an attempt to slow the fish. The rod throbbed and the line sang as it began to stretch toward its breaking point.

It often happened when you were trying to turn a fish that the line would snap at some weak point or that the hook would pull free from the fishes mouth. The rod would straighten and the line would fall slack on to the water.

Ed let the fish run, but he applied a little pressure to the edge of the revolving drum of the reel with his free hand, and he also held the rod sideways and low to put more line in the water so that both the drag of the reel and the drag of the river against the line would help slow the fish. Ed increased the pressure on the reel as the fish slowed. The fish stopped a moment, then turned. Now it began to speed downstream, forcing Ed to lift the rod and to haul the line in with his free hand to keep contact with the fish as it sped toward him. The fish ran past Ed, in to the tail of the pool, in to the fast white water with its noise and sudden rocks.

Ed chased after the fish, holding his rod high so the line would not snag around a rock and snap the leader. He slipped and fell over boulders as the fish took him down-river to the next pool.

The pool was long and and deep and there in the slow and heavy water Ed stopped the fish.

The fish made two more powerful runs, both of which Ed was able to check. The second run was less powerful than the first and at the end of it, after trying for another run, which Ed checked, the fish hung motionless in the stream. Keeping the line tight, Ed began to walk backwards towards the bank up the wide shelving beach. It was a huge fish, Ed saw: a hen, of perhaps twelve or fourteen pounds. It came in fast, the water bulging up in front of it as Ed walked faster up the beach and led it in to the shallows.

The line became taught and hard and its springiness vanished. Ed felt the full weight of the fish and in that moment the rod straightened, the line shot toward Ed and fell limp on the water. It drifted away, straightening out downstream, the rod tip pulsing, moving to the pull of the fast stream.

There was the chuckle of water amongst rocks, birdsong.

Ed sat heavily down on the river bank, and there he remained, staring at the water, back to the moment when he had lost his fish. Ed felt empty and desolate and a little sick. Because one moment he had everything, and in the next, nothing.

*

Natasha thought that if she followed the stream it would lead her up out of the trees and on to the moorland, where there was a minor road. According to her map if she followed the road it would return her to her car after a round trip of some ten miles. Natasha was looking forward to the moor. She liked wind swept spaces and barren crags. She had sketched the river and now she was going to sketch the mountains.

She was following the track through the woods when she came out in to a clearing, in to the hot sun, where there was a small cottage.

At first sight she thought that the cottage must be derelict. There were no windows and no door, and there were slates missing from the roof along one verge, exposing the timbers there. Ferns and a small tree grew from the top of the chimney. Then she smelt wet cement and new wood. She heard hammering. It was followed by a curse.

A tall, awkward looking character, his fingers covered in blood-spotted plasters, and with a bandage around one wrist, holding a spiked roofing hammer in the crook of his crossed arms and nursing his thumb, emerged in to view from behind the cottage. He was a strange sight. His forearms protruded from his jumper and his trousers were short enough to suggest that he had bought them in a charity shop. He disappeared in to the cottage for a plaster.

Natasha followed him as far as the doorway from where she stood looking in to the cottage.

In the left hand alcove between the wall and the chimney breast, and set lengthwise along the back wall, she saw a camp bed. There was a filthy, yellowed pillow on the bed and an old sleeping bag. Beside the bed there was an upended breeze block on top of which there was an alarm clock and a burnt down candle, the candle welded by its own wax on to a jam jar lid. In both cavities of the breeze block there were tattered books, notebooks, it looked like. Buckets, a hammer, a saw, trowels, a crow bar, an axe, a pick and shovel, lay heaped up in the corner to the right of the door. There was an open bag of cement on the floor beside them, the cement granular in places, hard looking in others. There was a stack of yellowed newspapers beside the fireplace, along with an untidy pile of sticks, broken and badly hewn logs. She saw a box of food, cans mostly. Clemence was stood beside the fireplace, head bent, putting on a plaster.

Natasha stood studying Clemence with a steady and dawning realisation, the kind that puts a person on the verge of a laugh. All it needs is for something funny to be said.

A slate skittered down the roof before smashing to pieces behind the cottage. Clemence, glancing in the direction of the noise, saw Natasha standing there looking at him, jumped from surprise and accidentally tore off his plaster. He winced.

Natasha laughed. 'Sorry,' she said, managing to stifle her laugh. 'Are you actually staying here?' she asked him.

The place was miles from anywhere. There was no running water, save for the river, no electricity, not even a toilet. And the roof had holes in it.

'Yes. Who are you?'

'Blimey. Why? If you're not a builder, I mean? I thought you were a builder.' Natasha had at first thought that he was salvaging the slates off the roof to use elsewhere.

'I live here, is why, I'm doing up the place.'

'Really?' Natasha looked at the ruin in a new light. She looked at Clemence differently. It would be easy for him if he were a builder. And it didn't look like it was going to be easy for him at all. Natasha liked to see unusual, unremarkable people attempt unlikely things.

'Okay, so if you're not a builder then what are you?'

Clemence shrugged. Though he had faith in himself and in his plans he became nervous and unconvinced of them in the presence of others. Other people had more iron ways and certainties, making his appear insubstantial.

'Nothing, really.'

'Nothing?' Natasha frowned.

Clemence noted her disappointment. 'I mean, people would say I did nothing. They do. I busk, I play the fiddle and tin whistle. I'm hoping to be a writer. In a way, it's why I'm doing up this place.'

Natasha's mood changed. Her face lit with a broad smile. 'That's what I am. I paint. I'm a painter and a street artist, I do caricatures. I charge £5 a time.'

It was possible even now to free yourself from work. There were ways of making money that meant that you did not have to work. You began by spending less, then everything else followed. Some people can get by on very little. The idea that you might free yourself from work was far too compelling not to be attempted.

Time, that was the important thing. That, and having somewhere to do your own work. Then you had a chance.

Clemence had bought the cottage using the cheque that his father had given him. He thought that if he owned a place that was his and his alone to come and to go from then things would be easier for him.

Natasha understood. The cottage seemed different to her now.

'You are so lucky to have this place. I would love to have a place like this. I could paint such pictures here, it's so peaceful. There are no distractions. Me, I always get distracted.'

But the world could not do that to her here. Cut off, as this place was, a person's work could remain important to them. They could keep their idea of themselves intact. Working at their idea they then had a chance to perfect it and to make it real.

'This is where I'm going to write my great novel,' said Clemence.

'I could help,' said Natasha. 'With the house, I mean.'

Natasha loved to immerse herself in new things. There was always something else that she would rather be doing. Some new thing would come along and in to it she would pour all her energies, till the next new thing.

Natasha moved in with Clemence. At first, she slept in her tent, on the square of flat ground at the side of the cottage where there had once been a vegetable garden. Inevitably though, she moved in to the house.

Sex with Clemence was comical, as Natasha knew it would be. He was overeager and without practice. Their teeth knocked painfully when they tried to kiss. He got sudden cramp.

Work on the house progressed slowly. Clemence replaced the slates, but somehow the roof still leaked. Natasha sketched. She used that house as a base, she was always nipping off to places. But having her help him with the house wasn't her attraction to Clemence.

At night, Natasha liked to party. Clemence, tired from working on the house all day wanted only to sit in the window at the rough table that he had made for the purpose and work on his poetry. Clemence liked to compress language, to fill it with meaning.

Natasha, though, needed to be doing things.

'Why not get down your fiddle and play us a tune? I've got a bottle of wine. We could party.'

Clemence declined and returning to his poetry he read over what he had written:

'Sad as the cloud hangs,

'Heavy in the sky before rain. . . .'

He picked up the paper and he crumpled it to a ball and he threw the ball angrily at the fire. The ball missed. Natasha picked it up, she unscrewed the paper and read what was written there. After a glance at Clemence - who had watched her anxiously, hoping for encouragement from her - she too crumpled it in to a ball and threw it on the fire. It landed on the fire, on the hot coals, where it blackened, before bursting in to flame.

Clemence took another piece of paper and he bent over it. Then he sat upright in his chair. He sat staring at the blank page.

You had to have the feelings first. The knowledge. The experiences. It was afterwards that you looked for the words. He should have gone travelling, he thought. Instead, he was mired in work.

'You should forget poetry,' said Natasha. 'No one ever got rich being a poet. No matter how good they were. You should concentrate on your music, really, you're a brilliant musician.'

It was true, Clemence played the instrument beautifully, both as a fiddle and violin. When he played, the music moved Natasha. It often possessed her.

'You really could make it as a musician, you know.'

But it wasn't what Clemence wanted. 'It's other people's music that I play, not mine. I want to do my own work, not copy other people's.' His mood darkened. He grew angry with Natasha, with his writing that would not come, and with the house, which was using up his time and eating away his money, threatening him with work.

'You'll be sat here writing that stuff for years.' Natasha grinned. 'Then, one day, when you're least expecting it there'll be a knock on the door. And you know what?' said Natasha.

Clemence sensed the change of mood in Natasha and his mood changed too. 'What?' he said, interested. He willed her to go on.

'It'll be someone from some record company. He will have heard you busking on the street and will offer you a contract to sign. And do you know what you'll tell him?'

'Yes!'

'No. "Go away," You'll tell him. '"I'm trying to be a poet here!"' Natasha laughed and laughed. She was bored and a little drunk on the wine and she blamed Clemence for her boredom and that made her cruel.

'You don't like poetry, do you?' said Clemence.

'No. I don't. It's too - whiney,' she said.

'Whiney?'

'Miserable, morose. And all that wishy washy shit about the countryside.'

'And when was great poetry ever cheerful? Dylan Thomas wasn't cheerful, if anything he was melancholy. Sylvia Plath was far from cheerful. Charles Bukowski wasn't cheerful, he was disappointed, because the world was disappointing, he felt let down. Unrequited love. Loss. Angst. Disappointment. Anger. They are the wellsprings of great poetry, everyone knows that. Poetry is about feelings and ideas, Natasha. But if it was cheerful then it would be a fucking limerick. I should write limericks, is that it? There was a young poet, or not. Whose poetry was nothing but rot, he wrote ditty after ditty, every one of them shitty, so he put a gun to his head and fired the shot. No, I don't think so, Natasha.'

Natasha was laughing. Only when she saw that she had angered Clemence did she finally stop. They spent the rest of the evening in silence.

Silence envelopes everything, eventually. Silence signifies acceptance of some things, and boredom and irritation with others.

It was another beautiful day. The sounds of running water and of birdsong and the bright, warm sunlight distracted Natasha. It made her want to go out.

'I might be gone a few days,' she told Clemence.

'Good,' he said beneath his breath. Natasha felt relieved too.

Some people can be like furniture, they get in the way. But then, when they have gone, it is like something is missing. There is too much space of a sudden, the place looks and feels emptier. People do all sorts of things to fill that emptiness.

Clemence worked. He worked because for all their disagreements he missed Natasha. Also, he needed something to show for his day. Writing wasn't doing it for him.

It was a glorious day. The sun was hot, the air still, there was not so much as a breeze. It was a perfect day for the beach. The sea had been calm for several weeks and the water was crystal clear.

Andy lay on the surface of the water, borne up and down on the gentle lulling swell as he drifted along the coast. The town was a picture postcard from this distance. He drifted north with the current past Constitution Hill, out of sight of the town, until all there was were tall cliffs to look at. He was about to turn around and swim for shore when he saw something in the water. Somebody. A head.

Andy rolled off his back and slid underwater, pulling himself down in to the cold, green depths. Silence, like a pressure, pressed in around him.

Blurry at first, but growing more distinct as he drew close, he saw a naked girl treading water.

She was like a lap dancer in space.

Andy dived deeper and he looked up at her from beneath. He circled her like a shark, looking and looking. He swam under Natasha.

He surfaced beside her in to the bright day to the sound of seagulls and the faint sound of the swell pushing up the shore.

Natasha had noticed Andy circling her so she was not surprised.

They treaded water together, staring. Andy lifted his mask on to his forehead. The suction of the mask had marked his face, disfiguring his face. Even so, Natasha could see that he was good looking.

She splashed water in his face, laughing, then she turned and swam away. She emerged naked from the sea, running up the shore toward some rocks, where she turned and lay back on a huge, smooth, sun warmed boulder and she waited for Andy.

The weather turned foul for a short time. There were storms, high winds, torrential rain. Natasha did not go back to the cottage. Inspired by the violence and the power of such elemental forces, she wanted to paint the storm. She bought nylon cord and several tent pegs to tie down her easel against the fierce winds.

Storm tossed coasts, wind blasted mountains, trees grown in to twisted and wind blown shapes. It were as though a great wind blew across her pictures. Rolling waves, rolling inland as hills, cresting as mountains.

She painted 20 landscapes in half as many days. She painted fast. She thought that by painting at speed she could bring life to her pictures. She painted movement: restless seas, living growing hills, soaring mountains, tormented trees. The land, it was not a solid thing at all. Natasha was evolving a style of painting without name or school or code or precedent but which was entirely new.

When Natasha returned to the cottage, a week and a half later, Clemence noticed the change in her.

'You seem different,' he told her. She was like someone with good news. Or a new lover, he suspected.

Guilt washed over Natasha, the smile dropped from her face. 'Of course I am.' Natasha's heart, lumpy and thumping, smoothed and grew quiet. What did it matter who she slept with? It didn't matter. They were just lovers in a growing string of lovers who would become jumbled in her memory over time anyway.

'You've been away a whole week.'

'I've been painting,' she said. 'Come and see.' And she had Clemence follow her up the overgrown track to the car.

One by one, Natasha removed her finished pictures from the car. She lay them out on the ground in the turning space in the bright sun until they formed a circle around her.

'Well?'

Clemence stared at the paintings. He stared at Natasha, he stared back at the paintings. He walked slowly around the circle of pictures until he had seen them all.

'They're brilliant,' he said.

'I've had them accepted for an exhibition. At the Great Hall in Aber. Okay, so it's not London, not yet, but it's a beginning.'

Natasha gathered up her things, stuffing them one after the other in to her pack, then she stood at the door looking around the cottage making sure that she hadn't left anything.

Clemence couldn't understand why Natasha had to leave.

'Because, that's why. I need to be near the exhibition. There's a heap of things to do, everything to organise.'

'We should talk about this.'

'What's there to talk about?'

'But I thought. . . .'

'What? That we were. . . .' Natasha laughed.

She felt the anger swell inside her. How could she be with Clemence, with anyone, when this is what they were like? People think they have a right to other people. That can stop people doing things. Natasha didn't want to be held back, not by anyone. It was better to be with no one.

'I'll send you a card, Clemmy, let you know how I'm getting on. Maybe you can come and stay with me in London sometime, in the new penthouse I'll soon be getting.' She immediately regretted saying it. Okay, so she wouldn't send him a card, but saying it just seemed to make getting away easier. Yet Clemence stuck to her like a limpet. It made Natasha cruel.

'I've had a wonderful time, Clem, thank you.' Natasha leant forwards and she pecked Clemence on the cheek. 'Look after yourself, and good luck with finishing the house. Oh, and good luck with the poetry.'

The car was old. It had low compression and had trouble climbing hills. The car overheated and Natasha had to stop to let it cool. It was late afternoon, early evening by the time she got to Aberystwyth.

Natasha tried for her old room at the Castle. But all the rooms there had gone. It was the school holidays. The student accommodation had filled with holidaymakers. There'd be a room tomorrow though, she was assured. She could have it first thing in the morning, promised the landlord, meaning ten o'clock.

Natasha drove to the furthest end of town, beneath Consti, where she turned, parking in the first space she came to, opposite the Public Shelter.

The weather was balmy, she had her sleeping bag, and so she decided to sleep on the beach for the night.

Andy was working on the day shift. It was hot work in the bakery, especially in the summer, and it was a relief to get out in to the cool of the evening and to walk home along the river and to sometimes have a swim. It was good to walk off the constraints of work, the stiffness and the pain, and to enjoy the space and freedom and fresh air. It was good too to wash off the heat and dust and smell of work.

It was the shouts that attracted him, the loud, vile swearing.

The town's football team were out practising, at Blaendoli fields.

Andy did not know that it was the town football team. He asked could he have a game. He had no kit, and no boots, and so they told him No. Andy stood on the touchline and he watched the game.

One of the players went down, hard, and he did not get up. Limping, he had to be helped off the pitch.

No one passed to Andy, not at first. They were not used to him. They would rather pass the ball to someone they knew that could use the ball. For ten minutes Andy did not get one touch of the ball.

'Ter me, ter me,' he yelled as he ran in to space, this time toward the edge of the penalty area. He was completely unmarked. The ball came to him from behind, a little from his right. He was running when he intercepted it. He took a swing at the ball with his right foot and the goalie dived to his right to save the ball. But Andy only stepped over the ball. He kicked it, on his next step, with his left, hammering it in to the top right hand corner of the net.

It was an incredible but such an unlikely goal that not one of the other players could believe in it. They called it a fluke.

Andy's second goal was more convincing.

The move started with a high crossed ball. Twisting, Andy caught the ball, deadening it on his chest, dropping it at his feet. His left foot knocked it to his right, then he ran on past the first player, then past two other players. He passed to a player on his right and ran to the left and in to space, taking the quickly returned pass on the volley, scoring another goal.

Two nil.

Andy's third goal was not of the same standard, it was fumbled and scrappy, but it was still a goal.

He had just dribbled past two players and was running at the goal. The goal keeper was running out at him to narrow the angle and block the shot. Andy chipped the ball high over the goalies outstretched arms as he dived, hitting the crossbar. The ball rebounded off the crossbar, hit Andy on the head, knocking him flat, and rocketed in to the net.

He was not only good, he was lucky too.

The opposition marked Andy closely after that and he hardly got another touch of the ball, but he did not need to. He had only to run to one side and he would pull defenders with him to create space. Andy understood football. It was all about movement on the pitch to create opportunities.

The two teams formed a crowd around Andy after the match. The referee, who was also the team coach, approached Andy. 'You should play for us. He should play for us, shouldn't he boys?'

'Us?' asked Andy.

'Aber Town.'

Andy felt a smile rush up from the very centre of his being.

Ole! Ole ole ole!

The pub was crowded. Everyone was singing, everyone was drinking. Andy was singing at the top of his voice, 'As we came in to Aber town, John knaker nacker tour eye eh. . . .' It was an old Liverpool sea shanty but he had changed the words. Jigsaw joined in with the chorus.

Ed was there, with YoYo. Meredith Hughes was there. Pints were being passed over people's heads. A glass smashed, then another. The jukebox was booming out Phil Collins. Andy was singing his serenading song to the tune of the cornetto advert: 'Give me your body, for just one night, we'll love so fast it will make you blind, give you nausea, early morning sickness and pregnancy, but in between, I'll rupture your splee-ee-eeen!

Three goths came in, two women and one male, their faces deathly white and their hair dyed so black that it shone with a blue sheen. They looked miserable, as goths are meant to. They seemed completely out of place amid so much gaiety.

Andy said: 'There used to be four of them but one of them just died.' Everyone burst out laughing. Andy glanced over at Meredith Hughes. Meredith Hughes was very blonde and very beautiful and she was laughing. It was Guinness promotion night, and the barman was pouring out slow pints. Pouring them out, then letting them settle, then topping them up again. 'Two pints of Guinness!' yelled Andy. 'And something to drink while we're waiting.' Soon everyone was saying it. People were knocking back their pints, shouting and getting drunk. The jukebox was booming: 'A working class hero is something to be. . . .'

There was a girl sitting in Jigsaw's lap, a friend of Meredith Hughes, one of those from the beach. 'He's always been a bit of a joker,' Jigsaw was telling her. 'Haven't you, Andy?' He had to shout to be heard above the noise. 'I was just saying. About that play in school that time.'

'Oh, yeh,' Andy laughed.

'We were nine years old or something. It was some scene from the Bible, where Jesus goes around curing the sick. Well, Andy was supposed to be this crippled kid and Jesus comes up to him and he reaches out his hand and he says: "Child. . ..." At which Andy backs off an he says, Andy says. . . .' Jigsaw was laughing already.

'He says: "Don't touch me! I'm on sickness benefit." Well, half the audience were.'

Meredith Hughes threw back her head and she burst out laughing. She had a wonderful laugh. Someone passed Andy a pint.

Jigsaw broke off from kissing the girl on his lap and he said: 'It's time's like these that you really know that you're alive.'

Andy disagreed. 'No. It's times like these that you think that you've died and gone to heaven.'

The Bangles, *Walk like An Egyptian*, began blasting out. Ed and YoYo began to dance.

Jigsaw was celebrating too. He had been celebrating all night. A local band, The Rage, had been playing that night at the Angel, and there had been over one hundred people in the audience. 'One hundred,' he told Andy, for the umpteenth time. 'And every one of them feeding on the energy and the power of the music. They've got it, Andy, they have fucking got what it takes. And they're interested in having me as their manager.' He pointed his thumb at his chest. 'I'm a manager, me. Can you believe it? I'm the manager of a band.' Jigsaw nodded, and he kept on nodding. 'And they're good, Andy, they're going places. You should have seen it. People were pogoing in the air, pushing themselves off of each other. They were dancing off the walls, man. It was really happening. You had to be there. You had to be there.'

Andy was laughing. For no reason. For every reason. He was happy. Happy for Jigsaw, happy for himself. He had a job, money, he lived in a beautiful place, he played football for Aber, and now there was a girl sitting on his lap. And it was Meredith Hughes. Andy sat staring at Meredith. Her face had lost its smile, her eyes smouldered. She had dark brown eyes. Her eyes narrowed and grew fierce. She held Andy's face between her hands and then she pressed her face against his and she kissed him hungrily. The music changed. Hazel O'Connor, *Will You*, began blasting out of the jukebox.

'Come on!' yelled someone, 'Next pub.' Everyone poured out in to the street in to the loud night.

Open doorways poured their parties out on to the streets. Gradually the streets fell quiet. There were just the odd few drunks staggering home, or stood in a doorway urinating or searching themselves for keys. Pogget traipsed the darkened streets.

A policeman, strolling past, saw, or at least he thought he saw - it could have been a shadow - a black clad figure flit across a lawn. The policeman stopped walking and he studied the house.

Pogget gripped the rough edged stone of the wall with his fingertips and he stood on the very edges of the stones on the edges of the soles of his shoes and he worked quickly up the wall. He could have been a climber, the best, but he saw no point in it, just the top of some mountain and the long walk back. Pogget climbed up the wall until he was beneath the open window and then he lifted himself up and vaulted in. The room was warm, Pogget sniffed the air: sleepsmell. He could tell immediately that there was someone there.

The policeman waited. He thought it was a student who had forgotten his key, but when no lights came on in the house he grew increasingly suspicious. He considered ringing the doorbell. Instead, he went and he stood in the shadows of the bushes edging the lawn.

In a short while the same black clad figure reappeared at the window. Something, a weighted pillowcase, was dropped from the window to land in a bush. Then the figure climbed backwards out of the window, attached himself to the wall and began to climb down. He was halfway down the wall when he pushed himself off and dropped in to the flower-bed. The policeman stepped from the bushes and grabbed Pogget around the waist.

Pogget bent over, straining against the policeman's tight grip, but he was not trying to burst from it. The policeman was too strong. Instead, he bent over as far as he could before he brought back his head, slamming it hard in to the policeman's face. The policeman let go of Pogget and staggered backward, clutching at his face, the blood pouring from his burst nose. Pogget kicked him between the legs and the policeman doubled over, then Pogget kneed him in the face. The policeman straightened on buckled knees, then fell sideways, turning, so that he landed in the flower-bed on his back. Pogget snatched up the pillowcase and ran.

Meredith Hughes kissed Andy goodnight outside the Pier at the corner of Pier Street and the Promenade, promising to meet him the following night. Andy was going to take her to a restaurant. Jigsaw was going to take Ffion, her friend, to see The Rage, his new band, who were playing at the Tavern In The Town. Andy wanted to go home with Meredith, but Andy was very drunk, and so was Jigsaw, and Meredith and her friend were not so drunk. Jigsaw and Andy wove home under the promenade lights.

Bam! Bam! Bam! The loud, insistent hammering woke Andy. It woke Jigsaw. It grew louder and more frantic. Bam! Bam bam bam! Bam! The front door of the pub rattled in its frame. The hammering woke Howard, the landlord, in the bedroom upstairs. There were two thumps on the ceiling above as he got out of bed.

It was 3 o'clock in the morning.

Pogget was crouched beside his bed, emptying the contents of the pillowcase in to his holdall when the hammering started. He slid the holdall back beneath his bed, crossed to the window and pulled back the curtains. Bright light from the street-lamps illuminated the room.

Jigsaw, screwing his eyes against the light, said, 'Christ, Pogget, tell whoever it is to fuck off or we'll call the police.'

'Irriz the police, is a fucken raid.' Pogget ducked down under his bed and he pulled out his holdall.

A raid. Jigsaw leapt out of bed, suddenly very sober, pulling on his clothes then grabbing up his shoes. Andy jumped out of bed too, because it was the police, because Pogget and Jigsaw were panicking. He knew that Jigsaw had drugs. Drunk and confused, he began to get dressed. Jigsaw dived under his bed. He pulled up the carpet square, then the plank, retrieved the money first, then the drugs, but then he replaced the drugs before concealing the hiding place. He didn't want to be caught with drugs on him. He stuffed the rolls of money in to one pocket, grabbed the rest of his clothes, and his shoes, and bolted for the door. Andy was still looking for his shoes. He found them. There was no time to put them on.

'Cum ed,' yelled Pogget, 'Urryup.'

Bam bam!

'Alright, alright,' yelled Howard from upstairs, his heavy footsteps thumping across the ceiling above. 'I'm coming, I'm coming!'

Pogget, Jigsaw and Andy ran down the stairs, just as Howard was starting down them on the floor above. They ran past the two locked bars and in to the gents toilets where they opened the window and squeezed through, out in to the yard.

Andy pulled on his shoes, then they scrambled through the back gardens and out on to Queens Street where, crossing the road, and keeping to the wall, they ran toward town, veering right through the public shelter and out on to the prom.

Pogget smashed the side window of the first car they came to with his elbow, flipped the catch on the door, pulled it open and swung in to the driver's seat. He reached beneath the steering column and he started the engine. Then he flicked up the catch on the passenger door. Jigsaw pulled the door open, threw in his bag, pulled back the seat and threw himself in to the back, pulling the seat down for Andy. Andy jumped in after him and he slammed the door.

'Go!' Pogget, 'Go!' yelled Jigsaw.

Pogget put the car in to gear, did a U turn in the road, and then drove off slowly down the prom.

'Faster, Pogget, faster for Chrissakes,' screamed Jigsaw.

'Wha, an draw attention to ourselves?'

It was not until he was safely out of town that Pogget put his foot down. The headlamps picked out the road ahead, a white tunnel between the hedges and overhanging trees.

'Okay,' said Andy, 'That's it, stop the car.'

'Yeh wha?' said Pogget, and he pressed his foot on the accelerator.

'I said stop - the - fucken - car.' His voice was hard, vicious. There was real anger in his face and in his eyes. 'Am going back to Aber.'

'Andy, we can't,' said Jigsaw.

'Youse can't, no, but I can. I haven't done anything, have I? What have I done? Nothing,' said Andy. 'Except hang around with youse two fucken pricks. Am going back. Come on, for all we know the plod might've been trying to catch Howard having another fucken lock-in.'

'A don't think so,' said Pogget, and he told them what had happened to him earlier that night, how he had almost been arrested. 'There's no fucken way am goin back there,' he said. 'Fuckers know who I am now, don't thee? Beat the fucken shite owrra me thee will if thee catch me. *If* thee catch me, which thee won't.' He pressed his foot harder on the accelerator and dropped a gear to try and coax more speed out of the car. It began to slow on the hill so he dropped another gear and he pressed the pedal to the floor, but when he saw the temperature gauge begin to rise dangerously he eased up on the revs. He turned the heater on full, to drain heat from the engine. The cab began to fill with hot air.

'We'll be back in the Pewel in a few hours,' grinned Pogget. He glanced down at his holdall, jammed against the seat behind his legs. 'An A'll be able ter pay off me fines now, woan I, soon's A fence this lot.' Ignoring the rising temperature gauge he went up a gear and pressed his foot on the accelerator.

'Gud olidee though wannit, eh?' He began to laugh.

Liverpool. They were going back to Liverpool. Andy felt sick and angry and scared. There was no way he was going back to that, not now, not when he knew that it did not have to be like that, not anywhere.

'Jigsaw rested back in to his seat. The seat and the boot space behind him were full of gear. Searching through it, he found an artist's easel, and a large artist's portfolio, and a satchel full of sketchbooks, a backpack full of clothes, a stack of canvases hidden beneath a barbour jacket. He began to struggle in to the barbour jacket.

Andy gripped his seat, he tore at it with his clawed hands as he stared out of the window in to the darkness ahead, in to nothingness. He thought of Meredith Hughes. His job. Playing football for Aber. Aber. . . . He gritted his teeth and, letting go of the seat, he balled his hands in to fists. Turning, he punched Pogget in the head.

The car swerved. It crashed through a hedge, landed on its side in a field and rolled on to its roof.

Andy staggered through the hedge in to the road, followed by Jigsaw. Pogget was looking for the holdall containing his stash, which Andy had taken and then flung in to the darkness. He was still searching for the bag when a flame, erupting from the car, illuminated the field. Pogget turned, there was a blinding flash, a rush of loud noise, and then a wall of air hit him that knocked him flat. A yellow-black cloud of flame and smoke mushroomed in to the sky then disappeared.

Jigsaw turned. 'POGGET!' he shouted.

Andy carried on walking.

The numbness and the shock passed, leaving nothing in its place for a time. Natasha was devastated by her loss. There could be no exhibition now, not without her pictures.

A climber takes certain safeguards when they climb. They tie a rope about themselves before they climb and they place pitons in the rock face as they climb so that if they fall they will not fall much beyond the piton but will hang there suspended until they can regain their position on the rock face and continue with the climb. Natasha's sketchbooks had been like pitons. But she had lost her sketchbooks. And she had no photographs, no records whatsoever of her work. She felt that she had fallen in to a deep abyss, at the bottom of which she lay broken and with no means of escape.

There was no way that she could repaint those pictures from memory. Those pictures had built up in her over time, as had the creative energy needed to paint them, and painting had released that from her. She would need new energies, new feelings to build up in her before she could paint in that way again. She felt that she could no longer be that artist. It seemed easier to give up.

Clemence tried to forget Natasha, by immersing himself in work. The cottage roof still leaked, there was the pointing to be done, a long drop to dig . . . yet he couldn't settle to it, he was too depressed. He missed Natasha.
Natasha was gone, and it was like a limb that is suddenly amputated. The body knows that the limb has gone and yet it still feels that limb.

He was overwhelmed by an acute feeling of loss. An emptiness opened up in him. He felt sad, lonely, upset. All feelings which, as a poet, he began to exploit. He had been right about the wellsprings of poetry.

He wrote poem after poem, some thirty in all.

Clemence typed his works up. He sealed his MS in a jiffy-bag and he posted it to a publisher in London. He got on with the house.

Back his work came. He sent it out again. Back it came.

Since his return to Aberystwyth Ed had fallen back in to his old ways. He fished, climbed the mountains, went on pub crawls, got drunk, partied. He was now working as a builder's labourer, after a stint at painting and decorating. He was going out with YoYo again. But things weren't the same, somehow. No, they were exactly the same, and so there was not the same excitement to them anymore.

Ed woke up in bed, hungover after yet another night on the town. He rolled over and nudged YoYo.

Ed had moved in with YoYo. He had sort of drifted in. It seemed the natural thing to do after waking up there so often.

It was a small flat in a run down property on South Beach. A place of worn out furniture and second hand carpets. Damp-stained curtains hung limply in the windows.

They sat up in bed, looking out of the big bay window at the view: Blue sky, the transverse bar of the window, blue sea.

'What shall we do today, Ed?' Asked Yoyo.

Ed shrugged.

They were dull and hungover, much too hungover to do anything.

'Lets spend all day in bed,' Ed suggested.

In the evening they would go out and get drunk. They would end up at a party someplace and then they would come back here.

YoYo threw back the covers and lay looking at her stomach. There was the beginnings of a pot there. She pinched a handful of flesh from it. The sight made her depressed.

'I know,' she said, levering herself upright, 'let's climb a mountain.'

YoYo was fit and healthy and had good strong legs. But Ed had stronger legs than YoYo and a greater stride. He loved a good walk. Walking fast over difficult ground was like flying to Ed. It liberated him, somehow.

Ed stood waiting for YoYo, but whenever she caught up with him Ed took off again. She had to struggle to keep up. He could be infuriating sometimes. Even so, she still wanted to make a life with him.

'Ed, what's the longest we've ever been together for?'

Ed stopped and turned. 'About a mile,' he said, taking off again.

The ground grew steeper and Ed quickened his pace. He felt the mountain resist him and he responded to that. YoYo hurried after him.

'We've been seeing each other, on and off, for five years and two months now,' she said.

Turning, Ed frowned. Five years and two months. Jesus, how do they know these things?

'So?' said Ed.

'So,' said YoYo, who had now caught up with Ed. He was stood there waiting for her. 'We either split up or we drift apart, but we always get back together again, don't we?'

'I guess so, yes,' said Ed. It was why he called her YoYo.

'Five years, you sure?' he asked.

'And two months. What does that tell you about us?' She answered the question herself: 'We've got something, Ed.'

'Perseverance?' he said.

'We're a couple. Me and you.'

Ed shrugged. 'I guess,' he said.

YoYo linked arms with Ed, and, pressing herself close, rested her head on his shoulder.

YoYo was in the kitchen making dinner when Ed came in from work. Something was different.

'You've changed your hair?' he said. It had been long and black that morning when he had left for work. Now it was short and dyed peroxide blonde.

'I felt like a change.' Opening the oven door she took out two full plates and put them on the table 'It's ready. Grab some forks.'

Ed did as he was told. They sat facing each other. There was an uncorked bottle of white wine on the table and two empty glasses. YoYo poured out the wine.

'Pasta?' said Ed.

'In white sauce,' said YoYo.

'But where's the rest of it?' Ed picked up his fork and he began poking around in his pasta. He put down his fork. 'I need meat, YoYo. I've been out working hard all day.'

Ed looked tired. He had not showered yet and he was still dirty.

'You work too hard. You should get a proper job. I mean, I don't want to live with a scaffolder. I hate having to tell people that you're a scaffolder.' YoYo worked for a solicitor as a legal secretary.

'It's never bothered you before,' said Ed. 'You've liked me in all my previous transformations.'

'Things are different now.'

'Different?'

Women change. Men change too, they adapt. But women change. They change their hair, or they buy a new dress, and they're a different person of a sudden. Now there was all this talk of Ed improving himself.

The flat was different too. YoYo had been busy. There was a new white rug in front of the fire, and new white curtains in the windows, and some of the furniture had been moved around. The place looked different but it was still the same place, and that seemed to rankle YoYo. She took her annoyance out on Ed, like everything was his fault.

'I want better than this. But we'll never afford something better unless you begin bringing in more money, Ed.'

What YoYo really wanted was for them to buy a place together. There were some wonderful apartments proposed for the new harbour development. She had set her heart on one. The developers were clients of her firm so she had seen the plans.

After dinner, YoYo went and fetched the local newspaper and she spread it out in front of her on the table. She flicked quickly to the situations vacant page. She circled several positions that she thought might be suitable for Ed.

'There, what do you think of those?' Ed picked up the paper.

Social security officer. Tax office clerk, Apply Human Resources.

Human resources? What kind of vile, blood stained machinery lay in wait for people there? Ed wondered. Something to separate body from soul, no doubt.

'They're not my usual job, YoYo. I mean...'

YoYo cut him short. 'You need to raise your horizons,' she said. 'You're not stupid, you can do anything if you put your mind to it.'

'That one would suit you,' she said, and she leant forwards, reaching over the table, and pointed out the job to him. *Shoe shop trainee manager.*

Everything was a trap, thought Ed, or could be, everything sucked you in, and then in to something else again, until you were tangled up in everything. Drink was an escape, drugs too, for some, and women, for the pleasure they gave, even money was a trap because you had to have enough of it. Getting enough of it, there was the rub. They all trapped you in something.

The shop was on the main street. It was a big shop that was always having sales. It was very bright in that shop. It stank of plastic and rubber. Nothing was made of leather in there.

'Have you ever worked in a shop?' the manager asked Ed.

'Sure,' replied Ed. He had helped to renovate one once, as a plasterer's labourer.

'Great,' said the manager. 'And how's your maths?'

Ed began to look uncomfortable. Numbers had never been his strong point. Ed had a theory about numbers. They were called numbers because they turned people like him numb.

The manager decided to test Ed. 'Are you ready?'

Ed nodded. 'Give it to me,' he said. He meant the job.

'Right. A man comes in to the shop, he buys a pair of size eleven loafers and then a pair of size eleven and a half training shoes. The loafers are forty seven pounds fifty, the trainers are fifteen pounds. There's a sale on, with a twenty per cent discount on certain lines. The customer gives you a fifty pound note. How much change will you give him?'

Ed stared in horror at the man.

'Nothing,' he said. 'You can keep your fucking job.'

Outside, in the street, Ed began to feel better. The panic and the nausea passed. My God, he thought, but a career, a job for life. It was an unfair exchange. He had been that close: the apartment, YoYo - it promised to be an easy life. He had to get out of there. He could not live the rigid and punctual life.

Ed moved from place to place, working. He did odd jobs. He picked fruit, he laboured on building sites, he built walls. Chance and opportunity determined his steps. He made plans, and chased after them, only to abandon them in the heat of some new desire. Each new place brought a fresh start. He never once saw his destination written on a signpost. So long as he was never in the same place twice that, to him, was progress.

Ed bought himself a squeegee and a plastic bucket. He stood at the traffic lights in towns and he cleaned windscreens for 50p a time. It seemed the perfect trade to Ed. At the end of the day he had only to ask for a lift and he was on his way, and to who knows where, he didn't care.

Ed's feet hurt. It was a hot day and he had been walking for some time. He sat down to rest on the low garden wall of a large ivy clad house. *The Old Vicarage*, said the sign on the iron gate, *Private Property*. Ed sat in contemplation of the afternoon. The heat shimmered off the corn fields. Crows called out from the surrounding trees. There was the sound of hedge clippers coming from around the side of the house, which sound now ceased. Turning, Ed watched a squirrel cross the neatly tended lawn. There was a movement of energy through its body like a Mexican wave. A portly, silver haired man appeared from the side of the house and he hailed Ed:

'I say! You there!' he shouted. He was red in the face and he carried shears. He wore brown corduroy trousers and a white checked shirt with a mustard tie. The man's wife was stood in the window, her arms folded, staring at Ed, looking indignant. When she saw Ed looking at her she unfolded her arms and placed them on her hips. A chaffinch, that had been hopping about Ed's feet, flew noisily away as the man approached.

'What are you doing here? he asked crossly.

'Good question,' said Ed, 'Why are any of us here?'

Everything changes. Lives created with difficulty disintegrate with ease. Lovers quarrel. Couples who had based their lives around each other find others in whom they are more interested. People you depend on suddenly disappear and you do not know why nor where they have gone. Communities lose their function and people scatter about the country in search of work. Everywhere, things fall apart and nothing is certain anymore. Everything that was once sure and predictable becomes either insubstantial or a threat.

7

The Dog's Bollocks

Jigsaw was in The Pig And Truffle, a wine bar in the City. He ordered a magnum of Champagne, paid the barman with a twenty then waved away the change. He looked the dog's bollocks, stood there, drinking champagne, dressed completely in black - black jacket, black turtle neck sweater, black jeans, a pair of black bespoke city-slippers, lace ups, hand made from calfskin by the Original Shoe Company, Pall Mall, on his feet – and with his long hair tied back in a pony tail.

Two girls came over and they positioned themselves either side of him. They were good looking, well-stacked girls. They wore high heeled calf length boots, short dresses and frilly tops and they showed plenty of cleavage. One was tall and blonde, the other slight and dark.

Jigsaw beamed. 'Ladies,' he said, and, raising his arm, he clicked his fingers: 'Barman!' he shouted, 'Two more glasses for my friends here.' The barman passed him the two glasses. Jigsaw filled them to their brims and offered them to the girls.

'What are we celebrating?' asked the blonde, taking her glass.

With a roll of his hands, that left them palms uppermost, Jigsaw presented himself.

'You're drunk,' said the dark skinned girl.

'To being drunk then,' said Jigsaw, 'on champagne.' Laughing, he raised his glass to the air, spilling a little drink. The girls raised their glasses. All three clinked their glasses together. The girls, downing their drinks in one, held them out for more.

Jigsaw took the bottle, together with its ice bucket, to a table at the window.

The girls followed. They sat either side of him, showing plenty of leg. Jigsaw recharged their glasses. The girls sat closer to him, touching.

Cigar smoke, laughter, the pop of champagne corks, Pink Floyd's *Money* playing through the speakers. And blue-grey, scented smoke, hanging in layers, billowing on the thick, wine fumed, drink saturated, sound filled air of the busy wine bar.

Everyone experiences moments of great joy now and then. Whether it is from personal success, a windfall, good news, drink, drugs, sex, good company, or just a short turn at brief money. Or perhaps all of those things. Right now, Jigsaw was having his.

'When I first came to London,' he was telling the girls, 'I had nothing, nothing. I lived in a doorway for a time. They wouldn't let me in to the shop. Ha! Haha!' He seemed to think it was funny.

'Drink up! Drink up!' he roared, toasting first himself and then the girls and then life in general.

The girls indulged Jigsaw. They even began to like him a little. They leant over and they kissed Jigsaw, each pecking him on the cheek. They helped themselves to champagne. 'Champagne! More champagne!' he shouted.

Jigsaw lit a cigar, his mouth working at it like he was performing fellatio. There was a loud POP! from the bar and a moment later the new bottle arrived, still ejaculating champagne, the pulsing foam avalanching down its sides. Jigsaw slipped the barman a crisp twenty and the barman vanished it. Jigsaw lifted the magnum of Champagne and he recharged everyone's glasses. When he replaced the bottle in the bucket it made a lovely sound of crushed ice.

'So,' he said, relaxing in to his drink, 'what do you lovely ladies do?'

They were dancers and they worked at Girls A Go Go, they told him. 'It's a pole dancing and strip joint,' said the blonde, her accent East European.

'With private cubicles,' said the dark girl, she sounded estuary, she was from the east end.

The girls reached down in to their handbags. They presented Jigsaw with their cards. Semena's, the blonde's, said Dominatrix and showed her dressed in a red and black basque, black stockings and high heels. She held a whip in one hand, handcuffs in the other. Ra's showed her naked, her back to the camera, staring over her shoulder wearing a jewelled face veil. *Egyptian Temptress*, it said. There were phone numbers on the cards.

Jigsaw took out his wallet, opened it - there were two twenties and a crisp fifty in there - placed the cards in his wallet and returned his wallet to his jacket. The girls watched that wallet all the way back to its resting place.

Jigsaw beamed at the girls, his eyes greedy for them. They had long legs.

They had wonderful legs. Their skirts were short, just narrow black strips, like strokes of a censors pen. Their breasts bulged out of their low cut tops. Dressed as they were their every movement was provocative. They taunted Jigsaw with their closeness. Straightening their backs, pulling back their shoulders to push themselves out whilst rolling on their buttocks as they sat and moved around those two essential goals of his like they were points of gravity and balance.

'You've got wonderful legs,' Jigsaw told them, admiring their legs, and, starting at the knee, he began walking his fingers up their legs. 'Real dancers legs,' he said. Then, gripping their legs, he slid his hands up the hot, damp, clammy insides of their smooth thighs.

Laughing, leaping back, eyes wide, mouths open, lifting in their seat, the girls grabbed a hand each and they pushed Jigsaw away.

Semena wagged a long finger at him. She pushed her beautiful, northern, high cheek-boned, long blonde face in to his much darker, soft face. 'No, we do business proper, later, okay?' she said huskily.

'We can do business now,' said Jigsaw, 'I'm a business man.' And he made a laughing lunge for Semena, and then for Ra. The girls twisted up out of their seats to get away from him, sliding back in to them a little less comfortable, a little further away; shifting, rearranging their clothes.

'Go on,' said Jigsaw, 'let me put us all in heaven for a time. We have to be nice to each other, it's the only way. Life would be too cruel otherwise.'

'Is there a problem here?'

It was one of the doormen. He was tall and heavily built and he was stood over the table looking questioningly at Jigsaw.

'No,' said Jigsaw.

The doorman looked at the girls. 'Ladies?'

'No,' said the girls. 'We were just leaving.'

They stood, knocking back their drinks, and, after thanking Jigsaw for them, they hurried from the bar.

Jigsaw blew air from his cheeks. He lifted the champagne bottle out of the ice bucket and he recharged his glass. The empty bottle banged on the table when he put it down. There was something final about it.

Jigsaw sat, glass in one hand, sloshing champagne, his cigar smoking in the other. He was smiling, laughing. He felt no sense of defeat, no sense of it at all.

He stood and he finished the champagne. Then he was across the bar and with an eagerness born of anticipation he pulled open the door on to the cold, hard city and plunged in to it without a second thought. He had a new band to go and see.

Several evenings later, after the necessary phone call, he took a taxi to Ra's place, a flat on the third floor of a four storey building in Hoxton.
'Okay,' Ra agreed, when Jigsaw showed her the money. She ushered him inside. Reaching behind herself, she began to take off her dress.
She stood invitingly before him in long black boots, thong, and suspender belt and stockings, but no bra. She had a slim, hard body. She hooked her thumbs in to her thong and she pushed the thong off.
She was smooth as a peach down there.
'Keep the boots on,' said Jigsaw, when she bent to unzip them. 'No, don't get up.'
Live music, Jazz, began blasting out from the flat upstairs.
The music distracted Jigsaw. A trumpet and sax. Whoever was playing was very good.
'Hey,' said Ra over her shoulder, 'we going to do this or what?'

Andy unlocked the alsatian from its pen, put it on its chain, and began his hourly circuit of the perimeter fence, flashing his torch along the tall steel fence that was topped with razor wire, before running it along its base to check for signs of entry. Thieves were always attempting to cut cut through the fence or scale the wire. They were after the copper and lead. It was locked in steel shipping containers, but they came after it anyway. Andy raked the beam across pyramids and towers of rusting scrap, sweeping it over redundant machinery, metal girders, beams, rusted cars, all waiting for the crusher. Broken glass, from numberless car windscreens, crunched underfoot as he walked the hard packed, oil sodden ground.
A cold east wind blew across the scrap yard from off the river across emptiness and dereliction, bringing with it river smells. The smell of sea-mud, methane, oil, petroleum, chemical smells, the smell of worked metal, of burning rubber and wood all mixed. The strength of its components varying, always the same. There was the sound of loudly throbbing ship engines from the river.
Somewhere, in all that din, Andy heard the smaller sound of dropped metal. Pricking its ears the dog stiffened. It barked, pointing itself, straining against its leash. Andy unleashed it.
There were three of them and they were climbing the fence. The dog leapt at them, it crashed against the fence, bouncing back off it and landing on its side on the wet ground. It writhed upright and leapt at the fence again, snarling,

barking in frustration. The hoodies were already over it, having draped a wrapped-up coat on the razor wire, and were dropping to the ground on the other side. They ran off laughing in to the dark.

Andy put the dog back on its leash and continued on his circuit.

Finishing the circuit he set the dog loose and returned to the caravan.

It was old, decrepit, and was streaked with dirt, spotted with mold and covered in graffiti. There was the odd botched repair.

Inside stank of unwashed clothes, stale tobacco and beer, curdling milk. It shook when Andy moved about in it, like a small boat on the water would.

Andy hated it, he had to keep himself small in there.

Andy took a mug from the pile of dirty mugs heaped in the sink. He tossed out the cold and curdled tea and he rinsed the cup. He opened a cupboard door, leaning back, first to avoid the door and then from the strong smell of must and mice that had concentrated there. Andy removed the box of tea bags, revealing a small and startled mouse sitting upright on its back legs, looking at Andy. Andy punched the mouse, dead, flattening it. He picked it up by the tail, opened the door and flung it out on to the mice pile.

He put on the gas and he filled the kettle and he put it on to boil. It soon heated up the caravan. Andy opened the door.

He returned to the cupboard and fetched down a box of muesli. Then he rinsed out a bowl and spoon and he put them on the table.

There was a high pitched whistling and the caravan rapidly began to fill with steam. Andy switched off the gas. He made his tea and he sat at the small table with it, banging his knees and spilling a little of his tea.

Andy poured some muesli in to the bowl. There was no milk. The milk in the bottle had separated. He turned the dry muesli over with his spoon, over and over, stopping to watch as one of the raisins struggled to the surface before taking flight. The bluebottle buzzed and bumped around the caravan.

Andy poured the muesli back in to the box and he returned the box to the cupboard and he closed the door. Then he hunted that fly and he killed it, smashing it against a window with a rolled up magazine, smearing the glass with its insides.

Andy dropped back behind the table and he sat there, staring in to space, in to nothingness, drinking his bitter, milk-less tea.

A car pulled up, its engine stalling. Its door slammed, then slammed again. There were footsteps on the broken glass outside. The caravan door was yanked open and in stepped Jigsaw, bringing with him a smell of aftershave and deodorant.

Jigsaw removed a cashmere overcoat from off his shoulders. He wore it like a cloak. Off it came, along with a cup from the table.

'An were the fuck were you last night?' asked Andy.

'Well, out. Obviously,' said Jigsaw.

'Yeh, out. Out all night. Out with that fucken slapper again, weren't yer? When yew were supposed to be here, working, with me.'

'No one noticed I was gone, did they?'

'Is not the fucken point.'

'One nil to the workers,' smiled Jigsaw.

'What d yer mean, workers? The worker,' said Andy, 'Me. You, your not a worker. You don't do any work.'

'I'm an entrepreneur. I procured those paintings, didn't I, remember?'

'You fucken stole them.'

'And it was me that found a buyer. £100 a picture. £500, not bad for a day's work.'

'It's all you've ever done.'

Andy kicked off his sleeping bag. He stood, hitting his head on the ceiling and his arse off the wall. Andy balled his fist. Jigsaw ducked just in time. Andy punched the wall, after first banging his elbow on the backswing. He kicked the wall.

It was two o'clock on a Friday afternoon and Andy and Jigsaw were propped up in bed in their sleeping bags. Crushed and empty beer cans, empty wine bottles, polystyrene trays, pizza boxes, chip wrappers, unwashed cups and plates lay scattered around them.

There was a loud clang from the yard as the crane grabbed up yet another car and fed it to the crusher. The noise was continuous: Metal grated on metal, banging on metal, metal clanging. . . .

Jigsaw said, 'A nice Mercedes came in yesterday. I think I'll swap the Rover for it. A Merc's got more kudos. Appearances are everything in this game.'

'We need to get out of here,' said Andy.

Jigsaw sat peering out through the grimy, fly smeared window at the car stacks.

'Some of these cars, I reckon you could sell them, you know, as cars, I mean. I could start a dealership. Resurrection Motors. What do you think?'

'Jesus, Jigsaw, don't you ever let up?'

Jigsaw sat staring out of the window. 'If we had an angle grinder,' he said, 'we could get in to those containers.'

'Fucksakes, Jigsaw. We haven't got an angle grinder. Besides, we'd need a van to shift the stuff.'

'We could get a van, easy. There's one, two cars under the Merc.'

'Forget it!'

Jigsaw rubbed his chin. 'I wonder what happens to all the petrol in those cars. That must be worth something.'

There were all sort of scams going that you could get involved in.

Andy picked the previous days newspaper up off the floor and he opened it on the jobs page.

'You won't find the solution in there, not on the slave pages. You think if you could make real money they'd be advertising it in there? They'd be doing it themselves. Besides, this is a cushy number, this. We've got a place to live, they're actually paying us to live here. And I'll get another band, soon. This city is full of bands. There's loads of people trying to make it here. I saw a great band last night. The Bizz. I'm in negotiations.'

'Oh yeh? Told yer to fuck off, did thee?'

'They'll come round. I'll get us a band, you'll see.' Another idea occurred to him. 'I should set up an art gallery. All we'd need are premises. There's loads of derelict properties and plenty of artists out there we could promote.'

Jigsaw could keep this up all day. He was full of ideas, full of optimism. He was certain that somewhere in this new Britain there was a place for him. Andy, on the other hand, felt that under the Thatcherite scheme of things they'd already been allocated their place.

Andy reached for his cigarettes. He lit up. 'Sling us a beer, will yer,' he told Jigsaw.

'We drank all the beer,' said Jigsaw. Picking a beer can off the table he gave it a shake. Nothing. He upturned it to show that it was empty, then he crushed it noisily.

Andy tried several of the cans himself, but there were no dregs, just cigarette butts. 'Jesus,' he said, 'no beer.'

5 o'clock and the noise of the yard ceased abruptly. Time passed. It began to grow dark outside. Time for Andy and Jigsaw to start work.

'Let's go out on the town,' said Jigsaw. 'This place is getting me down.'

But Andy did not want to go out. 'I hate going out. We go out and then we come back here.'

'We can let out the dog. The dog can look after the place.'

The car would not start and so they caught the bus. They had a few beers in a pub then they moved on to The Comedy Club. They needed a good laugh, and they could always heckle the performers, reckoned Jigsaw. He thought that Andy would be good at that.

Andy and Jigsaw left the Comedy Club sometime during the fourth act and they returned to the pub.

'Christ, what a waste a fucken money that was. I could have done better than that.'

Jigsaw agreed. 'Yes, Andy, you could.'

If they did not like you, and sometimes they were determined not to like you, if they thought it would be more fun, then they heckled you. Things could turn ugly then. They hurled abuse at you, they threw glasses. Either that encouraged you to perform better or it terrified you.

'What the hell happened to you out there?' asked Jigsaw, 'You froze. It was an absolute disaster.'

Andy was still shaking, he was ashen faced. It had been open mic. night at the Comedy Club and he had just come off stage after attempting to perform a five minute monologue on unemployment. He'd had it all prepared: *I see no ships . . . Thousands of jobs in Jeopardy. . . . What do you call enquiries these days . . . I'm not standing for another election. . . .* He had spent all week working on the material, but on the night, on stage, his nerve had failed him and his mind had gone blank.

'I see no ships,' he had said, but what kind of ships he could not remember. He did not even shield his eyes with his hand as though he were looking for ships. He stood, terrified, looking out at the disappointed, increasingly hostile and gleefully vindictive audience until he was booed off stage under a hail of plastic glasses.

'I didn't think it would be like that,' he said. He held out his hand, it was still shaking. 'I wasn't prepared for that.'

'Yes you were, I said: 'Get ready, Andy, you're on.'' Jigsaw laughed.

Andy looked like he would be sick. He felt sick. 'It was terrifying,' he said.

'It was just stage fright, that's all,' said Jigsaw. 'Everyone suffers it. You'll get over it, in time.'

'I am over it. It's work for me from now on.'

'You can't be serious.'

'Well I am not being funny, Jigsaw. No way. I am not going through that again, you can forget it.'

'So you'd rather be getting up for work every morning for five days a week, forty eight weeks of the year, every year for forty more years, would you? And for what? Nothing, that's what. Fuck all. Because work isn't going to do it for us. We're here because of work.'

8

Bolt for Home

Success was the 4,000 sq foot warehouse conversion with river views, it was designer clothes, it was shopping. These were the visible signs that you were living the life. Money was proof. All the sacrifice, all the trying, all that time spent, exchanged, you had to know it was worthwhile.

Natasha was living in a penthouse suite in an exclusive development in Docklands, she was working in advertising and earning £50,000 a year.

'No!'

The falling nightmare is what wakes most people. But giving up on yourself, turning your back on the life which you could otherwise have led, and becoming forgotten, and everything about you forgotten, that was terrifying. You wake, but you can't shake the fear that everything you do is pointless, that you will end up irrelevant.

With a sharp intake of breath, her heart pounding, Natasha wrenched herself from sleep. She sat upright in bed, hating herself for having given up. She shot out a hand and switched on the lamp.

A single wardrobe, a dresser and chair. A sink with a mirror above it. Damp-stained curtains. A pair of scuffed army boots. A midden heap of clothes on the floor and, beside them, an empty haversack. A collapsible easel resting against one wall. A black duffel coat and, beneath it, a leather satchel bag full of new sketchbooks hanging from a hook on the misshapen door, the doorframe twisted out of alignment due to subsidence. A low, bowed ceiling, with its paint peeling, the plaster cracked. The tiny bedsit room pressed in on Natasha.

Relieved, she dropped back on to the pillow and began to laugh, mocking herself for her relief.

Ed woke with a nasty beer and spirit and white wine and red wine hangover. It was the worst kind of hangover, the party hangover. He had been at a party in Aberdovey the night before and he had left with a girl and they had gone off in to the sand dunes together.

He lay there in the dunes, alone, on the damp sand, in the cold and wind, wanting only to sleep. The drunk sleep was not a restful sleep. Ed was still tired from his previous sleepless night of two nights before when he had sought shelter in a concrete drainage pipe, one of a stack of such pipes that he had found on the site of a large construction project. It had been a wet and windy night and the wind had whistled past those pipes making an orchestra of them.

His full bladder made him increasingly uncomfortable. The cold cut in to Ed, making him shiver. He was cold and hungry and hungover, and felt a little sick. The first thing that Ed did after relieving himself was to check his pockets. So long as the money lasted then he would last. He had almost ten pounds. £10 was not enough. Just two more days and then Ed would have to go and earn more money.

One of the great snags about the easy life was that it wasn't easy. It was no small feat being able to guarantee freedom from employment whilst at the same time maintain sufficient funds to purchase that which distinguishes leisure, that most easily borne of free times, from its more mundane manifestations, loitering and idleness. It required real knowledge, a sense of dedication, luck and skill in equal amounts, a momentum, almost, that could be readily and inexplicably lost, forever, and at any moment, because sometimes it was easier to be in work.

Shouldering his pack Ed left the dunes, sliding down their steeply worn face on to the beach.

High winds blew in from the west and there was a heavy surf running that thundered ashore in explosions of white water. The air was hazy with salt mist.

Ed looked north. There was a distant view of mountains on the horizon. He stared south across the estuary, past the straggled-out town of Borth, beyond the cliffs, toward Aberystwyth. He could just make out the seafront. He thought of YoYo, and the flat on South beach. It was a tempting prospect.

Though it is an illusion that causes two parallel lines to appear to converge over distance the road ahead did seem to be narrowing for Ed. There were fewer opportunities, he had less enthusiasms. Things had begun to lose their appeal to Ed.

He stood on the beach, the wind buffeting him, unsure of where to go, of what to do next. He tossed a coin.

Heads.

Aber.

His legs felt tired and very heavy. He felt that he was not walking so much as pulling the beach toward him with his feet, the beach and the distant town and the far off mountains. Ed was tired, tired of travelling, tired of the road. It would be autumn soon and he needed somewhere to winter over. He had gone to that party hoping to find someone with whom he could shack up. Because every day was a struggle when you had no place to rest. What Ed needed was somewhere where he could go to recover his energies. And, ironically, he needed to work, work built the energy up in him.

The dark days, the hungover days, the lonely days, the wet days, the winter; all those days wasted whilst harnessed to a job, when he was locked in to some other life - in to what felt like someone else's life, like being stuck in the wrong body: these were the bad times, the times when Ed questioned himself, when he questioned everything. He would not be free otherwise. Every day that he was restrained the resentment would build in him, as would the need to escape, until he could resist it no longer. In a way, Ed needed to be constrained and his freedom threatened, just as much as he needed space. Because there was no escape, ultimately. Escape was the goal, not a stopping place. Without purpose escape brought ennui, it brought boredom and suffocation. It could mean inertia. Escape was merely the moment you found release. What you relied on was its momentum. That was the useful thing. You left one thing or place for some other thing or place.

Either you ran from something, and you kept on running, or you worked toward something.

Natasha carried her equipment through the dunes and on to the beach. She drove several tent pegs in to the hard, wet sand and unfolding her easel she stood it upright on the sand then guyed it down. The fine cord sang in the fierce wind.

The surf was high and white and very loud. Huge waves exploded ashore with all the noise of their great weight. The air was full of salt-mist. The conditions were perfect.

Natasha clamped her canvas to the frame. The wind caught it, bowing it, like a sail, but the guy ropes held. She pulled a small canvas bag out of her pack, from which she removed several tubes of paint. After squeezing the paint that she needed on to her palette she chose a brush and started work. She began painting the mountainous backdrop to the surf, trying to transfer all the movement and violence of the sea on to the canvas.

The wind blew hard. It blew sand, snake-like, along the beach. It tugged at Natasha's clothes. It blew her hair out behind her and up in to the air before lashing it across her face. It pushed and pulled on the easel.

There was a desperation to Natasha's painting, she painted fast. She plied the paint on thick, each brush stroke bold and deliberate, but her picture was wrong, and it soon became apparent to her. Snatching up her palette knife she began scraping the paint off the canvas, flicking it away in great dobs. Then, just as she was about to begin again, a gust of wind caught the canvas, tore it off the easel and sent it cartwheeling down the beach.

Natasha screamed.

Ed bent and he picked up some cord. He tested the cord, then he coiled it and he put it in his pack. He found a small orange buoy with the number 7 on it, which he picked up and looked at but then threw away. He picked up a long length of thick rope, and he carried it a short distance, to test its possession, before discarding it as too heavy. He passed a bucket with a hole in it, and a single orange wellington boot, a green flipper. He found a burst football, which he then kicked ahead of him for a short distance.

Plastic bottles, lines, ropes, driftwood, planks. . . The shore was littered with debris. It lay in a long and tangled heap, marking the high tide line. . . logs, a dead sheep, a bailer from a boat, a piece of cargo-net, some canvas on a wooden frame.

Ed picked up the canvas. The canvas was a good find. He would use it to patch his haversack, which was in need of repair. Ed tore the canvas from its frame and he threw the frame away.

A little further up the beach Ed watched a girl bend to pick up an artist's easel. At first, Ed envied her her find, but then he recognised the girl, and, when she planted the easel upright in the sand and stood there, looking at him, Ed stopped dead. He turned and hurried back down the beach.

Ed held the canvas out in one hand, the stretcher in the other.

'Sorry,' he said, 'I didn't realise.'

Natasha snatched them from him, yanking his arms. She threw the stretcher on the ground then she rolled the canvas in to a tube which she stuffed angrily in to her pack.

She stood glowering at Ed. 'Well, goodbye,' she said. Then she turned her back on him and began to dismantle her easel. She undid a wing nut, and a leg slid down its housing until it hit its end-stop. Natasha cursed. It was a simple enough mechanism but it required patience to operate and Natasha was at her wits end.

Natasha fought with the easel, trying to make it do what she wanted it to do. It made her angry that she could not do such a simple thing. Then, catching her hand between two moving parts, she flung the easel away from her, screaming in anger and from frustration.

Ed bent and he picked up the easel. He loosened the wing-nuts, slid the extendable legs alongside of each other, re-tightened the nuts then folded down the wings. It was that simple. The easel folded up very small. Ed offered it to Natasha.

Natasha stood, close to tears, staring at Ed. She reached out her hand. 'I hurt my hand,' she said, her voice shaky, her eyes filling with tears.

She lifted off the loose cap of skin. The flensed skin was white, at first, but then red spots appeared on it. The whole area became red.

Ed grimaced, he sucked air in through his teeth, though it was only a grazed knuckle, 'That must hurt,' he said.

Natasha burst in to tears. Because of her hand, because painting was just too difficult. She poured all her hurt and her anger and her frustration in to concern for her hurt hand. Utterly miserable, she was suddenly very cold. A shudder racked her body and she began to shiver.

Ed found them a hollow in the dunes where they could shelter from the wind.

Natasha, with her back against the sloping sand, wiped the wetness off her cheeks, then her nose on her sleeve. Ed was searching his pack for a plaster.

'Here,' he said, as he pulled out a thin plastic folder of them.

Natasha held out her hand. Her hand was long, with long slender fingers. It was purple from the cold and stained with oil paints.

Ed pressed gently on the two wings of the adhesive strip, smoothing them out. The graze was in an awkward place and the plaster did not sit well, it would doubtless fall off, but that was not the point.

Ed left Natasha sheltering in the hollow. He returned to the beach and he collected up an armful of driftwood. He dumped several loads of driftwood in the hollow, then he built up a large fire. Very soon there was grey smoke twisting in to the air.

It was not long before the fire, burning with a fierce yellow flame, was throwing out heat. Natasha sat close to the fire, extending her hands to it.

'There's nothing like a fire to cheer you up,' said Ed. 'Except perhaps for a beer.' He reached in to his pack and he produced two beers. He handed one to Natasha.

The beer relaxed Natasha. Out it all came: her painting, the cancelled exhibition, how it had all come to nothing with the theft of her car.

'All they wanted was the car. It was joy riders out looking for kicks, or so the police reckoned. But it wasn't that kind of car. It was someone from out of town, must have been, someone who came in to get drunk and then stole themselves a lift home.'

Ed sat staring at Natasha. She had high cheekbones, dark brown eyes, long black hair which she now brushed from her face, hooking it over an ear with her long slender fingers. She wore faded and paint stained jeans, an old duffel coat, scuffed army boots. She was tall and slender. She was very beautiful. Ed was listening but he was mostly looking.

'The bastards burnt the car. They crashed it then they burnt it. I lost everything, all my paintings, my sketchbooks, my equipment, my clothes, everything. The exhibition. My chance of being discovered, gone.'

Ed could think of nothing to say. He was thinking of Andy, Jigsaw and Pogget, and of that day on which he had first seen Natasha when they had crashed in to her car and had not stopped because the car was stolen. But he dare not tell her.

'It seems to me,' he said, 'that a person can lose everything and it would still not matter to them, if everything they wanted was in the future.'

Natasha frowned.

They sat and they stared in to the fire, sipping on their beers. The sun had come out but the wind was fierce and it remained cold. Ed had been feeding larger and larger logs on to the fire. Now he straddled it with a huge log that he had dragged up from the beach.

The fire was soon blasting out heat. Natasha pulled herself away from it a little.

'I'm Natasha, by the way.' She offered Ed her hand. She seemed to have forgotten how upset she had been.

'Ed.'

They shook hands.

Natasha looked enquiringly at Ed. 'Ed what?'

Ed had been wondering about that himself, lately.

'Nothing,' he answered. 'Oh, I see what you mean. Larrikin. And yours?'

'Plane-Smith. Just plain Smith,' she said.

'And where are you from, Natasha Smith?'

'Oh, just some estate, in Norfolk.'

'I'd hate to live on an estate,' said Ed, 'No space. Too many people.'

'Oh there was space,' said Natasha, 'it was just the people.' Natasha stared off in to the distance, she seemed distant.

'You staying in Aber?' Ed asked. 'It's just I've seen you around the place.'

'Yes. I've got a room in The Castle, the Hotel. But I'm thinking of leaving soon. Of going back to London.'

'London?'

'I really don't know. Maybe. It depends. But I think so, yes.'

'How's that hand of yours?' Ed asked.

'Hand?' Natasha had forgotten about her hand.

'Your knuckle.'

'Oh, that.' Natasha looked at her hand. Ed had done a good job with the plaster. She smoothed it down anyway. She looked at Ed. 'Thanks,' she said, 'And sorry.'

'That's' alright. Pleasure.' Then he remembered the food that he had stocked up on at the party.

'You hungry?' he asked.

'Ravenous.'

Ed pulled a grease stained brown paper bag from his pack and he tore it open. Inside were two chicken legs, some cold potatoes, a thick slice of egg and ham pie, a jar of olives and a half packet of broken crisps. He also had several slices of thick bread, a jar of honey and a jar of peanut butter.

'Cup of tea?'

'You've got a kettle in there too?'

Ed pulled out a bottle of water followed by a smoke blackened billy that was wrapped in a polythene bag. Ed filled the billy with the water and he placed it at the edge of the fire on a bed of hot coals. He began to snap some thin sticks in to short lengths, which he then placed around the billy, to make a sort of nest. Steam began to twist off the water. Ed continued to feed twigs on the fire.

They ate the chicken legs, the potatoes, the egg and ham pie, most of the olives and all of the crisps. Natasha looked at the empty grease stained paper they had eaten off, reached forwards, pressed a piece of soft white pastry on to her finger and popped it in to her mouth.

'Dessert?' asked Ed.

Natasha nodded. 'What you got?'

'Sweet F. A.' Ed laughed.

He took two thick slices of bread and he placed them on the paper. With the blade of his knife he smeared honey on to both slices of the bread.

'Honey, turns ordinary bread in to cake,' he said. Then he spread peanut butter on the honey and pressed the two slices together. He cut the bread in two, and offered one half to Natasha. 'There,' he said, 'the cake you don't have to bake.'

The beer and the food and the fire relaxed Natasha. Sitting out of the wind, on the slope of the dune, hands wrapped around a tin mug of hot tea, she told Ed about her idea to paint the bigger picture.

'No one else seems to be doing it. Of course, there is so much I don't know yet. It won't be easy, and it might take a long time, but I want to take everything I've seen and learned about the country and put it all in a single picture. The bigger picture. I could really make my name with something like that. That's what I should be trying for. Anyone can paint landscapes, you might just as well take photographs.'

Ed thought how he would like to have something like that. From what Natasha was telling him you could create one image and it could see you through the rest of your life. It seemed to Ed to be the kind of thing to be trying for.

'It must be good to be an artist,' he said.

'I'm not an artist yet. You're not an artist until you can support yourself with your art. That's the real proof. Until that happens you're just struggling.'

Natasha stared in to her tea. It was blue from the smoke and there were bits floating in it, bits of ash and tiny lumps of creamy tasting dried milk that hadn't quite dissolved. She was hugging it for the warmth.

'So what about you, what do you do?'

Everyone wanted to know what it was that you did for a living. Was it possible to know a person through knowing what they did? Everyone seemed to think so.

'Me?' Ed shrugged. 'As little as possible, to be honest. Anything, really. Whatever. I sort of work my way around. Mostly away from places.'

Ed knew then that he had failed. Because all the alternatives scared him. Perhaps the one that scared him less, that would be the one.

'So where have you been?' asked Natasha.

And so Ed told Natasha about his travels. Like most travellers, Ed had lots of amusing stories to tell, some of which were true. Ed was a good story teller. Natasha thought so.

'You should write a book,' she said.

'You need a plot for a book,' said Ed, 'and I lost that years ago.' He laughed. 'Besides, I can't write. Not properly.'

'Just write it down like you say it, like you just told me,' said Natasha.

'Really.'

Being a writer. It was one of those things that Ed had once thought about and had just as soon forgotten. Like playing football for England. Or having a million pounds of a sudden. What would you do? Of course, you would never have such money. They were only dreams, games almost.

'I wrote a poem once,' said Ed. 'You want to hear it?'

'Not really, no.' Natasha grimaced. 'But go on,' she said, resigned.

'Ready?' Ed coughed to clear his throat and he changed his expression to what he imagined to be a lovelorn look. He clasped his hands to his chest. He began: 'If love is the full blossoming of summer joys. And the spring its sweet discovery. . ."

Natasha had to look away to hide the pain evident on her face.

'Then I don't want to be around in autumn when my nuts drop off.' Ed laughed.

Natasha pursed her lips and she punched Ed playfully on the shoulder.

It was late afternoon, the wind had died down, the clouds had moved inland and the sun was glinting off the sea. Ed and Natasha left the fire and they sat higher up the slope so they could look through the gap in the dunes and out on to the beach.

People were walking along the beach, couples, dog walkers. A solitary jogger ran past. She was tall and thin, gangly, and wore her hair in a pony tail.

'Fi!' Said Ed.

Natasha watched the jogger out of sight. Something, not the wind, narrowed her eyes. 'Friend of yours?' she asked Ed.

'No, I was just thinking of some character in a cartoon strip.'

Natasha frowned at Ed. 'That's not a nice thing to say.'

'What I meant was. Look.' Picking up a piece of driftwood Ed drew in the sand.

'Meet Fi,' he said and he drew a matchstick-like bendy limbed character with two long strands of hair protruding from a round head to represent a pony tail. Natasha laughed because the figure looked just like the jogger. Then he dressed her in high heels and a short, triangular shaped skirt. He crisscrossed the dress with a tartan-like pattern. 'McFi,' he said.

He erased the picture. Then he redrew it, this time Fi was wearing a bikini and was climbing a coconut tree. 'Fi-ji.'

'She could have a different adventure every week. Here she is in Cuba.' Ed put her in a pill box hat and beard. 'Fi'del,' he said.

'And here she is working as a masseuse.' He drew her with huge matchstick fingered hands reaching out before her to massage a foot. 'Fi-sio,' He said.

Next, Ed drew a stage on which there shone the conical cylinder of a spotlight. 'Here she is singing at the opera.' The Fi character was stood inside the cone of light, mouth wide open, tonsils showing, musical notes to denote singing littering the air around her. 'Fi-garo!' sang Ed, 'Fi-garo Fi-garo!'

Natasha couldn't resist it. Laughing, she sang along with Ed.

'Fi-garo!'

'Base Camp Billy,' he said.

'Where?' Natasha straightened to look up and down the beach.

'No. Another comic strip. He's an overweight adventurer, a total incompetent. There is no expedition that he cannot ruin.'

'So you do cartoons?' asked Natasha. 'You're a cartoonist?'

'No, they're just something I thought up.'

Natasha frowned. 'You should. You should send them off or something.'

A cartoonist? Ed didn't much feel like a cartoonist. It did not seem plausible to him. He was not that convinced of his ability.

'Nar,' he dismissed the idea. 'Besides, there's probably already a Fi or a Base Camp Billy out there. It's happened to me before, with all the books I've thought up.'

'What books?'

'*The Grapes of Wrath*, for a start,' said Ed. 'Only joking. Though I did have an idea for a book once,' he admitted. 'Well, not a book exactly, a sort of guide. More a survival manual.'

'I can see you writing that,' said Natasha. Ed looked like a survivor.

'I want it to be more than that though. It seems to me,' said Ed, 'that all the old skills are being lost. Who can bother to make anything anymore when everything is made for them? But useful things make useless people. And they cost money. And that traps you in work. Mankind has progressed, but have people? Individuals. And I wonder if society has really?'

'The world has moved on, Ed. Not everyone can live in the sticks.'

'No, but they can try.'

Ed reckoned that everyone should experience the basic human condition at least once in their lives. If it taught you how to look after yourself, if you could make do, then you realised just how much simpler things could be for you, that there was so much you did not need. You would know then what was necessary and what you could do without, because anything else was a distraction. Either you would learn what it was to live in the real world – the world of mountains, of running water, woods, fishing and hunting - the world that Ed inhabited, or tried to – or you would know how difficult that had become for you. Doubtless there would be some, many, who would grow bored long before they had a chance to become inconvenienced or uncomfortable.

'In this day and age?' Natasha frowned. 'Why? Who'd want to? '

'Nobody, I guess,' said Ed. 'Very few. People have grown soft. No one does anything anymore. Hardly anyone. They expect everything to be done for them. They press buttons, flick switches, tap keys, pull levers, and the things they want happen. Mostly though they spend money.'

Money was the key. Money provided what was wanted. Ultimately, money would decide. Having enough money, not having money, that made the decisions of most people.

'You can't get by without money, Ed. Even an anachronism like you needs money in this day and age.'

'True,' Ed nodded. 'All you can hope to do is lessen the need, otherwise all there will be for you is work. There is too much work. But you can subvert work. You don't have to work, not all the time.'

'Go on,' she said, 'I'm listening.'

Ed picked up a small stone from off the ground and he began to turn it over and over in his hand. He was thinking of his book.

He could see the chapters now: *Mending and making do. Lying low. Roughing it. Busking.* . . . The book's title would be *How To Construct A Temporary Shelter*. It would be much more than a survival manual. It would be about the method and principle of subverting work.

'It would be a book about escape, about exits and entrances. Maps,' Ed realised. He was drawing all the threads together.

'Maps?' Natasha frowned, confused.

There was the OS map of Britain and then there were Ed's map of Britain. Ed's maps varied according to his interests. When he had been in to sailing Ed's map of Britain had been one of coastlines and lakes, being the only places that he was interested in at the time. Later, when he developed his obsession with climbing, Ed expanded his maps to include the mountains. Then, when Ed took up trout fishing, he discovered a whole new world of rivers and fast streams, which were suddenly the only places that he wished to be. As Ed's interests and knowledge grew Ed's map of Britain grew. Some places, though small, made enormous maps. Each and every activity has its own map. Having a new interest creates a new map. There are maps within maps. You could live in a place all your life and you would still not discover all its maps. Some people live in a big country, others in a small one, though it is the same country. The world can be one thing, or it can be any number of things.

'You can own country simply by knowing it.'

Ed told Natasha how the nomadic Aborigines of Australia owned land, their knowledge of a track granting them access to it.

Ed explained how mankind had expanded outwards from his origins by walking, how he had mapped the world by naming it, by understanding it, thus making it his. That knowledge gave him access to the otherwise inaccessible. Sensing new possibilities he began to transform things. He turned inhospitable lands in to home. Though he later built upon and obliterated his first trackways, their remnants, the instinct for them, still remains They are etched deep in to the psyche and they influence our behaviour.

Everyone at some time or other suffers the urge to take a sudden and apparently pointless walk. It is a deep and ancient need and it causes paths to sprout up as though from nowhere, across fields and mountains and through woods, upon patches of grass in the centre of paved squares between high rise buildings. They are everywhere and they go nowhere yet they persist.

'Just suppose,' said Ed, 'if someone were to map such a thing, if they were to somehow discover those tracks ancient and still necessary intention.'

Ed asked Natasha had she read *The Songlines*. She hadn't. Had she heard of the Bush Tucker man? No.

Ed then talked about fishing and how immersed in it he became, how purposeful it felt to him. How it was like stepping out of one world and in to another much earlier and more essential world.

Natasha was slowly beginning to grasp what Ed was working toward.

Ed then related to Natasha a fable that he had once read. It concerned a town where when every time one of its citizens made a journey a line appeared. An actual physical line.

'There were lines for relationships between people, lines for almost everything that happened there. Pretty soon, people couldn't move for all those lines. They couldn't do anything. They had to abandon that town eventually and rebuild it someplace else and start over again.'

Then Ed asked:

'Do you ever get the urge to take a sudden and apparently pointless walk?'

'Well yes, but. . . ?'

'You ever wonder why?'

Natasha shrugged, turning down her mouth. There were lots of reasons why you would go for a walk, she said. Sometimes you just went. You couldn't explain it to yourself. It was just this need that you had that had gradually built up in you.

'Because sometimes you just need to get out,' she said.

'Exactly,' said Ed. 'You've just got to get out.'

The whole thing was right there. Ready. Waiting. Natasha saw it in a flash. Understood it perfectly.

'You've got to do it, Ed. You can't not do it now that you've had the idea.'

Ed had been toying with a stone whilst he had been talking, turning it over and over in his hand, smoothing it, polishing it. He reached behind himself and he flung the stone away from him. It smacked in to the side of a dune where it was buried in a slide of sand.

Ed shrugged. 'Maybe. One day.'

'That's what people say who never do anything. Then they start wishing that they had done it. But by then it's usually too late. You have to try, Ed. Either until you succeed, or until you find out for certain that it's impossible. Even then, you have to keep trying. If you don't try you'll only end up resenting whatever it is that you do instead.'

'What, you mean do it for the exorcise?' said Ed. Natasha laughed.

Ed shook his head. 'No. It would be too difficult. It was just some idea that I had.'

Writing was easy. And it was hard. It was not as easy as not writing.

Natasha knew that Ed would have to be pushed in to doing the thing. Encouraged.

'I like your book, really,' she said, 'but not as a guide. It could work as a novel though. You should think about it, really.'

They sat together, looking at the sea. It grew cold on that dune and they began to shiver. Ed looked at Natasha. Natasha looked at Ed.

Maybe they recognised something of themselves in each other. The female Ed, the male Natasha. Natasha pressed herself close to Ed. She rested her head on his shoulder. Encouraged, Ed reached an arm around her shoulder. They watched the sun set on the sea. The sea flared. The sky turned pale and then luminous.

It was almost dark when they returned to the hollow. The fire had long since gone out. Natasha helped Ed erect his tent. Ed put in his sleeping bag, stored their packs in the vestibule, then crawled in, squeezing himself past the bags. He was followed by Natasha. Ed turned, twisting himself over Natasha, as she twisted under him, then he pulled shut the zips.

It was morning. They had breakfasted, Ed had taken down and packed away the tent. Their backpacks lay at their feet. It was time to move on, to go their separate ways. But it was like they were waiting for something.

'I hate goodbyes,' said Natasha.

'There is nothing worse,' said Ed, 'than the long drawn out goodbye.'

'On your marks,' said Ed, and he crouched to the floor, like he was on starting blocks. 'Get set,' he said, tensing himself, forming his body to an arch.

'Gooodbyeee!' he yelled.

Natasha laughed as he sped away in a spurt of sand and ran leaden footed over a sand dune, and she was still laughing when he reappeared, racing over the taller dune behind. She only stopped laughing when he did not return. The skyline remained empty. There were just the dunes, standing empty against the sky.

Natasha stood alone on the deserted beach.

It happens. We emerge from the distance, we meet, we grow close, then we return to that distance which engulfs us, as, from being unknown at first we become a little later perhaps forgotten.

9

A Small Part of the Bigger Picture

All this aimlessness, all this wandering, all this unwillingness to work, it is not laziness, it is a questioning of work, of the work that is on offer. It is not the cause of their poverty. They would be poor in work too, harnessed to some poorly paid job of their desperate choosing. They would be poor even if they were paid well, these people of their kind. Only Jigsaw perhaps, who loved money, the numbering of money, would be happy with money. And Natasha, who with her background could so easily have money, could never be happy with money, not if that was all that there was. Money was not wealth.

It was not money they were after. And it was not work.

Work, you bastards, work, even when there is no work, just the threat of its absence to keep you pliant to that greater good, the flawless machine, that requires that carrot, this stick, these people to remain as they are, under pressure of change, who struggle and who attempt to change themselves. And the dole, that great breathing space, allowing of art and creativity, that helps nurture this wild and creative base, by definition disadvantaged, those who choose this life and who fill it with themselves, who use this device invented and fostered to other means, who misuse it to other ends who, when badgered in to line, in to Job Club, in to work, find themselves forced in to ever more desperate expressions of selfness so they might avoid that emptier and far more humbling and degrading waste, total work: forced in to a use that is not their use. Instead, they live for this hope, that dream, this necessity. This scrambling, hoping, tumbling free-fall of people:

Ed heads toward London in a removals van.

Clemence, after receiving yet another rejection slip, writes the name and address of a publisher on to an envelope in to which he puts his recently returned MS.

Natasha, stands in front of a canvas, paintbrush in hand, as she did yesterday, and the day before that. As she will do today.

Pogget, back in Liverpool, back at job club, artfully, slowly and with tongue in cheek, crafts yet another letter for another job that he does not want. He prefers shoplifting, taking and driving, house breaking, money with menaces, theft....

Clemence writes and writes, he reads what he has written, and grips his head, frustrated at this inability of his to write his book. The roof still leaks, he still shits in the woods.

Enzo works and works, the work flowing from him in a continuous and unstoppable stream because it is so easy. Moving from one easel to the next he accidentally flicks a speck of paint on to a blank canvas and he curses himself for his clumsiness. He is about to wipe it off when he changes his mind. He signs the canvas.

Clemence has his MS returned to him, again. He posts it off, again. Pogget is at job club, still.

Mister Guggenheim, the wealthy American art collector, purchaser of several landscapes by an unknown artist, searches the galleries and exhibitions of London for more of these works by this skilled and anonymous artist, but he fails to find any. Though there are numerous copies spawned by his interest he is in no way persuaded by them. They lack the obvious life, the originality and accomplishment so evident in the originals, for which he had paid £10,000. He flies to Paris, hoping to discover something there.

Clemence is celebrating, he is doing a sort of dance. Above him, the letter of acceptance from Backstreet Books, that he has thrown high in to the air, floats slowly back to earth.

Andy, stepping out on to the stage at The Comedy Club, stands nervous and bewildered beneath the spotlights. He lifts a hand to his forehead to shield his eyes from their glare. 'I see no ships,' he says. 'Only hardships.' Jigsaw, seated in the audience with his fingers crossed, breathes a sigh of relief.

The city grows. It is people giving themselves hope, getting even, getting theirs, getting their own back. Or just getting.

10

A Turn of Events

'Take a left here,' said Andy, looking up from his A to Z. 'It's off this road someplace.'

Jigsaw down shifted the gears to take the corner. The worn gears of the transit crunched in protest as he searched for third. He freewheeled around the corner.

Long before they saw the sign for the tip they saw sign of the tip. The sky appears different, emptier over some places. First they passed through a council estate, then, ahead of them, came the wide expanse of landscape under a big sky. Clouds of gulls filled the sky. There was that unmistakable tip smell.

In the distance, on the active edges of the tip, there were lorries tipping. Jigsaw pulled up between the recycling section, the two lines of yellow skips, and the tip itself.

ANDY RANT ON TOUR, said the amateurish paint job on the van's mostly white, partially mottled and rusted sides.

Everywhere you looked people were unloading things from their vehicles then throwing them in to skips just as others were picking through the rubbish and taking it away with them.

Jigsaw found a matching armchair and settee which they then loaded in to the van to join the mattress already there. The tiny box like interior of the van began to take on the appearance of a bed-sitting room as they loaded it up with furniture. A chair and table. A magazine rack. A bookcase. Everything they needed was here.

'Just look at this place, Jigsy, it's like the whole fucken country has been dumped. Hey, lookit this, remember these?'

Andy held up an old bakelite telephone. Jigsaw took the receiver and he placed it against his ear.

'It's Alexander Graham Bell. He wants to know if I can hear him.'

Andy picked up a broken television set and he put it in the van. He picked up an old boot and he stood studying it for possibilities. He threw it in the van. He found a pile of old bricks. 'Give us a hand with these, Jigsy, mate. Here, hold out yer arms.'

'Bricks? What do we need these for?'

'You'll see. Yeh need equipment. Yeh can't get through life without equipment, yer a fool ter even try.'

Jigsaw made a cradle of his arms and Andy filled it up with bricks. Andy returned to searching the tip.

'What else would be good? What else do we need?'

Andy found an old plastic bucket and he filled it with broken glass and he put it in the van. He found a burst football. A can of paint. . . .

The Blood and Bucket public House in Millwall was trouble. Most nights, starting at seven, there would be a band. Usually, the band was too loud, the small dance floor would get overcrowded, there would be pushing and shoving until, inevitably, a fight would break out that would then spill out in to the car park. There was always a ruckus in the car park and an active gathering of police. It was a kind of training ground for them.

Locals knew the pub as Sarajevo.

London was full of such rough venues. This was where new bands and comedians came to cut their teeth, and sometimes have them broken, along with their hopes.

The manager eyed Andy suspiciously, he seemed unsure about him. Cropped hair, bony face, angry eyes, sullen. Andy looked hard.

'He doesn't look like a comedian, he looks more like Security to me. And what's with the burst football?' Andy was holding a football, the one from the tip. 'I thought all comedians came with a guitar these days? Jasper Carrot. Billy Connolly.'

'He can't play a guitar,' said Jigsaw, 'but he can play football though. It's a prop. You'll see. Max Boyce has a leek,' he said. 'Dave Allen, a glass of whisky. Alexi Sayle, a small suit.'

The worry showed on the manager's face. He was a burly, bald headed character with a gold earring and tattoos who kept a baseball bat behind the bar. His customers would destroy the place if they didn't like Andy. They often destroyed it, and for much less. Every night they destroyed something they didn't like. Each other, usually.

'You sure he's a comedian? He doesn't even smile. Like Billy Connolly, you told me. He doesn't even look like Billy Connolly.'

'He's good, believe me.'

'He'd better be.'

'Trust me. They'll love him to bits.'

'They'll tear him to bits if they don't like him. Fire exit's over there. If you end up using it, don't come back. I'll have spent your money repairing the place.'

It was eight o'clock and the function room was empty. The stage was littered with half bricks, broken glass, lumps of concrete.

There was a canvas back drop to the stage that had been painted to look like a brick wall and it was covered in graffiti: *Giz A Job. Liverpool Twin Town Pompeii. One Hundred Jobs in Jeopardy: Liverpool man secures Arabian deal. Is There Life Before Death? Eat The Rich. . .* Running along the top of the wall was Liverpool's skyline: the two cathedrals, the restaurant tower. . . In the centre of the stage, beside the microphone, was a television set, a poster depicting Thatcher's face pasted on to the smashed screen. There was a boot embedded in the face.

By 8.30pm the function room was crowded. It was blue with smoke and loud with the buzz of anticipation.

Word had spread of Andy's performances at the Comedy Club. There were many present whose first time it was at The Blood and Bucket who had come especially to see Andy. There was a journalist present, a critic who wrote for the *Evening Standard*.

Andy stood to one side of the stage, smoking. He was nervous. He finished one cigarette then started on another. Jigsaw stood next to him, twirling Andy's football in his hands.

The lights in the function room dimmed. There was an expectant hush. A spotlight flashed on. It illuminated the stage. Andy appeared, carrying his burst football.

A glass came flying out of the dark that exploded on the casing of the television set. Andy ignored it. He lifted his right hand and shielded his eyes with it. 'I see no ships,' he said. 'Only hardships.'

Andy launched in to his routine: *A job to find a job. . . What do you call enquiries these days. . . The country as a hole. . . . The news.*

Andy stood behind the TV and he did the News:

'Unemployment today hit the three million mark.' Andy changed his stance, looking in a different direction to deliver the next bulletin: 'Another utility has been privatised with more job losses expected. . .' He concluded: 'Things are going from bad to worse. This whole fucken country is going to the dogs. The top dogs.'

Andy tore the country apart.

He attacked the bosses and the owners. He attacked money. He attacked work. 'All's it is is some poxy job like.' He attacked modern architecture: 'Tall buildings,' he said, and he stuck up his finger. 'It's like the planners got all the works on architecture. And stood them on end. There, we'll build that.'

'The Greeks and the Romans had carved marble, the Victorians dressed granite. What have we got? The fucken breeze block. It says it all.'

Andy struck a chord with his audience. By the end of the show Andy could have told them anything and they would have laughed.

He told them his Christ healing the sick story and they laughed.

They were still laughing an hour later when Andy left the stage. The laughter died, it petered out. It was replaced by silence, emptiness.

The audience remained in their seats. There was a certain uneasiness to the place, an edginess that was palpable.

Andy had taken every truth and belief that the audience had ever held and he had replaced them with laughter. And now the laughter was gone. The world seemed different somehow. Or maybe they did not want to go back to it just yet.

Then that now familiar voice shouted: 'Jesus, will yis fuck off!' and the silence was broken, and with it the unease. The audience laughed. They applauded.

Andy came striding back out on stage. 'What the fuck are youse lot still doing here? Don't yer know there's jobs goin' down at Tescos? There's jobs going everywhere,' he said. 'Soon thee'll all be gone.'

'Did you hear the good news? What Thatcher said? I am not going to stand for another election. . . . '

Andy came off that stage wired and angry, but he soon calmed down. After a few beers, all of which were bought for him, and after the manager had given Jigsaw their share of the take and Jigsaw had passed Andy his share, Andy forgot his anger. That was a response. For now, all there was was the money. Money was a balm, it makes everything all right for a time. Until the need for more money.

11

Yes!

It was a rough estate. There had been riots on the estate the year before and most of the ground floor flats in Andy and Jigsaw's tower block were boarded up. Some had been burnt out. Jigsaw and Andy lived in a flat on the fourth floor.

It was ten o'clock and Andy and Jigsaw were sat in the kitchenette having breakfast. The rickety Formica table which they had rescued from the dump was piled with the day's newspapers.

Every day Andy trawled the papers for new material.

Just as war correspondents and anti-war protesters need a war in order to thrive, Andy needed unemployment and hard times. The worse things got for the country, and the more controversial, then the better for Andy. He would turn it in to comedy. People need distraction from their troubles. It acts as a pressure valve.

As usual, the papers were full of bad news. But there was one piece of very good news.

Grinning, Jigsaw passed Andy the newspaper. Under the headline, Street Fighting Man, Andy read:

Working class hero, Street fighting man, the voice of our times? Angry young man, Andy Rant is all of these things. This is a hard-hitting entertainer with more than just a few one liners under his belt. This is a man on a mission. We will be seeing and hearing a lot more from this exciting new talent in the coming months. He is the unmatched witness to our times.

'We're on our way,' said Jigsaw.

'Come the revolution,' said Andy. He raised his fist. 'Burn it down!' he shouted. 'Burn it down!' He laughed.

'You mean half revolution, surely,' said Jigsaw.

'Half revolution?' Andy frowned.

'You don't want to end up back where we started, do you?' Jigsaw laughed. 'It's our turn to be on top now.' And he climbed on to the sofa and began jumping up and down on it. 'We're going to be rich,' he sang, 'we're going to be rich.'

'If there isn't a civil war first,' said Andy.

'After you with the brick,' said Jigsaw. He was laughing.

'No, after you,' said Andy.

It really did look like things were going to work out for them.

12

Going Places

It was first thing Monday morning and all over the city people were rushing off to work, no one wanting to work but everyone hurrying so as not to be late. People hurried along the pavements, traffic roared by. The whole city rumbled with noise: trains, cars, buses, lorries, motorbikes. . . . wherever you went in the city there was traffic converging there. Soon, the traffic was inching along. Drivers grew irritable, they needed to be elsewhere, earning.

Ed was seated in a removals van in traffic on Kingsway.

O'Doom, Ed's foreman, a huge and ruddy faced Dubliner, the driver of the removals van, gave vent to his frustration by blasting the horn. He roared in his loud and accented voice at the line of slowly creeping traffic: 'COME ON, MOVE IT WILL YIS. YOU CAN'T PARK HERE!'

They had left the depot in Camden at 8am, expecting to be in Peckham by 8.30am. It was now 9am.

O'Doom hated the city. It had become a much more crowded and frantic place than when he had first arrived, from Dublin, some twenty years previously. True, everything you could possibly want was here, but so was everyone that was after it.

'COME ON, MOVE. . . OH THAT'S ALL WE FUCKEN NEED!'

Several car lengths ahead, a bus edged out in to the traffic and the traffic stopped. O'Doom hit his horn, leaning his full weight on it.

Next to Ed in the window seat, resting his bare feet on the dash and listening to Bob Marley on his Walkman, was Bradley Parker, a West Indian. Like Ed, he was quite happy to be stuck in traffic if it meant that he was not working. The hours would pile up, but so would the money, and they wouldn't have to do anything for it.

The traffic began moving again, bumper to bumper, in a muddled line, vehicles attempting to edge in to it from the side roads and alleyways, taxis trying to pull out, buses pulling out, motorbikes weaving, braking. . . .

O'Doom fought them for every inch. He wasn't going to end up a car length behind in the race to get to work.

And then there were the lights. O'Doom slammed on the brakes.

'JESUS GODDING FUCK CHRIST! GOD FECKIN LIGHTS! CHRIST! HOW ARE YOU SUPPOSED TO GET ANYWHERE HERE!'

The van dipped forwards on its springs before bouncing up again. The *A to Z*, the clipboard containing the weeks itinerary, and O'Doom's copy of the *Star*, all slid off the dash and in to the footwell. Ed reached down and he picked them up. He kept hold of the clipboard and he flicked through the coming week's itinerary.

Though it could be backbreaking at times, Ed enjoyed working in removals. He felt that he was finally going places. Which he was. Every day was different, every day he went to a different place. The North, the South, Scotland, Wales . . . the whole country was on the move. Ed moved people in to and out of mansions, basements, warehouse conversions, converted farmhouses, terraced houses, semis, penthouse suites. . . . He met all sorts of people, and from all walks of life.

It sometimes depressed Ed, returning to his bedsit each night after all that escapism.

Bedsit: Home, but not like home at all, simply a refuge. A place to keep yourself when not in use. Like in a box.

Sometimes Ed felt that he was nothing more than a scene shifter, rearranging the props.

Today they were moving a client from Peckham to Wapping. Ed looked up the addresses in the *A to Z*. He knew both places well. One was a tower block, the other riverside apartments in a converted warehouse. Working in removals Ed had become familiar with the fashionable areas and those that were becoming fashionable:

'Someone's going up in the world,' he said.

'AYE, AND COME TONIGHT YOU'LL WISH THEY WERE GOING DOWN,' growled O'Doom, glancing Ed a scowl. BLOODY TOWER BLOCKS. AN' I BET YIS ANYTHING THE LIFTS ARE BROKE.'

Bradley Parker nodded, but it was to his music. Eyes closed, he began to sing tunelessly: 'No woman no cry. . . .' Ed nudged him quiet.

Ed passed the time looking out of the window, absorbing London. Ed liked

London. Living in London Ed sensed that he was at the very centre of something. All those important and impressive buildings somehow made him feel important: The Palace, Whitehall, Trafalgar Square, St Pauls, the Tower, Horse Guards, the Houses of Parliament, Number 10. . . . Some buildings can take possession of their occupants, and transform them, with some becoming like tiny gods.

Living in London, Ed reckoned, was so much more different than living in, say, Birmingham, for example. Something of the place, its energy, the vitality, rubbed off on you here. Here he felt if not important then most certainly energised. And sometimes a place changed you so that you felt that you belonged.

There is an Andy Rant joke: 'They did this survey, asking people around the country which did they think should be Britain's second city? In Birmingham the people answered Birmingham, which surprised everyone. But then in Manchester they had said Manchester. It was the same wherever you went. In Cardiff, they answered Cardiff, in Edinburgh, Edinburgh. Even Glasgow: 'Glasgee,' they said. Leicester, Nottingham, Coventry, Bristol, Oxford. . . . the answer was always the same. They asked the question in Liverpool. The answer: 'Well London, of course."

Of course, people were more often than not forced to move. The jobs market, like the property market, had become a kind of musical chairs.

The traffic began moving again and they were soon speeding down the embankment. As they passed Cleopatra's needle Ed saw Natasha in the crowd.

'Stop the van!' He yelled.

'WHAT? NO WAY!' roared O'Doom. The lights ahead were about to change against him and he was determined to beat them. 'YES!' he roared as they soared through on amber.

They began to fly it. Crossing out on to the width and openness of Waterloo Bridge they temporarily left the city in to light and space, only to plunge back in to it on the other side. Then the lights turned to red, the cars in front stopped, and O'Doom, who had just shifted up to third, had to slam on the brakes. Ed and O'Doom were thrown forward in their seats. Bradley Parker's head jerked down and his headphones flew off in to his lap.

Bradley Parker flicked open his eyes, 'What's happening?' he said, fearful that they had arrived at their destination. Then he saw that they were still in traffic. Relieved, smiling large, he replaced his earphones, closed his eyes and returned to his music, Bob Marley's *Exodus*, the music isolating him, just as it transported and protected him.

O'Doom leant on the horn. It was now 9.15am. 'FECKIN COME ON

WILL YIS!' he roared, 'YOU CAN'T PARK. . . .'

The teeming city slowed to another halt. It began to gather behind and to rage at the blockage. And the pressure built.

It was cold, a freezing easterly wind blew off the river.

Natasha placed her sign, *CARICATURES £5*, against the embankment wall, unslung her canvas shoulder bag, containing her artist materials and sketch books, and rested it beneath the sign, then she began to search the ground. But it had rained over the weekend and her pictures, from the previous week, had washed off, though they could have just as likely have been worn away by the continuous, inconsiderate passage of feet. In any case, it was better to start from scratch. She could change things, experiment. She slipped on a pair of fingerless gloves, pulled off her hat and placed it upside down on the floor, opening uppermost.

Then, crouching, she began to tape off a square of pavement using masking tape to provide a neatly defined area in which to work, and with an open sketch book beside her, from which she chose a composition, she began to copy it on to the pavement using coloured chalks.

She drew crowds, crowded streets. What she was trying to show was what made those crowds work. Crowds, if you could interpret them, revealed deeper energies. She was hoping to capture the defining spirit and mood of the country. For background, she drew the city as a barcode.

Her work soon attracted the interest of several passers by. A small crowd formed, and, being a crowd it began to draw attention to itself. Natasha's hat, which she had placed on the floor beside her, began to fill with coins; mostly 10p and 20p's, but there was the odd 50p and one pound coin. Someone approached her who wanted a caricature done.

Caricatures were like cartoons, they told a story. You exaggerated a persons features and personality in a caricature. They told a lot about a person, far more than the exact likeness of a photograph could ever tell.

Ed had been right. The address turned out to be that of a run down tower block on a rough estate. There was graffiti on the walls. The ground floor flats were boarded up and some had been been burnt out. Hoodies hung around on the street corners.

O'Doom parked the removals van as close as he could to the tower block, behind a rusted, white transit van that had *ANDY RANT ON TOUR* painted amateurishly on its sides. The van's tyres were flat and one of the wheels was missing. It was jacked up on bricks. All the windows were smashed and one of its rear doors had been ripped off. There was furniture in the van, arranged like a bed sitting room.

A cold wind blew across the estate. *No Ball Games,* said a sign. The place was desolate.

Bradley Parker was putting on his boots, slipping in his bare feet, then tying up the laces.

'Bloody hell, it's cold,' said Ed, jumping out of the cab after O'Doom.

O'Doom threw Ed his overall. 'DON'T WORRY, YOU'LL SOON WARM UP.' The flat was on the fourth floor.

It belonged to the brothers, Gary and Liam Ash, the drummer and keyboard player of the recently succesful new wave band, The Bizz.

There were amplifiers to move, decks, a synthesiser, a vast record collection, a 40" TV set, and the inevitable and much dreaded piano. A water bed had to be drained before it could be moved. Fridge freezer, boxes and racks of clothes, lava lamps, rugs, a huge white sofa still in its slippery plastic cover, more clothes, a cappuccino maker: all the detritus of sudden wealth.

It was three in the afternoon by the time they had loaded up the van. O'Doom had been right, the lifts were broken. They brought out a drum-kit last.

There was a small crowd gathering outside.

'KEEP YOUR EYES ON THE GEAR,' warned O'Doom.

But the crowd wasn't interested in them. Across the road, parked amongst the rusted white vans and the rotting ford escorts of the tower's residents, was an open topped sports car, a black BMW. Someone was stood in the car handing out fliers to the small crowd gathering around it.

'What's going on?' said Bradley Parker, pointing with his head, his arms full of drum kit.

'That's Andy Rant,' said a man as he came hurrying out of the tower block to join the crowd. 'Oy! Andee!' he shouted.

Ed's mouth dropped open. 'It's Andy and Jigsaw,' he said.

'That's James Truitt, our manager,' said Gary, seeing Ed point. 'He's a promoter, he also manages Andy. Andy's an alternative comedian. Comedy is the new rock and roll.'

'Andy's a comedian?' said Ed.

'Well yes.' Gary laughed. 'You know,' and, lifting a hand to shade his eyes, he did the now familiar signature impersonation of Andy Rant: "I see no ships, only hardships. Sailor: Land Ahoy! Christopher Columbus: What, this far out to sea?" That Andy,' he said.

Ed looked bemused.

'You know: "Masturbation. How gay is that?"' He looked questioningly at Ed.

Ed shook his head.

Gary tried again. He had Andy's whole routine off pat. He owned *Andy Rant The Video*.

"Super modern supermodel." He said: "Plastic this and plastic that, plastic tits and plastic twat, she's a super modern supermodel. She'll last for ever, like a plastic bag."'

But it was no good. Ed had never heard of Andy Rant. He didn't read the *Metro*, or *HELLO!* magazine. He didn't have a TV.

The symbols crashed and crashed again as Ed loaded them in to the van. Then he hurried across the street to join the crowd. 'Andy!' he shouted.

'ANDEE!' People were calling out Andy's name, pushing out pieces of paper, fliers, footballs, even money for him to sign. Pushed and jostled, Ed worked his way to the front of the crowd. Someone pulled him back.

'Andy!' he shouted. 'It's me, Ed. Andy!'

Andy looked over at Ed, he looked right through him like he didn't recognise him. Ed was just another face in the crowd.

Jigsaw threw the last of the fliers in to the air, dropped down behind the steering wheel and started the car. The crowd parted as it sped away, shedding fliers. Some people ran after the car.

Ed bent down and he picked up a flier. They were falling to the ground like snow, the car scattering them in its wake:

ANDY RANT LIVE AND LIVID, THE NEW TOUR, 90 SEPARATE VENUES IN AS MANY DAYS.

'COME ON!' yelled O'Doom, his huge and heavy hand pushing Ed from behind, propelling him forwards. 'WE HAVEN'T GOT ALL DAY! MOVE IT, GET IN THE VAN!'

The warehouse conversion was full of space and light. It seemed an impossibility in such a crowded and contested city. Huge windows looked out over an alley on to the brick walls and cell like windows of the neighbouring warehouse. Everything was white in the apartment – the walls, the wooden floors, the ceilings, the furniture, the carpets . . . there was even white art. It was very busy in there, delivery men were arriving all the time, moving stuff in. The place just got whiter. Then a huge flat screen TV arrived. It really stood out in there: a dark hole, like something you could fall in to, a portal. A mini gym arrived. An Emperor size bed arrived. Packaging lay everywhere. An interior designer directed operations: this here, that there.

Some people live in a prosperous city, others in a deprived one, though it is the same city.

It was freezing cold on the Embankment and the wind cut right through Natasha's clothes, making her shiver - she had not worn enough layers, but she did not like to be restrained. She needed to be agile for this work, limber, almost acrobatic, the drawing being a performance in itself. Natasha was like a gymnast when working: reaching out this way, stretching herself over her pictures - and not just physically - outlining them, filling in. But then there was the time after, when she'd finished - the long, lengthening period when she had to hang around, waiting.

People hurried by out of the cold and darkening day. It was only 3pm.

It had not been a particularly good day. Counting up her money, she found she'd earned only £16 and 37p.

Natasha blew on her fingers, they were blue and had turned numb. She was on the verge of packing up and going home when a middle aged and distinguished looking gentleman in a heavy woollen overcoat and red scarf stopped to look at her work.

He stood looking at the pictures for a long time.

'They're very good,' he said. He was pleasant faced and encouraging. 'Do you paint?' he asked Natasha. 'That is, could you transfer this material on to canvas?' He seemed keen to know that she could.

'Well, yes,' Natasha told him, encouraged, warming to the man. "These are just my compositions. I'm still working on them, you see.' She showed him her sketch books.

Natasha told him of her plans. She talked of her idea for the bigger picture. 'Have you thought of a title for the work?' he asked. Natasha shrugged. 'Well, The Bigger Picture.'

The man nodded. Then he reached inside of his coat and he took out his wallet from which he removed a business card. He offered it to Natasha. Natasha stared at the card: *Weldon-Veal, Gallery of Contemporary and Fine Art. Cork Street.*

Natasha stared dumbly at the card, then at Weldon-Veal. 'Well, take it, go on.' Natasha took the card. She continued to stare dumbly at the card.

'When you are ready, come and see me. I would very much like to represent you.' And, smiling, he walked off.

Natasha gripped the card, she held it to her chest. She kissed the card. She half-crouched and, laughing, leapt high in to the air.

There are points in time around which all other points seem to arrange themselves. They are like labels that we use to divide our lives and which then help us to describe them. They are the beginnings and they are the endings and they announce when they occur that a change has happened. Though life is fluid it is almost as though someone has taken a picture of a single moment and that this picture is how things are going to be or how they were for a long time until the next picture.

Natasha packed up her artists materials and hurried home to her bedsit. She dumped her gear and went right back out again to get a bottle of wine.

It was dark when Ed finally finished work. He had O'Doom drop him off on the Embankment on their way back to the depot. But Natasha was gone. There were just her pictures. He came back first thing in the morning before work. He did the same the next day and the day after that. Each day the pictures were a little more faded. By Saturday they were gone, worn away by the continual passage of feet.

Traffic roared by, planes rumbled overhead, boats plied the river, people hurried along the pavements. Natasha was off to book a plane ticket. Ed was on his way to work. Going their separate ways and headed in different directions it was inevitable that they should meet up.

Everything around them was in constant motion. People, traffic, time. Pedestrians hurried by, bumping Ed and Natasha. The streaming crowd bulged around them. The couple were a knot in its progress.

'It is, it's you.'

'I don't believe it. Fancy meeting you here.'

Their separate lives have just touched, but they are about to part again.

The couple want to stand and talk. But they have things to do. Ed was being pulled one way, Natasha another. They both sense that the other has to be elsewhere. There is a sense of urgency to them, an anxiety that makes them appear strained. When it should have been easy. Chance and circumstance have played their part, that magic has passed, it is working its tricks elsewhere now.

'I've got to go,' said Ed. 'Work.'

'Me too,' said Natasha. 'Things to do.'

They stood poised between two worlds. Then, with a final faltering farewell, they both turned and began walking away from each other.

Ed stopped and turned. 'Nat?' Natasha span around.

*

That same night, Ed and Natasha went out for a few beers. Afterwards, Ed walked Natasha home. They were stood in the dark street.

'Come in for a cofee, Ed.'

'I don't drink coffee.'

'That's okay. I haven't got any.'

It was a small and untidy room at the top of the house and it smelt of oil paint.

'Nat! Your hands, they're freezing.'

'Hold still then whilst I warm them up on you.'

Natasha pulled off Ed's jumper. Ed pulled off Natasha's top. They knocked over the easel, scattering tubes of paints over the floor.

Ed kissed Natasha's neck, he kissed her bare shoulders and her bare breasts. They fell sideways on to the sofa. They rolled off the sofa and on to the floor. Prussian blue, chrome yellow, Titian white, burnt umber squirted out from under them.

They woke several times in the night with an insatiable hunger for each other. They could have stayed in bed all the next morning, the whole of the next day together. But there were things they had to do.

'Ed, you've got work, remember.'

'Sod work,' said Ed, 'Man on a pogo. Man at work.'

Natasha grew irritable. She must paint. She had the irrepressible need to paint. Painting was everything. But now Ed was in the way of that. People were always in the way. Get rid of them.

'Ed. You should go, really. I have to work.'

'You're right.' Ed leapt out of bed. The change in him was noticeable. He was charged. 'We're off to Aber today. I really love this job sometimes.'

The moment that Ed left, Natasha began her preparations. But she could not paint. With Ed gone, a restlessness had opened up in her. Painting seemed so small and insignificant in the face of her new need. Not until she met Ed in Hyde park later the next day, as they had arranged, would she forget her need.

ABER 50 MILES, said the sign.

Ed's stomach fluttered as though from nerves. It was anticipation. Already he could feel the distinctive, disruptive pull of the place. He got exactly the same feeling when he saw it on a map. Ed once saw it on the destination board at Euston station, just that single word, Aber. But it was enough. His whole chemistry changed.

Scientists might not yet fully understand the migratory instincts governing the movements of animals across the globe but Ed can.

Aber.

Ed was periodically drawn to the place. Though he was wary of it too. And for good reason.

Croseo I Aber Welcome, said the sign.

'Take a left at the bottom of the hill. Llanbadarn's another mile,' said Ed. It took them three hours to load up all the furniture. They should have gone back to London right then but O'Doom wanted to see the sea.

The sea was calm. The prom was empty. Parked cars shimmered in the sun. The shops were all closed. The whole town seemed deserted. There was just the odd pedestrian. It was Wednesday afternoon, half day closing, quieter even than on a Sunday.

O'Doom decided on a pub lunch. They went in to the Boars Head and there were Ed's friends.

They were drinking, singing and dancing on the tabletops. Someone noticed Ed.

'Ed! You're back!'

'And I'm just going,' said Ed. 'Bye bye.'

Ed's friends surrounded him, blocking his escape.

'Ed!' cried YoYo. 'You remembered it's my birthday.' YoYo flung her arms around Ed and she gave him a big kiss.

Everyone was overjoyed to see Ed. They all wanted him to stay. They tried plying him with drinks. They forced drinks on O'Doom and Bradley Parker. They told stories to remind Ed of the good times, and there had been many. They sang him songs. They got YoYo to sing, 'Give me your body, for just one night. . . .' They promised him a chase pub crawl. 'Romans and slave girls,' suggested someone. 'Vikings and fair maidens. Executives and char ladies.'

O'Doom, a pint in each hand, got up on a table and he began to sing: 'AS I CAME IN TO ABER TOWN. . . .' He finished the song, lifted back his head and demolished a pint to appreciative cheers. Someone passed him another. But before he could down it Ed reached over and he grabbed him by the wrist.

'O'Doom, no!' he pleaded, 'Don't be a fool, man. Tomorrow?

They would wake up in the morning disorientated and feeling terrible. They would retire to the station cafe for breakfast from where they would watch the new arrivals step off the train, bewildered and disappointed by the town's smallness, which would nevertheless swallow them up whole. Family member missing presumed dead? Try Aber. Then, later, they would nip across the road to the Cambrian Hotel for a pub lunch, and the whole remorseless cycle would begin again. From that moment on there would no longer be a tomorrow for them. Each day would be the same.

Everyone was drunk, everyone was singing and dancing and laughing.
'STAY IN ABER. STAY IN ABER. . . .'
'O'Doom, stop it,' cried Ed, 'you don't know what you're saying, man.'
'JUST ONE MORE PINT,' roared O'Doom. 'WE'VE GOT TIME FOR ANOTHER.'

Ed cornered O'Doom and he tried to get him to see reason. 'No! We have to go now, whilst we're sober, whilst we've still got a chance.'

But O'Doom proved belligerent. He had discovered a little piece of heaven and he was determined to fight for it. 'LET GO OF ME, ED, I'M WARNING YOU.' He made a fist and he threatened Ed with it. 'COME ON, ED, WHAT POSSIBLE HARM COULD ANOTHER PINT DO?'

One by one, Ed pointed out his friends to O'Doom. 'Not one single person is actually from here. They came here on holiday, most of them, liked the place and stayed. Think of that, O'Doom, think of what that means. Everything you ever wanted from life, abandoned, then forgotten.'

Natasha had arranged to meet Ed in Hyde park. But after sitting waiting for Ed for almost two hours she knew that he would not be coming. She walked home across the park cursing Ed. She cursed herself. She laughed at her stupidity.

'Nat! Nat!'

It was Ed. He came running across the park toward her.

'You've been drinking.'

Ed nodded. Breathless, he bent over, clasping his knees. 'We lost Bradley Parker.'

'Lost?'

'To Aber.'

Ed watched her make her preparations.

Knickers from one drawer, tops from another. Natasha stuffed them in to her pack. She boxed up her artists materials. She made a parcel of her sketchbooks and she tied it with string. She sorted out her camping gear, her sleeping bag, tent, carry mat and cooker. Natasha was leaving London. She would spend the summer touring the country, gathering the material she needed for her bigger picture.

Ed and Natasha were stood outside in the street, beside her rusted Ford Escort Estate. It was a huge and lumbering vehicle that burnt oil and was often difficult to start. Certain that it would not pass another MOT Ed had christened it the Carasaurus. 'Carasaurus Rex.'

'What, you're going to travel around the country in shitty shitty bang bang here?'

'No. I'm leaving that with friends.'

She revealed, from behind her back, a pair of plane tickets. She waved them in the air. 'I was going to ask you anyway. I sort of hoped.' She made a little dance: Clippity clop, clippity clop. Clap clap.

'You're going to Spain?'

'Paris.' Natasha punched Ed playfully on the shoulder. Some can can. Some can't.

'Why Paris?'

'Because I'm not ready yet.'

There were things she must do, people and places to pay homage to, things she must see before she could begin to paint. The trip would provide her with a watershed. There would be the time before Paris, and then there would be that time after Paris, the uncluttered future ahead in which anything was possible.

'So, will you come with me?' asked Natasha.

'What, you want me to leave London, just like that?' Ed clicked his fingers.

'You want me to drop everything, abandon my job, my whole future, to run off with you to Paris, and to God knows where and to who knows what after that? Okay,' he said.

Natasha gave Ed her hard honed, narrow eyed, glittery as diamonds look. That hint of a smile, that sometimes meant sex, which always meant mischief, and which now was taken to mean, which now meant. . . .

That brief single moment of eternity with nothing beyond.

'Really!' said a passer by.

They celebrated with a fire in the back garden. They had a barbecue on the coals and then they partied. Two bottles of wine and a dance in the garden to an old Bryan Ferry number.

They lay on their backs, in the grass, in the dark. There was just the night sky above them. They were homeless, or soon would be.

Natasha poured out the last of the wine.

'To Paris,' said Ed, lifting his glass. 'And the world beyond.'

'To my painting the bigger picture,' said Natasha, lifting hers. They clinked glasses.

Natasha wanted success. Ed wanted Natasha. But wanting a thing can begin to take possession of you, it can harness you to its acquisition, trapping you in a job, a way of life, a single place, or in somebody else's future that was not necessarily your own future.

*

It was late, 10pm, and Jigsaw was still in his study seated at his desk, his face illuminated by the pool of light reflecting from the desk lamp. He looked tired. He had spent a long and exhausting day working the phone: making last minute changes to Andy's tour – checking up on hotel bookings, working out travelling times, organising, rearranging. Then there had been The Bizz's coming gig at London's Music Machine to finalise, promoters to ring, lawyers to contact, his new company to think about. He was trying to decide on a name.

He was doodling on his blotter, completely absorbed in the task.

Midas Promotions Limited, he wrote, that sounded good. No, he didn't like that word limited, why should he limit himself? Had he limited himself he would have gotten nowhere, he would be a plumber, like his dad, or on the dole still. He would not be the manager of Britain's most promising new comedian, or of its latest up and coming band, The Bizz, that was for sure. Let alone own a BMW. He would certainly not be renting a luxury apartment in a flash riverside development. Midas Promotions Unlimited then? Jigsaw crossed out the Unlimited. He crossed out Promotions. Midas.

13

Revelations, Insight and Inspiration

Flying was like stepping off the world for a time. It was like roulette. The plane hung in the air, the earth span and span beneath it, and when it stopped.

Ed and Natasha were in Paris.

Different language, different noises, different smells. The smell of fresh bread, of coffee, of Gitane and Gauloise cigarettes. The noise of mopeds echoing down narrow streets. The uplifting comedy of the French police siren. Paris sounded different, because the shape and pace of Paris was different.

The Hotel Bon Sejour, in Montmartre, was a tall building of long windows and iron railed balconies. The room, on the fifth floor, was small, clean and full of light. Ed threw himself on to the double bed. Natasha sprang across the room, pulled open the windows and stepped out on to the balcony. There were views across Montmarte.

Natasha was excited to be in Paris. To her, it was the capital of art, of painting, certainly. Or had been.

'Just think,' she told Ed, when he came to join her on the balcony, 'Van Gogh once walked these very streets. Picasso, and Braque, and Jean Gris, they invented cubism, here, in Paris. And the Impressionists. Cèzanne, Degas, Manet, Monet, Camile, Pissaro, Renoir, Sisley . . .'

They had all worked and exhibited in Paris, exchanging ideas, inspiring, competing against each other. There were numerous great artists buried in the cemeteries. But great artists were buried everywhere, and not just by earth, observed Ed.

Ed wanted to see the sights: the Eiffel Tower, Notre Damme, the Arc de Triumph . . . and to get drunk on cheap wine.

'We could get hold of some absinth,' he said. 'And absinth ourselves. Like those great painters of yours.'

Natasha frowned. She had come to Paris to pay homage to art. Something about Paris had been able to turn poor and struggling artists in to successful artists. In Paris, Natasha could walk the very streets which they had walked, sit in the same cafes, look at the very things which they had once looked at and had studied. She would be able to see, in the galleries and museums, the works which they had then gone on to create, and which had then inspired others to create. Perhaps she too would become inspired. She would, she hoped, soak up, first hand, whatever it was that had encouraged that art and she would grow strong on that. If nothing else she would leave Paris refreshed, knowing that great things could be small pictures.

Natasha visited the Louvre. She stood for a long time in front of the *Mona Lisa*. It was a great painting, certainly, but it did not inspire her. Whatever it was that she was searching for it wasn't there. She crossed the river to the Musee D'Orsay, to view the impressionists, particularly the Van Gogh's. But she was too familiar with the work for it to have any new effect on her. She visited the Musee Picasso. It made her head spin. She visited contemporary art galleries, dusty art rooms. . . . but whatever it was that she was looking for, it wasn't there.

It was evening and Ed and Natasha were sitting on the steps beneath the Sacre Ceur, looking out over Paris and eating dried bread and drinking cheap wine. They had a jar of olives, some tomatoes, cheese, spring onions.

Natasha took a drink of wine straight from the bottle. Then she poured a little wine on to the bread, to soften it. The bread had been slashed with a knife before it had been baked and the patterned, oven-hardened crust cut the roof of Natasha's mouth. Her mouth was torn and sore from eating baguettes. She was sick of baguettes, and olives, and cheese. And tomatoes.

'You promised me we were going to eat out.'

'We are eating out.'

'I want some proper food for a change. Cooked food. We haven't been to one single restaurant, not one, not since we got here.'

'Restaurants are a waste of money.'

Ed disliked restaurants. You didn't eat in restaurants because you were hungry. Just like you didn't drink alcohol in pubs to quench your thirst.

'I've had enough French stick to fill any woman.' And, snatching Ed's baguette from him, Natasha hit him playfully on the head with it, before flinging it, along with her own, in to some nearby bushes. 'We're going to eat out properly, in a restaurant, tonight.'

They went to several restaurants, but every place they went to was the same. They were much too expensive.

'We could live for a whole week on that,' said Ed, looking at yet another price list.

Natasha agreed. 'Yes. Best keep our money.'

'Maybe we could find a cheap workingmen's cafe,' Ed suggested.

'There aren't any. I haven't seen any. It's all shops and boutiques and expensive cafes and restaurants and stuff.'

Then Natasha knew. It wasn't Paris that had turned people in to artists. Paris had allowed them to be artists.

Paris had been cheap. Money had lasted in Paris then, and that had given artists their chance. It allowed anyone who needed it the time to work at their ideas until either they succeeded or they grew to realise that the thing was impossible for them. Even then, they would not have given up, many of them. Because, sometimes, poverty was far easier to endure than its moneyed alternative if it offered the time to work on the next idea. That was what Natasha was looking for, that, and the certainty you get when there is no other way but the way you have chosen.

Paris was no longer cheap, it was no longer the great workshop it had once been. That was elsewhere now.

Ed and Natasha left Paris. They hired a 2CV soft top and drove it to Bayeux. Natasha wanted to view the tapestry. She made numerous sketches, and took copious notes and photographs. She bought the book in the inevitable gift shop. Leaving Bayeux, they headed south.

Ed loved this carefree, roamer's life: having some far off goal, some distant place in which to put his faith.

'So, where to now?' he asked.

He needed to know where he was travelling to. It would feel pointless otherwise.

'The Dordogne.'

'Where the trampolinists come from?'

'Trampolinists?'

'Dordoing. Dordoing.'

They drove in to longer, warmer days. There were bluer and bluer skies. The land grew drier, yellower. The sun blazed. There were limestone outcrops, mountains. Everywhere was white and hot and luminous.

They stopped at Lascaux.

They parked the car in the carpark then followed the long line of people down in to the cave. There were handrails, a concrete path, dim electric lights. Coldness. Silence. Dark.

Sound did not echo here. Something pressed down, compressing even the air.

Then, there they were, the famous cave paintings.

A huge bull, an auroch, reindeer, numerous horses, bison. . . . The paintings were over 17,000 years old. It was some of the oldest art in the world, Natasha told Ed.

Natasha pointed out the figures carrying spears. 'People were nomadic back then, they were hunters. They followed the animals on their migrations. These here were what they hunted. I guess they painted what was important to them, what was necessary. And there, look, there are their handprints.' And she reached out, only to restrain herself.

Hunters, nomads. Ed's blood quickened as he felt that deep and ancient need stir inside of him.

Not for him the settled life.

There are television shows where the contestants are abandoned in the wilderness so that viewers can then laugh at their attempts to survive as they struggle to perform even the most basic of tasks. But Ed would survive. To laugh at Ed you would need to abandon him in an office with a form to fill out, a phone to answer, or a computer or a drinks machine to operate. But he could hunt and fish and sleep rough and be the better for it and love life.

At first, Ed had marvelled at the images but he soon began to grow depressed.

Inside, in the cave, everything remained as it had been, undisturbed, for over 17,000 years. It was the same. But outside.

Ed was disappointed when he emerged from the cave, annoyed to find tarmac, modern buildings, cars, people stood in queues. People queuing for the gift shop.

There was no sign and Natasha almost drove past the turn off. It was a long time since she had been there and she did not recognise the place. Pebbles spat out from beneath the tyres as she swung the car off the main road and on to the corrugated dirt track.

'You've been here before?' said Ed.

'A long time ago, on holiday.'

They drove up in to the empty, scrub covered hills. Finally, after passing between two steep bluffs, that came together to form a gorge, they emerged in to a large, natural amphitheatre, the remains of an ancient, long collapsed cavern. Steep encircling cliffs of white limestone towered above them. The dazzlingly white rock was hard to look at in the fierce sun. Above them, the sky was a blue lens.

Natasha pulled up in a cloud of white dust that took a long time to settle. She pointed out a gulley in the cliff to Ed.

The ground was steep and broken and the fierce sun made the climb difficult and they were soon drenched in sweat. It took them half an hour to reach the shade of the gulley and a further twenty minutes of climbing before they emerged out on to a hot, dry, sunlit plateau, where there were towers and mounds of tumbled limestone. The place was eerie, in the way that a deserted city can be eerie.

Natasha walked over to a low cliff and, bending, she disappeared in to a fissure in the rock. Ed followed her.

The cave, illuminated from above through a cleft in the ceiling, glowed goldenly in the diffuse light. The walls and ceiling were covered in handprints.

An exclamation of surprise and of awe was forced out of Ed. Wherever he looked there were handprints. To Ed, the hands seemed to be reaching for him. He felt compelled to reach out, to touch them. But the prints were strange and otherworldly too. Ed felt his flesh tighten and he shivered. He withdrew his hand.

'Isn't it amazing,' said Natasha.

'There must be hundreds of them,' he said.

'One hundred and twenty six.'

'You counted them?'

'I was curious. Isn't it incredible. It's the very first art, Ed. All around the world it is. It's like there's this deep-seated need in us, this impulse to create, to make our mark and leave some kind of presence behind after we have gone.'

They stood gazing at the handprints.

The primitive images possessed power. They reached out from and in to the rock, from past to present and back to past again. Almost as though they might cling on to something.

'Just think, these are the signatures of people who lived here ten, maybe twenty thousand years ago.'

'What happened to them, do you reckon?' Where did they go?' asked Ed.

'Go? Nowhere. They became us.'

Natasha reached out and she placed her hand on the faded red handprint of someone who had lived thousands upon thousands of years ago. She closed her eyes, and in the red glowing darkness behind her eyelids that distance was reduced, it disappeared. The same sun warmed her that had once warmed them. She breathed the same air. Touched the same rock. There was no difference. She felt the slowly increasing warmth of the rock return her warmth. Another body, another pulse reached out, even as she reached in, and, for a moment, something touched.

Natasha flashed open her eyes. 'Come on,' she said, 'I want to show you something.'

Making a search of the ground outside the entrance to the cave Natasha soon found what she was looking for. The crumbly red pebbles were scattered across the ground like an abandoned game of marbles.

Natasha found a hollowed out rock, and, using it as a mortar and a smaller rock as a pestle, she began to grind up the red stones until they were dust. Then she poured in some water from their water bottle. She mixed the dust and the water together.

'It's red ochre,' she said. 'Iron oxide. The same as in blood. Most handprints are stencils. That was how they did it, they placed their hand on the rock, filled their mouth with this stuff,' she pointed at the puddle of red water, 'then they sprayed it over their hand.' She placed her hand in front of her face and she demonstrated the technique. 'And when they removed their hand. . . .' she pulled away her hand, 'there was their hand silhouetted on the rock.'

'Fancy putting that stuff in your mouth. Why do you think they did it that way?' There were other ways. 'I mean, it was obviously deliberate.'

The method left a diffuse aurora around the print where the ochre had been sprayed, so maybe that was the reason.

It was a statement of absence, it seemed to Ed, rather than of presence, which was how he had first read the prints. Ed felt that he was starting to break the code: there was no code, just knowledge and understanding.

Natasha added more red ochre, thickening the water till it became a paste, then she smeared one hand with it. Crossing to an overhang of rock she pressed her hand on to the rock face. Ed did the same.

Their two handprints lay side by side, glistening, like freshly spilt blood, as in a sacrifice. Like strange flowers: kangaroo paws; stylised images of the sun.

'Eventually,' said Natasha, 'the iron oxide in the dust will permeate the rock and our prints will stay there for hundreds perhaps thousands of years.'

Ed did not say anything. He looked at the two handprints and he thought: They will be there long after we have gone. What will they mean to the people who will then see them? What do they mean to us? We are so alive in this instant and we will leave this place and go on living. What we have just done was but an instant's work, an impulse, yet it may well last beyond us, maybe forever. It will first identify us, then, perhaps, it could become more important than us, it might even define us.

A sudden breeze, like cold water, blew across their skin. The sun was lowering in the sky. It grew cold quickly on those exposed uplands. The white rock yellowed, then glowed. Slowly, it began to darken. Ed and Natasha scrambled reluctantly down the gully, back to their vehicle.

They drove off, disappearing through the cleft between the bluffs. And for a long time afterwards the land was alone again, left to itself, possessing no meaning.

It would have been easy to carry on travelling. Ed could do odd jobs, Natasha could paint, she would do caricatures. Until somewhere along the way things would be different for them. But Natasha was keen to return home to begin her preparations for the bigger picture.

'Later, Ed. When I've done my paintings.'

Everything was in the future. That huge and empty space for the storage of the undone. And sometimes the undoable.

Sitting, waiting at the airport, Ed and Natasha felt detached, divorced from their surroundings, that they were no longer involved.

They took their seats on the plane. The seat belt sign pinged on, there was the click of buckles being secured. The last of the overhead lockers were banged shut. The stewards and stewardesses took their places. The engines roared and the plane taxied down the runway. The plane stopped and the engines idled. There was the low, monotonous hum of the plane's air conditioning.

The jet engines roared and the plane accelerated down the runway, then the ground shot away as the plane soared in to the sky and when the plane levelled again, the distant ground slowed, like the plane was floating.

Ed and Natasha experienced a period of waiting that was like the suspension of time. In an hour everything would be different: it would be the same again. It was like sitting in the cinema waiting for a film to start. There were refreshments, you sat and you waited, you were between worlds.

Like Mister Ben after he had chosen a suit of clothes and just before he stepped out of the changing room.

14

Sudden Transformations

Clemence had signed the contracts, the galley proofs had been checked and returned and the first edition, a run of 500 copies, of his first ever volume of poetry was at that moment being run off the presses. Clemence locked up the cottage and travelled down to London on the train.

Experience and inspiration, and the workshop of hard graft that turn ideas in to reality might well exist anywhere, but it was to London that everything eventually must come before it could be said to have been discovered.

Here were the galleries, the exhibitions, the artists colonies and gathering places, the great publishing houses, the centres of media and entertainment, the headquarters of the corporations and advertising agencies.

The roar of the traffic was deafening. People hurried everywhere. Lights shone off the wet streets. Clemence hailed a taxi. 'Backstreet Books,' he told the driver, giving him the address.

The taxi left Euston, took a right on to Woburn Place, and then another on to Russel Square, taking Clemence in to the very heart of Bloomsbury, the London of Virginia Woolf, Lytton Strachey, Vanessa Bell, Duncan Grant, Roger Fry. The world of the literati. Continuous rounds of dinner parties, book signings, poetry readings, talks and interviews. . . . The London that he was about to inhabit. Here he was, a successful poet at last, on his way to see his publisher.

The taxi left the main drag entered Soho and eventually pulled up in a side street. As the driver pointed out the premises, several provocatively dressed women pushed themselves off the walls and began to converge slowly upon the taxi. Clemence paid the driver and, blushing at the women's lewd advances, he hurried across the pavement to the building. There was a plaque on the wall:

First floor: Gym will Fix It, Suppliers Of Keep Fit Equipment.
Second Floor: J Wyles. Osteopath. Third Floor: Backstreet Books.

Clemence took the steps two at a time to the third floor where, after unslinging his pack and putting down his violin case, he knocked on the door.
'Yes!'
Clemence pulled open the door and stepped confidently inside only to check himself.
The office was very small and cluttered and dimly lit.
An overweight, balding man with a comb-over and a bright red face, a drinker's face, looked up from behind a desk piled high with books and manuscripts.
'Well?'
'Mister Grenville-Jones?'
'Yes?' said Mister Grenville-Jones.
'Clemence Tartt.'
'Tartt? Tarrt? Ah, yes, Clemence Tartt, the young poet. Well, come in, come in.' Clemence reached behind him and he shut the door.
'Sit sit.' Grenville-Jones motioned to a chair. It was full of manuscripts. Clemence removed the manuscripts from the chair and he looked for somewhere to put them down. Grenville-Jones told him to dump them on the floor. Clemence placed them carefully, reverentially, on the floor and sat down. The leaning pile of manuscripts toppled and slid slowly across the floor.
Grenville-Jones sat with his clasped hands rested on the desk and he stared at Clemence and was just about to address him when the phone on his desk rang. Grenville-Jones eagerly snatched it up. 'Backstreet Books, Mister Grenville-Jones, manager and editor in chief speaking. 'Ahh, Timothy, so glad you called. Yes. What? Well yes, yes. Go on. . . '
Clemence sat looking at Grenville-Jones. He waited patiently. Then impatiently.
Waiting made some people angry. It depressed Clemence. He felt let down, unimportant, like he was on hold. When this should have been his moment.
Clemence sat looking around the cramped and dingy office. The room depressed him. There was an empty bottle of Chinese Four Dragons Whisky in the waste paper bin, and a dirty, almost opaque glass on Grenville-Jones' desk. There were wooden filing cabinets, with papers sticking up out of the drawers. Manuscripts stood in stacks along one wall. There was a battered

table, on which rested an old fashioned typewriter, a second telephone - it was disconnected – and a fax machine. Clemence noted that there were no computers in the office. An old clock with Roman numerals and a yellowed face hung slightly off centre on the wall. Grey light filtered in through a small grimy window from the narrow street outside. A single naked lightbulb lit the office.

It was not how Clemence had expected it would be. The office. His reception. His book lost a little of its powers for him.

Grenville-Jones put down the phone. Resting back in his chair, he placed his fingers on the edge of his desk and he sat looking at his desk. His eyes scanned the desk and his fingers began to tap on the desk, like it was a piano.

'Now, where were we?' he asked. 'Ah, yes. Mister, er. . . .'

'Tartt,' said Clemence.

'Ah yes, Tartt. Now, where did I put them?' Grenville-Jones looked thoughtful. 'Ah!' He reached down and he lifted a small stack of thin red volumes from off the floor and he placed them on the desk. 'Here we are, yes,' he said, 'your book. Five free copies.' He pushed them across the desk to Clemence. 'To give to friends and family. If you want more, you will have to pay for them.'

Clemence took a book off the pile. His very first book: Window On My Being, by Clemence Tartt. The title and his name were written in gold on the rib. He sat staring at his book, admiring it. He turned it over in his hands, hefting it to feel its weight, tapping it to feel its solidity. It was in hardback. A thin volume but his. He'd written a book. He was a real poet, at last, a published poet. Here was the proof.

Clemence leant forward in his seat and he took grateful possession of the other four books. He sat holding the books, waiting.

'So, what happens now?' said Clemence.

'Well, what have you brought me?' said Grenville-Jones.

'Brought?' Clemence frowned. 'Nothing, I. . . .'

'Nothing? No new poems?'

Clemence held up his books. 'This is it,' he said. 'The complete works of Clemence Tartt.'

'Ah,' said Grenville-Jones. 'I see. Well, it was nice to meet you, Mister, er, Tartt. Yes. Now, if you don't mind, I have work to do.' Grenville-Jones gestured toward the door. 'When you have something to show me, bring it around. Until then. . . .'

'But the book launch? The book signings?'

'Book launch? This is poetry not fiction. This is Backstreet Books.'

'And the poetry readings?'

'Readings?'

'Well, aren't there poetry readings I'll be doing?'

'I suppose, but who'd come?'

'What? no readings?'

'Look,' Grenville-Jones explained, 'you're a promising young poet, but you're an as yet completely unknown poet, and in a world that is not in the least bit interested in poetry. And we're a publisher, not your agent.'

'But I can't live off the profits from 500 books,' said Clemence.

'Well, no, obviously. No one is expecting you to.'

'But I thought. . . .'

'Yes, I know,' said Grenville-Jones. 'You thought you could be a poet and nothing else. Alas, a first edition of 500 copies, that is all we can hope for, at this stage. Poetry is a very small market, you must keep the work coming, you understand? New work, that's what's it's all about. Quantity and volume. Now, if you don't mind.'

Clemence made to protest, but he could think of nothing more to say. There was nothing to say. He still had everything to do yet. There was always that one more hill to climb. Then another. And another.

Clemence felt very tired of a sudden.

He got up out of his seat and pulled open the door.

So, that was it, this, his fifteen minutes of Warholian fame, over, to be followed later by whatever you could wring out of it. That, and the knowing that you could do it. That you had done it. And there was the rub.

But writers are tenacious. They have to be, or they wouldn't be writers.

'And please, don't slam the door,' said Grenville-Jones. 'Everyone these days slams the door.' He prepared himself for a door slam.

Clemence closed the door. He turned to face Grenville-Jones.

'Mister Grenville-Jones?'

'Yes?'

'I do have an idea for a novel.'

The publisher drew in a deep breath, which he then slowly exhaled. He was a large man but his sigh seemed to deflate him.

'A novel, you say?'

'Yes.'

'And what is it about, this novel?'

'Everything.'

'Ah, yes, the great novel. Look, I am sorry if I seem brusque, it is nothing personal, you understand, only I hear so much about what people are going to do, when what I need to see is what they have done. Frankly, their intentions exasperate me, their accomplishments, on the other hand, would be a pleasure to see. Whatever it is, then by all means go ahead and write it, then, maybe, we will have something to talk about. Until then, good day.'

Natasha was in London. Clemence had her address from the postcard she had sent him when she had first arrived.

Clemence found the street. He knocked on the door.

Clemence had dedicated his poems to Natasha. He hoped that Natasha would like the poems and tell him that they were good. She might, he hoped, tell him that they were brilliant.

He shifted his pack on his shoulders, the straps were beginning to dig in to him. He swapped his violin case to the other hand.

He knocked again.

An old woman, one of the building's tenants, answered the door.

'Who?' she said, 'Natasha? Oh, you mean that artist girl? Her. She just left.'

'Left?' Clemence's bag felt suddenly very heavy. 'Where, where did she go?' he asked.

The woman didn't know. She wasn't sure.

'Paris, I think.'

'Paris?'

'Yes. I think that's where she said. Paris. The two of them went.'

'Two of them?'

'Her and her boyfriend.'

Clemence stepped wearily out in to the street. He had very little money, nowhere to stay, and no return ticket for the train home. London had become a different city.

He sat down in a doorway to rest and to think things over. Someone tossed him a pound coin.

Clemence walked back in to town. In Covent Garden, he stopped for a while to watch the street performers. He saw a juggler, then a mime act and after that some clowns. But there were clowns everywhere, in every walk of life.

Clemence removed his fiddle from its case, placed the open case on the ground then began to play.

The city exists on various edges. Numerous levels in several dimensions operate at any one time. The interface is everywhere, generating energies. The city is a labyrinth: complex, intricate, a maze like structure of tunnels, pathways and sudden transformations. . . .

15

The More Real the Thing Gets, the More Unreal it all Becomes

Huge cranes loomed over the city. Metal flew down its crowded streets. People streamed everywhere. Workers. Shoppers. Even at this late hour. And it was raining heavily. City people are always busy. You won't find too many idlers in a city. There are the rich, of course, and there are down and outs, and any number of criminals: con men, fraudsters, all that sort, but anyone that holds down a job, they look downright pursued.

Jigsaw sped from traffic light to traffic light. He cut in front of a bus, narrowly missing a motor cycle. The car, a Porsche boxter, registration, *Midas1*, handled beautifully.

Andy gripped his seat. 'Christ! Jigsy, mate. Slow down will yer, fucksakes! You'll get us done for speeding.'

'Doing fifty miles an hour? That's not speeding, not in this car.' Jigsaw checked in his rear mirror. 'Besides, there's no police.'

'No?' Andy pointed out the numerous cameras. They were mounted on traffic lights. On lamp-posts. They were on the sides of buildings.

Jigsaw braked so hard that Andy was thrown unexpectedly forward in his seat. Cars stacked up behind the stopped car before speeding around it in to the oncoming traffic, desperate for the empty road ahead. Several passers by peered in to the suddenly stationary car. They became excited when they saw Andy.

Andy stared malevolently back.

Jigsaw sat complaining. 'All this surveillance, they should be using it to catch proper criminals, not busy people. You can't get away with anything, these days.'

It wasn't being under constant observation that angered him so much as the restraint he would now have to impose on himself.

'I'm surprised you haven't been caught speeding before, Jigsy, mate.'

'Of course I've been caught before, I drive a sports car. I'm a busy man. And now I'm only three points clear of being disqualified. I know, we'll say that you were driving.'

'I can't drive.'

'It's the perfect excuse. You didn't know any better.'

Andy laughed. 'Better move, Jigsy, mate, before we get a parking ticket. Just drive a bit more careful, that's all.'

'I am careful. It's not a question of being careful, it's a question of not getting caught. That's what careful driving means these days. But what if I run a red light? Or go the wrong way up a one way street? It happens, it's quicker sometimes. I can't be looking out for signs all the time. I might be punching in a phone number, or reading a text. And what about the scenery?' He meant the women. 'This is London, it's distracting out there. And how can I possibly be watching my speed if I have to look at the road? I'm driving a car. People make mistakes, they have accidents, they're not deliberates. We are being harassed for the purpose of generating revenue.'

'It's the law, Jigsy, you can't argue with it, it's against the law.'

'Right, they've got the full ignorance of the law behind them. But people should not be criminalised for having to be elsewhere, it – Don't they realise just how busy we are?'

There was a rap on the window. It was someone holding out a pen and some paper, wanting Andy's autograph.

Jigsaw hit the accelerator, snatching Andy away.

They'd just got in when the phone rang. It was Enzo, who lived in the Penthouse upstairs.

'That was Enzo,' said Jigsaw, putting down the phone, 'inviting us to an opening.'

He had an exhibition opening at White Cube and there was to be a party afterwards.

'Tonight?'

'Eight o'clock.'

Andy groaned. 'Aw no, I hate his art, it's shite.'

'There'll be a party afterwards.'

'A party? Nice one.' Andy brightened.

The phone rang again. Jigsaw snatched it up.

'Hello?' he asked. 'Who?' he frowned, 'Hello? Oh,' he exclaimed, realising, 'Hello!' he beamed, he sat upright. 'Hello, HELLO!' he said. Andy frowned at him, puzzled. Jigsaw put his hand across the mouthpiece. 'It's *HELLO!* The magazine,' he explained, before returning to the phone. 'Yes,' he said, Yes, yes absolutely. No...' Covering the mouthpiece again he addressed Andy: 'They want you for an interview with Bane Burke.' She was their main features writer. 'They want to do a feature on you. Comedy, the new rock and roll. The apartment, the cars, the whole lifestyle.' Jigsaw was excited.

'Tell them....' Andy looked thoughtful. 'Tell them to fuck off.'

Jigsaw returned to the phone. 'No, of course, yes. Yes, yes, absolutely. Okay. Bye , bye, *HELLO!*' he said, laughing. 'Bye,' he repeated. Delighted, he put down the phone.

'Andy sat glowering at him. 'You said yes, you cunt.'

'Well of course. Think of the publicity, Andy.'

'Bad publicity. I'm supposed to be an angry young comedian. A rebel. I'm not supposed to have all this.' Andy gestured about the room.

The phone began ringing again. Jigsaw snatched it up. 'Hello,' he grinned. 'Petra, hi!.' It was Petra Vane, Andy's supermodel girlfriend.

Andy waved away the phone, gesturing that he didn't want to speak to her, but the device was cordless and Jigsaw had already thrown it to him. Andy caught the phone.

'Petra, hi,' he said, 'so how you doing, babe?'

'Don't you babe me,' she said, 'it's been over a week now, one whole week and not one single word from you, not one word, no phone call, nothing, not even a....'

Andy recoiled from the phone, holding it away from him. Petra's voice became tinny and distant.

The tirade stopped and Andy returned to the phone.

'I've been busy, babe,' Andy told her, 'I've been away, on tour, you know that.'

'You said you'd call.'

'I did call.' Andy winced at the lie. 'I have been calling. Every night.'

'Liar,' she snapped. 'I've got voice mail.'

'I hate those things.'

'You didn't ring, did you?'

'You know how it is on tour. It's like when you go off modelling on assignment. You've never any time to yourself.'

There was a long silence on the other end of the phone. Doubtless, Petra was stoking up on past resentments. Andy readied himself for the onslaught.

'I see. Hotels and parties, was it? Too busy entertaining other women, that's what.'

'Other women? There's no one else, Pet, honest. Just you. Look, I'll make it up to you. I'll take you out shopping, someplace, yeah? I'll get you that new dress that you're after.' Andy was sure there was a dress. There's always some new thing that they're after. Otherwise, what was there to look forward to.

'Promise?' she said, her voice hurt but conciliatory.

'I said, didn't I?'

'And shoes?'

Andy breathed a kind of relief. 'Well of course shoes, you can't go around barefoot, can you? Not like the other way around. Look, I'll get you the whole outfit,' he promised.

'Really?'

'A sed, din' I?' His accent was always more pronounced when he was angry. Neither spoke for a time.

'Andy?' said Petra.

'Yes,' said Andy, warily.

'You do love me, don't you?'

Andy's head lifted and his eyes coursed about the ceiling. 'Jesus, Petra,' he said, grimacing. 'Well, yeah, course I do. Loads. A mean, Am goin out with yeh, aren' I?'

'Then say it, Andy.'

'What?'

'You know.'

Andy had to say it. And then he had to say it again, only this time like he meant it.

'Anyone can say it, Andy. You have to prove it. Prove it to me, Andy.'

All those stories of Princesses sending their suitors out on quests are not fables.

'Prove it to you, how?'

'Well I don't know. Somehow. Because I'm not going to be treated like a piece of arm candy, not anymore. I'm a real person too, you know, with a real person's needs.'

'Hey, you're more than arm candy to me, Petra. You look good on the end of me knob, too.' He laughed. 'Petra. Petra?' But the phone was dead. Andy looked at the phone. 'She cut me off,' he told Jigsaw.

Jigsaw shook his head. 'You should treat your women right,' he said. 'That way, they'll recommend you to their friends.' He began chuckling to himself.

Andy tossed Jigsaw the phone. He crossed to the mini bar and he poured himself a drink, a large whisky.

Jigsaw dialled voice mail.

'You have four - call messages,' said Andy. There were ten messages.

There were several from Petra: 'Andy, where are you?' 'Andy, call me.' 'Andee!' The rest were for Jigsaw as Andy's manager, requesting Andy's presence at supermarket openings, clubs, dinner parties. . . Jigsaw got out his work diary and scanned the pages, dropping the less lucrative appointments and replacing them with the more profitable appointments. He began working the phone.

Sipping his drink, Andy crossed to the music deck. He picked up a tape, it was The Bizz's latest release, *Vermin Zillionaires*. That sounded interesting. He put it on and he listened to that for a while: Boom boom, boom di boom, boom boom, boom di boom, boom. . . . Andy fast forwarded the tape: boom boom boom di, boom boom boom di boom. . . . He held the fast forward down for a full twenty seconds: baddle a baba, baddle a baba, baddle a. . . . What the f. . . .

'Jigsaw, there's no lyrics? It's all the fucking same.'

'The Bizz are going dance. House, it's called, acid-house. It's going to be big. There's lots of money in it.' Jigsaw pondered that. 'Maybe I ought to open our own club.'

Andy tried Joy Division. *Digital* came on. It was his going out music. He often used it to get up his blood: 'I feel it closing in. I feel it closing in. . . .' But it was too early. Filling him with its energy it only made him feel contained. He wanted to be out there, doing things.

Andy switched off the machine.

'So, what we up for tonight?' he asked.

'White Cube, for the opening, then the party, followed by some clubbing, yes?'

Andy nodded. He checked the clock. There were still two hours to kill. 'An' before?'

Jigsaw clasped then rubbed his hands. Smiling, 'Indian or Chinese?' he asked.

'Thai,' said Andy.

'Two Thais it is.' And, picking up the phone, Jigsaw rang WorldBabe.

Armageddon, the nightclub. Loud music, flashing lights. Crowds of people dancing. It was two in the morning and the place was packed. Loud music, thumping and repetitive, thudded off damp walls. Andy was with a crowd of

Enzo's friends – the sculptor, Petros Kouriakis, Sadie Sommers. . . . Everyone had disappeared on to the dance floor.

'ANDY!' someone yelled. 'It's Andy Rant!'

The man thrust out his hand. Andy ignored it. 'I see no ships,' said the man, snapping the hand to his forehead. 'Hey. Say something funny, Andy.'

'FUCK OFF,' shouted Andy in to the man's face.

The man laughed. He had been told to fuck off by Andy Rant. It was something he would always have that he could tell people.

Andy's attention was caught by a stunning wafer thin blonde in a tight, off-the-shoulder top and short dress that was sitting at a table opposite. It was Petra Vane. She was staring over at him. But when Andy lifted his hand to wave she looked away, deliberately offering him a steady view of her uplifted profile. Andy wasn't sure, but she looked different somehow. Thinking she was still angry with him, he pulled down his hand.

Petra was with a group of her air-friends: Stefan Preaer, the hairdresser, Veronica Vajamiinke, the clothes designer, and Vera Louche, the gossip columnist. They were out celebrating Petra's new nose. She glanced back in Andy's direction, to gauge its effect on him, but he was nowhere to be seen.

The dull percussive thumps of repetitive music shook the room. Andy could feel it inside him, thumping, urging him to dance. He resisted the music. Grabbing an unattended drink off a table he knocked it back. It was neat vodka and Andy grimaced. He swept up a bottled beer.

A hand rested on his shoulder that whirled him around, the sudden movement making the room spin.

'That's my drink you got there, pal.' Fighting talk.

Andy's punch completely missed its target, the momentum of it taking him elsewhere. He was in a different room, the air there more humid, the music louder, too loud. Angle limbed people danced too close, nudging Andy, making him angry.

Jigsaw was there. He was stood talking to a tall and stunning blonde in a short white dress and high heels. Jigsaw introduced her.

'Andy, this is Semena. Semena, Andy.'

Jigsaw had to shout to be heard above the music. Everyone had to stand very close in order to talk. Semena bent herself toward Andy - she was an inch or two taller than him. Now she was reaching out and touching him. Proof of Andy. He'd experienced this before, but not this. The girl gave off heat. And electricity.

'I know Andy,' said Semena, smiling, the smile almost a laugh. She had a husky voice, Eastern European. She smelt of musk. Andy felt her body heat embrace him. 'I have seen Andy on television.' She lifted a hand to her forehead. 'I see no ships,' she said.

'Only hardships,' mouthed Andy, grinning. It seemed like he mouthed it. All you could hear was music – noise. He did a bit of his routine: 'Sailor: Land Ahoy!' to which Semena then offered the punchline. They laughed. It was like mime, but to some other soundtrack.

Andy offered Semena a swig of beer. She declined, she was drinking water. Andy took a swig of beer.

'Semena is from Prague,' said Jigsaw.

'They call me the bouncing Czech,' said Semena.

Andy stared at her, puzzled. She wasn't buxom.

'I'm a call girl,' she explained. 'If ever you're interested.'

Andy pulled the bottle from his lips and he sprayed drink in to the atmosphere like he was some kind of air freshener.

The music changed, from dance to new wave. It grew louder, more bass. It was the first of the night's bands: The Right Fecking Eejits with their new number, *Incoming*. The music came screaming out of them with artillery barrage loudness: Scream bang, scream bang. . . . The place vibrated to it. Jigsaw went off to see the band. Andy stayed with Semena.

Her smile was beautiful. Her long capable fingers wove playfully in her hair. She lifted her arms, swaying her hips to the music, her knees bent, lips pouted she looked sexily over her shoulder at Andy.

Semena motioned with her head toward the dance floor, a sea of writhing, leaping bodies, pressing close. 'Dance?' she shouted, the words unheard. Scream bang, scream bang.

Andy shook his head. 'A never drink and jive,' he shouted, lifting up his beer. It only seemed like he was dancing. Drunk, he was just trying to stay upright. He looked robotic under the strobe lights.

Semena tried to match her movements to Andy's movements. When Andy's legs went out from under him, Semena responded with a shimmy. Like a limbo dancer, he flung himself backwards over a table. He was quite happy there for a time, until Semena lowered herself over him, hauling him upright. Her eyes were sultry, her lips pouting, her breath hot on his face.

Then she went flying away, was pulled away from him and a loud screech pierced Andy's eardrums. He actually heard it:

'YOU BASTARD! I'M NOT GOING TO TAKE THIS. IT'S OVER. WE'RE FINISHED!'

Petra raked his face with the nails of one hand and slapped it hard with the other. Then, grabbing a glass off a table, she threw the contents in his face.

Andy sat on the floor dazed and disorientated, temporarily blinded by the drink.

'What the fuck?' he said, wiping the drink from his eyes. He licked his lips. It was Bollinger. He'd had it before.

Petra began slapping Andy about the head before bursting in to tears. Her air-friends hurried over to offer her their support. A crowd gathered. Drawn to the commotion, several bouncers and a photographer began making their way over.

Jigsaw appeared and began to sort everything out. If there was going to be a photograph he wanted everything to be just right.

Semena and Petra got involved in a catfight. It started with abuse, then there were slaps, a whirligig of claws and then hair-pulling. Finally, each girl leant back against her restraining bouncer and went at each other with their shoes. They were wearing stilettos.

A bright pulsing flash stopped everything dead. Petra, offering her new profile, insisted on another photograph. Andy punched the photographer. Next thing he knew he was flying through the air, it felt like flying.

Jigsaw, Sadie, PK, Enzo and Semena bundled Andy in to a taxi. A whole crowd came back to the development with them. Everyone piled in to PK's. There was music and dancing, drink and drugs and pairing off.

Jigsaw found a large pair of decorator's scissors and he began running around cutting the dress and bra straps and then the girls knickers and g strings off them. There were loud shouts of ribald laughter and great roars of appreciation from the men, and screams and giggles from the girls. Then one of the girls commandeered the scissors. There followed more robust, and, this time, enforced protests.

Andy had a line, to counter the effects of the drink which had begun to tire him, then he needed another drink.

Mostly, when Andy got drunk, wonderful things happened. He woke up in strange beds with the most beautiful women, and sometimes the most unlikely women. It was a bit of a lottery, drink.

Andy woke, with his usual head-splitting hangover, in a strange and luxuriously appointed bedroom: gold painted fragile looking furniture, gilded mirrors, tall windows, heavy purple coloured drapes, pale blue and gold striped velvety wallpaper. . . . He looked around the room, trying to focus, fighting the need to be sick, noticing, scattered across the pink carpeted floor amongst his own clothes, a crumpled black dress, some skimpy black underwear, torn stockings, black high heeled shoes . . . he recognised none of them.

'Semena!' he shouted. There was no reply. He waited.

No one came.

'Er, Petra?'

Andy got up out of bed, staggered to the window and looked out. Knightsbridge?

Who did he know in Knightsbridge? Someone, obviously. Not Petra. She was Olivers Wharf.

Andy remembered nothing of the night before. He was completely lost in space and time. It was happening to him often. These blackouts and memory loss, these inexplicable appearances in strange places. Their effect on him was crippling.

Andy turned from the window. He found his shorts and put them on. He found and then put on one sock. He pulled on his jeans. A boot, and then the other boot. He found his missing sock and he put it in his pocket. He was pulling his T-shirt over his head when he heard the bedroom door open. He turned, just as a pretty young girl with a dark complexion stepped in to the room. She was dressed, provocatively, or so Andy thought, in a short black dress and white apron, exactly like a French maid.

'Aha!' grinned Andy. 'Role play.' He made a lustful lunge for the girl, who let out a shrill scream as he began chasing her around the bedroom and then over the bed. . . .

A tall and heavy boned blonde in red shoes and red dress, wearing a necklace of huge white pearls entered the room. She was very tall and very blonde, not beautiful, but statuesque, and not so young.

She stood, glowering, tight lipped, her eyes furious, pointing at the door. Submissive, shrinking, the maid squirmed out from between Andy and the wall, first curtseyed and then rushed past the woman and fled the room.

Andy recognised the woman immediately. 'Charlotte Champagne Hinton,' he said, clicking his fingers. She was always in the papers and celebrity magazines. She was the daughter of billionaire businessman, The Right Honourable Lord Jack – I'm all right – Hinton. But didn't she have a boyfriend? Miles Sackburn, heir to the Sackburn drinks fortune?

Andy smiled.

'I think you'd better go,' she said, pointing.

The first drink relaxed Andy. The second was to keep something of that first drink alive.

It was not a rough pub, not by reputation, but it was early and there were rough people in it. It was quiet.

It was effortless company, sitting there, alone, apparently unrecognised. Andy began to recover his energies.

It wasn't long though before he was recognised.

'Hey, it's that bloke on TV,' said a man. Andy sighed.

Someone shouted: 'I see no ships!'

Andy kept his back to the pub. He sat and he stared at his drink. He said nothing. He picked up his glass and, staring in to the drink, moved it in a circular motion. Lifting the glass he finished the drink.

Slowly, the mood in the pub turned against Andy. Andy knew that they hated him and not just because he had refused to join them in their banter. It was resentment. He had what they would never have: a way out. And being one of their own made him both traitor and enemy. Andy was about to get up from his seat, was pushing himself off the bar, when someone came up behind him. Andy stood, checked, watching it in the bar mirror.

The youth was large and shaven headed, one of four who had been sitting by the jukebox. Andy watched him roll his shoulders, like he was pulling on a jacket, then stretch out his chin, like he was adjusting a tie. The youth tapped Andy on the shoulder.

Andy turned.

The youth stared malevolently at Andy. Andy held his gaze. He noticed the scars, in the shape of half-moons, dug deep in to the youth's scalp. One eyebrow was disfigured by a scar.

'Think yer better than us don't yeh? Coming in here an ignoring people. Think your hard, don't yer?' And he pushed his face right in to Andy's face. 'Well yeh not. Yeh just a fucken soft cunt.' He poked Andy in the chest.

Most people will only fight when provoked, but not many can fight well. Either they can't fight, or, more likely, their heart is not in it. Mostly they are not angry enough. But if you were angry then you welcomed a fight. You fought until there was no more fight in you, or until it had been beaten out of you. Even then, the anger in you meant that you would only come back for more. Some people could be beaten almost senseless and they would still win because of their anger.

The anger built in Andy. It had been building in him for years. He balled his hands, tightening them in to fists. His eyes narrowed and his breathing changed. It became deeper. He felt the anger grow in him. Andy smiled. He laughed from the pleasure he felt.

He stared two feet behind the youth's head before he let fly. There was a sickening crunch of breaking bone as Andy butted him. The youth dropped. Something like that happens and everything stops, everyone falls silent. No one does anything, except stare. Maybe because they are so used to watching it on TV. It is good to see it for real for a change.

'Hey!'

Andy turned.

It was one of the thug's three companions. 'What do you just do to my mate, uh?'

'What a stupid question.' Andy laughed as he butted him. The youth staggered backwards clutching his face, doubling over. Andy straightened him, kneeing him in the face. He held him upright by his hair and he punched him, then he punched him again, harder this time so that he fell on to his back.

Andy stood over the two stricken youths, his fists balled, wanting more. But they remained on the floor, clutching their broken faces. He roared at their two companions, 'Come on!' and then to the whole pub, 'Al' take on the fucken lot a yis.'

The barman, a well-built, tough looking Scot, stared fiercely at Andy, lifted up the counter and stepped out from behind the bar. He passed close to Andy, bent, grabbed the two youths by their collars, lifted them to their feet and manhandled them through the door and out in to the street. Their companions hurried after them.

Outside grew dark and the graffiti began. The store lights burnt fiercely. People were streaming in and out of the shops, even at this late hour. The homeless stood waiting for the shops to close so that they could occupy the doorways. Cars sped from traffic light to traffic light. Bikes wove in and out of the stopped vehicles.

Eventually, the shops emptied, the offices disgorged the last of their workers and the pubs and the restaurants filled. Half-dressed women threw back cocktails. Young males downed loud laughing pint after laughing pint.

Andy bought round after round for the laughing pub. He put £50 behind the bar. And then £100. He gave out free tickets to his show, of which he had a pocketful. He told stories and jokes, sang the usual songs.

The whole pub was laughing and singing, people were dancing on the table tops. It was not long before they began falling over. Glasses were being smashed.

'Ole ole ole ole. . . !'

Everyone was singing, everyone was laughing, dancing, drinking. A fight broke out.

When people are straightjacketed by rules and by work, by the order of their days, by the relentless grindstone, the need for self expression grows and mutates. People cannot live within rules, be governed by practice, conform to restriction without it should generate other energies. The crowds burst out in to the night from the screaming pubs. . . .

Andy stumbled out in to the street, in to laughter and screams. There was the crash of a beer glass. A thrown bottle popped against a wall. And then another. Above it all, the wail of police sirens and ambulances, as the evening began clamouring toward its close.

Andy stood in an alleyway that stank of piss, one arm extended, rested against the wall as he retched up his drink. Then he staggered off to find a taxi that would take him home. Slowly, the crowds drained from the streets and the shattered night calmed.

There were only the alarms now, ringing, portentous. . . .

8am and the rattle of jackhammers and the scream of power saws rent the air. The heavy, rhythmic thump of pile-drivers shuddered through the building. The noise was intolerable.

Jigsaw got up from his desk and he crossed to the window. He shut the window, dulling the sound of the construction work.

The low, brick built, Victorian warehouse, that stood between their block of apartments and the river was in the process of redevelopment. It was being demolished. According to the board posted on the shuttering surrounding the site a 6 storey block of luxury apartments was to be built in its place. Once built, they would overshadow Andy and Jigsaw's building, cutting them off from their view.

Jigsaw loved London - there was always something going on, something more to be had from it. But it was loud and dirty and close, and full of sudden transformations, and so he was wary of it too.

Jigsaw left the window and returned to his desk.

He reached for the London Property Guide and was soon immersed in the publication.

It would be expensive. But money was no longer a problem. He only had to pick up the phone and make the necessary arrangements:

UP THE WORKERS. ANDY RANT. THE NEW TOUR. Including: Economic climate - it's raining money. London - mostly indoors. Civil War - after you with the brick. Fashion - Accessory to the fact. The body snatchers - fat burger and lard bar to go. Buy British - bye bye. Made in a hurry - brand new and broke already. Credit that - an in debt analysis. Half Revolution. Con-servative. UK for sale. British nuclear fools. . . . Now appearing: The 9th, Manchester Salford Quays, The Lowry. The 10th, Nottingham, The Playhouse. The 11th, Bradford, George's Hall. The 12th, Belfast, The Opera House.

The 13th, Colston Hall, Bristol. The 14th, Grand Theatre, Swansea. The 15th, Theatre Royal, Norwich. The 16th, Jongleurs, Cardiff. The 17th, Civic Hall Bedworth. The 18th, The London Palladium. . . .

Within days of their being advertised all the venues were sold out. Andy was on a roll. There had never been a more popular comedian.

16

On the Road

Returning from a trip anywhere can be difficult, it can leave a person unsettled. New things, new possibilities, new places, other lives, other ways of doing things make the old and the familiar appear dull and suffocating. There is, too, that time between returning and getting on with things when everything stops. One world ends and another has yet to begin. Work looms, there are bills to pay, that dripping tap to fix. . . . Ordinariness beckons. People feel cornered, they feel depressed. Everyone escapes for a time and then they are back.

Overcast skies, greyness, crowds, traffic, traffic noise. There was that constant roar of traffic in the air. Ed and Natasha were back in London.

Ed felt let down after his travels. Depressed. At some point in your life you achieve your goals and realise that you are still unfulfilled. You need new goals.

'So, what now?' he asked Natasha.

Natasha rummaged in her backpack. She produced a magazine and handed it to Ed.

'Festival Eye?' He frowned.

The publication was a list of all the festivals and fairs being held throughout the country that year.

Natasha intended to spend the summer travelling between those festivals and fairs. Following that circuit she would hear of those other more interesting events, the ones that weren't publicised: the acid house parties, the raves, protest marches and demonstrations that were gripping the country and which, some said, were tearing it apart. She might even, she hoped, get to see a riot. She had only ever seen them on TV. Then there were picket lines to visit, travellers' camps to see, the blighted manufacturing towns of the north. . . .

The country was changing and Natasha intended to make a record of that. At the same time she would support herself by selling caricatures.

'So what will you do, Ed?'

Ed felt sick and empty of a sudden. Alone.

'For work?' said Natasha, 'How do you intend to earn money?'

'Oh,' Ed grinned, relieved. He didn't know what he'd do, he shrugged. Ed was always happiest when he was doing nothing.

'You will have to do something, Ed. I can't support both of us, not all the time, I'll be doing other things. I'm going to need to paint, eventually. I won't be earning money then. I'm going to need to find a studio. We're going to need somewhere to live. That costs money, Ed.'

Ed shrugged. That was ages away yet. 'I'll think of something. Something will come up. It always does.'

If there was one thing about Ed that annoyed Natasha it was his complacency. His continual insistence that something would turn up was the only conviction he seemed to possess.

A camper van would have been more practical, but they were too expensive. Even the cheapest of them. Instead, they retrieved Natasha's Ford Escort estate, that she had bought from Resurrection Motors.

The bodywork was dented, and the yellow paintwork which had faded to lemon was full of rust spots. She put it in to the garage for a minor service and had it fitted with new tyres. She also had the garage install a radio. Natasha insisted on having a radio to listen to the news. She wanted to keep abreast of events, she told Ed.

'We'll only need the the car for six months,' she said.

Ed was dubious. 'Six months is about all it's got.'

They drove around the high streets of East London, stopping at charity stops, stocking up on what they needed.

For some it is how much they own that distinguishes them, for others it is how little. Ed prided himself on just how little he did need. People censured Ed for that. They said that he wasn't ambitious enough, that he would never amount to anything, because he would never have anything. Ed turned that argument on its head. He claimed that his lack of material possessions was proof that he was a success. He didn't need anything.

Parking up on a quiet bit of road they unloaded the gear they had bought out on to the pavement. Like Natasha, Ed had lived in cars before. They both knew how to organise a car to make living in it bearable.

'How much for the cooker?' asked a passer by.

As well as the small cooker, that ran off a gas bottle, there was a thin rolled up mattress that Ed had reclaimed from a dumped sofa bed, a square plastic basin for washing in and for washing up, some pots, a frying pan, chipped enamel plates and a bowl each, chipped enamelled cups, eating utensils, a bread knife and chopping board, two foam pillows and a duvet. There was also a box of tools, oily rags and half-full bottles of brake fluid, engine oil and antifreeze, as well as a hazard triangle and towrope. Ed folded down the back seat, unrolled the mattress out on to the platform, made a bed on it with the duvet and pillows, then began to pack everything else down the one as yet unfilled side. First, an empty box, for food, then, the washing up bowl loaded with cooking utensils, and, lastly, the cooker. There were numerous water containers to be stored too, and these Natasha packed in to one of the footwells in front of the folded down seats and besides the box of tools. In the other, she packed away her artists materials: her fold-down easel, some canvas, and her sketchbooks and paints. Finally, when everything was stored to their satisfaction they put in their packs: Natasha's back pack, that was full of spare clothes, and Ed's much smaller back pack.

Natasha started the vehicle. It started first time, but there was an explosion of black smoke from the exhaust.

'It's just a bit of smoke, Ed, don't worry about it.'

'I'm not worried about the smoke, Nat. That's just oil gathering in the cylinders. It's the revs.'

The car stalled.

Natasha turned the key in the ignition. Pressing her foot down on the accelerator she kept it down, first to burn off the oil, then to stop the engine from stalling. It had been set to a very low idle but when the engine heated up it ran fast. The rev counter rose and fell. Ed could not figure it out.

They drove south, out of the city, then they skirted the city and headed west. Natasha drove at a steady 50mph. She watched the gap between her car and the cars that overtook her increase. She liked to see the road ahead empty. It was like it was opening out before her. In part, it was this open space which she was driving toward.

Another car overtook that then filled the space.

Ed produced a pencil and a small red book from his pocket and he began to write in it.

'You keeping a diary, Ed?'

'No. Just writing something down. An observation.'

Ed had decided to keep a notebook. In it he would put his observations. Natasha would paint and he would write a book, not of their travels, necessarily, but of the picture that Natasha was setting out to paint, and how they figured in it.

Setting aside time, protecting it with money and giving it purpose, that was the greatest freedom, reckoned Ed.

Retail Park, said the sign. Natasha indicated to turn off.

Ed said, 'What are you pulling in here for?' He was repulsed by such places. 'You'll see.'

The sight of the huge hangar like buildings and vast car parks annoyed Ed. He grew increasingly agitated. He hated to see new development. It usually meant that something had been lost.

There were several roundabouts to negotiate, then a confusing intersection. The signs didn't help, there were signs everywhere.

Exit.

No Exit.

Natasha sensed Ed's unease. 'You know, I think that if society ended tomorrow you wouldn't even notice. In fact, I think you would be happier.'

'I'm not against progress,' said Ed, 'so long as it doesn't change anything.'

Natasha laughed, as much at the contradiction as at Ed's earnestness.

'Anyhow,' said Ed, 'You're wrong. People like us, we need society more than anyone. Where else would we get our cheap cars, second hand clothes and equipment?'

It was not possible to live outside of society. You could live on its edge, but you still needed that society, without it there would be no edge to live on.

Natasha parked the car in front of a huge store, the biggest in the whole complex:

WELCOMETOTHENUTTYPRICEHOUSEPROUD
CAR WORLD
BURGERDOMEMEGASTORECOMPLEX
Private Property
No Skateboarding. Roller-blading or Cycling.
No Ball Games. No Dogs. No busking. No loitering.
Images are being recorded for the purposes of: Public Safety,
Crime Prevention and Prosecution, Property Management, Marketing and Advertising.
Parking £2.00. Fee refundable when you spend more than £20 in the NuttyPrice
Megastore. Max. parking, two hours only.
Warning: wheel clamping in operation.
Toilets 20p

When Natasha switched off the engine the engine overran. It stopped with such a shudder that it rocked the car.

More signs were posted on the superstores windows, walls and doors: *Bread 10p. Beans 5p. Buy three get one free. Situations Vacant: Part Time Staff Wanted. Store Detectives Wanted. Car Park Attendants Wanted. Dishwashers Wanted. Must be willing to work flexible hours.*

Natasha fetched a trolley and began roaming the aisles. She stocked up on bread and beans. Ed picked up some cheap plastic plates, cutlery, new cups, and a cheap tarpaulin to make an awning with and to serve as a fly sheet, and some cheap nylon cord, 100 yards of it.

'I guess that's everything,' said Ed.

On their way to the tills, Ed picked up two black Andy Rant T-shirts with *ANDY RANT* on the front and *LIVE AND LIVID* on the back. They were only £1.

Natasha bought a long red skirt, for £4.99, and a baggy and colourful woollen jumper for £4.99.

'It's almost as cheap here as in a charity shop,' said Ed. 'And it's brand new. And look, cheap tents.' He became interested in the tents. They came fully accessorised. For £30 you got a tent and camping chairs possessing cup holders in the arms, as well as sleeping bags and sleeping mats. Ed loaded them in to the trolley. 'I guess that's it,' he said.

'There's just one more thing,' said Natasha.

She found the car accessories section and she picked out a spray can of red paint.

'The car's yellow, Nat, sort of.' Ed handed her a can of yellow.

Natasha didn't want yellow. 'It's not for the rust spots.'

'So what is it for?'

'Contrast,' said Natasha. 'You'll see.'

Ed got the yellow, two cans – it was cheap – for the rust spots.

Natasha put two pairs of Marigold gloves in to the trolley. Ed hefted in a twelve pack of cheap beer.

They loaded their purchases in to the car.

Natasha produced the can of red spray paint. She shook the can. The ball bearing rattled.

'Roll up your sleeve and put this on,' she told him. 'Just do it, Ed.'

Ed put the Marigold on his right hand. The glove was small and was very tight.

'Now give me your hand.' Natasha reached for Ed's hand. Ed pulled away his hand.

'Trust me.'

Ed held out his hand. 'Spread out your fingers.' Ed spread out his fingers. Natasha took hold of Ed's wrist. She placed his hand on the driver's door, just where she wanted it, slightly off centre of the panel. She placed her right hand beside it, then she sprayed a mist of red paint over their gloved hands. There was the chemical smell of paint.

Removing their hands they stood back to appreciate the work.

The two handprints lay side by side. It was the sign of welcome, and of presence. It said, I am. But it also said, here are we. It was a sign of unity and bonding. A sort of marriage.

Ed and Natasha were time twins. They were born on the same day in the same year and within two hours of each other.

They performed the ceremony on the front passenger door, then again on the bonnet. Ed had got paint on his arm. He wiped the paint off with a rag. He passed the rag to Natasha.

'With this spray can I thee wed.'

The couple turned. It was the car park attendant. He wore the uniform of a car park attendant. Blonde dreads poked out from beneath his hat. He pointed to the car. 'You guys off to a festival or something?'

The car marked them out. Ed knew then that it was going to be trouble.

'Stop the car!'

Natasha braked, pulling up opposite a church. They were in a small village. They had been arguing over where they should stay that night. Natasha wanted to camp in a proper camping ground for a change, one with showers. They had spent the previous night in the car, and the night before that camped in some woods. Ed reckoned that they should save their money. Natasha countered that they wouldn't need to if Ed earned some.

'Ed, I didn't mean. . . .'

But Ed was already out of the car. Running across the road he vaulted over a church wall.

The old Norman church was encircled by yew trees. Tree surgeons were pruning back the trees. They had lit a fire nearby and were preparing to feed the pruned branches on to the fire.

Natasha watched Ed approach the tree surgeons. One of the men nodded, he pointed to some branches. Ed walked over to them, picked up an armful and returned with them to the car. He opened the boot and he began to load up the car with these short lengths of wood.

'I told you that something would come up,' he told Natasha.

'You're going to sell firewood?'

'Burn yew? Are you crazy? Do you know what this could be worth?'

'Well they're burning it.' Natasha pointed.

Ed ran off to get more wood.

Little Poncey. Twin Town, Aspic, Minnesota, said the sign.

The village was typical of the villages of Southern England. It had a village green with a pond at its centre, a church with a lych gate, a thatched pub - The Cricketers Arms - and one small shop which doubled as a post office. The village had kept its red telephone box.

'This seems a nice place,' said Natasha.

'And it'll be full of the nicest people,' said Ed in a very nice voice. 'We'd best go.'

Most of the houses had names: *The Old Forge. The Old Schoolhouse. The Vicarage. The Mill house.* Just as the car, with its stencilled doors and cluttered interior, marked Ed and Natasha out, so did those houses, and the cars parked outside them - the Jaguars, Daimlers, Range Rovers, Volvos and BMW's - mark their owners out. They distinguished them.

People stopped in the street, in their gardens, and they stared at the old car as it drove by.

Natasha pointed out a cottage whose walls were draped in wisteria. 'Isn't it beautiful,' she said.

She stopped the car, parking it beside the village green where there were picnic tables.

The village fell quiet. The noise of lawnmowers, hedge clippers and strimmers ceased. The silence drew people to their windows to see what had changed. A woman, walking her dog, stopped in the street and she stared at the couple. The inhabitants of the village looked with suspicion at Ed and Natasha and their car.

Ed wore faded jeans, scuffed boots, and a multicoloured woollen waistcoat. His hair was long and he had the beginnings of a beard. Natasha wore boots and purple leggings, a red, yellow and green dress, and a baggy, green, red and yellow flecked woollen jumper. There were coloured beads in her hair.

In 1983, travellers had arrived in force in Little Poncey and had made camp on the village green. They rampaged through the village, damaging cars, smashing windows, trampling down gardens, even ransacking the village shop. They tore up fences to fuel their fires, caught the ducks off the village pond, killed them and then cooked them on the fires. They occupied the village for three whole days before police finally evicted them.

Ed and Natasha got out of the car, took what they needed from the boot – their cooking stove, water, food and chopping board, all of it in a box and two bags, and then carried it across the green to the edge of the pond to one of the two picnic tables there. Several ducks took to the water as the couple approached.

Ed set up the stove and he boiled up some water. Natasha cut the bread and cheese and made sandwiches. Ed poured the boiling water and made tea.

Curtains fell back in to place, the pub window emptied of its faces, people resumed their gardening and continued to wash and to wax their cars, though an occasional curtain did twitch in a window and now and then people looked up from their tasks to check on Ed and Natasha.

They watched the couple finish their lunch, saw them return to the car and then pack their things away. But the couple did not leave. Natasha took out her easel and a fold up chair, she set up her equipment on the green and she began to paint the house with the wisteria. Ed took a short length of wood from the car, sat on the ground, his back resting against a wheel, took out his pen knife and began to carve. The wood carved easily, it was like wax. At first, Ed carved the wood simply to enjoy the feeling of carving wood, to get an understanding for the wood - testing it for possibilities. Soon, he began to sense shapes in the wood.

In less than twenty minutes Ed had made a magic mushroom. He put it down beside him. Then he fetched a thicker piece of wood, 6" in length, and he began to work that. Within an hour he had carved an exact copy, from memory, of the *Venus de Milo*.

Ed was a craftsman. A craftsman was someone that could graft a tool on to his person so that the possibility he saw in his mind would appear in front of him at his fingertips. Ed used a penknife. Later, he would use sand paper, of various grades, to smooth the figure, he would finish it with fine wire wool and then emery paper then polish it with beeswax. People, their curiosity and interest, would do the rest. Ed had once carved a Venus for a friend who owned a pub and who placed the finished statue in the public bar. Within a month the breasts shone like headlamps.

Ed had a whole box of finished work in the car. Mushrooms, leaves, dolphins, and various statuettes: Michael Angelo's *David*, Rodin's *Thinker*, his *Kiss*, several Brancusi type heads, his *Sleeping Muse*, as well as some Henry Moore abstracts that were like shapes from a lava lamp, all of which he had carved and smoothed and then polished over the previous weeks but had not yet sold.

A mud spattered Range Rover pulled up in front of the village shop. A woman in jeans, a light blue shirt, the collar turned up, a green quilted waistcoat and tall, tight fitting green wellington boots, climbed down out of the vehicle. She looked at Ed seated on the ground whittling on a stick in the productive hours, took in his strong, tanned physique, smiled to herself and came over.

Ed mistook the woman's interest in him. He offered up his carving for her inspection.

'Five pounds,' he said, holding up the finished mushroom. 'The Venus is ten pounds. They're hand made. I've got a whole box full if you want to see.'

But the woman wasn't interested in the carvings.

She stared at Ed, at his well-toned, thickly veined arms, his broad chest. 'I came to offer you a job,' she said.

'Work?'

'Mucking out. I own a riding stables. There's plenty of work.'

'It just piles up, I imagine,' said Ed, and he returned to his carving.

'I pay cash,' she said. '£1.20 an hour. Breaks excluded, of course.'

'Of course,' said Ed, not looking up.

The woman reached inside her jacket and produced a card advertising the stables and on the reverse of which there was a small map. 'You can start work tomorrow, eight thirty, prompt.' She held the card out to Ed. 'Here's the address.' Ed ignored the card, he continued carving.

Ed already has work, of sorts. He can get money whenever he wants, conjuring it out of nowhere, almost. He literally makes money. He takes unwanted branches and driftwood and logs that people would otherwise burn and he crafts them in to shapes that they can appreciate and will want. And because they are handmade he can charge what he wants for them, within reason. So few things are made by hand now. There are few crafts and ever fewer craftsmen. People have lost those skills, and something else too. But Ed has not lost it. The world will have to find someone else to muck out its stables, to labour, to stack and re-stack its supermarket shelves, to place one brick upon another, to build its roads and work in its factories and make its money for it. The world despises Ed and people like him when it cannot turn his need for money against him in order to put him to use.

'I've got work, thanks,' he said and, holding up the carving, he smiled at the woman. He returned to his carving.

The woman grew angry at Ed's refusal and her face tightened, it became a contortion of knots.

'Your sort don't want to work.' And, turning on her heel, she marched off in the direction of the village shop.

Natasha came skipping barefoot across the green.

'Did you sell her a carving, Ed?'

'No, she didn't want a carving.'

'Never mind.' Natasha looked very pleased with herself. 'I sold my painting to the people in the cottage. For fifty pounds. '

They packed their gear in to the car. Natasha turned the key in the ignition. The engine caught. There was a cloud of black smoke. Natasha had to gun the engine so it would not stall. The car roared out of the village, destroying the peace and quiet and chasing away a dog.

The village breathed a collective sigh of relief at their departure.

Ed noticed a long line of trees snaking across the countryside. Several times, the line of trees came close to the road only to swerve away from it again, sometimes at right angles for a distance, at others running parallel with it. Ed knew that there must be a river there.

Eventually, they came to a bridge where Ed had Natasha stop the car. A sign on the bridge said *River Kennet*.

The trout streams of Southern England - the Kennet, the Test, the Itchen, the Avon - they were holy places, shrines to Ed.

It was a beautiful summer's day: blue sky, yellow cornfields, green trees. The land shimmered in the heat. Sunlight blasted off the surface of the trout stream. Ed peered over the bridge's parapet in to the river below. Long streamers of silkweed waved in the stream. In the clear water Ed saw a large trout hanging motionless in the water. Ed imagined dropping a fly in to the pool just above the bridge and taking that trout.

He decided to walk the river. It was a good looking river and he liked the feeling looking at it gave him. It promised to have a lot of good trout in it. He would find a bend in the river, someplace where he was hidden from the road, and maybe he would tickle a trout.

'We could take a picnic,' he told Natasha.

Ed crossed the bridge to where there was a gate in the hedge on the upstream side of the river. Just as he was about to vault the gate, Natasha pointed out the sign to him. It was nailed to the gnarled oak there.

Private. No Fishing, said the sign.

On the other side of the road, the downriver side, on another tree, there was another sign. *Private. No Fishing*, said the sign.

'I don't think we should, Ed.'

'We're only going for a walk,' he said. 'Come on.'

Natasha brought the picnic stuff and they headed upstream beside the river, beneath the trees, walking the rough ground.

Now and then, usually only in neglected spaces – in abandoned or blocked laneways, sometimes a neglected garden, often a railway siding, or a disused allotment or derelict factory, but most often only a yard or so square – appeared the real world: that tangle of tree and bush and briar and grass and flower.

To Ed, the river bank was such a place, a remnant, affording access: a narrow strip of shrunk back country running through well-tended farmland back in time to its source.

Ed moved slowly, staring in to the stream, stopping now and then whenever he saw a fish. He pointed the fish out to Natasha. He was just looking but in his imagination he was fishing.

Natasha picked a cornflower and she put it behind her ear.

They had not gone far, maybe 100 yards, when someone shouted at them from the road. The man had stepped out of a range-rover and was now gesturing at them. He climbed the fence and strode purposefully in their direction.

He stood, ruddy faced, furious, legs apart, his hands on his hips. 'This is private property,' he said. 'Didn't you see the sign.'

'We're only going for a walk,' said Ed.

The man stood pointing in the direction from which they had come. 'This is private property,' he repeated.

'Aright, we're going, keep yer fucking hair on.'

'Ed!' said Natasha.

'Well,' said Ed, and he glowered at the man.

Natasha snatched the cornflower from behind her ear and she flung it in to the stream.

The man remained in the field, regaining possession of it, as he watched Ed and Natasha get in to their car and drive away.

Natasha parked up on a wide, grassy verge in thick woods. There was no one for miles, no buildings which they could see.

Natasha cut the engine. Silence.

Just the sound of wood pigeons and running water from a nearby stream.

Ed got out of the car and he walked over to the stream, tripping on a tiny sign set upon a little white post hidden in the long grass there.

No Camping, said the sign.

'Christ!' roared Ed. 'It's not a crime. It's a fucking punishment!' He kicked the sign, hard, with his heel, snapping it off its post. Then, picking it up, and with a loud roar, he threw it in to the trees.

Wherever they went there were all these signs to contend with: *No Fishing. No Overnight Parking of Vehicles. No Camping. Camping £5.00. Private Property. No Access. No Exit. 50p to see the waterfall. . .*

It was depressing for Ed to meet with such restriction. They hemmed him in. Their continual insistence on compliance battered away at him. It collided against his every whim, every instinct, every urge to touch and to see and to investigate. No wonder there are madmen.

'Let's face it,' said Ed, getting back in to the car, 'People just don't want the likes of us around.'

'Can you blame them?' said Natasha. 'Well, we've taken things, haven't we?' Ed looked at her askance. 'We've taken wood that wasn't ours, for firewood and for your carving. We've trespassed. We've slept in barns and hayricks. We've camped in fields without asking for permission. We've helped ourself to things, and not just to firewood but to rabbits and fish. And we crap in the woods. It might seem alright if there's just us two doing it, but what if everyone did it?'

'You're right,' said Ed, 'There are too many people.'

It was making all kinds of things impossible.

'People are wary of travellers, Ed. Travellers are like refugees, they're people in need, and the needy take things. That puts people on their guard. Travellers, what use are they, really?'

'No use,' agreed Ed.

It was not easy to find a camping place in the south, not unless it was an official place. Ed and Natasha found huge rocks blocking the entrances in to picnic areas and lay-bys, making them unusable. Ground which they thought ideal to camp on they found spread with manure. Almost everywhere they went they found signs outlawing camping and the overnight staying in vehicles. People were expected to stay on proper sites under proper supervision and obey proper rules. That went against everything that Ed and Natasha needed. It wasn't always possible to enjoy the amenities when they were decided for you, especially when they cost money, when what you were trying to do by camping was to save money. Ed, particularly, didn't see the need for such places. Ed resented being channelled from one paying place to the next paying place, and he was becoming more determined to defy that. Because when you have to pay for everything then you have to work, and, inevitably, you end up having to work for them.

Sometimes though, it wasn't possible to find any kind of place to stay, even if you were willing to pay for it.

Natasha stopped the car in a small picnic area under a stand of birch trees. There was a toilets and rubbish bins and several picnic tables. The site seemed ideal. Located on the summit of a low hill there was a view of the whole county stretched out beneath them – low wooded hills, yellow cornfields, distant blue hills.

As usual, they waited until evening before they unloaded their equipment from the car. A woman, out walking her dog, a golden labrador, stopped to look at them. She looked at them for a long time. When Ed began to put up the tent she came over.

'You can't camp here,' said the woman, and she pointed out the sign:

*No Camping. No Fires.
No Overnight Staying in Vehicles.
By Order.*

The dog nuzzled Ed's hand, it wanted to be stroked. Ed stroked it.

The woman was very polite and helpful. 'The camping ground is that way,' she told them. 'Through the village, turn left at the shop. . . .' She proceeded to give them detailed directions. She was making it impossible for them not to leave.

Ed and Natasha loaded their gear back in to the car and, watched by the woman, they drove off. She waved them off, stick in the air.

They drove on through the village of High Dudgeon. People stared at the car as it drove by and they kept on staring at it until it had gone.

A tall leylandii hedge curved inwards to form the entrance. On either side of the entrance, each one surmounted by two white flagpoles, was a sign. Natasha stopped in the entrance to read the sign:

*All vehicles must book in to the office before entering the site. No animals. No fires.
No noise after 10pm. Max speed 5mph. Office. Shop. Toilets. Showers.
Laundry room. TV and games rooms. Amusement Arcade. Animalarium.
Model farm. Please Drive carefully.*

'Let's go,' said Ed.

Natasha drove in anyway.

She was tired of looking for a place. 'It's got showers,' she said, 'and a laundry.'

She pulled up outside reception.

The woman behind reception looked at Natasha, and then at Ed, who had remained waiting outside, leaning against the car. Arms folded across her chest the woman stared at the car, then she turned to look at her husband. He had been sat working in the back office but had looked up when he had heard the car and was now stood framed in the doorway. He narrowed his eyes to his wife, glanced at Natasha then he looked back to his wife, turned and returned to the office. That gesture communicated something.

The woman turned to Natasha. 'I'm sorry,' she said, 'the camp site is full.'
The couple got back in to the car.

'Who wants to stay in the poxy place anyhow,' said Natasha. She pumped the accelerator several times then she turned the key in the ignition. The engine caught first time and there was a lot of black smoke.

As they drove out through the entrance a huge motor home passed them on its way in. There were bicycles on a rack at the rear of the vehicle and a TV ariel on its roof.

'I bet they don't get turned away,' said Ed.

Some people are upwardly mobile, others are just mobile and that is not acceptable.

Ed and Natasha drove back through the village, the villagers watching them anxiously, from suspicion and with not a little dread, and they proceeded up the lane to its junction with the main road where they turned left and headed west. A huge Mercedes coach with tinted windows, *ANDY RANT ON TOUR*, written on its sides, passed by, going in the opposite direction.

People everywhere were on the move. The whole country was restless. It was a restless century. People had become gypsies, migrants, refugees - even if they did not know it. They left one place and they settled for a time in another, different place, or job, or house, and then they moved on, often at the first opportunity. Sometimes, whole lives can become caricatures of the society that is spawning them. Then there were those who lived upon the road, whose life it had become.

There are lots of people who think that because they are moving they are going places.

17

Kingdom Come

It was a brand new apartment and it smelt of paint, of new carpet, of the pungent smell of new leather, of oiled wood, the drapery-shop scent of new curtains. Numerous works of contemporary art, and several framed pieces of graffiti, hung on the white painted walls. The carpets, curtains, blinds, floors, ceilings and most of the furniture was white. A single dark space, a 72" flat screen TV hung on the wall, offering an infinity of distraction. There was a Bosch music deck, Bang and Olufsen speakers.

A mini bar.

A polished chrome and glass table, seating 12, the chairs leather backed and constructed of beech.

Several huge sofas and armchairs.

A huge stone built chimney breast with a massive slab-marble fireplace at its centre, containing a 40" x 40" digital fire, took up most of one wall. A remote-control operated the fire, turning on an image of dancing flames and at the same time altering the temperature of the room by employing the underfloor heating system.

The lights could be controlled by remote and were touch sensitive.

There was a huge kitchen with marbled work tops and a beechwood work island, a double fridge, a stand up freezer, a wine rack along one wall that was fully stocked with wine and champagne, a rack of kitchen equipment with knives by Svisk.

There were two huge bedrooms, both with double beds, each room having walk in wardrobes, ensuite bathrooms and toilet. There were rooms furnished as offices adjacent to each bedroom.

There was a guest room.

The 4,000sqft. apartment was on the fourth floor. Huge picture windows offered wide views south across the river as well as to the east and west at each corner. The windows were triple glazed.

From the lounge, French windows let out on to a large balcony where there was a table and chairs, and a small garden, with shrubs in pots - clipped and sculpted mulberry bushes, bay trees, laurel bushes: balls sitting on tall stems, some of the stems twisted, woven. The terrace was protected from the weather by a retractable red and white striped awning. Andy and Jigsaw had argued vehemently about that detail. Jigsaw had wanted blue, for Everton, but Andy had insisted on red.

A new development had been built in front of their old development, blocking out the view, so Jigsaw had bought an apartment in this new riverside development.

Jigsaw had a hunger, a greed for material possessions, as though owning them he could somehow fix the world in place with him firmly at the centre of. All his life he had possessed nothing and he had been treated as nothing, a nobody and now he was somebody.

'Can we afford all this?' asked an incredulous Andy.

The pictures alone, some of them by Enzo, had cost £25,000. They were by the latest up and coming names.

'Of course we can afford this. You're Andy Rant. But don't think of this as a home, think of it as an investment. Property and art prices are rising all the time. We'll make a fortune just being here We can't not afford it.'

Property and art, they were places to grow money and to put it out of reach.

Jigsaw suggested that they celebrate their move with champagne.

'Outside, on the terrace, I think.'

But it was too cold, there was a wind blowing, and it was very noisy.

Jigsaw was seated in his study, leafing through a wine catalogue, when the door burst open, slamming against the wall. Andy came storming in. He was clasping the mock-up flyer for his proposed new show.

'What is this!' he said, slamming it down on Jigsaw's desk.

ANDY RANT, LOOSE IN THE CITY, THE NEW TOUR

'It's the flyer advertising your new tour,' said Jigsaw.

'Exactly. Another fucken tour. An right after the last tour! It's been non-stop ever since we started. Well I can't do it. I need a rest, Jigsaw,' He snatched the flyer off the desk. 'An just look at this. Well go on, lookarit!' He shook it in Jigsaw's face.

There was a picture of Andy holding a microphone and howling at his audience on the top half of the page, with the three month itinerary listed beneath.

'Look at the dates. You've only gone an double booked us. See. And there. And there.' Andy pointed out one discrepancy after another.

'Those are matinees, Andy.'

'Matinees?'

'How else are you going to fit one hundred venues in to ninety days?'

'One hundred?' Andy grabbed at the flyer. 'I can't do this. One hundred in ninety days? It's impossible.'

'No it's not, there's motorway connections. I've worked it all out. Anyhow, we've no choice, we have to have another tour. We need the money, Andy.'

'I thought we were raking it in?'

'We are. But we're spending it too.'

'What, all of it? What on?'

'This place for a start, the payments on the cars and stuff.' And then there were the bills to pay if the thing were to be kept going. 'The overheads. The hotel bills, the various travel costs. Then there's the club owners. They take a big cut. And the lawyers fees for all the contracts that have to be drawn up. Then there's promoters fees to be paid. And agents fees too, of course.'

'But you're my promoter, you're my agent!'

'I still have to be paid, Andy. Then there's all the entertaining that we do, the partying, the eating out. It all costs money you know. It costs us a fortune to live like this.'

You had to live the life. It wouldn't be worth it otherwise.

'But you said we could afford this?'

'We can. If things keep on like this, we can. The tour, it's completely sold out.'

'One hundred venues? All of them?'

Jigsaw nodded.

'But some of those places hold five thousand people.' Andy sat. He stood right back up again. 'Jesus, Jigsaw.' Andy laughed.

Andy couldn't not do it, not now, not with the rewards.

'We can't stop,' explained Jigsaw, 'not now.'

Andy felt very tired of a sudden. 'What about new material? I can't keep creating, not at this rate. How do you expect me to create if it's going to be like this all the time?'

'No problem. We'll get someone to write your material for you.'

Andy was not so sure. He didn't like the idea of performing other people's material.

Jigsaw dismissed his objections. 'If we keep this up we'll soon be millionaires.'

'That's what you always say. First drugs was going to make us rich, then the band, then it was Resurrection Motors. Resurrection motors,' Andy sneered.

'It will,' said Jigsaw. 'It is. From now on, everything you do is going to make us rich – with careful management. I mean, just look at where we're we're living. Just look at what we've got. Or do you want to go back to how things used to be? You do want all this, don't you?'

Andy threw his hands in to the air in exasperation. 'More money, more things, more fucking work,' he said.

'More of everything,' smiled Jigsaw. 'It's what we want, isn't it?'

Another tour meant more money, but it also meant more work. It meant living in hotel rooms, grabbing meals. Work was wearing Andy down. Not in the obvious way. That too, but it went much deeper than that. It was the very idea of work. It was what work meant. Andy remembered how it was without work. He didn't want to be working all his life with the threat of having no work, no money, hanging over him. He wanted to be free of that fear, that fate. It was why he worked. You had to keep working. You had to keep working either to free yourself from work entirely or to earn the money that made working worthwhile.

Then there were the parties and the women too, the groupies that followed Andy everywhere. Andy was dreading the tour, but he was looking forward to it too.

Jigsaw suggested that they go out to a restaurant and celebrate.

The restaurant was Japanese. They had to take off their shoes. Koto music was being played, making the air tremble. There were brush paintings on the walls. The walls were opaque.

'Careful of the walls,' said Jigsaw. 'They're paper.'

There was a famous actor at one table, two famous footballers at another. They nodded to Andy. Everyone knew Andy.

The manager ushered them to the rear of the restaurant where two doll faced traditionally dressed geisha girls pulled aside a set of lacquered paper doors on to a small private dining room where there was a low table but no chairs, just cushions on the floor. The manager bowed and then departed. The girls bowed. Jigsaw bowed. The demure serving girls handed Andy and Jigsaw a menu each.

Andy was in a mischievous mood. 'I'll have the origami,' he said. Jigsaw ordered sushi for them both. And a bottle of saki.

A little apparatus, a burner, was brought in and set down on the table which was then used to heat up the saki.

Andy raised his tiny cup. Jigsaw raised his cup.

'Onwards and upwards,' said Jigsaw.

'Down the hatch,' said Andy.

They knocked back their drinks. There were loud gasps, followed by coughing. Andy had several more cupfuls in quick succession and was soon quite drunk.

He spoke through great mouthfuls of seafood and rice. He illustrated his conversation with jabs of his chopsticks and flourishes of soup spoon. Flying sauces, soup and egg yolk crazed the walls.

'Andy! Careful, will you, you're messing up the walls,' said Jigsaw.

'Is all right, Jigsy, mate, they're paper, they'll change them for the next crowd.'

The busy but unobtrusive servant girls bore Andy's loudness, they cleaned up his messes. Their fawning and servility made Andy angry.

Andy helped himself to more saki. He knocked it back, tiny cup after tiny cup , each time placing the empty, upturned cup on his head before holding it out for more. 'More!' he shouted. 'More!'

'Don't you just love Japanese food,' Jigsaw was telling him. 'I hear it's a very wealthy country, Japan. We should go there, on tour. Here's an interesting fact. The Japanese buy more luxury goods than anywhere else in the whole world. They're a hard working and very law abiding people.'

'Servile is what thee are, like bow and scrape here,' growled Andy.

'I'm just saying it wouldn't hurt us to be a bit more like them. Well, not us, not me and you. Everyone else.'

Andy narrowed his eyes and tried to touch his chin with his top row of teeth. He offered his new face first to Jigsaw and then to the two girls. He burst out laughing. The two serving girls, their heads bent, stood giggling at him behind their hands.

'Stop it, Andrew! You're being offensive. Remember where you are.'

'More like them?' Andy looked incredulous. 'Well here's an interesting fact for yeh, Jigsy, mate. Yeh won't find this in yer Ladybird book on Japan. Thee have death from overwerk, did yeh know that?' Karoshi, thee call it. And hari kari. Kill themselves all the fucken time. Why? Cuz they've had a enough, is why!'

Andy picked up the saki bottle, he put the bottle to his lips and, like someone blowing a trumpet, he filled himself with saki. Putting down the bottle he burst in to song: 'I THINK WE'RE TURNING JAPANESE, I THINK WE'RE TURNING JAPANESE, I REALLY THINK SO. . . . EVERYONE AROUND ME IS A TOTAL STRANGER...'

Jigsaw apologised to the girls and motioned for them to take away the saki.

'THE TROUBLE WITH CROWDED COUNTRIES,' shouted Andy, Jigsaw telling him to keep quiet. 'The trouble with crowded countries,' he said, resting an elbow on the table, only to have it slip off. Very deliberately he replaced first one elbow and then the other on the table before resting any weight there. He stared over the table at Jigsaw. 'The trouble with crowded countries,' he said, 'is that's how you get treated. As a crowd!' He leant backwards, almost falling off his haunches. 'This is what's coming, Jigsaw, this is the future, mate. We'll end up all crowded together living little Bonsai lives and eating measly amounts of this – shite,' and he spooned up his seafood and let it drop back in to his bowl, splashing the table. 'The place will be hell!' Andy hiccuped. He hiccuped again. He couldn't stop hiccuping.

'Here, try drinking some water,' said Jigsaw.

Andy gulped down some water, but to no effect. He tried holding his breath, but that didn't work either.

One of the Japanese girls instructed him to put his thumbs on his nostrils and his index fingers on his ear lobes and then to swallow.

'What? What kind a hocus pocus is this?' hiccuped Andy. 'Gerrof!' he said as the little Japanese took Andy's hand and began to place his fingers in the required places. She replaced his fingers, she was very gentle. Though sceptical at first after only four gulps Andy found himself cured.

'Fucking hell,' he said, surprised.

Andy was no longer comfortable sitting crosslegged. It was causing him circulation problems. He tried to shift his position, but one leg had gone numb. He undid his legs, pulling one leg out from under him. Then, when he tried to stand, his leg collapsed beneath him. His eyes widening, his mouth open in horror, he let out a scream as his calf muscles locked in painful spasm and his leg cramped. 'CRAMP! CRAMP! I'VE GOT CRAMP!' he bellowed. He fell backwards on to his elbows and he held out his leg in an attempt to relieve the pain, knocking over rice bowls, sushi dips, cups, and then the mini cooker, setting fire to the table cloth. He tried to stand, to scramble away from the flames, only to fall sideways, crashing through the flimsy lacquered paper wall and on to the table of a group of surprised diners in the next room.

'CRAMP!' he roared. 'CRAMP!' Then he threw up.

Next thing he knew he was outside in the street. Japanese people were walking back indoors, making little clapping sounds as they brushed their hands. Jigsaw was picking Andy off the floor for the second time. Now he was putting him in a taxi. Concerned for his upholstery the driver insisted on a carrier bag. Andy sang: 'Swing low, sweet chariot, coming for to. . . .' He blacked out.

ANDY RANT, LOOSE IN THE CITY, THE NEW TOUR. Including: Up the workers. The Body Snatchers. Taking Liberties. Turning Japanese. Simon Says. . .

It was the first night of Andy's new nationwide tour and he was opening at the Palladium.

Andy paced the stage. He harangued his audience. He gave them *Up the Workers*, with the one fingered salute. He moved angrily through his itinerary concluding with *Turning Japanese*. He told it exactly how it was. The audience responded with laughter. Their grotesquely laughing faces taunted Andy. It worked him into a fury.

Andy roared at the audience: 'How long are you going to let them push you around? You're all a bunch of slaves. Your whole life is bullshit. Yeh should be out there, all a yis, on the streets, burnen down their big houses, trashen their fucken cars, sinken their fucken super yachts. Not sat here laughing abowr it. So what are you going to do about it!' he shouted. 'What are you going to do about it! Bring it down! he roared. Bring it fucken down!'

The audience responded with a roar, they applauded wildly, making Andy angrier. Didn't anyone understand? It made him feel like an outcast at times. He really did take himself seriously. People thought that funny, that it was part of his act.

Throwing his hands to the air he left the stage. 'Fucken, tossers,' he cursed. People, they were just making everything worse, fucking things up with their ordinary, everyday lives.

Backstage, someone handed him a towel and he wiped his face with it. He threw away the towel.

Jigsaw came running up to him. 'Get back out there, you're not even halfway through your act.' The audience had begun stamping their feet rhythmically on the floor. The whole building shook to it. 'For Christ sake, before they start tearing the place apart.' He had to shout above the noise.

'It'll be a start then, won't it? Ha! Nah, they won't do anything. Not unless you sell it to them.'

'You're losing it, Andy.'

'No, they are. Thee already have. Just listen ter em.'

'BEIGE NATION! BEIGE NATION!'

'ANDEE! ANDEE! ANDEE!'

'I never thought you'd give up so easy,' said Jigsaw.

'Me, give up?'

Andy was wired, he was angry. He came striding back out on stage.

'A man goes in to a bar. . . .'

The audience fell silent, people turned to look at each other, puzzlement on their faces.

'Only joking,' said Andy.

'Beige Nation,' he said. And the audience erupted. He followed with *Money Go Round*.

'Bring it down!' he shouted, punching the air. 'Bring it down!'

Andy's star was on the rise, he was appearing at larger and larger venues, to bigger and more enthusiastic audiences.

He appeared on television and on radio, hosting his own TV shows, BBC's *Andy Rant Live* and ITV's *This Week's Rant*. He was special guest star on quiz shows. He had a column, Andy's Rants, in one of the national newspapers. He opened supermarkets and out of town Mega stores. He attended gala performances, he was invited to dinner parties, he attended openings and shows.

On stage Andy continued to hammer away at the iron ignorances.

Off stage, he drank, took drugs, got in to fights, smashed up hotel rooms, went on blind drunks. It all went to fuel the Andy legend.

He appeared at the Edinburgh Fringe Festival and swept the board of the awards.

Chauffeur driven cars, a show-for driven car dropped Andy off at the awards ceremony. He walked the gauntlet of flashing lights. So many smiles. His name called out.

He remembers the ceremony, and the drive to the party afterwards. He doesn't remember what happened at the ceremony, or to the award, nor what happened at the party. Nor does he remember the fight.

He remembers the various waitress, and bar girls, the girls from Worldbabe, other women: models, reporters, numerous actresses, showgirls, waitresses, but not their names. They are just numbers to him. 197. 198. He keeps count.

His life had become a whirlwind of performances in different cities, staying in different hotel rooms, of TV appearances, openings, first nights, film premiers, He had standing reservations at the very best restaurants, was offered front row tickets to all the shows, and found himself whisked through VIP lines at trendy nightclubs. Everyone pointing at him, shouting out his name. He began to party like there was no tomorrow. All too often there wasn't.

*

Andy liked a drink before a performance. It helped him to loosen up. It calmed his nerves. Sometimes Andy got so nervous before a performance that he threw up. When that happened he had to boost up on drink all over again.

Andy had the quarter bottle of whisky in his hand and he was knocking back the drink. He drained a third of the bottle in one go. He rested the bottle on the dresser to light up when Jigsaw snatched up the bottle, along with the cap. He replaced the cap.

'Hey! What are you doing?' said Andy, watching Jigsaw pocket the bottle.

'Give it back. I need it, Jigsaw,' he pleaded.

'You've had more than enough,' said Jigsaw. 'Just look at you, Andy. Christ! You're on stage in ten minutes and just look at the state of you. You're drunk, you're a fucking mess.'

'Yeh? Well, I've been putting a lot of work in to this new look of mine, haven't I?' Andy laughed.

Andy made a lunge for the bottle, which Jigsaw easily sidestepped.

'I'm warning you, Jigsaw. If you don't give me that bottle back, right now.'

'No.' Jigsaw was adamant. 'If you drink, Andrew, then you can't perform. And if you can't perform?' He left the question hanging. 'After the performance, okay?'

There was a loud knock on the dressing room door. 'TWO MINUTES!' shouted someone.

'Here, take this, said Jigsaw. And he reached in to his pocket. 'It'll counteract the drink.'

Andy bent over the dresser and he snorted up a line. He snorted up another line. There was another loud knock on the door.

'You're on!' came the shout.

Andy stormed out in to the lights to wild applause. The performance began and Andy lost himself to the adrenaline.

After two hours Andy left the stage. He was exhausted, but he was exhilarated too. He pushed his way down the crowded corridor toward his dressing room. People congratulating him, reaching out, slapping him on the back, thrusting out pieces of paper, tickets, footballs, even paper money for him to sign. Andy was on a high from his performance, but already he could feel himself coming down. He quickened his pace. Behind him hurried Jigsaw, updating him on the following week's itinerary:

'The 9th, Cambridge, The Corn Exchange, we've got a supermarket opening that afternoon. The 10th, we're in Southampton, so we can stay in London the 9th. . . . The 11th, York. . . .'

That night, back in his hotel room, with Jigsaw and two girls, Andy produced a full bottle of vodka. Placing it on the dresser he unscrewed the cap, placed the cap beside the bottle, then, making a fist and staring hard at Jigsaw, he flattened the top with his fist.

'Ha!' he said, 'Now we drink the whole bottle.'

Jigsaw laughed, then Andy, and then the girls. Everyone was laughing. It would be some time yet before the laughter would stop.

It was late and Jigsaw was seated in his study, going through the accounts. He sat staring at the numbers. His eyes stung. Closing his eyes, he pinched the bridge of his nose between his forefinger and thumb and he squeezed shut his eyes. Numbers, income streams, sub totals, totals, deductions, costs, danced on his retina and whirled through his aching brain. His mind reeled at the numbers. Jigsaw blew out a long breath, pushed away his books and threw his pen on them. Then he got up from his desk and he went and poured himself a whisky and crossed to the window with it. He stood staring out of the window. He felt tired and was worried and not a little scared.

He had let an incredible sum of money slip through his fingers that he had never really had the use of.

Jigsaw left the window, returned to his desk and sat heavily down. He pulled a ledger toward him and he flipped it open:

Annual income twenty pounds, annual expenditure nineteen nineteen six, result happiness. Annual income twenty pounds, annual expenditure twenty pounds ought and six, result misery.

It was the greatest line in literature to Jigsaw's mind and he had written it on the fly leaf of his accounting books, as well as on a card, and he had framed the card. The frame stood in front of him on the desk where another person might have placed a picture of a girlfriend or wife or family or, having none of those things, an executive toy. Jigsaw picked up the frame and, looking at the quotation, he began to wonder whether in this day and age the statement actually rang true. Some people lived very happy lives all payed for by debt, lives that would not otherwise have been possible.

18

Financing the Lifestyle.
The Great Money Trick:
Money from Nowhere

The room was blue with cigar smoke. Jewellery and silverware glittered beneath the lights. There was the loud buzz of conversation, laughter, the chink of champagne glasses, the crash of cutlery. Tables laden with food and drink. With magnums of Moet, platters of pheasant and grouse, crayfish and lobster, oysters, salmon, caviar. . . .

Andy and Jigsaw were at the businessman of the year awards where Andy had been invited to perform his *Up The Workers* routine. There were over 1,500 people present. Multimillionaire retailers and financiers, the heads of corporations, billionaire fund managers. . . . some of the richest people in the country were there. They were people with Monaco tans, Davros tans, Capri tans.

Jigsaw pointed out Sir Peter Grey to Andy. 'He's a billionaire retailer,' he told him. 'And there, sat next to Sir Peter, that's Dick Fault, CEO of Lemmon Brothers, he's a multimillionaire. And that,' he said, his voice low, almost reverential, 'is Sir Geoffrey Plane-Smith, he manages his own private equity fund, Phoenix. He buys and sells companies. He makes more money buying and selling companies than he could ever make by selling what those companies produce. And it's all done on borrowed money. The banks are falling over themselves to lend him money, he makes that much for them.'

There is a slide rule of greed, and those who possess it think they know the value of everything. Andy seethed. He hated money: the people with money.

It made such shits. It created bosses and owners and deities.

According to Jigsaw, there were only two kinds of money, and that made two very different kinds of people. There was the money that the rich dealt and thought in, that bought and sold companies, which they then invested in property and in art, and there was what was left over which was what everyone else worked for and built their lives around. The big money, the money that was used to make more money, that was what money was for, Jigsaw reckoned. The small money, that which everyone else slaved for and fought over, merely underpinned that, keeping the thing fed. It was why money worked for some people, and why most people worked. It was why there were millionaires, multimillionaires, billionaires. Because for everything there is the chances are there is a millionaire.

Jigsaw pointed out numerous people that had made their millions through the sale of all sorts of mundane things: vacuum cleaners, a new kind of can, buttons. . . .

Andy balled his fists. His teeth grated. There is nothing like money to stir up the emotions.

'How come the people that need a thing the most always get the least of it, eh?' he asked. 'How come?'

'Shhh,' said Jigsaw, sheepish. People were beginning to stare over at the pair.

'Yeah, an how the fuck can there be billionaires, eh?'

Jigsaw ignored him. He took a gulp of champagne from his glass, refilled it, then, reaching over, he lifted more pheasant on to his plate, then some of the grouse. 'More grouse, Andy?' he laughed, dropping a large portion on to Andy's plate.

Andy scowled back at him.

With the main course finished, dessert was served: bee bread and ambrosia pudding. It was delicious. The room fell silent for a time.

Coffee was served followed by brandy. Cigar smoke filled the air. There was loud talk and laughter. Then the master of ceremonies rapped a knife against a glass and gestured for silence.

A City financier then took the podium to give a talk on corporate finance and the need to deregulate the banks.

'Deregulation will create fantastic new hierarchies of existence,' he concluded.

The audience stood and they applauded the financier. Jigsaw stood and he applauded. Andy hauled him down. 'Christ,' he hissed, 'whose side are you on?'

'Shush!' snapped Jigsaw, 'You'll get your turn.'

Next, two economists, Skutt and Hames, gave a talk on the need for easy credit. It would stimulate the economy. Skutt explained:

On the one hand, labour was required, the cheaper the better. On the other, there had to be purchasing power, to keep the thing going. Though there were less and less jobs, there had to be more and more money.

'Easy credit will create billions,' he promised.

'Trillions,' offered Hames

'Future money, now!' they both demanded, to loud applause.

With the aid of diagrams and complex financial formulae Skutt and Hames proceeded to talk up a brave new world of easy credit. Rising consumer confidence coupled with an ever buoyant housing market financed by cheap and easy credit would make everyone wealthier. It would fuel consumption, ushering in an era of unprecedented economic growth. There would be more money, more work, more of everything. Everyone would benefit.

It would be money first and everything else would follow.

Because when all the ordinary ways of making money are used up, when things are working at full capacity, there is always future money. Money can be invented, it can be imagined. It's just symbols, it's just numbers. The numbers whirl around and they underpin everything.

It was all lies and falsehoods, reckoned Andy. He felt an intense anger toward the men and to their nodding and appreciative audience.

'Money happens,' explained Skutt, to rapt applause.

'No more boom and bust,' promised a grinning Hames. The audience stood and they applauded the two men. Jigsaw stood and he applauded.

Andy seethed: The rich fucken bastards. The smug idle cunts. Just look at them, the twats. They sit around and they do nothing and they get rich. The value of their shares, property and art increase and they tell us that they are creating money? Anyone would think there could not be money without them. They don't create money, there are tricks they perform that conjure up money, that dictate the money that has yet to be made. With an eye for the main chance the owners and the rabbit farmers of money were playing fast and loose with the structure of everything.

Andy knew what was going on. He read the newspapers. They were a constant source of new material to him. Some papers though have more than just the news in them. You can learn a lot from reading between the lines. You can learn everything eventually: Rising property prices are an engine of economic growth. The private banking system creates most of the country's money supply as debt with interest. This money does not exist until it is loaned in to existence by the banks. It is money which the banks have created out of nothing. But money has to come from somewhere. Someone has to pay. It was the reason for all the work.

Andy fumed.

Work you bastards work, even when there is no work.

Because, for the rest of us, we have to console ourselves with the hope that if we work, and work hard, then we too can enjoy the good life. And what is the good life if not a superabundance of material things? Andy knew exactly how they accumulated all that money, all that power, and got everyone to do their bidding. The new car that lasts only so long. The latest fashion that is as fleeting as this years colour. The new device for which there will be no conceivable use tomorrow. Everyone is working to get the money, the things, that tell them that they have made it, that say finally that they are safe. More things, more money, more fucking work. Because when all the money gets spent you have to go out and earn more money. Life is getting harder and more expensive because of such games. It made Andy livid. People were tools, they were dupes. We're the ones that should be raking it in, we're the ones doing all the work. If it wasn't for us there wouldn't be all this money. We worked it out of the world. We turned whatever it is that we do for a living in to money, and they creamed it off by working it out of us. And now here they are living the good life on it. Angry, Andy picked up his glass, gripping it tight in his hand and tighter still until the wine in it trembled. These fucking cunts have got our money, he snarled. The glass smashed, spilling wine over the table.

Andy's accident passed virtually unnoticed. Everyone's attention remained directed at Skutt and Hames who, expanding on their model, were now proposing to convert loans in to marketable securities.

'Parcelling up debts and then selling them on to investors as securities would,' Skutt claimed, 'become a major source of corporate finance, providing the insurance necessary to guarantee an ever expanding supply of cheap money.'

'It would be the ultimate free lunch,' promised Hames.

Jigsaw paId the most careful attention to what was being said. He hung on their every word. He took notes, writing everything down on a paper napkin. There was such a lot to know and he needed to know everything. He wanted for himself what the people gathered here had come to celebrate. He wanted money but more than anything he wanted power over money. These people were manipulators, they controlled the numbers that said that there was money. They owned the banks and the trading houses. They ran the politicians. They made and destroyed companies, economies, countries, communities, whole lives. Jigsaw was at the puppet show and he was being shown the strings.

It was all being made clear to him. Everything seemed possible.

'We stand poised on the brink of a new era,' said Skutt. He finished the talk to a standing ovation.

Now it was Andy's turn.

He ascended the steps to the podium. 'Up the workers!' he shouted, snatching the microphone from its stand.

The audience cheered his rallying cry, expressing a far different sentiment, some giving him the finger, they applauded, everyone laughing: at the tuxedo printed on his T-shirt, and at the battered guitar waiting there for him on its stand which had just one unbroken string and five broken ones. Normally, Andy carried on a football that he had signed. He would do tricks with the football then he would kick it in to the audience.

Andy picked up the guitar. The audience roared with laughter as the several broken strings sprang about, flashes of silver in the bright lights. Andy plucked the single taught string as though he were tuning the instrument. He twisted the screw then he plucked the string again.

'A minor,' he said. 'Remember them?'

'Up the workers!' the audience shouted to its own rapt applause.

Andy retaliated with his *Off To Hell In A Shopping Trolley* song.

'You've knocked down our factories and sacked all our pals, you needed the space to put up some more malls.

'Let's all go shopping, let's all go shopping. Shop, shop, shopping,' he sang.

'An we can rant and rail abowr it, whoop and holler, but what's the point, I wouldn't bother.'

Unprompted, the audience joined in with the chorus:

'Let's all go shopping,' they sang at the top of their voices, 'let's all go shopping. Shop, shop, shopping!'

When the song finished the audience responded with wild applause.

Putting down the guitar, shading his eyes with one hand, Andy stared in to the audience. 'Millionaires,' he said, pointing them out, just as Jigsaw had done for him earlier. 'Multimillionaires,' he pointed. 'Billionaires! Greed,' he said. 'You just can't put a price on it.'

Andy harangued his audience. 'We spend eight hours of the day at work. Another eight hours asleep. Come on. Wake up. Think of what we could be earning here.' The audience roared with laughter.

'The weather, brought to you by Powergen. . . ' laughter.

'Fashion, accessory to the fact. . . ' laughter.

'This whole country is going to the dogs. . .' more laughter.

People just didn't get it.

They got it all right. They just did not care. They cared, but in a different way. Disgusted, Andy left the stage.

'More!' cried the audience, 'More! More!' It was a rallying cry and the more they shouted it the harder they laughed.

Bastards, swore Andy, they get the last laugh, every time.

Andy sat. He poured himself some wine. He tilted back his head and he drained the whole bottle.

As soon as the audience had settled, Sir Peter Grey stood up behind the microphone to announce the winner of the Businessman of the year awards.

The room fell silent.

Jigsaw leant forward in his seat.

'And the winner is. . . .' A smile broadened Sir Peter's face, pleasure shone from his eyes. 'Sir Geoffrey Plane-Smith! For having overseen a record rise in share price for the Wyles Corporation with its NuttyPrice chain of retail outlets.'

Sir Geoffrey received a standing ovation to loud applause.

He was then presented with a three foot high celebratory cake, topped with a bust of himself. The cake was carried in by four models who can't have been wearing 20 sequins and 20 black beads between them. About to cut in to the cake Sir Geoffrey stepped back astonished when the lid lifted up and a petite young beauty emerged from inside. Jigsaw recognised her immediately.

Ra leant forwards and she kissed Sir Geoffrey. The girls surrounded the businessman.

It was late, Sir Geoffrey was working the room. A press of people surrounded him. Everyone congratulating him, feeling blessed by his presence, everyone wanting his advice.

'What about gilt-edged securities?' he was asked.

'One should never feel guilty when it comes to making money,' he smiled.

Jigsaw laughed with the rest of them.

'Well done, Sir Geoffrey,' he shouted. Squeezing through the crowd, he extended his hand to the businessman.

Sir Geoffrey turned at the shout. He smiled broadly, reached out his hand, passed by Jigsaw and shook hands with Dick Fault.

Sir Geoffrey continued to work the crowd, the crowd parting for him. The shock of his shoulder striking Andy's shoulder almost knocked him off his feet. Andy had given him a shoulder barge, a sudden roll of the shoulder like a boxer might use to power a knockout punch, or a footballer to unbalance the opposition.

Sir Geoffrey glowered at Andy, but then he regained his composure. The superior smile returned to his face.

'If it isn't our good friend the comedian,' he said. He stood staring at Andy in his printed tuxedo.

Andy was shorter than him, he was lean and wiry, but muscular too. Andy was scarred. Scarred from work, scarred from fighting. He looked hard. His face vicious. He was that product of most British inner cities, a much smaller version of what, if things had been different for him, he would otherwise have become.

Sir Geoffrey was tall and unblemished and well-fed. He was well-dressed and manicured. He smelt mildly of aftershave, of toothpaste, freshly laundered clothes, of freshly purchased clothes.

They were two separate species entirely. Certainly, they were from two different worlds. Sir Geoffrey would not have considered himself to be a member of the public. They own land, they own grouse moors, mountains, rivers, streams, people. . . . they lift up their heads and they look down their noses at you. Sir Geoffrey peered down his nose at Andy.

'You know,' he said, his upper lip curling in to a smile, the smile filling his face, 'you don't much look like a comedian.'

'Appearances can be deceptive,' said Andy. 'Yew don't look stupid.' Jigsaw vomited out a laugh. He was the only one that did laugh.

The smile left Sir Geoffrey's face. His eyes met Jigsaw's eyes. They narrowed. The successful businessman glared icily at the very much less successful one. He saw fear and uncertainty and need and longing there. He laughed out loud at Jigsaw and at the joke. Laughed it right back in to Andy's face.

Sir Geoffrey was immune to insult. When you've got money you have no doubts whatsoever about your own worth. Millionaires, multimillionaires, billionaires. It was what some people used to keep the score.

People began pressing in, slapping Sir Geoffrey on the back, offering him their congratulations. Andy wandered off toward the bar. Jigsaw was left standing on his own, feeling alienated and miserable.

He plucked a full glass of champagne from the tray of a passing waiter and he knocked it back. He picked up another full glass and was about to down it when he caught sight of Skutt and Hames.

He went over and introduced himself. 'James Truitt,' he said, extending his hand, 'Andy Rant's manager.'

At that moment, their attention was drawn toward a loud commotion at the bar. It was Andy, giving out.

'In another country he'd be a revolutionary,' said Skutt.

'Luckily in this country we've got shopping.' Hames laughed. The three men shook hands.

'I enjoyed your talk,' Jigsaw told them. 'I found it uplifting.'

For the next ten minutes the men discussed finance. They were ebullient and over-talkative as people are when they discover a shared enthusiasm.

The talk eventually turned to Andy.

'Andy's very successful then?' said Skutt.

'Oh yes. Andy Rant the Roadshow is a multimillion pound industry. We grossed over four million this last year.'

The two men were impressed.

'There's serious money in comedy then?' Hames grinned.

Jigsaw let out a nervous laugh. 'The money pours in, virtually non-stop. And just as quickly goes out again.' The smile dropped from his face.

It is never your money, not for long. Money belongs to those who do not need money. That is how money is accumulated.

Jigsaw found himself staring in to his glass, in to the champagne. People often stare in to their drink for what it can tell them about things. The curved lens of the glass reflected back an image of Jigsaw and his surroundings that appeared warped. Jigsaw realised that he had stopped smiling and so he forced another smile.

There was a desperation to Jigsaw, something between panic and over confidence that made him appear manic. He was that peculiar mix of laughter and terror you often see in anxious people. Of an energy contained, then brimming over, then contained again.

He told Skutt and Hames about the overheads. Then there was the money that was continuously being creamed off by other people. There were all kinds of middle men and facilitators. Andy Rant the Roadshow was being preyed on by a long list of takers. Club owners, promoters, lawyers, producers, recording companies, insurers... they all took their cut.

What Jigsaw needed was a way of breaking in to the money flow that stopped it dead.

It was so frustrating. All that money that was slipping through his fingers. It had Jigsaw in despair thinking of what he could do with that.

And what would happen to them when the gravy train stopped, as it eventually must, and Andy stopped making money?

His grip on the life remained precarious. Everything depended upon Andy. And fate or the next comic superstar could come along at any time and take it all away.

Skutt and Hames agreed that it was a problem. There was though, they told

Jigsaw, an obvious solution.

'There is?'

'You could have all that money and more,' said Skutt. 'You should put money to work. You could stop working.'

'I could? How? Give it to me,' said Jigsaw, and he gulped down his drink.

Just then, a loud commotion from the far end of the room caught everyone's attention. It was Andy arguing with the financier that had given the talk earlier. A fight broke out and Andy was ejected from the building.

The city is full of the angry, the grasping, the desperate, the disadvantaged, the forever dispossessed. The city runs on such things. Here are the rich and the soon to be rich in all their nakedness and need.

New things were appearing in the apartment all the time. The bigger TV screen, the better music system, the personal computer, the new kitchen, more contemporary art. . . . Andy picked up a small glass snow scene that appeared one day upon a shelf. He flipped the snow scene over. Handmade personalised designs, said the sticker on its base. There was something familiar, almost unnerving, about the object. It was the tiny figure. It was Jigsaw alright, stood there, smiling, the cityscape behind him, with his arms outstretched like some mini Messiah. Andy gave the thing a shake. Who can resist it? His laugh was involuntary, out loud. The Jigsaw-like figure had become lost amongst a snowstorm of swirling banknotes. Money fell on Jigsaw, it formed in drifts around his feet, he was covered in money. Andy slammed the gewgaw down.

Andy felt compromised, he felt trapped. Trapped in work, trapped by money. He needed money to get out and he had to work to get it and that trapped him in work. It was the same for everyone, he knew, he just expected that it would be different for him. He was successful, wasn't he?

Jigsaw was in his study when the door burst open and Andy came storming in.

'Where the fuck is it? We are earning a fortune here, must be, with all this fucken work, I'm working like a dog here, but I'm not seeing any of it, am I? So where the fuck does it all go?'

Jigsaw put down the wine catalogue he had been perusing.

'I've invested it.' Jigsaw smiled. He really did think that Andy would be pleased.

'Invested it, what on?' Andy grabbed at the catalogue. 'Wine? Old fucken wine?' He flung the catalogue back at Jigsaw.

'And on the stock exchange.'

'What? We can't afford to invest money on the stock exchange.' He felt like he was being led toward some precipice.

'Yes we can.'

'No. We hate those fucken bastards, remember. Am meant to be anti-capitalist, me, yeh stupid twat.'

'Andy, we can't afford not to. We are on a roll here, but what about when there is no work? When the work dries up? We need to safeguard against that, because it could all end,' Jigsaw snapped his fingers, 'like that, tomorrow.'

A premonition of doom hangs over the city. There is a need to secure everything before everything crashes.

'But if we put that money to work, we can stop working.'

Andy went quiet, thoughtful. Walking off in to the lounge he went straight to the drinks cabinet and he poured himself a drink, a triple scotch, then he slumped down on the sofa with it. He looked exhausted, worn out. Jigsaw followed him.

'Am sorry, Jigsy, mate, you're right, it's just I can't keep this up, you know, not without a break, I can't. I need a fucken holiday, mate.'

'Sure you do,' said Jigsaw. 'You've certainly earned it. Which is why. . .' A broad smile broke across his face as he reached inside his jacket. 'Tara!' he sang as he produced two airline tickets. He handed one to Andy.

'Australia?' said Andy.

'Six weeks, eight different venues. Perth, Adelaide, Canberra, Melbourne, Sydney, Cairns, Darwin, Alice Springs. We travel through the outback in a land rover. You discover Australia. You meet the local characters, have scrapes, that sort of thing. A camera crew will film your shows and all your experiences. The sun will do you good. It will do us both good.'

'It's another fucking tour!' said Andy.

'A change is as good as a rest,' smiled Jigsaw, 'And just think of the money. We need the money, Andy.'

You need more and more money, so you work more and more hours, and you work harder. You work yourself in to the ground. Karoshi, the Japanese call it, death from overwork. It used to be that you worked to live, now you live to work. How did that happen? How do you think? The rabbit farmers of money need you to work so that they can farm you for money. Those who don't or won't work need those of you who do work so they don't have to work. You've become a wage slave. Why else would you have to slog and sweat and put in the hours but never get the lion's share? Those cunts have got your money.

19

Lost. Then Found Again

Ed had the road atlas open on the correct page but he had lost their place on the map.

'We're lost, aren't we?' said Natasha, 'I told you we should have stuck to the main road.'

'Lost? In England?' Don't be daft, Nat, you've only got to put one foot wrong here and someone will come along to put you in your place.' Ed laughed. Natasha too, reluctantly. 'Just keep driving,' Ed told her. 'We're bound to come to a signpost or a village soon. There', he said, pointing. 'We could ask at that farmhouse.'

'It'll have dogs,' said Natasha.

They were wary of dogs. They were sometimes chased away by dogs, to the satisfaction if not the encouragement of their owners.

They continued past the house. Ed held his face out the window, enjoying the warm breeze. They drove through a ford. Then there were ducks on the road that Natasha had to stop for.

They came fast around a corner. A policeman was stood in the centre of the road, his arm raised. Behind him, a police car was parked across the road, blocking the junction. Another officer was stood beside the car, on its far side.

Natasha braked, the car stopping just in time. Ed hit his head on the window frame.

'Here we go again,' said Ed.

'They can tell us where we are,' said Natasha. She smiled out of her open window at the approaching constable. Ed made to get out of the car.

'Please remain in the vehicle.' The officer then told Natasha to cut the engine.

'What's up? What's going on?' asked Ed.

'Just remain in the vehicle, sir.'

The officer walked slowly around the vehicle. He checked the tax disc, then the car's tyres. He tugged at the bumpers. He checked the lights. The second officer stood watching from the patrol car.

The officer finished his check on the car. He peered in to the car and saw the bedding. 'Living in this car, are you? Travellers, eh?'

'We're just passing through,' said Ed, squinting in to the sun that was shining in to his eyes, the officer a silhouette.

The patrol car's radio came to life in a burst of static and the officer waiting there bent in through the window to answer it. 'We're on!' he shouted, climbing in to the car...

In seconds, four police cars drove past the junction with their headlights ablaze. They were followed by a long queue of ramshackle vehicles: old ambulances, trucks, double decker buses, coaches, minibuses, converted vans. Vehicle after vehicle clattered past. There were about thirty in all.

Once the convoy of travellers had passed, the two policemen climbed quickly in to their patrol car and reversed it out of Ed and Natasha's way. The officer that had spoken to them waved Natasha on. But Natasha hesitated. The patrol car blazed its lights at them.

Ed told Natasha to turn right, in the opposite direction to the convoy, but there were two police cars waiting there that were blocking the road.

'They want us to join the convoy, Ed.'

'I don't like this,' said Ed. As Natasha fell in behind the convoy, the police cars closed in behind them, two abreast, blocking the road. 'First chance you get, Nat, pull off the road.'

But every junction and turnoff they came to was blocked by police. Whenever they tried to stop or to pull off the police waved them on. A police helicopter clattered overhead and both Ed and Natasha leant forwards to stare through the windscreen at it.

'Maybe the convoy's going to a festival,' said Natasha. 'It's just a lot of vehicles going to a festival, that's all, that's what this is, and the police are protecting them. People attack convoys, don't they? Maybe the convoy got attacked,' she said.

The convoy slowed. The vehicles were turning off in to a field.

'What did I tell you? Look, they're stopping in that field,' said Natasha, relieved.

'Drive on,' Ed told her, 'Don't turn in to that field, whatever you do.' He had seen, through gaps in the hedge, the lines and squares of police waiting in the field that were armed with truncheons and riot shields.

But Natasha couldn't drive on, a lorry load of gravel had been dumped across the road. The line of police stationed there waved them in to the field.

One after the other, as the vehicles turned in to the field, the police descended on them. Vehicles began speeding off in all directions across the open fields. There were police everywhere. Some of the convoy vehicles stopped, others found themselves cornered. The police swarmed over them, smashing in windscreens, tearing open doors, hauling out the occupants and dragging them off to the waiting police vans.

Natasha, whose first instinct had been to stop, sped off across the field.

'DRIVE! NAT! DRIVE. FUCKING DRIVE! THERE. THERE.' Ed was roaring at her, pointing out the way to go.

The police were running about, smashing windscreens, descending on stopped vehicles. The vehicles were being busted open and the people inside hauled out. A screaming policeman came at them, he swung his baton at the windscreen. Ed pulled on the wheel. Natasha screamed as they crashed through a hedge, the car hitting the road at an angle on the stretch of road beyond the police barricade. Ed leant across Natasha and he steered the car up the road.

'DRIVE! NAT! FUCKING DRIVE,' he roared, as Natasha gripped the steering wheel, pressed her foot to the accelerator and tried to engage a higher gear, the gears crunched.

Ed kept glancing over his shoulder, peering out of the window, looking up in to the sky in case they were being followed or tracked by the helicopter. There was a helicopter, but it remained hovering over the field. The road behind them stayed empty. Ed began to laugh from relief.

Natasha was shaking. 'What did we do? We did nothing wrong. What have we done? Nothing. Why should we be in trouble? All we've done is to get out of trouble. What do the police want with us?'

'We're not wanted by the police,' said Ed. 'We're not wanted by anybody.' Ed laughed, but it was not his usual laugh. Forced, it was cold and cynical.

They left the B road - there might be police on it - and for the next ten miles or so they lost themselves down a network of narrow country lanes.

Ed had Natasha pull up under some trees so he could check the car over. One of the headlights was broken and there were scratches to the bodywork down both sides of the car. There was a piece of hedge jammed in the bumper. Ed pulled it out. Then, getting out a can of yellow spray paint, he began to obliterate the scratches.

Miles from anywhere, the lay-by seemed a good place to stop for the night, and Natasha wanted to do just that. She was numb with shock still. The world had changed for her and she had not yet come to terms with that. Ed cautioned against it.

'We need to fix this light first. Find a scrappie, someplace. Or a garage. We might get stopped again and they'll stop us for sure if they see this.'

They drove down narrow country lanes, passing yellow cornfields, green pastures, shaded woods. It was another peaceful afternoon in midsummer. It was hard to take in what had happened.

There were no scrap yards. They found a garage, only it did not have what they wanted.

That night, parked up on the edge of town, Ed wandered the streets. He found a similar make of car and, breaking in to it, he took what he needed.

Salisbury Plain shimmered in the heat. They were at Stonehenge. Natasha wanted to sketch the stones. Ed wanted to touch them. They promised him a connection with something, in the same way that fishing did.

But the stones had been fenced off.

'The bastards,' said Ed.

'Why won't they let anyone touch the stones?' asked Natasha. 'They are our stones, aren't they?'

They were everybody's stones, and so they had to be protected from everybody.

The police stopped Ed and Natasha often, because of the car, not because of who they were, but of what they were suspected of being, and they questioned them about this or that theft, and about drugs and raves and the festivals which they had attended and which they intended to attend, or whatever, though they had committed no crime not as far as anyone knew. And they always gave the car a thorough going over. And they always found nothing. The police kept after them anyway. They would say things to them like, 'Sooner or later we're going to have you.'

They were continually moved on. Everywhere that Ed and Natasha went they went in fear of discovery. The trick was to arrive late and to leave early, so as to avoid confrontation.

The sun beat down on yellow cornfields and green fields and it lit up the woods. There was a sluggish feel to the day. Ed knew of a place not far off, up in the hills, where there was a waterfall with a deep plunge pool. It was in a natural amphitheatre and it caught the sun. No one ever went there, he told Natasha. It was miles from the road along a winding narrow track and it was surrounded by thick oak woods. They could be naked there. And it was a good place to camp, though it was years since he had been there.

First there was the sign: *Waterfall Cafe and Gift Shop*. Then they saw the car park. The old house, at the access to the waterfall, had been renovated and its garden, its orchard and lawns, had been tarmacked to provide the car park.

Natasha pulled in to the car park.

There was a gate across the path that led to the waterfall. A sign on the gate said, *50p to see the Waterfall. Tickets from the Waterfall Cafe and Gift Shop*.

Ed swore.

Natasha drove out of the car park.

It wasn't possible to take that place seriously any more. Someone had turned that waterfall in to a gimmick.

Where there are rivers, the rivers must pay. Where there are woods, the woods must pay. Every last penny was being extracted. Great things have been constructed by such means.

Angry, frustrated, increasingly contained, the country contracting around him, the anger built up in Ed. 'FUCK IT!' he shouted, and he punched the dash.

He felt an overpowering need to escape, he was propelled by it. But there were increasingly fewer places in which to escape. No unexploited, unknown, uncontested, limitless, boundless territory in which to break free. Everywhere was known. Everyplace, and everyone, had a use. Everything was limited.

This was Ed's terror. Not being locked up, but being in a locked up country: ungiving, fortified, with neither access nor opportunity. With no means of self expression there occurs the motionless death. But the striving individual has to test his new shape.

They drove to Wales. Here, in the west, in the mountains, they felt they could live with less restriction. There were few if any instructions written in to the landscape here. Things were less certain, were more natural, more human, less restrained. There was possibility in these unused, uncontested places. But things were changing here too.

Aberystwyth had changed. It was busier, more built up. Aberopolis, Ed called it.

'You're back!' said Ed's mother.

'And forth,' said Ed.

Natasha came in behind him.

'Everybody,' said Ed, 'I'd like you to meet. . . . ' Ed hesitated. What was she, his partner, fiancé, his girlfriend, what?

'Natasha,' she said, introducing herself. The family stared at the couple.

They were deeply tanned from the sun. Ed was dressed in a colourful waistcoat, his hair in dreads. Natasha wore scuffed boots, red leggings and a rainbow coloured dress, her hair was braided in to strands and there were coloured beads woven in to it. To Ed's family they looked exactly like those people that were travelling around in convoys that everyone was being warned against.

'My God, it gets worse,' said Ed's dad, 'there's two of them now. So, what are you doing with yourself these days? Nothing much, I'll bet.' He shook his head.

Ed went to the car to fetch his carvings. His father was not impressed.

'When are you ever going to get a proper job?'

Natasha showed everyone her sketchbooks, which seemed to impress them. Then, at Ed's insistence, she drew everyone's caricatures, to each of her subject's individual discomfort but to much general amusement. Ed then told them about her offer of an exhibition and how, needing new material, they had taken to the road.

'So, you're living in a car now?' said Ed's dad. 'I just can't understand you. You've no jobs, no place to live. Why do you do this to yourselves?'

'It's not like it's going be for ever,' said Natasha.

'No?' Ed's father remained sceptical. Some lives, once you started out on them, you just couldn't escape.

'Of course it isn't,' she said. She would never be trapped. She knew what she wanted, and she was going to get it. There were all sorts of worlds that it was in her power to make possible. She told them about Enzo, and Sadie Sommers, PK, and their success.

'Enzo sold a painting for one million pounds,' said Ed. 'And Natasha's a much better painter than Enzo.' He made it sound possible.

What a life it was going to be for them. You needed a house, you painted a picture. You needed a car, you painted a picture. Whenever you needed money to get a thing you painted a picture. This idea of conjuring things out of nowhere was too appealing not to be tried. There was much more to it than that, of course. That was just how it had to be explained to people who could see no other reason for doing things. Ed did not want money so much, not yet anyhow. It was not money that motivated Ed, it was having no need of money. That was how he would occasionally be made to want and to need money.

The family looked at Natasha and at Ed differently now. All the travelling, the apparent homelessness, began to make sense.

Ed's dad produced a bottle of whisky and some glasses and he poured them all drinks. Large ones for Ed, Natasha and himself, a small one each for Ed's mum and gran.

'A toast,' said Ed's dad. 'To Natasha.'

Ed's gran downed her drink in one. She held her glass out for another.

'Now, now,' chided Ed's mum. 'Everything in moderation.' She confiscated the glass.

'That's the trouble with moderation,' snapped Ed's gran, 'some people take it to extremes.'

Ed's dad topped up Ed and Natasha's glasses.

'You're welcome to stay as long as you like,' he told them.

'Just until we get back on our feet,' said Ed. And, though the joke was wholly unintentional, everyone laughed heartily at its implication.

They drove to the Midlands, to Birmingham, Liverpool, Manchester, the North, the North East. Scotland. They attended raves and anti road protests, street demonstrations, festivals, fairs. Natasha sketched. She sketched new age travellers, anarchists, graffiti artists, the unemployed, the restless, the police, shoppers, revellers, crowds. Wherever there were crowds there was Natasha. People behaved differently in crowds. It was the reason for all the signs.

They began to follow the open-air market circuit, Natasha selling caricatures, Ed his carvings.

At one of the local agricultural shows which they visited Ed entered a dry stone walling competition There were seven competitors in all and Ed came third. He won a white rosette and ten pounds.

Laughter and drunkenness. Friends made and as easily forgotten. People meeting up, then parting later. Paths crossing and uncrossing. . . .

3rd - 4th, A Little Folk Festival, Penzance. 7th, Brighton Fringe Festival. 12th, Keswick Jazz Festival. . . .

The nights began to draw in. There was a distinct chill to the air. The leaves of the trees had begun to turn. There was the sound of a dog barking. It was far off. But noise carried far in the cold, autumnal air.

The couple were parked up for the night in some woods, beside a stream. Natasha was sat in the car going through her sketchbooks. Ed was sat in front of a smoking camp fire on which he was boiling water to make tea. The blue smoke from the camp fire rose in a column in the still air. He sat flicking idly through the festival guide. It was dog eared and disintegrating. 'How about a horse fair?' he suggested.

Natasha shook her head. 'I've had enough of horse fairs, Ed. And drum camps. And folk festivals.'

She returned to her sketchbooks. She was picking them up, one after the other, and flicking through them, the pages flipping past, each picture a frame in the continuous film of their travels. It was a way that she had of trying to see the bigger picture: *A crowded high street. People shopping. A derelict factory. A boarded up shop. Wasteland. A skip full of old doors. A new development. Wastelands, construction sites. An empty warehouse. Abandoned docks. An out of town mega store. Traffic. A retail park. New roads. Surveillance cameras. A festival. Signs: No Trespassing, Private Property. Cars stuck in a traffic jam. Tall buildings. Barcodes. A derelict pit. Miners. A derelict drunk in a crowded street. Dockers. A homeless person in a doorway. Graffiti. A steelworker. New age travellers. The City. A skyline of cranes. New construction. A rave. A police raid on a squat. . . .*

A picture was emerging, but what kind of picture Natasha remained unsure. Change was sweeping the country making everything uncertain. There was so much that was deemed unnecessary of a sudden. It was not a progression as such, the old giving way to the new, but more an abandonment – a separation. It were as though two nations were being created. Something was coming apart. But how did you paint that, and in one picture? Natasha continued to flick through her sketchbooks, trying to make sense of them.

'What about a green fair?' suggested Ed. 'Or how about.' Ed made his voice strange, he wiggled his fingers in the air and enlarged his eyes: 'A Cosmic Consciousness Gathering? It'll be good for a laugh that. Or there's that antiroad demonstration I was telling you about.'

The sound of a car, its engine noise rising and falling, mapping out the geography, the bends and straights of the road it was travelling down, drifted to them on the still air.

Natasha turned to face Ed.

'Aren't you tired of all this travelling, Ed?'

'Tired? No.' Ed loved this life.

'I am.'

Ed's face fell.

'Well don't look so surprised,' she told him. 'We said, remember, that's what we agreed.' She lifted her sketchbooks. 'It's what this is all about. Besides, we can't live like this, not in the winter. How can we live like this? I need a place, Ed. Somewhere where I can paint.'

Ed did not know for certain what he wanted, but he did know what Natasha wanted. Wanting Natasha, wanting her to succeed, made Ed want that too. Sometimes, a person can want a thing so badly that they will stop at nothing in order to get that thing. That can lead people to all sorts of places.

20

Down Under

Blue sky. Yellow parched land. White sun. The empty land trembled in the fierce heat.

Andy appears, walking out of the shimmering heat haze. He is wearing shorts, boots, singlet and a sweat stained bush hat.

A voiceover, the accent Australian, says: 'Australia, it's a hot country, an unkind country at times, and an empty one. A person can go for days without seeing another soul.'

The camera pans away to show Andy at the centre of an empty and treeless landscape. Everywhere shimmers in the heat.

The voiceover continues: 'Then you see another person.'

The shot focuses in to show a beautiful tanned blonde dressed exactly like Andy emerging out of the heat haze. Looking Andy up and down she runs her tongue across her dry lips. Andy returns her look. It seems that both of them are after the same thing.

'Got any water?' they ask each other.

The camera crew burst out laughing. The girl laughs, then Andy. Andy beams. He is enjoying himself out here in this difficult place.

A featureless and almost treeless landscape crossed by a seemingly endless, straight, tarmac road. The road shimmered in the hot sun.

The yellow sun hammered the yellow earth in to yellow dust.

Andy and Jigsaw were driving across Australia, travelling up from the yellow plains and bleached white wastelands of South Australia in to the vast red centre of the Northern Territory. The land was so vast the horizon curved.

As the morning progressed the sun grew fiercer, hotter, it turned white.

The Land Rover pulled in to the side of the road. Andy, dressed in the same sweat stained slouch hat, black singlet and shorts, and elasticated boots that he wore earlier, and Jigsaw, wearing a well pressed safari suit, climbed out in to fierce heat. Jigsaw fanned himself with a map which he then unfolded and spread out on the bonnet. He bent over the map. The map was yellow, it was featureless. There was just a single black dot on it. Jigsaw tapped the dot.

'A town?' said Andy. 'In this place?'

Town. The word meant pubs, beer, women. But it also meant law and order, shops, shopping, suburbs. That removed a little of the word's magic. Town. Andy had an anticipation of the place, but also a wariness of it.

Andy took off his hat and wiped the sweat from his forehead with his forearm. It was ten o'clock in the morning and already it was searing hot. The hot dry air reminded Andy of the bakery. Andy's eyes stung from the glare of the fierce heat. He shaded his eyes and he stared down the road in the direction of the town. The road shimmered in the heat haze.

Somehow, he could not imagine there being a town in a place such as this. Town had to have some other meaning here.

Jigsaw looked the place up in his guide book. He read it out to Andy, for the benefit of the camera. 'Godsown. Population, 12. Former mining town, mostly underground. The houses, called dug outs, are carved in to the bare rock. One pub, The Willy Willy, serves as a watering hole for travellers.'

'Great,' said Andy, 'We can have a beer.'

The Willy Willy was a ramshackle building with a zinc roof, its windows taped over, like those in the blitz. The single, sparsely furnished room was full of rough looking characters who gave them the hard-eye. The barmaid, a tough yet good looking blonde, greeted them with a sharp nod.

Andy ordered a beer.

'Vodka and orange for me,' said Jigsaw.

'We only got tomatoe juice,' said the barmaid.

'A Bloody Mary then. Yourself?'

'I'll have a fucking beer.'

'Australia,' said Andy to camera, 'Where men are men. And the women are men too.'

'Oh, and, have you got any ice?' asked Jigsaw.

'What kind of ice do you want?' asked the girl. 'We got vodka an ice, whisky an ice.'

'Just ice, for the eskie,' said Jigsaw.

Dressed in salt stained hats, shorts and singlets and wearing salt stained and scuffed elasticated boots, the locals stood idly around or were seated on bar stools, leaning on the bar, drinking beer from foreshortened bottles, stubbies, that were inserted in to polystyrene or neoprene sleeves to keep the beers cool. The beer was ice cold and the bottles were wet with condensation.

'You making a film?' someone asked.

'We're travelling the country, meeting the local characters,' explained Jigsaw. 'I'm kind of the production manager. This is the comedian, Andy Rant.'

There was a shout: 'Hey Wal!' Someone to see you, mate.' A well built man detached himself from the crowd.

'Show him your tatoo Wal.'

Wal turned his back to the camera. Dropping his shorts and pants he exposed his bare arse. There was a large blue W tatooed on each of his buttocks.

'Why's he got W's tatooed on his arse?' asked Andy.

'Show him, Wal,' said the barmaid.

The cockie bent over, touching his toes.

'WoW,' said Andy.

The land rover slowed and, turning off the road, it edged on to the dirt. It bounced as it left the bitumen, as though on a wave, lifting, then bowing low as it crossed that threshold.

The land slowed. It was brought in to focus. It could be felt.

Dropping in to hollows, bouncing over rocks, the wildly lurching land rover shook its occupants, throwing them in to the air, their heads hitting the ceiling.

'Disco drive,' laughed Andy. Jigsaw looked uncomfortable, cowed.

Andy squinted in to the too bright sun. His face glowed. He was with Les Hiddins, the Australian survival expert. Les, like Andy, was dressed in bush hat, sweat stained singlet, boots and shorts.

'People actually lived out here?' said Andy.

'The Aborigines, they owned all this once, but not in a way that we would recognise. They knew all the plants, the animals, all the waterholes. They had this whole continent mapped out. That meant they could go anywhere, I reckon.'

The voiceover said: 'The land gave, it gave freely, it gave its animals, its fruits, its plants, it gave water. It gave life itself.'

Les, a Major in the Australian army, was currently travelling the continent, interviewing aboriginal elders. He was gathering information, using ancient aboriginal knowledge of the land to create bush tucker maps, before that knowledge and the access which that conferred, died with them.

Les explained how life had once been a continual search across the landscape in the form of a track. It was not possible to stay in the one place, not for long. There could not be that kind of ownership.

'But what's there to eat out here?' asked Andy.

Andy looked around. The land seemed empty. He could see no emus, no kangaroos. There were just lizards and snakes, the occasional scorpion.

'Lizards and snakes,' said Les, 'and the occasional delicacy,' He walked over to the stumpy, sun bleached remains of a wattle tree. He bent to one knee and he began to pull it apart, digging around in the rotten wood until he found what he was looking for. Gripping the huge translucent grub between his finger and thumb he offered it up to the camera.

'Ugh,' grimaced Andy. 'What is it?'

The fat white grub writhed slowly in a motion that was almost hypnotic. The grub curled to a finger. It beckoned to Andy.

'It's a wittchety grub, mate. The larvae of a moth. You can eat it.'

'No,' said Andy, 'You can eat it.'

Les shot a hand in to the long grass. He withdrew his hand and held up a snake. Andy jumped back. 'These are good tucker too,' said Les. He grabbed the snake in both hands, holding it close to its head, and snapped its spine, like you would break a stick. He dropped the carcass on to the ground. It fell with a heavy thump.

'What does snake taste like, Les?' asked Andy.

'A bit like lizard, I reckon.'

'So where are the aborigines now?' asked Andy. He stared out across the land. The land was empty. The featureless landscape shimmered in the fierce sun.

'Gone.'

'Where?'

Les toed the ground, pushing up a ridge of red dust. 'Back in,' he said. He crouched to one knee and he dug up a handful of the red dust. He spilled the dust slowly from his hand. The dust was red, blood red. 'Iron, iron oxide,' said Les, 'The exact same thing that colours blood, the same thing exactly.'

A chill ran up Andy's spine and he shivered, despite the heat.

It was late. The sun was setting in a blaze of yellow light. Gallahs, cockatoos, crows and kookaburras let out their cries. The sun dipped beneath the horizon and the ghost gums became black silhouettes as the land fell silent. It cooled.

The director and the driver set up lights, powered by a generator. The lights dazzled Andy. Other, much tinier lights, of various sizes, and in pairs, the reflections of the eyes of bush-rats, mice and snakes, glared at them from the pushed back darkness all around.

'The Southern Cross.' Les pointed to the cruciform pattern of stars in the blue-black, luminous sky. He explained to Andy how you could navigate by it.

'And that one,' asked Andy, pointing to a bright light flickering through the trees. 'Right there, low down, on the horizon?'

'That's my camp fire,' said Les.

'Great,' said Andy, 'camping.'

'It's a wrap!' said the director.

'Well, it's been a pleasure meeting you, Les.' Jigsaw shook him by the hand. He turned to Andy. 'Come on, we're spending the night at Hotel Australia.'

'But I thought we were camping. The tent, all the equipment?'

'They're just props,' said Jigsaw.

Hotel Australia had green lawns, air-conditioned rooms, room service, house-boys, restaurants, a casino, swimming pool, golf course, tennis courts, numerous bars, and a shopping arcade complete with a hairdressers, a supermarket, a souvenir and an outdoor apparel shop. There were tiny electric buggies to ferry guests between the facilities to save them from having to walk in the fierce heat. There were also guided tours. Every morning a column of four wheel drive vehicles left the complex to bump off in to the surrounding desert taking tourists on the trip of a lifetime. They ran several such trips of a lifetime every day from Hotel Australia.

Andy sat in the air conditioned comfort of the Dreamtime bar, sipping cold shards of beer, watching, through the tinted windows, the production crew load up the land rover. Jigsaw climbed in to the land rover. The director signalled to Andy. Time to go.

A waiter, an aborigine, in the starched white livery of Hotel Australia, looked up from his work and he watched them leave. He stared out from beneath his heavy, creased brow and he glared at them with his sullen, sorrowful, yellow eyes as they drove off in to a land of low bleached scrub and yellow cracked earth that was like iron.

The road cut through the centre of the continent, one straight un-metalled road that was like a scar, allowing trespass to the unsuited, to the unseeing, in to the unknown and sometimes the unknowable.

The land shimmered in the heat. Low hills seemed to detach themselves from the land and hover in the blue air. Everywhere was illusion.

The heat grew fiercer, the land stranger, more alien.

They stopped at the intersection of two dirt roads. One was a road, the other a dried up creek bed. There were tyre tracks in both. It was hard to tell which was what.

They drove for hours.

Finally, the land rover pulled over and the scenery stopped.

Flies, trapped between the windscreen and the dashboard, hoolahooped around, fizzed and then died.

The engine ticked and cooled. The bonnet thumped.

They climbed out of the vehicle in to the fierce white sun.

The cameraman and the director and the guide bent over the bonnet of the vehicle on which they had spread a map. It was no more than a yellow sheet of paper folded in to squares. There were no lines, no features, no dots with names that might have been towns. Because there were no roads, no towns, not one single house. They had no place in this featureless, timeless desert. It was the same in every direction.

'So where the hell are we?' asked Jigsaw.

The guide looked up from the map. He looked at the land, at the sun and then at his watch, and then he looked at the map again. It was a convincing performance.

'Buggered if I know,' he said.

Shielding their eyes, they stared in to the hot dry interior, in to the fierce white sun.

Jigsaw scratched at his chest, where a rash of prickly heat had appeared.

Scorpion,' said Andy, pointing to it as it scuttled away.

Jigsaw jumped. 'Kill it,' he shouted, leaping back.

'Hey, what's that over there?' said Andy, pointing.

Jigsaw started, then jumped at the sight of a snake-like line of caterpillars as they crossed the desert floor, each one attatched somehow to the one in front. The director bent down and, using a stick, he manipulated the line, attaching the leading caterpillar to the one at the rear. The caterpillars continued to wander in a tight circle.

'I hope we're not driving round in circles,' said Jigsaw.

'Nah,' said Andy, 'We've had the sun to our left all the time.'

'That way I reckon,' said the guide, pointing to who knows where.

Andy wanted it to be the wrong way. He didn't want to leave just yet. He wanted to camp.

A few hours later the land rover left the dirt and regained the bitumen.

Andy's face, small and round in the window, lost its anticipation.

The vehicle accelerated, snatching them out of the landscape. The bitumen sang. The land flashed by, yellow and blurred, distant and alien.

The hard metalled road cut through the land, tearing them through it.

21

Taking Root

The house stood on in its own in an overgrown garden at the end of a rutted lane and looked derelict. There were slates missing from the roof. Its windows were curtain-less. Inside, the house smelt of pin mould and damp. There was no furniture, just broken and rotted away chairs and a collapsed dining table, a gutted sofa. The house had not been lived in for many years, but someone at some stage had broken in and had lived rough in one corner of the living room. There was a kind of nest there, made of newspapers, blankets, curtains and rugs. There were cigarette butts, empty bottles and beer cans scattered everywhere. The half burnt remains of a chair rested in the fireplace.

'Well?' asked Ms Evans-Jones, the owner of the property. 'Will you take it, do you think?'

'I don't know,' said Ed as he and Natasha made their way up the creaking wooden stairs, the occasional strip of wood-chip wallpaper wafting in its entire length off the wall to some draught. 'It needs a lot of work doing to it.' Ed stopped and he shook the wobbly bannister. Natasha continued on up the stairs.

'A good sweep out is all it needs,' said Mrs Evans-Jones. 'A few coats of paint and it will be like new. Nice and homely, once you get that stove going.'

There was an old Aga in the kitchen. The kitchen was squalid. A Belfast sink stood on pillars of old bricks. It had a rotted wooden draining board. And just one tap: cold. There was a free-standing cabinet with a drop down work surface – the only work surface in the kitchen – but which did not quite drop down because of the broken and poorly repaired chain that had been fixed with a granny knot.

Ed could hear Natasha exploring upstairs, heels hammering on the bare boards, doors opening and closing.

Natasha stepped in to the bathroom. There was black pin mould on the walls, a stained cast iron bath and a brown toilet.

'How much?' Ed asked the landlady.

'200 pounds. In advance,' said Mrs Evans-Jones.

200 pounds. It was more than they could comfortably afford. In only a few short months it would eat up their savings. They needed that money to pay for Natasha's artists materials. Ed would have to find work.

Ed hesitated.

'You won't find anywhere as cheap, not for a whole house you won't,' said Mrs Evans-Jones.

Natasha continued to investigate upstairs. At the rear of the house, next to the bathroom, there was a small box room. Opposite was a spacious bedroom lit by two huge sash windows. There was no bed, no furniture, nothing, just bare floorboards and a fireplace. The room smelt of damp and of chimney soot. But it was full of natural light, and the windows were north facing. It would make a perfect studio.

'Well?' asked Mrs Evans Jones.

Natasha shouted down the stairs. 'It's perfect, Ed.'

Mrs Evans-Jones smiled.

Ed shrugged. 'We'll take it,' he told her.

'A rat! A rat!' screamed Natasha.

She had been sweeping out the kitchen and something huge had raced out from behind the Ann Twack – Ed's name for the drop down cabinet – and run in under the sink.

'It was a rat, a big fat rat, Ed! A rat,' she screamed.

'Calm down, Nat. It can't be a rat, not in the house. It's a mouse, surely. A big fat mouse. Where was it now, show me. Jesus Christ! A fuckin' rat! Fetch down the frying pan, hit it with that. Okay, I'll hit it, give it to me then. You poke it with the broom, flush it out. Don't point at it, Nat, we know where it is, prod the fucker. Get him out in to the open. Here it comes. Jesus Christ! the fucker's after me.'

Plang! Ed missed. Plang! He hit a plate. Plang plang! The kettle and two cups. He finally cornered it behind the kitchen door. Plang! He gave it another hefty wallop for good measure.

Ed held the flattened creature up by its tail. Natasha shuddered at the sight of it. 'It's enormous,' she said.

'It's certainly much bigger than it was. Jesus, will you just look at the bloody thing. It's almost a rug. I hope it didn't have family?'

'It's too late to feel sorry for it now, Ed.'

'I'm not grieving for it, Nat. I was just wondering if there were more.'

'More! Where?' Natasha span around, she peered under the sink and discovered what she thought must be a rat hole.

'I heard,' said Ed, 'that there is a rat within ten yards of everyone in Britain.'

'But that's everywhere in the house. We have to fill up all the holes, lay poison. Buy traps. We need to get a cat, Ed.'

'We had a cat, once. It was ferocious. We called it Genghis. Genghis Cat. He provided us with security.' Ed laughed. 'And acupuncture. He tore the furniture to ribbons. Believe me, Nat, we're better off with rats.'

Ed bought several large rat traps from the local ironmonger in Montgomery. They were huge wooden affairs, like Japanese sandals. Ed knocked them together and they clonked.

Ed put a little lump of cheese on the wire pin. Gingerly, he levered back the spring. His hand shook as he reached in and placed the baited trap under the sink and in front of the suspected rat hole.

Natasha screwed shut her eyes and pulled a face against the trap springing on

Ed's fingers. 'Careful, Ed,' she grimaced.

Ed lay the trap gently down on the ground and he pushed it closer to the hole. He smelt black pin mould and the rotten egg smell of the trap water from the leaky S bend. 'Nicely does it,' he whispered. 'There,' he said as he let go of the trap.

Snap!

Bright and glorious pain blazed through Ed's body like he'd been electrocuted.

'Jesus godding fuck Christ! ' he yelled, 'My fucking fingers!' he jumped to his feet and shook his hand free of the giant trap. There was a loud crash and the sound of falling glass as it flew straight through the window. There was the sound of birdsong. A fresh breeze.

Ed found a set of aluminium ladders, and a home made wooden roofing ladder in an old and sagging shed in the garden that was hidden amongst the trees. He made repairs to the leaking roof and he cleared and repaired the gutters. There were all sorts of things in that shed. A butter churn, mangles, iron bars, a pick, shovels, garden forks, scythes, hammers, a rusted lawnmower, a steel framed bicycle. . . .

Ed and Natasha threw themselves in to working on the house. They swept out the house, gutting it of every last bit of rotted furniture. They lit fires, to dry out the house. They washed the black pin mould from off the walls and ceiling with bleach and water and hard work. Then they painted the walls white. Natasha concentrated most of her efforts on her studio, painting not just the walls but the ceiling and the floorboards a brilliant white. They obtained some furniture from the local recycling tip and from charity shops in Newtown and Welshpool. After a month of hard work the house was habitable. Natasha felt herself ready to begin painting.

Natasha was wary of beginning painting. She was afraid of the process. She knew how obsessive she would become. 'Nothing will be as important to me as my work,' she told Ed, 'Do you think you can handle that?'

'You've got your painting and I've got my carving to do. See you in the spring, Nat.'

Natasha prepared herself to paint. Ed carved. He sold his carvings at the markets that were held once a week in the nearby towns. He made the same kind of money that he had always made but it was no longer enough. There was rent to pay now, and council tax, and electricity and water bills, as well as artists materials – paint and canvas – to purchase. Natasha intended to paint huge canvases, and that was going to prove expensive. Ed knew from experience how Natasha ate up paint. She ladled it on with a palette knife at times. And scraped off just as much. He soon realised that he would not earn the kind of money which they needed by doing carvings.

Ed stared at the picture, trying to work it out. Puzzled, he angled his head. That action angered Natasha. She knew then that she would have to prompt Ed's interest with an explanation. But if you had to enter in to an explanation it meant that you had failed.

'It's London, Ed'

'It's nothing like I remember it.'

Nothing was fixed. Nothing was certain yet.

Ed and the old farmer were stood looking at the tumble down walls. They stretched for miles, like veins across the hillsides. He had been out walking and he had met the farmer and now they were looking at the walls.

There are two things that people say whenever they see a dry stone wall and the farmer said them now:

'They last for ever, don't they, dry stone walls.' And: 'Nobody builds walls these days.'

'I do,' said Ed.

Ed followed the farmer up through some woods and on to the bare hillside. The two sheepdogs ran on ahead. Ed and the farmer crested a hill where there was a view of country that Ed did not recognise. He searched out and followed the windings of a river. The water shone in the sun through the bare trees.

'What do you reckon. Can you do it?'

Ed walked around the tumbled down sheepfold. The sheepfold, built of huge blocks of stone, was of a roughly circular construction. Some of the stones in it were massive. Ed tried shifting a huge stone, but it would not budge.

'No problem,' said Ed.

'How long will it take?' asked the farmer.

'Six, maybe seven weeks,' said Ed. 'Depends.'

This seemed to please the farmer. 'And how much do you charge?' he asked.

'£30 a square yard.'

'The job's yours, if you want it.'

Ed stood. He returned to staring down the valley, trying to make out the river there. He could not place it.

'What river's that?' he asked. He was hoping that it was a new river to him, one that he did not know.

'Banwy,' said the farmer.

Ed knew the Banwy. He had fished the Banwy.

'Oh,' he said, disappointed.

'If it's fishing you want, you should fish my stream.'

The farmer turned in the opposite direction and he pointed out the stream with his stick. Ed could not see the stream, but he saw the thick belt of trees that marked its course.

'It's only a small stream, nothing like the river. But no one fishes it, so you'd have it to yourself.'

Ed's heart sank. 'Nobody fishes it, why not?'

'I won't let them.'

'Are there fish in the stream?'

'Oh yes.'

'Big ones?'

'Yes.' The farmer nodded.

'How big?'

The farmer had to rest his walking stick in the crook of his arm before he could show Ed how big the fish were.

Ed burst in to the studio to tell Natasha his good news. He stopped dead. Natasha was stood before her easel. She was deep in thought. Ed turned and he left the room. He closed the door quietly.

Natasha was busy. She was always busy.

Ed began work on the sheepfold at eight in the morning. Apart from gloves, the only equipment that he brought with him that day was what he called his heaven and earth moving equipment: a long metal bar, to help him shift the big footing stones, and a shovel and a pick axe. He brought sandwiches, and a flask of hot water to make tea. Ed ran on tea.

For a while Ed stood and he looked at the wall.

Before Ed could rebuild the wall he had to dismantle the partly tumbled, bulging wall, stone by stone. The farmer had offered to dismantle the wall using a mechanical digger, to save Ed time, but Ed had refused the offer.

Ed needed to touch the stone with his hands and to sort the stone himself in order to know the stone. Used in a wall, certain shapes and sizes of stones perform certain functions. A wall built with cement relies solely on the cement to keep it together but a dry stone wall relies on its structure. Dismantling the wall by hand, and by sifting through the tumbled and spilt stones where the wall had collapsed, Ed, by judging the size and the shape of each stone, discovered the nature and the use of that stone, and he stacked it accordingly.

When Ed began to rebuild the wall he would not expect to place the stones exactly as they had been placed in the wall before. He simply stacked the stone so that the right size and type of stone would be available to him when he came to place it in the wall. All this preparation took time, but it saved time too: it made rebuilding easier.

There are difficult stones, and there are impossible stones, but there are no useless stones. Every stone has its use. Even impossible stones. They can be smashed apart with the hammer and used as fill.

Ed stopped to eat a thick meat and cheese sandwich, an apple, a banana, two biscuits, and a piece of cake, and he was still hungry. He vowed to make more and bigger sandwiches in future and to bring more cake.

It took Ed three and a half days to dismantle the sheepfold in preparation for his marking it out. It should have taken him only two days, but halfway through the second day Ed had to go home. The stones were too big and he had had enough. His legs, his back, his arms and shoulders all hurt, even his hair hurt, or seemed to.

He came home slow and bent over.

'Ed,' said Natasha, 'what happened?'

Ed did not answer. He was far too tired. He sat on the sofa and soon fell asleep there.

Natasha had created several fine pictures but they did not please her. There was something lacking in them.

'Have a rest, Nat,' advised Ed. 'You've been working too hard. Let'a go for a walk. It's lovely outside.'

It was one of those crisp days of clear blue skies in late March. There was still snow on the distant mountains. Maybe they could take a trip to the mountains. Ed felt their pull on him.

'Things will look different after a rest, come on.'

'No!'

Natasha was adamant. She was sure that she would solve the problem, if only she kept at it. She was close. There was an edge in her work, and she was painting around that, when what she wanted was to go beyond that boundary in to the transformation. Her work said nothing still, she knew.

Ed understood. He hated to have work hanging over him. That was as much a burden as the work itself. Some people put work off. They spend all their time not doing it. And it hangs over them. And they still have to do it.

Natasha returned to her painting, Ed went fishing.

As soon as Ed stepped off the roadway and in to the woods he forgot the world. He stooped low as he approached the stream. He did not want to frighten off any fish. Ed heard the stream long before he saw it. Already he could tell what kind of a stream it was.

A fast, shallow stream, but with occasional deep pools.

At first, Ed saw no fish. But it was not easy to see fish in such water. The water was clear, and the glare of the sun, where the water was not shaded by trees, made a mirror of the water.

Ed walked upstream, pushing through the trees and the undergrowth. It was difficult to make progress in such country, and the stream proved hard to fish. The trees made casting difficult. Ed caught trees, bushes, ferns, bracken, brambles, grass, tree roots, boulders, himself, everything but fish. He lost dozens of flies. He fished the stream right up to where there was a gorge surrounded on both sides by craggy cliffs. A waterfall plunged in to a deep pool there. Ferns clung to the cliff, to its black, cold sides.

Ed loved barriers. Push beyond a barrier and you discover new things. Worthwhile things. Things that have remained undisturbed because of the barrier.

Ed scrambled above the gorge in to wild and open countryside. He found that the stream was fed by two smaller streams running off the moor, both of which proved shallow and unfishable.

Ed did not catch a fish on his next trip to the stream either, nor the trip after that. He did have one take, but he tightened too late, or too early, he couldn't tell.

People laughed at Ed because he caught no fish and yet still went fishing. They told him in the village pub that he would never catch a fish, and certainly not from that stream. No one had ever heard of anyone catching a fish from that stream.

'Face up to it, Ed, you're no fisherman.'

'You can buy fish, Ed.'

You can buy anything.

'The thing about fishing,' said Ed. And the pub fell quiet. Everyone needed to know what it was that could be so compelling about fishing that cushioned Ed so completely from failure. 'Is that it has got absolutely nothing to do with catching fish, and everything to do with fishing.'

'Ed just pretends to go fishing. What are you up to really, Ed?'

'He's got a woman up there, haven't you, Ed?'

'Fishing's cruel,' said the barmaid. 'It should be banned. Like hunting.'

'Ed doesn't harm the fish, do you, Ed?'

'Are there any fish in that stream, Ed?'

They were big fish, and they were proving impossible to catch. That made them the only fish worth fishing for, as far as Ed was concerned. Ed would learn a lot about fishing from such fish, he reckoned.

Ed had heard enough. 'You want to watch what you say, wars have been fought over fishing,' he warned.

'The cod war,' said someone.

'Yom Kipper,' said another.

The whole pub laughed at the joke and at Ed.

Ed continued to fish and to not catch fish, and people continued to taunt him about that.

As far as Ed could tell the sheepfold had once been a perfect circle.

To mark out the new footings for the sheepfold Ed placed his metal bar upright in the centre of the sheepfold, which he discovered by measurement. Then, using a length of string attached to the bar by a loose loop, he walked a full circle, marking out the circumference of the sheepfold.

Ed did not possess much in the way of tools. He had his heaven and earth moving machinery: a pick and shovel, with which he redug the footings; and the long metal bar, which he then used to prise and position the big stones back in to place. And he had his hammer, to break up stone and to persuade others in to place.

Ed set up his frames, wooden battens which he hammered in to the ground and then braced to determine the walls dimensions. He had to place the frames close, no more than two metres apart because of the walls curvature. He positioned his frames symmetrically with a plumb bob.

Ed relaid the footings, on which he placed and levelled off the first course. He did not bother with strings on the wall. Instead, he checked the dimensions of the wall by holding a batten to the first two courses and eyeing it up against the frame.

Later, when he had built up enough courses, Ed would line up the face of the stone which he was placing on the wall with that of those beneath.

Ed laid the larger stones first. He placed their long axis in to the wall, each stone sitting on two other stones, each stone wedged from beneath so that it sat firmly on the wall. Ed built up both sides of the face at the same time. He had constantly to clamber from one side of the wall to the other because the stones were so heavy. As he worked, Ed filled in the gaps between the stones with the much smaller hearting stone, using as large and as few stones as possible for each gap, and he packed them in tight.

Ed sat on the hillside, with the landscape stretched out before him, and he ate lunch. Ed smiled to himself. The irony of his trade was not lost on Ed. Ed liked freedom and space, and here he was erecting boundaries, constructing walls.

Eighteen inches up the wall Ed built in a layer of through stones. There would be three such courses of these stones in the wall eventually, each course staggered over the one beneath so that every bit of wall would be covered at intervals by a through stone. Their purpose was to stretch across the wall to tie both sides of the wall together to stop the two sides separating under the weight of the stone above. Ed marked the stones.

Stones do not want to be arranged to make a wall, they want to be stones littering the fields. Structure must be built in to a wall. There are no stresses or strains in a good wall. All there is is the right stone sitting in the right place. The wall is not clenched, like a badly built wall is clenched, full of tensions and things waiting to happen.

After a fortnight of hard work Ed had managed to rebuild one quarter of the sheepfold.

Often, when placing the bigger stones, Ed let out a vile curse just to get the things to move. He spoke all sorts of things in to the air up there. There was no one to hear him.

His back ached. He stood upright slowly and he leant backwards. He looked at the wall. He stood studying his wall.

'It looks good,' he said to himself.

Sheep bleated. Rooks called down from the nearby crags. The wind sounded through the long grass. Silence. And he clonk and clatter of stone, of slow wall building being resumed.

'It's a dying trade, walling.'

That was another thing that people often said about dry stone walls.

'It's killing me,' Ed would reply.

Ed had sprained his wrist, hauling on the big stones. He had a cure for that.

'Horse liniment?' said Natasha.

'I got if from the vet.'

'It's for horses, Ed.'

'And dogs. I work like a dog.'

Natasha grinned. She offered to massage the liniment in to Ed's wrist.

Ed reached out and he touched Natasha. He ran the back of a finger down her hair. He held her gently by the shoulders and he kissed her shoulder. He kissed her neck. He was gentle with her, she became a fragile construction between his hands.

It was easier to satisfy a woman when you were gentle with her. When you were gentle a woman moved around her point of satisfaction, embracing and encouraging it. Being gentle, by taking note of all the various signals of arousal, Ed found it was possible to direct that arousal. After a time, Ed no longer needed to be gentle with her.

'Ed, you're all hard. Your arms are hard. Your chest is hard. Even your stomach is hard. And your head,' Natasha made a fist and she rapped it on Ed's head, 'Thonk!' she said. 'It's like a great big rock. Are you my rock, Ed?'

Ed loved Natasha. At first it was for the pleasures which they could have together, and then it was for other things. There was too, the time which they had spent together, the things they had done. Over time a couple develop a history of shared things which, if they are good things, binds them together. They expect more good things.

Ed had found a penny amongst the stones of the wall when he dismantled the wall, a 1727 King George I penny. He had pocketed the penny, so that when he had rebuilt the wall he could return it, together with a pound coin.

Ed placed both the coins beneath one of the ties in the wall-head at the sheepfold's entrance. The two coins, which Ed placed beside each other, would date the wall. The coins would no doubt interest whoever found them in years to come. Maybe the person who found the coins would stop in his intentions and be made to think. It might cause him to cherish the wall. He might protect it, even against those changes he had intended.

There are a number of tests you can make to a wall to see that it is a good wall. You can kick the wall, to ensure that the stones in it are firm, that the hearting is tight and does not rattle; or you can stand on the top of the wall and walk along it, to see that both sides of the wall are tied together and won't push apart. Ed kicked his wall. He took a running jump and he kicked it hard. Ed climbed on to the wall and he jumped up and down on it. He walked along its top.

It had taken Ed eight weeks to rebuild the sheepfold. But it is not how long it takes to build a thing, it is how long it lasts that matters.

A good wall lasts, maybe forever. If people like it, if they find the idea of it at all useful then they will maintain it and rebuild it if ever it falls down. That is what people mean when they say that such walls last forever.

Ed gave thousand year guarantees on all his walls.

Ed cleared up, flattening the mounds of earth left over from his excavation of the new footings, and he gathered up all the unused pieces of stone and made a pile of them. They might prove useful in some future time, Ed reckoned.

Ed stood back from the sheepfold and he looked at the sheepfold for a long time. First from this angle, then from that. He climbed to the top of the hill and he viewed it from there. He liked to walk around the wall and watch the wall curve. It was perfectly smooth, perfectly proportioned. He loved the way the wall appeared rough when you faced it, and smooth as glass when you viewed it side on. Ed spent quite some time alone with his finished wall, walking around and around it. Then he picked up his tools, his hammer, his frames, and his heaven and earth moving machinery, and he walked away. Just as someone had last done in 1727.

Ed fished most evenings, now that there was light enough to fish. One evening, Ed finally caught a fish, a 2lb brown trout, on a gold ribbed hares ear that he fished as an emerger. Though he was pleased to have finally caught a trout, and from so difficult a place, he was acutely disappointed at its small size.

They celebrated Ed's capture of the trout in the village pub. They made Ed stand on the table and drink a yard of ale. They sang rugby songs and sea shanties. They stood on the tables and they drank and sang until they fell off the tables.

There is a demon of parties and once it is conjured it is difficult to shake.

'Ole! Ole ole ole!' they sang. 'Ed caught a fish! Ed caught a fish! E aye adio, Ed finally caught a fish!'

It slowly dawned upon Ed that they were taking the piss.

Ed was digging a hole. Beside him were two fruit trees that he had bought. An apple and a pear.

'They were half price so I bought two,' he told Natasha.

'Sort of buy one get one tree.' Natasha laughed. 'Are you taking root, Ed?'

'It is nice here.'

'Yes, it is, isn't it?' said Natasha.

Sometimes, it wasn't what you were after that was important, it was what you found upon the way, finding it and knowing it when you'd found it and not walking past.

Natasha painted larger and more troubled and more violent pictures.

Ed advertised and he found more work. He built more walls. He fished. He could imagine no other life.

Take an empty jam jar and place inside it a small handful of soil. Fill the jam jar with water and replace the lid. Give the jar a vigorous shake then observe. As the murky water begins to clear you will notice that first the big things, the gravel, and then the smaller things, the sands and the clays, and then the finer things, the silts, will gradually settle to the bottom and in strict arrangement. It is always the same. No matter how hard or how many times you shake the jar the same pattern will result. Life is like that. Just as you begin to get used to things, just as a pattern or a routine becomes apparent, something will come along that will shake everything up.

People put their heart and soul in to a place. They put so much of themselves in to it that eventually it feels like it is theirs. Then money changes hands and the ownership shifts. Builders experience this phenomena all their lives. As do artists with their pictures. Ed experienced it with the walls that he built, and not just walls.

In the short time that they had lived there Ed had transformed the cottage. It had become home.

He had painted the outside of the house brilliant white, and he had repaired the roof, as well as fixing and repainting the rotten window frames, splicing in new wood.

Now, Ed began to transform the garden. It was no longer the wilderness it had once been. Ed had cut back the undergrowth and dug the ground over intending to plant a vegetable garden. He loved the feel of the soil. He liked to see dirt on his clothes, and on his skin, particularly his hands. It seemed a proof of something.

'You've transformed the place,' said Mrs Evans-Jones, thrilled at the numerous improvements. It was why she was putting up the rent. She wanted to double it.

'You won't find any cheaper, not for a place like this, not around here you won't.'

Ed could not believe it. 'We can't afford that,' he complained.

'I was paying less than that in London,' said Natasha. 'Well, we weren't going to stay here forever, anyway.'

22

The Street Poet

The rumble of traffic overhead, the footfalls of pedestrians passing by, someone hawking. . . . Clemence lay in his bash, in the dark, in the cold, clinging on to sleep, the slats of the two wooden pallets that protected him from the damp concrete floor of the underpass, digging in to him. But it was too cold to sleep and so he forced himself upright, his head pressing against the ceiling of his sagging bash, the ceiling bowed under its own weight, the weight of the carpet and tarpaulin stacked there pulling the walls in on themselves. Stacked newspapers, an upturned waste paper bin that was both seat and bedside table, a backpack, an untidy midden heap of clothes, his fiddle case, all were now visible in the grey light filtering through the threadbare, yellowed blanket that was his door.

Clemence reached in to the heap of clothes and he retrieved a sweatshirt, which he pulled on over his vest, then he struggled in to a hoodie, then a baggy jumper. Kicking off his sleeping bag and lying lengthways on his bed he pulled on a pair of jeans over his long johns, kicking over his combination seat and bedside table as he did so.

The sound of the traffic and the easing off of pedestrians that were hurrying through the underpass, told him that it was after nine o'clock.

His stomach growled. He reached in to the polythene bag hanging on the bent nail banged in to the frame of his bash and he took out some plastic wrapped cheese-slices followed by several slices of white bread. He unwrapped the cheese, folded the cheap white bread over the slices, jammed one in to his mouth, biting off a good half of it, and wrapped the rest in some newspaper, slipping the parcel in to the hip pocket of his donkey jacket which he then struggled in to, his elbows hitting the walls. Finishing off the other half of his sandwich, he put on his boots, grabbed his violin case and, pulling aside the blanket, he crawled out in to the Bullring in to the piss-smell and chaos that was cardboard city.

Boxes, tents, humps of tarpaulin and polythene . . . hundreds of these low, crude shelters lined the underpass leaving just a narrow avenue between them. A few of the occupants of those shelters - bearded, dirty, hooded, bundled up against the cold and bulked out by overcoats - were seated on chairs outside the entrances to their shelters, smoking, some drinking beer as they stared at the commuters on their way to work. Clemence joined them.

Time passes. It flies. You set out to do one thing only to find it easier to do another. Other opportunities present themselves, offering alternative escapes.

The lock-up was situated beneath some railway arches. There was a huge set of padlocked doors in the arch, the wood weatherbeaten with neglect, the hinges rusted solid, but in one of them there was a small door. Clemence pushed open the door within a door and, crouching, lifting his foot over the wooden threshold, he stepped inside. It was gloomy inside the lock-up, bare walled and cold. Trains racketed overhead. It had once been a workshop of some kind and was black and grimy and smelt of oil, old metal, damp brick. The machines, the stamps, drills, presses and lathes, had long gone, but their shapes, ghostly imprints, were still present on the walls. The band were sat waiting for Clemence on benches and old crates.

'You're late,' said Keith, from behind his drum kit. 'Nine o'clock, we said.'

'Yeah, where the fuck have you been?' said Will, pushing himself upright off a bench.

'I overslept.'

'You look like shit,' said Bernice. 'And what happened to your face?'

Clemence lifted a hand to his face. 'I got butted by a dog,' he said, touching the still tender flesh of his bruised cheek. 'I bent to stroke a dog and the dog leapt up at me.'

Nobody made any comment. The band had become used to Clemence and his explanations.

Getting to their feet the band picked up their instruments. Clemence shouldered his fiddle, he ran the bow across its strings, he tightened a string. They played *Leaping Leonardo*. But their hearts were not in it. They were out of time. They were like anyone going back to work on a Monday morning. They had little enthusiasm for it. One by one, they stopped playing. There was just

Clemence playing.

'What's up?' he asked, stopping, dropping his instrument to his side.

The band glanced at each other but said nothing.

'Come on, we won't get anywhere if we don't practice.' Clemence was itching to play. 'How do you expect to get any gigs if we don't get our numbers perfect?'

'It's not working out, is it?' said Bernice.

'What do you mean?' asked Clemence.

'Do you know how many bands there are out there?' Will asked. 'I mean good bands? Hundreds. Thousands.'

It was a depressing thought, and it could be off putting: if you weren't driven enough or talented enough or sufficiently desperate. After all, they were just a chance gathering of buskers that had come together to form a band simply because they enjoyed playing together. Then they had had their big idea, because maybe it was possible for them. Clemence made it seem so. He was their driving force.

Street Fighting Man, Leaping Leonardo, Chaos Chaos . . . Clemence had written them some truly original numbers. But the band had been trying to make it on to the North London pubs circuit for several months now. It was just too difficult sometimes. You needed more than the right sound. You needed drive, you needed conviction, and you needed the breaks. And you had to put in the hours. You had to practice until you were the best you could be, until either you were good enough to succeed, or until you realised that you would never get any better and that it was pointless trying.

'We're never going to get a gig, are we?' said Louis.

'Yes we are,' said Clemence. 'Look, I wrote us a new number last night.' He had been up most of the night writing it. It was why he had overslept. '*Our Nation*. Maybe this could be the one that will get us noticed. Do you want to hear it?'

'We got enough numbers as it is,' said Will.

'But it's got some real good hard-hitting lyrics. It goes: Our nation the separation nation. . . .'

'Lyrics,' said Will. 'Who cares about lyrics? All they want to hear out there is loud, something they can throw themselves around to.'

For Clemence, there had to be lyrics. Without them there was no point. Lyrics were everything. 'What would Hazel O'Connor be without lyrics?' he asked. 'Or David Bowie. The Sex Pistols? Ian Dury and the Blockheads?'

'An there's another thing, we haven't even got a name, have we?' said Louis.

'How are we going to get gigs without a name?'

Will laughed. 'We can't go on calling ourselves The Band, can we? What band? We could be any fucking band. "Hey, did you see the band last night?" "No? What band?" "Oh, you know, The Band."'

'So we'll think up a name,' said Clemence.

The reason that they called themselves The Band however was because they hadn't been able to think up a name.

'The Who, Led Zep, Black Sabbath, The Doors, The Beatles, The Grateful Dead, Joy Division, New Order, Sex Pistols, Ian Drury and the Blockheads, The Bizz. All the best names have gone,' said Keith.

'The Purple Saxifrage,' said Clemence.

'Never heard of them,' said Will.

'Purple,' said Louis, 'that's royal, innit?'

'Saxifrage?' Keith frowned, 'what's that, a fucken instrument?'

'It's a rare plant,' explained Clemence. 'It grows in wild places.'

'I like it,' said Bernice.

'Yeah, it sort of sums us up,' said Louis.

Will nodded, thoughtful.

What did it matter what they called themselves? If the music was good then any name would do. It would become the name, the band that everyone wanted to be.

Bernice picked up her microphone. 'Tonight,' boomed her voice, 'for the first time ever, I give you: The – Purple Saxifrage!'

'Right,' said Will, 'what shall we play.'

'What about *Leaping Leonardo?* said Louis. It was his favourite. 'And real loud this time, yeh?'

Clemence loved playing in the band. He loved the spirit of the band. Sometimes, when he played, he got the strangest feeling. Even when the music was not good it was still good to play music. There was something uplifting, even holy, in the process of making music and in the togetherness of a band.

Keith hammered on the drums, like he was making drums. Louis blew hard and shrill on the trumpet. Bernice shouted herself hoarse. Will boomed away on bass guitar, and then on lead guitar. Everyone danced as they played. Clemence, sawing away at his fiddle, span and bowed and jigged. They gave it everything.

The sound was not that much different to when the place had been a workshop.

'That was brilliant, fucking brilliant,' said Will, when they had finished. 'Only, Clem, you need to saw a little louder on that fiddle, mate. Didn't hear a single fucking note. Bernice, don't sing, howl, we're supposed to be a riot, remember.

Louis, loud is great, but not so harsh. Right, let's play *Street Fighting Man*. Is everyone ready? Okay. A one, a two.... And remember, we're not just jazz, we're all that jazz. We're urban punk jazz.'

'With strings attached,' said Clemence.

The band's first gig was in the Students Union of a small technical college. The college was old and run down. There were twenty seven people in the audience. The band started by playing *Street Fighting Man*, the audience not impressed, remained talking and drinking. It wasn't until the third number, *Leaping Leonardo*, with its long and repetitive introduction that steadily built up in volume, that anyone got up to dance. Then everyone was up. People were pogoing in to the air, leaping sideways. As the music intensified so did everyone's reaction to it. They began to throw themselves in to each other.

Someone threw a chair, then everyone was throwing chairs, first at each other, and then at the band. They put out the windows, and the lights, before they ran rioting in to the street. Windows were smashed. Car alarms sounded.

One person remained. Clemence thought that he recognised him from somewhere. He stood at the back of the room and he began to clap:

Clap clap clap.

Some of those claps were echoes.

Jigsaw offered the band a regular spot at his new club. He had opened a club, in an old warehouse in the East End and, intending it to become a show-house venue for all those untried bands on the music scene's raw and noisy edge, where British music could reinvent itself, he had called it The Door. Here, he would promote promising new talent, committing it to contract whilst it remained commercially naive. Most of the bands he employed were talentless, some though, like The Saxifrage, had a highly assured and individual sound that might one day fill stadiums. From here, in time, would emerge Terwang, The Van, and the award winning Betty Barry, as well as his most successful discovery, the money spinning rock band Kerching! Then there was brand-band. Jigsaw intended to create a whole new genre-independent commercial pop, sponsored by corporate UK. It would be a real money-spinner he reckoned. With their snappy repetitive lyrics and glamorous image devoted purely to product these predominantly girl brand bands would exploit the twin worlds of music and advertising in one cynical stroke.

As he did with all his bands, Jigsaw promised The Purple Saxifrage a recording contract with Midas Records.

At this point in time Midas Records had just established itself as a label, signing on the Irish punk band, The Right Fecking Eejits, with its problematic and troubled lead singer, Flonny Kerhediggan.

The band were only too keen to sign.

Jigsaw made everyone he handled sign complex and binding management agreements, like the one that he had with Andy. It would, he assured them, outline their separate responsibilities to each other and avoid any messy recrimination later on. Lawyers were worth their weight in gold. They tie people up in all sorts of obligations, and in a language that few can understand.

The Purple Saxifrage was, however, lacking that one essential ingredient that was to eventually make the band great, and it was Jigsaw's, and the band's, good fortune, that he knew exactly what that missing ingredient was.

Ra looked much thinner than how Jigsaw remembered her.

'Well?'

'Breakfast at Tiffany's,' said Jigsaw. 'To start with.'

Ra undressed to her stockings and g string then she climbed on to the table on all fours. Jigsaw slipped down her g string, stretched forwards and extended his tongue but he could not reach. His hard-on had caught under the table.

Ra turned, her face sullen and provocative. But then a trumpet started blowing: So-Ho! So-Ho! over and over, from the flat upstairs. Ra got down off the table and, maddened by these short bursts of music, she picked up a broom that she kept specifically for the purpose and began hammering on the ceiling with it.

A bad jazz player was the worse kind of musician, a bad jazz band the least sufferable noise imaginable, it was a kind of musical migraine. Jazz was the Picasso and Dali of the music world. But there was also Bix Beiderbeck, Duke Ellington, Louis Armstrong. And Barry Daker and Dave Bass.

'All that banging, that fucking bitch downstairs is getting on my tit, Dave.'

'Well it is a knocking shop, Barry.'

Dressed in army greatcoats and thick woollen balaclavas the two lank haired, bearded, skinny and sunken cheeked men sat on the bare floorboards, Dave cradling his trumpet, Barry staring in to the fireplace at the ash piled grate there. It was freezing in the room and, except for two single mattresses, the room was bereft of furniture. Couch, table, chairs, fitted cupboard doors, cupboard shelves, wooden bed frames, had all long ago been fed in to the fireplace, along with the skirting and the architraves. There was also a piece of moulding missing from the ceiling from one of the corners above the fireplace which, on the off chance that it was painted wood, Barry had torn down to throw on the fire.

Barry picked up a pair of socks, the heels gone in them, and, with purple, shaking hands, he resumed his darning. He could barely grip the needle, his fingers were that cold. Dave was sat writing a musical score, making corrections to it, occasionally blasting out on his trumpet what he had written. From downstairs came the thump and groan of wild love making. Barry, unable to complete the repairs to his socks, slipped them back on to his hands and, folding his arms, he stuffed his hands under his armpits.

Dave began humming to himself, trying to get back in to what he had written. He lifted the pen and he made time with it.

'This is ridiculous, Dave. This is getting desperate.'

'We can handle desperate, Baz. We've always been desperate.'

'I'm cold, I'm hungry. What if it'll always be like this?' It was beginning to freak him out. 'I'm going to get a job. Bar work. I've had enough. Don't look at me like that. Just part time, to tide us over. We'll have money, Dave. Heat, food, alcohol. Those things really are possible for us,' and he began to laugh.

If you wanted something then you either had to make it happen or you had to go to where it was happening. Baz and Dave had had no illusions about London when they had first arrived, from a depressed and gutted Leeds, hoping to break in to the music scene, and they had prepared themselves, psychologically, for a long and difficult haul. For one whole year they had scraped by on the dole and by busking, sustained by the occasionally gig in a pub - usually for free beer.

'You want us to work? Us? Are you crazy? We can't give up now, not after all we've been through. It will all have been for nothing. We will make it, Barry. We must.'

'When though? I can't take much more. The cold, the hunger. The fucking suspense. We haven't had anything lately. Not one thing. We'll never get discovered.'

'You want us to give up on ourselves?'

It wasn't that they did not want to work. If they worked it would be the end of them as musicians. All their life they had avoided proper work. The threat of work hung over Daker and Bass like the threat of unemployment hung over others. They could not work, not as others worked. Work would take up their time, it would sap their energy and determination. So long as they could avoid work there was always that chance that they would find success. Work stifled talent, it hindered purpose. Work promised you freedom, and then it trapped you in work.

'You can't get a job, Baz, you mustn't. It will happen for us. Someone will hear us. They just have to.'

'But what if they already have? Have you considered that?'

Dave said nothing. He had begun to fear the same thing of late, though he always fought the fear down, being far more terrified of the alternative.

In the long silence that followed they could hear the repetitive banging from downstairs that told them that someone was getting theirs.

Dave stared at Barry. Barry stared back, both of them shivering, cheeks sunken, eyes sad, pleading, watering from the cold.

'Well they haven't heard this,' said Dave. 'Listen to this. Play it. Come on. I've written you in a great solo here.' Dave pushed the piece of paper across the floor to Baz. 'Another month, Baz, we'll give it another month.'

Barry pulled the socks off his cold, purple hands, his fingers itching from chilblains, his toes too. He picked up his sax. The metal was cold.

'So-Ho!' they played, 'So-Ho-oooo!' They played to keep out the cold, to push away their thoughts of failure, and because it made them feel good to play. Music was hope. Music liberated them. They escaped on their music. It was sex and warmth and food to them. And music too. They put their whole heart and soul in to it.

The knocking shop sounds stopped, just as the music stopped, but then they started up again: 'Yes! Yes! Yes!' taunting Bass and Daker. It was more than they could bear, those cries of triumph.

Despite Jigsaw's promises The Purple Saxifrage did not cut a record. At first, Jigsaw told them it was because they were not yet ready, that they needed to refine their sound, which was still raw. He provided them with a pub gig almost every night and, once a week, they got to perform a few numbers at The Door. He kept stringing them along, assuring them that they had potential. They were going to be big, he told them, but they would have to work at it first. There would also, he decided, have to be certain changes.

They were at the lock-up, they had been practising their new number, *Our Nation*, when Jigsaw confronted them with the news.

'No,' said Will. The band were all agreed. 'You can't get rid of one of us, not like that you can't. Clemence, Bernice, Loui, Keith, me, we're the band. It's what the band's all about.'

The band was what held them together as friends. It was the name that they gave themselves.

But Jigsaw was adamant. 'I am doing this for the band, and believe me the band does not need a fiddler. What it needs is a sax.'

'But Clemence writes all our numbers,' protested Bernice.

'I can pay people to write numbers,' said Jigsaw. 'I can get songwriters any day of the week. That's not what the band needs right now.'

'And the band's name, it was his idea,' said Louis.

'He's kind of like our manager,' said Will. 'You can't sack our manager.'

'It's my band,' said Clemence, finally. The others nodded.

'I'm the band's manager now,' said Jigsaw. 'You signed a contract, remember. And you signed all your songs over to me. Look,' he reasoned, 'you want the band to be successful don't you?' They nodded. 'Then you need to change,' he told them. 'You don't want to hold the band back, do you?' he asked Clemence. 'You don't want to deny your friends their chance at success? You don't want them to fail because of you, do you? Do you? Is that what you want? Do you want to deny the band their success? Do you want the band to fail?'

The band turned and they looked at Clemence.

'Well, no,' said Clemence, 'of course not.'

'Well then,' said Jigsaw, and he gave Clemence that look of his: head angled, eyebrows lifting on his forehead, the faint trace of a smile on his face.

Clemence looked to the band for support. The band looked away.

Clemence put his fiddle in its case, and he closed his case. The sound of the clasps snapping together resounded about the lock-up. No one tried to stop him as he left. He climbed out through the tiny door within the bigger door, shutting the door quietly behind him.

Moments later, the door creaked open again. Two men, in their early thirties and dressed untidily, ducked in to the lock-up.

'Everybody,' said Jigsaw, 'I'd like you to meet Barry Daker and Dave Bass. Daker and Bass. The new members of the band.'

Louis looked at the trumpet in Dave Bass's hands and he knew then that his days were numbered. Will didn't look too happy either. Barry Daker played sax, but strapped to his back was a 1950's Telstar. It would be between Will and Barry now.

Clemence unrolled the length of threadbare, stinking carpet he had found in a skip and he tugged it over his bash. The more that he could heap on it, the more layers that he could put between himself and his surroundings the more secure that he felt, despite the extra weight that it put on the structure.

Heartsick, he climbed in to his bash, where he sat in the dark, drinking. Nothing ever went right for him. It was like he was cursed. Even his success as a published poet felt like a failure. Poetry? Pah! No one bought poetry anymore. His degree was a mistake too. He had never wanted to do mathematics or economics. What use were they to a writer and musician? And that was another cruel joke that he had conspired to play on himself. Writer and musician, he sneered. He was filled with regret for not having done things differently. But how could he have? He should go back to Wales, he decided. Or home, to Chestnut Avenue. Yes, but then what? He would only be running away. But from what? Nothing. He could see no possible future for himself.

He drained his last can of Tennants Super as he left the Bullring, the insistent flow of the rush hour crowd drawing him in to the crowded station, in to the homeward milling horde, where, turning, he had to fight against it to get out again, past the shining ranks of cabs, in to the brightly lit night.

His first reaction when it had all gone wrong had been to get a job. Working, he could have had it all by now. But it would have meant nothing to him. From that point on his whole life would be one continuous attempt at escape. Living for the weekends, the holidays, his eventual retirement. It had him waking up in a sweat at night, his heart pounding.

The night was cold. Lights glistened like hard gems off the river's dark surface. Car lights sped by. Illuminated trains crashed across the railway bridges. The city was beautiful at night, full of light. Full of life and living.

Drunk, he found himself on Waterloo Bridge. It was cold. There was a wind blowing. The cold brought him to his senses. He was holding a quart bottle of whisky and he was leant over the bridge's parapet, staring down at the river, at the volume of water that was flowing there. He felt the flow pull at him like a force of gravity, as the crowd had earlier drawn him with it in to the station; just as the collective momentum of the times pulled at him, pulling at everyone. The river, the whole world was on the move. But to what end? he wondered. And what was the point, when everything was impossible. His fingers tightened on the bottle, on the bottle's cap. Then he was throwing the cap away, flicking it over the parapet, watching it descend slowly on the air until the dark river snatched it away.

Clemence downed the whisky. He let the empty bottle fall. There was a splash. Then he pushed himself off the parapet.

Stood in the centre of the pavement, his fists clenched, staggering slightly, passers by gave him a wide berth.

For two whole days he lay immobile in his bash like he were stricken by some illness. He had no energy for anything, no interest in anything. He felt that he had run out of chances. All he wanted was to sleep. Clemence told himself that he was resting, that he was renewing his energies, when really he was hiding. He felt that there was no point to anything. He was all out of chances. And so he lay there, in the dark, in the stink, in the end-place that was cardboard city.

Clemence drank. He slept. He wandered the streets aimlessly, the crowds, the traffic, the brightly lit shops sustaining him somehow.

THIS IS ENGLAND.

The graffiti was scrawled on the walls of an underpass. Clemence later saw it scrawled on a derelict factory. He saw it on empty warehouses, on the boards surrounding a new development, on high rises, sink estates. . . . The tag was sprouting up everywhere.

Why not? he thought.

What better way was there to communicate seditious and subversive ideas than to incorporate them in to the very fabric of the city. People, passers by, in the very act of looking would then have those ideas planted in to their consciousness. He'd force people to read his stuff whether they wanted to or not. You don't decide to become a rebel. One day everything gets that little bit too much, you get that little bit too angry and you find that this is what you have become.

Clemence began to spray slogans and angry poems on to the city's walls: *THE ONLY FREEDOM BIG BUSINESS RESPECTS IS THE FREEDOM TO DO BIG BUSINESS. . . . EAT THE RICH. . . .*

He made stencils of his slogans and poems so that he could execute them quickly and neatly. He worked in the dead of night, always in secret, always alone. He dreaded being caught. There were hefty fines and long jail terms for those convicted of graffiti. Graffiti defaced things, it degraded them. No one liked to look on such things:

Those poor degraded things,
Curled up on pavements, begging.
They move you.
On.

The square seemed deserted. It was 9pm, and the offices had shed all but the most pressed of their workers. Clemence walked across the square, his footsteps slip-slapping back to him off the walls. Above him the glass and steel building soared twenty storeys up in to the night-time, yellow, urban sky but here at ground level the wall was concrete, a blank concrete wall, solid, impenetrable, unassailable. Almost.

Reaching the wall, Clemence set immediately to work. He chose the spot right beneath the array of golden metalled letters bolted to the wall announcing the corporation's name, only feet from the entrance. Crouching on one knee and flipping off his back-pack, unzipping it, then dropping it at his feet, he produced a spray can of paint, a pot of gum, a brush, and several sheets of folded paper. He unfolded a large sheet out on to the floor, gummed the paper, lifted and pressed the paper to the wall, then, flattening it out with his palms to remove any creases, and picking up then shaking the spray can, grimacing against the ball-bearing rattle of it, he began spraying a fine mist of gold paint over the stencil:

Insider traders,

He heard footsteps approaching across the square. Clemence's heart slammed at his chest. But it was just someone crossing the square on the opposite side, the footsteps hurrying down the steps there before trailing away. London continued to hum in the background. There was always that constant noise of traffic in the air.

Wheeling and dealing, playing the futures market, with ours.
Take a bath. It stinks.

Finished, Clemence peeled off the stencil and he folded it in on itself, balled it up and dropped it at his feet. He took a step back and he stood admiring his work.

The letters each twelve inches tall and right beneath the company sign.

'Impressive,' said a voice.

Clemence whirled around. A tall West Indian, his long hair fashioned in to dreads, the dreads poking out from beneath a dome of woollen hat, and wearing a combat jacket and scarf, his hands stuffed deep in to its pockets against the cold, was stood looking at the work. 'You should be a poet,' he told Clemence, grinning, the grin lighting his face. It was a pleasant face.

Relieved, Clemence blew out a long breath. 'Jesus,' he said, still coming down from his fright. His heart hammering at his chest, he bent and began to gather up his things.

'Hey, you know what?' said the onlooker.

'I should be a poet?' said Clemence, 'You already said.'

'No, you should get the hell out of here.' He drew Clemence's attention to the approaching security guards.

Clemence ran. He was the flying poet, the Triathlon Thomas of the streets, the capital's most wanted unwanted poet. He began to enjoy his new role. He played cat and mouse with security guards and the Metropolitan Police. He became hooked on the danger. Uncaught, he grew bolder:

You won't stop anything, I'm the one with the words.

He wrote it on the walls of police stations and magistrate's courts. In the coming weeks, his poems spread throughout the city.

They appeared on the walls of sink estates, particularly those where there had been rioting:

Our Nation, A stagnation.
The separation nation like a lamination
of alienation and indignation.
Consternation. Conflagration our destination.

At the entrances to cardboard city:

Mind the poverty gap.
Once you fall
In the city
You keep falling.

On the headquarters of developers, the windows of estate agents, the business premises of landlords:

Hey rack renter,
Spare a thought for those adrift on the middle passage.
Don't cram us in,
to your forges and factories,
Toiling to keep you from our door.

And on walls and pavements everywhere:

Whoa, city slicker, in your city slipper, hurrying with the crowd.
Slow down. Blinkered sight set tunnel vision-wise on the goal ahead.
Like a race horse, a big dipper, a white-water raft ride. Hanging on,
Tight.
You're thrilled by the ride. Ambition is the current,
and life turns out to be scenery.

Clemence wanted to pull the world out from under people's feet by telling them how it really was.

There is a feat that tricksters can perform. They stand beside an overburdened table laden with plates, dishes, tureens, cups, saucers, cutlery, candlesticks, bottles, glasses, and, with one deft movement, they remove the tablecloth – leaving everything the same.

23

Business as Usual

It was front page news in *The Standard*: *Phantom Poet Strikes Again*. There was a picture of the offending poem and a short article about the spreading scourge of graffiti in the city.

Andy read the article then he folded the paper in to a baton and began to tap his leg with it.

He remained standing in the window.

It was one o'clock on a winter's afternoon and all over the city the lights were blazing.

Andy turned from the window. He began pacing the lounge like some caged beast.

He was restless. He felt trapped, contained.

He was two days away from the start of his next tour. And he had a stack of new material to rehearse. There always had to be new material, especially now that the old had been televised.

At three o'clock Bane Burke was coming to interview him for *HELLO!* magazine.

Then there was his weekly column for *The Press* to write.

He hadn't written anything yet. And he had a deadline to meet.

This period after a tour was to have been a time to rest up and to recharge his creative energies. Writing, with all its uncertainty and hard work, had Andy missing its alternative, the end result, the excitement of being on tour with all the possibilities that offered him. And the freedoms.

It was hard to come down from that. But work was wearing him out too.

He felt sucked dry. The anger in him had ebbed draining him of creative force. The months of endless touring, coupled with the continual outpouring of ideas had emptied Andy.

He picked up the TV's remote unit from where he had left it on his sofa and he pointed it at the TV. The huge flat screen flashed loudly in to life: *THE COURTS AND THE POLICE ARE TO BE GIVEN ADDED POWERS TO CONTAIN PICKETING AND VIOLENT DEMONSTRATIONS. THE GOVERNMENT ALSO ANNOUNCED NEW MEASURES AGAINST TRESPASS.'*

The news: War. Inflation. Privatisation. Unemployment. . . . Here were the triumphs and the catastrophes, the great events that held everything else in suspension. The news rescued you from smallness. Here was the world's purpose, here were its possibilities, its hopes and greatest fears. 24 hour news. Breaking news. Anything otherwise incidental or occasional could become huge and overwhelming. International news, business news . . .

Jigsaw entered the room, working his phone. He sat down on his sofa.

'Andrew! Do you mind. I am on the phone here.'

Andy switched off the set.

Jigsaw tried the number again. But all he got was the answering machine. Art Soless, the American promoter's office wasn't taking calls. What time was it in Vegas anyhow? Jigsaw checked his watch.

Andy went and he stood in the window for a time. He left the window and he crossed to the mantelpiece where he stood looking at his awards.

He picked up the Golden Grin, a pair of golden grinning lips mounted on a golden stick. He held it to his face, covering his mouth with it. 'Ho ho ho!' he said. 'Tee hee hee!'

He placed the Grin back on the shelf. He picked up the Angry Young Comedian Award, a golden fist and forearm on a wrist-like plinth. Doing the Muhammad Ali shuffle, he began throwing punches with it. 'Boosh! Boosh boosh! Boosh!'

Jigsaw cast him a censuring glance. Andy returned the award.

He walked to the window, then to the door, then to the window again. His constant to-ing and fro-ing began to annoy Jigsaw.

'Andy! Go out and walk will you. It's wearing me out just looking at you.'

Andy stopped mid-pace. 'I would go out, only I can't can I?'

He would be mobbed by the press and by his fans. He would be hassled for autographs. Photographed. Chased. He was too well known.

His face was in all the papers and magazines. It was plastered on billboards across the city, like a wanted poster.

He continued to pace the lounge. He felt suffocated indoors. The apartment was triple glazed. The fire was blasting out heat. The underfloor heating was blasting out heat. He began tugging at the collar of his T-shirt. He needed fresh air, but more than anything he needed space.

'I have to get out,' he said, and, crossing to the French windows, he began pulling at the doors. But they wouldn't open. Andy kicked the doors.

Jigsaw pointed a remote and the doors opened.

Andy stepped out on to the balcony in to the cold and smell and noise of London. There was the loud roar of traffic, the clang of construction. He was soon banging on the doors to be let back in.

The doors shut behind Andy with a noise like something being sealed.

He went straight to the table and sat down. Snatching up a pencil he bent over his pad of A4 and began to write:

Automated doors. Automated lights. Automated barriers. Automated tills. Automated cash dispensers. Automated checkouts. Automated voices at checkouts informing of check out availability. Automated trains. Automated factories. Automated phone answering services. Automated speed signs that flash up to warn you off your speed. Automatic direct debit payments. Soon everything will be automated and you won't have to do a fucking thing. When no one has to do anything what will be the point of anyone?

He sat staring at the page. He sat staring at it for some time. He was soon pacing the apartment again.

'Andy! For God's sake! Look, go out and see some friends, why don't you.'

'Friends? What friends? We haven't got any friends, Jigsy, mate, in case you hadn't noticed. Not real friends, anyhow.'

There was a chasm between Andy and the world, Andy and people. He had moved between worlds and that, and fame, had set him apart. He could not return to the world that he had left, but the world he now inhabited didn't feel right to him either. He was from some other place, some previous time, another people. Who was there to hang out with on street corners or to have a kick-around with now? People change, they move on. Mostly though they drift apart.

And there was no longer any time for friends, not in the old way. Andy's friends were people he met on tour, at parties, in clubs, in the directors box at football matches, at first nights. . . . People sought out Andy not because he was Andy but because he was Andy Rant. Andy had friends, he knew lots of people, but friendship had changed. Everyone knew Andy and Andy knew no one.

'Only real friend I got is you, and you're a cunt.'

'Andy, we know lots of people. Enzo. PK. Sadie Sommers . . . Everybody who is anybody, anyway. Go up and see Enzo or something.'

Andy sighed. 'We know lots of people, sure. But they're not our kind a people though, are thee, eh?'

Jigsaw shrugged.

Andy resumed his pacing.

Then he was making for the minibar.

'Fancy a drink, Jigsy, mate?'

'At this hour? It's far too early.'

'Early? We've been out drinking at two in the morning before now. Just a small whisky, yeh?'

'No.'

'Vodka then?'

'No.'

'We could do a line together?'

'No! Haven't you got a column to write?'

Andy grabbed a glass from the cabinet, removed the top from the decanter and poured himself a large whisky.

'Hey! Easy on the scotch,' said Jigsaw.

'Why? There's loads.' Andy hefted the decanter.

'I don't want you drunk for the interview. And I don't want you smelling of drink.'

'Fuck the interview,' said Andy, and he knocked back the scotch. 'Fuck Bane Burke, fuck *HELLO!* magazine. Have you ever read the shite that she writes?'

'Of course I have. It's in *HELLO!* magazine.'

'It's obscene. Just rubbing it in, thee are. There's more important things we could be discussing. Unemployment. Class war. An she'll be going: "Who does your hair, Andy?" an, "Where do you buy your clothes?" Fuck that shite. A hate reading that an A don't want her writing me up like that an havin everyone hatin me. This interview, it's not a good idea, Jigsy, mate, Am telling yer, it's not. It won't do me image no good at all.'

'People won't hate you, Andy, they'll envy you, that's the whole point. They will want to be even more like you. They'll all want the T-shirt then. It will open a whole range of retail opportunities.'

It was Jigsaw's latest idea He was planning on introducing a whole new product line: Andy Rant T-shirts, Andy Rant jackets and jeans, Andy Rant boots. The whole Andy Rant look. Rough Stuff, he planned on calling it. The logo would be a rhinoceros.

'Jigsaw, we're supposed to be on the other side, not helping them promote all this. . . . ' he searched hard for the right word, 'shite!'

The phone rang, making Jigsaw jump. He lunged for the phone, thinking it might be Art Soless. It was Tamsin, the manager of Galleria, Jigsaw's latest business venture. She required a decision on a new artist.

Andy took his drink to the window. He stood looking out at all those other people in other apartments that were stood in their windows. He lifted his glass to them. No one returned the gesture. Andy knocked back his drink.

Jigsaw finished his phone call then he began sorting through his mail that lay piled on the coffee table. He picked out an official looking envelope and turned it over. It was from the Metropolitan Police. He tore it open, cursing.

Andy turned from the window. 'What's up?'

'I've only been caught for speeding.'

Andy laughed.

'I'll be banned.'

'So contest it.'

'You can't contest these things. If you do they find you guilty anyway and they increase the fine. It's a kind of punishment for calling them in to question.'

'So pay the fine.'

'And admit that I was speeding?'

'It's the law, Jigsy. You shouldn't break the law.'

'The law. The law is nine tenths of the problem. That's the problem, right there. There are too many laws, you can hardly move for them. Let me tell you about the law, Andrew.' Jigsaw began to fulminate against the erosion of his liberties.

Andy bent over his notepad and took down Jigsaw's tirade, word for word:

Every year there are more laws, bringing more constraints. But the more laws we have the more law breakers there are going to be. People feel hemmed in, their instincts and passions are being checked, and it's happening everywhere. People are hurried, they are stressed, and now there are all these laws that they have to contend with. I'll tell you, there must be something very wrong with a country when it requires so many laws. If a thing worked properly it would work without them. Something, the whole thing, must be wrong. There is too much law and too much order, and we do not have law and order, all we have are all these attempts at control. . . .

His article finished, and with Jigsaw now on the phone to his solicitor, he left the lounge, intending to go to the mini gym and work out his anger on the punchbag. Instead, he went to his bedroom and lay down.

*

Bane Burke came striding in through the front door, her long blonde hair flying behind her. She was all long legs, short skirt, and smiley enthusiasm.

'Wow! Will you just look at this place. And the views.' The massive windows filled the apartment with light, and with London. The whole city was there. Then she saw the artwork on the walls. 'You've got an Enzo!'

Accompanying Bane was *HELLO!* magazine's photographer, Gavin Maxwell, who immediately set to work taking pictures of Andy. Of Andy with his awards. Of Andy stood in the window gazing out at the city. Of Andy and Jigsaw together, Andy scowling, Jigsaw grinning. Of Jigsaw in front of the Enzo. Next, Bane wanted pictures of them in the various rooms of the apartment. Andy in the multi-gym, Andy working at the punch bag. Jigsaw in his study, seated behind his desk, and in front of the picture windows, laughing, holding a cigar, his arms apart as though he were embracing the city. Gavin used up his film and then left, despite Jigsaw's offer to ring out for more film.

'It really is amazing what you've achieved for yourself,' said Bane.

'Well, you work hard you get the rewards,' grinned Jigsaw.

How many times had Bane heard that on her visits. 'To the victor, the spoils,' she countered.

It was another of those things which they said that she knew they liked to hear about themselves and which put them immediately at ease with her.

Andy scowled.

He and Jigsaw were seated on Jigsaw's sofa. Bane was sat to one side of them, on Andy's sofa. She placed a tape recorder on the coffee table in front and she pressed play. She took a pencil and pad from her case and she placed it on her lap. She had a whole list of questions she wanted to ask Andy.

'Andy, you have inspired a whole generation of angry young men. They are taking to the streets, unshaven, wearing faded jeans and black T-shirts, the streets are full of Andy look-alikes. What our readers want to know is where do you shop? Which brands do you wear?'

Andy stared out of the window, he looked at the clock.

'Actually,' said Jigsaw, 'we're in the process of merchandising the look. We intend to bring out our very own product soon. AndyBrand, under the RoughStuff label. If you could,' he suggested, 'mention that. It has a rhinoceros logo.'

Bane began scribbling in her note book. She noted that Andy's T-shirt was Gap, that he was wearing Levi 500's, that he wore boots by Shoe of Pall Mall. She made a list of all their possessions. The clothes, the Enzo, the Porche, the BMW, the wine collection, the knives by Svisk, the Armani jacket that Jigsaw wore, its sleeves rolled up on his forearms . . . her articles were a compendium of such observations.

Andy continued to stare out the window. It was almost dark. The lights were coming on.

Bane asked about the apartment's square footage? She wanted to know who did the interior design? She asked which clubs they frequented? Which hair stylist did Andy use? Who was he dating?

Bane Burke wrote superficial articles on celebrity and the super-rich. She was a journalist to the stars and a minor celebrity herself. She wrote about the lives, the fast cars, the luxury homes, the extravagant furnishings, the expensive clothes and extensive wardrobes of the massively rich, the well-connected and the famous. Thinking that she was joining them in a celebration of their wealth they showed her everything, but what she was really attempting was to use that wealth against them by holding them up for derision. In her articles, she presented the over-wealthy, overfed and overindulged as precisely that: over-wealthy, overfed and overindulged. She revealed just how greedy they were, and how vapid. The very idea that a small class of people should expect to be feted, praised for their shallowness and greed, quite frankly, it astounded Bane. Here were some of the most big headed, sociopathic, up-tight people on the planet. Their very existence was an insult. But it was a reporting style that had backfired on her. It had turned the magazine, and others like it, in to a ridiculous parody of itself. The lifestyle of the rich and famous was now being celebrated wholesale, promoted everywhere as *the* lifestyle. The whole aspirational thing was a lie, Bane knew, it hid an ugly truth. But, like everyone and everything else, Bane had found herself harnessed to its promotion.

But here, in Andy, supposed street fighting man of the people, was someone she could undermine.

'Andy. You are currently the best known face in British comedy. Tell me, how does it feel to be feted wherever you go?'

Andy scowled at Bane.

'Fan-tastic,' said Jigsaw, chuckling at his wit. 'We love our work. It's not like work at all. Men with a mission us.'

'I'll say,' agreed Bane, 'you are constantly on tour, forever playing to packed houses. You must,' she said, 'be laughing all the way to the bank.'

'That won't be the title of your piece, will it? Jigsaw frowned, the smile dropping from his face. 'I couldn't possibly countenance that.'

'Of course not,' said Bane. She fixed Jigsaw with a smile. She drew a line across her notepad. It was a theatrical gesture.

Jigsaw returned the smile, the smile wavered and died in him. The interview didn't seem like such a good idea anymore. Andy was going to come over as some kind of playboy.

'We haven't discussed Andy's deprived background and his struggle for recognition,' noted Jigsaw.

'And what a fabulous success story yours is. You've escaped the fate of so many people of your generation. The dole queue, the sink estate, the dead end job. Maybe even prison. It's incredible what you have achieved for yourself, both of you, coming from your background. Which reminds me, do you have any pictures of you from before, in Liverpool? I did mention it in our phone call.'

'Certainly,' said Jigsaw. He went off to get the photographs he had prepared earlier. Returning with them he spread them out across the table.

There was one of both Andy and Jigsaw stood on waste-ground in front of a row of boarded up terraced houses. Another of them playing football on the same wasteland. One showed Andy and Jigsaw with Pogget. The three looked tough, mischievous, even a little malevolent. Though Andy looked very much the same, he even dressed the same, Jigsaw had changed.

'Can I take this one?' asked Bane, picking out the group photo.

'I'll send you a copy,' said Jigsaw. He retrieved the photos.

Bane smiled at Andy. 'Andy,' she said, 'on stage and in your weekly columns for *The Press* you come across as the champion of the disaffected and the unemployed and yet here you are living the life in one of the city's prime riverside developments? Isn't it the case that you are profiting from that discontent? Isn't that a little, well, hypocritical?'

'Bane, really!' Jigsaw protested.

Andy grinned, maliciously. 'Hypocrisy,' he said, 'is what saves us from ourselves.' And he laughed. 'Up the workers!' he said, and he made the militant fist, from which he flicked up his middle finger. 'The redemption is in the struggle, Bane.'

Jigsaw, smiling, placing his hands on his knees, made to stand. 'Well, he said, 'I think that's everything, Bane. Thank you.'

'Just one more question. Andy, I'm curious, about your act? There you are, you have everyone roaring with laughter, they are like putty in your hands, everything you say they laugh at, and you just leave the stage, you storm off, abandoning the performance? Why?'

Andy said nothing. He sat glowering at Bane.

'Andy?'

'No one understands,' he said.

'It's to build up the tension,' said Jigsaw, and, leaning forwards, he switched off Bane's tape recorder. 'Now, if you don't mind,' he said, standing.

'No one understands what?' pressed Bane. She shrugged, the palms of her hands uppermost, the question in the angle of her head, in her raised eyebrows.

'Nothing, no one understands nothing. Fuck all. They do not give a shite. They're all fucken sheep. Everyone. All a yis. The whole fucken lot.'

Andy wanted a revolution. Blood in the streets. Their blood. The owners and bosses blood. He wanted revenge. No more getting fucked around. It was time to fuck them round.

'You,' he stared hard at Bane, 'you think Am some kind of a fraud, don't yer, eh? A traitor to me class. Well Am not, a'right. Me an him,' he pointed to Jigsaw, 'we been through it, alright, aint we? Tried everythin ter get out we did. Only we couldn't get out, could we? There want no way out, there weren't no fucken jobs, were there? No good jobs anyhow. An what good would a poxy job have done us, eh? A mean, the fucken wages are shite, an there's no unions to organise around, not any with any clout, not any more. There aren't those kind of jobs. There aren't those kind of people. So how the fuck are yeh going to change things? Voting won't do it for yeh. There's no point. There's no one on your side to vote for. Can you imagine that, Bane, going through life with no one on your side? No, if yeh want ter change things then yeh have to threaten the bastards, yeah? Yeh have ter take ter the streets.'

Jigsaw disagreed. 'You have to fight money with money,' he said.

'You have ter hit them where it hurts,' said Andy, with an accusatory glance at Jigsaw: 'Yer have stop buying all this fucken shite they're selling us. Only it's not going to happen though, is it? A mean, there's a war goin on out there, between us and them, the bosses and the workers, the rich and the poor, everyone out for what they can get, an we're fucken losin it. We're being handed over to the owners and the bosses all over again. We're handing ourselves over.'

The struggle had been going on for years, the main players changing over time with the money and the power forever accumulating, making some lives worthless and elevating others, and all that some people knew or cared to know about it came from publications like *HELLO!* No wonder Andy was angry.

Certainly, people agreed with much of what he said, but they simply shrugged it off as part of the business of living. People had to live, they said. Besides, you couldn't stop progress. Everyone knew that. You could protest all that you liked about it and it wouldn't change a thing. But things were changing all the time. And this contempt for the rich that he had, how could anyone accept that, when he was rich himself. Besides, who didn't want to be rich? When money would solve all of their problems.

'An you,' he said, his gaze at Bane hardening, 'this fucken lie all youse promote with your fucken *HELLO!* magazine. We're being used, Bane, can't anyone see that? They tell you that if you work hard you'll have it all, eventually. Bullshit! That's just turning people in to slaves. All this shit they buy, it isn't wealth, it isn't culture, it's just a sign of their enslavement. We're being used, Bane. We're making millionaires. An those cunts, they've got it so that everyone is clamouring for more work. But people aren't happy, Bane. A mean, why do you think they want all this stuff all the time? Need? No. Dissatisfaction.'

'Sometimes,' said Bane, 'there's an emptiness growing in people that's just too big to fill.'

'Yeah, an sometimes, you can be so full of want that you forget what you do want. Fucken werk, they hold it up to yeh like it's some kind a holy fucken grail, when all's it is is some poxy job, like. An what would werk ever a done for us, eh? Nuthin, that's what. Fuck all. Except to push us in to ever tighter corners. A whole life spent, wasted, in a succession of dead end jobs. An us shit scared a fucken losing them? An the bosses and the owners takin everything, an everything disintegrating around us. Can you imagine that? the nothingness of it? Alcohol and drugs ruining our lives instead of enhancing them. Ha! Ha ha!' Andy barked out a laugh. He just could not help himself. He was his own worse enemy at times.

Bane's eyes softened. She had warmed to Andy, though she hadn't expected to. It had not occurred to her that he would be anything like his stage image. She had reckoned that that was an act. But Andy really did care, she realised. And all those stories that she had heard, the partying, the clubbing, the women – some of them prostitutes – the drink and drugs. They were true, she was certain. Money had affected Andy, of that there was no doubt, but not in the way that Bane had imagined. He wasn't anything like all those others she had interviewed.

Bane had a sudden urge to hug Andy, to tell him that she understood. That he wasn't alone anymore, that he had a good friend in her. That everything was going to be alright.

Still grinning, Bane asked him if he always knew that he would become a comedian.

Andy exploded. 'Christ! Doesn't anybody listen to a word I say? Look,' he said, 'if A cud a bin somethin other than what I am, A would a bin, okay? A mean, is like this, A tried, right. An I'll tell yer, is no fucken fun being famous, like. An all these fucken bastards,' he indicated Jigsaw, 'fucken sucken us ter death thee are, treat us like circus animals, thee do. I resent performing for fucken idiots who don't really know, who haven't gorra fucken clue wharrit is

Am tryin ter tell em like. All thee ever do is laugh. How would you feel, eh? Just look at it out there. Well go on, lookarit!' He jabbed his chin towards the windows.

24

Stranded

Today, the city roars and races with rage. The anger is everywhere. Cars hurtle at death speed down the city's rat runs. People fight for space on crowded streets. The frustration is everywhere. On the barren estates, with their gutted buildings and scorched walls. And in the graffiti scrawled livid across those walls, that says *FUCK*, the protest stifled, unaddressed. There is no protest, just unemployment and the alternative of total work, with all its stresses and discontent. Now the pressure is building. All this drive, all this spending, all this discontent. People are overworked, and still they are in debt. Property prices rocket and the rich get richer in their sleep. Oh you fuckers, you greedy, grasping, fucking twats, just look at what you've gone and done.

Every day, the city awoke to more city. There was building on all fronts, and in every direction. A whole new city was being flung up. Needles, spires, blocks, towers, domes. . . . The sky was overcast with new construction. The overcrowded sky bristled with building.

Ed and Natasha were back in London, sitting on Hampstead Heath. Beneath them stretched the city, a mix of the new and the familiar, the unknown and threatening. Natasha had a sketch book open. She had been drawing the scene.

'The place is different,' she told Ed. 'It feels different.'

The new building, the constant sound of construction, and of traffic, the continuous roar of it; the place appeared busier, faster, much louder than she remembered.

Ed agreed.

London had changed, and that change was accentuated because it had happened without them. They had become unused to the city, forgetting just how frantic things could be here. It had always been a busy, changing city, but its pace had increased. It was why they had retreated to the Heath.

'Everything's changing, Nat. The things we base our lives on, the rules we live by, the places we know, that we thought we knew.'

'But how do you paint that?' asked Natasha.

'Can you?' Ed shrugged.

'I'm going to try,' said Natasha.

They fell silent for a time. Natasha staring out over the city, Ed at the grass stem that he had plucked and was now twirling between his fingers and thumb.

'It's funny, isn't it?' said Natasha.

'What is?' asked Ed.

'Well everything. All this.'

Natasha was thinking of the millions upon millions of people that were at that moment surging through the city, making it work.

'All those people down there, all of them busily working away in offices, factories and shops, how many of them really want to be there, do you think? Not many, I'll bet. They would all prefer to be somewhere else, to be doing something else. You don't want to be here, Ed. I know that. You want to travel. Me, I want to be a great artist. And yet here we all are. So what keeps it all together do you think?'

'Money,' said Ed flatly, throwing away the grass stem.

Natasha was not convinced. 'No, it would be terrible if it was just money. There must be more to it than money. There wasn't always money. I mean, we're not here because of money.'

They fell silent for a time, thinking.

Ed laughed. 'Everyone wants to escape,' he said, 'that's what keeps all this together.'

Natasha smiled. 'We're all dreaming of something,' she said. 'We live out our dreams, we test them against the world, and, if they're convincing enough, then we achieve them.'

'We get away with them,' said Ed, 'because people believe them.'

'Because we believe in them,' said Natasha. She understood. 'We can be anything we want, just so long as we keep at it.'

The city moved, and moving it was changed.

Natasha returned to her sketching. She drew London as a barcode.

Ed plucked a fresh grass stem and he popped it in to his mouth and he chewed on the stem.

It was peaceful up here on the heath. But they could not stay here.

They began to grow edgy. Ed was the first to give in to it. He threw away the grass he had been chewing and climbed wearily to his feet.

'Come on,' he said, 'we'd best make a move.'

They got back in the car and drove to the East End where they intended to find a cheap place to rent.

They barely recognised the place. New apartment blocks, posh cafes and wine bars, cappuccino bars, restaurants, and an upmarket art gallery: *GALLERIA*, its huge neon sign visible from a long way off had taken over the high street. The whole district, once semi-derelict, and the haunt of impoverished artists, was in the throes of a transformation.

'The launderette's gone,' said Ed, 'it's a restaurant. The betting shop's gone.' It was now an estate agents. There were numerous estate agents on the high street. The off-licence, the greengrocers, the newsagent, the charity shops, they were all gone. They passed a new supermarket. 'Isn't that where the corner shop used to be?' asked Ed, pointing across the road to a trendy looking wine bar: *Mr Barrantoe's Neon Bar* written in snaky pink and orange neon above its plate glass windows.

Natasha took a right off the high street in to her old street.

'This isn't the street?' said Ed.

Expensive cars lined the street that was full of For Sale and To Rent signs. There were numerous yellow skips between the cars. Most of the houses were in the process of being renovated. Natasha pulled up outside the house where she had once rented a bedsit. For Sale, said the sign outside the smartly restored house.

They made enquiries at those houses with rooms for rent signs. There were places to rent, certainly, but the prices had sky rocketed.

'We can't afford that,' said Ed.

They were told they'd be lucky to find anywhere half decent for less in the area.

All that afternoon they drove around flat hunting, but they found nothing that they could afford.

'You've got friends in London, Nat, couldn't we stay with them?' said Ed.

Natasha frowned. 'Enzo and Sadie, you mean?'

They found a call box and Natasha rang them. No one was answering.

'I'll try them again, later. What about your friends, Ed?'

Ed didn't have any friends, at least no one that he'd kept in touch with. They were all alone in that city, though they did not know it until later.

'We can sleep in the car tonight,' said Ed. 'Try again tomorrow.'

The city moved. And moving, it was changed.

There was a loud bang, like they had driven over a rock. Immediately the car lost its power. Natasha steered the car to a halt, the tyres squeaking against the kerb.

'Try the ignition,' said Ed.

Natasha turned the key in the ignition but the car would not start.

'Maybe we've just run out of fuel,' said Natasha.

Ed pointed to the fuel gauge. It was quarter full. 'I think the timing chain's snapped,' he said.

'You can fix it, can't you, Ed? You've fixed this car before. You've virtually built this car.'

'Isambard Kingdom Brunel built this car, Nat. No, I can't fix it, not this time. That bang? It was the cam shaft busting. The pistons will be jammed in their cylinders. It's just scrap, Nat.'

One moment everything had been fluid, and the next. . . . It was a strange feeling to have the city close in on you like that. The city was a different place of a sudden. From now on everything would be a little more difficult. But it took time to readjust to this new reality.

Natasha pumped the accelerator, she tried the ignition again.

'What are we going to do, Ed?'

'Well we can't stay here, that's for sure.'

'You mean we're going to leave the car here? We're just going to abandon it?'

'Hell no, we can sell it for scrap. We should get at least a couple of hundred for it, maybe.'

Natasha brightened. 'Enough to get a place.'

A traffic warden appeared. She rapped the window with her knuckle. Ed wound down the window.

'You can't park here,' she told Ed.

'We're not. We've broken down.'

The warden was insistent. 'You can't park here,' she said.

They had to pay £20 to have the car towed away and another £20 to have it scrapped. They also had to pay £50 to put Natasha's pictures in to storage. A van came and picked them up. They took from the car only what they needed and could carry. All the other stuff they abandoned.

They shouldered their packs and began to walk. The packs were bulging with gear and were very heavy. Natasha carried her sketchpads in a leather satchel which she held tight against her chest.

They came to a phone box. Natasha tried Sadie again. No answer.

'We could stay in a hostel tonight,' she told Ed.

'You mean like for homeless people? With drunks and junkies and that? No fucking way. I'd rather sleep on the street. We'll get a place, Nat.'

They carried on walking. They stopped at a newsagents to check out the Rooms To Let notices.

'Ed? You know, before, what you said about sleeping on the street? Did you mean it?'

'We'll find somewhere,' said Ed. 'Don't worry.'

'I'm not worried, Ed.' They carried on walking.

Ed was hungry. He was tired. His feet hurt. His shoulders hurt where the weight of his heavy pack pulled down on them. He didn't think that this was something they should be doing.

'I don't mind sleeping on the street,' said Natasha. 'It mightn't be so bad. I mean, I'll get to find out what it's like, won't I? I'll be able to paint that then.'

'Don't be ridiculous,' said Ed. 'We are not living on the street. Okay?'

'I meant just for now, Ed, for tonight, just until we found a place. Oh, look.' Natasha pointed out a poem that was stencilled on a wall beneath a railway arch.

Mind the poverty gap.
When you . . .

She stopped to sketch it in to her book.

It began to grow dark. The street lights came on. The city blazed.

'First thing tomorrow,' said Ed. 'Early. I'm going out to Camden, to see O'Doom. I'll get my old job back. Then we can get a proper place. A flat.'

'Cool,' said Natasha, we're going to sleep rough tonight.'

She sang: 'Old mother Hubbard she went to the cupboard to fetch her poor doggie a bone, but when she got there, the cupboard wasn't bare, two squatters had set up a home.' She laughed. She sang: 'I am a mole and I live in a hole.'

She knew that Ed would sort something out. 'I'm with the expert, aren't I?' she said. Singing: 'There was an old woman who lived in a shoe. . . . '

'We could maybe even find a squat,' she said.

An hour later they arrived in the Strand. The shops had shut and the vagrants had taken over the doorways.

It was pointless walking any further, any further and they would be on their way out of the city.

Ed and Natasha hunkered down in the entrance to a shop.

It was like they were waiting for something, but without any of that expectancy that comes when you know what it is that you are waiting for.

Suddenly, everything was changed for them. People looked at them differently. They felt different.

They became different. It did not take them long to realise it.

'We're Stranded,' said Natasha, and she laughed.

'Jetsom,' said Ed, offering her his hand.

'Flotsam,' said Natasha. They shook hands.

The streets emptied. It grew darker. But it was never fully dark in the city. The city lights blazed.

They sat and they waited.

There was a loud and drunken shout that made Ed and Natasha jump. It was just another derelict, sheltering several doorways down, in the direction of Trafalgar Square.

People think that the streets of London are paved with gold. They're not. They're paved with homeless people.

You catch a glimpse of the world, a version so unlike your own that it holds your attention. It is as though there are two worlds. But what if you are attracted to this other world, what if you could swap worlds? Suppose, whilst you are looking, that the world shifts. Something changes and you get stuck in that world.

People change. They change to suit the world, and the world changes them. And the world changes. . . .

25

Mind the Gap

Ed and Natasha were on the Strand, stood outside a telephone kiosk, waiting for it to become vacant.

'I heard that Enzo sold a painting for one million pounds.'

'One million?' Ed whistled. 'It must have been some painting.'

'It was, it was two yards by three yards.' Natasha laughed. She obviously did not think much of the work. 'It consisted of two blocks of colour, light blue above dark blue. Sea and Sky he called it.'

'A million pounds for a piece of colour chart.' Ed shook his head.

'People pay for the concept. Apparently he churns them out. I heard that he has a whole studio of people making them for him. But I don't believe that. People are just envious.'

Ed was still shaking his head. 'What do the critics say?'

'The usual mumbo jumbo.' Natasha opened the copy of *Scene*, a free publication that previewed the latest goings on in the arts and entertainment world. She had found it in a bin at Charing Cross train station when she had gone to use the toilets there. She read out the relevant passage: "Enzo is a truly radical artist whose work pushes at the boundaries of painterly possibilities to create an alternative world of conceptual arty conceits."'

'What the hell does that mean?'

'It means,' said Natasha, 'that Enzo is a genius.'

'He certainly has a talent for separating people from their money.'

The two of them fell silent. They were thinking of all that money and what they would do with it.

*

The phone rang.

Sadie ignored it. She was painting. She was trying to paint.

The phone stopped ringing, allowing Sadie to return her attention to the canvas. The blank white canvas.

She was consumed with frustration. It should have been easy, she was an artist, dammit! So why couldn't she paint? She had not produced one single painting, not for several months, not since her last exhibition.

That exhibition of *Big Women Paintings* had been poorly attended and Sadie had sold only the one work, *Big Women Partying*. It seemed the public had tired of her paintings. The world had moved on. Now the critics were saying that she had lost it.

Sadie stood staring at the blank canvas, the frustration at not being able to do this once simple thing building up in her. Gripping her brush in both hands, she bent her brush. With a loud dry crack the brush snapped.

'I'VE BROKEN MY BRUSH. MY VERY BEST SABLE. I CAN'T FUCKING PAINT AND NOW I'VE BROKEN MY BRUSH!'

Sadie flung the brush away from her and, turning, she swept her arm across her work bench, knocking over pots filled with brushes, scattering the brushes and sweeping tubes of paint on to the floor.

The noise brought Enzo in from his studio next door. 'Sadie, what's up?' He was holding a palette with a dot of paint on it in one hand and a brush in the other.

'Nothing. Absolutely nothing!' said Sadie, throwing her arms toward the object of her frustration.

'Ah, right.' said Enzo, taking a deep and preparatory breath as he searched his mind for the right thing to say that would extricate him from this predicament. 'Best get back then,' he said, and he turned to leave. He had an exhibition coming up that he was working on.

'Going well, is it?' Sadie asked, glowering at him, before fixing him with a forced smile.

Enzo turned, grinning. 'You know me,' he said buoyantly, ducking out of the room just as Sadie's palette came whirling at him, frisby-like, hitting the slammed door. The loaded palette stuck to the door, slowly peeling itself off under its own weight and leaving what appeared to be a painting by Enzo on the white paintwork.

'Well anyone can do your work!' roared Sadie. Then she threw herself to the floor and began frantically searching amongst the jars she had knocked over earlier, tipping them upside down, scattering further the scattered brushes and tubes of paint, sorting through them, sweeping them away. She eventually found what she was looking for on the floor beneath the easel. Snatching up the bottle she unscrewed the top, rattled several pills in to her hand, threw her hand to her mouth and tossed back her head.

Natasha stepped back out of the phone box. 'No one's answering, Ed. Isn't there anyone you could try?'

O'Doom. The removals firm. But Ed couldn't remember the number and there was no directory in the phone box. 'Tell you what, I'll go out there, see if I can get my old job back. We can stay with O'Doom tonight.'

'Good idea. But we don't want to be lugging our bags across the city so I'll stay here and keep on trying Sadie. Knowing her, she probably isn't even up yet.'

Sadie returned to her canvas, but she was soon gazing toward the windows. Crammed full of buildings, it felt like the city was pressing in on her. The city was always pressing in. Sadie stared at the view, yet it was not that which absorbed her. An idea had begun to form which she was on the verge of giving shape to.

Sadie snatched up her brush and palette, loaded her palette with red paint and was about to touch the brush to the canvas, to make that first bold stroke, when the phone rang, making Sadie jump, causing her to slash a line across the canvas. The line, like a wound, began to dribble red paint.

Sadie flung down her brush, strode across the studio and snatched up the phone.

'What!'

'Hi, Sade, it's Na. . . .'

'I'm working. Fuck off!' Sadie slammed down the phone. She unplugged the phone and was hurrying back to her canvas when Enzo came in, breaking her train of thought.

'Hi, Sade, how's it going?'

"Going? It's gone!' she screamed. Grimacing, she began slapping her head with her palms. 'It's all right for you,' she told Enzo, who was backing away. 'You don't have to try, you can paint anything you can, anything you like! They'd even let you paint that!' she roared, pointing at her spoiled canvas.

Enzo stared at the canvas. Nodding, he turned down his mouth. 'Not bad, Sade,' he said, ducking as Sadie hurled a jar of brushes at him.

Natasha stepped out of the phone box and on to the cold street, her breath was like smoke in the air. She sat disconsolately on her pack, knees pressed together, elbows on her knees, hands clasped, waiting for Ed to return. The traffic roared by. She clutched a foam cup, it was half full of lukewarm tea, and she was clutching it for the warmth that it still held. She was cold and she shivered. People hurried by. One of them dropped a coin in to her cup.

Arriving at the removals depot in Camden Ed asked to see his old foreman, O'Doom.

'O'Doom?' said a driver, whom Ed did not recognise.

'You must know him,' said Ed. 'Big bloke. Irish. Tattoos.'

'Oh, him. He went months ago. Moved to Wales.'

'Wales?'

'To. . . .' The driver hesitated. 'Ah. Ab. A. . . .' He knew the name of the place alright but he had trouble pronouncing it.

'Aber?' said Ed.

'That's the place! Opened a pub there.'

Ed asked about work, but there wasn't any.

Passing a building site Ed decided to try there.

The foreman looked Ed up and down. Dirty jeans, scuffed boots, faded donkey jacket, weather beaten face, calloused hands. 'You look like you've seen plenty of work,' he told Ed.

'I have,' said Ed. 'From a distance.'

The foreman laughed. He understood. But he didn't have any work either.

'Come back tomorrow,' he said. 'Better still, come back next week.'

'Any luck with Sade, Nat?'

Natasha shook her head. 'No. You?'

'Nothing,' said Ed and he recounted his experiences. 'There's plenty of work but there's even more people looking for it. But something'll come up. Bound to. Always does.'

'Who else do we know in London, Ed?'

Andy woke, dazed and confused, in to another black hangover unable to remember anything of the night before. He checked the bed, but there was no one there? And he was in his own room?

He felt sick and claustrophobic. The underfloor heating was blasting out heat. Clutching his mouth, Andy jumped out of bed and ran to the toilet.

His head throbbed, he was dizzy and his gut churned. No more drink, he promised himself. It'd be just drugs from now on.

He took two paracetamol, drank them down with some water, then poured himself a second glass.

Andy showered. He decided he'd work off his hangover in the multi-gym.

Jigsaw was in the multi-gym, stood before the mirror, gazing at his reflection. A spare tyre of pale white flesh hung over his boxer shorts. He pulled in his stomach then he gave it a loud slap. A judder ran through his thick fleshy waist and on to his hips.

Each time that Jigsaw grew concerned about his weight a new piece of gym equipment would arrive at the apartment. So far, he had bought a treadmill, an exercise bike, a bench press and weights, an aerobics step, and now a rowing machine.

Jigsaw clambered in to the rowing machine.

He pulled on the oars, his awkward pulls pressing his knees in to his face as he slid back and forth on the seat. It was two full hours to dinner and Jigsaw had decided to spend the time working up an appetite.

The Romans had vomitariums, we have the treadmill, the exercise bike and the rowing machine.

Don't diet, do it! read the slogan on the apparatus. It was the latest keep fit mantra from the advert promoting the brand: *SpeedyFit clubs, SpeedyFit club wear* and *FatBoySlim apparatus.*

'One two three four, burn off those calories so you can eat more,' sang Jigsaw in time to his rowing. Pulling harder and more determinedly on the oars he farted loudly from exertion.

'I'm in perfect rude health,' he laughed.

Minutes later exhaustion, followed by chest pains, forced him to stop. He climbed out of the rowing machine, his face bright red, and he stood clasping his knees, gasping for breath, the sweat dripping off him, his heart hammering at his chest.

Andy entered the room.

'You should cut down on the exercise, it's killing yeh, Jigsy, mate. What you need to exercise is some self-restraint. Look at yeh, your like a fucken air bag gone off.'

Red faced, Jigsaw stood upright. He patted his bulging waistline. 'This is the new body shape, Andrew, get used to it. Anyhow, this isn't fat, it's potential. I'll soon work this in to muscle.'

Jigsaw wiped the sweat from his face with a towel then he went and he lay on the bench press. He just lay there.

Andy went and stood in front of the punch bag. Bare fisted he landed it a hard punch. He punched fast and hard: left, right, left, right, left. He ducked and punched, he danced and feinted and punched: left, right left. . . . He aimed a quick flurry of fists at the punchbag: Left left left, right right right. Left right. Left right. . .

The buzzer went, followed by loud knocking on the door.

'Get that will you, Andy,' said Jigsaw, trying and failing to get up off the bench press.

Enzo walked right past Andy in to the apartment, he crossed the lounge and he dropped down on to the sofa. He just dropped and then he sat there like there was no Enzo in him, just clothes draped across the furniture.

'What's up, mate? You look beat,' said Andy.

'It's Sadie, the bitch.'

Andy frowned. 'I thought you two had ceased hostilities?'

'No, we're back together again.'

Andy laughed. 'Ah, right. Danger UXB?'

'Unexploded? That bitch blows up all the time. Everything I do winds her up. I can't do anything right, not as far as she's concerned. You must have heard her, screaming and shouting, throwing things around the place. She smashed a window the other day, a fucking window, threw a fucking chair at it. She can't paint, see, she's having trouble painting, it just won't happen for her and so she takes it out on me.'

'What you need is a drink,' said Andy, pouring a triple whisky. "Those men's magazines,' said Andy, handing Enzo the drink, 'they've got it all wrong. They're full of advice on how to turn your woman on when what you really need to know is how to switch her off.'

Enzo grinned. He laughed out loud. 'I like coming down here, Andy, you cheer me up.' Enzo knocked back his drink.

'Another drink?' Andy asked.

Drink, that oil of song, harbinger of good times and comradeship. If someone offers you just one drink they go against the very essence, the symbol of drink itself.

Enzo smiled. 'Do ducks float?' He held out his glass for another.

'Is Enzo a great artist?' said Andy.

The fire went out of Enzo then. He looked deflated of a sudden. He slipped down in to the couch and he sat looking at his drink. He stared at his drink for some time.

'To be honest, Andy, it's not Sadie that's bothering me, it's everything.' He was an artist so by everything he meant art. 'You know, I sometimes think that I can't paint either.'

Enzo painted dots. He painted canvases of light blue and dark blue.

Anyone could paint an Enzo, Andy reckoned. Trying to understand them, listening to explanations of why they were good, that was hard. Andy had never understood why Enzo's work was so highly prized, other than the fact that it was by Enzo. Owning an Enzo was like owning a Picasso or a Pollock or a Van Gogh.

'Thing is, once you're a name people will buy anything you churn out, and pay ridiculous prices for it. So how can I know if I'm any good if people will buy anything that I do. I've no way of knowing anymore. I could paint shit and people would still buy it because it's an Enzo. Do you see my problem, Andy?'

'Problem? I wouldn't mind your problem, mate.'

'Can you believe that there is never one single criticism of anything I ever produce, not ever?'

'You want criticism?'

'I just need to know that my work is good. But how can I know that if people praise it simply because it is by Enzo?'

Enzo was frustrated by success. He wanted his art to be judged on its own merits.

'Do you understand what I'm telling you, Andy?'

'Your work's not shite, Enzo, mate. Okay, so the critics and the gallery owners talk a lot a shite about it, sure they do, yeah, but that doesn't mean that it is shite. A mean, it must be good, mustn't it? People wouldn't buy shite work, would thee, not for a million quid.'

'No?'

'Course not. No way, it'd be fucken stupid, wouldn't it?'

Enzo laughed. 'Andy, you don't understand. The thing is, I have been doing deliberately shite work for several years now.'

Whatever Enzo produced it was received with acclaim, because it was by Enzo. He slapped paint on to a canvas and the critics applauded the results for the textures and ideas which they claimed to find there. One time he even exhibited a blank canvas, with just his signature on it. There seemed little point in painting anymore. And the critics and the gallery owners reacted in the only way they knew, by acclaiming him for his genius: 'Enzo has done it again. He teaches us to see right through the sham that modern art has become. Just when everyone says how it is time to kill art Enzo kills it dead, and in so doing he brings it immediately back to life. What an instillation!'

Enzo then set out to single-mindedly destroy his reputation. Without his reputation, he reasoned, there could be only his art. He had been trying to destroy his reputation for some time now, several years in fact, such that it formed the greater body of his work.

'It just proves what a racket contemporary art is. And no one can see it,' he said. 'They daren't.' Enzo balled his fists in frustration. 'Making things, making them yourself, making them sacred to you like that, it's an incredible feeling. You know that. When you're on stage and the audience is responding to you, you know when it's going right, you know when it's good, the audience laugh. Well, that's been taken away from me. Because when everything that you do is met with applause, even when it is shite, especially when it is shite, then that calls everything in to question. I mean, maybe it is all shite. I don't know. I no longer know if I'm any good any more.'

'You're not, Enzo mate, your pictures are shite. Really. They're nothing like pictures. I've never liked them, not ever, not one. Even Jigsaw wonders about them. Everyone I know does.'

Enzo smiled. 'Thanks, Andy. You're a mate, you're a real friend, you know that.'

'Hey, anytime, everyone needs mates, yeah?'

Enzo knocked back his drink. Andy offered him another. 'No,' he said, getting to his feet, handing Andy the empty glass, 'I'd better be going. Switch her off somehow before she destroys the place.' He lifted his gaze to the ceiling.

It was very quite in the apartment after Enzo left. Quiet and empty. Andy took a chair and he set it down in front of the Enzo and, glass in hand, he sat staring at it. Sure, anyone could have done it, he realised. Only they hadn't. Enzo had.

Andy was sitting there contemplating the picture when Jigsaw exploded in to the room. He was breathless with excitement.

'Andy! That was Art Soless the American promoter on the phone.' Laughing, Jigsaw crouched and made fists. 'He's offered us a two week tour of the States. Big bucks, Andy. Big bucks.'

Jigsaw leapt up from his crouch and in to the air. He ran from the room to fetch cigars.

Andy drew in a deep breath, making him large, and blew it out again, so that he deflated.

Ed dug deep in his pockets. Natasha went through her pockets. Ed held up a 20p. He put it with Natasha's 10p.

They were sitting on the steps outside a shop.

'But how are you going to get his number? We don't even know where he lives,' said Ed.

Natasha put her weight on her left hand, lifted herself up off the step and pulled the magazine she had been sitting on out from under her. 'Hello!' she laughed, holding aloft a copy of *HELLO!* magazine. There was a picture of Andy on its cover.

'I'm not so sure,' said Ed. He was thinking of that time in Peckham when he had been working in removals and they had moved the keyboard player of the Bizz. Andy had looked right through him, like he didn't know him, like he was nobody.

Whilst Natasha went in search of Andy Ed remained guarding the bags. One of them always ended up having to look after the bags.

Andy barely recognised her. He was crossing the car park to his car when she accosted him.

There was how he remembered her, and then there was how she appeared now, and, for a second, they were like two different people.

Face pinched. Gaunt. She looked completely worn out.

'Ra?'

She was nothing like the vivacious and bubbly Ra that had attended his after show parties.

She scratched herself then sniffed. She stood hugging herself, shivering.

Imagine losing everything: your job, the flat - the bailiffs are there now, distressing your possessions. You sit up in bed, screaming, but it is just a bad dream, your subconscious working through your deepest fears. All you have to do is to wake up. But Ra lived that nightmare. An addict, she had lost her job and with it her flat. Now, escape was the dreamlike state she experienced on crack and amphetamines.

She was desperate for a fix.

'Is Jigsaw in?'

Jigsaw was always good for a couple of hundred.

'He's out,' said Andy. 'On business.' He opened his car door and got in, making to close the car door.

Ra grabbed and pulled against the door. She shouted.

Andy slammed shut the door and drove off.

Pogget travelled down from Liverpool on the train. He was hoping to cash in on Andy's success. He had their address from the article in *HELLO!* magazine. He arrived in Euston and took the underground to London Bridge.

Emerging from the concourse and onto the bridge Pogget was awed by London. Huge buildings peered over the tops of their much smaller neighbours, smaller buildings peered around the sides of those bigger than them, the buildings at the front appearing to hold them back. It was like they were all straining to see Pogget.

There was a busker on the bridge, dressed in an old fashioned tailcoat, playing a fiddle, singing: 'Made of wood like you'd find in a tree...'

He had poetry for sale, a stack of photocopied sheets held down by a stone, as well as a small stack of thin poetry books. There was an upended top hat at his feet with his day's takings in it. Some Japanese tourists had stopped to have their picture taken with him. Putting down his fiddle Clemence began to recite poetry to them.

He coughed to clear his throat.

'May-we-regret Thatcher,' he said.

'Grabbing, grasping, dull-slogging, amass. Slow shuffling, clot-cloying, mad mobbing populace.
Gut clutching mess of the mass of this maze. Reeking and retching of wretched wrecked ways.
In-vice. Invoice. Sacrifice all. Shouting, babbling, hoarse screaming brawl.'

The Japanese applauded then dropped coins in to the upturned hat. A small crowd began to gather, attracted by the applause.

Pogget pushed through the crowd, grabbed the hat, several books, even the sheaf of poems and ran off with them.

It was a warehouse conversion with a walled car park but no gate. There were signs on both gateposts, however: No Entry. Private Property. Jigsaw's car was in the car park. Natasha recognised it from the pictures in the article.

Natasha was stopped at the entrance to the development by a uniformed doorman. Navy blue serge jacket and trousers, silver buttons, white cap. He stopped Natasha and turned her away.

'We've had more than enough trouble from your kind lately' he told her.

Pogget dumped the poetry books in a bin. After tipping out the money he threw the top hat in the river. Then he went to the first cheap cafe that he found.

He ordered bacon, sausage, eggs, beans, fried bread, several buttered slices and a pint mug of tea. He hadn't eaten since leaving Liverpool the previous day and he was ravenous.

He ate the bacon rinds that he had cut off earlier and then the tomato skins and then he wiped his plate clean with the bread. Still hungry, he squirted out a quarter bottle of red sauce on to his plate and he mopped it up with the remainder of the bread.

Watching him, the proprietor made to protest but he checked himself. Pogget's shaven and scarred head, his broken nose and broken jaw, giving him a permanently malevolent grin, made him look like trouble. He sat and he drank his tea then he counted out his money. He had twenty one pound fifty left of the twenty seven pounds fifty he had stolen from Clemence's hat. And he had Clemence's poems:

The hate of the city, its shouts and its cries. The crowds push and surging.
A shuffling murmur of blank downcast eyes.
No love nor compassion. No selves but them-self.
No ties nor relations. No time and no help.

Pogget wiped his greasy hands on the page and then deposited it in the ashtray. He went to the toilet. . . .

Tight strangling traffic in snarled arteries wrangle. Massed crowds of the street, whose relentless mass movement will knot, block and entangle.
All peace of the country and calm of the park is banished by. . . .

He crumpled up the paper in order to soften it and then he used it to wipe his arse. There had been no toilet paper in the cubicle.

'Pogget?' said Andy. 'You saw Pogget? That twat is here in London?'

Jigsaw nodded. 'Yes.'

He had seen him coming toward him down a crowded street.

'He didn't recognise me. I hardly recognised him. He was the last person I expected to see.'

Or wanted to, he realised, having turned and gone in to the nearest shop. A vintner's as it happened.

'Stroke of luck, really. I found this.' He lifted up the bottle. A vintage chablis.

Andy laughed. 'You did right, Jigsy, mate. Don't worry about it.'

'Still, I should have said something. I should have given him something, some money. I could have given him a job.'

'A good working over is what I'd a fucken given him if I'd a seen him, the fiucken cunt. A fucken good kicking. He's nuthin but trouble, him. Always was, always will be. We're well shut a the cunt.'

Pogget was turned away from Andy and Jigsaw's place. The uniformed doorman threatened him with the police. Pogget tried to push past him, and was pushed back. Pogget pulled out his pen knife and he stabbed the doorman in the leg with it. Now he was on the run.

It was late by the time he reached central London. He was in Covent Garden on his way to Soho when he saw the Outdoor Shop. Ten minutes later, he came running out of the shop wearing brand new trainers, a black puffa jacket and carrying an expensive down sleeping bag. He ran on to the Strand, headed down the side of Charing Cross Station and disappeared in to the Underground.

It was freezing on the street, and as dark as it ever gets in the city.

Ed and Natasha wore sleeping bags over their shoulders. They were dressed in hoodies and heavy coats.

They were sheltering in a doorway. Natasha sat hugging herself. Ed stood, hands in his pockets, shuffling his feet in an attempt to keep warm.

A cold wind blew up the street. But at least it wasn't raining.

It started to rain.

Cars passed by on the wet street.

A car pulled up opposite. A black sports car, a Porsche, registration *Midas2*. Sweeping the car in to the kerb Jigsaw came to a halt outside the bank. 'I won't be a sec,' he told Andy. He jumped from the car and he ran over to the ATM. He inserted his card, tapped in his details and the amount that he wanted then waited impatiently for his card to be returned. He took it, and then his cash, all new twenties, pocketed the money then climbed back in to the car. 'I feel naked without money,' he told Andy.

Andy was looking across the street, staring at the homeless couple in the doorway.

'That looks like Ed,' he said. 'It is, it's Ed and Natasha.'

'Who?' said Jigsaw, as he put the car in to gear, and, with a quick look over his shoulder, he sped out in to the traffic.

You couldn't get a job without an address. You couldn't get an address without a job. Homelessness was often a simple case of economics.

'We can't get a flat without a deposit but how are we ever going to get that if we can't get jobs?' Natasha was close to tears. 'What are we going to do? What the fuck are we going to do?' She was scared.

'This living on the streets, it's impossible! I hate this! Hate it! I hate being dirty. I hate being cold. There's never any privacy. And the looks that people give us. I hate being stared at like a piece of shit. I'm cold all the time, and tired. I'm wet through. But do you know what the worst thing is? Everything is such an effort, every little thing. Keeping clean is an effort. It's impossible. Living like this is impossible. How can people live like this? We must have been crazy to do this. Are we crazy?'

'Thinking we were sane, that would be crazy.'

Here is what scared Natasha most. That they would not get anything unless they could pay for it.

'We've no money, Ed. I can't even afford chalks. How are we going to get money if you can't get a job and I can't do my caricatures or street art.'

Her chalks had been stolen, along with her brushes, collapsible easel and paints. It wasn't easy keeping possession of things on the streets.

'I'll get a job. Somehow. Or I'll steal you chalks.'

'No. Ed, don't, what if you get caught? I'll be on my own.'

Ed found some wood, an old chair leg, in a skip, and he took the wood and he went and he sat in a park beneath a tree and, taking out his pen knife, he used the saw blade to cut the leg down to six inch long pieces. He took up one of the pieces and he began to carve.

Ed was a craftsman. A tool took an initial force or movement and extended its possibility. The simpler the tool that the craftsman used then the more control that he had over it and the more of a craftsman that he was, the more there was of him in the finished product.

Within an hour Ed had carved a magic mushroom.

'Perfect,' he said, admiring the finished product. He placed it beside him on the ground in front of a small sign that he had made: *MAGIC MUSHROOMS £5.00*. He had enough wood for three more. Four mushrooms a day, that was twenty pound. Smiling to himself he began work on the second.

Two policemen came strolling across the park. Seeing Ed and his sign they came walking over.

'Not real magic mushrooms,' Ed assured them, 'just carvings. See. Wood.'

They asked to see his pen knife. Reluctantly, Ed handed it over. It was an ordinary pen knife but Ed lived on the streets, that much was obvious, and he would maybe use that knife for other things. The policemen confiscated the knife and when Ed protested they cautioned him.

Ed wandered the city. He just wandered around trying not to look homeless. He wanted work, he was still looking for it, but it was a half hearted search.

Ed and Natasha ate at soup kitchens. They looked for out of date food in the wheel-y-bins and skips found behind supermarkets and restaurants. They slept in doorways. They were moved from doorway to doorway.

Ed placed his hat on the ground. He sat on the floor, his back against the wall. He folded the square of card - the same one that he had written *MUSHROOMS £5.00* on - and he propped it in front of him. On it was now written: 'No money, no job, no place to stay.'

He sat and he waited.

Waiting is emptiness. It confines you within invisible boundaries, restraining you with whatever it is that you are waiting for. But if you are waiting for nothing, when there is nothing to wait for? Ed felt like he was just waiting. He sat waiting for time to pass, which was the worst kind of waiting.

Ed sold the mushroom that he had carved. For £2.00.

The more that you needed money, if people knew that, then the less that you got.

But he had also earned £15 and 32p from his begging.

He bought Natasha some chalks so that she could to do her street art.

There was a log fire burning in the pub. Ed and Natasha ordered a pint of beer each. They put on the jukebox. Hazel O'Connor, *Who Needs It*. They went and they sat by the fire together. Their damp clothes steamed in the heat releasing smells so that people moved away from them. Their food came: egg and gammon steak and peas with extra chips and a bowl of soup each and a plate of buttered white bread. They wiped their bowls and their plates clean with the bread until all there was on the plates was the yellow egg stains showing on the cracked glaze. They drank a second pint of beer. They sat facing the fire. They were content for a time. The cold, all the waiting and the trying was elsewhere, it could be forgotten, though they knew that it waited for them. For now, it was enough to be warm and well-fed. But it would never be enough. Not for Natasha, with her dreams. Ed too wanted more from life than its few comforts. The beer made Ed a little drunk. It made him confident. 'We'll get money, Nat, we'll find somewhere. Somewhere you can paint. You will have that exhibition.'

Our certainties are so insubstantial. They are like a thin crust that has formed over everything that is uncertain. But if you tread too hard on them then you are through, in to the deep and swirling hells beneath.

Ed and Natasha left the pub and retired to their doorway with a few cans.

Ed had found a huge cardboard box to shelter in and they had set it up in a disused service entrance down an alleyway off The Strand.

Natasha had decorated the doorway with pictures of furniture. There was a window looking out on to green countryside. It made the surroundings more tolerable.

She stencilled their handprints on the wall.

The police came by, saw the box, and the pictures on the wall. They questioned Ed and Natasaha. They made them turn out their pockets.

50p. 20p. Some chalks, the stubs left over from when she had decorated the doorway.

The police threatened to book the couple.

Natasha protested. 'But it's not graffiti, it's just chalked on. It rubs off. See.' And she rubbed the wall with her sleeve, smearing colour across the wall. 'We'll rub it off. All of it.'

The officers confiscated the chalks, then they cautioned the couple. They told Ed and Natasha that if they were seen hanging about the streets in future they would be arrested for vagrancy.

'We're not vagrants,' said Natasha.

'We're just waiting for things to get better,' said Ed.

Ed and Natasha sat on a bench in the rain sheltering beneath their box which Ed had flattened and folded in half and now held over their heads like a roof. Rain poured off the box and down Ed's sleeve, soaking him to the elbow.

'At least we've still got the box,' said Ed.

'We'd have been alright in that doorway if it wasn't for your box. Fucking box. It made it look like we'd settled for something. Now look at us. We're even more homeless than we were before. We've been kicked off the streets. How the hell can that happen?'

Natasha slid further in to her coat until it covered her face completely. There was just her forehead poking out. Inside her coat was warm and dry and private. There was nothing outside, everything was inside. Natasha became resentful of everything that was outside. She pushed her hands deeper in to her pockets, and her face deeper in to the warmth and darkness of her coat.

'Come on, Nat. We can't stay here. We'll catch our death if we stay here.'

'Where can we go? Nowhere. No one wants us. You heard what the policeman said. We're vagrants, Ed. We're against the law. There are things that other people can do that we can't now, and they're the same things. You can sit on a bench someplace and that's okay, but if they so much as think that you're going to stay there then they move you on. I can't take any more of this.

I can't. I've had enough, Ed, enough.'

'You can't give up, Nat. How can you give up?'

They sat in the park, in the open, on the bench, sheltering beneath the cardboard, shivering. The rain came at them in squalls. The wind grew fiercer.

'Okay, ' said Ed, 'have it your way, let's give up. I give up.' And, throwing aside the cardboard he had been trying to shelter beneath, he adopted the same pose as Natasha, thrusting his hands deep in to his pockets, hunching his shoulders, his head slipping down in to his coat.

'Satisfied?'

The rain came in, hard. The wind blew away the cardboard.

'See, nothing's any different, is it?' said Ed. 'We're still broke. We still haven't got a place to stay.'

He jumped to his feet. 'Well you might want to sit here and catch your death of cold but I don't.' And, grabbing Natasha by the hand, Ed yanked her upright. 'Come on.'

'But where to? Where are we going to go?'

'Wherever. Now come on!' and he walked off, pulling Natasha along with him.

Ed was like a tiny clockwork soldier. You wound him up, placed him on the ground and he set off marching. Even when he came to a brick wall he would continue marching.

26

Exit: No Exit

It was the night before Andy and Jigsaw were due to leave for a two week tour of the States and Jigsaw was in his study catching up on the paperwork and doing his accounts.

He was still seated at his desk several hours later.

A pool of yellow light reflected off his desk top illuminating his face. Jigsaw was tired. His eyes stung and his brain reeled at the sums.

Balled up paper and used AAA batteries lay scattered about the floor. He did the final sum one more time to be absolutely certain.

He stood up, knocking over his chair. He walked as though he were in a trance, bumping in to the doorframe, hitting it with his shoulder as he left the room.

Andy was sat on the sofa in the lounge reading *A Rock And A Hard Place* - Bane Burke's article on him in *HELLO!* The long years of unemployment, the crap jobs, the battles with authority. It was a flattering piece. There were pictures of Andy and Jigsaw, and a picture of the two of them with Pogget on some wasteland in Liverpool.

'Andy.'

Andy lowered the magazine.

Jigsaw was standing looking at him, his face pale.

Andy sat up on the sofa. 'Whasup Jigsy, mate? What's wrong?'

'I was just doing the accounts.'

'And?'

'We owe quarter of a million in tax.'

Andy's face dropped. He leapt off the sofa and made gestures of departure in each of the cardinal directions.

'What? What the fuck have yer done? We can't pay that! '

A smile broke out on Jigsaw's face. 'Oh yes we can. That is just the tax.' Jigsaw half crouched then he sprang up and he threw his calculator, his papers, everything, up in to the air. 'We have done it! We have fucking done it! We are fucking millionaires!'

Andy stared at him, incredulous.

All that hard work had finally paid off, the balance had tipped in their favour. Somewhere, in various banks and offshore accounts, were the numbers that said that they were millionaires. And that was just the cash. There were the investments still to take account of, the art work and property too.

Relief washed over Andy. He laughed and laughed. 'We've fucken done it!' he said.

'What did I tell you? Didn't I tell you, didn't I say I was going to make us rich. Didn't I, didn't I?' said Jigsaw.

Jigsaw pulled out his wallet and tore it open. He removed a thick wad of fifties and threw them up in to the air. There was a blizzard of descending banknotes. Then he grabbed Andy by the shoulders and he began to dance around the apartment with him.

'We're rich, we're fucking rich,' they sang. Jigsaw raced off to the kitchen for champagne, returning with two bottles. Bollinger.

He gave Andy one of the bottles. They shook the bottles vigourously. There were two loud POPS! The corks rocketed across the room. One of them breaking a light fitting the other a window. London appeared caught in the web of cracked glass.

They drank. They shouted. They sang. They laughed and danced. Every light in the property blazed.

Upturned furniture, newspapers, magazines and books lay scattered across the floor.

'We are fucken millionaires,' they shouted. 'Millionaires. Us. Can you believe that?'

Linking arms, they began dancing a Scottish reel, swapping arms and changing direction several times before they collapsed, laughing, on to the sofa where they sat drinking champagne.

Jigsaw lifted his glass. Andy raised his glass. 'Millionaires,' they said. Andy grinned. He couldn't stop grinning.

They had escaped the common fate. No more getting fucked around.

'You know,' said Andy, 'I read somewhere that there is enough money in this country to make everyone a millionaire.'

Jigsaw shook his head. 'Don't be ridiculous,' he said. 'It would make being a millionaire meaningless. There would have to be multimillionaires.'

'There are multimillionaires.'

'No. It could never happen. Not in the way that you mean.'

'Why not?' Andy's tone was belligerent.

'Well, think about it for a minute. If everyone could be a millionaire in the sense that you mean then no one would have to work. But if nobody had to work then nothing would get done. It just wouldn't work. People with money, who need something done, require people without money whom they can employ to get it done. Somebody has to work, otherwise those that don't have to work would then find that they did. Everyone would have to do everything for themselves. Can you imagine what things would be like if we had to do everything ourselves? I wouldn't have this fine cigar.' Jigsaw waved the cigar at Andy. 'You wouldn't be drinking that champagne.'

Andy, who was just about to take a sip of champagne, lowered his glass.

'Certainly not out of that glass you wouldn't. And we most definitely would not be sitting on this sofa. There wouldn't be a sofa. You'd be sitting on a rock. We'd be back living in the stone age. Money is power. It allows great things to be created. But not if it loses that power. And that power comes from inequality. And inequality, properly managed, is the engine of production. It is what gives us all these wonderful things. It is what creates wealth. It is what, by definition, makes us millionaires. You can only have so many millionaires. Or so few, to be precise.'

Jigsaw lit his cigar. He blew smoke at the ceiling. Andy took a drink of his champagne.

'Don't knock inequality, Andy, you wouldn't be a millionaire without it.'

Jigsaw had read all the great works on the subject, books by Keynes, Hayek, Friedman, Marx, Malthus, Schumaker, John Stuart Mill, Adam Smith, JK Galbraith, Skutt, Hames. . .

'And let me tell you something else, Andrew. Call me a cynic if you must, but the purpose of materialism is the consumption of the produce of human labour. The purpose of human labour is the production of material for consumption. The need to consume creates the need to work. The purpose of the promise of wealth is to ensure the desire to work. The purpose of want ensures the necessity to work. The need and desire to work creates wealth. Of course, not everyone can be wealthy, there is percentage rake off.'

Jigsaw knew exactly what too much money in the wrong hands would mean:

'Only the few can get rich, Andrew, it's not for everyone. If it was it would ruin everything. Imagine it, all that money around, everyone getting what they want and more besides. God forbid. Better everyone stays poor than that. The place would be hell. Well it's impossible, so forget it. Besides, all that money has to come from somewhere. Someone has to make it, otherwise there wouldn't be all that money. Money can only be accumulated by those who don't need money.'

'Fuck work, then,' said Andy.

'But if you don't work, Andrew, then you will never have anything.'

When it comes to getting every last bit of work out of a person there is no better encouragement. And there is so much to work for that you need never stop. No century has created so many willing and efficient workers as this age of plenty. People have to throw stuff away they get so much, and it's not only because it's fallen out of fashion.

'There is more money around though, isn't there?' said Andy. 'Millionaires are being made, every day. Look at us, we're millionaires. People are getting wealthier. They are better off.'

'Are they?' Jigsaw smiled. He took a pull on his cigar, exhaled a long column of smoke. 'I'll let you in on a little secret, Andy. The growth rates of incomes are far lower than productivity growth rates.'

'What the fuck does that mean?'

'It means,' said Jigsaw, 'that workers get no share in the benefits being generated by economic growth. In fact, their share is getting smaller. Workers exist to create wealth. If they want a share of that wealth then they will have to invest.'

'Good job we're millionaires then,' said Andy, and he laughed, relieved, glad that he was now free of all that.

He held out his glass to Jigsaw. Jigsaw filled it with champagne, then he filled his own glass. He lifted his glass. Andy lifted his glass. 'Millionaires,' they said, and they touched glasses. The glasses rang.

They knocked back their drinks, then they jumped up on to the table top and began to dance to show just how very happy they were.

They were millionaires. They could do anything, have anything that they wanted. Beautiful women, fast cars, big houses in the country, in any country, in the sun, a whole life spent in the sun. The ordinary happinesses cannot exist when there are all these new, extraordinary happinesses.

Several times that night Andy woke himself with his own laughter.

He was still in bed, smiling to himself, at three o'clock the next afternoon when Jigsaw exploded in to his room and flung open the curtains, filling the room with bright light.

Andy threw an arm across his face to shield his eyes. 'Jigsaw! Shut those curtains, will yeh.'

'Andy, get up! It is three o'clock in the afternoon. We have to be at the airport in four hours and you haven't even packed. The tour, remember.'

Andy pulled the covers up over his head. 'Fuck the tour,' he said. 'I don't have to work, me. Not anymore. I do not have to do a single fucking thing. I'm a fucking millionaire, remember.'

Jigsaw pulled back the bed covers and he tried to haul Andy out of bed. 'Get up and get dressed. Like it or not you are going on this tour.'

Andy fought Jigsaw off. 'What was it you said: When money works people can stop working? Well, from now on, I'm taking it easy me. I'm going to enjoy life.'

'And what kind of a life do you think that will that be? A million is nothing these days. After the yacht and the overseas apartment there will be nothing left.' Jigsaw pleaded with Andy, he tried to make him see sense.

'America, Andrew. Big Bucks. Just think, this time next year we could be multimillionaires.'

'I'm a millionaire, that's good enough for me.' Andy gave Jigsaw the vees. He placed his hands behind his head, closed his eyes and lay there smiling.

'Well you won't be, not for long,' said Jigsaw, 'not if you don't go on this tour, you won't.'

Andy's eyes flashed open. The smile dropped from his face. Pulling his hands out from behind his head he sat upright. 'What d'yer mean, I won't?'

'We have to go on this tour, Andy. We've no choice. I've signed the contracts. Do you want Soless to sue us for breach of contract? Because he will, he'll set his lawyers on us. You will have to go on tour just to pay him off. We might never pay him off. The legal fees alone will cost us millions. We won't be millionaires anymore.'

'I've got to carry on working?'

Jigsaw nodded.

Andy dragged his hands down his face, disfiguring his face. He felt sick and despondent.

'What have you done to me, Jigsy, mate, what the fuck have you done?'

'Come on, Andy, you'll love America. California, Andy. All that sun. Surfing. Las Vegas. The Hollywood Bowl. Carnegie Hall. New York. Look.' He pulled a baseball cap out of his back pocket. 'I bought you a hat.' It had, *I Love NY*, embroidered on it. He placed it on Andy's head.

Andy didn't look like he'd love New York.

27

The Rainmakers: Making it a Better World

And then it was the best of times.

It was the dawn of a new era, the twentieth century was about to take its giant leap forward in to the coming age. The energy and expectations of a whole eager nation were finally to be unleashed as the doctrine of cheap and easy money began to take hold. There was a powerful overriding sense that the country had at last broken free of its long decline, that if only we could keep this up then we would finally if not always pull through. At last, the dream seemed certain of becoming a reality. There was growth on all fronts. The economy was booming. A great future was up for grabs for anyone with the balls for it. We were making it a better world. . . .

It was first thing Monday morning and there was that familiar loud rumble in the air.

Bane, who was at home, haunched over her laptop, wrote:

Do you hear that loud roar out there? That is the sound of work, and of people hurrying to work. The world is teeming with furious activity. We swarm around and we make such a noise and a commotion. As for this better, braver world we are constructing? We have trampled the world and drowned it out.

She paused for a moment's reflection, but was soon back hammering at the keys:

Today, everything dies of poison and unleashed steel. This continuous search for possibility has unearthed every locked up death there ever was. And everything carries the contamination. The evil spreads dangerously. Unchecked growth has turned the familiar and the loved ugly and unrecognisable. Everything must be new. Only in the future can anything be complete. Everything is in the future. Change, constant change, growth, more growth, it is the new stability.

Bane found herself staring at the screen at what she had written there, hands balled in to fists, her face contorted.

It was driving Bane crazy. What the hell was going on out there? What, really, was going on on this planet? Was the global village being run by its idiots? Was the future out of control?

She poured all her venom and frustration in to the piece:

All this new development, this constant growth, it does more damage than any amount of good honest destruction could ever wreak.

Pylons, chimney stacks, cooling towers, tower blocks, shops, shopping centres, cars, car parks, roads. . . . The undeveloped countries, they're the beautiful countries. My country's a fucking shit hole!'

There are so many changes, they are relentless. It is just one new thing after another. And though improvement follows upon improvement there is never a resolution. The great evolving mass continues to unfold. One thing seems certain though. One by one, we are all of us losing touch with the fundamental realities. We are cutting ourselves adrift. In time, there will be only the city, city ways, and laws, and city opportunities. And city work.

All this hurrying about, all this frenzy for possession, all these people possessed, unattached, lonely, searching. . . .

Bane stopped writing. She went over what she had written, highlighted it then pressed delete. The words disappeared off the screen. The piece had been far too emotive. The facts, she told herself, stick to the facts. What she needed were facts, numbers, statistics.

Bane reached down a file.

The tiny room was stacked with files, heaps of newspaper cuttings, piled up newspapers.

Numerous notebooks and scraps of paper cluttered her desk. There were press cuttings and pictures pinned to the noticeboards on her walls.

She had more than enough facts. What she needed, what she was searching for was the story, that one essential thread that would draw them all together.

The elite create false aspirations to exploit the masses.

Where did that come from?
Andy Rant, his column in *The Press*. Bane reached for the article:

A country in thrall to the pursuit of wealth coupled with a governing, moneyed elite promoting relentless hard work as the panacea to all difficulties is creating a subjugated people for the purpose of being exploited by big business. We are being handed back to the owners and the bosses. We have handed ourselves over. The emergence of a new moneyed class with their capacity to outbid others in the competition for houses, space and possessions are pushing people to the fringes and redefining the meaning of success. . . .

A feeling of anxiety gripped Bane, a sense of urgency which she could not control. It threatened to immobilise and overwhelm her.

She took a valium, to fight down the fear. She was afraid most of the time now.

8 a.m. and the sudden thump of pile-drivers starting up for the day made Bane jump.

The construction was coming closer. New offices and luxury apartments were going up in the area. A better class of people were moving in and rents were sky rocketing. Bane's rent was being raised. She could no longer afford to live in her apartment. She was being forced to move out to a much smaller apartment in a far less fashionable area.

Bane had resigned from her job with *HELLO!* magazine. Her increasing contempt for the rich had made her position there untenable. She was now working freelance. What she wanted was to be a serious journalist and to win awards.

For some time now she had been pursuing hedge fund managers, venture capitalists, economists, corporate bosses, politicians, developers, media moguls. . . . following them around, asking uncomfortable questions and getting thrown out of offices. They said that Bane was crazy. Bane said that it was everyone else that was insane. What she was attempting was a wholesale expose of big business. She was looking for the story that would bring it all together and blow the lid on everything. She wanted everyone to know how the world really worked.

She claimed that the country was being run for the benefit of a small, moneyed elite with the result that whole sections of the population were becoming alienated, pushed toward the margins in to ever tighter corners on the fringes of society. As far as Bane was concerned, the pursuit of wealth was pushing mankind to the brink, filling the world with shite and enslaving everyone in its creation. It threatened to destroy everything.

But few of the papers would publish her work. Her opinions were far too radical. They found her pieces too defiantly out of step with the times:

The world is being stripped of its resources. Warming and acidification are killing the oceans. The planet is being impoverished. Whole ecosystems are being destroyed. Whole ways of life are being abandoned and not just abandoned but destroyed. We are destroying everything. Progress is taking people off the land, out of the countryside, the villages and towns, fields and workshops, and it is moving them in to cities. And progress and constantly shifting capital will abandon them there.

Eventually, everyone will live in a city and then everyone will be alienated. From the land, their origins, their sources of sustenance, their ancient human past. From each other. People have been drawn in to the city and now they are bound up there. Other ways and livelihoods, new existences are constantly having to be found for them.

We are being dispossessed, and no one seems to realise it. No one seems to care. Imagine, a world without hunters because there is nothing left to hunt, everything is farmed. No fishing, because the seas and rivers are poisoned. No access, because of ownership. No vast open spaces, because everywhere is built up. No time, because of work. It will be just money and work from then on.

It is a future in which everything will be done for money. People will set up in business not to make things but to make money. Restaurants will make food, not to provide food but to obtain money. Mechanisation will make money better than it makes things because it makes them cheaper. It makes labour cheap. People will operate presses, stamps, levers, buttons, keys. The artisan and the craftsman and the engineer will become operators of machines. When work is no longer interesting people will lose interest in work. Only money and the things it can buy will have any importance then. A complex interplay of want and fear and need will keep people in work. Ownership and work and money will become, by necessity, the new virtues.

Money gets things done and that is becoming a problem. Money has become its own reason. Once money becomes the principle then anything that isn't money gets ignored. Nothing becomes so necessary, so inevitable as money, except perhaps for work. Once you unleash money on a place it releases the potential in everything. Everything can be turned in to money, in to something else. It is like watching locusts at work. And all the while it is getting worse. Population is increasing. Emissions, pollution, traffic... everything is increasing. The trouble is that whilst such things are accelerating that is multiplying the forces that will ultimately have to be brought under control.

The golden years are still ahead of us, we are forever being told. But what if they are just a myth? What is really lying there in wait for us beyond this hopeful illusion of the dream we pursue? The tragedy is that what is being destroyed by this whole desperate lifestyle that we are so keen to create is the very thing we all seek. It seems certain now that few of us understand the essential material purpose of such an impossible myth. Everyone is caught up in it, we are all rushing headlong in to that future now.

What is needed is an economic collapse sufficient to force humanity in to remission long enough for things to recover.

Bane sat staring at the piece. Putting down the copy, she turned to her notebooks:

Advertising creates new needs, new wants, new desires. . . . Fashion. Accessory to the fact. Like a drug. . . . Diclofenac: given to working animals to reduce joint pain so as to make them work longer. . .

Her notebooks were full of such random, apparently unrelated facts but Bane was convinced that they were linked. A pattern was emerging and she was beginning to form a picture from them.

Bane spent most of the day working, only breaking off at lunchtime to grab a sandwich. Her eyes stung from staring in to the screen. The words burnt in to her retina. Her brain whirled with ideas. She could no longer think straight. And still she had not got a handle on the thing.

Bane was tired. It was now late in the evening. Outside, there was the most amazing sunset. Chemical reds, sulphurous yellows, petroleum blues. The incredibly stained sky glowed over the city.

Bane bowed her head, ran her fingers through her scalp, inflated her cheeks as she exhaled a lungful of air. It had been yet another all too long and frustrating and fruitless day.

She tried to recover the piece, but she was tired and confused. Dammit! she cursed.

Bane got up from her laptop. She crossed to the window and she stood there looking out in to the night at the bright city. But it was never really night-time in the city. The bright lights burnt fiercely, staining the sky above with their orange glow. The eerie orange glow was like a perpetually setting sun on almost every horizon. Soon, it could not be night anywhere. There was no longer any need for night. The world had gone too far, and no one had realised it yet. No one was rich enough yet nor still enough to appreciate that.

Bane turned from the window and returned to work. The city never stopped. Stop and you got left behind.

8am and the thump of the pile drivers starting up for the day shook the building.

Bane jerked her head upright off her folded arms, blinking at the light, the light hurting her eyes. She scrunched shut her eyes then she rubbed the tiredness from them. Dazed, she sat yawning, caressing her stiff neck, kneading it with her fingers, staring dumbly at the blank, black screen of her laptop.

She still had a story to concoct. She powered up the machine, moved the cursor to the menu and brought up a new file.

EXCLUSIVE, by Bane Burke: ANDY RANT AND SUPER MODEL PETRA VANE WEDDING BUST UP.

She moved the cursor and typed a single word in to the headline, breathing life back in to the story:

EXCLUSIVE, by Bane Burke: ANDY RANT AND SUPER MODEL PETRA VANE DENY WEDDING BUST UP.

Bane had not forgotten her gutter press, gossip column origins. The story had been flogged to death but Bane was doing what she did best, giving it the new angle.

There was an easy story here and she needed to keep it running. She had to make a living somehow.

She tapped away at the keys. The words raced on to the screen:

Since the bust up with millionaire comedian Andy Rant, super model Petra Vane has desperately been trying to make up their differences. She had earlier sold the rights to their planned June wedding in a £50,000 magazine deal with HELLO! . . . .

It was vintage stuff. Just the sort of the thing the editors at *The Press* loved. Bane printed the piece out, sealed it in an envelope and then addressed the envelope. She reached for the phone intending to ring the courier but then she changed her mind. She decided to deliver it herself. She needed that cheque. Bane glanced at her watch. No time for breakfast. She grabbed her notebook, her coat and phone and then hurried off to deliver her piece before her next assignment. She had arranged to meet a photographer at cardboard city at ten to do the groundwork for an article on homelessness. Bane climbed in to the lift. It was occupied by a young City trader on his way to work. Bane didn't recognise him. He was one of the many new tenants that were gradually taking over the building. Bane stared straight ahead at the closing doors, blanking him out. As the doors shut the man reached forward for the control panel. 'Going down?' he asked.

'All the way to the bottom,' said Bane. And she fixed the impeccably dressed yuppie with such a stare that he felt the need to take a cautionary step back from her.

28

Cardboard City

Worldwide, over 1 billion people live in shantytowns. In the future, the vast majority of homes won't be made of glass and steel, brick, breeze-block, or stone, they will be made from whatever: corrugated tin sheets, oil drums that have been cut open and beaten flat to form walling panels and to provide roof tiles, scraps of old wood, polythene sheeting, tarpaulins, cardboard. . . . People will live in caves and crypts and beneath underpasses.

In London it is possible for the curious of the city to visit the Bullring at Waterloo station and see amongst the various crude shelters that have been erected in the underpasses there, a far more brutal and desperate world than that which otherwise surrounds us. Here is what we would become if we rejected the city, or if the city rejected us. Here we are at our most ape-like and removed. This is what it would mean to be stripped of work and possessions and to be reduced to that most basic of functions, survival, but without many of the resources that would enable us to survive. Here we can catch a glimpse of what would happen to modern urbanised man - deskilled, dispossessed, dysfunctional, increasingly unemployed – if everything, the city and its functions, were to collapse.

29

Rock Bottom

It was a cold wet night of rain and howling winds. There was ice in the air, stinging shards of it. Ragged clouds flew across the sky. Winter was piling in out of the cold white east. And the city was burning, blazing. The fierce white electric of it lit up the night sky.

Ed was blown on to Waterloo bridge. He was followed by Natasha. They were cold and exhausted, tired from lack of sleep and worn out from walking. They had tramped for miles through the storm in search of shelter. Air roared down the wide open space, a constant cold blast of it. It held Ed in place. It pushed Natasha backwards. They were in an avenue of pure wind. It took their breath away. They could barely hear each other shout. Air filled out their clothes. Off went Natasha's cap. Out stretched their scarves, and their hair. Away in a blizzard of white went Natasha's sheet of polystyrene.

The air was full of debris: speeding papers, cardboard, leaves, a hat, reluctant birds, flying sky and stars, torn clouds. It were as though the city was racing through space, everything torn to shreds and the air turned to thundering wind. But there was a corridor of still air behind the bridge's parapet. Ed ducked down in to it, followed by Natasha. Loud air, litter, hail, flying ice, tore overhead. The wind pulled at the very stones. Ed and Natasha sat slumped against their packs on their flattened and folded over box on the cold wet ground and they looked up in to the fast sky.

'Fucking hell,' said Ed.

Natasha said nothing. She folded her arms across her chest and buried her hands in her armpits, hunched up her shoulders and slid her face down in to the up-turned collar of her coat.

They soon began to grow cold again.

'Come on,' said Ed, 'we have to keep moving.'

Neither of them stirred. They remained sheltering from the weather, from the fierce wind, the cold rain, the hard hail. Natasha could barely talk she was that cold. The cold was inside of her.

There was relief from the wind here. All she wanted was to sleep. She stopped shivering, her eyelids began to droop and she drifted off in to a warm and pleasant doze. Then Ed was shouting and shaking her to get up. The cold and the damp shot back in to her. Ed grabbed her by her coat with both hands and he shook her awake. He kept shaking her.

'We can't stay here,' he shouted. 'We'll freeze to death if we stay here. We have to keep moving, come on.' He pulled Natasha to her feet.

'Look!' Natasha pointed down the bridge.

There was an eerie glow to the sky to the left of the station. The light of it danced in their eyes. It flickered off the buildings. There was the smell of smoke on the air.

'Fire!'

'Come on!' said Ed.

The air was fast and cold, like racing water, it had all the force of water. Ed and Natasha could barely stand.

It was like a huge bomb blast. Red smoke was rolling up out of it. Sparks from numerous fires were tracering in to the night sky only to be torn away by the wind. It were as though a hole had been punched in to the city, a great black pit that formed the entrance to some underworld.

Sounds of exploding glass, the crack of splintering wood, savage laughter, insane shrieks and shouts rent the air.

'Fucking hell,' said Ed.

'It's like something from Heironymous Bosch,' said Natasha.

They stood peering over the wall in to the Bullring's concourse, the firelight illuminating their faces as they stared in amazement at the scene.

People were drinking, they were staggering about the place drunk, dancing and shouting, attacking stacks of wooden palettes, tearing them apart with their bare hands, kicking them, smashing them to pieces and then throwing them on to fires. Their grotesque shadows leapt and danced off the walls.

A boom box blasted out loud techno. There was a brief frenzy of fiddle playing.

Empty bottles smashed and popped against the walls in explosions of glass that were like fireworks.

Vicious fighting dogs, snarling and spitting foam, leapt in the air, flying around each other.

Someone dropped to the floor under a carelessly thrown bottle.

There was the loud wail of police sirens, but they were headed elsewhere.

An end of the world party had burst forth. It was giro day and the homeless were celebrating.

Natasha leapt back from the parapet as a hurled beer bottle crashed against the wall only a few feet below her. A loud, brief fire-fall of reflected light cascaded down the sheer cliff-like walls.

Natasha crept back to the parapet, she peered cautiously over it.

'It's like Picasso's *Guernica,*' she said, 'his *Charnel House*. It's. . . .'

'Fucking insane,' said Ed.

'Like Munch's *Scream.*' Natasha pointed. Someone was shouting up at the walls, at the flying sky, cursing God, the government, the encircling city and all its inhabitants.

Another bottle smashed against the wall, this one only inches beneath the couple.

Ed leapt back. Natasha was completely oblivious to it. 'It's the city gone mad,' she said.

She slipped off her pack, swung her satchel off her hip and undid the buckles. She got out a sketch book. She had forgotten just how cold she was and found she could barely grip the charcoal.

Ed shivered. 'Come on,' he said. 'We have to find somewhere to shelter.'

Natasha put her book back in to her satchel and, with numbed, clumsy fingers, she fastened the buckles. She swung her satchel off her hip on to her front and then she shouldered her pack. Then she began walking toward the ramp that led down in to the concourse.

'Not that way.' Ed tried to stop her. He grabbed her by the arm and he tried to pull her back up the ramp with him. 'Are you fucking insane? We are not going down there, not with that lot. We'll be torn to pieces down there.'

It began to rain.

Natasha ran down the ramp in to the Bullring. Ed chased after her.

A drunk made a lunge for Natasha, missed, and landed in a heap on the hard ground. Another, a woman, made a grab for the flattened, folded up box that Ed was carrying. Ed yanked the box free, pulling the woman over. She went sprawling across the floor. People were falling over, were struggling back to their feet in every direction.

Whirling and jigging, a fiddler came hurtling toward them from between the fires. He was followed by a conga-line of drunks. He saw Natasha and stopped dead.

When the music stopped some of the craziness stopped too. The conga line piled in to itself. Without music to keep the dancers upright it became a crowd of staggering drunks trying to maintain their balance. A few dropped to their arses on the floor, as only drunks and infants can.

The fiddler stared at Natasha.

'Natasha?' he said.

Natasha stared back. It took a moment for her to recognise him.

'Clemence?'

His hair was long. He had grown an untidy beard and moustache. He was much thinner than Natasha remembered. Natasha was thin too. Tired looking, worn out, shabbily dressed.

Clemence hadn't noticed Ed. He had been so intent on Natasha. Then he saw Natasha's backpack, and then Ed and his backpack and the cardboard box that he was carrying. Understanding crept slowly across his face.

Someone shouted for sounds. A bottle smashed. And then another. There was a loud shout of anger, but it was just someone running out of drink. The boom box resumed blasting out loud techno.

Another, heavier, squall of rain swept across the concourse that sent people running for shelter.

'Come on,' said Clemence and he led Ed and Natasha in to one of the underpasses.

There were over one hundred shelters in the underpass, mostly crude constructions made of pallets and old doors that had been propped against each other and angled in to tents, or leant against walls to make lean-tos. There were tents. There were caddis like accretions: benders – humped structures of heaped canvas, polythene, carpet and tarpaulin . . . whatever their builder could pile on to the frame.

There was a whole stinking shanty town spread out before them.

Ed and Natasha seated themselves down on their packs outside Clemence's bash, a misshapen dome of tarpaulin and carpet with a blanket for a door. Clemence, reaching inside, fetched out some cans of cold beer.

'Room temperature,' laughed Ed. He was just happy to be out of the weather, happy to have beer. He knocked back his beer.

The beer was too cold. Natasha shivered. She put her can on the ground. Natasha stared at Clemence. Clemence stared back. They sat opposite each other, staring, saying nothing.

It was awkward to be met with in such a place. It was humiliating. It spoke of failure, of unravelled plans, unsolvable problems, the un-lived life.

They were trying to get the measure of each other, both of them a little afraid of the other's darker side, that terrible shortcoming, or event, which each suspected had pushed the other over the edge and which, if it were ever mentioned, might unravel them further.

It made even friends wary of each other.

It was Natasha that broke the silence. 'What happened, Clem?'

'I'll tell you,' said Clemence, 'Nothing. Fuck all. So what happened to you? You used to paint. You were going to be an artist.'

Natasha narrowed her eyes. 'And you were going to be a poet.'

Clemence reached in to his hip pocket. He pulled out a slim book. It was dirty and creased, cupped - bent out of shape by his hip - and he threw it to Natasha. It opened in flight, landing in her lap, fanning her with its pages.

Natasha picked up the book. A book of poetry. Clemence's second. Natasha looked at its title: *Modern Twentieth Century Verse. Introspect II, by Clemence Tartt*. She looked sharply up. Clemence forced a cynical smile. 'I'm one of Britain's great starving poets,' he said. 'So what's your excuse?'

Natasha stared wide-eyed at Clemence. 'You did it? You actually did it, you're a published poet, Clem.' She laughed with joy for him.

Clemence shrugged. 'Yeah, well, you can't live on it,' he said.

'Everyone knows that, Clem,' said Natasha. 'You do it for other reasons.'

Natasha flipped through the poems. There were other, more recent poems, working copies, written in longhand on the book's flyleaves. She recognised them immediately. 'The graffiti on the walls, they're your poems.' She looked surprised.

Clemence nodded.

'But they're brilliant, Clem.'

Clemence was suddenly very angry. 'Well don't sound so fucking surprised. Christ, why does everyone sound so surprised when they discover that I can do these things?'

'But what are you doing living on the street? I mean, the cottage? You've still got the cottage, haven't you?'

Clemence nodded.

'So what are you doing here?'

'That's a good question. Do you know what? I've forgotten.'

A long time had passed since his arrival, time that had seen everything undone and the future uncertain again.

Ed reached out and wiggled his empty can between the pair. 'You haven't by any chance got another beer?' he asked.

Clemence, after reaching in to his bash, passed Ed another beer.

Natasha remained curious. 'But what are you doing here, in London, I mean?'

'It's the place to be when you're successful.' He offered a wry smile. 'The moment I heard that I was going to be published I thought, I've done it! I'm made. I came straight down here. I was attracted by all the book signings, the readings, invitations to appear on radio, the prizes, the awards.'

'You did all that?' said Natasha.

'No. I'm just saying. It's just what I thought would happen.'

And then there was the Saxifrage. Clemence told them all that had happened.

'They kicked me out. And it was my band.' Ed and Natasha exchanged glances.

'So what about you?' Clemence asked, before they could question him further. 'You haven't given up on your painting have you?'

'Me, give up? God no.' The very thought horrified Natasha. 'I'm here because I won't give up. Does that make sense?'

Clemence nodded. 'How could you expect to live here in this city and do your own work otherwise? You can't. It's just not possible. When I first arrived I thought I'd get a bedsit but I soon realised what a waste of money that would be. You'd need to get a full time job just to pay the rent. Only I didn't come here for a job. I came here to write, to do my work, not theirs. You're better off without a place if it means you can do your work.' Clemence's eyes narrowed. He tightened his lips. 'They're the failures, them. The people with jobs. Not us. Particularly not us, whatever anyone thinks. They're the ones that have given up on themselves.'

'I tried to get a job,' said Ed and he took a sip of beer.

'We needed a flat,' said Natasha. 'For a studio. Only we didn't have enough money.'

'We couldn't even afford a bedsit,' said Ed. 'We've been living in doorways up to now. But we got kicked out.'

'We even got kicked off the streets,' said Natasha. She shot Ed a glance.

'Well you can stay here,' said Clemence. 'No one gets turned away from here, you can't get any lower than this.' And he hammered his boot on the floor. 'This is rock bottom.'

'We don't intend staying,' said Natasha. 'Not for long.' She couldn't contain it any longer. 'I've been promised an exhibition.' She grinned. Out it all came. Every hope and enthusiasm.

'So, it really can happen for you,' said Clemence, and he forced a smile.

Natasha nodded. 'It can happen for you too, Clem.'

Clemence looked at Natasha. 'Aren't you forgetting something?' he asked.

'What?' Natasha shrugged.

'It already has.'

Natasha looked down at Clemence's book of published poems. She wanted to say something encouraging. She handed Clemence back his book of poems.

Clemence refused the book 'Keep it,' he told her. 'They gave me five copies at the publishers, to give to family and friends. I've got plenty.'

Clemence stood and, taking his fiddle, he returned to the concourse with it. He began to play.

Ed and Natasha sat listening to the music. 'You really went out with him?' said Ed.

Natasha shrugged.

Ed frowned. 'Do you believe him? About the Saxifrage, I mean?'

'Why not?' Natasha shrugged. 'He's a brilliant musician.'

'Yeah, but the Saxifrage though? I mean, they're number one.'

They sat and listened to the music for a time. Natasha drumming her fingers on her thigh, Ed tapping his feet.

Natasha yawned.

'Come on,' said Ed, finishing his beer. Standing, he unfolded the cardboard box. It was damp, all bent out of shape, so that when he tried to erect it it would not stand.

They lay out their sleeping bags on the length of cardboard. They struggled in to them, keeping their boots on, just in case. Their packs were hard beneath their heads.

They could hide from the city here. There was protection for them here. Of sorts. For all its squalor this place was a refuge. It would always be that, so long as Ed refused to give in, and Ed was determined, and Natasha refused to give up.

They lay in their sleeping bags on the cardboard on the floor and they listened to the partying.

The fires burnt low. They went out. The Bullring fell silent. The city rested.

Night mutes the city, which seems distant, though no matter where you are in it there is always that far off rumble in the air that tells you you are in a city. The streets empty. Lights blaze. They seem redundant in the cold grey dawn of the new day. The rumble turns in to a roar. Traffic tears by. Buses. Cars. Motorbikes.

Morning saw a brand new city again.

The roar of traffic and the feet of passers by hurrying to and from the station woke Ed from his sleep. Ed woke Natasha.

A loud yell, 'FUCK!' echoed down the underpass, making Natasha jump. It was just someone waking up to another day in cardboard city.

'Did you sleep well, Nat?'

Natasha yawned. 'Not at first, no.' She rubbed her eyes. 'Some of those noises, Ed.' Natasha shuddered as she recalled the shrieks and screams. 'I thought I'd never sleep. But you went to sleep right away. You must have been exhausted.'

'I even dreamt I was asleep.'

The couple struggled out. of their sleeping bags and climbed stiffly to their feet. Their bodies ached from sleeping on the cold, hard ground. Despite their time on the streets they still had not got used to that.

They stared about the underpass. At the shelters. At the concrete roof, that was stained black from fires. At the graffiti strewn walls.

The place stank of urine and woodsmoke.

A woman sat up amongst a pile of black rubbish bags and began to argue with herself. A man with a haunted look hurried past. A woman was seated outside her bash rocking to and fro. Someone stood pissing against a wall. It was a shock to wake up in such a place. It took time to come to terms with that.

Natasha swung her leather satchel on to her hips from off her front and off her hips on to her back. She wore that satchel everywhere. Even to bed. Then she folded up her sleeping bag and she put it in her pack. She sat down on her pack, pulled her satchel on to her hip, undid the buckles and took out a sketchbook. She began to sketch. She intended to get something more than shelter from her hopefully brief stay here, but sketching was also a kind of refuge for her.

Someone passed by carrying a tied up plastic bag. Several people passed carrying similar bags.

In the Bullring, if you were caught short and did not want to or could not pay to use the public toilets, or if you cared less for the walk, then you pissed against a wall, or in to a can or bottle. As for that other and often more urgent function some did that in their bash, on newspaper or straight in to a carrier bag, which they disposed of later, sometimes in a bin, sometimes carelessly. They were called flying toilets.

Like most of the men, and a few of the women, Ed went behind a pillar.

His hands were freezing cold and he rose in to the air on his toes.

Ed folded up his sleeping bag and he put it in his pack. He folded up the box. He put the box on the ground beside Natasha and he placed his pack on it. He sat down on his pack.

Ed and Natasha sat and waited for Clemence to get up. He was the only friend they had there.

There were others too, sitting, waiting. Like the crocodile waits. Waiting for the opportunity to satisfy an appetite, be it the next drink of alcohol, or cup of tea, or another pull on a cigarette, even if it was just on an old dog end. Anything can be a hope if you want it badly enough. They sat and they stared at the new arrivals, searching Ed and Natasha, checking them out for things of use, and for strengths and weaknesses.

Ed busied himself by building up a small fire, using the remains of the bonfires in the concourse. He and Natasha were sat warming their hands on it when Clemence emerged from his bash, red-eyed, in his slept in clothes.

He went straight to the fire. He crouched down on his haunches and he extended his hands to the flames.

'I was thinking of making a shelter,' said Ed.

'You can get palettes from the warehouses round the corner,' said Clemence. 'Most of the building sites will give you wood.'

A girl, short dress, high heels, hair pulled back in a pony tail emerged from a bash and came walking down the underpass. Slightly built, but big breasted, she was pulling at her skirt, shrugging her short wooly jacket in to place on her shoulders, tugging it down around her midriff, fumbling in her pockets, and then pulling out a box of cigarettes. The click of her high heels echoed along the underpass, drawing attention to her.

Clemence reddened and his heart missed a beat, as it always did whenever he saw Ra. She was one of the girls on the cards that he found in public phone boxes. He had amassed quite a collection. He always got that hot lovers flush whenever he saw her in the flesh.

He waited for her to pass. Then he gestured with his head to that part of cardboard city from which she had just emerged. 'That lot down there.' There was a gang, six of them, stood around, lolling against the wall, smoking. They were thin and weasel like with hard pinched faces. 'Keep well away from them,' he warned. 'They're just piss heads and junkies. Whenever the police raid here it's usually because of that lot. They'll steal anything that lot if they think they can trade it for a quick fix. They will rob you blind.'

Ed stared at the group. He thought that he recognised one of them.

Pogget stared back. He pulled hard on his roll up and he stared at Ed. Ed looked away.

Clemence said: 'Most people here though, they leave you alone. And believe me, you do want to be left alone. Just mind your own business, keep to yourself, and you'll be alright. It's how I survive.'

'Hey, we're just two more homeless people looking for a place to stay,' said Natasha.

But she had no intention of minding her own business. She returned to her sketching.

'Jesus!' Said Ed, and, pointing with his head, he asked 'Who the fuck is that?'

'That is Alexander Hero. Don't look. If he catches you looking at him he'll be over here wanting to know what the fuck you're looking at. And if he ever does ask you, whatever you do, don't say nothing.'

Hero was six foot tall and heavily built. He had long black hair, a black beard, wore denim and leathers and a pair of torn boots with shiny metal toe caps. He had emerged from the same bash as Ra and was now stood, arms hanging at his sides, onion in one hand, hunk of bread in the other. His knuckles seemed bruised. They were tattooed. *Love*, across the knuckles of one hand. *Hate*, across the other. 'Choose,' he would say. And when you did he hit you with it. He took a bite out of the bread. Chewed. Took a bite from the onion. Chewed. Chewing, he looked over in the direction of Clemence, Ed and Natasha. He stopped chewing. Clemence looked quickly away.

Hero threw away his bread. He threw away his onion.

'Shit!' said Clemence, 'Now we're for it.' He picked up his fiddle case and held it protectively to his chest.

A gang fell in behind Hero as he walked over. It was the group that Clemence had warned them about, that had been eyeing them up earlier.

People shrank away from Hero as he approached, they stopped what they were doing and they eyed him cautiously.

Right then Ed knew that he was in for the worst kind of trouble. It was clear what it would be about.

The gang surrounded Ed and Clemence and Natasha. They stood too close. They were filthy and they stank.

'Alexander,' said Clemence, subdued.

Natasha had closed and covered up her sketch pad. She sat on her sketch pad.

Ed stared up at Hero. He held his gaze.

'What you looking at?' said Hero.

'Just looking,' said Ed.

Alexander Hero walked behind Ed. He looked down on Natasha. His huge fists swung close: Love. Hate.

'More new arrivals, eh? Friends of his are yis?' he asked, indicating Clemence by prodding him in the shoulder. 'Here visiting him, are yis?'

'We're here looking for work,' said Ed.

'He's going to get a job on a building site,' said Natasha.

Hero frowned at Natasha's accent. He hated that accent.

'Full up at the Hilton, were they?' he said.

'No self catering,' said Ed.

Hero stood in front of Ed. He had huge hands. Demolition ball fists. Love. Hate. 'A job. On a building site? You? You'll be lucky. It's hard work, labouring.'

'Suit me then, won't it?'

'Reckon so, do yer?'

'Yeah.'

'Cocky cunt, aren't you? Think you're better'n us don't you, with your fucking job?'

'I haven't got a job.'

'No, you haven't.' Alexander Hero laughed.

He turned on Natasha. 'An what you doing here, uh? With your posh fucking accent.'

'Leave her out of this,' said Ed.

Hero whirled on Ed. 'An you!' He pointed. 'What you bringing a girl to a place like this for, uh?'

'I can look after myself,' said Natasha.

'Shut it, you! I wasn't talking to you!' He spoke right in to Natasha's face. His breath stank of onion.

'She's got me to look after her,' said Ed.

A cruel smile broke across Alexander Hero's face. He clenched his fists. Love, the left hand. Hate, the right.

Ed's mouth turned dry. His pulse raced. He stood. He clenched his fists. He readied himself to hit Hero. He knew that he had to get in the first punch, a good hard one, and that it had to be in the throat. He was trying to summon up the courage. Ed was determined to fight. Even if he was beaten he would fight, and he would keep on fighting. He had to. Because once people discovered that they could intimidate you then you would always be pushed around by them. He focused beyond Hero. Aimed two feet behind his head.

There was a shout. 'Wales!' It was Pogget. He pushed to the front of the gang. 'I know im!' He pointed to Ed. 'An her!'

Hero turned to Pogget. 'They're friends of yours?'

'Well A know 'em lyke. Yeah.' Something changed.

'You should have said.' Alexander Hero landed a glancing slap across the top of Pogget's head. He eyed Ed and Natasha, snorted down his nose at them, turned on his heel and left. The weasels nodded to Ed, and to Natasha, before following after Hero.

'You made yourself some nice friends there,' said Clemence. He grabbed up his violin case, fetched a battered top hat from his bash and left the bullring.

Until only a few weeks ago they had been four separate and unsuccessful buskers working the same square, their music clashing. Then Clemence had suggested that they play together. They now each of them earned twice as much as before and in just half the time. The Euston Square Quartet met most weekdays at 10am. in the square in front of Euston station.

'What shall we play, Clem?' asked Jane. She plucked at the strings of her cello: Thrum. Thrum thrum.

'What, right now? In this cold?' Tamara, on viola, was always complaining. She cupped her hands together and she blew on her fingers. 'Can't we grab a coffee first, I'm freezing.'

'Shostakovich,' said Clemence, ignoring Tamara's pleas. 'Okay?'

William nodded. He lifted his violin. Jane positioned her cello. Tamara sighed.

The four musicians arranged themselves in to a tight little group facing the entrance to the station.

'Now, when you play this piece,' said Clemence, 'you have to create silences. There has to be absolute stillness in those moments, understand?' The group didn't quite understand but they nodded anyway. They just wanted to play music. 'Okay then, after three. A one. . . .'

Clemence's hair flew. His hands were birds.

Pigeons flew up from the busy square. People hurried to and from the station. You could hear traffic noise, the sound of construction. Clemence's upturned top hat, sitting on the floor in front of them, remained empty. Clemence stopped playing.

'No no no,' he said.'

'What? What's up, Clem?' frowned Jane.

William shrugged.

'Hey! I was enjoying that,' complained Tamara.

'Look, let's try it again. Right from the beginning. Only this time stop when I stop. Okay? I want the music to stop. Suddenly. Pause for several beats. Then carry on again. Create anticipation. That should do it.'

They resumed their playing. Just as the music was building up to something, the music stopped, unexpectedly. There was only the city, and city noise. The sound of pigeons flying. People looked up. They turned to see what had happened. They saw a group of musicians they had not previously noticed until that moment. The quartet resumed playing. They played fast. The music quietened, then became calm. Some of those that had stopped remained to listen. A small group formed around the quartet. That crowd drew others.

A passer by, Art Fontainbleu, an employee of the Deutsche Gramophone Company, on his way across the square to catch his train, was struck by the talented playing of the group of young, untidily dressed musicians. He checked his watch. Then he took out his newspaper, placed it on a nearby low wall and sat down on it to listen. It were as though he were listening to the great man himself, he considered. He became so immersed in his enjoyment of the music that he missed his train. He had, he grinned, been otherwise transported.

A bash was a shelter that you made as best as you could from whatever materials that you could find. In a city that meant cardboard, wooden pallets, sheets of polythene, old newspaper, carpet, discarded doors. . . .

Ed found a swivel chair. He found a wind up alarm clock. It was only the minute hand that didn't work. He found a typewriter with a snapped ribbon. Battens. Screws. Planks.

A sofa, and sofa bed. Various chairs. Several large window frames.

He obtained a hammer and a saw. Numerous lengths of used 2x2. Wooden pallets.

He found several doors. The skips were full of them. Nobody wanted old doors anymore, they wanted new doors opening on to new things.

Ed, and people like him, they are like dung beetles. They pick up what everyone else considers to be rubbish and they put it to use. And the rubbish is gone.

Most bashes were no bigger than a large box, but what they did was to mark out and to make personal a particular space.

Clemence's bash was made from several large window frames nailed to a base of wooden pallets which which he had then covered with carpet, old canvas and polythene, for insulation and draught proofing.

Ed laid six wooden pallets out on the floor - two deep, three long - to form an oblong. He built a simple wooden frame out of 2x2 by nailing it to the wooden pallets, then he nailed the old doors to the frame to form the walls and roof. He cut up an old hoarding that he had found and he nailed it to the floor to fill in the gaps. Inside, for the walls, Ed secured sheets of hoarding to the frame, first stuffing the cavity with old newspapers, which he laid down in layers. He painted the walls white. Ed cut a square hole in one of the walls and he nailed some thin canvas over it, to let in the light, what little of it there was in the underpass.

'Well, what do you think?' he asked Natasha when he had finished.

Natasha studied the new construction. 'How do I get in?' she asked.

'The red door, Nat.'

The door squeaked open on un-oiled hinges.

'It's a bit dingy inside.'

'It's light enough once you get used to the dark. Anyhow, we can always burn candles. If we had proper windows, we'd lose our privacy.'

It was small and it felt claustrophobic.

'Clemence was right, it's no different than a bedsit,' said Natasha.

'This is much better,' said Ed. 'This is free.'

The shelter was big enough to stand in and long enough for the two of them to lie down. One half of the floor space was occupied by the narrow foam mattress that Ed had rescued from the sofa bed.

Ed went off to get some beer to celebrate the fact of their new residence.

On the walls, using poster paints, Natasha drew a bed-frame, tables, chairs, a full bookcase, pictures hanging on the walls and then a four paned window, showing a view of countryside under a rising sun. She finished the whole thing off with a door opening on to what seemed to be another much larger, far sunnier room that was similarly well-appointed.

It proved quite a surprise to Ed on his return to find himself crowded and uncomfortable amongst all this space.

Ed promised to make it more comfortable. But Natasha didn't want to be comfortable.

Ed surrounded his bash with furniture: a sofa and chairs, a bookcase complete with books. There was even a brazier for warmth that he had made from an old bin. Ed and Natasha and Clemence were seated on the sofa, warming themselves on the brazier.

Natasha was sat sketching. Clemence tuned his violin. Ed just sat.

Pogget turned up. He stood warming himself in front of the brazier. He held his hands over the brazier. 'Fucken cold, innit, eh?'

No one said anything. They were wary of Pogget.

Passers by were streaming past on their way to work.

'It's like people an anti-people, innit?' said Pogget. 'Us and them. We av ter be kept apart. Otherwise,' Pogget clapped his hands together. 'Boom!' he said.

Natasha looked up from her sketching and she stared at Pogget like she was seeing him for the first time. She abandoned her sketch. She turned a page on her sketch book and began a new sketch. She worked furiously.

Clemence tightened a violin string. He plucked it: Dink! He plucked another string: Thromb! He tightened the string.

It was morning, 10am, and Ed had just got up.

Reluctantly, he pulled on his boots. He put on his donkey jacket with its yellow square. The charity shops were full of them.

'You'll find a job, Ed, if you keep looking. I'm sure you will. You just need to keep looking.'

Ed grunted. Now that they had a place he no longer felt the need to work. Life promised to be easier from now on.

'It's money, I want, not a job. I don't need no job. Clemence gets money. He doesn't work.'

'He's a musician, Ed. What can you do?'

'Carve.'

'I'm talking real money. The kind that will get us out of here. That will get me somewhere where I can paint.'

That did it. Ed pulled open the door. 'I'm going out!' he said, slamming the door behind him. It bounced back off its frame.

'You are out, idiot!' shouted Natasha, 'Down and out!'

It was stupid and demented in every way but there were benefits to be had from living in the Bullring. There was a certain irony, not to mention a deep satisfaction, in being able to survive here. The seduction of money, the power of capitalism, these forces could be defeated. It was just the kind of thing that someone like Ed could make a convincing argument for, a powerful and continuous knowledge that he could use to drown out all doubt. Living in the Bullring, Ed reckoned, they could survive without work. It was just a question of the means.

Ed was seated on his sofa, warming himself before the brazier, studying the tin whistle that he had bought.

Clemence emerged from his bash to go busking, saw Ed on the sofa inspecting the tin whistle, came over and sat down next to him.

'I didn't know you played the tin whistle, Ed?'

Ed put the whistle to his lips and blew out a jangle of foul noise that caused Clemence to grimace.

'Peeeep! Fweeeeeeee! Teet!'

Sound like that got inside of you, it clattered around.

'Stop it, Ed! Fucksakes?'

'What?'

'Give it here.' Clemence snatched the instrument from Ed.

He pulled out a length of sleeve and he wiped the mouthpiece then he put the instrument to his lips.

He played jigs, reels, waltzes. He played slow melodious airs. He played hauntingly, stirringly. He played *Fool's Jig, Sheebeg Sheemore, The Rising of the Moon, Kevin Barry, My Lodging's on the Cold Ground.* . . .

Listening to the music Ed's spirits soared. He was transported. How, he wondered, was it possible to create such sound from so simple an instrument? Then his spirits plummeted. The playing had nothing whatsoever to do with the instrument. It was all down to the musician. The instrument's simplicity, its one great attraction for Ed, was at once undermined. How would he ever master this? A chasm opened up between what he felt he was capable of and what he knew the instrument could be made to do.

Clemence returned the instrument to Ed.

'Keep it,' said Ed.

Clemence insisted on teaching Ed, despite his protests.

Slowly, patiently, he went up and down the scale of notes several times, trying to get Ed to remember them.

Ed took reluctant possession of the instrument. He was become afraid of it. Either it would elevate him, as it had Clemence, or it would broadcast his inadequacy and destroy his confidence entirely.

Already the instrument was presenting Ed with problems.

Clemence re-positioned Ed's fingers. 'There, like that, in your left hand, with your index, middle and ring fingers over the top three holes. No, what did I just tell you? Like this. Here.' Clemence took Ed's fingers and he repositioned them, reshaping them until they were exactly right. 'That's it, nice and relaxed.' To Ed though they felt unnaturally cramped in that position.

'Now,' Clemence told him, 'whisper out a steady stream of breath. Don't blow, just whisper.'

Ed's face was tense and dark with concentration. He put the whistle to his lips, hesitated, eyed Clemence for reassurance. Clemence nodded a go on. Ed looked down the length of the whistle, took a deep breath, then blew. There was a loud ear splitting squeal and the pitch wavered: 'Pwee - ee - eeep!'

Clemence repossessed the instrument. Ed gave it up gladly. He felt depressed.

Clemence spent the next twenty minutes or so explaining the instrument and the rudiments of music to Ed. He showed Ed all the finger placings for all the notes across the whole scale, when Ed had hoped to be playing jigs and reels already.

'Okay,' said Clemence, 'Now you try.' He handed Ed the instrument.

Ed took a deep and calming breath. What would he play? Would it be the stirring Irish rebel piece, *Rising of the Moon*, or the jig, *Blarney Pilgrim*?

'E,' said Clemence.

Pweep! Ed blew an A.

Already he was forgetting things.

Clemence reorganised Ed's stiff and reluctant fingers over the holes. 'Now try.'

Ed took a breath, hesitated, then whispered: 'E!'

Ed beamed, he was immensely pleased with himself. Ed blew another E, then another.

E!

A passer by flipped Ed a pound coin.

Ed held it up, triumphant, then he sat grinning at it.

Busking, you couldn't live any other way and have the same power.

The whole thing was mad. Natasha was wired up to some strong, uncontrollable force that she could not quite understand. But she had real ability, and that made the thing believable, sucking her in. Clemence had it too. Even Ed reckoned he was going to succeed at something someday. Everyone had their hopes and dreams and ways of coping. Or maybe they feared what might happen to them once they stopped chasing the thing.

It was late, maybe two, three in the morning. Natasha woke suddenly. People were singing. It was just another crowd of drunks arriving back at the Bullring. There were angry shouts for them to pipe down. The singing stopped and the fighting started.

There was shouting, the odd curse, the sound of a bottle smashing. Then silence. Or what passed for silence in the city.

The loud traffic rumbled overhead. Natasha lay listening to it, her heart pounding.

It was like she was cut off from the city, with everything, all life, thundering overhead.

It was not the shouting that had woken her. Natasha was scared, afraid that she would be trapped, here, in this place, in cardboard city, and become forgotten, and everything about her forgotten. It was like her life had stopped, that the world was passing her by.

You needed to keep up the hope. Hope sustained you, it was all that kept you going at times. You needed to believe in something, and it did not need to be real nor obtainable so long as it sustained you. Nothing else mattered.

Because without hope there was nothing, only what surrounded you. You had to be out there, working toward some goal. And all the time the world was racing away ahead of you.

The rumble turned in to a roar. Traffic tore by. Buses. Cars. Motorbikes. There was the hurried footsteps of people streaming past on their way to work.

Natasha woke with a start.

Ed woke. Though he tried not to.

Another day to face. Another day to begin to make things right. The days sapping their energies, dulling their enthusiasms.

Ed and Natasha remained lying in their sleeping bags in their bash, listening to the traffic and the footfalls of the pedestrians hurrying to work.

It was a viciously cold day. There was a thick mist. Ed blew on his hands to warm them up.

'See you two later,' he said and he left Natasha and Clemence at the Needle and, carrying his tin whistle, he walked off in the direction of Big Ben, disappearing in to the mist.

Clemence headed off in the opposite direction.

Natasha crouched down on the pavement and, using coloured chalks, she began to copy out a composition from one of her sketchbooks, changing it slightly as she did so. She wore fingerless gloves but it was bitterly cold and her fingers were soon numb. She blew on her fingers. She pulled her scarf up around her face so that her breath would be warm and it would no longer hurt her to breathe. Natasha coughed, grimacing at the sudden pain in her chest.

Natasha glanced at the single silver coin in her woollen hat. She picked out the coin. 20 cents, Australian. She flipped the coin over her shoulder in to the river. She didn't even bother to make a wish.

Clemence appeared out of the mist. He rested his violin case against the wall and he stretched out his hands. They had turned blue and were shaking. He jammed his hands beneath his armpits.

He stood looking at Natasha's pictures. Next thing, he was bent down, snatching up a chalk, and before Natasha could stop him he had written: *Monday makes people do what they don't want to do,* beneath Natasha's picture of people hurrying off to work.

The annotation transformed the work, making its meaning immediately apparent.

It was powerful stuff. The picture had acquired an impact it had not previously possessed. But a picture shouldn't need words. Natasha wanted her work to stand on its own merits.

'What the hell are you doing?' she said.

Clemence was busy annotating another picture. He had taken out his notebook and he was copying a passage from it on to the pavement.

'Your pictures, my observations. Just imagine it. We could create huge murals together. On every wall, every gable end, underpass, bridge. Every building in the city. Think of the impact that will have.'

'No!' she shouted.

This was about her work, not his. It was about her place in the world, about her getting noticed.

'No,' she said.

Clemence fisted the chalk. 'You're right,' he said, standing. He handed Natasha the chalk.

'I need to do this on my own,' she said, taking the chalk.

'It was a stupid idea,' said Clemence.

Artists can be so naïve. They get some new idea and suddenly they are going to change the world. They suffer such delusions all the time, they get carried away on them. They rely on the imagination, so it's no surprise. They don't live in the real world. Besides, what difference would a few slogans scrawled on walls ever make? or art, or literature, for that matter? Who was going to pay any attention to some unknown writer and artist against the everyday business of making money.

Ed appeared out of the mist, smiling, holding up five pounds.

'Maybe somebody dropped it,' said Clemence unkindly.

But Ed's attention was on the pictures. He stood twisted, head bent, reading what was written there. Then, removing his notebook from his pocket he began writing everything down.

'Hey! What are you doing?' said Clemence.

'It's for my book,' said Ed.

'You're writing a book?'

'No. But I might.' Ed told Clemence about his book. He grew enthusiastic whenever he talked about it.

'But that's my book!' said Clemence and he told Ed about his book.

'I don't fucking believe this,' said Ed.

Novel, my arse, it happened to him every fucking time. Someone always got their first.

Writing a novel seems an impossible thing to do when you start out on it. Clemence had been planning his book for years. It is beginning it that is most difficult. Maybe the secret once you have begun is not to stop.

Twenty eight tins of oxtail soup, twenty eight cans of chilli beans, 12 cans of sweet corn, 12 onions, four sticks of salami, twenty eight packets of noodles, four bags of pasta twirls, four packs of pre-sliced wrapped cheese, four large boxes of assorted breakfast cereal, one container of dried milk, a large box of tea bags, two jars of instant coffee, several large containers of water, a small portable cooker, several bottles of meths, polythene bags, toilet paper, newspaper, a bucket, several reams of A4 paper, typewriter ribbons. . . .

Usually, when you attempt a thing so big everything conspires to get in your way. Writers need space and time in which to write. They need to devote their best energies to it. They need to insulate themselves from the world. Some even cut themselves off from it entirely.

Clemence finished stocking up his bash, he borrowed Ed's typewriter off Natasha, barricaded himself in to his bash and set to work.

He sat cross-legged on the floor before the typewriter. He fed in a page. He sat staring at the blank page.

Clemence thought long and hard about what he wanted to say.

His typing was slow at first, and full of mistakes and that interfered with the free and easy flow of his ideas. But he soon got the hang of it.

Genius is crazy. It can be. All that work, all those ideas building up, just waiting to explode out.

Clemence worked at his book from early in the morning till late at night. From being immersed in work he became obsessed. He worked in to the night. He worked all night. Night after night, day after day. He only emerged from his bash to dispose of his flying toilet.

Ed lay in bed listening to Clemence typing. He cursed Clemence. He pulled the covers over his head. The typing stopped. Ed held his breath. He pulled down the covers. The typing started up again. It seemed faster somehow. Louder.

The typing stopped.

'Yes!'

Clemence leapt back from his typewriter, collected up the pages of his manuscript, shook the thick weighty wad of them in front of his face, as though requiring proof of their existence, kissed the pages, hugged them, then jumped to his feet, hitting his head on the ceiling and making himself bow. It was an appropriate gesture.

Oh, people can laugh if they want, but this damned book had imprisoned him for years, yes, years. And it had taken him just two weeks to write. Two weeks!

Clemence came bursting out of his bash. Blinking and red eyed and foully dressed. He was shouting, clutching his violin case in one hand and waving his finished manuscript in the air from the other.

Ed came rushing out to look. Followed by Natasha. Alexander Hero appeared. A crowd began to gather.

Clemence was laughing, laughing. 'I've fucking done it. I've finally done it,' he roared. 'I've done it! At last, I can get the hell out of this place. I've seen the last of you fuckers!'

Hero broke from the crowd. Clemence ran. Hero chased after him.

Backstreet Books. The door exploded open.

Clemence was fighting for breath, but it looked like apoplexy to Grenville-Jones.

The publisher had not seen the young poet for some time, but he recognised him immediately. He recognised everyone that he owed money to. It helped with avoiding them.

'Your royalties are in the post,' he told Clemence.

Clemence wasn't interested in royalties. He slammed his manuscript down on to Grenville-Jones's desk. Then he dropped backwards in to a chair and he refused to leave the office until Grenville-Jones had read it.

Grenville-Jones glanced at the first page. He picked up the page. He read it to the end then he looked sharply up. He studied Clemence, then he reached for the next page. He read the page.

Some books you cannot put down. There are others that get abandoned after only a few pages. There are many books put aside and eventually returned to the shelves with bookmarks wedged in them a third or perhaps half way through that have been lodged there many years. They are like arrows through the heart of a book telling you that it is a dead book. Good books, however, offer a door in to another world.

It began to grow dark outside.

Grenville-Jones got up from his desk and, still reading, he walked across the room and he switched on the lights. Reading, he walked back again. He sat down and he put down the page and he picked up another page.

Grenville-Jones burst out laughing. Clemence, who was sat studying him, watching him for his every reaction, grew concerned for his book.

Grenville-Jones stopped reading. Lost in thought he stared off in to space. Then he went back to the book of a sudden. Next thing he was nodding in agreement. There was music in the book and Grenville-Jones began to hum along to it. He completely lost himself in the book. Several hours later he finished the book.

'Well?' Clemence was on tenterhooks.

'Incredible,' said Grenville-Jones.

At the end of the day though it's not about books.

It's impossible. You think that you are on to something original, something so unusual, so imaginative that no one else could possibly have thought of it and then someone comes along with the exact same idea.

'You can think up another book, surely,' said Natasha.

'Where do you think he went?' Ed asked.

'His publisher, I imagine.'

'You reckon?'

'Well of course. He got his poetry published, didn't he?'

They were walking beside the river. It was bitterly cold. The wind cut through them. Natasha was rigid from the cold.

There was a row of yellow skips in the road. Some warehouses were being renovated. In one of the skips Ed found a white puffa jacket. He handed it to Natasha. There were dark spots of oil on it in places. Natasha took it from him anyway. She was cold and the coat promised to be warm and it had a hood. She put it on over her duffel coat.

She did a model's twirl. She looked over her shoulder at Ed. Pressing her palms to its hem she paraded up and down, showing it off to him.

'It's a bit dirty, Nat.'

'Well I like it,' said Natasha, 'it keeps me warm.'

Few books change the world, but they can change the world of those who write them.

'Right,' said Grenville-Jones. 'Here's the deal. £10,000. Take it or leave it. Well?' he asked.

Clemence laughed. He reached forward and he snatched up his manuscript. 'That's all I needed to know,' he said, and he made to leave.

Grenville-Jones, who had been resting back in his chair, sat bolt upright.

'What are you doing?'

'I'm taking this to another publisher.'

Grenville-Jones jumped to his feet. 'You can't. You can't come walking in here and show me this and then snatch it away like that? Do you know what this is?' He pointed to the manuscript. 'This book could have print runs running in to millions. There will be several new editions, every year. Manifold translations.'

'Backstreet Books can do all that for me?'

'No, I can't possibly offer you what the big publishing houses could offer you. Of course not.'

'Then you're wasting my time.' Clemence turned to leave.

'No! Wait! This book stands to make millions.'

'£10,000, you said. You tried to cheat me.'

Grenville-Jones gave a palms-up shrug. He began to laugh nervously.

'That's it, I'm going.'

'No!' shouted Grenville-Jones. 'It's dog-eat-dog out there. If you go somewhere else you'll end up with nothing, just your name on a book. They employ lawyers that will eat you alive. You want money, don't you?'

Clemence nodded.

'Then you need someone to represent you.'

'An agent?'

Grenville-Jones nodded. 'Someone who knows their way around the publishing world. Someone with contacts. Someone,' he said, 'that can get you the best deal.'

'You?'

Grenville-Jones nodded.

Clemence narrowed his eyes. Grenville-Jones was right, publishers could be tricky. What he needed was an agent, someone who knew the ins and outs of the publishing world.

'I can play those people off against each other. We'll be able to name our price. I won't settle for anything less than one million.'

Clemence stared back at Grenville-Jones. Grenville-Jones swallowed.

'Agreed. But I want an advance.'

'How much?'

'£10,000.'

Grenville-Jones wrote out the cheque.

As Clemence took it from him, Grenville-Jones snatched the manuscript. He placed an elastic band around it and he locked it in his battered briefcase.

'What happens now?' asked Clemence.

'You go out and celebrate. I'll do the rest. Come and see me first thing Monday morning.' It was Thursday. 'I should have the makings of a deal by then. I'll also have some papers drawn up for you to sign.'

Clemence went out and celebrated.

Alone, Grenville-Jones poured himself a glassful of whisky. He knocked back the whisky. Checking his watch he picked up the phone and dialled New York.

*

Winning the lottery, the big killing in the City, being discovered, the blockbuster novel. Today, anyone can be plucked from obscurity and have sudden wealth.

Clemence could not decide between the veal steak, a back-cut, cooked in a red wine sauce, or the lobster, landed that very morning and flown down from Scotland. He ordered both. Also a bottle of champagne.

He went rushing in and out of shops. He bought new clothes, a pair of shoes, a hat and gloves, a woollen overcoat, a fancy silk scarf. He threw his old street clothes away. He wouldn't be needing them anymore.

Clemence booked in to an expensive hotel for the weekend. Everyone called him sir: Yes sir. Certainly sir. This way sir.

Grenville-Jones danced a jig around his desk. He picked up and kissed the manuscript. He cradled it to his chest. He fetched the bottle of whisky from his filing cabinet, poured himself a drink, and lit a cigar. He did another little dance. But he was soon out of breath and had to sit down, his heart racing.

Clemence soaked himself for hours in the hot scented water of the bath, draining it then topping it up several times, the bathroom full of humid, scented steam. He cut then shaved off his beard. Looking in the mirror he barely recognised himself.

'Very pleased to meet you, sir,' he said.

He dried himself, dressed, then drank everything in the mini bar. Why stop at the mini-bar?

He went out.

He visited several wine bars. He toasted himself in champagne.

Next thing he knew he was sliding along the walls, bumping in to lamp-posts, cars, trees. Pillar boxes, litter bins, buildings. Whole streets came flying out of the darkness at him.

The publisher sat slumped in his chair. Short of breath, he loosened his tie. He needed air. Gripping his desk he pushed himself to his feet, knocking over his chair. He staggered to the window and, with clumsy scrambling fingers, he undid the catch. He pulled down the sash.

Cold air flooded in around him. Gripping the window frame Grenville-Jones took several deep breaths of fresh air. He saw the bright lights of the city, his city now, and his heart swelled. He felt a pain in his chest and there was a dull numbing ache in his left arm. The human heart can hold only so much happiness.

Clemence woke with a start in a shop doorway, surrounded by a scattering of empty beer cans and clutching a half-full, half-empty bottle - he couldn't decide which - of 12 year old malt whisky.

He climbed stiffly to his feet, hailed a taxi and returned to his hotel.

It was only when he pulled out his wallet to pay the taxi driver that he discovered that he had just £300 left of the £1,500 which he had saved from his time busking on the streets.

Natasha went and she retrieved Ed's typewriter from Clemence's bash. She returned for the mattress and sleeping bag.

There was a shout. It was Ra, accompanied by Pogget. She came tottering over on high heels. 'You put those things back. Them's my things. It's my bash now.'

'Yours? It's Clemence's.'

Ra pushed her face in to Natasha's face. 'Coming back is he? I don't think so. Hero'll kill him if he comes back. You heard what he said. Fucken kill him he will, the lanky streak a piss.'

'You know what?' Natasha flung the mattress and sleeping bag on the ground at Ra's feet. 'I hope he doesn't come back, he doesn't belong here.'

'None of us do,' said Pogget. 'I shud be in prisen, me.'

First thing Monday morning, after depositing the cheque at the bank, Clemence returned to Backstreet Books. He raced up the stairs, turned the handle on the door and pushed on the door. But the door was locked. He hammered on the door. No answer. He returned to the street from where he looked up at the windows. The lights were off.

'You should have made a copy of it,' said Natasha.

'I know. I know.' Clemence felt sick to the pit of his stomach.

His manuscript was missing. Grenville-Jones was dead. He had had a heart attack on the tube on his way home. He had sat on that train for several hours before anyone noticed. The manuscript had been in the publisher's briefcase but there was no sign of the briefcase. The police presumed that he'd had a briefcase. According to those who knew him, he always carried one. His wallet was missing too. There was no sign of the manuscript in Grenville-Jones' office. And the cheque had bounced.

'You can write it again, surely,' said Ed.

Clemence shook his head.

The energy needed to write the book had been all used up when he wrote the book. Besides, how could he recall a whole book.

The book was dead in him. Clemence's face twisted in to tears.

He lifted the whisky bottle to his mouth, but it was empty.

Clemence was no longer clumsy, it was true, but his life had become clumsy. It was nothing but a series of accidents, failures and missed opportunities.

'Even my successes are failures,' he said.

Clemence went in to a state of dumb shock. Emptiness throbbed in him like a dull pain.

The world is full of checks and balances. It is what stops us from becoming gods.

A boom box blasted out loud Techno. It was giro day. And there were fires burning in the concourse. Bottles smashed against the walls.

A passer by stood staring over the parapet looking down at the party there. Ed shouted abuse up at the man. Natasha threw an empty beer bottle. The man leapt back as it smashed beneath him against the wall.

Clemence sat staring in to the fire, the empty whisky bottle in his lap, cradling his violin case.

Clemence lifted the bottle to his lips, remembered that the bottle was empty and let it slump back in to his lap.

He reached for his fiddle case and undid the clasps.

The music soothed Clemence. The sound was soaring, yet sad. Uplifting, in its own strange way.

Everyone stopped what they were doing. Everyone sat listening to the music, staring in to the fires, in to their drinks, their gazes distant.

It spoke to something deep inside. Listening to it, something swelled up in people. Hero smiled when he heard it.

He came striding out of the darkness, curled back his arm and bowled his great balled fist in to the back of Clemence's head, sending him sprawling.

The violin shrieked, the bow rasping across its strings. Ed leapt to his feet. Fists balled, ready to hit Hero.

There were three clear yards between Hero and Ed. Hero covered them in two strides. He hit Ed square on the side of the head, knocking him to the floor.

Natasha leapt to her feet, yelling: 'You piece of fucking shit!' She threw a bottle at Hero which missed. Hero came at her. Natasha slipped her satchel off her shoulder and, holding it by the strap, she swung it through the air with all her might.

It hit Hero on the side of his head, tearing his ear on a buckle.

Hero roared with pain. Natasha swung it at him a second time. But Hero grabbed hold of the satchel and he pulled it toward him, yanking Natasha off her feet. She let go of the satchel.

Ed was no use. He was sitting on the floor, his legs spread out in front of him, looking dazed and confused and shaking his head.

Natasha screamed: 'Give me that! Give it to me!' and began to sob.

Hero held the bag from its strap and he dangled it in front of Natasha, but when she lunged for it he pulled it away. He taunted Natasha. 'It's never out of your sight, is it bitch? Got money in it, have you?'

Hero tore the satchel open, the flying buckles catching in the firelight, and he peered in to the satchel. He looked up disgusted. 'Sketch books?'

He strode over to the nearest fire, upturned the satchel, and emptied its contents on to the flames. He threw the empty satchel on the fire too. A shower of vicious sparks exploded in to the air.

Natasha launched herself at Hero, tearing at his face with her bare hands, raking her nails down his cheeks and trying to hook out his eyes. Hero pushed her away. She landed heavily on her back on the floor.

Ed staggered to his feet, he rested his back against the wall and he pushed himself off the wall and flung himself toward the fire.

He grabbed the books and began to beat out the flames with his bare hands. Now Ed was on fire. Ed dropped the books. Natasha was hysterical. She ran forward, took off her coat and began to beat out the flames with it.

Clemence remained curled on the ground around his instrument. People were stepping over him, tripping on him. Clemence watched as the crowd closed in to surround Hero.

'Cunt,' someone said.

'Fucking arsehole.'

'Fucking cunt.'

'Get the bastard.'

Pogget hit Hero with a bottle. Hero turned and dropped him with a head butt. Ra took off a shoe and she hit Hero repeatedly on the head with its stiletto. Hero dropped her with a punch to the gut. Then a brick came flying out of the darkness that hit Hero in the face. Hero staggered backwards, his hands clutching at his face, blood pouring through his fingers and down his arms, blindly kicking out at everything in his path, cursing and roaring that he was going to tear Ed and Natasha, and fucking Clemence, in to fucking shreds when he got hold of them.

*

St Thomas's Hospital. Casualty.

The burns to Ed's hands were painful but not dangerous, the doctor told him. A nurse cleaned them, covered them in gauze and then dressed them in a bandage. The nurse told Ed that he must keep his burns clean if they were to heal properly.

'You'll live,' the nurse told him.

'Why does that frighten me right now?' said Ed.

The nurse was more concerned about Natasha.

Natasha's pallid complexion, harsh cough and spare frame also drew the attention of the doctor. Natasha dismissed his concerns. 'It's just a cough,' she said.

Clemence paced to and fro outside the cubicle.

There were raised voices and casualty exploded as other victims of the fight began to arrive.

The nurse disappeared, followed by the doctor.

'Fuck this,' said Clemence, 'I've had it with all this.'

'Come on,' said Ed and they left the cubicle.

Natasha said, 'It's all turned to shit. We're right back where we started.'

Euston Station. A cathedral to comings and goings. A lone pigeon flew across the square. It shat on Clemence.

'Good omen that,' said Ed.

'Come on,' said Natasha. 'We'll miss the train.'

They stood on the platform beside the train. Natasha hugged Clemence, then she hugged him again, tighter this time. Ed and Clemence shook hands. They stood there looking at each other. Each of them trying to think of a suitable comment that would capture the moment, making it exceptional.

'Soon be off,' said Ed.

'Look after yourselves,' said Clemence. 'Look after each other. And good luck.'

The whistle blew. Clemence climbed aboard.

'Keep in touch,' he said.

Thunk! the door slammed. Thunk! Another door. Thunk-thunk!

Another shrill whistle, a roar of diesel engines and the train departed.

Natasha threw her hand in to the air and she watched the train curve out of Euston and disappear in to the night.

Slowly, hesitantly, Natasha brought down her arm.

'What now?' asked Ed.

'Now?' said Natasha. Natasha was tired, she was worn out, but her face was stony and her eyes were fierce.

'You don't think we should have gone with him?' said Ed.

They had no money and nowhere to go. But as anyone who has ever wanted anything knows. They have a look that the rest of us will never have. Natasha had that fire in her eyes too, and it burnt fiercely.

'Any sensible person would give up,' she told Ed. 'But you know what?' Natasha smiled but there was no warmth in it, this was something else.

'Come on,' she said and she strode purposefully down the platform, back in to the city.

They say that you can do anything if you want it bad enough. All you have to do is to take your chances and to work like a dog.

Well they'd had their chances.

Clemence sat alone between two unclaimed reserved seats, unwashed, reeking of drink, woodsmoke, and stale body odour.

He was more scared than he had ever been. The emptiness gripped him. What was he going to do now? There was no longer any alternative. The alternative was work.

The train continued its headlong rush in to the night. Everything rushing out of darkness, then torn away, torn in to emptiness, because the past was irretrievable. And the whole world changing, everything getting faster and with no going back.

And Clemence, trapped, trapped on this train, this symbol of life itself. Trapped in the hours, the years, and time speeding away and all life with it. Clemence stared through the window at the flying world.

There was a loud scream, but it was just the sound of the train.

Ed sat in a doorway in the Strand, staring blank-faced at the traffic. Beside him sat Natasha, staring at a sketch book. Its charred, fire damaged pages possessed a yellowish tinge. They were black and brittle about the edges. She crumbled the carbonised paper between her fingers and watched it fall.

She held the spine cupped in her left hand, the four fingers of her right hand holding the back cover, the thumb holding back the pages, the book bending, pieces of it flaking off. Then, lifting her thumb, she let the pages fly: *Strange Buildings Unusual Shapes. Tall Buildings Giving Everyone the Finger. Wastelands and Construction Sites.* . . .

It was the city alright. All the images were there. The question was how to arrange them on the canvas.

30

The Cost of Water

Clemence's cottage was much the same as he had left it. There were several slates missing from the roof, the gutters were blocked with leaves and were overflowing, and the garden was overgrown.

Clemence had to push hard on the door, the wood having swollen in the frame. The door ground on the floor as he forced it open, before trapping itself on the stack of mail that lay piled there.

As he stepped inside, the coldness of the place gripped him and he shivered. There was the smell of pin mould. He could see his breath.

Building materials, bags of rock hard cement, lengths of wood, burst bags of nails, scatterings of wood shavings, pots of rock hard paint brushes, paint tins, tools....

Clemence cursed.

He could have finished it by now. Instead he had it all to do still.

Clemence put his violin case on the table, along with his stack of mail. He pulled out a chair and sat down.

The mail was damp, some of it mottled with pin mould. It was junk mail mostly, just adverts and inducements. There were a few official looking envelopes. There was a postcard from Paris, from Natasha. A letter from Backstreet Books.

Clemence tore it open.

Inside was a cheque from the sale to date of the copies of his poetry - the grand sum of fifty two pounds and twenty five pence.

Clemence sat staring in to space. It was some time before he could open any of the other letters.

The first that he opened was a demand, in red, from the water authority, for £370.

Clemence laughed. He could get all the water he wanted from the stream, they could hardly cut him off.

The next letter he opened was a court summons for non-payment of those water rates. Clemence balled up the letters and, as with the junk mail, he threw them in the fireplace.

The final letter that he opened was a notice from the local planning authority, recently dated, informing Clemence of his obligations under the relevant section of the local town and country planning acts concerning the restoration of listed buildings. The letter informed Clemence that there were two serious infringements concerning his property. First, Clemence did not have the necessary planning permission for his improvements. Second, and more importantly, under the relevant public health legislation, which they were empowered to enforce, the lack of adequate sanitation facilities at the property rendered it unfit for human habitation.

It took some time for the relevance of this to sink in.

Clemence bowed his head. He ran his fingers through his hair. He sat with his head in his hands. The tears welled up in his eyes. He felt sickened and numb and empty.

He reached for his violin case. He undid the clasps and opened the lid. He picked up his violin and, holding it by the neck like a cricket bat, he smashed it to pieces against the wall.

It was just one thing
after another.
And it all added up to
nothing.

Art Fontainbleu of the Deutsche Grammophone Company returned many times to Euston Square. He would arrive off the train and go straight to the square and he would sit and listen to the quartet. He liked the sound which the quartet had created. The lush chord voicings laced with spiky, dissonant improvisation and gently swinging lead lines bore little resemblance to the usual gypsy jazz that he so liked to listen to. This was amazing stuff, he believed, and it was going to be cult. The four young musicians had turned a compelling mixture of East European folk music, Bartok's string quartets and Shostakovitch, into a richly textured, rhythmical and propulsive jazz.

It was some time since Art Fontainbleau had last visited the square. There had been a lot to organise. People to sound out. Now, finally, he was in a position to make them an offer.

The quartet had already found a replacement for Clemence, another music student.

'That other violinist?' asked Art Fontainblueau. He was especially interested in that particular violinist.

But no one had seen Clemence, not for several weeks.

'He just disappeared,' said Tamara.

'Like that,' said William with a click of his fingers.

No, they didn't know where he lived, he'd never said. To be honest, they knew nothing at all about him. He'd kept himself to himself, they said. They didn't think that he lived anywhere, particularly. They thought that he lived on the streets.

31

Not another Bill Hicks, this Guy is Much Angrier

Completely Sold Out, the first show of Andy's American tour, performed at Carnegie Hall in New York, turned out to be a big mistake. The Big Apple was the city at the heart of the American Dream. Here were the owners, the bosses and money men, the big players that decided everything, and Andy had subjected them to an hour long assault on their whole way of life, delivered at furious pace and with a great deal of anger. They had not expected it and they denounced the show as un-American.

But if New York was the city at the heart of the American dream then Boston, where Andy was due to appear next, was its conservative centre. Soless panicked. He told Jigsaw that he had no choice but to cancel the remaining shows, offering him in its place a tour of struggling working mens clubs in America's decaying industrial heartlands and run down inner cities.

In truth, Soless would not care if he never heard of Andy Rant again. He'd rather Andy concentrated on his free-styling.

'Now that is showmanship. If he dropped the act and concentrated on those tricks with the football I could run that in Vegas at The Happy Crassus,', his hotel and gambling complex.

Sometime in the night the laughter stopped and the good times ended.

It was one, maybe two in the morning and Andy was staggering down the centre of a dark Las Vegas street, his clothes torn and with puke on his pants, trying to remember the name and the location of his hotel. He didn't know how long he'd been searching, all he knew was that he had to keep walking.

He turned another corner on to yet another unfamiliar street. There was a brightly illuminated building at the end of that street where it joined the main drag: Topless Bar and Casino, flashed the sign. It looked strangely familiar to Andy.

Andy staggered out on to the busy and brightly lit strip with all its enticements: Casino. Strip club. Topless Lounge. Bar, Bar, Bar. Naked swimming girls. Girls. More Girls. Girls A Go Go. All you can eat all day and night Diner and Girls. Until, finally, he came to The Happy Crassus Casino and Hotel Complex: Naked Dancing Girls, Hundreds Of Beautiful Girls And Two Ugly Ones.   That was all Andy needed to know.

Vegas, it was what happened when all there was was money.

12:00 am. And with an audible click Andy's alarm clock went off with a loud blast of sound, waking Andy:

'Y'awl get up now, do your thing. We gonna put one over on you, ain't no sin. It's called working you over, this is the American Dream. We gonna work you hard, you motherfucker! Motherfucker!'

It was the lyrics from Andy's song, *I Got Life*, which he performed as RapperD, a character in his American show, *Completely Sold Out* which Jigsaw, who knew a niche when he saw one, had marketed as an alarm call.

'Mother fucker! Mother fucker! Mother Fucker...!'

Andy's eyes flashed open. Bright sunlight, streaming in through the thin white curtains, illuminated the room.

Andy shot upright with fright. There were two big girls in bed beside him: a black one and a white one. They were massive. Obese.

The girls mumbled as they began to wake. One of them turned restlessly on her side and Andy rose to the air on a section of displaced mattress.

'Motherfucker! Mother...!'

Andy brought his hand down on the alarm and the room fell silent, and not a moment too soon. The girls sighed and their faces softened as they fell back to sleep. Andy blew out a loud breath of relief. He sat staring at the two girls, at their huge heads, vast bellies, and gargantuan breasts. He wanted more out of life, sure, but this was ridiculous. It had to be some kind of dare that had gone horribly wrong. And then he remembered: Hundreds Of Beautiful Girls And Two Ugly Ones.

Andy groaned. He held his head in his hands. His head hurt. He felt sick, hungover. More than hungover. It was just too horrible to contemplate. He dropped his head back on to his pillow and he shut his eyes, and he kept them shut. But then he was drifting back off to sleep, in to unconsciousness.

12:10 am. The phone rang. It was Jigsaw. 'See you in ten.'

Andy leapt out of bed, dressed hurriedly, and was just leaving the room, was in the act of pulling the door shut behind him when Jigsaw appeared in the corridor. Andy shut the door. He locked the door. Jigsaw frowned at Andy's nervousness. 'Everything alright?' he asked. 'You seem edgy.'

Andy stepped away from the door. 'Well I would be, wouldn't I? Soless? What did he say?'

First in Schenectady, then in Pittsburgh and Chicago and again in Detroit, Andy had begun to play to larger and more enthusiastic audiences. He was given a standing ovation in Baltimore and again in Cincinnati. By the end of the tour Andy was playing to riotous full houses. He had found his audience. Inner city youths, blacks, Hispanics, disaffected vets, the unemployed, those in low paid and part time employment, blue collar workers, miners, car and steel workers, white trailer trash, hippy drop outs, students . . . all across America people found a champion in Andy. Angry, disillusioned, here, finally, was someone who understood them, who spoke their language. Or something like it.

'Soless has only offered us another tour,' said Jigsaw. 'Full advertising. All the original venues.'

They walked fast, Jigsaw's words juddering to his footfalls. 'We'll have a ninety day tour of the states. There'll be a show every night. You'll be on chat shows, TV, the radio. Soless is going to get you on all the major networks, maybe get you your own show.' They entered a lift. Jigsaw pressed ground. 'And he wants you to do more free-styling, maybe just a free-styling act, to widen your demographic.' They emerged from the lift, Jigsaw still talking. 'Here.' Jigsaw handed Andy a pair of shades. 'Your own shades.' *RoughStuff* was printed on the arms. Andy hung them on the collar of his T-shirt. 'That's right,' Jigsaw nodded, 'we're going to launch RoughStuff in the States.'

Merchandising. Not just videos and dvds, but the whole Andy look. The T-shirt, the jeans, the boots, the jacket, maybe even a hat. A complete RoughStuff range, the whole Andy way of life. Or at least the appearance that you were dressed and up for it. People didn't just want to see Andy perform, they wanted to be Andy. Hard frugal living and a dose of real life could now be offered to poor America as a marketable alternative. Andy offered a new kind of opportunity in this land of opportunity. The disadvantaged and disaffected offered a vast, virtually untapped market. There are so many ways that you can milk a thing.

Jigsaw hefted his attaché case. 'I've got some papers for you to sign. We'll do it in the car.'

They hurried down another corridor, burst through some doors, trotted down a flight of steps. The steps were concrete, uncarpeted, the ceiling low, the passage harshly lit. Service ducts ran at head height along the painted cinder-block walls. There were hampers full of laundry. Deliveries of cleaning materials. They arrived eventually at the hotel's rear doors.

There were two men stood there guarding the doors, solid, sombre looking men, square jawed, jar headed, ex-marine types. They stood with their hands held clasped in front of them, each of them wearing an ear piece, wires coiling down from the devices in to their suits. One of them touched his earpiece, he angled his head. He looked at Jigsaw and nodded to him.

Jigsaw turned to Andy. 'Ready?' he asked.

Andy unhooked his shades from his T-shirt and he put them on. He ruffled his hair. 'Ready,' he said and he began to limber up, shifting his feet, shaking his hands at his sides, like a boxer before a fight, or a footballer waiting in the tunnel before coming out on to the pitch.

Jigsaw nodded to the doormen. 'Let's do it,' he said.

The men opened the doors on to bleaching white sunlight.

Cameras flashed, the media pack surged forwards, the fans surged forwards, there were loud shouts: 'Andy!' 'There he is!' 'Andy!' 'Andy Rant!'

A huge crowd surrounded Andy. He was jostled and pushed. Microphones and cameras were thrust in to his face. On the edge of the crowd several correspondents from the major networks stood speaking direct to camera, reporting on the event even as it was happening.

Soless owned the TV station, 24Hour7News, StateWide Radio FM, and the magazine, *Lives of the Stars*.

A stretch limousine with tinted windows pulled up. Jigsaw's minders bundled Andy in to the car. Jigsaw climbed in to the car after him. They were driven off, fast. It was going to be metal for breakfast from now on.

Jigsaw opened his leather attaché case, pulled out some papers and handed them to Andy. 'Sign here,' he said. Andy signed. 'Sign there.' Andy signed. Jigsaw checked the documents before returning them to his attaché case.

There was an open bottle of champagne in the car, sitting in an ice bucket.

There were two glasses in the ice beside it.

Jigsaw filled the two glasses. He handed one to Andy. They raised their glasses.

'To champagne socialism,' said Andy.

'To Andy Rant,' said Jigsaw.

'Andy,' they said.

Andy laughed. Being yourself, it was the ultimate victory in this modern age. There was a loud Ching! As their glasses touched.

Andy had escaped the common fate. He was Andy Rant, angry young comedian. The angry young comedian. Not a victim any longer, but a part of the process: the property, through contract, of Soless Global Entertainments Corp, of A. Soless & J. Truitt Proactive Agents plc., and of 50/50, a subsidiary of Midas, the company at the centre that controlled everything. These were the vested interests, corporations with the rights to the Andy image, with interests in the brand, in RoughStuff: The Andy Rant T-shirt, the Andy boots and jeans, the Andy shades, the whole Andy look. A whole industry was being spun around his image, propelling Andy.

They loved Andy in America.

Whatever venue he appeared in he filled to capacity. Relayed live on to giant screens, he performed to over one hundred thousand enthusiastic fans in stadia used for international sporting events. Videos of his concerts sold millions of copies. Comedy was the new rock and roll.

Andy appeared at the Aspen, Canada, the Melbourne, Australia, and the New Zealand Comedy Festivals.

He had to be in London, on the 5th, for a performance, and in Vegas on the 7th, followed by LA. Jigsaw organised everything, guiding him through the complexities of his various engagements.

He crossed multiple time zones multiple times. Seasons no longer passed on their meaning to him. It was summer in one place on a particular day, and winter in another the next. His grip on reality loosened. It seemed that there were various realities, all liable to abrupt change.

Increasingly, Andy's relationship to people was in terms of their function to him. They were stewards and stewardesses, waitresses, bar girls, drivers, doormen, roadies, agents, managers. He had managers for everything. Everything had to be managed because of these complexities of time.

Most people work all the time. Some, a few, play all the time. Andy worked hard and he played hard too. Inevitably, he fell in with a bad crowd.

Drink brings out the passion in people. It offers companionship, laughter, song. It is how some people bolster themselves, how they are able to keep their faith in the world and in the work that holds it all together. And because drink helps people to bear those things which they might otherwise find unbearable it brings out the worst in them too. It releases the monster in people. The world is full of things that promise you one thing and deliver another.

The Big Bucks drank, and they drank hard. They were a group of fast living young actors, writers, rock stars, artists and their privileged hangers on, all of them millionaires, who inhabited LA's wild party scene. They gathered together, often at each others houses, and they played drinking games involving a moonshine whisky from Arkensaw which they called Deep-Six, on account of its affects. It was known by numerous other names too: Four Star, Battle Juice, Skull Attack, Destroying Angel, Betty Ford, White Man's Wobbly, Alzheimers, Time Machine.

Loud music. Flashing lights.

Andy was wired on speed. He was drunk on moonshine, to offset the effects of the speed. And now he was coked up, to counteract the effects of the drink.

He was in a club, then he was in a strip joint, then he was in another club.

Whenever Andy was in LA he would hit the town with the Big Bucks, yet he rarely ended the night with them. Inevitably, he would meet with some woman – usually a stripper or barmaid or waitress, and she would often be someone who was trying to be a poet, or writer, a sculptor, a painter, a musician, an actress. Andy often woke in some would-be artists studio surrounded by her paintings, or by carvings, metalwork, a drum-kit, or in some room in some cheap lodging house downtown, the tiny room scattered with balled up rejection slips, discarded drafts and empty bottles and dog ends.

Or he would wake up amongst the derelicts beneath an underpass, or, more often than not, on Venice Beach.

Dawn. And a fierce white sun exploded on the horizon.

Andy woke with a start on Venice Beach. The sun shining in his face. But it was the smell that woke him. The smell of unwashed, pissed on clothes and bad breath.

An old, grey bearded derelict was bent over Andy, trying to prise a half-full bottle of whisky from his hands.

Andy shot up on to his elbows. Then he was propelling himself backwards on his heels and the palms of his hands.

'I just want a drink,' said the derelict.

Every day now Jigsaw awoke to a better world. He was much richer than the day before, and happier, and more experienced.

He lay looking at the girl, admiring her long blonde hair, her tanned back and bottom, her long tanned legs. He reached out and he touched her. He ran his finger down her long long back.... The girl woke.

They did bouncy castle, then reverse cowgirl, and finished off with his most recent favourite, orbiting astronaut.

Jigsaw lay exhausted on his back on the damp bed, his chest rising and falling.

The blonde slid out of bed and began putting on her clothes: red dress, high heels.

She picked up her overnight bag. She placed it on the dressing table. She unzipped the bag and took out a card swipe machine. She picked Jigsaw's credit card off the dresser and she inserted it in to the machine. She pulled back the block, removed the slip, and returned Jigsaw's card to him, together with the counterfoil. She kept the original for her records, placing it in her pocket book. She wrote something in the pocket book, put the pocket book and the machine back in to the bag and zipped up the bag. She gave Jigsaw a little left handed, clam-open clam-shut, wave and then she left.

Her name was Jenny Taylor. She was Jigsaw's latest recreational sex partner, supplied to him by Jezebels.

Jigsaw showered, dressed, then ate a hearty breakfast. He checked his watch. It was 9:30am. He was seeing Seena at ten. He rang Andy.

Blue skies, turning yellowish. Hot sun. Traffic sliding along the freeway. Talking Heads, *Once in a lifetime*, blasting from the car stereo. Andy was driving out of LA. up in to the hills.

The wind pulled at his blonde hair. The warm dry wind. His sun bleached hair.

This was the life. No more grey skies, no more rain. No more getting fucked around. He felt godlike, on top of the world.

Coming round a bend in the road the sun dazzled Andy. He flashed his lights.

Tall cypress trees, fan palms, oleander bushes, flame and jacaranda trees, orange and lemon trees surrounded the property, which was fronted by well-tended lawns. Peacocks strolled across the lawns. The house, with its white walls, orange tiled roof, arched doors and windows, and long colonnade, had been built in the Spanish Mission style. Beside it, and built right to the very edge of a precipice, was a large infinity pool. There was a miniature Greek temple beside it.

Music by Tim Wheater was playing on the the pool's sound system. There was the heady, pleasant scent of marijuana on the air.

Jigsaw was lying on a sun-lounger beside the pool and smoking a reefer, a smile fixed on his happy, tanned face, his eyes glazed. Beside him, on another sun-lounger, lay Seena Dollar, psychoanalyst to the stars and something of a minor celebrity herself.

'Are you in a relationship, James?' she asked Jigsaw.

'Yes.' Jigsaw nodded. 'Loads.'

'I mean a meaningful relationship, with a single person. Isn't there someone special, someone that you want to spend the rest of your life with?'

Jigsaw shrugged. 'There's just me, I guess.'

A jeep came racing in to view up the long drive. It slid to a halt in front of the house, the wheels locking, the vehicle continuing on the gravel for a short distance. A cloud of white dust drifted across the lawn toward the infinity pool. Andy leapt from the jeep and disappeared in to the house.

He emerged five minutes later, barefoot, drinking a beer, dressed only in his shorts, his hair sun-bleached, stiff with sea salt and full of sand. He headed straight for the infinity pool, intent on throwing himself in, and he was just about to do so, his toes gripping the pool's edges, his thumb covering the neck of the beer bottle, when he noticed, from the corner of his eye, a blonde stunner stretched out on a sun lounger wearing a pink bikini and sky blue sarong that was parted to show off her beetle-bonnet.

Andy windmilled for balance, but he fell in anyway. The water was cool and refreshing.

Jigsaw and Seena sat upright on their sun-loungers. They stared at Andy. Andy stood in the pool, waist deep in water, the sun blasting off the water, illuminating his tanned face.

Seena looked Andy up and down. She took in the hard knotted muscles, the sinews that were taught as hawsers, his clenched fist, with its grazed knuckles, the tensely bowed arms. Andy stared back, he took a swig of beer. Jigsaw made the introductions.

'Andy, I'd like you to meet Seena. Seena is life goals consultant at The Wellness Resource Centre for Designed Life Change.'

'The? A what?' Andy almost sprayed out his last gulp of beer.

Jigsaw took a long pull on his reefer. He held in the smoke. When he next spoke his voice had changed. 'Seena here is my psychoanalyst,' he said, hoarsely.

'Are you crazy?'

Jigsaw turned to Seena. 'Andy's a comedian,' he told her.

'Oh, I know all about Andy,' smiled Seena, 'Andy Rant the angry young comedian versus the rest of the world, yes?'

Andy narrowed his eyes at Seena. He made a gesture for Jigsaw's reefer.

Jigsaw leant forward. He rose languidly off his sun-lounger and he handed Andy the reefer.

Andy took a long pull.

Seena sat smiling at Andy. 'We were just discussing the therapeutic benefits of optimism,' she told him. 'Maybe you'd like to join us.' And with a nod of her head she indicated the empty sun-lounger beside her.

'I don't need no psychoanalysis, I got all the therapy I need, right here.' Andy held up the reefer and his beer. He took another long pull on the reefer, before handing it back to Jigsaw.

Seena smiled at Andy. 'It's okay, James here has told me everything. Coming from such deprived backgrounds as you do can mess you up for life. But you can do something about that. James is. I mean, are any of us really happy? Deep down, are any of us content?'

'So he wants that too, eh?'

Seena smiled at Andy. 'You know, I could help set you free from yourself.'

Andy's face darkened. 'Hey! A don't need no fucken shrink. A'right!'

Seena smiled. 'You want to watch that anger of yours, it really could make you ill, you know. You should come and see me sometime, professionally, I mean. I could help teach you to relax, like I have with James here.'

Andy narrowed his eyes, he clenched his teeth, breathed in deeply through his nose. 'Relax! Me? When do I ever get the time to relax! I'm too fucken busy working, aren't I?'

'Then you need to make time,' smiled Seena.

The anger built in Andy, and the rage. He flung his beer bottle at the water then he punched the water with his clenched fist.

'Just fuck off, aright? Leave us alone, yeah?'

'Wow!' exclaimed Seena, smiling. 'You really do need help, you know. This whole social isolation thing of yours, it is so maladjusted.'

Jigsaw smiled dreamily. Lifting his reefer to his mouth he dropped his reefer. He bent forwards to retrieve it and rolled over in to the swimming pool.

Dawn. And a fierce white sun exploded on the horizon.

The sky was cloudless. The air polished and still. Bright sunlight blasted off the surface of the infinity pool.

The radio said: 'It's another great day in paradise.'

Andy had just finished a three month tour of the States: *U.S. and Them*, and he now had two whole weeks before the start of his next three month tour, *Andy Rant Completely Sold Out II*. For Andy, who had been working virtually non-stop for years, it was his first real break. He could experience the promised land of rest and recreation for a time.

Andy and Jigsaw were relaxing on their sun-loungers when the alarm on Jigsaw's watch told him that twenty minutes had passed since he had set it. He sat upright and put on his Hawaiian shirt and a beanie hat. Then he stood and unfurled the large umbrella that stood mounted on the low table between them, putting Andy in the shade.

'Oy! What the fuck you up to, Jigsaw? The sun, mate. I'm working on a tan here.'

'It's not good for you, you know, all this sun.'

'Says who?'

'Everybody. The experts. You're not supposed to get more than twenty minutes of direct sun a day now. It says so on the bottle. Here.' Jigsaw tossed Andy the bottle of sun block, Factor 30. 'Stick some of that on.'

Andy caught the bottle.

'Sun block? But we came here for the sun?' Andy looked incredulous. He threw the bottle back at Jigsaw. 'Fucken typical, innit,' he said, disgusted. 'Just when we get to live the rest of our lives in the sun, what happens? They tell us it's fucken not good for you.' Andy got to his feet, picked up his sun-lounger, removed it from the shade and placed it defiantly in the sun.

'Very clever,' said Jigsaw, 'Get cancer.'

'Before it gets you,' said Andy.

Clear blue skies, hot sun. It was another great day in paradise.

The sun grew grew hotter, fiercer. It blasted off the surface of the infinity pool, the white walls of the house.

'This is the life,' said Jigsaw, taking a sip of his tequila sunrise.

Andy and Jigsaw, both seated in inflatable easy chairs, were drifting about the infinity pool. Jigsaw was reading the business pages of a newspaper. Andy was propelling himself around, flexing his ankles idly underwater. The pair were completely drenched in sweat. It was ten o'clock in the morning and already it was too hot.

Andy tipped himself from his easy chair in to the cool water below. He sat underwater on the bottom for a time.

He swam underwater in the cool blue silence to the pool's furthest edge. He surfaced in to bright sunlight.

Andy swam the whole length of the infinity pool. He swam fast, churning up the water, destroying the peace and quiet and splashing Jigsaw as he sped by.

'FOR GOD'S SAKE, ANDREW!' shouted Jigsaw, now bobbing up and down in Andy's wake.

Andy stopped swimming. He stood in the infinity pool, the sun, flashing off the water, making bright patterns on his dark face.

Water lapped at the pool's sides for a time.

The sun climbed higher in the sky. It grew hotter, fiercer. The rattle of cicadas became deafening.

Andy and Jigsaw retired to their sun-loungers.

'This is the life,' said Jigsaw.

Andy picked up the magazine, *Lives Of The Stars*, and flipped idly through its pages: the women, the fast cars, the luxurious houses, the whole extravagant lifestyle, before flinging it back down again. 'Smiling Jerkoffs,' he cursed.

Andy was bored. He was irritable. He felt strangely dissatisfied and he didn't know why.

He thought of cracking open a cold beer. But he didn't want a beer. He considered going for a drive. But the mood just as soon left him. He had neither the energy nor the inclination. But he didn't want to hang around the pool doing nothing all day either.

He sat upright on his sun-lounger. 'Is this it? Is this what it's all about? Is this what we've been working so fucking hard for? So I can do nothing all day?'

Jigsaw smiled. 'Isn't that what you wanted? Enjoy,' he said, 'Chill.'

Andy sighed. He didn't know what he wanted anymore. 'Do you know what I miss?' he told Jigsaw.

'What is there to miss?' frowned Jigsaw. 'You can have everything, anything that you want, Andy.'

'That's it exactly. I miss not having things, Jigsy. I miss the edge that needing a thing gives you, that going for it and giving it all that you've got gives you.'

'And haven't we just,' said Jigsaw. 'We have taken everything that life has thrown at us. And we have kept it. Ha!' He burst out laughing.

'But don't you ever get tired of it?'

'What?' Jigsaw laughed. He sat upright he was so surprised. But he was soon lying down again. 'You never get tired of making money, Andrew. Other things, yes, but never money. You can always have more money. It's like sex in that respect. You can never have enough of it. I can't.'

The thing with money, as Jigsaw was so fond of explaining, was that the more that you acquired and the wealthier you became then the more that you needed. Because in order not to need money then the more you had to earn so that you could continue in that happy state.

It was the ultimate paradox.

Smiling, Jigsaw lay on his sun-lounger, comforted by his certainties. He would never be bored.

Andy lay back on his sun-lounger. He lay staring at the empty blue sky.

The day grew hotter. The white walls of the villa whiter. The sky bluer, emptier. The sun more fierce. The cicadas louder until it became even too hot for them.

Andy couldn't bear it a moment longer. He leapt up from his sun-lounger, kicked his leisure shoes off his feet and in to the infinity pool, then raced in to the house to fetch his car keys.

Andy tried to walk off his frustrations. But wherever he went he was recognised and mobbed.

He drove out in to the desert, intending to walk there.

The desert in the late afternoon light possessed an intense beauty all of its own. The bare rock glowed orange in the sun.

Blue sky, purple horizon. The intense stillness of everything. It was deathly quiet.

Nothing was happening. Just the distance, shimmering in the heat.

Andy was not happy if nothing was happening. Something had to be happening, all the time. He got back in to his jeep and sped off. Since nothing was happening then at least the scenery could be happening.

It wasn't possible to do nothing. An emptiness opened up in you. Earning a living, being comfortable, it just wasn't enough. Not even the the rich can stay idle, it eats away at them. They need drink and drugs too.

On stage, Andy continued to rant at the world, and he was hailed as brilliant and subversive.

Off stage he could be violent and abusive, smashing up hotel rooms, punching out photographers, getting in to fights.

Andy was mugged in New York late one night after a performance. He head-butted the young Hispanic that pulled the knife on him and he threw him in the harbour. He didn't know if the man drowned and nor did he care.

He joined a boxing club, hoping to work off his frustrations. He had a go at the punch bag. He punched like a professional. He punched hard. He feinted and punched. He punched with both hands, till his hands hurt. He butted the bag. He began kicking it. The other gym users stopped what they were doing and they watched Andy butt and punch and kick the bag till its seams split, dumping its sand on the floor.

Andy woke with a start, in to yet another black hangover in yet another unfamiliar room. He found a pair of torn black lace panties in the bed.

The toothpaste smelt of whisky. The bathroom smelt of puke. Looking in the mirror Andy pulled from the gaps between his teeth several strands of black lace. The find puzzled him at first but then he began to laugh. Andy grimaced. Laughing only made his head hurt.

He shuffled back in to the bedroom, crossed to the window and opened the blind. He staggered backwards. Bright sunlight blazed in to the room, blinding Andy. He stood, shielding his eyes from the red glare, but he was also a little perplexed. The sun was doing strange things. Now it was bathing the city in orange light. It was some time before he understood.

Andy hurried about the place, getting ready to go out. He felt a rising excitement at the coming dusk and the brightening neon lights.

Andy continued to live the Dream life, dating Dream women, driving Dream cars, living in a Dream house.

He could have anything that he wanted: more women, more money, more things. More of everything. And it was like something was missing. There had to be more to life.

The superabundance of everything trivialises the necessities, so that only the unique and the superfluous seem necessary. And sometimes the grotesque. Somehow, the world had slipped through Andy's fingers.

Andy felt trapped, hemmed in by his obligations. He was being squeezed smaller and smaller by Andy Rant, superstar. His life was spinning out of control.

Andy dreamt that he was playing football for Liverpool. He was running with the ball toward the goal, but the faster that he ran the slower he went and the further away the goal became. It began stretching away from him, and at a faster pace, becoming smaller and smaller in the distance; the pitch becoming larger, immense, so that it actually curved. Andy took a desperate kick at the ball, and the ball burst, waking Andy.

With a sharp intake of breath he sat upright in bed, heart pounding, his body covered in a cold sweat.

He lay there for a long time in the dark listening to the traffic passing by on the freeway.

He was drifting back to sleep when his alarm went off: 'Mother fucker! Mother fucker! Mother fucker. . . .' Andy grabbed the alarm and he flung it across the room where it exploded in pieces against the wall.

It was getting harder to start the day alive.

*

The lives that people lead are driving them crazy. Every day you read in the papers of someone going off the rails.

STOP! said the hexagonal sign, the white letters on a red background.

There was the smell of burnt rubber in the air. Skid marks led off the road to where Andy's car, a bright red Ferrari open top, Registration, *ANDY3*, its engine still running, had come to a screeching halt. It was parked at a slant, two wheels up on the sidewalk, the driver's door open and the boot flipped up. Andy was stood on the sidewalk with a car-jack in his hand, swinging it at the road sign.

The sign had informed him of a restriction and something in him had snapped.

There he was under every encouragement to live a busier, more competitive, more productive life, and then there were all these restrictions compelling him to slow down. He just wasn't going to take it any more.

He swung the jack wildly at the sign, swearing incoherently, cursing the world and the whole coming age as he continued to beat the car-jack against the sign.

A crowd gathered. The media appeared. 24Hour7News, and StateWide Radio FM. The crowd urged Andy on, each resounding blow he delivered to the sign meeting with loud and appreciative cheers. Now the cameras were rolling.

By now the sign was so bashed up it was no longer recognisable as a sign. It was just some beaten shield of torn up metal clinging to a pole by a single bent bolt.

The police car gave a short whine on its siren as it pulled in at the kerb, lights flashing.

The two officers climbed slowly out of the patrol car, they put on their hats, rearranged their belts and began pushing back the crowd.

'Okay folks. Come on, everybody move back! Let's give the man some room. These people are trying to make a film here!'

Andy punched away at the beat up metal. His swings were becoming less frequent, more frantic. He missed with a swing, spinning himself around, and was forced to stop for a moment. He stood there, the jack hanging from both hands, breathing heavily, his shoulders heaving. He flexed his hands, then he gripped the jack tightly, his knuckles turning white. Focusing his eyes on the sign he took careful aim. Summoning up the last of his strength, and with a loud and animal roar, he let fly. To loud applause and cheers from the crowd the torn remnant of sign fell clattering to the ground. Even the policemen cheered.

32

People Need their Struggles

Either work rescued you, or it did not. You could commit yourself for years, trapping yourself. The years pass and still you have not done what you set out to do. What you want to do.

Natasha acquired her studio, a draughty lock-up located beneath some railway arches in London's east end. But rather than begin work, she seemed instead to do everything possible in order to avoid work, preferring instead to immerse herself in its preparation. She seemed reluctant to begin, being apprehensive of committing her ideas to canvas. She hesitated over her compositions, changing them constantly. She preferred the continuous flux of new ideas to the all too disappointing results of their crystallisation. And so she reworked her ideas, hoping to improve on them. But the ideas became lost in the reworking, forcing her to begin again. She underwent innumerable false starts. Her stacks of discarded compositions began piling up. The walls of her studio filled with studies. She felt hemmed in by the clutter, physically and mentally suffocated by her surroundings and this burden of work.

Natasha excused her lack of progress, knowing that she was not yet ready, that she needed more time.

She took to touring the galleries, forever attending exhibitions of new work, searching for inspiration and encouragement, hoping to find the least confirmation of her novel ideas, and at the same time dreading ever making such a discovery, fearful that her work was already being done and by someone far more accomplished and certain of their ideas, those ideas being refined and polished to perfection.

When Natasha finally began work she painted people, she painted festivals and fairs, she painted raves. She painted the city, city crowds. She painted six finished canvases in all, each picture some 4'6" high and 6' long.

Natasha cleaned and then put away her brushes.

But an artist rarely thinks of their work as finished. A picture, though it may take weeks, even months to complete, is of a moment in time. It is seen in a moment, and it captures but a moment in the subjects life. The two things together are what make a picture, or any piece of art. The subject pauses, momentarily, then moves on, and it continues to move on, as does the observer. If the subject changes, if the times change, if the artist's perception of things change then the artist, to capture that, must change with them.

Natasha was not happy with her work. She wanted to paint the bigger picture but how could she do that when with everything changing so fast it meant that so much was missing still. The frustration built in Natasha, creating tensions. She felt the need for release.

Just a little dot, a stain on a piece of paper. Natasha gulped it down. Nothing. The same as the last time.

Van Gogh smiled down at her from his portrait on the wall where Natasha had hung beside her easel. The yellow straw hat, the fur like face, the blue blue eyes, one of them sad, the other piercing. He was an inspiration to Natasha, a kind of guardian to her.

'Hard isn't it?' he said.

'Yes,' said Natasha,

'Hang on in there.'

'I will.'

'Try yellow, more yellow. Yellow's good. I always liked yellow.'

Natasha unburdened herself when she painted, she became full of brief enthusiasms that she failed to curb.

She painted suns. Suns rose and rose.

She painted sun flowers and laburnum trees. She painted blossoming acacia branches. She purged herself of yellow, and still it came. Yellow cornfields, yellow flowers, yellower and yellower suns.

The pictures blazed and vibrated with energy. They were masterpieces of colour. But they were not what Natasha wanted to paint. She was simply purging herself of all those energies and notions that had built up in her that had nothing to do with those other less understood energies and notions which she wished to convey. She was easing herself in to the work, waiting for the ideas to come.

She painted crowds, crowded streets, when what she was trying to paint was what made those crowds work.

She painted the city as a barcode.

She tried painting in black and white in an attempt to simplify her ideas, hoping to discover that essential quality that made her subject what it was, that point at which it ceased being one thing and became some other. Her works became abstract, their meaning lost to her – mutated, far too symbolic.

She ended up confused.

Her finished work all too often disappointing her, she discarded canvas after canvas of finished work, scraping the canvases clean and then painting over them, removing from her sight anything she considered to be inadequate. Those pictures were like a barrier to her, they were holding her back. They were the evidence of what she was trying to do and could not.

She kept her work in flux, hoping that the idea of it might survive in to some better thing.

Natasha loved the flux and the flow of new ideas, of endless possibility. It was where she wanted to be, on the border between the known and unknown, where there was so much to explore and be discovered. And yet she needed to bring that to a resolution. But whenever she viewed a finished work it felt incomplete. She was not ready to be finished. She was attempting an analysis, yet it was one that she could never quite grasp. There was always some new interpretation, yet another possibility there. She would no sooner finish a painting than some new thing would occur to her that would turn everything on its head.

Natasha loaded up her brush and made a change. But once one thing changed then everything had to change. Next thing, she was slapping on paint, and in any old fashion, and with bolder and more aggressive strokes until her canvas was obliterated. Staring at what she had done, Natasha screamed. Frustrated, she threw down her brush, and not for the first time that day she felt like giving up.

It is sometimes difficult to understand why an artist must work. The process is difficult and more often than not it ends in failure. Most artists, even successful ones, are rarely happy with their work. Art is a continuous attempt to overcome limitations and to break through barriers.

It was why Natasha's work always disappointed her. She was struggling to give form to ideas which she felt a need to express but which she did not yet fully comprehend.

Natasha became fatigued and depressed. She began to doubt her work, to despair of her ability. She felt that it would be years before her finished work would be anything near what she wanted it to be.

33

This England.
It Wears you Down

Monday morning. 6:29:57. 6:29:58. It was the city's iron heartbeat. 6:29:59. Its unwavering pulse. 6:30:00.am. Ed's alarm went off.

Grumbling, still half asleep, Ed reached over and he switched it off. Just five more minutes, he told himself.

Ed felt tired, and it was not because he had not slept well. This was the kind of tiredness that you never shook. Ed would wake up just as tired tomorrow, and the day after that. No amount of sleep would cure this tiredness. He felt heavy, far heavier than the day before, and less able. There would be years and years of it.

Ed was getting up for work.

The Monday to Friday routine wears everyone down. The weekends aren't long enough. The tiredness gives way to new energies but then it is Monday again. You should be refreshed and keen and you are dog tired instead. It is the dread, the sum weight of all that time you still have to do bearing down on you. Monday is the beginning without end. Monday makes people do what they don't want to do.

All over the city people were reluctantly forcing themselves out of bed and dragging themselves off to work. Unless they were late, in which case they ran.

Ed burst from his tent in to Lincoln's Inn Fields. It was a glorious spring morning and many of the Field's inhabitants were seated outside their shelters. They greeted Ed as he hurried past. But there was no time to stop and talk, no time even to say hello. Ed raced on to Kingsway to catch his bus.

*

Two Rastafarian buskers, working the square, broke off from their routine to serenade Ed as he hopped of the slowing bus and went hurtling past:

'Speedyman, speedyman, racing down de street, got to get to work ten minutes ago.'

Laughing at Ed they resumed their routine, shouting: 'Tin - can - melody!' and tapping-out loud and piercing notes on their steel drums.

Ed burst in to The Popodopulous Cafe, slamming shut the door and cutting off the music. The smell of cooked bacon and the aroma of coffee made Ed's mouth water and his stomach growl. Ed was hungry, but the cafe was busy, there was a long queue at the counter and the tables were all taken, and there was no time.

First there was the rubbish to put out, then there were tables to clear, the dirty dishes and cutlery and mugs to wash and then dry, the ashtrays to empty, then more tables to clear and to wipe down, more cutlery to wash, more dishes, cups, ashtrays.

'A woman's work is never done,' grumbled Ed, muttering it to himself as he cleared yet another table.

'Then she should do it properly the first time,' said a voice at Ed's shoulder.

Mister Adopolopolis, Ed's boss, a balding, heavy featured man in a stained, white vest and white apron, snatched from Ed's hand the rag which he had been using to wipe down the tables, and, holding it at arms length between the tips of one finger and thumb, he looked at it in disgust. The cloth was gelid and dirty and it stank.

'How many times do I have to tell you? Use hot water not cold. Hot! You understand?'

Ed preferred cold water. Though the burns to his hands had healed, the scars, still red and livid, remained sensitive to heat.

'Here.' Mister Adopolopolis flung the stinking rag at Ed, spreading it across his chest. 'And you were late again today.'

Ed frowned 'Me? No.'

'You were late. Ten minutes late. That is two days running now.'

'Ten? I don't think so, Mister A'. Five, maybe, not. . . .'

'Why am I talking to you about this? Am I paying you for conversation? No. Go clean the toilet.' Mister Adopolopolis pointed Ed to a mop and bucket. 'There's been a complaint.'

'But that's Ashok's job, not mine,' complained Ed, grimacing.

'I had to let Ashok go. From now on you do his job also. Now get to work.'

Ed told Mister Adopolopolis exactly where to stick his mop, and his bucket. And his fucking job.

Mister Adopolopolis laughed. 'Why you want to leave? Where else would you get two jobs,' and, throwing back his head, he burst out laughing. 'Well go on, get on with it.' Then, repeating his joke to himself, he walked away laughing.

Ed cursed Mister Adopolopolis. He cursed the job. Mostly though he cursed Natasha. If it wasn't for Natasha he wouldn't need a fucking job.

Ed opened his mouth to protest but he gave Mister Adopolopolis the vees instead.

Ed stared in utter disgust at the clogged toilet bowl. He flushed the toilet, slopped the brush down the bowl, to remove the stain, then flushed the toilet again. He had to flush it twice. Then he swept out the toilet, emptied the bin, cleaned the sink, polished the mirror, then the taps, and then he refilled the toilet roll and soap dispensers. He mopped the floor, emptied the bucket of dirty water down the bowl, flushed the toilet, twice, and then he returned his equipment to the utility room.

He undid his apron, threw it on the chair, then stormed out of the cafe. He turned left along the high street, turning the corner in to a street running parallel with the railway line.

There was a long line of lock-ups in the street, built in to the arches there. One was a car repair shop, another a furniture restorers. Most however were derelict, their wooden doors covered in graffiti. Ed stopped before the last lock-up in the street, pulled open the small door set in one of the huge double doors and stepped inside, slamming the door shut behind him.

The lock-up smelt of oil paint, linseed oil, turpentine. The studio, such as it was, was poorly lit, illuminated by a row of grime stained windows that were located high up the wall at the rear, as well as several 100 watt light bulbs. The lock-up had once been used as a storage room and several broken armchairs, a sofa, a broken bed, broken tables, chairs and numerous boxes lay piled in a bonfire-like stack against one wall. In the centre of the room stood Natasha's easel, on which there was a large, partially finished canvas.

The floor around the easel was covered in splashes, drips and multicoloured dollops of trodden in paint where Natasha, in her previous attempts, had thrown it after scraping it off the canvas.

Natasha was stood, deep in thought, scrutinising the canvas:

Broken furniture, wrecked and burning cars, screaming flowers, broken and screaming rocks, broken trees, half bricks, screaming skies, empty waste-grounds, busy construction sites. . .

Ed found the work a little disturbing, but, being all too aware of Natasha's need for encouragement, said: 'I like it.'

'You like it?' Natasha looked at Ed as though he had let her down. People always let you down. 'You're not supposed to like it. You're supposed to find it disturbing. It's meant to be disturbing.'

Natasha grew angry. At Ed. At her picture. At herself. She felt incapable of getting her work to convey exactly what she wanted it to.

'I just can't do it. Why can't I do this?' she asked, flinging out her arms, gesturing around the room with them. 'Everything I need is here.'

Blu-tacked to the walls were her numerous studies and compositions: *Strange Buildings Unusual Shapes. Tall Buildings Giving Everyone The Finger. The Mad Scrabble City. The Relentless Grindstone.*

For inspiration, there was a postcard of Picasso's *Guernica* propped against a jar on her work table. She was trying to replicate the enormity and impact of that work in her own work and she could not do it.

Ed was about to reassure Natasha that her picture was indeed disturbing, and in the way that Picasso's picture was considered to be disturbing, and Natasha, for her part, was about to make yet another drastic change - she had her palette knife in her hand poised ready- when, with the knife barely touching the canvas, a train clattered noisily overhead, sending vibrations through the building and causing the lights to flicker.

Natasha flung down her palette knife.

'How the hell can I work here?' she shouted.

'It's all we can afford, Nat.'

'It's a fucking shit hole. Look at it! The light's crap. There's rats.'

Ed shrugged. 'It was either this place or a bedsit, Nat.'

'Fucking bedsit. I can't work in a bedsit. Are you crazy? It's bad enough here. Fucking trains clattering overhead, the fucking lights flicking on and off every five minutes.'

Another train clattered overhead and the lights flickered and went out.

When they came back on again, several seconds later, they were much brighter. Ed decided not to mention it.

Natasha held her brush up to the canvas, hesitated, hardened her resolve and reached back toward the canvas, only to be gripped by indecision again. Ed turned away, he walked over to where there were twenty or so finished canvases stacked four deep to face one wall. He lined several of them out along the wall before standing back to view them: *Sun Flowers. Laburnum Trees. Blossoming Acacia Branches. Yellow Cornfields. Yellow Suns.*

Ed couldn't understand Natasha's problem. As far as he was concerned, the solution was simple.

'I don't know why you don't just go ahead and have the exhibition,' he said. 'You could exhibit these. Look at them. You've got more than enough here. Why not? They're good, these are.'

Natasha didn't care for the suggestion. 'You just don't understand. Look, they're just pictures. They don't say anything. They just don't say what I want them to say.'

She had started off painting pictures of festivals, fairs, construction, regeneration. . . The Fairground of Life, she had called the collection. But her experiences had changed her, altering her perceptions. Life it seemed was increasingly being lived in a kind of shooting gallery. If it could be lived at all.

As far as Natasha was concerned all Ed was interested in was having an exhibition. The pictures were just money to Ed, a ticket out. But to Natasha they would be her way in. She had to get them right. Exactly right.

She insisted that Ed return the pictures to their original positions facing the wall. She didn't want to be reminded of them.

Ed did as he was told. He looked again at the picture she was working on.

'You know why I like it, Nat. It's this city, alright, but it's the city gone mad.'

Natasha however was still far from happy with it. First there had been her idea for the picture, and then there was the picture itself. And they were two different things. To Natasha, it was yet another proof of her shortcomings as an artist.

'It's no good,' she said, 'I'm going to have to do it all again.' And she reached behind her for her palette knife.

Ed stood for a moment in the doorway, watching Natasha scrape her picture in to non-existence. He knew then that she was never going to finish her work, that she would never have that exhibition. She was too afraid, he realised. Afraid that her work was not good enough.

Ed returned to his work, a little less certain of it. Less convinced.

Another picture ruined.

In a maddened rage, Sadie grabbed her canvas in both hands, wrenched it from the easel and sent it flying across the room.

The picture was box like and clumsy yet it flew gracefully, defying all the known laws of aerodynamics. Its four corners were like a vicious whirling star. Sadie knew, the moment she released it, that it was looking for something to destroy. The canvas skimmed a table, narrowly missing several jars of brushes, glanced a light shade and embedded itself in one of her finished works.

One thing goes wrong and then everything goes wrong. It is as though there is a law governing such things, that the world, whenever it is thrown out of balance, has somehow to reconfigure itself.

Sadie screamed. Unable to control her rage she began picking up canvases, hurling them about the room, smashing them against the walls, putting her fists through them. They were no good anyway, she decided.

There is a fascination with destruction once it has begun. It is like pulling out a lynch pin. Maybe it is nature's way of forcing us to abandon our mistakes and to start over again, right from the beginning.

The next picture, knowing that it's going to be the one, and then doing it, that is what keeps an artist going. All the artist's hopes and ideas can be transferred in to the new picture. Natasha finished scraping her failed canvas clean, picked up her palette, her paintbrush and began to paint:

Girders, breeze blocks, pillars, windows, doorways, doors, scaffold. . . a tsunami of component parts all jumbled up, kaleidoscope like, forever changing, with never a resolution.

She spent several hours immersed in the work.

But as the euphoria of the idea began to wear off, she became all too aware of the work's shortcomings. She grew increasingly uncertain of it. Her pace, fast until then, began to slow, she hesitated often. She stopped painting, stepped back from the easel and shook her head.

She'd had a firm idea of what she had wanted to achieve, but she had lost that idea somewhere in the execution.

Natasha felt that she was always on the edge of breaking through, but without ever doing so. Getting the picture to work, making it understood, that was the problem. Sometimes it depended on the tiniest change of detail, or it could be the very idea itself that was wrong.

It would take a lot more hard work and a great deal of artistry to pull this off now, she decided.

Over the next three hours, Natasha made several changes to her painting. But it soon began to feel overworked. Careful painting was bad painting, she knew. She could see the hard work in it. It appeared contrived.

She just wasn't sure what she was trying to say anymore. What she needed, she reckoned, was a title. A title would help tie everything together, directing her thoughts in to some kind of order.

She considered using, *This England*, but dismissed it as unsuitable. Far too all encompassing, it hardly helped to focus her ideas. What she wanted was something like *The Grapes of Wrath*. It was the title used by John Steinbeck for his novel about the great depression, the phrase taken from a line in the battle hymn of the American Republic:

> *Mine eyes hath seen the glory of the coming of the Lord:*
> *He is trampling out the vintage where the grapes of wrath are stored. . . .*

It was the perfect title, suggesting in those few words that there would be consequences. It was exactly the kind of title which Natasha needed. Something concise but with a larger meaning: a funnel in to which she could pour and concentrate her ideas, that would conjure up the essence, the message of her work and serve as an epigraph.

She decided that she would go to the library and look at all the titles of the books there. She would pick a book down from the shelf and there it would be, the succinct phrase, the all encompassing line from a poem or song that would serve as her theme.

Natasha was known at the library. They had once refused her application to join on the grounds that she did not have a home address. Now here she was searching through their shelves. Suspicious of her intentions they threw her out.

Natasha wandered the streets. Walking helped her to think. She needed to think. She was so deep in thought that she walked right past Ed.

Ed continued to work in the cafe. He payed the rent on the lock-up, he bought Natasha her canvases and paints. He even tried to find her a better studio.

The gallery was carpeted and brightly lit. Garishly coloured pictures hung off the walls. Weldon-Veal's face darkened when he saw Ed and he came right over, intending to throw him out.

Ed explained who he was and what he wanted.

'They're ready? You've brought them?'

'Not quite.' Ed explained what the problem was: 'She needs a better studio. I was wondering if you knew of anywhere, whether you could help?'

'But of course,' said Weldon Veal.

He gave Ed the address of an artists co-operative in Chelsea and of another in the docklands, assuring Ed that both had very good studio space and were reasonably priced.

The studio was in a fashionable warehouse conversion in Wapping not far from Tower Bridge. Huge picture windows filled the studio with light. With London. There was a view of the river, of the city in one direction and Canary Wharf in the other.

'It's like being outside,' said Ed, 'but with all the comforts of home.'

The studio was full of canvases. Canvas was the only description Ed could think to use to describe them.

There were light blue and dark blue canvases. Single dots on canvases. There were hundreds, and they were all signed, Enzo.

Enzo offered Ed a drink.

Whisky. Full to the top of the glass.

Ed's eyes lit up. 'Bit early though, isn't it?' It was 11am.

'Early? I've been up all night,' said Enzo. Ed knocked back his drink.

Enzo knocked back his drink, then he picked up a brush and he went and stood in front of a canvas. He was a little unsteady on his feet.

'You paint drunk?' asked Ed.

'Course I do, it helps fuck up the perspective.'

Enzo slapped a few daubs of paint on to the blank canvas, then he signed the canvas. The work took him longer to sign than it had to paint.

Ed told Enzo why he had come.

'Help Natasha? Me?' Enzo frowned. He seemed surprised. 'How? How can I possibly help?'

'By helping her to get a studio. Maybe let her use here. You two were good friends once, she told me. She's having a really hard time.'

'All the great artists went through hard times, it's what made them great, Ed. Struggle is everything. It's the prerequisite of great art. The longer Natasha remains undiscovered, and the harder that she has to try, then the more chances she'll have of developing as an artist.'

'You're telling me you won't help?'

'But I am helping, this is the best help I can give. Once you're discovered, Ed, once you get known for a thing then you have to keep on doing it. If you try something new your public will never forgive you. Look at what it's done to me.' And he made a sudden open armed gesture toward his finished work that flung a splash of red paint across a blank canvas. He didn't even hesitate, he signed the canvas.

Enzo stood, the tip of the brush pressing against his chin, and he stared thoughtfully at the signed canvas. 'You know, the ancient Chinese calligraphers they used to change their name, mid-career, that way they could start out as someone else.'

But Ed wasn't interested in Enzo's problems.

Ed tried Sadie, but with the same result. She did tell him one thing though. He was getting to hate these people.

There were times when Ed could handle being homeless because he was living in the Fields. The park, with its giant plane trees and shrubs, and the magnificent buildings that formed a quiet and welcome square about the Fields, took away some of the degradation. It was particularly beautiful at night: the illuminated buildings; the green and yellow and blue and red tents all glowing from within.

It was late in the evening, just after dusk, and Ed was seated on one of the park's benches, waiting for Natasha.

Someone was singing. It was a girl's voice, a magnificent voice. The voice soared up out of the Fields: 'One day I'll fly away. Like a bird from these prison walls. I'll fly. I'll fly away. I'll fly away, fly away. . . .'

Ed was like someone who had given up on waiting but who had nothing else to do. Ed was not even waiting anymore. He was just sitting there, alone. He knew that Natasha would not be back any time soon, that she would be working in her studio.

Ed looked glum. He sat, his forearms resting on his knees, his hands clasping a vodka bottle, staring at the ground, at nothing in particular, at himself perhaps. At this life.

Ed was trapped in a job he did not want, in a life he had come to hate. Natasha was never going to finish her pictures.

Poverty was a steady process of reduction. Gradually, it took everything away from you. It took your self esteem. It took away your dignity. Hope turned to despair. Anticipation became waiting. That emptiness had to be filled.

Ed cracked the top off the vodka bottle. He threw away the top and raised the bottle to his lips.

Laughter, drunken shouts and singing drifted across the Fields. There was a party going on in the bandstand.

'Fuck is she?' He wondered.

Ed drained the bottle. He threw the bottle in to the bushes. He reached beneath him and he pulled a six pack from beneath the bench. He pulled the tab on a can of Tennants.

Ed looked across the Fields, past the bandstand to where there was another group of drinkers by the old brick shed.

The old brick shed was the hangout of a hardcore group of drinkers. It was not a pleasant place and you did not go there for the company so much as for what you could get. There was always someone in the shed from whom you could cadge a drink, or at least a smoke. The people there could be passable company so long as they had a drink and provided they did not drink too much. Since there was little else to do in the Fields everyone drank too much.

It was how they passed the time.

'Fuck her,' said Ed, the anger building in him, and, climbing unsteadily to his feet he staggered off in the direction of the shed.

It was early in the morning and Natasha was just about to begin work when there was a loud hammering on the lock-up door. Someone tried the door. It was jammed. You had to lift it.

'Natasha!' It was a woman's voice. 'Are you in there? Natasha!' It was Sadie. Ed's visit had galvanised her in to action.

'Natasha! Open up. I know you're in there! I can see you. Let - me - in!' She kicked the door. 'I've brought flowers!' she shouted.

Quickly, Natasha threw a dust sheet over her easel, covering her work.

Natasha did not want Sadie to know what she was working on. But there were her studies scattered everywhere. And her compositions. The stacks of newspapers, the newspaper cuttings, even her artist materials were clues to another artist. Natasha rushed to the door, intending to intercept Sadie. Keep her outside.

The door lifted. It opened.

Sadie stepped in to the lock-up. It was poorly lit. It smelt of oil paint and linseed and turps. Sadie sniffed the air, her eyes narrowing as they searched the room.

The place was a mess. Flattened paint tubes were scattered across the floor. There was a table full of paint streaked pots that were stuffed full of brushes, tubes of squeezed paint, open sketch books. There were studies pinned to the walls. Compositions. Her eye was drawn toward the dust sheet covering the huge canvas on the easel.

'Natasha,' beamed Sadie, and, she opened her arms.

Natasha was forced to step in to them for a brief air hug. Sadie grimaced at the smell. She stepped out of the embrace and held out a bouquet of flowers.

Bright yellow daffodils.

'You're favourite colour. You could paint them. Here,' she said, stepping back, thrusting the bunch of flowers against Natasha's chest and then leaving them there. She stared around the studio, her attention drawn to the huge and concealed canvas which she then pretended to ignore. 'They'll need water.'

The river, thought Natasha, placing them for the moment on a nearby chair. The two girls stood staring at each other.

Natasha looked tired, worn down by work and from lack of sleep. There were dark circles beneath her eyes. Her face was pinched, the cheek bones prominent. Her lower lip was split and swollen and she had a large cold sore in one corner of her mouth.

Sadie was more like herself than ever. Her hair was redder, she was better dressed, bustier. She had put on weight. But her face had aged, it had become lined, and there was a tiredness there too, and anxiety in her eyes.

'So what are you doing back in London? You should have got in touch.'

'I did get in touch. I rang. I left messages. I came round, Sade.'

'Well here we are, together again.' Sadie flashed her a smile. 'So, what are you working on?'

'What do you want, Sade?'

'Nothing. I came to see you.'

Sadie began to prowl the studio. She picked a sketch book up off the table and she flicked through it. Put it down on a chair.

All the time she was working toward the easel. Natasha watched her, willing her to leave.

Sadie picked up a composition.

Strange Buildings Unusual Shapes. The buildings were distorted, as though they had passed in to another dimension. Sadie frowned at the work.

Then she made a move toward the easel.

Natasha stepped forward and blocked her way.

'What are you working on, Nat. Show me.'

'No. It's not finished yet.'

It was not good to show your work until it was finished. Before a work is finished it is incomplete. Some people cannot conceive of a things beauty or possibility unless they can have a thing in its fullness right there before them. They are usually the kind of person who to look at a thing must also pick it up. And having picked it up they always put it down in a different place. Everyone knows a person who will pick up a thing and play with it until they can find its fault. They are the sort of people who never give you any of the encouragement which you need in order to continue with your work. And some take advantage of that. You needed to protect yourself from such dangers and so you did not show your work to anyone.

'Go on, just a peek.'

'No!'

'Okay, Nat, okay. I was just curious.'

Sadie walked over to the canvases that were stacked along one wall. 'My, you have been busy.' She flipped back a canvas. She flipped back canvas after canvas: *The Relentless Grindstone, Exit: No Exit, Alien Environments, Tsunami Of Development. . .*

Sadie stared open mouthed at the works. Wherever she looked there was something new, something different. Ideas came flying out at her. She became gripped by a feeling of great urgency.

'Well, it was nice seeing you, Nat. And if ever you are in Wapping do come see. Bye. Got to go.'

Natasha closed the door on her. She bolted the door.

Sadie looked left and right for a taxi. Her head was whirling with ideas. They were like a disease she had. She began to walk faster, to run. 'TAXI!' she shouted in to the racing traffic.

Natasha returned to the Fields sometime later that morning. She went straight to the tent but Ed wasn't there. She crossed the Fields and, passing the bandstand and the old shed, she disappeared in to the bushes. There was a large shelter there, built of palettes and old doors. Natasha knocked on the construction.

An elderly man with long white hair, beard and moustache, and wearing John Lennon glasses, appeared in the entrance. He was holding a book that he'd been reading. Camus, *The Rebel*.

'What do you want?'

'Can I come in?'

Natasha crouched in to the bash. She left the door open. It smelt strongly in there of unwashed clothes and bedding, stale urine, and old books. All four walls were lined with books. There was just this gap for the door, another for a window. Books were a compulsion with Somerset, in the way that alcohol had once been.

Somerset sat down on a large bean bag. Natasha had to make do with sitting uncomfortably on an upturned metal bucket. She could have sat on any one of the numerous book stacks – there was, for example, a sturdy stack of encyclopaedias - but that would have been seen as a sacrilege by Somerset and she needed his help. She sat with her satchel rested on her lap, her fingers working at the buckles.

Natasha had brought Somerset a present, a sketch which she had made of him days before. She held it out to him. Somerset marvelled at the likeness. The wild hair, unkempt beard and moustache, creased face, the crazy staring eyes, magnified by the pebble lensed glasses.

'Good god! It's me alright, but it's me gone mad,' he said. He propped it up on a stack of books.

'Well?' he asked, 'what do you want? You want to borrow a book, is it?'

'Not exactly.' Natasha glanced around the shelves. 'It's just, I've been having trouble with my painting.'

Somerset began reaching down books. Books on Van Gogh, Picasso, Munch.

'Everything you need is in books,' said Somerset. 'Books....'

Natasha sighed, her spirits sank. She looked very tired of a sudden. Once Somerset began talking about books he could go on for hours.

Natasha took the books from Somerset, making a stack of them on the ground beside her. That made Somerset uneasy seeing his books abandoned and out of category like that. He started to twitch.

'It's not a book I want exactly, it's a title,' said Natasha, 'to help me with my work.' Natasha explained. Out it all came. Her offer of an exhibition, her idea for the bigger picture.

'I know what I want to paint, but I just can't do it. I started with landscapes. I thought I could make a record of the country through its landscapes. But a country is nothing without its people, so I set out to make a study of its people. A completely different picture began to emerge. The more I saw, and the more I learned, then the more I had to change it. Now I can't stop changing it. It's become – I don't know what it's become. It's confusing. I just don't know what I'm trying to do, what it is that I'm trying to say anymore There are just too many changes everywhere.'

It was driving Natasha mad. Lifting her hands to her head, she ran her fingers through her hair, pulling back her hair. What she needed was some kind of handle on the thing.

'The country is changing alright,' agreed Somerset. 'There's a whole new Britain out there for sure. Busier, wealthier, more modern. I read somewhere that we were making it a better world.' His laugh was sardonic. 'You know,' he said, eyes drifting to the distance, 'all my life things have got better. When I was born people didn't have televisions, they didn't even have fridges, let alone cars. Then, suddenly, we got televisions and fridges. We got cars. We got better cars. Every year things just got better and better. We had a national health service, pensions, unions, better pay.' Somerset who had fallen dreamily silent snapped out of his reverie: 'Now, though!' The shout made Natasha jump. 'Now,' Somerset fixed her with a hard stare, 'every day I get more and more disheartened. I'm afraid of the future now.'

Somerset shook his head and sighed. 'What a country it has become, and is becoming, a place where people shit in their pants about trifles, where every day there is some new law to contend with, yet another restriction, more restraints. The law abiding citizen has nothing to fear, they say, except to stay within the law. That citizen has become neurotic, nervous of the world in which he lives and liable to explode at any moment. And the pressure is building. New things have to be learned all the time when a year can see everything undone and the future uncertain again. When people are uncertain they can be easily led, they can be controlled, they become dependent on instruction. There are instructions everywhere. Signs everywhere. Every day there are new isolations to endure, more controls, more restraints, and it is happening everywhere. Wherever you look there are instructions written in to the landscape. You can hardly move for them. We have become afraid, afraid of people, and of life too. And in a world that is growing safer by the day: it is less wild, more controlled, more fully understood. But we are more timid still. We need more help, more gadgets, more protection, more laws. More of everything, in fact. Life would be too difficult otherwise.'

'It's become a much different world for sure,' said Natasha. 'But there is certainly more money about than ever before. You'd think that people would be happy with that.'

'Some people are very happy.'

'But are they, though, really? And are there more freedoms or less? You'd think there would be more, but I'm not sure. Maybe they're just different freedoms.'

'You're no one without money,' said Somerset, 'that's for sure. It's all down to money. And look what that's doing to the place. Offer a man enough money and he will poison his water and his land and the air that he breathes. He will destroy everything that he loves, and he will watch it as it disappears and he will call it progress, because it puts money in his pocket and fills his house with things. And we've let it happen. And for what? Everything is being taken from us. The powerful are rewriting the rules and dictating the law and making things just the way they want.'

'You're right,' said Natasha. 'People are scared. Everyone is scared of losing what they've got, of not getting what they want. I'm scared. It's like something is closing in on us. Wherever I look I find people trying to escape, and from every walk of life. But that's just making things worse. Everyone is out for what they can get. All this work, people think they are setting themselves free, when all they're really doing is creating everything they are trying to escape from.'

'You can't escape, Natasha. Every great book there is tells you that. And nor can you hope to buck the system. You can try, certainly, but look at what happens to you if you do, you only end up here.'

'Everyone talks about the system. We accept there is a system. It's a frightening thought. But there has to be a way out. There just has to. There have to be alternatives, or we'd go insane. It would be just too crazy otherwise.'

'It drives you mad alright. Look at what it did to me.'

'No, it's society that's gone insane,' said Natasha.

'Yes,' said Somerset, 'and you have to go insane along with it. You have to conform, Natasha, otherwise? Well, otherwise they will despise and reject you. They will lock you out. They will take away your chances.'

Natasha despaired. 'All I ever wanted was to be an artist, is that too much to ask? Now look at what has happened to me. I've ended up on the streets. How the hell did that happen? And my work, it has ended up as a, I dunno, a kind of Picasso's *Guernica*. Which can't be right, can it? And look at what's happened to Ed. All this is destroying him. He doesn't belong here. We should never have come here. And it's all been my fault.'

'Surely not,' said Somerset. Like most people Somerset thought that it was Ed, with his dead end job and his drinking that was the problem, not Natasha.

Ed woke with a start. He felt terrible. Hungover.

He was lying on the hard concrete floor of the brick shed. He had the eyes and face of someone who had not slept well, who had had far too much to drink the night before.

'You look like shite.' It was a woman's voice, not Natasha's.

Marie!

Ed sat bolt upright. He moved too quick. The walls of the shed moved with him, making him ill. He lay back down on the cold hard floor.

Marie. Gap toothed and with a shaven head. Earrings hanging from torn cauliflower ears. A broken nose. Broken in some fight. Broken teeth. Different fight. Pierced lip. Cold sores.

'You were an animal last night, a fucking animal, Ed.' Marie let Ed suffer, but only for a short while. 'Only joking,' she said. 'You couldn't manage it. Ha!' She laughed again, cackling.

Ed sat upright, this time propping himself against the wall. He felt terrible. He surveyed the floor. The floor was scattered with bottles and cans. Ed reached for one. Most of them would be empty, but there could be dregs in some.

Another body stirred. Marie kicked it. It groaned.

She picked up a bottle, reached forward and passed it to Ed. 'Here.'

Ed put it to his lips and took a swig. He pulled the bottle away and grimaced.

'A fucking bottle bank, Christ!' Full of all sorts of dregs. Ed took another, longer swig.

'I was hoping that you could help,' said Natasha.

'Help?' said Somerset. 'How?'

Natasha undid the buckles on her satchel. She took out the sketch book containing her compositions and another book containing some studies and she offered them to Somerset. The books had been burned, they had singed and blistered covers and the pages were yellowed. Some were brittle and had cracked. Somerset took the books.

He turned the pages slowly, each page more carefully, more slowly than the page before, his gaze alternating at times between the pages and the person that had created them. He sat gazing at each page for a long time.

Half an hour later Somerset put down the books. He removed his spectacles and he rubbed his eyes. He appeared exhausted, blowing air from his mouth in the manner of someone that was too tired, that had seen and felt too much.

'Well?' asked Natasha.

'It's powerful stuff.'

'It's what I've seen.'

'And you say that what you need is a title?'

'Yes, something to help hold it all together. Something that I can use to organise my ideas and give them meaning. As it is I can't make sense of anything.'

A good title held a work together. With a title everything else would follow. It would tell Natasha what she had to do.

Somerset looked to his books. 'Something from Shakespeare, I think. Almost everything there is can be found in Shakespeare.'

'I already thought of Shakespeare. *This England.* Only—'

'That's it!' cried Somerset, cutting Natasha short. *King Richard II, John of Gaunt, Act Two.* Perfect. Well done, Natasha. Well done.'

Natasha sighed. She blew air from her cheeks, inflating her cheeks.

This England. It seemed a good title, but it was a flawed title. England was changing. Things would not always be as the title might suggest they were. Everything changed, could change, and would change. That was the problem. Once things had changed the title would no longer be relevant. Her work would become obsolete, redundant. This England would become That England, it could be dismissed, either as history or as someone else's experience. And people were different, they lived different lives, inhabited different worlds. No, there were too many Englands for that to work.

Somerset reached down the book without even looking for it. He knew the exact location of all of his books. He had them indexed in to his consciousness in every way. He even opened the book on the correct page without having to search for it. He fixed Natasha with a hard stare to silence her objections. He

began to read:
'This royal throne of kings, this sceptered isle, This earth of majesty, this seat of Mars, This other Eden, demi-paradise, This fortress built by nature for herself. . . .'

Listening, Natasha grew impatient.

Oblivious to her increasing irritation Somerset continued reading. He became immersed in the flow and beauty and meaning of the words:

'This precious stone set in the silver sea, Which serves it in the office of a wall, Or as a moat defensive to a house, Against the envy of less happier lands, This blessed plot, this earth, this realm, this England. . . .'

Natasha expected Somerset to stop there but to her surprise he continued to read, and it was something that Natasha had not heard before, because people rarely quoted the speech in full. It would not have served their purpose otherwise.

'This land of such dear souls, this dear, dear land . . . . Is now leased out . . . . With inky blots and rotten parchment bonds: That England, that was wont to conquer others, Hath made a shameful conquest of itself.'

Somerset closed shut the book with a loud thump.

A shameful conquest.

There it was. In that moment, everything fell in to place. Everything made sense of a sudden. Natasha knew where she was coming from. She had her angle.

A few drinks were something to look forward to. Somehow they sped the day up. They erased days. It is not good to drink alone, perhaps, but it is better than not drinking. Drink insulated you from the world, you always faced things better when you'd had a drink. You always took the more cheerful view.

It was eleven o'clock Sunday morning and Ed was drunk.

He was stood on a bench and he was singing at the top of his voice: 'Why why why, Delilah? Wa wa wa wi wa wa wa wa. . . .' He paused to take a swig from a champagne bottle, finishing off with a loud: 'I can't take any morrrrrre!'

Natasha snatched the bottle from Ed.

Ed made a grab for it, missed, and fell sprawling on to the floor. Natasha upended the bottle and she poured its contents out on to the ground.

'Just look at you, Ed. You are blind drunk. How do you ever expect to get out of here if you spend all our money on drink. You're a fucking waster, Ed.'

There were maybe ten people stood around and they were all of them drinking. They laughed at Natasha, they told her to fuck off.

Ed pulled himself to his feet. He rolled on to his side and he stood upright, staggering. 'Waster? Me? I never wanted nothing in the first place.' He raised his arms in triumph. 'I'M A ROARING SUCCESS! HA!' Ed laughed. His audience of drunks laughed, they applauded Ed. Ed began to sing: 'Down down, deeper and down. . . .' He burst out laughing again. It was the kind that should have ended in tears. Ed laughed and laughed.

A sash window from a building across the street rattled open. Someone yelled: 'SHUT THE FUCK UP! TOSSER!'

Ed gave the man the vees.

The window slammed shut.

'Wanker!' shouted Ed.

'Stoppit, Ed, stoppit! You're making a fool of yourself. You're making a fool of me. Well I've had enough of your antics.'

Natasha turned and headed off to their tent. Ed staggered after her. He hadn't finished with her yet.

'So where were you, last night? You didn't come home?'

'You call this place home? Jesus, Ed, you are such a fucking loser. Just look at the place, it stinks. Just look at you.'

'Fuck this,' said Ed.

Ed grabbed his pack. He began stuffing in his clothes, shirts, socks, trousers, his sleeping bag.

Natasha turned pale, she looked frightened. 'Ed, what are you doing? What's happened? What's wrong, Ed? Tell me. Stop, stop it Ed, you're frightening me.'

Ed had had enough.

Maybe there is no such thing as freedom, not absolute freedom, but there can be freedom from something. Freedom from tyranny. Freedom from work. Freedom from Natasha. From all this.

'You don't need me, Nat. You never did. You fucking lied to me.'

'Lied, to you? About what?'

'About you. About everything.'

'Me? I never told you anything about me.'

'No, you didn't.' Ed stopped packing. He stared at Natasha.

'I saw Sadie. She told me all about you. Fucking plain Smith, my arse.'

'I can explain, Ed.'

'You lied, Nat.'

'No!'

'You fucking lied. You made me get a shite fucken job that I fucken hate in a place . . . Christ, you had us living in the fucking Bullring, fucksakes. Fucking Bullring. And all the time we could have got out of there anytime you wanted. You could have had money anytime you wanted. You still can. But you don't! You make me work for it! Christ! What the fuck are you playing at? Well I'm not doing it anymore. Fuck you. You are on your own from now on.'

Ed resumed his packing.

'Ed, no. Stop it! You don't understand. Anyone can have money, it's not an achievement. You can be born rich, I was. But not everyone can be a painter. You can't be a painter if you can't paint, can you? Do you think my parents would have helped? They wouldn't help. You don't know them, Ed, what they're like. They cut me off. And yes, of course I want money, who doesn't, but I want it on my terms. And I can. I have that chance. Do you understand? Some things you just have to do for yourself or else they mean nothing, and that means that you mean nothing. I don't want to be Natasha Plane-Smith. I want to be me, Natasha, and not just any Natasha, but *the* Natasha. I want my own life. Do you understand that? Being an artist is my only chance to break free.'

But Ed didn't want to understand, he was too hurt, too angry to even try. Just as he was too tired, too disillusioned, too drunk to leave. Where would he go? There was nowhere.

Ed pushed aside his pack.

'I knew you'd understand, Ed. Ed?'

'You used me, Nat. Well I am sick and tired of being messed around. Go on, fuck off. This is my tent, I bought it, with my money. That I earned. Me. Well? Go on, what are you waiting for? Fuck off, I've had it with you. It's over!'

Natasha's resolve strengthened. She had grown sick and tired of Ed, of listening to what he would do when he never did anything. Well fuck him. She didn't need him. She didn't need anyone. She had her painting. It was all that she did need.

'Christ, Ed, you are so pathetic sometimes. You were no one when I met you, you had nothing then and you've got even less now, if that's possible. Just look at you, at what you've become. Are you going to live like this all your life? Tell me that you haven't settled for this. Go on, tell me. You can't. You're nothing Ed, no one, and you never will be, because you'll never have anything, you'll end up with nothing you will, you'll be all alone. Is that what you want? Is it?'

Natasha grabbed her things, her clothes, her sleeping bag and pillow, stuffed them in her pack and left the tent. It was like a burden had been lifted from her shoulders.

You can get caught up in other people's lives. They want this from you, then that. Eventually, they clog your life with their own, then neither of you are happy. How can you do anything under such scrutiny? Really, you can't. You daren't do a thing sometimes. There's always someone you'll upset. It has you screaming in frustration. You can see why people break their ties with other people. They think that they are setting themselves free. Maybe it's the only freedom left.

Ed lay in his tent, drinking. He remained lying there, drinking all that day, and the next. He saw no point in getting up, certainly not to go to work, he saw little purpose in it anymore. There didn't seem to be much point to anything. He felt empty and alone.

But the drunk is rarely alone. He converses, he shouts, he sings. Whenever he has a drink the drunk is in company.

Ed reached for a fresh can, but all the cans were empty. He would have to go out and get more cans.

Alcohol preserves the living and the dead.

34

The Bigger Picture:
A Shameful Conquest

Now that Natash knew how to approach her subject she threw herself in to the work. She worked feverishly. Time passed quickly when she worked. She grew cold and hungry, without knowing that she was cold or hungry. She ate little, she had no time to eat, and nor did she wash nor change her clothes, not for days at a time. She often slept in her clothes. She slept only when she was too tired to work, flinging herself down exhausted on to her makeshift bed on the floor. But the moment she awoke she went straight back to her painting. Dark whorls, like bruises, appeared beneath her eyes. She looked exhausted, yet she did not feel exhausted. She was exhilarated. Her work was easy now. There was no longer any hesitation. Things finally had begun to fall in to place with the result that picture after picture were committed to canvas. No sooner did she finish one canvas than she started on another. She created thirty canvases in just over four weeks, almost one every day:
Strange Buildings Unusual Shapes. Tall Buildings Giving Everyone the Finger. Alien Landscapes. Tsunamis of Development. The Last Day of the Sales. Here Comes Everyone. The Mad Scrabble City Speeds and Roars. . . .

She was now ready to start work on her great centrepiece. At 20' long and 12' tall the canvas was vast, just a little too tall by several inches to fit vertically beneath the rafters. Natasha had to stand it on the ground, propped at a slight angle against the wall. It was a huge blank space yet she doubted that it was big enough. She had so much to fit in to it, so much to compress. And then there were all those numerous other puzzles to be solved: problems of angle, problems of perspective, problems of context, of juxtaposition, of colour and line.

Natasha threw brushes, she kicked easels, tables, chairs.

She climbed ladders, walked planks, balanced, stretched. She painted in blacks and whites and shades of grey.

Then, getting deeper in to the work, she let rip, and all order and symmetry collapsed.

It was early in the morning, just before dawn. Natasha loaded her brush with dark colour. She lifted the brush to the painting, holding it poised over the canvas. She stood like that for some time. There was nothing more that could be added. The picture was finished.

Natasha stepped back and she stood staring at the finished work, completely dwarfed by the enormity of her vision:

Darkness. Light. Colliding worlds, waste grounds and construction sites, everything twisted, distorted, as though forced in to another dimension. And all life lived on that precarious edge.

She had finally succeeded in giving form to those ideas that she had for so long wished to express but had not known how to. She was presenting a picture of the world that was radically different to that shared by most people. She was offering up an analysis, yet it was one that the observer could never quite grasp, there was always some new interpretation, some new possibility there.

Her work was exactly as she had imagined it. Now everyone would see what she could see, everyone would know.

Tired but exhilarated, she left the studio.

It was raining outside, a fine drizzle. The rain was cold and refreshing. Natasha lifted her face to the cleansing rain. Let it wash it all away. All those years spent trying. They were over at last.

'Mind the step,' warned Natasha.

Weldon-Veal, bending low and mindful of the shin-high wooden threshold, followed Natasha in to the lock-up where, standing upright, he stopped dead.

'Good God!' he said.

The space was full of huge canvases. Completely surrounded by them it was like he had stepped in to one vast picture.

Weldon-Veal gasped. One work, a mural, the centre-piece of the collection, took up an entire wall. He had not expected this. How could anyone have painted this? He had never seen anything like it before:

Screaming skies, broken and screaming rocks, broken factories, wastegrounds, construction sites. ...

'This is where worlds collide and are torn apart,' explained Natasha.

Weldon-Veal shot her a sideways glance. He approached the mural.

The work was executed in stark black and white with muted greys, a colour scheme it shared with most of the other works.

The dealer gazed from picture to picture, there were pictures everywhere: *Strange Buildings Unusual Shapes. Tall Buildings Giving Everyone the Finger. Tsunamis of Development. The Relentless Grindstone. The Last Day of the Sales. Here Comes Everyone. The Mad Scrabble City Speeds and Roars.* ...

Taken separately, the pictures seemed to him to be fragments of something. Weldon-Veal stared opened mouthed at the collection, he was transfixed.

Natasha, almost tiptoe in anticipation, couldn't bear it a moment longer.

'Well?' she asked.

Weldon-Veal stood shaking his head. The collection was a masterpiece. Certainly, it was highly accomplished. Yet the pictures disturbed Weldon-Veal. They were too big, too dark, too — dystopian. He actually felt threatened by them. They threw his whole world in to question. Natasha had reached deep in to the modern nightmare: chaotic, terrifying, alienating. And there seemed no way out.

'Natasha, what have you done? Whatever were you thinking of? I can't accept these. This, it's not what I expected. It's far too dark and dystopian. I couldn't possibly exhibit this.' The dealer swivelled around, his eyes darting from picture to picture, searching. 'Where are all those other works? The ones I saw you drawing on the pavements?'

Natasha felt sick to the pit of her stomach.

And Weldon-Veal had other reasons to dislike her work.

'They are hardly original, are they?' he said.

Natasha threw her hands up to her head and she began pulling back her hair, exposing her forehead. 'What are you telling me? ' she screamed at him.

Weldon-Veal pointed to the vast mural and he correctly identified its influence. 'Picasso,' he said, 'Just like his *Guernica*. And that one, it's reminiscent of his *Charnel House*. But we have had Picasso, Natasha.' He pointed to another picture: *Yet Another Fucking Monday: the Treadmill of Work*. 'Van Gogh,' he said. He went from picture to picture and he identified the influence behind each one. 'Munch,' he said, 'And there, Kirchner, and that one, Bosch. And there, Bruegel.'

'There is even a Sadie Sommers. Her *Opulent Interiors*.'

'What?' Natasha felt numb.

Weldon-Veal wanted only cheerful pictures, bright pictures, pictures that would sell. He wasn't interested in the bigger picture. That was much too stark and disturbing.

'Go back to your easel,' he told Natasha, 'take your ideas and remould them. And be original,' he advised her, 'but above everything be cheerful.'

Success was difficult. Unless you possessed exceptional talent and were very lucky then success was a door that would remain barred to you. You might have most things necessary for success but you would not be successful unless you had them all. An artist has sometimes to create a considerable amount of work before they can become successful. Often, it is the best that they will ever produce. Everything that they know and are capable of has gone in to that work. A few burn out and many of them end up with nothing. The opportunity to profit from their talent can be very short. There is always some other artist somewhere producing the next new thing.

Natasha flung herself at a canvas. She punched the canvas. She tore it off its stand. She picked up canvas after canvas and she flung them across the room. She kicked a hole in a canvas. Then she was ripping the pages from her sketch books, balling them, tearing them apart. Finally, exhausted, her anger spent, she flung herself to the floor where she sat in a heap crying.

She could not start over again. Her work was finished. Finishing her work had separated her from it, putting her outside of it. She did not have the energy nor the ideas to begin again. Natasha was all used up, her ideas finished. She had run her course. Because when the work is done, the artist is done too, something dies inside.

Natasha wept. She wept because overwork had made her weak and because there was comfort in tears. She wept because she was weary, because she was sad and disappointed and full of bitterness. Her whole life had been a preparation for this one single moment which, when it came, had only disappointed her. What had she to hope for now? It was all too much for her to bear.

'I tried, I did, I really tried,' she wept. She wept and wept.

Natasha had educated herself, studying all the great masters, immersing herself in the works of Bruegel and Bosch and Van Gogh, experimenting with their styles, their palettes. She had then adapted her work, incorporating everything she could learn from the likes of Sickert and Degas and Picasso. There were also traces of despair and isolation, the despair and isolation of Edvard Munch and Ernst Kirchner in Natasha's work.

Yet for every Picasso and Bruegel and Van Gogh, there were all those that could not be Picasso nor Bruegel nor Van Gogh, and nor were they Sickert, nor Degas, nor Cèzanne. They had failed, as they would always fail, because there already was Picasso and Bruegel and Van Gogh. Everything had been done. You could not, it seemed, even surpass yourself. You could only be different.

Natasha felt sick, physically sick. She didn't know what to do. She just did not know what to do. She could not think straight. She could no longer imagine any kind of future for herself.

She felt isolated and empty and alone.

Ed. He would know what to do.

You needed someone. A friend. The world would be too empty otherwise.

'What did he say exactly? What?'

'He said he couldn't possibly have an exhibition because he couldn't sell them. He could only sell a few. He didn't like them, he said,' Natasha sniffled. 'He said they were too dystopian, too unsettling. But they have to be, they have to, otherwise what would be the point? Then he attacked me for my influences. He told me that I was wasting my talent. Oh, Ed, all that work, all that time wasted. Everything I've done, that we've done, it was all for nothing. I am such a fucking idiot!'

Natasha sat on the floor in the lock-up hugging her knees her head rested on them, and she cried and cried. Her sobs racked her body.

Ed put an arm around Natasha. He held her as she cried. He held her tight.

'It's not wasted, Nat.'

'Yes it is. There's no point to anything anymore. I've got nothing, Ed, nothing. Fuck all!' Natasha cried. 'There was so much I wanted, that I was going to do,' she sobbed.

Ed held her tighter. 'Yes, and you went and did them,' he said. He wiped a tear off Natasha's cheek. 'And you know what the most incredible thing that you did was?'

'What?' Natasha looked up.

'Those paintings.'

'They're finished, Ed. I'm finished.' Natasha burst in to tears again.

'You're not finished, Nat. Those paintings are finished, yes, but you've only just begun.'

Natasha untangled herself from Ed. He pushed him away from her.

'No, Ed, no. I can't paint another thing. I just can't.'

'You don't have to. You already have. So what if Weldon Veal doesn't like your work. There are other dealers, aren't there? There are hundreds of other galleries.'

There was the flicker of a smile across Natasha's face.

'Nat, I want you to go to the post office on Kingsway and get hold of a yellow pages. Here,' he gave Natasha a notebook. 'Make a list of all the Art Galleries that you can find. I'll meet you there in say, half an hour.'

'What are you going to do, Ed?'

'I'm going to get us a camera. We'll take pictures of your work. We'll make a portfolio to show around the galleries.'

London was teeming with galleries. There were hundreds of them, with new ones opening all the time.

Art Firsts, Art Futures, Art Investments, Art Now, Art To Go, Expensive Art, Forward Art, Galleria, Intangible Tangibles, Massive Art Attack, The Portentous Gallery, Tomorrows Art Today. . . .

There were so many that rather than copy them all down Natasha ended up tearing the pages out of the directory.

Ed stole several disposable cameras and a large *I-Love-London* photograph album from a Tourist shop in Trafalgar square.

'You stole them?'

'From a nick-nack shop, yes. Did you make that list of galleries I asked you to?'

'No, there were too many. I tore out the pages instead.' Natasha handed them to Ed.

Ed grinned. 'One of these is bound to be interested in your work,' he said. They tidied up the studio, lifting the pictures off the floor from where Natasha had flung them, propping them back up against the walls. Ed sent Natasha out to get some duct tape and he used it repair the torn canvases. No one would notice from the photographs that they had been repaired.

'I'm really sorry, Ed. For what I said about you. Before. I didn't mean. I – It's just. . . .'

'Yeah. Me too.'

First they had to get the photographs developed. Natasha then spent a whole day arranging them in to her album. She took great pains over this. She had insisted on three copies of each photograph. One set she kept as security. Another, which she had enlarged, she put on each page of the album. The last set she taped together in one long strip with the mural at its centre to create the bigger picture. It gave her immense pleasure and satisfaction to see her idea in all its fullness in this way.

They targeted all those galleries of repute first.

The pictures aroused a great deal of interest. Everyone wanted to know what the pictures meant.

One after another, Natasha explained her pictures and the ideas behind them. She was bright, bubbly, enthusiastic.

'You see why the title is important? You understand why they have to be shown together in this way?'

The manager of Galleria nodded. 'These are not just big pictures, this is the bigger picture,' she said.

'Exactly.'

Natasha beamed. Finally, here was someone that understood. 'So you'll exhibit them?'

The manager smiled sympathetically. 'The whole thing is far too big. Maybe just one or two. The more saleable pictures. The yellow ones?'

Galleria was exhibiting Damien Hirst's work. Art a Go Go was exhibiting Tracy Emin's work. Massive Art Attack was exhibiting Grayson Perry's work. White Cube were exhibiting the Chapman brothers. The Portentous Gallery were exhibiting Enzo. Art To Go were exhibiting Sadie Sommers. They didn't want Natasha's work.

Ed lay spread-eagled on the ground in Green Park. Natasha was sat on the grass beside him. She was plucking at the grass, pulling it up, one blade at a time then throwing it away.

Ed sat upright, took off his boots and socks and began to caress his sore feet.

'I'm getting a blister,' he said, 'look.' There was a fierce red swelling on the pad of Ed's foot.

Natasha picked up her portfolio. She began turning the pages of her portfolio, slowly back and forth. She sat with her head bowed. She slammed shut the portfolio and she threw it away from her. 'It's no good,' she said, 'It's hopeless, Ed, fucking hopeless.'

Ed reached over and he retrieved the portfolio. 'I don't understand it,' he said, flipping through the pages. 'You tell them about your idea, they look interested, and then they turn you down. Why?'

Natasha's face darkened. 'Well how the fuck should I know? I don't know.'

'We've just been throwing ourselves at galleries. We need to be more methodical. We need to find a gallery that exhibits your kind of work.'

'I haven't seen anywhere like that,' said Natasha.

Time and again Natasha had her work rejected. It became hard to go on. Ed urged her on. Encouraging her. Reassuring her. But wherever she went she met with the same response. Everyone who saw the work acknowledged that it had impact. But they rejected it nonetheless. Natasha knew that her work was good. But it meant nothing to her if she could not get her work accepted.

'What do these people know anyway?' said Ed. 'They're not artists, they're just fucking shopkeepers is all. All they're interested in is the sale. This art world, it's a con.'

'That's it, Ed. We've tried every gallery.'

Natasha held up the stained and folded sheaf of yellow pages. She flung away the pages.

'Don't think that we're giving up just because we've run out of places to try,' Ed told her.

'Face up to it, Ed, it just isn't going to happen for me.'

'Yes it will,' Ed reassured her, 'but only if you keep trying. It won't happen if you give up. Look, none of the great artist's had it easy, did they? not to begin with. They became great precisely because they didn't give up. Look at Van Gogh, no one liked his work to start with. It was too original. He was pushing at the boundaries, like you are now. Didn't you tell me yourself that he sold just one painting in his lifetime, one.'

'Well thank you for reminding me, Ed.'

'Yes, and now his pictures are some of the most sought after and expensive in the world. And the Impressionists, they were all rejected at first. But they ended up turning the art world completely on its head. They didn't give up, they persisted, and just look at them now.'

'They're all dead.'

'You know what I mean, Nat. Their struggles were the makings of them.'

'Yes.' Natasha laughed. She began to cough. Each cough giving her a sharp thumping headache. She could not stop coughing. She could barely breathe.

'I'll be alright,' she said, pulling her scarf up over her face. 'It's just this cold air is all.'

'We are not giving up, we haven't even begun yet.' Ed reached in to his back pocket and he pulled out a copy of *Scene*. He turned to the relevant page and, grinning, he handed the paper to Natasha. 'There you go, read that.'

Wealthy investors have developed an insatiable appetite for new art. Billionaire hedge fund operators, City professionals looking to spend their bonus, corporate bosses wishing to impress new and important clients, and professional collectors and dealers keen to cash in on this new interest in contemporary art are scouring the art schools and makeshift galleries of the capital, some of them set up by the artists themselves in empty hairdressing salons, abandoned shops, old yards and warehouses. . . .

'We can have our own exhibition,' said Ed. 'Well, what have we got to lose?'

'Nothing,' said Natasha.

'That's the spirit,' said Ed.

Crippled animals drag themselves on. Successful athletes think the movement through then perform it perfectly. Maybe nothing more than curiosity draws the mudskipper, a small fish, out of the water and on to land. The mind sees the object and it constructs the solution. Maybe anything is possible.

35

Jigsaw's Satori

On the 22nd of the month, at 1pm, NASDAQ released AndyBrand for trading. By the time trading closed AndyBrand had become the most actively traded stock in the US with more than 10 million shares changing hands. It closed at $25 per share, up 500% on the day, making it the largest percentage gainer on any stock exchange in the world. Jigsaw's share of stock had risen in value by $120m.

Money from nowhere.

A party, poolside.

Clear blue sky, no wind, hot sun. It was another great day in paradise.

TOPDOG, A1MINE, SOLESS4, GELDT7, SEENA D... the cars left the city and tore up in to the hills. Porsches, Bugattis, Ferraris, chauffeur driven limos, a Rolls. They came racing up the long curving drive toward the house.

A marquee had been erected in front of the house. Inside were numerous tables heaped with food and drink. People were stood around laughing, congratulating each other, slapping each other on the back and shaking hands. A party was being held to celebrate the successful launch of AndyBrand and everyone was dressed in the same black T-shirt, faded jeans, scuffed boots and AndyBrand shades. All the major AndyBrand shareholders and those associated with the company and with its launch had been invited.

Jigsaw was stood, drink in hand, amongst the cars, welcoming his guests and looking like a man who had just conquered the world. 120 million dollars worth of it.

Seena Dollar arrived in her BMW, registration, *SEENA D*. She looked very fetching in her pair of figure hugging jeans and a tight AndyBrand T-shirt straining under the twin pressures of her conical breasts.

Jigsaw beamed at the sight of her. 'Seena, hi! You look like a million dollars.'

'That's what I'm wearing,' she laughed. Everyone was laughing.

Champagne corks popped, there was the clink of glasses, of toasts being made.

Seena and Jigsaw air kissed. Seena apologised for being late. 'Getting out of the city is becoming impossible,' she said.

'It sure is crazy down there,' said Jigsaw.

Brownstein, Soless' lawyer, arrived in a bronze Jensen. Dick Fault and his wife pulled up in a stretch limo. The Bilderbergs arrived in a limousine with tinted windows.

Jigsaw smiled. For the first time in his life he felt truly safe. He had created something big and the people that mattered had bought in to it, wedding his well-being to their own. No one could take any of this from him now. He had locked himself in to the system. Because it wasn't just Andy Rant plc and AndyBrand that he was celebrating. Jigsaw had shares in WorldCorp, and they were earning him money. He had shares in Enron, in Halliburton, in Unilever, Beecham-Klein. . . . From now on, whenever anyone pushed ahead, that would push him ahead too.

Sir Leonard Choice, the multibillionaire head of the retail chain Mor4u, arrived in a chauffeur driven Rolls.

'This sure is some place,' he told Jigsaw, shaking him firmly by the hand. Everyone when they arrived stood marvelling at the house – a classical roman villa, complete with red tiled roof and arched collonade – and at the gardens and the well tended lawns, at the blue wonder of the infinity pool. They inhaled the clean air, with its heady scent of flowers, wandered through the gardens amongst fruit and blossom trees, phoenix and fan palms, cypress trees, olive trees. They stood gathered around the infinity pool, staring across it, searching the view, looking for LA., hidden now beneath its yellow stain of smog.

The two matt black Buggati Veryons, registrations *MIDAS3* and *ANDY2*, attracted a lot of attention too. Everyone wanted to know how much the cars cost.

'$1.4 million,' said Jigsaw.

The rich spend an awful lot of money on otherwise ordinary things in an attempt to make them extraordinary. They assume that any ordinariness in them will be elevated too. It was yet another way they had of distinguishing themselves.

Jigsaw offered Sir Leonard, Seena and Dick Fault and his wife a tour of the house. There were several statues by PK, numerous Enzos and a small Picasso that he wanted them to see.

My PK. My Enzo. My Picasso. Jigsaw introduced the works as though he had created them himself. My Dali. My Pollock. . . You can be a graceless fucker and still benefit from all the graces.

Everyone was impressed with the works. They were impressed with Jigsaw.

'You work hard and you get the rewards,' said Art Soless, chugging on a cigar.

A twin engined Bell Jet helicopter clattered overhead. It drew everyone out of the house.

The helicopter made a circle of the property before landing on one of the lawns.

Al Geldt, billionaire businessman and media tycoon, stepped out. He was accompanied by a young dark haired woman.

'This sure is some place,' he said, shaking Jigsaw's hand. 'So where is he, Andy?' Geldt stared around.

'I thought he was here,' said Sir Leonard. Everyone laughed.

'There he is, with Senator Doe,' said Soless. 'Andy!' he shouted, waving Andy over.

But it wasn't Andy, it was Brad Hollows the actor, the Andy look-alike from the AndyBrand adverts.

More cars arrived, bringing more guests.

Stephen Miloff, the industrialist, arrived in a dark windowed limo. His factories made most of the AndyBrand products.

'Which one of these people is Andy?' he asked. 'I want to shake that man's hand.'

Laughing, everyone checked everyone else out again.

Champagne bottles popped. Glasses chinked.

'Did you see him on the news the other week? Hey, what a stunt. That sign thing. Brilliant, brilliant. I wonder what he will come up with next?'

Andy was in the house, in his bedroom. He was sat on his bed, cleaning a hunting rifle. Jigsaw had bought it in Walmart, intending to use it to hunt quail.

Andy slid forward the bolt. He heard it click. He locked the bolt. The rifle felt good against his shoulder, like it belonged there. He eased it out of the window. He scanned the gathering through the telescopic sights. Everything was blurred. Andy adjusted the sights. There were crosshairs.
Andy centred them on Jigsaw.

Jigsaw was laughing, holding a drink in one hand, a cigar in the other. He was talking to Art Soless. Art Soless in his white hat. Art Soless in his white jacket over his black Andy Brand T shirt. Andy centred the cross hairs on Soless. On his white cowboy hat, his fat temple, his big fat grinning mouth. Andy surveyed the gathering through the scope. He centred the crosshairs on Dick Fault, the financier.

His finger tightened on the trigger. He pulled the trigger. There was a loud, click!

Andy lowered the rifle. He picked up a bullet, pulled back the bolt, placed it in the breech, slammed shut the breech and slid forward the bolt. He pulled back the bolt and ejected the cartridge. He loved to see the cartridge leap in to the air like that. He liked the noises which the rifle made. The clicks, the heavy clunks. Metal clunk, metal click.

Andy picked up the cartridge, pulled back the bolt, placed it in the breech and slammed shut the breech. He returned to the window. He leant the stock on the windowsill, took a deep breath and held it. His heart beat fast. He could feel the pressure of it in his throat.

A bead of perspiration rolled down off his forehead and in to his eye. It stung his eye. Andy wiped his eye.

Fuck comedy. What was needed was a massacre, a series of shattering attacks on the owners, their property and institutions. Those bastards had to be stopped. They needed to learn that there were consequences.

Andy curled his finger around the trigger.

All he had to do was to squeeze the trigger. Just curl his finger and then squeeze. It was such a simple thing to do. Andy squeezed the trigger, increasing the pressure on it until he felt it resist his efforts. Of course it took much more than that.

'Pitchoo!' he said.

'Mmmm' this salmon is good,' said Soless.

'Try the crayfish. It's delicious,' said Al Geldt

'Any more pheasant?' asked Ed Pilk. He was stood talking with the architect, Gilyotorerk Eesher. The men were old friends, from their millionaire days. The men, now multi-millionaires, shared a passion for sailing, currency trading and property and art. Ed Pilk owned works by Paul Kelpe, Kandinsky, Mondrian and Eliasson. He was the largest collector of Paul Kelpe in the world. 'I sometimes think that Kelbe actually works for me,' he said.

'Kate here is an art advisor,' said Al Geldt and he introduced his companion, Kate Rungle, to the men.

'I used to advise Mister Gold,' said Kate Rungle.

'The Sam Gold? Pyramid Gold?, the financier?' asked Ed Pilk.

Kate Rungle nodded. 'Now I advise Mister Geldt.'

'Maybe you'd like you to see my art collection,' said Jigsaw. Everyone followed him in to the house.

They stood looking at the Enzo, *Light Blue and Dark Blue*, from his sea and sky collection.

'How much did you pay for it?' asked Kate Rungle. It was the question on everybodies lips.

'Half a million. Sterling.'

There were low whistles, knowledgeable and appreciative nods.

'I should insure it for two,' said Kate Rungle. Jigsaw smiled.

'I'm after a painting,' said Dick Fault, 'for the boardroom at Lemmon Brothers'

'You should be looking at contemporary art, Mister Fault,' Kate Rungle told him. 'You seem the kind of person who would appreciate it.'

'So long as 'it' appreciates,' laughed Dick Fault.

'It does,' said Kate Rungle. 'There are exciting new opportunities in contemporary art.'

'Kate here has been telling me about a collection coming up for exhibition in London soon,' said Al Geldt.

'The subject is the city,' said Kate Rungle. 'The works are magnificent, the canvases vast. The artist a relatively young unknown.'

'She is going to be big though, right?' Geldt looked to Kate for confirmation.

'This time next year she will be worth twice, three times more than what you can get her for now,' said Kate Rungle. 'The interest in her will guarantee that.'

'You'll have to give me her name,' said Jigsaw. Dick Fault agreed.

'Now now, gentlemen,' said Al Geldt, 'she's our discovery.'

Taking one last look at the Enzo they made their way back in to the garden where Stephen Milloff was showing off to a young blonde advertising executive who had just confessed an interest in mountaineering.

'I own a mountain,' he was telling her, 'Well, not a mountain exactly, a ski resort. But there are mountains in it. You should come take a look sometime.'

Andy emerged from the house.

Everyone turned, everyone applauded, they stood aside to form an avenue for him to pass down, slapping him on the back, grabbing him by the hand. Everyone wanting to shake him by the hand.

Andy took it as he always did, like someone walking through bad weather.

He hurried in to the marquee where Brad Hollows was stood chatting up

Linda Farrs, the beautiful platinum blonde advertising executive who had orchestrated the highly successful AndyBrand advertising campaign.

'So, who have I got off with?' he asked Brad.

'He's some act, isn't he,' said Soless. 'That reminds me, James, Bringmeen wants Andy at a bash he's giving at his place in Beverly Hills end of next month. He's putting on something special. He want's the Saxifrage there too.'

'Bringmeen? Max Bringmeen? The Max Bringmeen, the multibillionaire?'

'The very same,' said Soless.

A pink Porsche Boxter, open top, registration *462236*, arrived. The actress, Candice, 46, 22, 36, stepped out. Everyone stared.

She was the girl in the AndyBrand adverts.

The day grew hotter.

People lazed around the infinity pool. They lay stretched out in the sun on the numerous sun loungers; the three Mexican maids – Carmen, Miranda, Consuella - hurrying to and fro, fetching everyone drinks.

The sound of the cicadas was deafening.

Sir Leonard talked to Dick Fault about retail. Dick Fault talked about finance. Ed Pilk, the plastics tycoon, told whoever would listen about plastics. 'Plastic is the future,' he said. 'There'll be plastic money even, and when the oil runs out we will make plastic out of plants.'

Senator Doe talked politics.

Seena talked about happiness and contentment.

Brownstein went about telling anyone that would listen about tax breaks.

Their affairs and their concerns were the things of importance. What they were doing was clearly more important than what anyone else was doing.

'Word is,' said Dick Fault, 'Max Bringmeen is creating the world's biggest buyout fund. 50 billion dollars. Every company will be a target.'

Jigsaw stood alone at the edge of the infinity pool, staring out at the view. Clearings were being made in the scrub and platforms cut in to the hillside to provide yet more building space. Everywhere he looked the hillsides were filling up with new building.

'Here comes everyone,' he said.

Jigsaw lifted his glass to take a drink. But the champagne had gone warm. He tossed it over the precipice.

'Earth to James,' said a voice.

Jigsaw turned. 'Oh, hi, Seena,' he said. He returned his gaze back down the valley.

'Some view, uh?' said Seena.

Jigsaw nodded. 'They say that on bad day you can see LA.'

Seena laughed. 'Come and have a drink,' she said.

Jigsaw rejoined his guests.

Dick Fault was saying: 'Theirs? It's us that finances everything. And what thanks do we get? The ungrateful pricks spray *Thief mobile* on your limo.'

Someone had tagged his limo.

Brownstein, the lawyer, said: 'Someone burgled my place the other week.'

Everyone had a horror story to tell. They were all agreed that it was getting worse down there.

'There are places you daren't go,' said Al Geldt.

'I wouldn't go if you paid me,' said Dick Fault.

'It's a problem alright,' said Senator Doe.

'Everything is — for them,' said Dick Fault. Al Geldt agreed. 'Always complaining that they're not paid enough. So get a better job, fella. I'll tell you, they turn the easiest of things in to the most desperate struggle.'

'More aggressive policing, that's what's needed,' said Dick Fault.

'We have aggressive police,' said Senator Doe.

'That are backed up by firm laws. And the political will to enforce them.'

Dick Fault stared at Senator Doe.

'Just build a wall round the neighbourhoods,' said Ed Pilk. 'Wouldn't even need a wall to keep them in. Just give them a factory to work in, a bar, pizza parlour and a Blockbusters and leave them to it. Like in the old days.'

'It's us that'll end up having to live behind walls under armed guard,' said Art Soless. He already did. Most of them did.

Everywhere you went these days people were unloading on each other. And it wasn't just the small things either it was the big things, everything: the economy, the environment, the very future of the human race, of the planet itself. People were conjuring up this dystopian horror of the future which they had now to escape.

Seena said: 'James has got the right idea, moving up in to the hills here. The air is so wonderful here. And it's so peaceful.'

Jigsaw took a deep breath. He knew that what he was about to say wasn't going to be popular.

'The problem, as I see it,' he said, 'is there are too many people.'

Dick Fault, Senator Doe, Al Geldt, Ed Pilk, Soless, Seena . . . everyone frowned.

Too many people?

Okay, sure, the cities were overcrowded. Yes, the roads were congested. Okay, so people were being marginalised. Pollution was a problem, yes, they knew that – you couldn't breathe in LA somedays because of it. Everyone agreed there was environmental damage. The climate was being altered, yes. But there were benefits too.

'I would have thought that the more people there were then the better,' said Al Geldt. Dick Fault nodded. The Bilderbergs nodded. Senator Doe nodded. Everyone agreed. People were the source. The source was important.

But Jigsaw was emphatic. 'There are too many people, and they all want what we've got. Now, ordinarily that wouldn't be a problem, but they are beginning to get it. Just look at what that's doing down there.'

A ripple of unease ran through the company. Something changed.

'He's right, you know.'

'Just look at LA.

'Like, where is it?'

'The pollution, it just gets worse.'

'It's all those frikin cars.'

'Like, everyone's got a car now.'

'You can't move for them.'

'Yeah. What possible use is a sports car if all you can do is to inch along in it? I want the roads to be empty.'

Everyone began talking at the same time: 'The oceans are dying.' 'The beaches are full of shit.' 'Now the ice caps are melting.'

'That's polarisation for you,' said Brad Hollows.

'Here comes everyone,' said Jigsaw.

'James is right,' said Soless, 'There is less space, not more.' Everyone agreed.

'They're ruining it for everyone,' said Dick Fault. 'Everything they touch they turn to shit.'

Everyone fell silent for a time, thinking.

A degraded and overcrowded world was not something they could enjoy. Soless looked at Jigsaw. Senator Doe looked at Dick Fault. Dick Fault looked at Al Geldt. Al Geldt at Brownstein. Ed Pilk glanced over to the Bilderbergs. An understanding passed between them. The Bilderbergs nodded. Dick Fault nodded. Al Geldt, Brownstein, Steven Miloff, Gilyotorerk Eesher, Ed Pilk, Sir Leonard, everyone was nodding.

'It wasn't meant to be like this,' said Sir Leonard. 'Where, when, did it all go wrong?'

'But what can you do?' shrugged Senator Doe. 'You can't stop progress.'

Everyone agreed. No one could think of an objection to counter the fact.

Though several people opened their mouths to object they immediately thought better of it and did not. They felt compromised, trapped in their own argument, by their own need.

There was silence.

It was Jigsaw who broke the silence.

'The way I see it,' he said, 'sooner or later we are going to have to embrace a new asceticism.'

The suggestion brought forth howls of derisive laughter.

'Somehow, James,' said Seena, 'I just can't see you as an ascetic.'

'An asshole, maybe,' said Dick Fault.

Jigsaw ignored the insult. 'I was,' he said, 'referring to them, to everyone else, to society in general.'

'Ah, them,' said Dick Fault.

They were threatening to spoil everything.

'Six billion people,' said Jigsaw. 'Think about that. We've never had six billion people on the planet before using all the earth's resources and to their limits. They will all want a car. They will all want more of everything. The place will be hell.'

Everyone experienced a paradigm shift in their assumptions.

Senator Doe stood. He cleared his throat. When he spoke it was to offer a new raison d'etra for the coming era.

'The egalitarian era it was a blip,' he said. 'What a few of us in this great nation of ours may enjoy in freedom the crowd necessarily destroys. It is my firm belief, as a Republican senator, that if we are to maintain these great and fought for freedoms, these privileges that we enjoy in this country, then it is not enough that everyone should be granted them by right, a person should have to earn them, right?'

'Right!'

Everyone was agreed.

'Of course,' said Al Geldt, 'it will be more necessary than ever to be a millionaire.'

'A multimillionaire,' said Art Soless, justifying his own position.

'A billionaire,' said Dick Fault.

'A trillionaire,' said Jigsaw. 'Imagine.'

It was an exciting prospect, everyone agreed.

Money, it would be the final frontier. Soon, it would be the only frontier. In this coming age of great and spreading wealth people will by necessity have to purchase their freedoms. Because the more that you had and could control then the less there would be for everyone else to use to gain access.

'We'll be alright,' said Art Soless. 'No matter what happens, we'll stay ahead. We've got percentage rake off.'

'And whenever things get to be too much,' said Seena, 'then I can show them the way, I can be there for them.'

They are masters of the game, of the quiet word in the right ear. Everyone else has to work out their struggles in a world that does not work for them and never will.

It is like this. They gather around pools, like this one, as they are here, or on yachts, and in executive suites in corporate tower blocks, in gentlemen's clubs and on ranches, and, like the Ancient Greek gods, they look down on the world and discuss where to throw the lightning bolts that fuck everyone else around.

More wine was provided, more champagne, more food called for that was then piled up on plates.

Everyone ate and drank eagerly.

The day grew hotter. The sun fiercer. Bright sunlight exploded off the surface of the infinity pool.

The smell of sagebrush, and of distant forest fires, drifted down from the hills.

Consuella-Maria-Carmen unfurled umbrellas and angled them over the sun-loungers to create patch-marks of shade. They brought out ice buckets and placed opened bottles of wine and champagne in them. Music by Jean Michelle Jarre drifted on the air. People began to strip down to their swimwear. They swam, slowly, languidly, like hippopotami.

Consuella-Maria-Carmen brought everyone towels. They removed the empty bottles from the ice buckets and they replaced them with fresh bottles. They replenished the ice.

People stood in the pool, drinking, cooling off.

The distant hills trembled. The earth shook. Light continued to explode off the infinity pool. The white walls of the house were too bright to look at.

By mid-afternoon it had become so hot that everyone had retired to the shade.

A line of ants marched to and fro, carrying off in to the brush anything that might be of use to them. Sticky drink drips, crumbs, leaves from the garden.

It was evening before people began to excuse themselves. Then, suddenly, they were all leaving.

The last of the red tail lights disappeared down the drive. Al Geldt's helicopter clattered in to the sky.

Andy, Jigsaw, Art Soless and Seena stood watching the sun as it dipped beneath the lip of the infinity pool. The infinity pool flared.

The sky filled with colour: red's and oranges, yellows, chemical blues.

'It's like a painting by Turner,' said Jigsaw.

'One of his Van Goghs,' said Soless. 'Isn't it beautiful?'

'It's like neon,' said Seena. 'It's even better than neon,' she said.

'It's pollution that causes it,' said Andy.

Seena shook her head. 'Who'd a thought that shit could be so beautiful.'

'It's caused by aerosols,' said Jigsaw.

'You can say that again,' said Andy.

Stars appeared. First Venus, then the constellations. The Big Dipper hung like a question mark over everything. It was reflected in the infinity pool.

Darkness, and the sounds of insects filled the air.

36

Work Takes Much More than Five Days a Week from You

Clear blue sky, hot sun. It was another great day in paradise.

Jigsaw was sitting beside the infinity pool, listening to the business news on the radio:

'Another day, another record. The stock market soared to a new high yesterday, up 100 points to close at 7895.81 on the Dow Jones Industrial Average, to date the highest finish ever.'

Day after day the news had been the same. For months now the market had been undergoing a bull run. The upswing was the second largest ever in American history.

Jigsaw switched off the radio and, reaching for his tequila sunrise, raised it in a toast to himself. . . .

AndyBrand, posting a near 30% jump in second quarter profits, was creating multimillionaires out of its stockholders. The quarterly reports were pumping up the stock price, and there was every chance that the price would double again over the next twelve months.

Money from nowhere.

Jigsaw bought a beach house. He bought a Jensen, registration *Midas5*. He bought more art, more vintage wine. There were more poolside parties, more extravagances.

Then, sometime in the next financial quarter, the market slowed, it stagnated, as speculators reached the limit of their confidence and wariness took over. There were fears that the bubble would burst any day now, that growth would slow and the economy stagnate plunging the country into recession.

But there were some, those like Max Bringmeen, who were convinced that there was more money to be made still, and he was determined to get everything on the move again.

Max Bringmeen was at the headquarters of his fund in Wall Street, the huge trading floor crowded with desks, the desks manned, stacked with computer terminals. A vast bank of computer screens ran the length of one wall, in effect creating that wall. The screens showed listings, numbers, graphs. Green and yellow listings, yellow and blue numbers, green numbers, green and blue graphs. It was Christmas-like, but that was not what made it so exciting.

THE BUCK STOPS HERE. It was written in huge gold lettering on the wall above Max Bringmeen's office. He was stood in the doorway there, looking out at the trading floor. He checked his watch.

It was 8.55am and everyone was waiting for the market to open. There was an atmosphere of tension in the room.

Max Bringmeen walked out of his office and on to the trading floor with the greeting, 'Morning everyone.'

Fifty voices in unison replied, 'Morning boss.'

Max Bringmeen folded his arms. 'Today it happens. What happens?' he asked. He asked the same question every day before trading.

The fifty voices chanted their reply enthusiastically: 'THE BUCK STOPS HERE!'

Max Bringmeen then gave his usual prep talk: 'We stand on the brink of a new hierarchy of existence. Now some people think that we have arrived at that promised land, but not me. And I know that you don't either. Anyone that believes otherwise can leave now. You need balls of steel for this work. Not everyone has such balls. But we do. It's why I chose you for this. We have power and we have ability and we are going to create deities. You are going to become deities. But out there they are faltering. They are getting scared. They are weak players and they are holding us back and they need to be weeded out. Because there is only one way that this thing can go: our way. The market needs leadership, our leadership. It is just resting. Things need a gentle nudge in the right direction is all.'

For some time now Max Bringmeen had been secretly buying up shares in target companies and in sufficiently small amounts so that their listings remained stationary. Today he would abandon that strategy.

Max Bringmeen checked his watch. It was 8.59am. He brought his hands together. 'So, let's get to it.'

He turned to face the screens.

The moment trading opened his staff began to buy up large blocks of shares in an attempt to shift the market and drive it upward. Max Bringmeen stood to make billions on his previous purchases. But it was a risky strategy.

'One hundred and fifteen point nine,' said a trader. 'One hundred and fifteen point nine,' he repeated. Then: 'Sixteen!' he shouted. 'It's moving.

The price of WorldCorp was rising.

Max Bringmeen ran a finger inside his shirt collar.

'One hundred and sixteen point one.'

"Are we driving it? Is anyone following?' Asked Bringmeen.

'Point two. Three. They're going for it. They've bit.'

Max Bringmeen chopped the air with a hand. 'Stop buying,' he commanded. 'Sell our holdings in yen, sterling too,' he said. 'I want to be ready for this.'

'It's still rising. One hundred and sixteen point four,' said the trader. 'One hundred and sixteen point five.'

Max Bringmeen stared in to the screens: at the numbers, the listings, the charts and graphs. AndyBrand was up. WorldCorp was up. Shares right across the board were rising. 'Come on,' he urged.

'One hundred and sixteen point six. Still six. Six. It's stopped.'

Max Bringmeen continued to stare in to screens. He pinched the bridge of his nose, dug the points of his fingers in to the wet corners of his eyes.

'Five,' said the trader, 'it's dropping.'

Max Bringmeen smiled.

We should make our move now, he thought. He lifted a hand to his face, he rubbed his face.

'Point four'

'Now, Max!,' urged Tamara, Max Bringmeen's secretary, 'Now! Do it now!'

'Point three'

Max Bringmeen watched the money disappear: the falling, flowing numbers, the plummeting graphs.

He loved this moment. The very edge. Now, when he was most alive. 'Do it,' he said. 'Sell our holdings in the Brand. Dump WorldCorp.'

And then it happened. And there was nothing anyone could do about it. All over the world trading floors exploded in a flurry of selling.

Jigsaw was sunning himself beside the pool when his mobile went off: Pink Floyd's *Money* filled the air.

'James?' It was Soless and he sounded panicked. 'Switch on your TV. Just do it!'

'What's going on?' asked Jigsaw as he made his way indoors.

'Are you looking? Are you looking? It's a disaster, a fucking disaster.'

Indoors now, in the cool, sun blind, his eyes readjusting, he switched on the TV.

A sombre looking newsreader stared out at him from the screen. A block of highlighted white text on a black background, a ticker tape of breaking news, the text un-scrolling itself beneath the newsreader, read: *Wall Street Shock. Dow Jones plunges 1000 points as stock market crashes.*

'It was the biggest ever fall in history,' said the newsreader, 'and it happened in just 8 minutes.'

The camera angles changed, and the newsreader readjusted her position to face the camera: 'Traders were left stunned when shortly after 2.30 pm this afternoon the Dow which had been down 3% lifted for a short time but then suddenly tumbled an incredible 650 points sending the whole market in to freefall.'

Pictures of a frantic trading floor filled the screen. People were up on their toes, shouting, waving frantically in the air. There were people screaming in to phones, sat staring dumbly at screens, stood with their hands on their heads, holding their shocked faces, every one of them looking helplessly on, unable to staunch the falling number flows. Everyone trying to pull their money out in an attempt to salvage something, anything.

Then it was back to the newsreader. She looked grave. 'For a full eight minutes the market haemorrhaged money with traders trying to come to grips with a market that seemed to be in free-fall as key stocks like AndyBrand and Worldcorp for a time fell to zero.'

'Did you hear that? James, are you there? James?'

Jigsaw did not answer. He sat staring at the screen. He felt sick to the pit of his stomach.

He lunged forward in his seat and threw up.

Max Bringmeen rubbed his face with his right hand. He loosened his tie, undid the top button of his shirt. He looked like a man outside of a club at four in the morning. He returned his attention to the screens.

'Everything's falling! Everything. WorldCorp's gone, AndyBrand's gone, they've zeroed and they're pulling everything down with them. Jesus!'

Just look at that money go, thought Max Bringmeen.

The market was haemorrhaging money.

Investors had begun dumping shares all across the board, triggering a stampede as dealers responded to the falling market by offloading shares in an attempt to rescue their investments. Prices plummeted in response, triggering the dumping of more significant blocks of shares as more thresholds came in to play. People couldn't dump their shares fast enough. For some it was already too late.

Personal fortunes vanished. Sir Geoffrey Plane-Smith's fortune vanished as WorldCorp's share price was wiped out. Jigsaw's fortune vanished. The money simply disappeared.

Max Bringmeen bent over the screen. He was mesmerised by the falling numbers.

He stood upright.

'Okay,' he said. 'Buy!' he shouted. 'Buy everything back.' The trading floor exploded.

Dollars came flooding on to the market, restoring confidence and setting off a feeding frenzy. Currencies tumbled. Companies were bought and sold, their assets to be stripped. There would be speculation. Mergers and acquisitions. The god, money, was on the rampage again.

It was the lead story on the news, pushing out the build up of tension in the gulf, pushing out the encroaching forest fires.

A sombre looking newsreader stared out from the screen:

'Tonight, the tremor on Wall Street that was felt around the world. US regulators are still trying to determine the cause of the dramatic sell off that hit Wall Street like a tsunami earlier today and which saw the Dow Jones industrial average plunge 998.5 points within minutes as share prices were swept away in the deluge, to end the day down 347.80. US regulators are still trying to determine the cause of the dramatic sell off. It seems that the market, nervous at its slowing in the last few weeks and its subsequent dip, had thought the bubble had burst. The sell off was apparently accentuated by recently installed computer trading programmes which can sell shares in a split second. But that is not the whole story.'

The presenter, turning her attention to a different camera, appeared from a new angle: 'Bogus trades and market manipulation may have been the cause of the fall.'

A bald man in glasses, a financial analyst, then appeared on the screen:

'The fall was triggered by a massive dump of shares,' he explained. 'Now this can be a big dump off of shares, a jittery trader, one with a short hair trigger, even a misplaced finger, someone pressing the wrong button. That sets off a reaction and with the market the way it was these computer programmes that are designed to sell after a specific decline, either in the market generally or in a specific stock, then triggered off the panic. The volumes were almost twice the normal daily volumes, very high volumes of selling and very broad based, not just a few.'

The newsreader reappeared, centre screen:

'Some stock, the high sellers, AndyBrand and WorldCorp, for a time fell to zero. AndyBrand finished the day at $20 a share after the recovery, still $5 down on its earlier price. WorldCorp however did not recover.'

The newscaster appeared at a different angle.

'And now the main points of the news again. Earlier today traders were left stunned as...'

That night Max Bringmeen held a celebration at his mansion in the Hamptons. Rockets went rushing up in to the night sky. Huge explosions, like palm trees, like brief chrysanthemums, burst continuously overhead. Glasses clinked. Corks popped. Champagne came everywhere.

And Jigsaw was on a plane to London.

From his seat in business class, Jigsaw looked down at LA. At the freeways, full of slow moving traffic, at the blue swimming pools, at the red tiled roofs of all the villas, at all the numerous white buildings like his own that were clinging to the surrounding hillsides. There were thousands upon thousands of them, but there were millions more people.

The plane finished its ascent, levelled off and began to bank eastward, away from the setting sun toward darkness. Far below, the tall buildings of the business district gave everyone the finger. Jigsaw returned the gesture.

Overcast skies. Cold winds. The threat of rain.

The City of London filled the horizon like a barcode. The mad scrabble city speeds and roars. Lives run faster here than in other places.

About the first thing that Jigsaw did when he got to London was to buy a newspaper, *The Press*:

CITY JITTERS AS WORLDCORP CRASHES

The pound plunged to a record low as stock markets from Tokyo to New York took an initial pounding yesterday. The run on the markets resulted in the collapse of the British based global concern, WorldCorp. Rumours circulating in the City claim that the jittery market, stable until this week's panic, was apparently initiated by speculators. The American billionaire, Max Bringmeen, who has offered a rescue package to WorldCorp, at $1 a share, dismissed the rumour, arguing that the frenzy of trading had precipitated a much needed shakedown of the market, ridding it of inefficient players. The events of yesterday, he said, had been in the best interests of investors who had become increasingly concerned about *diminishing returns in the stagnating market, a claim later backed up by the rallying market and by leading City traders who responded positively to his support. 'If the market is doing well then we are doing well,' he said at a gathering being held in his honour, adding, "We are doing God's work."*

The offices of *The Press*, in Wapping.

A meeting was being held amongst the various editors. Present at the meeting were the editor, Niall Fitzgerald; the deputy editor, Bill Harris; the financial and business news editor, Jeremy Stanford; the general news editor, Bill McDonald; and the features editor, Sue Platt. A computer stood on the editors desk, its screen showing the outlay of the next day's front page with the headline:

RECORD RECOVERY. STOCK MARKET EXPERIENCES ITS BEST DAY EVER.

A glass partition separated the editors office from the news room. Through it could be heard the clatter of keyboards, phones ringing and the beehive murmur of voices from the busy news room.

The mood in the office was tense.

'I heard he celebrated his coup with a bottle of the Dom Ruinart Rose,' said McDonald. 'The smug little shit.'

'God's work? Jesus, did he actually say that?' asked Fitzgerald. 'Or did we make it up?'

'He actually said it,' said Jeremy Stanford.

Fitzgerald thumped the desk. 'These people, they are taking the piss. Look at this. Look at it.' He picked up then brought the previous day's paper, with its full page headline, *CITY JITTERS AS WORLDCORP CRASHES*, down on the desk. 'Who the fuck do these people think they are?'

'The masters of the universe?' said Harris.

Fitzgerald scowled. 'They think they can do what they like. 'They sit there in their villas and on their super yachts, stroking their bimbos, smoking donkey dick cigars and drinking magnums of champagne, laughing their cocks off at us. Well this is not some fucking game. Real people have lost real money here. It's high time we nailed these bastards?'

'I thought that we were for these people?' frowned Stanford. 'Wasn't our brief to cut them some slack and just let them get on with it?'

Fitzgerald thumped the desk. 'Times change. Attitudes change.' He snatched up the paper and he waved it in the air, before slamming it back down on the desk. 'This can't go on. Someone presses a button in New York, a company gets sold, and the jobs and the money just disappear.' He jabbed his finger at the newspaper. 'Are we going to let them get away with this?' Fitzgerald got up from the desk and went and stood in the window. He looked out at the city, at its busy streets.

'People have had enough. They have been working their balls off, day and night to get ahead, but they are fast beginning to realise that all that hard work just isn't going to deliver it for them. There is genuine resentment out there. Those bastards think that everyone else exists to make them rich. So what are we going to do about it? Come on.'

Fitzgerald began pacing the room.

'Well?'

'These people are billionaires,' said Harris. 'They're protected. They have friends in government.'

'How can there be billionaires?' asked Platt.

'That is exactly what we should be asking.' Fitzgerald went and stood behind his chair. He pressed a key on his keypad. The screen changed. Fitzgerald swivelled his computer screen around so that everyone could see it:

RECORD RECOVERY. BEST DAY EVER.

'You call that a headline?' he exploded. 'It's just encouragement for these bastards. Well I want something better.' His eyes settled on Harris. 'Bill?'

'These are very powerful people we're talking about,' said Stanford. 'Wealth creators.'

'Bollocks.' Fitzgerald thumped the desk. 'They're not creating wealth they're just hoovering it up. We're going to let them get away with that, are we?'

'How about, 'Those Bastards Have Got Our Money',' said Harris.

'That's the spirit,' said Fitzgerald.

'It's Trough At The Top,' said McDonald.

'Brilliant. Now we're getting somewhere.' Fitzgerald rubbed his hands together. He was beginning to enjoy himself.

Platt said, 'Hostages to fortune?'

Stanford said, 'Near Collapse Threatens World Economic Order. Market Rallies But We're Not Out Of The Bretton Woods Yet.'

'Lets stick to vitriol,' said Fitzgerald. He liked what he was hearing though. 'It's time to tell everyone how it really is. I want a barrage of articles attacking the super-rich. We'll run a series of profiles on billionaires, fund managers, City fat cats, their extravagant lifestyles, their privileges and excesses, all the tax dodges they employ. The whole fucking lot. We need to demonise these people. Reign them in. We might even bring some of the bastards down. Ideas?' he clicked his fingers. He made gathering gestures with his hands. 'Come on. Come on.'

'There's a company called Midas,' said Stanford. 'It might be just the angle that we're looking for.'

'Midas. Perfect. Perfect. Get someone on to it. We need to give the public some hate figures. Get them behind us on this.'

'Bane Burke,' said Platt, 'She's been filing copy with us on this sort of thing for months.'

'Get her. Give her anything she wants. Tell her to get out there and to start digging the dirt on these people.' He turned to Stanford. 'Jeremy, I want you to run an expose on every financial trick these people employ to turn over a quick buck. You can bet that right now there is some young gun out there toying with a new investment strategy that is going to cause the next crash. Well, what are you all waiting for? Come on! Let's get busy on this. Let's nail these bastards.'

Max Bringmeen had manipulated the market to his own ends, single handedly threatening to plunge the world in to a recession, only to pull it back from the brink at the last moment. That had almost destroyed Jigsaw. It had shaken him to the core. He hated Bringmeen, and all those like him, not because of what they had done to him but for what they could do still.

They made and broke companies, brought whole corporations, even currencies to their knees simply for the money in it, and it was like a game to them. Jigsaw wanted revenge. He wanted to drag their whole world to hell. But revenge was impossible against such people. They possessed so much money it made them untouchable. They were even ranked according to the money they commanded. And that, Jigsaw realised, was their one and fatal weakness. Some people would be nothing without money. *He* would be nothing, a nobody, without money. He had to protect himself, insulate himself from what he knew must be coming.

Jigsaw began to conceive of a plan so audacious and daring that he dismissed it as impossible. But it would remain at the back of his mind, motivating him, informing his every move, as all the time he worked quietly toward creating the conditions that might one day make it feasible.

His decision made him nervous. But he was excited too.

Catching a taxi from the airport he went straight to the apartment. Seated in his office he began working the phone, ringing around, trying to secure the funding he urgently required.

There was no time to lose, with every passing hour the market was rising against him.

He contacted banks and clearing houses, corporate lawyers, finance houses. He talked to multimillionaires, to billionaires. He consulted with wealth managers. He contacted the analysts, Skutt and Hames, putting them on the payroll.

By the end of the month Jigsaw had transformed himself in to a player. He created a buyout fund. He made a move on the market every day. He used complex derivatives trades to hide the fact that he was buying shares in struggling businesses.

He acquired controlling interests in a sportswear chain, a travel company, storage facilities, a property development company. He bought in to fitness clubs, travel companies, petrochemicals, iron, steel, retail. . . .

And it was all done on borrowed money. You could buy anything using such methods, even the unaffordable, particularly the unaffordable. All you needed was the desire. If you wanted an employment agency you bought one, a supermarket chain you bought one, a water company, an electricity board, a football club you just went out and you bought one.

The banks were offering huge borrowing levels to anyone with balls enough to ask for it. Jigsaw borrowed and leveraged extensively, creating new tiers of debt to provide him with unlimited supplies of cash.

Now he was driving across the city, racing between the speed cameras to his new offices in Knightsbridge.

He stood before the black painted door, brass plaque shining in the sun. He breathed on the plaque, pulled his jacket sleeve over his hand and then he polished the plaque. He stood back to admire it: *KRYTEN*.

As a corporate raider Jigsaw would become the creator and destroyer of companies, of whole worlds. Of certain people's worlds. And he was going do it with the help of those he most despised.

Then he was on a plane to New York.

The world is a diminishing place. The city spreads, eating in to farmland, forests, streams, hills, mountains. Every single moment that passes there is more city. Nature has been confounded and its laws understood, man has conquered that restraint. So cities grow and the natural laws are replaced by financial formulae. It is the desperate moment when the balance tips and civilisations fall. Great Zimbabwe, the Indus Valley, Easter Island, the ancient Maya. . . . everywhere our triumph precedes our undoing. One single point is knocked off a share price and the whole world is blown sky high.

Bane was at home in her bedsit, working, trying to make sense of the thing:

$$\frac{1}{2} Q2S2 \frac{a2V}{aS2} + rS \frac{aV}{aS} + \frac{aV}{at} = 0$$

Key:
Q = volatility of returns of the underlying asset or commodity
S = its spot (current) price
a = rate of change
v = risk free interest rate
t = time

The Skutt-Hames equation, designed to help turn liabilities in to assets, was the financial instrument underpinning the new capitalism of derivative investment instruments. Supposed to guarantee safe investment by eliminating risk it had led to a boom in options trading, releasing a flood of new money in to the world. It was complex, and Bane found it difficult to understand. It surpassed understanding:

The size of the world economy was 50 trillion, yet the amount of derivatives being traded was 85 trillion? That was more than the entire economic activity of the whole planet? How on earth was that possible?

Exasperated at her lack of progress, Bane rested her elbows on her desk and, exhaling a long breath that blew out her cheeks, she placed her head in her hands.

Where does it all come from all this money? Money has to come from somewhere. Someone, at some time has to do the work.

And how could money just disappear? It had on the day of the crash. And then just as suddenly reappear again?

Bane reached down some rejected copy of hers:

THE RAINMAKERS
Growth, More Growth, Growing the Economy.

The private banking system creates 97% of the country's money supply as debt, with interest. Bankers love debt because it grows and grows. New loans create new money which is used to pay the interest on previous loans. Without this new money interest could not be paid, banks would not lend, there would no new money, and the economy would crash.

Such an economy needs growth.

But unrestricted economic growth is removing the world's biodiversity at a rate faster than that of the last great extinction. And all the time population and consumption continues to grow, and at a rate faster than technology can find new ways of expanding what can be produced. Each year humans use 30% more resources than the planet can replenish.

Growth is going to create a lot more wealth, but for who? We are going to create a lot more jobs, but for how long? How long before they are replaced by technology, how long before those jobs move elsewhere to where labour is cheapest, abandoning everything in their wake?

Growth only makes the problem worse because everything is accelerating and that is multiplying the forces that will ultimately have to be brought under control.

She had said it many times before:

It is not poverty that we should worry about, it is wealth.

There were all these separate strands to the thing and they were linked. What Bane was trying to do was to bring them all together in one coherent argument to show where all this was leading.

Bane was still working when she got the call. She had been trying to complete her piece on the crash. The crash had raised false hopes in her. But the markets had rallied and it was business as usual again.

Bane put down the phone. She sat staring at the phone. Yes!

Bane punched the air.

She bent over her keyboard and went straight to work:

There isn't going to be a catastrophe, not yet, no financial crisis so big that it will stop us in our tracks. Instead, the world is going to become grottier and faster and more crowded, a much less wild and interesting place, where the air is stagnant and stinks of oil and it rains all the time. On the other hand, if you like cities, shops, shopping, Prada, Versace, bling, Nuttyprice, One Size, McJobs, Midas, new things, fast and faster travel, and you want to see them wherever you go, then what's coming is for you. The future is Midas.

Bane switched off her computer, printed out the copy, placed it in an envelope and addressed the envelope to her new editor, Sue Platt, at the offices of *The Press*.

ANDY RANT, RAINING MONEY, THE NEW U.S. TOUR, *opening the 7th, New York at Carnegie Hall, Sold Out, the 8th...*

Andy comes on stage, an aerosol can in each hand. He tells the audience that he's campaigning for a better summer. He holds up the aerosols. Pisssh!

'Fuck the climate,' he says. Pissssssh! Pissssssh! 'It's that other climate I'm worried about. The economic climate.'

A backdrop comes rolling down behind him: a searing hot sun, red skies, the skyline of the City.

Eyes closed, hands out in front of him he begins to walk zombie-like across the stage. 'Buy. Buy. Buy. Buy, repeating it, Dalek like, over and over. He throws the aerosols in to the wings. 'Bye bye,' he waves.

The backdrop changes. A new backdrop rolls down:

Rain, floods. The upper storeys of buildings, church spires, the tops of trees poking from the water. A super yacht floating on the rising waters. Two Max Bringmeens on board. Two Dick Faults. Two. . . . The audience get the picture.

And the rain falling, falling. . . .

There are people on jet skies, on water skis and in motorboats, one hand in the air, waving, enjoying the flood.

Other people, crowds of them, sit huddled together on the rooftops in the rain. Silhouettes.

Andy bursts in to his climate change song:

> 'It rains all day now, it rains all night.
> It rains all summer, but that's all right.
> Let it rain, let it rain, it's raining money.'

Paper, a blizzard of money, dollars, begins to fall from the ceiling on to the stage.

'It's raining money, it's raining money, more, more and more money,' he sings, lifting his face to the blizzard, holding out his arms to it.

There's a road sign, *The Future*, stood on the stage. Andy snaps off the sign. He makes like he's paddling a boat with it.

'I bought a waterproof coat, wet suit and wellies.

'A jet ski and boat, and several flat screen tellies.

'Let it rain. . . .' Andy gestures for the audience to join in. 'Let it rain, it's raining money,' they all sing, 'It's raining money, it's raining money, more, more and more money,' the audience are roaring out the chorus now.

Andy makes like he's jet skiing towards the super-yacht, he waves to the audience, singing:

> 'I'm one of the lucky ones, I'm all right.
> I own a super yacht, it's not my plight.'

'Let it rain, let it rain,' the audience roar: 'it's raining money. It's raining money, more, more. . . .'

The audience stood and they applauded Andy. Bane stood and she applauded.

Financed by *The Press*, Bane, having flown out to America to pursue her inquiries, had been at that first night's performance.

She was stood naked in her hotel room window, looking out past the rain washed glass at the grey and waterlogged city.

She hated New York. The gridlock, the crowds, all this constant rain. She had been in New York a week now and it had rained every single day of her visit. It had rained non-stop.

It was three o'clock in the afternoon, the sky was overcast and all across the city the lights were blazing. The weather was driving people crazy. Everyone was cooped up indoors. Without light, without air, without exercise they had become edgy and depressed.

Bane thumped the glass. 'Look at it out there. People can't control their spending and now it's raining forever,' she said.

Andy lay in bed, staring at Bane. He had met her the previous night at the party after his show. There had been drink involved. Next thing he knew he was waking up in a strange and unfamiliar bedroom and there she was. Andy lay on his back looking at her.

Bane left the window and she walked over to the bed.

'What are you thinking?' she asked.

Thinking? Andy said nothing. Bane was a beautiful woman and she was naked. It wasn't possible to think.

Bane pulled back the covers. She slid in beside Andy. Andy was warm. He was all hard.

Bane straddled Andy. Her face changed as she began to work off on him.

Then it was no longer sufficient to have straight sex, they needed that other kind.

After, they lay in bed, on their backs, looking up at the ceiling. Satisfied, once again back in full possession of themselves.

They finished their cigarettes.

Bane felt an affinity for Andy. It was good to have someone on your side.

'We're on the same side, me and you,' she said.

Andy doubted it. No one understood him. It was like he was on a completely different planet to everyone else.

'Andy and Bane versus the rest of the world,' said Bane and she smiled.

She placed a hand on Andy's shoulder.

Andy shrugged it off.

'That piece you wrote about us? Changed your mind now, have you?'

'What piece?'

There had been several.

'The last one, the Judas piece. Bane Burke columnist. Fucken fifth columnist, more like. What piece? That fucken piece about exploiting youth culture. Layed right in to me, didn't you?'

In the article Bane had claimed that Andy Rant, angry young man, rebel and working class hero, had been turned in to an engine of capitalism, the cornerstone of the whole MidasCorp Empire:

Andy Rant, working class hero, so called rebel, is nothing more than a young capitalist in the pay of capitalists who, for the purpose of capitalism is exploiting youth culture – the sole remaining mainstay, after the crushing of the unions and excluding environmental activism, of protest and dissent - which he does by promoting fan worship, the mindless pursuit of the AndyBrand and wholesale passive consumerism. In this he is like The Beatles and Bob Dylan before him. . . .

The article then went on to attack consumerism in general and wealth in particular.

'All I wrote, Andy, was that you were being used.'

'Yeah, well, they use everyone, Bane. Anything to make them money. And no, before yeh say it, there's no conspiracy, it's just the way things are.' Andy laughed.

'I thought you cared,' said Bane.

'I do. Did. Too fucken much. Only it was too depressing, wasn't it? So I stopped. Forget it, Bane, the planet is fucked, okay. It's off to hell in a shopping cart. Best you just go out an enjoy yourself, get a bit of it for yourself, before it's too late. I am. Everybody else is. What difference can you make? One person.'

'What difference? Every difference. Every single one of us can make a difference if we all changed.'

'No, because nobody gives a shite. You're up against a mindless rampaging herd. Like fucken locusts, thee are. You know what they want, everyone? Everything. And they don't even think they're being materialistic, because everyone knows someone who has got more than them. And they want it. And they're not going to stop until they get it, either. They want their barbecue kit, and patio heaters, their flat screen TV. They want to to be warm all the fucken time. They want the latest fashion, the next new thing. They want, Bane, to be happy. And they won't be happy till they get all those things. And believe me they won't be happy then. You can't fight that. How can you hope to win against people like that who are fucking things up simply by leading ordinary, everyday fucking lives? You can't.'

Bane's eyes turned fierce and her face hard. She became a different person.
'Fuck you!' she said.

She was angry. Angry at Andy, angry at the world, at the way things had turned out for her. Everything was about to turn to shite and she hadn't secured a single piece of it for herself yet. She took all her fear and loathing and resentment and she vented it on Andy.

'You really don't give a shit, do you? You and your fucking half revolution, all your: 'Where's my land? My rivers? My lakes? What the fuck can I hunt? Jobs? Am a fucken job hunter, me.' It's just an act, that's all, a front. You've been bought, Andy. You've sold out.'

'Yes, Bane, I have.' Andy was up on his knees, flexing his arms, beating his chest, balls swinging, dick swinging. 'And just look at me, I'm fucking king. Me. It's my party, Bane. I can have anything I fucking well want. Who would turn their back on that, eh?'

'King? I don't think so. You're just another fucking commodity,' Bane said it with such contempt that it soured her whole face, making her ugly. What she was looking at was ugly.

'Well, yeah,' said Andy, grinning. 'It's called counter-culture, innit?' and he laughed. He laughed and laughed. Andy blew out his cheeks, pushed out his stomach and made himself fat. Or tried to. 'We're all Americans now, Bane.' Andy laughed. He laughed and laughed.

'You people make me sick.' Bane leapt out of bed. She found and picked up her knickers then pulled them on. She found and put on her bra. She looked for her dress. She couldn't find her dress. She found a T-shirt. It was an Andy Rant T-shirt, retailing at $9.99. It smelt of Andy. Bane pulled on the T-shirt.

'Oh, I know all about you, Andy, living the good life over there in California up in that huge fucking villa of yours with your swimming pool and your art. What do you care about anything, you people? The worst it gets for everyone then the better it gets for you, isn't that how it works? You want it all to yourself, you lot, and everyone else can go to hell.' She pulled the shirt down over her head, un-trapping her hair. 'As far as you lot are concerned we're just cluttering the place up. You lot think that everyone else exists just to make you rich. You're a fucking hypocrite!'

'And you are a pain in the fucken arse. I don't have to take this from you.

From anybody. Go on, get out!. Go back to your own fucken room before I kick yer out.'

'Me get out? You go. It's my fucking room.'

'Your room?' Andy's face dropped. He'd thought it was his room. Andy got out of bed and he began putting on his clothes.

Next thing, Bane was pulling off her T-shirt. 'An you can take this piece of capitalist shite with you!' She flung it toward Andy. It missed and landed on the bed. 'It's not a T-shirt, it's exploitation.'

Andy smiled. 'Let me tell you something, Bane. Do you know who the successes are, or who should be? The ones who've got nothing, who can get by on nothing, they're not fucking anything up. But they are getting fucked up. Big time. Do you want to spend your life getting fucked around, surviving on nuthin? 'Cos I fucken don't. I already had that life, I already been fucked around, good an proper. All my fucken life. Aright!'

Bane jumped: Andy had shouted it right in to her face.

Andy finished lacing up his boots. Bane picked up her shoe, a stiletto. Andy stood, he made for the door. Bane pulled back her arm. Andy pulled open the door. 'Well, thanks for the fuck. Fat girl,' he said as Bane threw her shoe at him. Andy slammed shut the door just as the shoe hit it, the stiletto piercing the false mahogany laminate and lodging there.

Andy opened the door. 'Oh, and good luck with the revolution,' he said. He slammed shut the door.

Bane stared at her shoe in the door.

Well what the hell, the room was in Andy's name.

'Idiot,' she said.

'IDIOT!' she shouted.

Bane reached under the bed and she retrieved her dictaphone.

She found her dress beneath the bed. She went and stood in front of the mirror. She looked at herself sideways in the mirror, then full on, then sideways again. She turned her bottom to the mirror and slapped it. Her buttock juddered and a shiver of flesh ran across her hips and on to her belly.

She swore, picked up her other shoe and she flung it at the door, at the last place where she had seen Andy. It bounced off the door.

'Bastard!' she shouted.

Bane pulled on her dress, grabbed her Dictaphone, retrieved her shoes, put them on and left the room.

Back in her own room, Bane locked the door and sat down with her dictaphone. She rewound it a distance and pressed play:

'Come on, get those clothes off. Ha! Ha ha!' Laughter, followed by the sound of a long zip going down. Her dress.

She fast forwarded the tape.

'Jigsaw is the only real friend I've got. If it wasn't for Jigsaw I wouldn't have all a this.' More laughter. 'Nah, you're right, he's a cunt.'

Eventually Bane found the place that she was looking for. Bane strained to hear. The voices were crackly, distant:

'Tell me about Midas, Andy.'

'It's Jigsaw's company.'

'It's a corporation. Who's behind it?'

'Jigsaw, who else? I dunno. How the fuck should I know?'

'What do you know, Andy?'

'Nothing. Fuck all.'

'Dick Fault, he's a member of the Kryyten fund, isn't he?'

'The what?'

Bane fast forwarded the tape.

'Tell me about James.'

'Jigsaw? He's sick, y'know. Really sick. He's got the big C. It's terminal. There's nothing anyone can do about it.'

'He's got cancer?' Bane sounded shocked. 'I am so so sorry, Andy, really I am. I didn't know.'

'Cancer? What the fuck are you on about? Not cancer, you idiot! The big C. Capitalism. He's got it bad. I'm going to have to kill the fucker. Put us all out of our misery. Ha! Ha Ha!' Andy fell silent. 'Maybe it is cancer. Cancerous.'

There was the sound of drink being poured, of glasses being knocked together, then Andy singing: 'Give me your body. . . .' Bane forwarded the tape. She was still searching for that one essential piece of information.

'Why Midas?' she asked.

'Cos everything he touches he turns to gold. That's a laugh. Shite more like. It's just the wrapper on the present, innit? Like Christmas is elsewhere, get it? Yeh, we've all got the Midas touch now, haven't we eh? We've all got something of that turning everything that is beautiful in to fucking shite touch.' He burst in to song: 'It's raining money. . . .' There was the sound of Andy falling over.

'Hey, are we going to do this or wha?' There was the sound of him pulling off his pants. Followed by silence. The sound of bed-squeak. Bane switched off the tape.

Bane smiled. Everything was falling in to place.

37

Another Bigger Slice of the Cake

THE MIDAS TOUCH
by Press reporter Bane Burke.

... The fund bought Shoe for £150m and the Kwik Fit chain for £600 million, increasing their joint debts from 100 million to 1.9 billion, which was raised from loans, creaming off £1.2 billion in dividends. The fund sold the freehold of the stores for £500 million and leased them back to itself through overseas holding companies to avoid tax. Cost were slashed by reducing the work force by 3,500 allowing the fund to take the savings in dividends. The fund floated the business and took another £600 million. ...

The offices of the Kryten Fund, Knightsbridge. The air blue with cigar smoke. A celebration.
   'More cake, anyone?'
   Jigsaw was in effusive mood.
   The fund had just been voted Private Equity Fund of the year for the second year running by the financial trade press and the funds select group of investors had gathered together to celebrate as well as to introduce four prospective members to the fund: Sir James Tindall, billionaire retailer; James Bankroft, billionaire; Myles Pimm, billionaire; Roger Gott, developer, another billionaire. Jigsaw introduced Skutt and Hames to the men. The analysts had been brought in to give the technical lowdown on the fund.
But there was no need.
   The funds performance had everyone convinced. Its success, in its first three years, had been prodigious. Employing financial analysts and mathematicians,

and using computers running algorithms to spot trends and price anomalies in everything from equities to commodities, futures and options. Kryten had, since its launch, made an annualised average return of 40% on initial investments.

The four prospective members were already convinced. They were there to sign.

The men signed.

Kryten was proving to be the ultimate free lunch. Certainly it was attracting all the usual free lunchers. Jigsaw was offering partnerships in Kryten to the world's wealthiest men. The money was flowing in. Kryten now managed a total of £25 billion in two funds, KrytenEquity and KrytenFutures, and Jigsaw was aiming to increase that amount to £100 billion.

Investors were so eager to obtain a stake in Kryten that Jigsaw had raised the entry requirement to 2 billion, the money to be locked in for a period of two years, with all redemptions after that period requiring a notice period of 45 days.

Jigsaw stood. He addressed the gathering:

'These are wonderful times we are living in. There is no limit to what we can achieve, to where we can go from here. This government knows how to help business. They are removing restrictions on business and free trade. They have deregulated finance. We are now freer than ever to make our profits as we see fit. We have now what we have always wanted. We can do what we want.'

Jigsaw raised his glass.

The partners raised their glasses. Champagne corks popped, glasses clinked.

Jigsaw flew to NY.

With the backing of several of the big American banks and investment houses and with the help of Skutt and Hames, his economic and financial advisers, he set up Midas Loans for Homes, offering cheap loans to low income families.

He flew back to London. He had an exhibition of new paintings to attend.

38

The Exhibition

Andy woke with a start.

L.A. had been all sunlight and blue skies. But it was deep winter in London. It was dark and it was raining.

The city blazed with light.

The headlights of oncoming cars; brightly illuminated buildings, streetlights, signs; and of rain caught in the cars' headlights like fragments of flying light, flew at him from the darkness.

Jigsaw drove fast. 70. 50. 30. The signs were blurs as they sped in to the warped and warping city.

A huge banner, proclaiming, *TOTAL ART TODAY*, hung over the entrance to the warehouse conversion.

Rotting cows heads complete with flies. A sheep in a tank of formaldehyde. A row of girls in brand name trainers with dicks protruding from their heads. A tent, with the names of the artist's lovers tallied on its sides. Blank canvases with a solitary dot at their centre. . . Something extraordinary was happening in the art world.

British art was suddenly the most exciting in the world, and the most expensive. Damien Hirst, Tracey Emin, the Chapman brothers, Marc Quin, Angus Fairhurst, Matt Collinshaw, Michael Landy, Sarah Lucas, Enzo, Sadie Sommers . . . names were being made all the time. And they were attracting investors from all over the globe.

Mister Guggenheim, the rich American collector, Larry Gargosian, the world's leading art dealer, Charles Saatchi, collector and gallery owner, and the

Directors of the Tate Modern, the New York Museum of Modern Art, Madrid's Prado, and the Hayward Gallery, London, had all signalled their intention to attend, as had Dick Fault, of Lemmon Brothers, the retail king Al Geldt, and Max Bringmeen, reportedly the world's second richest man. Ferraris, Porches, Daimlers, Buggatis, Bentleys, numerous Rolls Royces, many of them chauffeur driven, packed out the car park. They had been arriving at the exclusive warehouse development in London's Docklands since early that afternoon. It was the last night of Enzo's, Sadie Sommers' and Petros Kouriakis' respective exhibitions and the collections were now going up for sale.

From a small fenced off enclosure at the rear of the development, and hidden amongst the wheel-y-bins and mini skips, the three friends, Pogget, Munted and Mullah, watched the rich guests arrive.

'Wunuvum's bound ter wander over ere, sooner or later, ter avver smowke or summat lyke, an then will av the cunt. Fucken minted thee are, doan go no place wirout a wad, yewel see.'

A Daimler pulled up, parking close by and Max Bringmeen stepped out. Then Mister Guggenheim's chauffeur driven Daimler arrived. Al Geldt, accompanied by the art advisor, Kate Rungle, pulled up in Kate's BMW.

Ra arrived, emerging from a taxi cab. She was wearing an expensive fur trimmed woollen coat and a Russian style fur hat. She looked like a size zero super model. She hurried out of the spitting rain up the steps and in to the building.

'Is your ex, innit?' said Munted.

Pogget stared. 'Wha the fuck? Wha she doin heer, wir awl thees fucken cunts?'

'Obvious innit?' said Mullah. 'Fucken slag prossy, int she?'

Pogget took a swipe at Mullah's head, knocking off his hoodie.

More cars arrived, bringing more people. A taxi pulled up. A tall blonde stepped out. She was accompanied by a photographer.

'Willyer look a tha,' said Pogget. 'A wooden mind sum a tha, juz lookerit.'

Bane Burke bent and she passed money in to the cab. The photographer took a package out of the cab and handed it to Bane before they hurried up the steps and in to the exhibition.

The exhibition was being held in three of the four huge workshops making up the ground floor of PK's two floor apartment complex in the development. PK lived on the first floor. Andy and Jigsaw on the fourth. Enzo and Sadie Sommers had the penthouse upstairs. A hedge fund manager lived on the third and the media mogul, David Pinwang, owned the other apartment. It was a very exclusive development.

The entrance foyer and the several studios were crowded with impeccably dressed people drinking wine and champagne, talking, viewing the art on offer. Bane recognised some very successful artists amongst the gathering. There were architects, lawyers, fund managers, financiers, company directors, retailers – many of them millionaires, multimillionaires. There was even a billionaire present. Rich, well paid, well connected, here were the people everyone wanted to be. It was their city now and they had the money to turn ideas in to hard reality. Bane experienced a shudder of revulsion at the thought. She stood scanning the gathering, clutching her package as she searched out her target.

Signs set on tiny easels indicated the subject being exhibited in each studio:

Studio 1 - Enzo: Art. Period
Studio 2 - Sadie Sommers: Opulent Interiors
Studio 3 - Petros Kouriakis: Mona Lith: the Road to Perdition

There was a large crowd gathered outside studio 1.

Enzo was stood at the entrance to the studio talking with Andy. They were surrounded by a group of admirers. Andy was telling the gathering a joke:

'A rich merchant hires Leonardo Da Vinci to paint a portrait of his wife. When the portrait is finished the merchant comes around to view it. He stands in front of the finished painting. He walks to the left and the eyes follow him. He walks to the right and the eyes follow him. He's so made up with the picture that he slaps Leonardo heartily on the back an he says. . . .' Andy was trying to stop himself laughing. 'He says. . . .'

Jigsaw excused himself, slipping off in to the studio.

'He says, "That's great, Leonardo. I'll take ten.'

As Jigsaw entered the studio the room fell silent. People turned to look in his direction. They pointed him out.

'It's Mister Midas himself,' said someone.

Dick Fault waved, raising his glass to Jigsaw. He began to make his way over. Max Bringmeen and his group looked across, nodding their hellos. Jigsaw offered them the slightest nod of his head. Several people lifted their glasses to him but Jigsaw, his attention drawn exclusively to the new Enzos, appeared not to notice.

The works, consisted of no more than a small black dot on a white canvas. The paintings were in no way remarkable, and yet they were in every way extraordinary, because they were by Enzo. There was even one depicting the name, Enzo, signed, Enzo, that was entitled, *Enzo*.

The works puzzled Jigsaw and he was a little disappointed by them, though he remained intent on their purchase.

He checked his catalogue: Reserve price, one million pounds.

'What do you think?' asked Dick Fault.

Just as he was about to answer, several slow hand claps resounded about the gallery. Someone was offering their applause and in a distinctly jeering way. The room fell silent, everyone turning in the direction of the sound.

Jigsaw turned, saw Bane Burke. His face fell.

She had been harassing him for months, appearing at crowded press conferences and shareholders meetings, even accosting him in the street, and, once, in the lobby of MidasCorp itself, shouting out accusations, bombarding him with questions and demanding answers.

Now, she was crossing the room in his direction, holding out a life-size model of a dodo, its polished golden plastic reflecting the bright lights. People moved aside to make an avenue for her.

Jigsaw glanced around the room, hoping to catch the eye of someone in security. There was no one.

Bane stopped in front of Jigsaw and held out the dodo to him.

'Congratulations,' she said. 'On behalf of the readers of *The Press* newspaper I would like to present you, as head of MidasCorp, with this year's Dodo Award for MidasCorp's services to the planet.' And, thrusting it against his chest, she let the two foot tall, hollow, plastic trophy go.

Jigsaw found himself holding the dodo. Several people applauded. The photographer took his picture.

Producing the certificate accompanying the award Bane then read off a list of accusations against the corporation:

'MidasCorp drills for oil in environmentally sensitive areas. MidasCorp clear-fells tropical rainforest. Whole ecosystems are being destroyed by MidasCorp activities. . . .' The list went on and on. 'Its industries are polluting the planet, it is downright criminal what is being done.' Bane held out the certificate to Jigsaw.

Jigsaw waved it away. 'There is nothing criminal about our operations, Bane, I can assure you, MidasCorp operates entirely within the law. We have all the necessary licences.'

'All paid for, no doubt,' countered Bane, rubbing her fingers and thumb together.

Jigsaw ignored the accusation. 'And there are,' he said, 'acceptable levels of pollution.'

'No pollution should be acceptable!'

Jigsaw shrugged. 'But it is, and it is the price that we pay for development, and are prepared to pay, because MidasCorp, like many a global corporation, is creating wealth. You only have to look at the statistics. The GDP of every country in which we operate has increased as a direct result of our operations. And that means jobs. Midas is creating millions of jobs, worldwide, every year.'

'Pointless menial jobs on minimum wages. Part time jobs. Short term contract work. You call those jobs?'

Jigsaw smiled. 'Hundreds of millions of people depend on them for a living, Bane. You have heard of trickle down, I take it?'

'That's it's a trickle, yes.' Bane's eyes, narrow and hard, narrowed even further. 'You're not creating wealth, you're only interested in making yourselves wealthier by cutting costs, realising assets, increasing your profit margins and raising share value.'

Bane had the facts to back up her accusations:

'Workers in MidasCorp companies earn next to nothing, you employ people on minimum wages on zero hours contracts, yet you personally will receive £12m in bonuses this year, half of it as stock in the company. Then there is the retained incentive opportunity, worth £25 million, which you recently set up for yourself. And the £10m you are paid annually for providing an advisory role to MidasFinance. Not to mention the £25m in share based performance plans in which you are enrolled. You also receive £15,000 a week in benefits, and to top it all you have just set up an equity acquisition plan which will provide you with over £350m worth of MidasCorp shares over a three year period. You also own I don't know how many properties, a private jet, a yacht, all of them secured for you by MidasCorp.'

'Bane, if MidasCorp was not doing well then I would not be doing well, it's as simple as that. Spectacular remuneration only kicks in when there's spectacular performance. And you can't deny that it has been spectacular. Look at the MidasCorp share price. I and my executives are being rewarded for that.'

Bane glared at Jigsaw. 'Midas is doing very well, yes, but at what cost? Only this week Midas bought yet another major British company, sacked its workers, sold off its assets, looted its pension fund and sent its manufacturing operation overseas. At the same time it inserted a holding company based in the British Virgin Islands between MidasCorp and the new business in order to avoid paying millions of pounds in UK taxes, effectively denying that money to the exchequer.'

Jigsaw made to answer, but Bane pressed on with her attack:

'Britain is losing control of its key industries. We live in a country that no longer owns the productive processes that create its own wealth. Crucial economic sectors have been handed over to private and to foreign corporate ownership. The utilities have been handed over. One company changed hands a total of five times this last year. It was bought by your fund, you sold it on to a French consortium who passed it on to a German company who sold it back to MidasCorp. MidasCorp makes more money buying and selling companies than it makes from selling the very things some of those companies produce. A company gets sold, its assets are stripped, and then it reappears in Peking. And the jobs go with it.'

'We're not in business to make things,' said Jigsaw, 'we're in this business to make money. And money goes to where it can find the greatest return. It's the same with jobs.'

Jigsaw liked to tell it exactly how it was. He came across as someone driven by his convictions. Certainly he spoke without equivocation. He had no doubts, no uncertainties. His single mindedness and obstinacy angered Bane. It pleased her too. It just might, she hoped, anger everyone, eventually. Her method was simple. She would provoke Jigsaw in to making ever more unequivocal statements. She wanted to attack big money by turning opinion against it before it was too late. In this respect Jigsaw proved the perfect adversary. He was just the kind of businessman, rich enough, greedy enough, endlessly overconfident, to make the problem of his type abundantly clear. All too often he came across as an arrogant, uncompromising and uncaring neo-liberal, the very worst.

'As for jobs, Bane, they go to wherever labour is cheapest. It's sound business and economic sense. It makes things cheaper. In the global economy you can't have a British exception. There—'

Bane cut him short. 'And when wages are cheap no one will have the money to buy anything.'

'I suppose you would prefer astronomical commodity prices?' said Jigsaw, reframing the perspective: Bane, enemy of the people. Bitch.

Bane narrowed her eyes.

'Isn't it true,' she said, 'that in Alaska, MidasOil and Gas, along with several other major oil companies, is threatening to take out a lawsuit against the US government in order to stop it from listing polar bears as an endangered species to prevent them initiating measures to protect them in their habit?'

'Well of course we are. You have to understand, there are a lot of valuable resources beneath that ice. Oil, gas, maybe even coal. And it's just a wasteland up there. All there is are these couple of hundred polar bears. The world needs energy far more than it needs a few bears. It's the same with the Athabasca tar sands. It's just wilderness. But Midas is developing that. Or would you prefer it if the world ran out of energy?'

Bane's silence answered the question for her. 'Midas isn't creating wealth,' she countered, 'it's destroying it. At the present rate of development, in less than thirty years, we will need two planets to provide the materials necessary to maintain our lifestyle and provide people with the money to pay for them. But we haven't got two planets.'

Jigsaw grinned. 'No, but we do have the third world.'

There was quite a crowd stood around listening and every one of them laughed. Dick Fault, Max Bringmeen, Al Geldt, Kate Rungle. . . .

'There are huge unexploited reserves and vast untapped markets out there still,' said Jigsaw, 'and we are going to develop them.'

Like a lance stabbed angrily in to the ground, Bane stood, arms rigid at her sides, her hands clenched in to fists, her knuckles whitening, quivering with indignation. Would she ever make these people understand?

'There won't be any kind of a world if we carry on like this. There will be less wealth, not more. Less space, less forests, less clean water, less wilderness, less land. The place will just get more built up, more overcrowded, more polluted. Constant economic growth will result in shortages of everything. Water, fuel, food, space. It will end up with everything and everyone having to be controlled. There will be less freedoms then. There will have to be more laws, bringing more restrictions, more constraints. There will be shortages of everything. People will need more money, meaning more work.' Bane threw her arms in to the air. Not in defeat, from exasperation. 'Midas isn't creating wealth, it is destroying it, and on a vast scale. Midas is no more than an asset stripping locust. It creates wealth solely for the purpose of creaming wealth off. Your companies are milking the economy. And you are milking those companies. The world is being plundered. It is being run solely for the benefit of a greedy and unaccountable elite.'

In her column for *The Press*, Bane wrote that the corporations were taking over, that powerful elites were moving the planet toward a new world order by transcending national boundaries and passing control to themselves. And they were using government to do it, creating a business friendly environment which they would then be in a position to dominate. A synergy was being forged between government and big business that was bent on creating a worldwide commercial utopia serviced by a locked in client workforce.

Jigsaw smiled at Bane. 'There's no conspiracy, Bane. That's just the way things are.' He laughed.

'Isn't it true that MidasCorp recently made a £1m donation to the Tory party? And, in America, a staggering $12 million to the Republicans.'

'We make donations to all the parties, Bane. We're very democratic.' Laughter. 'And how did you get that information? It is supposed to be confidential.'

Someone had been sending Bane confidential information. And not just about MidasCorp. Details about private meetings in the Hamptons, in Corfu and in Davos between financiers, economists, equity fund managers, corporate bosses and politicians, which Jigsaw, as head of MidasCorp, had attended, had all been leaked.

They revealed that Jigsaw was a member of the multinational chairmen's club, an elite group that Bane claimed had access to the White House and to Downing Street. Downing Street documents leaked to Bane and then printed in *The Press* revealed how the secretive lobbying group, which consisted of the heads of Britain's most powerful corporations - including BP, Unilever, HSBC, Shell, British American Tobacco, Vodafone, and GlaxoSmithKline – had used their connections to successfully lobby government on issues ranging from environmental and labour law to taxation. According to the documents Jigsaw also sat on a secretive committee of business superstars brought together to advise government on how to improve the competitiveness of the UK.

'Tell me about Kryten,' said Bane.

'Kryten?' For a second Jigsaw appeared uneasy. 'It's a private equity fund, everyone knows that.'

'Who funds it?' Bane wanted to know.

'I couldn't possibly tell you that, Bane. The partners are very private persons. I can assure you however that they are all high net-worth individuals.'

'Isn't it true that Kryten has borrowed and is leveraged so extensively that it is now holding contracts worth 1.3 trillion dollars?'

'You're wrong. It's 1.5 trillion. And the sum is only going to increase.' Jigsaw was obviously delighted by the fact.

Bane frowned, puzzled at his reaction.

Jigsaw's ultimate success depended on just how much debt the markets could take on. The strategy had already become so complex that it was impossible to know exactly how much debt a particular asset might be carrying.

Employing radical new securitisation technology, financial instruments, designed to turn debt in to a security, were being traded on the financial markets, bought, sold and then hedged against and continuously reinsured. This had stimulated and allowed borrowing to reach incredible levels. And it was being used to fund massive private equity deals. Kryten Equity bought and sold whole companies but, through Kryten Futures, it also dealt in commodities, shares, bonds, currencies, debt, credit default swaps and collateralised debt obligations.

'You're very good at conjuring up money out of nowhere,' said Bane. 'In fact, you've created a whole corporation virtually out of nothing.'

'Money happens, Bane.'

According to statistics provided to Bane by Jeremy Stanford, finance and business editor at *The Press*, the size of the world economy was 50 trillion, yet the amount of derivatives being traded was 85 trillion?

'Just how can that be possible?' Bane asked. 'That is more than the entire economic activity of the whole planet?'

'It's capital's natural progression,' answered Jigsaw, beaming. 'What's being created here is pure money. It's capitalism without the capital, Bane. It's future money, now. Just imagine what all that money is going to do, it's going to make everything possible. There won't be anything we cannot do.'

The prospect horrified Bane. 'The City is warped,' she exploded, 'It's become warped. The whole thing is grotesque. Capitalism has set money loose on this planet.'

Bane had come to realise that in its ceaseless search for wealth capital, by expanding in to new areas, new technologies, new countries, new industry, by creating new fashions, new needs, new desires, must inevitably, by definition, abandon everything in its wake. It constantly generates old technologies, jobs, fashions, skills, industries, communities, towns, entire wastelands as whole ways of life, whole countries, even, become obsolete. Capital is fluid, it is ephemeral, it is everything there is distilled. When everything can be bought and sold for money, then everything can be destroyed for money. Everything can be sold, abandoned, and then money makes it reappear elsewhere. Once you understood that, then the whole world made sense: Capital existed to create money. Not food, not shelter, not the necessities. They were just the by-product of money. Wherever you looked, capital was extending the limits to what was possible, it was making some lives impossible. Life from now on was going to be lived on that edge.

'It's insane!' she burst out, 'You're insane.' She pointed a finger at Jigsaw. 'You all are. All this money, it will destroy everything eventually!'

Jigsaw, Dick Fault, Max Bringmeen, Al Geldt . . . everyone threw back their heads and laughed. They just could not see a problem let alone share her concerns. The City was doing well, the economy was booming, big business was in control and the money was flowing in. Rising consumer confidence financed by cheap and easy credit was making everyone wealthier. And the mood amongst the public was for more money. But what Bane was saying was that there should be less money. It made her appear deranged. That brought everything she said in to question.

To Bane, furious with rage, their laughter seemed a kind of celebration. 'You people make me sick. Money is destroying this planet. All this growth, it does more damage than any amount of good honest destruction could ever wreak.'

Bane had said it before and she would go on saying it until people understood: 'The pursuit of wealth is pushing mankind to the brink, it is filling the world with shite and enslaving everyone in its creation.'

Those listening sighed and shook their heads. They sniggered at Bane, mocking her for her conviction.

The laughter, the condescending smiles, they made Bane fume. These people were so smug and self assured, and no wonder, she realised. They owned the argument, because there was no argument, all the language was for growth, anything less meant failure. They owned the money. And money was power. They owned the jobs. They owned the politicians, and the media. They even owned the language. They say one thing and mean something else entirely, the opposite. They offer liberty, and we get rules and regulations. They talk of law and order, when what they mean is control. They offer freedom, through hard work. They're not talking about our freedom, they are talking about their freedom, the freedom to make money, and at everyone else's expense. They offer credit, and people end up in debt. Indebted. Debt is traded as a security and a liability becomes an asset. They claim that they are creating money, when all they do is to provide the numbers that say that there is money, dictating the money that has yet to be made. It was the reason for all the work. They promise a brave new world and all most of us ever get to see of it is some expensive, poxy T-shirt saying: *A Brave New World*. People were being used. The whole thing was a con and everyone had fallen for it. Wherever Bane looked she saw ignorance and collusion.

'Consumer confidence is destroying this planet!'

Her statement was met with groans. People began to move away. They had heard it all before, they were tired of hearing it.

Jigsaw rolled his eyes. 'There have always been prophets of doom, Bane. Yet here we still are,' he grinned. 'Do you really think that people care about the natural world when they no longer live in it?' Bane made to answer but Jigsaw continued: 'The world is changing. People are changing, and the world is being changed to suit them. People like living in cities, it makes life easier for them. They want things to be easy. It's not more green space that they want, it's more retail and leisure choices. They want retail parks, not the other kind. As for their concerns about the future, what is the economic climate going to be doing in the next financial quarter, that is what everyone wants to know. As for that other climate, well, that's just the weather.' Jigsaw laughed. But he just as soon stopped laughing. His face grew serious.

'Climate change does present us with some serious problems, though,' he admitted.

'You agree that it is happening then? Why it is happening?'

'Bane, if what the scientists are saying is true then rapid climate change will threaten the whole economic development of the planet.'

Bane groaned, she threw her hands to the air, claw like, from frustration.

Jigsaw went on, 'Which is why we at MidasCorp have set up Midas Emissions Trading. We believe that carbon offsetting will become the single biggest commodity being traded on the world markets, bigger than both the bond and the equity markets combined. We stand to make billions, possibly trillions from it. Just think of what we can do with all that money.' He was goading Bane, and he knew it. 'And MidasCorp is rising to the challenge in practical ways too. MidasCorp is setting up a development fund to bankroll initiatives in alternative energy and the emerging green industries. Green consumerism is the future, and what a future it promises to be. Electric cars. Passive houses. Solar energy. Clean fuel. Sustainable growth is the way forward and we at MidasCorp intend leading the way.'

'How can continuous growth be sustainable?' asked an incredulous Bane.

'That is the question we are all asking ourselves,' said Jigsaw. 'And MidasCorp is rising to the challenge.'

Bane felt sick to the pit of her stomach. She shook her head. 'When is it ever going to end?' she asked.

'End?' said Jigsaw. 'Bane, it isn't ever going to end. The whole point of sustainability is that it will never end. It will go on and on. The world will continue to get wealthier, and more modern. Think of it, Bane, there will be nothing that we cannot have. Everyone will have a jet ski. The future is Midas,' he grinned.

Bane could have wept.

Jigsaw shrugged at his victory. 'Bane, there are some things about which nothing can be done. Trying to change them in the way that you are is just a waste of time. You can write all the articles that you like about it, you can give every corporation in the land a dead as a dodo award, and it won't change a single thing. An austere future, like the one you're offering? It's not what people want. People want the good things in life, they feel entitled to them, they've worked hard enough for them, after all, and they are going to get them, otherwise what would be the point? And when they get them they will want more. They will want something else. And if you don't give people what they want then you are going to have to tell them that they can't have it. And who is going to do that? The politicians?' Jigsaw laughed.

'As for this award,' he said, holding the Dodo up for inspection, 'I'm afraid that I can't possibly accept it. It belongs to the consumer, to the customers of MidasCorp. It is the consumer that has made Midas in to what it is. Midas could not exist without the consumer. Present it to your readers, Bane. Here.' And he thrust the dodo in to Bane's arms.

The dumb look on the long doomed creature's face taunted Bane. It was the same dumb and smiling look she saw everywhere.

In the speech that followed that presentation Jigsaw told of a coming brave new world of unlimited economic growth. He promised more money, more work, more of everything. Jigsaw smiled. He beamed for his photograph. 'We are doing God's work,' he said.

Bane lost what little self-control remained to her then. She began shouting at Jigsaw, hitting him on the chest with the award, beating him on the shoulders with it, before breaking it on his head.

People looked on, horrified, several of them rushing forward to restrain her. Max Bringmeen grabbed her by one arm, Dick Fault by the other.

'Is this woman bothering you, sir?' It was security.

'Yes,' said Jigsaw, rubbing his head where Bane had hit him, 'she most certainly is. Could you have her escorted from the building, please.'

'Certainly, Mister Truitt, sir.'

As the men dragged her away through the crowd Bane struggled to free herself from their grip.

'Why,' she screamed, 'why are you doing this? What for? Haven't you got enough already? What is it that you want exactly? What?'

'Money, of course,' said Jigsaw. 'All the money in the world,' he laughed.

'She's quite mad, of course,' said Max Bringmeen, 'Have you read her column.' He drilled a forefinger in to his temple.

'Some people are plain nuts,' said Dick Fault, 'They want us to go back to living in the stone age.'

'God forbid that it should have to come to that,' said Jigsaw.

Max Bringmeen extended a hand to Jigsaw. 'Max Bringmeen,' he said, introducing himself. The two men shook hands like old friends, Bringmeen clasping Jigsaw's hand inside both of his hands.

'James,' he said, smiling, 'I've been tracking the progress of your fund, the numbers are impressive. You've got the Midas touch, alright. Look, I'll come right to the point. I want a piece of Kryten. 20 billion worth.'

'It's an extraordinary sum,' said Jigsaw.

'We live in extraordinary times,' said Max Bringmeen.

Jigsaw agreed.

Bane sat outside on the steps of the building in the cold and rain and she wept tears of anger and frustration.

She had never felt so miserable nor so alone. Jigsaw was right, she could say whatever she wanted and it wouldn't make a single bit of difference. You couldn't fight money. You could fight it, but it always had you beat. You needed money. Everyone did. It had everyone trapped.

What was it that Jigsaw had once said to her? 'You have to fight money with money, Bane.'

How though? And why would he of all people say that. It began to niggle her. Bane frowned, she narrowed her eyes, convinced that she was missing something.

Then it came to her as she recalled a story that she had once heard that people liked to tell about Jigsaw: Three men go in to the Adelphi Hotel in Liverpool and ask for a triple room for which they are charged £30. The bellboy, the young James Truitt, when he returns from carrying up the men's bags reminds the registrar that the room, at the rear of the building, should have cost only £25. Reluctantly, the registrar hands Jigsaw the difference, which he then returns to the men. The men are so grateful to Jigsaw that they allow him to keep two pound as a tip. The men are happy for a time but they later grow troubled by the transaction. They go over it and over it, and still they cannot work it out. Because £30, which was what they initially paid for the room, minus the £3 they were given back, makes £27, plus the £2 tip they gave to the bellboy adds up to just £29? The men bring this to the attention of the management and Jigsaw is sacked for financial irregularities. It is just a story that people in the financial world like to tell amongst themselves. The point is that a clever accountant or financier or economist can make numbers do whatever it is that they want them to do. It was the reason for all their laughter.

Bane experienced a moment of insight of the purest clarity. Pure money, wasn't that what Jigsaw said was being created? Yes, and it could just as easily disappear up its own fundament.

'Oh you clever bastard.' Bane laughed. She laughed out loud.

She had begun to think that nothing could reach those hundreds of millions of people living by the dollar. But people can be forced in to doing things. One way or the other. You can take way their capabilities. Bane laughed and laughed. Money was lies. It was falsehood and illusion. Money can be invented, it can be imagined. It's just symbols, it's just numbers. The numbers whirl around and they underpin everything. It was the greatest trick in the world. Without it the City would grind to a halt.

Mister Guggenheim was puzzled. He stood staring at the canvas, wondering whether the dot on it was supposed to be an e. He supposed it had to be, on reflection, it being the new drug for the new era. Or was that cocaine? He consulted his catalogue for an explanation of the work. What he read there caused him to raise his eyebrows.

There was no explanation, just the title: *Enzo. Period. The End Of Art*. What surprised him most though was that each picture had a reserve price of one million pounds. Disgusted, he snapped shut the catalogue.

What he was looking at, he felt, was the artist's ultimate revenge on an increasingly gullible clientele. Enzo was offering, at great expense, things which people were all too capable of producing themselves. It was a joke, surely, and perhaps a very clever one, but Mister Guggenheim felt intimidated. He shook his head. He despaired of contemporary art. The pictures said nothing to him. They explained nothing. It was just art for art's sake, for money's sake. Contemporary art, it was nothing more than artifice and so he dismissed the works as entirely symptomatic of the age, the product of too much liquidity coupled with no cultural judgement.

A frisson of excitement then ran like a charge through the studio as Enzo appeared. He was a compelling sight, with his long uncombed hair, one of his shirt fronts hanging out, his trademark shiny black suit crumpled and disarranged.

'He looks crazy,' said a voice.

'You know what they're like, these artists, they neglect themselves.'

Enzo looked like a drunk, like someone who had emerged backwards from a pub brawl. He had not even shaved.

Mounting the podium Enzo stared in to the crowd. The crowd stared back. They were waiting for the auction to begin.

'Art,' said Enzo, addressing the gathering. 'What is it exactly? That is the question that art most raises today. And I've heard it myself asked many times, here, tonight.'

There was some laughter from his audience. Uncertain looks were exchanged.

'What is it all about really though?' he asked.

'Monet,' he said, 'Cèzanne, Van Gogh, Picasso. Art is always pushing at the boundaries. It is experimenting with new ideas all the time. Mankind too is pushing at the boundaries. We are entering interesting times, we are possibly about to shape our future for the rest of eternity and what are we as artists doing?' Enzo shrugged. Glancing over his paintings, he shook his head.

'Art, today, is dead. Only it does not know that it is dead. We have spent the best part of the last fifty years deconstructing art and so successful have we been that it has become almost unintelligible. Is this what art is all about, people trying to make sense of what we have made? Possibly. It is symptomatic of the age, perhaps. But art should not raise questions about itself.'

'Is he drunk?' whispered Max Bringmeen to Jigsaw.

'I wish he'd get on with the auction,' hissed Al Geldt through gritted teeth, 'I didn't come here for a lecture on aesthetics.'

'Where are our Van Goghs?' asked Enzo, 'Where are our Brughels? Our Hogarths? Our Picassos?' Enzo paused. 'Where even, it might be said, dare I ask it, are our John Stuart Mills' and Karl Marxes? Who, now, is striving to make sense of the world today? Or are we just adding to the confusion?

'Art died with Picasso. Picasso took it as far as it could go. And in doing so he killed it. Everything we have done since is just more proof of that. We are more like Frankenstein than artists, forever mutating art in to newer and ever stranger forms in an attempt to give it new life, but all we get is distortion.

'Well I, too, feel that I have taken my art as far as it can go. That is why I have welcomed you here today, to Period. Or, as we say here in England, Full Stop. Because Enzo is over,' he declared, 'he's finished. The end,' he said.

The statement was met with stunned silence.

Everyone glanced to the person next to them. Their shocked faces looked at Enzo. It was a few moments before the full implications of his statement became clear.

No more new Enzos, ever. They were being offered his very last works, and, given his speech, perhaps his most definitive yet. Prices for existing Enzos would hit the roof.

A murmur rose up from the excited audience. They were keener than ever to acquire an Enzo.

Enzo had to call for silence.

'I would just like to say,' he shouted. He waited for the room to quieten. 'I would just like to say, in farewell, that my career, my success could not have been possible without you. It has been your support, your patronage that has made Enzo in to the artist he has become. And is still yet to become.'

Enzo bowed away from his paintings, presenting his paintings. He stood to one side and began to applaud his audience. His audience stood and they applauded. The applause was thunderous.

'From now on there will be no more Enzos,' he declared. 'Not ever. I'm done.'

Enzo had executed his signatures in biodegradable paint. In time, the signatures would disappear. The very things which made the canvases unique would cease to exist. It would, Enzo felt, provide the ultimate comment on his art, on what art had become.

The first lot, Enzo, signed, Enzo, entitled, *Enzo*, went to Max Bringmeen, for £7.5 million.

Disgusted, Mister Guggenheim left the auction at that point.

Rain lashed the building. Water gushed down its drainpipes.

Pogget looked up in to the darkness, the rain falling in to his face, in to his eyes. He squinted in to the rain, gripped the drainpipe and he pulled on it, hard, tugging it several times to check that it was securely fixed to the wall. The drainpipe was metal and it was very cold.

Pogget's hands were cold, discoloured and swollen by chilblains, cut and scabbed. Pulling on the drainpipe, gripping it, he lifted a foot to the wall. He began to scale the wall.

Opulent Interiors. Mister Guggenheim checked his catalogue.

'The artist offers the ultimate escape from the increasingly crowded and chaotic city in these vast and well-appointed interiors that will be familiar to so many of us. . . .'

The canvases were large, 8ft by 12ft. They showed huge, well-appointed rooms, with tall buildings crowding in at the windows. The pictures were rooms in themselves.

Though they were highly accomplished there seemed, in Mister Guggenheim's opinion, to be something missing from the works. It were as though they were copies of something. They were just pictures, like you could take with any camera.

Mister Guggenheim left the exhibition.

It was at that point that the auction at Enzo's finished. A charged and excited crowd exploded in to the hallway.

The room was dark. There was a humid heat to the room, the smell of toothpaste, soap, after-shave and of used damp towels that told Pogget that he was in a bathroom. He waited until his eyes had adjusted to the darkness, then he crept silently across the room to the door and he eased it open.

He could hear muffled music thumping up from downstairs, the deep biorhythmic drum beats of Iggy Pop's *Lust For Life*: Beat beat beat, beat-beat, beat-beat. . . .

With the auctions over a party had kicked off.

Loud music hit him like he'd walked in to a wall. The place was crowded with people. A seaswarm of dancing people pushed Mister Guggenheim deep in to the room, pressing him against a cold statue.

Mister Guggenheim walked around the 8 foot, five ton mass of misshapen carved stone. He caressed the hugely distended belly, ran his hands across its stump like arms and truncated legs, the featureless rounded head and oversized breasts.

According to the brass plaque fixed to its base the work was entitled, *Mona Lith*.

Stepping back to view the work he knocked over a beer bottle, smashing the bottle.

He was bumped and jostled from behind. Someone spilt drink over his shoes. He stepped in some vomit.

He was pushed this way and that, from statue to statue by the heaving crowd. One particular work, it looked cubist, caught the collector's eye. It was a frieze of the city but fractured in to blocks, in to shards, the various pieces sitting at unlikely angles to each other so that the scene, though familiar, appeared distorted and chaotic.

There was something called *The MultiBeast*, made up of a horde of intertwined screaming mouths, grasping hands and trampling feet.

There was a mouth and arsehole arrangement that was like a huge shitting scream.

All the works were massive.

Petrous Kouriakis was renowned for working on a heroic scale but it had always, until now, been in the classical style. Mister Guggenheim was appalled at the change. These works were grotesque. Everything about them was a distortion. The exhibition was no more than a celebration of sheer size and otherness as well as of the depraved.

There were leering satyrs, couplings of men and of women, of men with men, of women with women, and of men and women somehow coupled with themselves.

Mister Guggenheim stared. There were people in that dark inferno of a studio that were actually engaged in such things. The low, red lighting, the darknesses, the dry ice, the wild dancing, it was like he was in a painting by Heironymous Bosch. Semi-naked women, pole dancers, girls from WorldBabe, danced grotesquely in the strobe lights. A grinning bacchus lifted a wine glass in salute. People were entwined around the statues, dancing with them. Mister Guggenheim could no longer tell what was real from what was unreal. He fled the studio and hurried down the steps in to the cold and sobering night air.

It had stopped raining and the sky had cleared. The night sky glowed sodium yellow.

From their hiding place amongst the rubbish skips Munted and Mullah watched the elderly, slender gentleman walk over in their direction. Their faces hardened, their eyes narrowed to slits and their lips drew tight.

Mister Guggenheim's sweat cooled on his skin, making him shiver.

He pulled his overcoat tight around him and he lit a cigar. He stood at the water's edge, looking at the brightly lit city, blowing smoke in to the night air. All around him the bright city blazed, its reflection wriggling to him across the water.

Mister Guggenheim became lost in a contemplation of the city.

The city appeared warped to him, like the art was warped, it had become warped. Strange buildings, unusual shapes, of the kind once envisioned by science fiction writers and the illustrators of comics had become the considered creations of architects. They were all too real, and the city had become unreal. The city was being deconstructed, reality was being torn apart, one piece at a time, and then reassembled, and in a way that was no longer familiar to him. Those new buildings were too tall, too close together, too ugly, too unrestrained. They made the future seem ugly and deranged. There seemed to be no end to what was possible.

Mister Guggenheim knew then that there were no boundaries anymore, because there were no longer any restraints.

Why wasn't anyone painting that? he wondered.

The sound of footsteps closing on him from behind snapped him out of his reverie. Mister Guggenheim whirled around.

'Did you see anything you liked, sir?' It was Mister Thimblebaum, Mister Guggenheim's personal assistant.

'Nothing,' said Mister Guggenheim. 'Do you know, I think I have just viewed the worst kind of art from its worst ever period.'

The two men were crossing the car park to their car when Mister

Guggenheim stopped suddenly. The warped and distorted city, the equally warped art, in that sense alone it had captured the very ethos of the age. It struck him then just how brilliant Enzo and PK were and he cursed himself loudly for not having picked up a piece.

Flashing lights, lasers pulsing off the walls.

Night changes the place completely, the lid comes off. It was Friday night, the end of yet another week of hard work and, for some, several months of hard work, and an occasion for wild and drunken revelry. All the passion and need and want that life locks up in a person gets to be unleashed. People let themselves go and some forget themselves entirely.

Bane Burke was drunk, she was in PK's and she was dancing, waving the half destroyed dodo above her head. She danced with Andy. She danced with PK. She danced with Max Bringmeen then Al Geldt. She even danced with Jigsaw, until Jigsaw snatched the dodo from her and then refused to give it up, claiming that it was his dodo. Jigsaw, Sadie, Enzo, Ra, Max Bringmeen, PK, Dick Fault . . . everyone was dancing, everyone was celebrating. A fantastic energy, a sense of power and celebration filled the room.

Depeche Mode's *I just can't get enough*, was blasting out, thumping off the walls.

Champagne bottles were going off, foam ejaculating high in to the air.

Andy was drunk, he was stoned, he hadn't slept for almost twenty four hours and he was having trouble keeping upright.

The music got louder, the dancing faster, less restrained.

When David Bowie's *Fashion* began blasting out, everyone did what the music instructed them to do: Fashion, turn to the left. Fashion, turn to the right . . . the dancing seemed choreographed.

The music changed.

The Bangles' *Walk Like An Egyptian* filled the studio and everyone began to walk like an Egyptian.

Then it was Iggy Pop's *Nightclubbing*, then Joy Division's *Digital*, then Bryan Ferry's *Love is the Drug*, followed by David Bowie's *Ashes to Ashes*, followed by the Flying Lizards' *Money That's What I Want*, then. . . .

Andy was on the dance floor. He was in the toilets snorting up cocaine. He was on the dance floor again just trying to stay upright.

PK had removed his belt from his trousers and had fixed it around the neck of one of the lap dancers and he was leading her about the studio on all fours.

Now Andy was stood with his arms at his sides and was leaning forwards, pivoting on his ankles at an impossible angle, as far as it was possible to go before falling over. He leant even further forwards and he held the position to wild applause. And fell flat on his face.

Jigsaw tried, then PK, followed by Ra, Enzo, Bane.... Everyone was caught up in the same madness.

People began to pair off, to disappear for a time and then to reappear.

The night began to fracture. Time sped up, it slowed down, then sped up again. Events would later become confused. It was eleven o'clock. Then midnight, then two in the morning of a sudden.

It was eleven o'clock:

Loud music blasting out: Soft Cell, Mark Almond singing: *Say Hello, Wave Goodbye*. . . .

Pogget found a pocket watch. He pocketed it.

He searched the dresser, the bedside cabinets, but found nothing.

He left the bedroom and entered a study, there was a large desk. He was sliding open the drawer when loud music, Soft Cell, from the party downstairs, filled the room as someone opened the door. Pogget froze.

'Not the study, the bedroom,' said a man's voice. A woman giggled.

He heard another door open then close. Then there was the sound of clothes being pulled off, of shoes being kicked across the wooden floor of the bedroom next door.

He smiled. Cautiously, he stood up. Carefully, quietly, he returned to searching the desk drawer. He flipped on his pencil torch. Stationary, note pads, pencils, pens, a roll of fifties. A bag of ees. Two small bags of cocaine.

Joy exploded in Pogget's head.

Pogget pocketed the roll of fifties, the bags of ees and cocaine. He slid shut the drawer, then he crept back toward the bedroom and he eased the door open a crack.

There was a struggle going on on the bed. He heard choking sounds.

It was dark in the bedroom but there was just enough light shining in through the thin curtains from outside for him to recognise Ra.

There was a man between her legs.

She was tied to the bed posts by her wrists and the man was pumping away at her and strangling her with a belt.

Ra was pulling frantically at her restraints, kicking out her legs, pushing away the bed sheets with her heels.

Pogget pulled open the door. Then he was across the room, launching himself at the bed, hauling the man off Ra, throwing him headlong on to the floor.

It was a roll clasp belt and Pogget had to pull on the belt to release it. Ra's eyes bulged, her choking halted and her body stiffened and arched up.

She bucked and kicked, pulling at her restraints, her legs kicking out and kicking out.

She pissed herself.

Then a fist smashed in to the side of Pogget's head and strong arms grabbed him around the shoulders.

They fell crashing to the floor, punching, butting, palms pushing at each others chins, fingers in nostrils, in eyes. Pogget felt his head being pushed back and pushed back till he thought that his neck would snap.

Then the choking stopped, the fighting stopped and the room fell silent.

It was two in the morning when Andy staggered out in to the cold night air and threw up. Quite a few people, as soon as they got outside reeled and threw up. Others were being carried between friends, helped in to cars and in to taxi cabs.

Rockets went racing up in to the night sky.

Reluctant to go home a large crowd began to gather along the quay at the water's edge. People are attracted to edges. Eventually, inevitably, someone fell in.

Andy woke, in to yet another black hangover. He leapt out of bed, hurried to the bathroom and threw up. With his hands holding the sink he stood looking at himself in the mirror.

There was puke in his hair, he washed it out. Bruises on his legs and arms, and a large bruise on his forehead. He supposed he must have been in a fight. He combed his hair down over the bruise, hiding it.

Back in the bedroom he pulled on jeans and a black T-shirt. He shuffled in to the lounge and from there in to the kitchen.

He shuffled to the sink. He poured himself a glass of cold water and he downed it in one. He poured himself another glass and he walked, drinking it, in to the lounge. Passing the table he put the empty glass on the table and he went and stood in the window and he rested his forehead on the refreshingly cold pane and began to roll it to and fro.

It was raining outside, a light drizzle.

Staring down in to the car park Andy saw several police cars and men in white paper suits. He watched on as PK, dressed in a track suit, was brought out of the building between two uniformed police officers and led toward one of the badly parked patrol cars. One of the officers put a hand on PK's head, forcing it down as he pushed him in to the car, slamming the door after him. The car sped away through a gathering of reporters.

'Fucking hell!' He shouted: 'Jigsaw! Jigsy, mate!'

Pogget woke in a skip with a sharp throbbing headache and a deep gash in his skull. He winced when he touched it. His whole body ached.

Puzzled, he sat looking at his feet. He was minus one trainer.

But there was a roll of fifties in one pocket, and a bag of ees and several bags of cocaine in the other.

There was a loud knock on the door. Jigsaw answered it.

Two men in suits, holding up their warrant cards, were stood there.

'Police officers,' said one.

'Mind if we come in, sir?' they said coming in.

'These men are police,' Jigsaw told Andy.

Detective Sergeant Johnson and Inspector nugent introduced themselves. Andy was sitting at the table, nervously smoking a cigarette.

'What's going on?' he asked the men. 'Why've youse arrested PK?'

'Petros Kouriakis is helping us with our enquiries, sir.'

'Why? What's happened?' asked Jigsaw.

'There's been an incident,' said Nugent. 'We're trying to get a clearer picture of Mister Kouriakis movements last night, of what happened last night.'

'What incident?' asked Andy.

Andy and Jigsaw exchanged glances.

They suspected it was drugs. There were drugs at the party. Cocaine, E, Crack . . . PK was always good for drugs.

'If you could just tell us what you were doing last night?' asked Nugent.

Andy shrugged. 'Dunno, I was drunk. So, drinking, I suppose.'

'We were at the party, inspector,' said Jigsaw.

The Inspector and the sergeant exchanged glances.

Jigsaw explained: 'As you know there was an exhibition here last night. PK had just had a very successful exhibition. He was celebrating being a millionaire. We all were. There were hundreds of people there.'

'A friend, is he? Petros Kouriakis?'

'No, inspector, not as such, we just happen to live in the same building. Also he's a very successful, a very well known and respected sculptor. I happen to own several of his pieces. I bought another at the auction yesterday, his *Mona Lith*, for the lobby of MidasCorp.'

'Returning to last night, did either of you see anything suspicious or at all unusual last night? Anything out of the ordinary?'

Andy almost answered yes. The night had been the craziest yet. The set of his face said yes.

'No,' said Jigsaw. 'Nothing. Look,' he said, 'just what is all this about?'

'Someone was found dead last night, sir,' said Inspector Nugent.

'Dead?' Andy paled.

'Who?' he asked.

'A young girl. We think that she was murdered.'

'Murdered?' Jigsaw was incredulous. 'What, here? At the party?'

'What, PK murdered someone?' said Andy.

'We don't know,' said Nugent, 'it might well have been an accident. We don't know for sure.'

Andy picked up his packet of cigarettes. He lit one. His hands were shaking.

The Inspector walked over to the window and he looked out. The sergeant looked between Andy and Jigsaw. The Inspector turned from the window.

'Petros Kouriakis, who was he with last night? Was he with anyone in particular?'

Jigsaw shrugged. 'It was a party, inspector, there were hundreds of people there.'

'Last I saw of PK,' recalled Andy, 'he was leading some woman around on a dog lead. Not a dog lead, his belt.'

'He did this, here?' said Nugent, 'in public, last night? You saw this?'

Jigsaw said nothing.

Andy nodded. 'Well, yeah. He did it to quite a few of the girls there.'

'To who exactly?'

Andy shrugged. 'Dunno, they were just girls. It's just something that he does, at parties, like.'

'Look, what has all this got to do with us, precisely?' asked Jigsaw.

'That is what we're trying to find out, sir,' said the inspector.

The inspector walked to the wall and he studied the picture there, an Enzo, *Dark Blue and Light Blue*. 'Tell me,' he said, turning, 'what do you know about asphyxiophillia?'

'She was strangled?' said Jigsaw. 'It was an accident then?'

The detective sergeant and the inspector exchanged glances. They stared at Jigsaw.

'As I said before, we don't know. But late last night a man was attacked, here on the quays.'

Max Bringmeen had been assaulted. He had gone out for some air, he had been stood on the quay when he was bludgeoned from behind. An ambulance was called. The police were there, briefly, and then they left.

'And at around ten, eleven o'clock, the witness is unsure, someone was seen gaining access through a window at the rear of this building. We believe that whoever it was was involved in both incidents in some way. We found a dirty trainer in one of PK's bedrooms. It isn't PK's trainer, it's a size 8. We also found a number of restraints. We think the burglar interrupted something. That is what we are trying to ascertain. The girl was strangled, there was that tell tale mark around her neck. And deep cut marks around her wrists. She had been restrained. She had been strangled alright, certainly, but that wasn't what killed her.'

'No?'

'Tell me, what do you know about a girl called Ra?'

'Ra?' said Andy.

'Who?' asked Jigsaw.

'She was a prostitute,' said the inspector.

'A prostitute?' Jigsaw looked shocked.

'Ra, it's her that's been killed?' asked Andy.

'Drowned, yes,' said the inspector.

'Drowned?' Something exploded in Andy. He recalled rockets racing in to the night sky. Light on the water. He was stood at the water's edge, looking at the water. At the light there. Someone fell in.

'Drowned?' frowned Jigsaw. 'But you said she was strangled?'

'No, but we believe that someone did think exactly that. They thought that they had killed her, they panicked and so they dumped her in the river. To make it look like she had drowned. People when they panic they don't think, do they?'

'Did Petros Kouriakis use many prostitutes?' he asked.

'I don't know,' said Jigsaw. 'There was always girls around. PK was a sculptor, he used the girls as models. I don't know anything about their being prostitutes though.'

Nugent nodded to Johnson. The detective sergeant who had been making notes closed his notebook.

'Well thank you both for your time. Mister Truitt, sir, Andy. We'll be in touch.'

'Well, what do you think?' asked the detective sergeant. The two officers had just reached their car. They were stood either side of it, looking back at the building.

The inspector shook his head. 'Different world, innit. I don't know, probably was an accident. It was that kind of party. All that drink and drugs. Maybe the assault on her, those injuries, happened earlier and are unconnected. She was drunk, fell in the water and drowned.' He looked back at the building. At the figures in the windows there. 'They knew her though, I'm convinced. Sick, isn't it, us calling it an accident. As though that excuses what was going on here. And something was going on.'

'Drugs?'

'Prostitution. WorldBabe.'

'Sir?'

The sergeant pointed. He had seen the press pack and it was descending on them.

'Come on. Station.'

Andy turned from the window. He crossed to the drinks cabinet and he poured himself a drink, a large whisky, emptying the glass in one gulp. He immediately poured himself another.

'It was an accident,' said Andy. 'It must have been.'

'An accident? You call putting someone in the river after you thought that you had killed them a fucking accident? This does not look good, this does not look good.'

'Christ, Jigsaw, Ra's fucken dead an all you can think of. . . .'

'Shut it, Andrew! I can't think with you jabbering away at me. I need to think.'

Jigsaw crossed to the window and he stared down in to the car park at the gathering of journalists there. Someone saw him and pointed. Jigsaw stepped smartly back. He drew the blinds.

'What a fucking mess. You know what the tabloids are going to make of this? A prostitute, drugged up and strangled for sexual gratification and then dumped in the Thames like she was so much rubbish. Can you imagine the speculation they will indulge in? The enquiries that will be made?'

The whole excessive lifestyle would come under scrutiny. The drink, the drugs, the women. The money that supported all that. The source of that money.

'We can't afford to get involved in this.'

'Yeah, well we are fucken involved, aren't we?' said Andy.

'What are you saying?'

'We were there, weren't we? An can you remember what you did last night? Cos I fucken can't. I can't remember a thing about last night. I'm afraid to remember, me. It could have been any one of us.'

'No. It was PK,' said Jigsaw. 'It has to be. It has to.'

'Fucken hell, Jigsaw, Ra is dead, she was drowned, out there, right in front of us. Someone dumped her in the river thinking she was dead and she didn't have to be dead. And all you can think of is how that will make us look? You make me sick, you!' Andy felt sick. 'Don't you feel anything? You used to go with her, you did.'

Jigsaw's soft round face became uncharacteristically hard. 'Don't you ever dare tell anybody that. She was a crack whore, Andy, a fucking nobody. And we are somebody. Do you understand?'

'Oh yeah. Perfectly.'

Andy hit Jigsaw, hard, punching him in the face, sending him sprawling.

He stood over Jigsaw. Jigsaw wiping blood off his face, looking at it on his hand.

'We could have saved her, Jigsy, if we'd wanted. Anytime. We could have given her money. But no, we didn't, did we? We wanted her just as she was, so she'd do what we wanted, and now look. We did this to her, us! PK. Me. You. Everyone. We all did. Because that's how we treat people now.'

Liverpool 120 miles said the sign. Pogget had had it with London.

He was high on cocaine, driving a stolen BMW up the M1, music blasting from the car stereo: *I got a lust for life*. . . . Pogget sang along to the music, his hands beating out the rhythm on the steering wheel.

The car was a soft top. Pogget had dropped the roof and the wind was tearing at his hair. It had already ripped off his baseball cap.

Pogget pressed his foot to the accelerator. He gave a gentle touch to the steering wheel. The car responded beautifully to the pressure, sweeping in to the outer lane at 100mph.

110. 115.

He tore under a bridge. There was a brief flash of concrete as the bridge exploded momentarily overhead. A gantry exploded overhead, and was snatched away from behind.

Pogget checked in his rearview mirror.

The police were coming up fast, blue lights flashing, headlights ablaze.

Pogget slowed the car to 80 and he slid over to the inside lane. A police car sped up alongside, the officers pointing for him to pull in.

Pogget hit the accelerator, the police cars keeping pace with him.

There were road works up ahead, and a slip road, and barriers. A new bridge carried a stream of cars across the motorway.

Pogget span the steering wheel and he steered the vehicle off the motorway, crashing through barriers and speeding up the steep approach road. 'So long, fuckers,' he yelled, laughing, giving the police the vees as they continued up the motorway.

Cones flashed past like red and white tracers. There were earth works, huge yellow earth moving machines, and men in hard hats scattering in every direction. Pogget gripped the steering wheel and pressed himself back in to his seat. He swerved to avoid the bank of earth, aiming the car through the gap between two yellow diggers and at the road beyond. He went tearing, screaming through the gap, amongst exploding metal and fire and smoke, torn flesh and bone.

There were not that many people at the funeral. PK was there, handcuffed and surrounded by detectives. And Enzo was there. And Andy, who had flown in from America. There were a crowd of paparazzi, come to photograph PK, to witness him break down at the graveside. There was also a small gang of homeless people from the Bullring.

During the brief ceremony Andy noticed a mechanical digger stood waiting at a distance.

After the service Andy suggested the grave diggers fill in the grave by hand. The gravediggers refused. They had a mechanical digger to do that now. Besides, they didn't have shovels.

Andy began to fill in the hole himself. He kicked in the dirt, then he began pulling at it, pushing it in with great sweeps of his forearms, clawing at it with his bare hands. He was joined by a huge and bearded youth with a scarred face wearing black leathers and who had the words love and hate tattooed on his huge fists.

There had to be effort involved, always. If only to show respect. People just couldn't be disposed of. They weren't landfill.

Ra's mobile rings and rings. It is clients, offering her modelling work, drugs, wanting cheap sex. And for a time there is a Ra shaped hole in the world.

Jigsaw was sat reading the newspaper:

SCULPTOR CHARGED IN WHARF SEX MURDER

Police have charged sculptor Petros Kouriakis in connection with the death of known prostitute and drug abuser, Ra Hassan, whose partially clothed body was found in the Thames on Sunday morning last. The 27 year old prostitute, who had been attending a party at the home of the renowned sculptor, is thought to have been the victim of unusual sexual practices. Police, in a further development in the case, are investigating the existence of a prostitution ring in which women, smuggled in to the country illegally have been forced to work in the sex trade. Police have arrested a number of women in connection with the case, all of them associates of Ms Hassan.

He showed no emotion at the news. Finishing the article he turned to the business pages. The MidasCorp stock price had risen again, by four points. Jigsaw made the calculation and smiled.

He turned the page, and another page. He was searching for something.

But there was not the usual articles by Bane Burke, someone else had taken over her column.

Andy shook his head. He looked with disgust at Jigsaw.

'Jesus,' he said.

Jigsaw looked up from the paper. 'What?' Andy was staring at him, scowling.

'You,' he said. 'That's what.'

'Me? What have I done?'

'Nothing,' he said. 'Fuck all!'

'Andy, what is up with you?'

'Up with me?'

'Look, stop it, will you. It's done. Okay. Over. Things are exactly as they should be. PK does these things. This was always going to happen to him, sooner or later.'

'Fucken business as usual, innit? All you think about. Well they're fucken usen yeh, Jigsy, mate.'

'Using me? Who?'

'Them. Your fucken partners. Those so called rich friends of yours. They're just out for what they can get, thee are.'

'Of course they are. We all are.' Jigsaw laughed. 'As for them being friends? What friends? I haven't got any friends, Andy. Apart from you. They're just associates, business partners, is all. And yes, they're using me, of course they are. I'm very useful to them. Kryten certainly is. And they're useful to me too.'

'Yeh can't see it, can yeh. Christ, Jigsaw, they'll manoeuvre yeh out with all these multibillion dollar investments of theirs. They'll own the fund and the fund owns MidasCorp. It won't be yours anymore. Just look at yourself, look at us. We've become Them, we have. Us! But we hate these bastards.'

'I know what I'm doing,' said Jigsaw. 'I'm looking after our interests by keeping the money machine rolling. And so must you.'

MAN AND BALL. ANDY RANT, HIS NEW TOUR: ONE WHOLE

HOUR OF FOOTBALL FREESTYLING IN WHICH THE BALL DOES NOT TOUCH THE GROUND ONCE.
The 10th: London Wembley Arena, Sold Out. The 12th: New York Carnegie Hall, Sold Out. The 14th: LA, Hollywood Bowl, Sold Out. The 15th: Las Vegas, The Happy Crassus, Completely Sold Out. . .

Andy took his show to Chicago, to New Orleans, to Montreal, to Tokyo, Peking, Moscow, Berlin, London. He flew to Mexico City. He flew to Acapulco. He flew back to LA. He attended a film premier. And woke up the next morning amongst the derelicts on Venice Beach. He flew back to Acapulco. He flew to London. He flew to Dubai. He crossed multiple time zones, multiple times. He appeared at the Aspen, Canada, the Melbourne, Australia, and the New Zealand Comedy Festivals. He appeared at the Edingburgh fringe festival. Time and the things it brought with it began to repeat itself. There was no time. He had to be in a certain place one day and in a different place at a certain time the next. He flew back to LA. He flew to Vegas. He flew to L.A. He flew back to Vegas. Back to LA. To NY. To London. Back to LA. He woke up hungover in artists' studios, in the rooms of struggling writers, poets, musicians. There were more women, there was more more drinking, more drugs. . . . He went on ever more punishing drunks, often for several days. He bankrolled parties, hired yachts and whole hotels for wild weekends away. He rented a whore house in Nevada for a night, for himself and the Big Bucks. He had more women, weirder sex. He drove faster, took more risks on the road. He drove drunk. Took more drugs: speed, acid, e, cocaine, crack. . . . He got high on almost every drug imaginable.

He was just pushing at the boundaries, trying to break through so that everything would be different for him, just like everyone else. Except that for him there were no boundaries.

Andy had more run-ins with the press, smashed up more hotel rooms, there was more partying, more women, more drinking, more drugs.

People began to say that it was all going to end badly for him.

Then, one night, in LA, as he was driving between parties, he crashed his car. He was arrested by the police. He was done for drunk driving. He was done for possession of drugs, for leaving the scene, for assaulting a police officer, for criminal damage, for causing a disturbance. . . .

Andy shouted at the iron door, his voice echoing: 'The road of excess leads to wisdom! Are you listening to me out there!'

Andy laughed. He shouted. He laughed and laughed. He kicked the cell walls. 'Let me out!' he roared.

'I see no ships,' he shouted. He began to laugh.

He hammered on the cell door. 'Let. Me. Out!'

Andy pushed himself in to the corner and he slid down the walls. 'Let me out,' he sobbed. 'Let me out.'

The Wellness Resource Centre for Designed Life Change. Downtown L.A.

'Andy Rant to see Seena Dollar.'

This isn't Andy's voice. Something has changed.

The receptionist looked at Andy differently than she would have done say only a week before. There was uncertainty in her face, a look of disgust and contempt mixed with a feeling of superiority. She directed him to Ms Dollar's office.

Andy looked tired and unwell. His eyes were red and his face drawn. He finished yet another cigarette, stubbing it out in the ashtray on the table in front of him. He seemed nervous and on edge.

'The fights, Andy. Tell me about those,' said Seena.

'Hey! it's not my fault I get in to fights. I don't go looking for trouble. Aright?'

Andy stared at Seena. Seena stared back.

There was the sound of traffic through the open window.

Andy got up and he crossed to the window. He closed the window. But the room seemed tighter, tenser somehow. He felt closed in. He opened the window. Returning to his chair he sat down.

'Tell me about the shoplifting, Andy?'

Andy's face darkened. 'Fucking press, they blow everything out of all proportion. I refuse to talk to them so they make things up about me in the press.'

'Andy, I can't help you if you won't co-operate.'

'Look, I didn't ask to come here, right! They made me come. No custodial sentence, they said, so long as I came here for counselling. They said I had a condition. Okay, I said, so isn't there a cream I can use? So they made me come here.'

'The shoplifting, Andy? Why did you take those things?'

'I didn't take them. I just forgot to fucking pay for them is all.'

Seena stared at Andy. Her stare made Andy uncomfortable with his answers.

'There was a fucking queue, aright! Look, it gets tedious paying for things. Everyone knows I can afford them. It was just cents, fucken pennies, yeah?'

Seena made a note in her notebook.

'Was it for the adrenaline rush, Andy?'

'No! I got drugs for that. Look, alls I wanted was, I dunno. I dunno what I wanted. Something that I wasn't supposed to have, I suppose.'

'But bottled water, Andy?'

'Yeh, well, it used to be free once, water, didn't it, eh? There used to be springs you could drink out of and streams. There used to be drinking fountains all over the fucken place, until they got rid of them. Yeah, an' there used to be free toilets too, once. It doesn't seem right, having to pay for things when they should be free. What's that all about, eh? They want us to pay for everything? If you have to pay for it then it's not free, and that means you're not free, I mean, how can you be? You have to work all the time to get the money. Paying for fucken water? Fuck off.'

'But, Andy, someone has to bottle the water,' reasoned Seena, 'they have to manufacture the bottle. You're paying for the bottle, Andy.'

'Who wants the fucking bottle? You can get fucking cancer from it!'

'From a bottle?'

'From the fucking plastic. Jesus!' Andy grew irritable. He became animated. There was a manic sparkle to his eye. 'An' it's just fucken landfill, innit. Look,' he said, 'when they provided the public drinking fountains, when they built those beautiful brass and ceramic toilets all those years ago they understood that they were replacing something, something beautiful and essential and free, because it was everyone's by right, don't you understand? An now they're claiming it for themselves an sellin it on to us. Sellin us what's ours.'

Seena frowned. What Andy was saying was, well, un-American, it went against everything that she had been brought up to believe in. 'Plastics Andy, you were telling me about plastics.'

'Fucken plastic.' Andy was off again. 'It's the plastic fucken age. We have isolated plastics, dangerous metals, poisonous chemicals . . . what will we isolate next? Our fucking selves? We've created an artificial world for artificial people. Just look at it out there. We are filling the place with shite. Even the fucken food is shite. They tell us to wash an peel everything now because of all the dangerous chemicals on it. And then they tell yer not to waste water? I let the tap run me, I'm dilluting the pollution. Ha! An all this stuff about climate change. It's another fucken stick they'll use to beat us with, you'll see. Austere fucken future my arse. Not for them, it won't be. Brave new world, it's a fucken con. Con-quest. It's not our country, it's their country. Work like dogs for them, we do. And for what? More of everything? It's just more fucken shite. More work. More money. For them, anyhow. More rain, more—'

'Rain?' Seena cut in. frowning.

'It's this economic climate, innit.' Andy laughed. 'Let it rain, let it rain, it's raining money,' he sang. 'They even found a way to sell that.'

'Money?'

'Of course, money. No, I was talking about rain. Pay attention.'

'Rain?'

'Bottled water! Christ!'

He was back to that. Seena's sigh expressed annoyance, she rearranged herself in her seat. She had heard enough. 'Andy,' she interrupted him, 'tell me, why are you so angry all the time?'

'Wha? You're not fucken listening to me, are yeh, eh? You haven't heard a fucken word I've said. No one ever listens to a thing I ever say. What's the fucking point talking to youse anyway? You're fucken not interested. Nobody is. It's just questions questions questions. Only you're not interested in the answers, are yeh? No. Youse just wan' us ter start questioning ourselves.'

Andy grew angry, he hated being asked questions, like he was forever having to justify himself.

All his life he had had to justify himself.

What are you doing with yourself these days? What have you been doing to find work? Work you bastard work, even if there is no work. Andy, why are you so angry all the time?

Questions are alright, so long as there are answers, provided, that is, that you had nothing to hide. But when there are no answers, if the answers hurt, or are humiliating, when they hint at defeat, when all there is is emptiness, loneliness, not belonging - deficiencies which the questions serve only to draw attention to – then you can't always laugh or shrug it off. In slips a little more anger. And the anger builds.

Inside, in-side, Andy seethed.

He hadn't made any mistakes. They had all been made for him. He was owed, that was what this was all about, he was fucken owed, big time.

'Fucken questions? Youse dowanna hear no answers though, do yer, eh? Youse think yer got all the answers.' Andy sat glowering at Seena.

Seena looked up from the notes she had been making. 'Andy, tell me about you and James, Jigsaw, tell me about him?'

'That cunt!' But the anger just as suddenly dissipated. 'We did everything together. It used to be just us two, just me an him versus the rest of the world.'

'Then?' prompted Seena.

'Then what? Nothing, that's what. We became rich, didn't we? We got it all. It all became so, I dunno . . . ' Andy shrugged, 'so fucking meaningless.'

'I see,' said Seena, 'interesting. So you wanted out?'

Andy shot to his feet. 'I'm a celebrity, get me out of here!' and he began to laugh. It was a delirious kind of laughter and it scared Seena. 'Only I can't get out. How can I get out? I can have whatever I want. Money, fast cars, drink, women, drugs. . . . You can't get out of a thing like that. It's what you work for all your whole life. I love my life, but I'm trapped in it too.'

Andy stopped laughing, he just as suddenly sat down.

'What's it all for, Seena, what? Cos I just dunno anymore.'

Seena wagged her finger at Andy. 'We don't ask those kind of questions here. A lot of the people that come here are here because they have asked themselves exactly that. It's not a healthy thing to do, it can undermine your faith in everything. It can dismantle your whole world.'

Andy looked crestfallen. He hung his head. 'It's been dismantled. A mean, yeh can't go back, can yeh eh? How can yeh, it's gone. I got sucked in to this. The alternative was just too horrible to contemplate.'

'Andy, listen to me. Andy?' Seena reached out and she lifted Andy's chin, till she was looking him full in the face. She lowered her voice, her voice was soothing: 'Everything you want and could be you already have and are.'

The walls of her office were covered in such sayings:

You are the centre of your own universe. Love your life. God grant me the strength to change the things I can, and the money to change those I can't.

They hung in little framed signs amongst Seenas certificates.

Andy's anger flared. 'You can quit the psycho babble, aright! It isn't going to work on me. I'm not one of your run of the mill nutcases. Okay!'

'I can see that Andy.'

'Don't get clever with me, bitch! Sorry. Sorry,' he said.

'It's okay, Andy, it's okay. You're tired, you've been working too hard.'

'Too fucken right, and for what? Nuthin. Everything, it's all fucken shite, it is.'

'But, Andy, if we didn't have those things to show for it all then what would we have?'

'There you go again, scaring the shit out of me.'

Andy jumped to his feet, he began pacing the room. He went and stood looking out of the window.

'Tell me about your disappearance, Andy.'

Andy turned from the window. He came and sat opposite Seena. 'I had to get away. The plan was to hitchhike through South America. Walk the Inca Trail, see Macchu Pitchu, the Amazon rainforest, the Andes, all that. Cos I never had the fucken time too before, did I? So I drove to Mexico, dumped the car at the border. Walked over. Left everything behind. Grew a beard an everything. The plan was to pay my way busking, doing free-styling, like. I was just going to disappear.'

'Free-styling? You mean tricks with the football?'

'I did the clubs and bars, market places, promenades, city squares. They fucken loved me thee did, down there.'

Andy fell silent. His mood darkened.

'They hunted me down. Like a dog. Found me in a small beach-side bar in Acapulco. Dragged me back to LA. I had contractual obligations, they said. I made $270 on that trip, and Jigsaw and Soless took most of it. Turns out almost everything I earn belongs to them. Fucken shaftin me, thee are. Bastards!'

'I'd like to talk about the kidnapping, Andy. That must have been very distressing for you.'

'The kidnapping?' said Andy.

'Yes. If you can. I know it's difficult, but it will help if you talk, you know.'

Andy looked down at his feet, he stroked the back of his head, he stared at the floor for a time.

When he looked up Seena was surprised to see that he was smiling.

Andy laughed. 'I did it, me. I kidnapped myself. Well I fucken had to, didn't I? I had to get out, to get away from those fuckers. Working me in to the ground, thee were. I sent them a note for two million dollars for me. Could've lived the rest of me life on that, I reckon.'

'James didn't pay the ransom though, did he?' said Seena.

'No, he didn't, the cunt.'

'He suspected?'

'He just refused to pay. Said it would encourage other attempts in the future, if he gave in, like.'

'He did negotiate for your release though.'

'He tried to bargain me down, the cunt. He wanted an ear, for fucksakes, as fucking proof!'

'Tell me about the dreams, Andy.'

'Dreams!' Andy leapt to his feet. 'I've had it with dreams. I want to live a real life for a change!'

'The dreams, Andy?'

Andy sat. He ran his fingers through his hair.

His mood changed. He grew calm and he smiled, his gaze distant. 'I used to love playing football, me.' His eyes lit. 'I could have played professionally, for Liverpool, you know. I could have played for England, I reckon.'

Seena made some notes on her pad.

'I used to dream about it all the time. Made me feel good, gave us a real buzz it did. Kept me going, you know. Better than drugs, it was, better than drink. Better than sex, even, yeah.'

The goal scoring, the roar of the crowd, the crowd chanting his name: Andee! Andee! Andee!

'I meant those other dreams?' said Seena. 'The more recent ones?'

'Oh, those.' The light went out of Andy's eyes. 'Well, this one dream, I'm playing in this match, right, an I get possession of the ball when this girl she runs out on to the pitch. She's got the other side's colours on, only she's not wearing kit, the strip's painted on. She's stark naked. Well, the play stops, doan it. We all stop and stare at her. Anyhow, she gets the ball and off she runs up the pitch to our goal with both teams chasing after her. Well, anyhow, she shoots and scores. Everyone mobs her. Her side. Our side. Then we're in bed. No! Not all of us, just me and her. Only she's not naked, she's wearing this body-suit, see, she just looks naked. So I peel it off her. And underneath the body-suit there's another bodysuit, and another, and another. . . .'

Andy peeled body-suit after body-suit from the girl. But the more he undressed her the less of her there was until finally she disappeared.

Seena frowned, she shook her head.

'What about your latest dream?'

'The same, in a way. I get the ball, I dribble it up through the midfield and past the defence. It's just me and the goalie, right? I can't miss. I shoot, and the goalie saves it, or the ball goes wide, or I hit the bar, the ball bursts, or it turns in to a balloon that just floats away when I kick it. No matter how hard I kick it it just floats away. So I kick it harder and then it bursts. ' Andy grew agitated. 'That's when I wake up in a cold sweat, my heart pounding.'

'Hmmm.' Seena had made a church spire of her hands. She kissed her fingertips. She stared at Andy. Then she dropped her hands. 'I think I see your problem, Andy.'

'You do?'

'You feel that your life is out of your control, that you are powerless to change it.'

'I'm trapped! My life's become a prison. I can't take any more.'

Andy leapt to his feet and he began to pace the room. He crossed to the window, he seemed drawn to it. He stood looking out of the window for some time. There was a distant view of mountains on the horizon.

Seena scribbled on her pad. She tore the scrip from the pad and she offered it to Andy. 'Here,' she said. 'Take these. They will help to calm you down. We'll have you back to your normal self and in work again in no time.'

Andy stared at the paper being offered him.

'WHAT? CHRIST! HAVEN'T YOU BEEN LISTENING TO ME? HAVEN'T YOU HEARD A SINGLE FUCKING WORD I'VE SAID? DO

I HAVE TO SPELL IT OUT TO YOU: I – DO – NOT – WANT – TO – WORK! NOT FOR THOSE BASTARDS. UNDERSTAND? CHRIST, DOESN'T ANYBODY EVER LISTEN? AND I DO NOT NEED TRANQUILLISERS. OR A FUCKING SHRINK! I DO NOT NEED ANYTHING. I HAVE HAD IT WITH EVERYTHING. ENOUGH, OKAY! I AM SICK OF ALL THIS. I AM NOT A HAPPY BUNNY! DO YOU UNDERSTAND?'

Andy resumed his pacing of the room. He needed to walk. The anger was building up in him and he needed to walk it off. He would have to smash the place up or beat the shite out of someone otherwise.

Seena sat staring at Andy, offering him the scrip. She just did not understand Andy's predicament.

'But, Andy, why would you want to escape, and from what? What else is there out there? You are living the life, you are who everyone wants to be. You've got everything, anything that anyone could possibly ever want?'

'That's it exactly,' he said. 'There is nothing I do want.' It was driving Andy crazy. 'Don't you understand? No one understands. What I want is. What I need. I don't need anything. I want something only I don't know what it is because there is nothing I do want! Christ, there has to be more to life. I have to get out of here!' Andy made a lunge for the door.

Everyone wants the good things in life, but what are they? A Gucci handbag, an Armani suit, the bigger house, the new kitchen, the flash car, the boat, the mobile home, a flat screen plasma TV, matching luggage, the collection of fine wines, property, the property portfolio, expensive art? If you think that those are the good things, then, yes, it's worth it, otherwise it isn't worth shit. Shit is all it is.

Brad Hollows drives a Buggati. Tamara Mellon wears Jimmy Shoo heels. Wear AndyBrand: Break Free, Like Andy. The world had gone mad.

It was driving people mad. It was producing madmen, killers, thieves, addicts, suicides. . . . And no wonder.

39

Getting On

Natasha held her exhibition. But there was no mention of it in the art pages of the press. No critics covered the exhibition and no major collectors or dealers had been present. There had been other, important exhibitions in the city that weekend. All the talk in the art world that week had been about Enzo's exhibition and his subsequent retirement. It put everything else in the shade.

But Natasha did sell several pictures: *Sun Flowers. The Festival. The Last Day of the Sales.*

Natasha's share of the proceeds, after paying for the hire of the venue, a derelict school – she used the assembly hall - and for the printing of flyers advertising the event, was just £500, half of the paintings sale value. Finally, they could get off the streets.

For the price of £35, London Flat Brokers – a subsidiary of London Properties incorporated, a company managed by the private equity firm Kryten Equity - provided Ed and Natasha with a single page list of available bedsits.

Small rooms. Empty rooms. Broken rooms full of broken and abandoned things. Rooms of peeling wallpaper and flaking paint. Dark rooms. Damp rooms. Rooms filled with the sounds from other rooms: of toilets flushing, of water gurgling in the pipes, of echoing stairwells and busy corridors, TV's and loud music blasting out, slamming doors, babies screaming for attention, of couples at the end of their tether shouting and arguing with each other. Other peoples lives pressing in from every direction. Small, cold rooms in shared houses in run down streets, in cramped and subdivided flats in draughty tower blocks. Constructs of delineated and reduced and reduced space brought to its ultimate and inescapable conclusion: the bedsit.

They had gone through every property on the list and were now at the last available bedsit, more of a small flat really.

Ed and Natasha stood in the open doorway looking in at the property.

'It's a fucking shit hole, Ed.'

'It is the biggest shit hole we've seen so far. The other places were much smaller.'

But neither of them laughed.

Pin mould crept across the ceiling. There were no carpets, no curtains, not even a bed. The room was on the first floor of a large house in a run down area of London's Docklands, and was virtually bereft of furniture. There were just the silhouettes on the dark stained walls where there had once been furniture: oblongs where there had previously hung pictures, a circle that had doubtless been a mirror, the tall outline of a wardrobe, the low outline of sofa, the long outline of a bed. There was just a single wooden chair set in the centre of the room beneath the naked light bulb.

'Dostoevsky' said Natasha, 'said that hell was a room with a chair in it.'

'We can get rid of the chair, Nat. And it is the last shit hole on the shit hole list.'

And it was in a proper house in a proper street with proper gardens. Also, it had its own kitchen and bathroom.

'It's ours if we want it,' said Ed. Their spirits sank.

A loud thumping, like approaching footfalls, shook the building. The bedsit door creaked open on its hinges then slammed shut, making Natasha jump.

'Pile-drivers,' said Ed.

Natasha went to the window. The glass was grey with grease and grime. Natasha wiped the window. She peered out.

Tall cranes, scaffolding, lattice works of steel: the skeletons of partly built towers, of phalluses, domes and spires filled the horizon.

Cold blades of air cut in to her eyes through the cracked glass.

Ed tried opening the window, but the sash wouldn't budge, the joints having been painted over. He hit the frame with his hand, several times, but the paint was solid.

'Who wants fresh air at this time of year anyhow. It would only kill us.'

An open doorway, without a door, led off in to the tiny kitchen. There was a sink in the kitchen with a small draining board and an empty rubbish bin underneath. There were no cupboards, no work surfaces, no fridge. There was a small portable cooker possessing a single electric ring and grill. A door led off the kitchen in to a narrow, cramped bathroom.

The bath was cast iron. There was no seat on the toilet. The cistern ran. Ed fixed it by bending the arm on the ball-cock to put pressure on the worn washer. There was no curtain in the window. One of its four panes had been cracked and the crack had been cello-taped over to stop the draught.

They celebrated their getting off the streets with a bottle of cheap wine. They didn't have glasses so they drank from empty jam jars. The wine was cold.
'Room temperature,' said Ed. They could actually see their breath.
'Fuck. It's freezing in here. My head's gone numb.'
There was an electric fire in the boarded up fireplace. Ed put 10p in the meter on the wall. The lights came on, but the fire did not work, not even when Ed kicked it.
Ed fetched the cooker from the kitchen and he placed it on the floor and he plugged it in, turning it on as high as it would go. The ring began to smoke filling the room with an evil stink. Then the caramelised stains caught fire. The cooker burst in to flames. Natasha pulled the plug from the wall. Ed dropped a foul smelling tea cloth on to the cooker, extinguished the flames.
Ed crossed to the electric fire. He gripped the fire on either side, preparing to rip it off the wall. 'I'll rip this fucker out and open up the fireplace. Then we'll have a proper fire.'
There was a loud click from the electric meter and the lights went out.
It was seven o'clock but it was dark and cold and so they went to bed. The only illumination in the room was the light from the developments shining in through the curtain-less window. A trellis work of shadows, cast by the cranes and emerging high rises filled the room.
Ed and Natasha lay on the floor in their sleeping bags on their backs wearing their hats and coats. They lay awake for some time. They had slept easily in such circumstances when they had been living on the street now however they found it a discomfort. Though they were no longer homeless something had crystallised. They had expected something much more.

Natasha continued to paint.
Ed continued to work in the cafe.
They bought a small yellow van, for £50, from Resurrection Motors in the East End. The legend, *DAKER & BASS ON TOUR*, though overpainted, and very faint, remained discernible on its sides.
At weekends Natasha loaded the van with the smaller of her paintings. She took them to the Bayswater road. Hundreds of artists took their work there to exhibit and to sell.
She didn't have a stall. She propped her pictures against the wall or hung

them from nails which she worked in to gaps in the crumbling mortar.

The strange dystopian pictures aroused a great deal of interest. Everyone wanted to know what the pictures meant. But they were dark and foreboding and she never sold a single one. She lived on the money she earned by drawing caricatures.

One day she returned home determined to become a cartoonist. She drew a series of Fi cartoons - it had been Ed's idea. She thoroughly enjoyed doing them, she even toyed with the notion of a graphic novel. She had great hopes for the project and sent a portfolio of finished strips off to various comic publishers. But she heard nothing and after a time she gave up.

She continued to hawk her portfolio around the city, but without success.

40

The Business of Living

Heavy rain was holding up the work. Something had gone wrong with the weather. It should have been sunny, instead it rained and rained. It was the wettest summer on record. It had been raining non-stop now for almost six weeks.

The stream beside the cottage, normally low and crystal clear, was aloud raging torrent. Heavy rocks clanked and rolled along its course, pushed along by the force of the water.

Clemence sat in the window of his cottage with a mug of hot tea looking out past the scaffolding at the falling rain. Behind him a fire of dampwood smouldered in the grate giving off very little heat but plenty of smoke.

He returned to looking at his mail.

The pieces of junk mail Clemence twisted up tight and threw on the fire. He kept the return envelopes which he would post, empty, later. He liked the idea of this small revenge.

Clemence stared at the letter from Midas Homes and Loans. He had mortgaged the house for £15,000, in order tocomplete the work on it.

The demand for water rates and that for poll tax he balled and threw in to the fire.

He reached across the table for the local paper and he opened it at the jobs page: *Shelf stacker wanted. Part time labourer wanted. Security guard wanted. Assistant librarian wanted. . . .*

Busking wasn't going to do it for him.

Clemence had failed as a musician, he had never really made it as a poet, but the prospect of losing his cottage had galvanised Clemence.

First, he had protested to the council.

But the council were adamant. His living in the building as it was and without the necessary planning permission was against the law. Unless he applied for retrospective planning permission allowing for a change of use and for permission to put in a septic tank, a toilet and bathroom, electricity and running water, the council informed him that they would be forced under current planning regulations and public health legislation to take action against him in the courts.

You couldn't fight them and Clemence soon realised it. They would disrupt your whole life. They would throw you out on to the street if necessary. They would not be doing their job otherwise. And there was the rub: this was what they were paid to do, whereas you needed to be doing other things. You needed them on your side, or you had to be on their side, if only to get your life back. What you could salvage of it.

Clemence was forced to apply for retrospective planning permission – after payment of the appropriate administration and planning fees – agreeing to instal running water and a proper toilet and bathroom – requiring a further planning application, and yet more fees – which he was then granted. It also meant that he had to hire an architect to draw up the plans to submit with his application. Clemence would have liked to have done the building work himself but since there was a strict timetable involved, the work having to be completed within one year once begun, he was forced to hire builders.

Clemence got the job in the library. He learned to drive and he bought himself a car, a battered Morris van. He also got himself a girlfriend.

Beatrice was tall, thin, and flat chested, with long straight brown hair and she wore glasses. She ran the bookshop at the Centre of Alternative Technology - an alternative community and exhibition centre sited at an old slate quarry several miles outside of town.

Within the year the cottage had been transformed. It was no longer recognisable as an old smithy. It had a new roof, there was a loft conversion with a dormer window, as well as a small extension at the rear, housing a kitchen and bathroom with a bed room above. There was running water, electricity, a television – necessitating a television licence – a cooker, a fridge, a double bed, sofa and chairs, a proper table, blanket boxes, vases, curtains, cupboards, a set of drawers.

Bee had moved in with Clemence. She helped him choose curtains and soft furnishings. She arranged the furniture, bought matching sets of crockery.

Finishing the house and then furnishing it left a vacuum in Clemence. As the changes stopped, everything settled. His life crystallised. He looked about him and took stock. This was it from now on. And that disturbed him.

Clemence had grown bored with his job, not bored, as such, more — disappointed.

Dissatisfied.

And not with the job so much as with himself. He was the town's assistant librarian, one of them, and it wasn't what he wanted to be, to be known by some job, he wasn't a librarian. He was a writer and musician.

Everyone is someone. Either they were going to be someone, they had been someone, or they were someone because they had been going to be someone for so long that they had somehow convinced themselves that they had been or possibly were. This kind of has-been who never was was the worst kind of thing to be because you could never really convince yourself of your own worth. You could fool others, for a time, perhaps, but you always knew yourself that you were a failure. The hope was there, but the reality was always beyond your reach. But it was hard to accept that, if it meant giving up. Even when it had been proven to you time and again that you had failed there was always the hope that it was still possible. Life would be too empty otherwise.

The house, the car, the job, the steady girlfriend, they all helped. But there remained in Clemence that underlying dissatisfaction that undermined everything. Without writing, without music, Clemence felt empty and unfulfilled.

Everyone needs something to ward off the boredom, the uselessness that negates everything – ambition, drink, drugs, work even: something to fill life with meaning.

The Black Lion in Derwenlas was a traditional, oak beamed, stone floored pub with a huge inglenook fireplace. Every Thursday evening those working at the Centre of Alternative Technology gathered there to play music and to get drunk. They were a young, long haired, scruffily dressed crowd, full of fire and enthusiasm. And they were going to change the world. Clemence looked forward to these evenings, and not just for the music. He played fiddle in a folk group called Catastrophe. The group consisted of Jacko, another fiddler; Colm, a bodhran player; Matt who played tin whistle and the uileann pipes; and Bee who sang.

It was 9pm and Clemence, surrounded by a large, laughing crowd, was letting everyone know how he felt: 'The planet has got nothing to fear from me, I spend hardly anything. I get paid hardly anything.' Clemence was obviously quite drunk. He had been there since seven, being one of the first of his group to arrive, and he had already downed five pints of beer in that time. Clemence was a little contemptuous of the conservation movement, with all their talk of sustainable growth and alternative technology. As far as he was concerned, they were the solutions of someone who had given up the fight.

To Clemence's way of thinking, there could be no such thing as sustainable development, not in a finite world of finite resources, but there could be sustainable non-development.

The problem, as he saw it, wasn't so much how you generated power so much as the notion of power itself. It was a question of what was being powered and why. The whole system was wrong in his opinion. The world didn't require more development, it required equilibrium. The world wasn't just cities and transport systems and retail outlets. Though you could be forgiven for believing so. It was oceans, deserts, ice caps, mountains, forest, savannah. It was weather systems and ocean currents. It was rivers and lakes of clean water. It was a life support system.

'Sustainable growth will obliterate everything, eventually. Think about it. You might save the odd historic tree here and there, but as for the rest of it, it's going to gradually disappear.'

Bee hissed at him under her breath. 'Clemence! Don't. I have to work with these people,' and she fixed him with a malevolent stare before returning her attention to Colm, the handsome bodhran player, who was at that moment telling the group about the wind farm project he was involved in.

Loud music: fiddles, bodhrans and pipes, filled the room. Someone had even brought a bullroarer, though there was no space to play it in. Though doubtless later, when its owner was drunk, he would try. There was drinking, laughter, singing. Everyone was enjoying themselves. They were having the time of their lives saving the planet.

A tray load of full pints was lowered on to the table. Clemence drained the last of the beer from his glass, slammed it down on the table, and was reaching out to pick up a fresh one when Bee grabbed his wrist. 'Don't you think you've had enough?' she asked him, fixing him with a stare.

'No,' said Clemence, and he picked up the fresh pint with his free hand. Disgusted, Bee threw him back his other hand.

Wild Cat finished playing and the Late Harvest Lunatics took over. Clemence found himself tapping his feet to the lively reel. The room was crowded and hot. There was a sudden cold draught as the pub door opened and more people crowded in. In passing, one of them nudged Clemence, spilling a little of his beer.

Hemingway frequented Bullfights and war, Bukowski went to the race track to study humanity, whilst Clemence, for his part, saw all that he needed to in a crowded pub. All that pushing and jostling, all that money changing hands, the laughter and guzzling, this was the future, this was what was coming.

'We're the problem,' said Clemence, 'we just can't be stopped.'

But no one seemed interested. Everyone was intent on the moment. They were enjoying themselves.

Clemence sat and he brooded:

We are the problem. And the problem went hand in hand with the condition. And the condition was this: Mankind was just too clever, too inquisitive and far too capable at pushing back the boundaries. We would never stop behaving the way we did because we could never be satisfied.

'We weren't happy living in the trees, we weren't happy roaming about the wilderness, and we aren't all that happy now, living in cities,' said Clemence. 'Maybe the condition is terminal. Maybe it's something that apes catch when they stop being apes. They can't go back to how they were, to how things used to be, and so they keep on going forward, constantly changing things, until everything, themselves included, have become quite another thing entirely.'

Clemence, being an economics graduate, thought he knew just what was needed.

'What we need,' he said, 'is to cut the thing off at source. We need to destroy money.'

'Destroy money?' said Colm. 'Are you crazy?'

'What we need is money,' said Jacko.

'What? You mean, blow up a bank, like?' asked Matt Varnish.

Clemence laughed. 'No, have a sort of bonfire of the vanities. In the City of London, say.'

'What, burn money?'

'Not real money, obviously. We haven't got any. Counterfeit money. Photocopies. To make our point.'

'The point being?'

'There is too much money.'

'How can you have too much money?'

Everyone laughed.

'You're talking bollocks, you are.'

'Too much money? Where? Not round here, there isn't.'

'And let's keep it that way, yeah?' said Clemence.

People shook their heads.

'Look, it's just something to get people's attention, then we hand out leaflets explaining our position.'

'Which is?'

'Didn't a rock group burn a million pound once in protest at western civilised greed and the tyranny of work?' said Matt Varnish.

'My point precisely,' said Clemence. 'If there wasn't all this money to finance it then there wouldn't be all this rampant development. What's needed is a paradigm shift in our thinking.'

'You can't destroy money, Clem,' said Bee. All her life she had needed money.

'They won't let you, for one thing,' said Matt. 'They'll lock you up in a lunatic asylum.'

Late Harvest Lunatics finished playing. It had everyone round the table shifting in their seats, reaching down and picking up their instruments.

Clemence reached for his instrument. They were on.

They held the protest in Aber. Their activities drew the attention of a large crowd. There was a riot. People objected to their burning money. The police intervened and several people were arrested for causing a breach of the peace.

Everyone has doubts and anxieties about their ideas, which is why so many ideas that are good ideas get abandoned. People, when they have doubts, need encouragement. Properly encouraged an idea can blossom into something brilliant, or it can fail, but at least you have tested your idea and maybe next time around you'll do it better somehow.

'I was published before,' Clemence told Bee, 'I could be published again. I was the flying poet. The Che Guevara of the streets. I wrote a book. It was going to be an international best seller. I could write another book. Maybe this time it will be different.'

Clemence was fishing for encouragement. He wanted someone that was on his side, that would support him in his endeavours.

'I thought you'd already had a book published, Clem.'

'A poetry book, yes. Two books, actually. Only they weren't that successful. Poetry isn't that popular anymore.'

'Well there you are then,' said Bee, pressing her certainty on him. 'Besides, I thought you gave all that up.'

'I did. Things just got too difficult.'

'You want to change things, Clem, and that's good, but nothing anyone wrote ever made a difference, not to anything, not anywhere. Besides, like you said, you already did those things. You wanted to be a writer, a published poet, and you were, you are, you got published, you achieved that ambition. Then you had the good sense to move on. Some people though they go on trying, they spend their whole lives trying, they refuse to give up even when it's hopeless. They just carry on trying when they could be making something of their lives.'

'I suppose,' said Clemence.

The way Bee saw it, there were far better ways to profit from writing. Bee was ambitious. She had other plans.

Clemence looked incredulous, like he would laugh. He did laugh.

'Sell the cottage?'

'To buy a bookshop, yes. We would be our own boss, Clem. You don't want to be a librarian all your life, do you? working for someone else? Because I know I don't.'

Clemence was wary of the idea.

'What if we split up?' he asked.

'We won't do that, silly.'

'But what if we did?'

'We won't.'

'But what if we did?'

'Look, the cottage is your place, Clem, and I want something that's ours. I want us to have a business together that we can grow. So we can grow.'

Clemence wasn't sure. He said he needed time to think about it.

'You don't want to do it.'

'No. I'm not saying that, Bee. I'm not saying no, just that we should think about it.'

'Then you'll do it?'

'I said I'll think about it. There's no hurry, is there? Just let's not rush in to this, okay? Anyhow, I thought you liked it here.'

'I do. It's lovely here. But it's a hideaway, isn't it? It's like you've settled for something when you could have so much more.' Bee began to work herself up in to a state. 'Clem, if we don't do this now, soon, if we leave it too long, we might never do it. Property is going up all the time. And that means the difference in value between this tiny cottage and something more suitable will just increase. It'll be ten thousand, then twenty, then forty thousand, we'll never be able to afford our own bookshop then, not on our wages. We'll be stuck in our jobs. Do you want us to spend the rest of our lives working, living in this poky little cottage miles from anywhere. Because I don't.'

All Bee wanted was for them to be happy together. It's all anyone wants. Bee went and fetched her bag. She pulled a huge sheaf of papers from it that she had acquired from the local estate agents. Then she and Clemence sat down and they began to work their way through the details of all the suitable properties that were for sale in the area.

Property was like a drug. Once you saw the place you wanted it became necessary to sacrifice everything in order to get that place. What a difference it would make to your life.

The shop was on the main street in to town. There was living accommodation on the two floors upstairs, and a cellar, for storage, and a large attic, and it had a large garden at the rear with an outhouse.

The place was perfect. And it was just £55,000.

Clemence sold his cottage for £25,000 to a couple from London who intended to use it as a holiday home.

Clemence and Bee took out a joint mortgage for £45,000.

ABC Books, said the sign above the black painted door. Clemence carried Bee in over the threshold, tripping there, almost throwing her inside. Bee thought it was eagerness.

It was not a busy shop, and they just about made a living from it, but Clemence enjoyed the business of selling books. He particularly enjoyed touring the country, going from book fair to book fair in his old Morris van. He stocked the bookshop with all his favourite writers. Their very names were an inspiration to him. He discovered new writers. Clemence also began to resuscitate his lost novel. The missing pieces of it were beginning to fit back together again.

Happiness lies in believing that everything is still possible.

He was working late in the shop. Someone had brought in several boxes of second hand books and he was placing them on the shelves. It was seven pm. and Clemence was moving the last of the now empty boxes into the cellar when Bee came in from an afternoon spent shopping in Aber. She kicked shut the door with her heel and she dropped down in to the nearest of the chairs which Clemence had placed amongst the bookshelves, kicked off her shoes, dropped her bag off her shoulder and let if fall to the floor.

'You look exhausted,' said Clemence. 'I'll make you a nice cup of tea.'

Bee said nothing for a time. She sat staring at Clemence.

'It's not working, is it?' she said.

'What isn't?' Clemence felt the fear rise up in him.

'The bookshop,' said Bee.

'Yes it is,' said Clemence.

'We barely get by on what it earns.'

'But we're in business for ourselves, aren't we? That's what you wanted, to have your own business, to be your own boss? It pays the bills, doesn't it?'

'But look at us, Clem, look at the way we live, in a crummy old flat over a crummy old bookshop that stinks of musty old books. And just look at that old van we have to drive. And that ridiculous sign you put out, *Old and interesting books*. You should be trying to attract custom. You're not interested in the shop, you just like books, you do. You want me to run the shop so that you can slope off and write yet another book. Well you can forget it. I'm going to need you to help run the café.'

'Café?'

'Yes, an Internet cafe and bookshop.'

'Yes,' said Clemence, nodding slowly, 'that could work.'

'It will. Everyone's getting connected. Times are changing and we have to change with them. It's the information age.'

'I thought it was the Age of Aquarius.' Clemence was an Aquarius.

'You were misinformed. We're going to transform this place, Clem. You'll see. We'll need to take out a loan, to pay for the alterations. We'll sit down together, tonight, and we'll write up a new business plan. I'll take it to that nice man at Midas Homes and Loans. I've already made an appointment.'

The cafe was a great success.

There were people who used that cafe who were surprised to discover that it was also a bookshop.

Bee purchased a stamp saying ABTea Internet Cafe and Bookshop and she had Clemence stamp the inside cover of every single book in the shop.

Clemence worked harder than ever, he was working six days a week, serving, clearing tables, washing dishes, preparing meals. He moved about the place like he was on a powerful stimulant. At night he and Bee worked in their tiny kitchen baking the date and apricot slices, lard bars, and chocolate shortbreads that were to make the shop famous.

He no longer had the time to work on his book, and very little energy. Nor the inclination. It no longer seemed real to him, there were far more tangible things to attend to.

Tired and overworked, Clemence became clumsy again. He forgot things, he knocked things over, he dropped plates. Cut himself and got blood on the sandwiches. Scalded himself doing the washing up.

Clemence missed the slow and easy life of the bookshop, with its peace and quiet, the long idle moments when he could sit and think and jotdown his thoughts. There was no time for that now, no time even to think. The cafe was always busy. It even began to open evenings. No matter how hard they worked it seemed they could always work harder. They went to bed tired. They woke up tired. Yet they told themselves that they were happy. They were better off than most people, that was the measure of it. They were certainly better off than they had ever been before,. The business was doing well. They had a nice flat. Bee drove an Audi. And they were earning good money. But where did it all go, all that money? It was the bank's money, most of it. It was Midas Homes and Loans. The electricity companies, the gas and water boards, the local councils, the revenues. . . .

Clemence became increasingly dissatisfied. He was just someone that worked in a cafe, cleaning, serving, preparing meals. He could have had that job anywhere, and for the same pay, and with none of the worries, he reckoned.

First, there had been the tyranny of property ownership, with its mortgage to be serviced and all its bills. Then there was the tyranny of work. Now, with an internet I and bookshop to run, those tyrannies combined. There was the added tyranny of rules and regulations to be observed: health and safety, hygiene. . . .

Even Bee began to question the point of it all.

What, she asked, was the point of anything? If you weren't a mother, or a father, for that matter, then what were you, life-wise, what had you got? Bee told Clemence that she wanted to start a family. It was time, she said, for them to stop thinking only of themselves.

Life had become a struggle for space and time.

It was a struggle that took away the hours. It took away the days. It took away the years. Even when you were successful. Particularly when you were successful. You become immersed for a time and then the years are gone.

And time was growing short.

Clemence stared in to the mirror at his lined face. He found the first white hair.

He felt very tired and scared and unhappy. Life was closing in on him. Where did it all go? he wondered.

He had it all to do still. He would never do it. It's impossible, he said.

One evening after work Clemence got in to his Morris van and he drove out to his old cottage.

A metal gate had been erected across the lane that led down to the cottage.

A sign on the gate said, *The Old Smithy. Private Road.*

Clemence parked the car in the lay-by beneath the farm. Then he walked back up the road to the lane way. He vaulted the gate and he walked down the recently widened and tarmacked lane. At the bottom of the lane he came to a large flat area that had been gouged out of the hillside. There was a people transporter parked there with kayaks and a surfboard on the roof and mountain bikes on a rack on the back door. Parked up beside it was a jet ski on its trailer. A chain suspended between two posts across the space bore a sign declaring, *Dim Parcio: No Parking. Private Property.*

Clemence barely recognised the cottage. There was a second large extension at the rear, that completely dwarfed the original cottage. And there was a large conservatory, that was full of green plants, built on to one gable end. There was a large paved area in front of the new extension and huge French windows to give entry in to the house. On the patio was a barbecue set and patio heaters and a round metal table and chairs as well as a covered chair swing. There was a gazebo erected on the lawn. Battery operated solar powered night lights marked out a path from it to the house and from the house to the gate. A low dry stone wall ran around the cottage. A sign, hung on the wooden gate, proclaimed, *The Old Smithy. Private Property.*

Clemence felt alienated from the place. Not a trespasser, exactly. And it was not because the cottage was no longer his. That too, certainly. No, it was because it was no longer what it used to be. It had once stood for something, something essential, and now it stood for something else.

It would never again shelter a struggling poet and his dreams. Or a blacksmith, for that matter.

There was no way back, and even fewer ways out now. Things had become much too expensive. It depressed Clemence. What would a person have to be to own such a place now?

Clemence passed between the cottage and the stream, intending to continue down the path to a good swimming hole that he knew. It had been Natasha's favourite place. Ed had once lost a big fish there.

There was a gate across the path that made Clemence uneasy. As he pulled it open, its hinges squealed and a curt, well-spoken voice, sounding from the house, confirmed his worst fears.

'Yes? May I help you?'

Why do some lives work out and others don't?

Clemence lay in bed, staring at the ceiling, unable to sleep. He was all twisted up inside, scared in a way that he did not understand. Panic gripped his insides.

Careful not to wake Bee he crept out of bed.

He dressed himself in the hallway. He put on old jeans, a faded donkey jacket and old boots. He took some food from the kitchen and he put it in his pack. Then he shouldered his pack, containing his sleeping bag and the unfinished manuscript of his book, picked up his fiddle case and took them out to his van.

He drove to the coast, where sweeping hillsides ended in abrupt drops at this edge of the world place. Clemence parked the van between the dunes and the grey sea, manoeuvring it to face the ocean as close to the dunes as he could whilst remaining on the hard sand

The dawn was cold and windless and grey. The ocean was grey. The sky grey. The ocean was calm but there was a huge swell. Heavy waves crashed wearily ashore.

Clemence sat looking at the sea for a time.

Hemingway said that the only proper end to any story is the death of the central characters. In films it's different. And maybe in life too. Death is much too final. Charlie Chaplin's tramp always walked off in to the distance. After removing his fiddle case and his pack, Clemence locked the van, shouldered his pack and left the beach. He took the steep and winding path that led up on to the clifftops. Once he was on their summit he got out his notebook and he wrote:

I am walking down a road and I am thinking as I walk how alike it is to all those roads I ever walked, not in sight nor in sound but in feeling. For I have a feeling about this road on which I walk, a feeling of great hope and expectation, as though I know to where it might lead and the people to whom it must bring me. . . .

There would be years of struggle yet.

Clemence stood at the cliff's edge, staring down through the gliding gulls at the sea, hundreds of feet below. It was mid-morning and a stiff wind had gotten up. It blew out his hair, his open coat and scarf. It blew the long tussock grass first one way and then another, turning it silver then green and back to silver again.

Far below, the sea churned around the surf whitened rocks. The tide forced the water this way, sideways, then dragged and churned it back. It washed white over the boulders. Waterfalls poured off the boulders in to the lowering sea, before the sea lifted again and engulfed them. In the gulleys between the rocks the disturbed water spired in to the air, then plummeted, then spired in to the air again.

A young family, a mother and father and their two young children, a boy and a girl, emerged on to the clifftop behind Clemence and proceeded to fly a large kite.

'What's he up to?' asked the man, trying to control the kite in the stiff wind. He pointed with a jab of his chin toward Clemence.

Clemence was stood on the cliff edge looking out to sea, his arms apart, like he was embracing it. He was enjoying the wind, the openness, the space. The feeling of infinity. He was stood on the edge of the world. Balanced.

The woman turned, half closing her eyes to the wind. Pulling the hair from her face she stared squint eyed at Clemence, frowning.

There was a loud flapping sound, the woman looked up and saw the kite drop from the sky and swerve violently toward her. She ducked down but the kite was already shooting back up in to the air where it hovered for a moment before wheeling viciously toward Clemence.

Clemence turned in time to to see the kite soar back up in to the sky. He seemed to hang there for a moment, leant back, looking at it, his arms outstretched as though the very act of reaching for it would stop him from falling. He fell backwards, head first, feet in the air, and plunged, like a cormorant, in to the sea.

The wind ruffled the tussocks. Seagulls lifted to sight before gliding back beneath the cliffs.

Shocked, the woman burst in to tears. 'Bloody Hell!' said the man. He stood staring at the now empty cliff edge. He let go of the kite strings. The kite plummeted to the ground. The children ran to the cliff edge. 'Get away out of that!' roared the man, his concern shaking him from his inertia.

It was not safe to have this thing that could so possess a person. When it was gone what comparable thing could ever take its place? Van Gogh, Hemingway, Plathe, Woolf . . . and all those others like them, they filled the world with works and it left them empty.

41

The Next Picture

A train clattered overhead rattling the paint brushes in their jars and causing the lights to flicker. Natasha barely noticed.

'Cheerful. I'll give them cheerful. And bright. They won't ever have seen anything so bright.'

Natsha found the tube of chrome yellow, unscrewed and then blindly threw away the top, squeezed the entire contents on to her palette and flung the tube over her shoulder, then she snatched up a tube of black and did the same with that. Grabbing up a brush, she threw herself at her work:

Tall buildings, blazing with fierce light. A yellow night sky. Yes, yellow. Because it was never really night-time in the city.

She worked furiously, completely immersed in what she was doing.

A cold draught made Natasha shiver. She stopped and stood looking at her work.

Strange Buildings, Unusual Shapes. Tall Buildings Giving Everyone the Finger. The Mad Scrabble. . .

It was the same hard city.

Natasha was still trying to paint that one great picture that would catch the art world's attention and get her noticed. She felt that she had to keep painting, if only to keep that idea of herself alive.

But try as she might, she could not change her style. It was the sum total of all her experiences and observations and it ensured that every attempt ended in the same conclusion: a glass door leading to the city, a window crammed full of tall buildings, a grim and subdued crowd of commuters, a horizon filled with new construction. . . . The achievement in these pictures lay not so much in their execution, which was often raw and unpolished, but in the imagery, which Natasha felt was perfect. Natasha could tell at a glance what those pictures were telling her. The titles were perfect too. Acting like directives, they told those looking exactly how to view what was being shown. But there are some things that people don't want to be shown.

And trying was wearing Natasha down. Because if you tried, if you gave it everything that you had and still had to keep on trying then you had failed. Every hardship, all the pain and the hope and the trying was wasted if you did not have success. You could distract yourself, you could lose yourself in drink and in drugs, but it would never be enough. Nothing protected you nor was so accommodating as success. Without it all your faults and the hardships that you endured were just the proof that you had failed.

Prostitutes used the house. Alcoholics gathered on its front steps.

A loud noise like approaching footfalls shook the whole building. Causing the wardrobe door to creak open on its hinges, before slamming shut.

Pile-drivers. Jack hammers and drills. Stereos, blasting out loud music. Couples shouting and screaming at each other. They were the usual sounds of the house.

Somehow, Ed dozed through it all.

But when a door slammed loudly it made him jump, causing his tin whistle to roll of his lap on to the floor. He had fallen asleep on the sofa practising, waiting for Natasha. A new gallery had opened up in town and she had gone to try her luck there.

Ed checked the clock. It was 1:30pm.

She should have been back by now so maybe the gallery had shown an interest in her work.

Ed went out to fetch the paper, *The Press*, a scratch card and a six pack of beer. He stopped in the pub for a time. Two pints.

On his return, he snapped a can from the six pack, putting the others in the fridge. He sat down on the sofa, opened his newspaper and took a long sip of beer. Then he remembered his scratch card.

Ed scratched at the windows with his thumbnail.

Nothing. Fuck all.

He scrunched up the ticket and he threw it in the fireplace. He got up off the sofa, left the bedsit and crossed the hallway to the window on the stairs where he stood looking out over the front garden in to the street. But there was still no sign of Natasha's van.

Across the street, a young couple were carrying their possessions out of the house, they were piling them on the pavement then packing them in to a car, a run down Volvo estate. People were leaving the street all the time. Ed watched them pack the car.

When the volvo drove off a group of workmen, who had been leant against a white transit, unloaded several sheets of ply from the back of the vehicle. They began to nail the sheets over the ground floor windows and the front door of the recently vacated house. There were numerous similarly boarded up buildings in the street. The workmen finished their work and left.

Ed remained stood in the window, drinking his beer. He was looking at the sky. Yellows, oranges, blood reds, chemical blues. Exactly like in Natasha's pictures.

'I got those ooooh-ooo-ooh! chem-i-cal blues,' he sang.

Someone shouted for him to shut the fuck up.

Ed left the window and he returned to the bedsit. He opened another can of beer and he dropped down on to the sofa with it. He hadn't been sitting there long when the door burst open, Natasha swept in to the room, slamming the door behind her. With a sweep of her arm she sent her portfolio flying across the room. It hit the wall opposite, spilling photographs on to the floor and setting in motion several finished canvases that were propped up there: *I'm In Here Somewhere: Just Me and Everyone Else. Alien Environments. The Last Day of the Sales. Vermillion Skies* . . . the works flipping over, one after the other, to land face down on the floor.

The pictures were faded, yellowed from exposure to the sun, some stained by rain, others covered in bird shit from when she had last taken them to the Bayswater Road. She had not yet gotten around to cleaning them.

Natasha dropped heavily on to the sofa beside Ed.

'Here,' he said handing her his beer, 'have a beer.'

She pushed away his arm. 'I don't want a beer. It's not beer I want.'

'I know,' said Ed.

'They didn't like them, Ed. They just weren't interested.'

Natasha sat staring at her hands. Her hands were shaking. Holding her hands, she began working at her fingers with her nails. 'Wherever you go it's Enzo, Enzo, Enzo. He doesn't even paint anymore. And if it's not Enzo it's fucking Damien Hirst, or Sadie fucking Sommers and her *Opulent Interiors*. She stole that idea from me, Ed. She did! She ruined it for me. I could maybe have broken through with that one. I was working on that one long before she was. But she's a name and I'm not so now it's her idea.'

Ed said nothing. He had grown used to these outbursts. They happened every time Natasha returned from submitting her work to a gallery.

'You'll have other ideas,' he reassured her. 'Better ones.' He offered her the beer.

Natasha took the beer. She drained the beer. Then she stood, crossed the room and began picking up the canvases she had knocked to the floor earlier, re-stacking them, slamming each one hard against the other. She collected up her photographs and her portfolio and she thumped them down on the table, scattering the photographs.

'You'll get there, Nat.'

Natasha's face darkened. 'I'm going to be a great artist. I'm always going to be a great artist, but I'll never actually be one. WILL I?' she shouted.

'Yes you will,' Ed reassured her.

Natasha turned her back on Ed. She walked to the window where she stood looking out at the new developments. Pile drivers shook the building.

'They're coming closer, Ed. It will be this street soon, we'll be next. What will we do then? Where will we go? Another fucking shit hole.'

Natasha didn't know how much more of this she could take. 'Face up to it, Ed, it isn't going to happen for me, no one's the least bit interested in my work.'

'They will be, you'll see.'

'I'm a failure, Ed.'

'No! You're not a failure. You're only a failure if you give up. You're still painting, aren't you. You're still an artist. You don't have to go to work every day, not like they have to, like everyone else.'

That, to Ed, was the greatest victory. No matter what the hardships.

Natasha did caricatures and sold the odd painting: Sun Flowers. Laburnum Trees. Blossoming Acacia Branches. Yellow Cornfields. Yellow Suns . . . and for £150 each sometimes. These were the works that people wanted, but they would never make her name for her. She could have churned them out, one a day, but she did not want to work on that production line. Ed busked. He signed on. It was how they paid the rent. How they were able to keep on the lock-up, and buy the canvas and paints so Natasha could work.

'Well maybe we should get proper jobs.'

Ed only laughed.

'Don't you want money, Ed?'

'Of course I do, yes. And if they paid me enough then I'd work for it, but they don't.'

Ed wanted money, of course, not to buy things with, necessarily, but rather to buy time. Having the time to do what you wanted, that, Ed reckoned, was real wealth. As for those with money, the owners and bosses, and millionaires generally, they were often as not overfed, self pleased people who looked at other people working and who lived off the money which they spent. They were inadequate, as far as Ed was concerned, and in so many ways. Money could make you rich all right but it didn't necessarily mark you out as being accomplished. It was just a compensation that people sought. Ed wasn't ready to make that compromise, not yet. Not whilst there was still hope.

'And what kind of a job do you think you're going to get?' he asked. 'Because you've got fuck all qualifications. You'll end up waitressing in a cafe, or working behind the checkout in some supermarket someplace. When you could be painting your way out of all this.'

'I could work in an art gallery.'

'Selling work that isn't your work? Seeing other people enjoying what you wanted for yourself. That you won't ever have because you gave up?'

'You don't want to work, do you?'

'Not to live like this, I don't. No. And this is all we'll ever have with the kind of work that's on offer. Don't you see? You have to keep trying, Nat. It won't ever happen if you stop trying. If you give up, then what else is there? What have we got? Nothing. Just this.'

Ed could never give up, no matter how hopeless the thing seemed. Hanging on in there was the only way he knew. It was better than quitting because it kept the hope alive. It carried the thing from one time and place, when it could not happen, to another time and place when it might. Because what else was there? Work wasn't going to do it for them. Painting was the only protection that Natasha had against her becoming a waitress, a checkout girl, a shop assistant, a receptionist. . . . How could anyone face a lifetime of such work when there was every chance they did not have to? Ed couldn't. Art, to Ed, was the only real safeguard against a life spent working that there was. It was the last refuge of the craftsman, and of the vagabond too, perhaps.

'You're just disappointed, is all, Nat. All this trying is wearing you down. But it's not your work that's the problem, is it? It's them. They haven't caught on yet. But they will. You've got to stick at it. All this trying will be the makings of you, you'll see.'

By a strange twist of logic Ed calculated that the harder things got for her then the more successful she was likely be in the end.

'People need their struggles,' he said. 'The poverty, the hard dirty living, it strips away the bullshit. Look at Van Gogh, at the hardship and the poverty in his life, and look at what that produced.'

The hunger would build up in her. The anger would build up, and the rage. It would come exploding out in painting. Her work would have depth, it would have feeling.

'Did Van Gogh have it easy?' he asked. 'Did he give up?' Natasha looked incredulous.

'Jesus, Ed, you fucking idiot! His failure drove him insane. He had a breakdown and cut off his ear. He was committed to an asylum. And then he fucking well shot himself.'

'Yes, but if he'd hung on that little bit longer he'd have been a success.'

Natasha gripped her head in her hands, her hands were claws. 'Van Gogh, Van Gogh. Will you shut the fuck up about fucking Van Gogh. I have had it with Van Gogh. I wish I'd never heard of Van Gogh. I am not fucking Van Gogh. OKAY!'

Someone shouted: 'Shut The Fuck Up!' There was hammering on the wall from next door.

'And what about all those other struggling artists who weren't Van Gogh?' she asked, 'who no one has ever even heard of? Who no one ever will hear of. Natasha fucking Plane-Smith, for example.'

'Natasha Plane-Smith painted landscapes,' said Ed, 'she could never have painted the bigger picture. But you did.'

'Stop it, Ed! Stop it! It isn't going to happen for me, okay? Can't you get that through that thick fucking skull of yours? But it's not the failure so much, I can handle the failure. It's the hope. I can't go on living like this. All this trying. I want things to be easy for a change. I just want it all to stop. I'm not like you, Ed. You might be able to live like this, but I can't. I want an ordinary everyday life, full of ordinary everyday things, just like everybody else. Is that too much to ask, to have a proper job, a house, things, maybe even a family one day? God, I have been so stupid. How could I have been so stupid? All those years, wasted when we could have worked. We could have had it all by now. But we still can work, it's not too late. We can still have those things.'

'And live out our lives according to social expectations, in a deranged pursuit of trophies.'

'I want those things Ed. Idiot!.'

'I can't believe that you'd settle for that, Nat. You have to see this thing through, otherwise you'll never know.'

'Christ! Why are we doing this to ourselves, Ed? Why? Why? We'll never get out of here, never. Not doing this we won't. It's just too difficult. It's impossible. Because if this is what it takes then I just can't do it, not anymore.'

'I'll tell you why we're doing this,' said Ed. 'Us. It's so's we can carry on being us. It's about our not becoming them. This, it's our only defence against all the bullshit. From work, for a start. Other people's values. Being pushed around, and in to ever tighter corners, and in to dead end jobs. In to a life spent doing their work, of doing everything that they tell us to do.' Ed grew angry. No one was going to tell him what to do. 'Simon says no more living on the road, so we stopped living on the road. Simon says you can't live on the street, so we stopped living on the street. Now he says, get a proper job. He says, put your hands on your head. So we put our hands on our head. We give up on ourselves.'

Natasha put her hands on her head.

'No, Nat! You can't.' And, throwing up his hands, Ed clutched his head.

'I'm a failure, Ed.'

'No you're not. You're only a failure if you give up.'

'Then I'm a failure.'

It might be years before Natasha became successful, she might have to paint hundreds more pictures before that could happen. The very thought of it exhausted her. All that time, and the work involved, and the inevitable frustration, and still she might not be a success. When you started out on a thing, if you knew the amount of work that was involved, if you thought about all that you had to do, then you would never do it. People become tired, they lose their enthusiasms.

Loud music, Talking heads, *Once In A Lifetime*, from their album, *Remain in Light*, began blasting out from the bedsit upstairs. Here was someone else that had rejected the materialistic world, or were revelling in their disappointments. It was just another way some people had of inuring themselves, of coping with disillusion. But those lyrics taunted Ed and Natasha. It would, they knew, be followed by *Road To Nowhere*, then *Houses in Motion*. That music was the cause of a lot of dents in their ceiling. And a good many cracks too. The music stopped. They waited. New Order's *Blue Monday* came on. That did it. Up went the broom, and yet another dent appeared in the ceiling. It was soon accompanied by a crack, and several flakes of falling plaster, as a heavy footfall came down on them from above in quick response. Then the volume went up, drowning out their protests.

People get trapped in all sorts of things. They can get trapped in work, trapped in poverty, or in a relationship. And they can get trapped in wanting a thing. They can get trapped because they did not try for something else, something achievable.

Natasha found work with Midas Homes and Loans at their call centre in

Docklands, working the switchboard as a receptionist:

'Hello, Midas Homes and Loans, how may I help you?'

She still painted, she still kept something of the hope, but she was no longer going to be a martyr to it. There were other things to work for.

'Midas is giving out 90% mortgages,' Natasha told Ed at the end of her first week. 'And to people with MidasJobs. People ring up that get mortgages who have only been in work for one week.'

'What? You mean, you're saying that you could get a mortgage?'

'If I had the down payment I could, yes.'

Ed thought about that. 'Couldn't we borrow it?' he said.

Natasha smiled at Ed's cunning. 'I don't think so. But if you had a job, then we could save the money.'

'You want me to get a job?'

'We won't get a place otherwise.' Natasha pleaded with Ed. 'Will you, Ed? Please.'

Ed could not work. Not to live like this, he couldn't. But he could work to escape this. He could work for a better life.

The idea of property ownership can do strange things to people. Once they know that it is possible for them they grow addicted to the idea. You had to have something to show for it all.

People change. They change to suit the world, and the world changes them. And the world changes.

'It seems to me,' said Ed, 'the way the housing market is going, that even properties like this could be a real investment. Get them cheap too, I bet. Real cheap. And we won't be paying out on rent,' said Ed.

'We could rent out a room ourselves,' said Natasha. She grew excited at the possibilities. 'We could rent out several rooms. It might even pay the mortgage.'

'It'd be like being given a free house.'

'You could do the renovations, me the painting and decorating. We could buy place after place.'

They could think of any number of reasons why owning a house was preferable to not owning one.

'God, Nat, what idiots we've been. We could have had it all by now.'

All it takes to wipe something out is to put it in the corner of some bigger picture. But the bigger everything else becomes the more we shrink by comparison.

'I'll work nights,' said Natasha, all too aware of a new urgency to their lives.

'Weekends. I'll sell the van. Whatever it takes. We can do this.'

The Midas Employment Agency's new offices on the Strand glistened in the sunlight. Ed stood looking at the job advertisements in the window:

Fed up with your old job? Then get yourself a new job, said one poster. *Flexible Employment Opportunities: Supply Teachers Wanted. £35,000 p.a. pro rata. Machine Operators Wanted. £25,000 p.a. pro rata. Labourers Wanted. £15,000 p.a. pro rata. Temps Wanted. Waitresses Wanted. Bar staff wanted. Electricians, Plumbers, Bricklayers, Blocklayers, Carpenters. . .*

It was an Aladdin's cave of jobs. Here was that much sought after and universally promoted panacea for all problems and ills, the means of escape presented in every guise and variety.

Start work today and you could buy your own property tomorrow. Ask one of our receptionists to refer you to Midas Homes and Loans for a Midas Homes and Loans mortgage.

Need a loan? Big or small, Midas Homes and Loans can meet all your immediate and future financial needs. Saving up for that new kitchen? Why wait? You can have that money today and the kitchen tomorrow. Tomorrow's world today: Talk to Midas.

Ed pushed open the heavy glass door and he stepped inside.

The offices were warm. There was the smell of new carpet and fresh paint. There were leather chairs to sit in. Potted ferns lined the walls. Huge prints, cityscapes, hung on the walls.

Ed was impressed. He felt that he could believe in work in a place like this.

He approached the desk and he enquired about registering. The girl handed Ed a form.

Ed filled in his details, writing down all the jobs he had ever done. Ten minutes later he handed back the form.

The girl raised her eyebrows at Ed's employment record. 'Exactly what kind of work were you looking for?' she asked Ed.

'Whatever,' Ed shrugged. 'Just work, you know. Anything. I've done most things.'

The girl looked Ed up and down. Long greasy hair, donkey jacket, jeans, holed boots. She typed manual work in to the computer.

'How much will I get paid?' Ed asked.

'That all depends on the work,' said the girl.

There was a printer on her desk and in a short while a page slid out of it. The girl checked it then she handed it to Ed.

'Report there first thing tomorrow morning,' she said. 'Seven o'clock, prompt.'

Ed looked at the page. The page was warm and it smelt of ink. At the head of the page there was an underlined address and a large arrow pointing out its location on the accompanying map.

Ed looked questioningly at the girl. The girl shrugged. 'They will tell you there where you will be working,' she told Ed.

Ed pulled open the heavy glass door and stepped back out in to the city. Crowded pavements, traffic, traffic fumes, traffic noise. He should have felt different, he knew.

The Midas Employment Agency's yard was nothing like its offices. It had once been a foundry but had long since fallen in to disuse. It was surrounded by a high wall of dark brick on one side and by derelict buildings on the others. There was a port-a-cabin in the yard. Parked beside it were four rusted and beaten up transit vans. A crowd of men were stood waiting in the yard. East Europeans, most of them.

At seven o'clock the door of the port-a-cabin opened and a man in a suit appeared in the doorway. Men that had been slouching against the walls now pushed themselves upright. Cigarettes were drawn on one last time and then extinguished. The agency man walked toward the vans and he handed each of the van drivers a clip board. The drivers walked to the rear of their vehicles. Pulling open the doors they then began to shout out the names on their lists. As their names were called out the men began to pile in to the vans.

Ed was driven to a paint factory on an industrial estate.

The smell of paint was overpowering at first. Something in the air stung Ed's eyes and caught at his throat.

The men had to stand either side of a conveyor belt and pick off tins of enamel paint then pack them neatly in to boxes and stack the boxes on to palettes. As each pallet was filled, when it reached the height of a man, a forklift arrived to take it away.

The boxes were heavy. It was not easy to pick up a box and then load it on to the stack of boxes and to do that, box after box, for the full eight hours.

That day Ed would have to work twelve hours. The men had been hired to fill a rush order and they would not leave the factory until the order had been filled.

The tins slid past on the conveyor. Ed picked tin after tin off the conveyor and he placed them in the box.

Even boring jobs are tiring. They wear you down. They overwhelmed you with their pointlessness.

Ed looked a the clock. It was 9.30 am.

The men were not allowed to talk. They were not allowed to smoke, to eat or drink, to wander off, to take a break, not for any reason, not even to go to the toilet, not without permission, not unless someone replaced them first.

During the shift the men were given a half hour lunch break and two quarter hour breaks, one mid-morning, the other mid-afternoon, for which they were not paid.

The breaks were staggered, at no time during the shift was the machinery left unattended.

The only time the work stopped was if something went wrong with the machine. Nothing went wrong with the machine that day. It was just something that the men working there looked forward to and hoped for.

At the end of the day the men trooped out of the factory and in to the waiting vans which then returned them to the yard.

Ed worked only two days at the paint factory. When the rush orders the men had been hired to complete had been filled they were let go.

Ed was next sent to work in a supermarket to help stack the shelves in a refit. He worked in a warehouse after that, and then in a toilet roll factory, then a box making factory, then a printers. It was lifting work mostly.

The work suited Ed. It was good to finish work in a place you detested and to start work in another place knowing that you would not be working there for long.

The hours were long and the pay low so that it was necessary to put in the hours. You had to work the hours. If you did not work the hours, if the employers complained, if at any time you refused any job which the agency offered you then they would not hire you in the future. The system weeded out trouble makers. It weeded out the sick, the unsuitable and the work-shy.

The work was hard. It exhausted Ed. At the end of the day he was good for nothing. It was the same with Natasha. Work was wearing them down. Whenever they were not working, they were resting from work.

Work took 8 hours a day from you. But it took more. The need for money changed everything. Poets, writers, musicians, artists . . . . because of their need for money, became receptionists, shop assistants, labourers, shelf stackers, factory hands, security guards, dishwashers. . . . You became trapped then. You had very little time for anything else.

*

The employment agency took 15% of Ed's earnings. But it was much more. The agency also charged the employers a fee of 15% of the total earnings of everyone that the agency sent to them.

Ed worked six days a week. He worked overtime. He thought that the more hours he put in then the sooner he would save up the money which they needed for a deposit. Only it did not work out like that.

'It's so fucking frustrating. We can't get a mortgage until we get our downpayment, and we won't get that on these poxy wages. We're spending all our money on rent.'

'We're spending almost as much money on rent as we would be on a mortgage. We're throwing money away, when it could be our money, Ed.'

'It'll never be our money, Nat.'

It was the landlord's money. And if they ever got a mortgage then the money would be the bank's. It would be Midas' money.

'They're advertising for part time staff at the 50p shop. I could work there in the evenings,' said Natasha.

'For 50p?' It was a weak joke in the circumstances and neither of them laughed. 'It still won't be enough though, will it?'

'Can't you get more hours, Ed?'

'It's not up to me, is it? And I can't take on an evening job in case I get overtime. I can't turn down overtime, I'll get the sack. Flexible employment opportunities? Too fucking right. We have to bend over backwards to please those cunts.'

'We should move,' he said. 'Get some place cheaper.'

'Cheaper than this? Somewhere worse, you mean.'

'What I meant was, look around for a squat.'

'And what if we get evicted. We'll end up back on the streets.'

'We might end up on them anyway. I heard they're going to knock these houses down.'

'Everyone knows that, Ed. It's just a matter of time.'

Ed and Natasha's street was one of those earmarked for re-development. It was why no one ever came to fix anything. Not the leaking roof, nor the rotting window frames, nor the cracked and broken window panes. Not even the smashed in front door and splintered frame from the last drugs raid. The tenants had had to fix those things themselves as best they could themselves

'We'll never afford our own place.'

'House prices can't go up forever, Nat. There'll be a crash, all this property that's coming on the market.'

448

*

The shops on the high street began to close. The corner shop, the laundrette, the off-licence, the pound shop.

One by one the houses in those streets separating Ed and Natasha's street from the new developments became derelict. The moment that a house became abandoned gangs of workers moved in that commenced to strip the building of everything of use: cast iron fireplaces, stone steps, floorboards, skirting and architrave, doors, doorframes. . . . Every evening after work Ed, along with many others from the street, went scavenging in the buildings after dark. He acquired a solid table and chairs, a small sofa, a bedside table and lamp, and he sold them on to junk shops.

Whenever a street became empty, and within days of the last tenants being cleared from the buildings, a huge yellow machine arrived that tore off all the house fronts in order to deter squatters. The buildings, with their rooms of abandoned furniture and torn wallpaper now visible from the street, had the appearance of dolls houses. The street was demolished soon after. Now there was just wasteland separating Ed and Natasha's street from the new developments.

Shuttering was erected around the site. Large signs were fixed to the shuttering: Luxury Apartments.

The pile drivers, like approaching footfalls, sent shock waves running through the house. Windows, that had for years been sealed tight with paint, freed themselves and could be opened again. Cups crept to the edge of tables and were smashed on the floor. Doors swung open then slammed shut.

Natasha lost her job with Midas Homes and Loans. The company had shifted their operation to a call centre in India. She worked on the checkouts in a supermarket for a time. And then as a waitress in a cafe. She moved from job to job, in the hope of bettering herself. She felt that she would never better herself.

Ed was sitting on a bench in Lincoln's Inn Fields. He was drinking. The sun had just set and the park and the buildings were illuminated by the streetlights.

It was very pleasant in the park. There were no drunks, nor junkies, no loud singing, no tents nor shelters to spoil it anymore. It had been cleared of the homeless by the authorities.

Ed was working for a painter and decorator, rubbing-down, in a building around the corner from the Fields. It was a rush job, a renovation. He was clearing his head and lungs after ten long hours of this hard and dirty work.

Ed reached in to his jacket, in to his poachers pocket, and he produced a brand new 3" Harris paint brush and he threw it in to the bushes.

There was a secret campaign being waged by the workers against their work. Tools, machinery, the product itself, anything that had anything to do with the company became a target. If it stopped work, or gave time or dignity back to the workers then it was considered a small victory.

Ed drained his can. He put it on the ground beside him then he cracked open another can.

Ed pulled a scratch card out of his jacket pocket. Jackpot, £1,000,000.

It was a con, he knew. But he had to believe that it was possible. There was a need that grew in a person in proportion to the desperation building there.

Ed scratched away the windows.

Nothing. Fuck all.

Ed felt empty and depressed and a little sick inside. A little less able to carry on. The chance at the easy money ate away at the ability to earn the hard money, the little money. One moment there was every chance that you wouldn't have to, and the next, that possibility was snatched away.

Ed had another scratch card in his pocket, but he resisted putting it to the test. You had to keep the hope.

Ed had always considered himself to be lucky. But winning wasn't down to luck, it was down to numbers. It was a simple case of percentages and probabilities. Improbabilities. The odds of winning were tens of millions to one against winning. When winning seemed improbable, that was when Ed would scratch that card, he decided.

Ed took another sip of beer. It was cold in the park and Ed shivered.

A girl walked by. She was very tall and slender and very beautiful. Her long black hair flew behind her as she walked. Ed stared at her. She was like most girls in the city. Hundreds walked past Ed every day that did not give him a second glance.

On the way home he called in at an off-licence. He went straight to the wine racks and he chose a bottle of white wine. Natasha's favourite. The shop was busy. There was a long queue at the counter. Ed walked past the queue, out of the shop and up the street.

He walked down unlit streets and back alleyways, past abandoned houses and the hulks of burnt out cars, across rubble strewn wasteland and the occasional bonfire.

He was stopped by a gang of hooded youths who were stood warming themselves around a fire.

They pointed to the wine. 'Give us,' they said.

'Fuck off,' Ed told them. 'Go and steal your own wine.'
'Pass, friend.'

A piano went off, someone playing honky tonk. The stairs were a cataract of running children. Television sets and stereos were blasting out noise. The constant heavy thumps of the pile-drivers shuddered through the building. There was a loud click as the wardrobe door sprung its lock and swung open.

Natasha tore at her hair, she kicked the furniture, she beat the walls with her fists. The neighbours hammered on the walls back at her. Someone hammered on the ceiling. There was hammering from beneath. Natasha stamped her heel hard on the bare floorboards, several times. She switched on the stereo at full volume: Hazel O'Connor, *Breaking Glass*. She switched on the television set.

Ed came in. He switched on the lights. No electricity. He put a pound coin in the metre and the lights came on. The television exploded in to life. The news, at full volume.

The walls started hammering, and the ceiling, and the floor. Ed raced to the television and switched it off.

'Blimey, Nat?'

Natasha was sat on the sofa, staring in to space.

Ed lifted up the bottle, 'I got us some wine,' he said.

Ed poured Natasha a glass of wine. He handed her the wine. Natasha knocked back the wine. Ed poured her another glass.

Ed pulled a scratch card from his pocket. He sat looking at the scratch card.

'Jesus, Ed. What the fuck do you buy those things for? You know they're a waste of money. You never win anything. You're not meant to. That's not what they're for.'

Ed shrugged. 'You never know.' He held it out to Natasha. And he remained holding it out to her until Natasha took the card.

She sat staring at the card. Jackpot £1,000,000.

What the hell. Natasha scratched off a window:

£1,000,000.

She scratched off another window:

£1,000,000.

She sat upright. 'Christ! Ed!' She was soon scratching at the remaining windows.

Nothing. Fuck all.

'What did I tell you!' she shouted and she tore up the card and she threw the pieces on the floor.

'We'll never get out of here. Never!' She looked close to tears.

'We'll get out of here,' Ed assured her.

'How? The fucking lottery? Because work's not going to do for it us. Christ, Ed, I hate this! I hate this life. I hate what I've become. Nothing good ever happens to me anymore. Why can't things ever be easy? Nothing's ever easy. Things used to be easy for me. I used to have everything, I could have whatever I wanted, once.'

'Yes, and you wanted to be an artist.'

'It was all I wanted. I had everything else.'

Everyone has hopes of getting what they want. Only if a thing were certain would there be no hope. Certainty would kill hope. And a great many people too perhaps.

'It isn't going to happen for me, is it? It could take years more trying, Ed.'

'So what's a few more years? Some people go a whole lifetime and never get what they want.'

That did it. Natasha's face showed real fear then. What if there was nothing out there for her, that this was how it would be for the rest of her life. Her mouth twisted and her eyes filled with tears as the terror of it gripped her. She fought the rising panic down, but it just grew and grew in her. This wasn't the life that she had dreamt of, that she wanted to live. She saw no possible way out. She could no longer imagine any kind of future for herself.

'I can't go on living like this. I can't take it anymore. I can't.' Natasha tore at her hair. She gripped her skull. When she looked up it was with the wild and terrified eyes of a cornered animal.

Natasha did the only thing that she could think of. She ran through the kitchen and in to the bathroom, bolting the door shut behind her. She yanked open the medicine cabinet.

She pulled the lid off a bottle of paracetamols, lifted the bottle to her lips, threw back her head and gulped down the pills, only to gag on them and cough them noisily back up.

Ed booted in the door, splitting the doorframe.

Natasha turned from the wall, she fell back against the wall and she slid down the wall. She sat on the floor, pressed in to the corner between the toilet and the wall, her forehead on her knees, hugging her knees, crying.

Ed was scared. 'Nat! Christ! What the fuck are you thinking of?'

'I can't do this, Ed. Not anymore. I can't. I can't.'

Ed stood staring at the pills in the sink. At the pills scattered over the floor. He felt sick to the pit of his stomach.

Natasha sat on the floor in the corner, her arms over her head and she cried and cried.

'I tried, Ed, I did, I really tried.' Her face streamed with tears. She was all used up. There was no more fight in her.

'I know,' said Ed.

Ed put his hands under Natasha's arms. He helped her to her feet and he walked her in to the bed-sitting room and led her gently toward the bed. He sat her down on the bed and he reached out a hand and he rested it on her shoulder and he caressed her shoulder.

'It's hopeless, Ed.'

'Nothing's ever that hopeless, Nat.'

Every life was a victory. And you had to see it through, right to the bitter end.

Natasha flung herself down on the bed and pushing her face in to the pillow she burst in to tears.

That night Natasha dreamt that she was trapped inside her paintings. She had to paint. If she did not paint then she felt that something terrible would happen to her. But the more that she painted, the more paintings she surrounded herself with, the more trapped she became.

Natasha woke up in to her worst nightmare:

Tall Buildings Giving Everyone the Finger. The Mad Scrabble City. The Relentless Grindstone. Exit : No Exit . . . there were paintings everywhere: paintings hung on the walls, leant against the walls, stood upright against the furniture, on the furniture.

Natasha screamed.

She woke up screaming.

The white glare from the developments cast shadows in to the room. The light shone off her paintings. She was surrounded by paintings.

People were hammering on the walls, banging on their ceilings and floors for Natasha to shut up.

'I have to get out!' she was screaming. Ed had his arms around her, Natasha was struggling to get free but the more that she struggled the tighter Ed held her.

'I'm here. I've got you. It's all right. It's just a nightmare,' he told her, 'that's all. Just a nightmare.'

Natasha was feverish. She was covered in sweat, her hair was plastered to her forehead. She could not breathe, her heart was hammering at her chest and she could not breathe.

First thing in the morning Ed called out a doctor.

A psychologist would say that Natasha's illness and depression were the manifestation of her inner torment. A doctor that she was underweight, that she had asthma and bronchitis and that she was in danger of getting pneumonia. A good doctor would read the signs in those previous diagnoses. He would know that Natasha was suffering from anxiety and the effects of overwork and that her body was run down. He would prescribe ventolin and becotide for the asthma, along with plenty of rest and quiet. He would tell her that not eating properly and living rough in a damp bedsit was wearing her down. People died from less, even in London.

The doctor who came out to see Natasha prescribed antibiotics for the bronchitis, and ventolin and becotide for Natasha's asthma. He gave Natasha tranquillisers for her anxiety and he put her on antidepressants.

On his way out he told Ed: 'Living in a place like this would get anyone down.'

Natasha was forced to take several weeks off work. When she went back it was to find that she had been sacked. Natasha told them where they could stick their fucking job.

Without work to force her out of bed Natasha began to sleep-in mornings. She showed no interest in anything. Whole days went by when she did not get up out of bed. All she wanted was to sleep.

'I'm tired, is all,' she told Ed, 'I just need to sleep.' But she could not sleep. The room reeked of her illness, of stale sweat, of damp hair, of slept in, lived in clothes, unwashed bedding.

Ed hung a thin yellow curtain in the window, so that even on the dullest of days the light shining through it illuminated the room, turning it yellow. The yellow light helped to cheer Natasha. Encouraged by this first sign of recovery, Ed bought a yellow vase and some flowers, sunflowers, from a florist, to help brighten the room. He thought they might help lift Natasha's spirits. They might, he hoped, even inspire her. He bought her several large tubes of chrome yellow paint to that end.

The flowers wilted and died.

Natasha painted the drooping limp stalks and fallen brown petals. She left the work unfinished.

She did not paint the vase, other than to outline it. And nor did she paint a background. There was no point.

The painting was a masterpiece of implication. All that effort, and the work involved. All those years wasted.

Natasha destroyed the painting. It depressed her.

She hated to be reminded of what she could not do, of what she had been incapable of achieving.

Natasha's painting the dead flowers gave Ed an idea. He thought that if he could provide Natasha with something that resonated with her situation then it might stimulate her interest. He knew that her interest would grow. That the need to express herself would build up in her. It would build up and build up.

It was eleven o'clock on a Saturday morning and Ed had just returned from the newsagents with his Saturday edition of *The Press*, a *HELLO!* magazine, for Natasha, and his now daily scratch card.

Ed scratched off the windows, balled the ticket and threw it at the fireplace. Loud music, The Flying Lizards, was playing from the bedsit upstairs.

Oblivious, Natasha sat reading her *HELLO!* Ed sat on the couch flipping through the pages of his newspaper. There was an article by Bane Burke about the Criminal Justice Bill. He read:

As well as cracking down on travellers and ravers the criminal justice act will ban most forms of protest. From the moment the bill becomes law it will become illegal to be anywhere that you don't own or rent even if you have permission to be there. . . . The bill is an attack on dissent itself, and on alternative culture, on any alternative to the mainstream.

'It says here,' he said, looking over at Natasha, 'that there's going to be an open air rave next week, in Hyde Park, in protest at the Criminal Justice Bill. They reckon there'll be 50,000 people there. There'll be music, Nat, and dancing. You could bring your sketchbook.'

'What for?' asked Natasha. She returned her attention to her *HELLO!* magazine. 'And what's the Criminal Justice Bill got to do with us? We're not criminals.'

'No, but if this bill goes through we will be. It's not only raves and rave music they want to ban. If they push this thing through then there'll be no more free festivals. And no more living on the road either. There'll be no more squatting too. They want to cut off our escape routes. It'll all be criminalised. And we're not safe here either. Landlords will be able to kick people out on to the street anytime they want. They could kick us out on to the street.'

Natasha turned the page of her magazine. 'It's still okay to live on the street then?' she said. She returned her attention to her magazine.

Ed had hoped to engage Natasha's interest, instead he had only made himself angry.

'Anyone can be a criminal now, all these fucking laws they keep passing. An all this surveillance, what's that about, eh? They're looking out for us? Too fucking right they are.'

Ed was against what authority represented, what work represented, and had come to mean. He was against big money, the money that accumulates. He was against development. People were being hemmed in. He felt that he was being hemmed in, and from all sides. There were fewer ways of escaping, and less places to escape to. And there were all these new laws to contend with. And there was nothing that he could do about it.

'They're eroding our freedoms, Nat.'

Natasha looked up from her magazine. 'What fucking freedoms? There aren't any. Not unless you've got money, Ed. As if you hadn't noticed. It's the only escape there is, and even then it's just another way of trapping you that they have.' She returned to her magazine.

'They're just putting a lid on the thing, is all,' said Ed. 'This country, it will explode, you'll see.'

'Not whilst there's shopping, it won't.' Natasha did not even glance up from her magazine.

Ed lifted his paper in the air. 'Well here's 50,000 people that won't be shopping this weekend, that's for sure.' He waved the paper.

Natasha stared at Ed. 'Will any of them be armed, Ed?'

'Armed?' frowned Ed. 'No.'

'Then no one will pay any attention to them.'

'They will if we riot. I hope there is a riot. It'll be the poll tax all over again. We got rid of that, didn't we?'

'And now we have council tax. You can't fight them, Ed.'

'But you have to, all the time.'

'Because they win every time. But you're right, there will be a riot. The police will see to that.'

'The police?'

'Of course, the police. To justify the need for legislation. Ed, what do you think it is that keeps a world like this together?'

'Money,' said Ed. Without a doubt.

'Rules,' said Natasha. 'But do you know what's more important than rules?'

Ed shrugged, he didn't know anymore. He didn't want to know.

'Enforcing them. Imposing law and order. It's got nothing to do with justice, Ed. You make the rules, you enforce them. You make everyone do what you want them to do. Simon Says put your hands on your heads. And if you don't.' Lifting her magazine, she threatened Ed with it.

'To hell with rules,' spat Ed.

'And where will that get you? This isn't your country, Ed. You only work here. Freedom is just some notion in a book. Haven't you learnt that yet? It isn't our world anymore, it's their world. It always was.'

'You know what. They're trying to scare us, Nat, but I think it's them that are scared.'

'Of what? Us? Ha!' Natasha laughed.

'Of what we represent. They want to get rid of the independent people and replace them with dependent people.'

'They already have. You know what people fight for these days? To keep their fucking jobs. Think about it, Ed. They smashed the unions, and now they are going to smash dissent. They want it so that no matter what they do you can't protest against it. If they want a big development then they will go right ahead and they will have their big development. And you can protest all you like because protest never changed anything. If it did then they would only ban it.' Natasha laughed.

You can get very depressed about the whole thing. Or you can get angry.

It made Ed furious, that there was nothing that he could do about it. He got so frustrated at times. It was like an urgency growing inside of him, and it was twisting him up. Anyone would get frustrated in the face of such constraint. Even if you had the words, even if you knew and understood the argument, it would do you no good. They owned the argument.

'They own us, Ed.'

'No one owns me,' said Ed.

'You work for them, don't you? And they pay you fuck all. You earn their money for them. They own you, they own everything. And now they are going to prove it to you. From now on there are going to be increasingly more things that you cannot do and more places where you cannot go. It'll be like in my pictures. And who the fuck paid any attention to them?' She went back to her magazine.

Ed was right, there was a riot.

Natasha did not go to the demonstration: not interested, no point. And nor did Ed, he had to work.

Things were becoming exactly as Natasha had painted them. The city faster, more frantic. The barcode skyline of the 80's, that had emerged from the loads-a-money ethos of that era was now giving way to something far more alien and unreal, as though all the old boundaries had been revoked. Imbalanced, precarious, the emerging city seemed to be growing out of some mad design.

Forces were at work that were distorting its buildings, fracturing them and bending them out of shape. There seemed a definite lack of structure and restraint. Things were being governed by different laws now.

It made Weldon-Veal fearful for what remained. Increasingly, it was like visiting another planet, and he was beginning to feel that he longer quite belonged here.

And just as Weldon-Veal was being surrounded by Natasha's vision made real he had also begun to see more and more work like hers emerging from the art schools. It was by no means as accomplished, and it was not popular, even though it embodied the accompanying shift in the public mood against a future of which it was growing wary and apprehensive. He himself would never like that kind of work, but his attitude to it was changing and he felt that he had a duty to the art world to bring it to the public's attention. And so he decided to give Natasha her chance as the very best of that school of painting.

But Natasha showed little interest in the proposal. 'Whatever,' she said, when he tracked her down. She had begun to hate those pictures.

And the pictures had been in that vermin infested, damp lock-up for so long that they had begun to suffer from neglect. Weldon-Veal, took possession of them nevertheless.

One morning, whilst Ed was at work, Natasha took her remaining pictures and drawings out in to the back garden and she made a large bonfire of them. She threw her portfolio in to the flames. She threw her easel in to the flames. Her sketchbooks. Her brushes.

She stood looking at the flames.

'There,' she said. 'Finished.'

Ed continued to work with the employment agency. He bought two lottery tickets every day with his newspaper now. He bought a 27 inch flat screen TV with quadraphonic sound, for Natasha. And a video, and dvd.

Ed left the employment agency. He found full time work labouring for a construction company, Midas Developments.

He began to write short stories in his spare time. *The Armchair Revolutionary, Rebel Nights and Days.* . . . In to them he poured all his anger and frustration. He bought a second hand Amstrad and a daisy wheel printer and he printed his stories out and sent them off to publishers and to magazines, he entered short story competitions.

Back they came. He sent them off again. So long as they were out there there was every chance he would be successful. Back they came.

It was hard to adjust to change when you were a dreamer. Reality has no bearing on such lives. But Ed began to feel that he had used up all the options, that he couldn't do it anymore.

42

The March of the Makers

6 a.m., Monday morning, and Ed's alarm went off: 'Mother fucker! Mother Fucker! Mother Fucker. . . !'

Natasha reached over and she switched it off. 'Ed!' she said, shaking him, 'Ed, wake up.'

'Uh?' Ed woke, tired and full of dread, in to another much too-soon day.

'You'll be late for work.'

Ed only groaned.

He remained lying there, in the half-light, thinking of the hard week ahead and feeling dog tired and scared.

Endless waves of driven people keep rising on the wheel every day. And every day they come right back down to where they started, which is in the shadow of the wheel, and that turns the wheel. It wears you down after a while.

It was a bright winter's day of frost and clear blue skies and Ed was working in deep shadow, in the damp, in the mud, at the bottom of a deepening, steel sided crater. The crater resounded to the noise of pile-drivers, diggers, pneumatic drills, hammering, banging. The air there stank of diesel fumes and the rot that is wet clay.

Ed was labouring at the new developments, helping to prepare the foundations for a block of luxury flats.

It was hard, bone grinding work.

Ed swung his pick, he lifted it high in to the air and then he pulled it back down again, barely driving its point in to the ground. The heavy, compacted clay resisted his efforts.

The work, its difficulty, made Ed aggressive. He worked in short, furious, bursts of angry activity. Get angry, it makes you stronger, he muttered.

His back was soon screaming at him.

Ed threw down the pick, like he blamed it for all the work. He stood upright, pressing his hands in to his aching back. He grimaced from the pain. And the dried mud cracked on his face. His hips, elbows, wrists, knees all hurt. Ed rested his hands on his hips and he pushed out his hips and he bent backwards, as far as he could go in order to straighten his back. He stared up at the circle of clear blue sky.

There was a shout. 'Hey, you! Get back to work.' It was the foreman, stood, hands on hips, staring down at Ed.

Ed bent and he picked up his shovel. Pushing it in to the loosened clay, he began to transfer it in to a barrow. He had to beat the shovel hard on the barrow and then scrape it clean on the barrow's rim to free it of the glutinous clay. He transferred shovel upon shovel load in to the barrow, until he had filled the barrow.

Bending, he gripped the barrow's handles, steeled himself, stood upright, and then pushed with all his might. His feet went out from under him on the slippery clay. The clay clung to his boots, making them heavy. It clung to his gloves.

Ed was exhausted. He felt strangely light headed and his hands began to shake.

He threw down his shovel, took up his pick and began to attack the ground with it. Next thing, he was hacking at the ground with angry, ever wilder and more careless strokes. 'Fucking wine cellars. Fucking games rooms. . . .' It was like he was attacking the notion of work itself.

They tell you that success comes from working hard. Bullshit. Ed didn't believe it, not anymore. There were no rewards, not for the man who does the humping and carrying and the hands on making of things. The rewards accrue in the bank accounts, property and stock portfolios, the garages and drives, and on the walls and in the wine cellars of the increasingly rich. The working man receives only what is sufficient to keep him in need and the system fed.

'Fuck it!' he said, and he threw down his pick and then kicked it away from him. What were luxury flats to him? He would never have one, no matter how hard he worked. And why the hell should he do their work? He wanted to do his work, not theirs. If they wanted something doing then let them do it themselves.

'Hey!' yelled the foreman, 'Where the hell do you think you're going?'

Ed was already at the ladder. Cheered on by his work-mates, he raced up it and leapt out of the hole. Then he was running past the port-a-cabins, out through the gate and in to the street where he kept on running. He began to laugh.

Natasha had just got in from her shift at the petrol station, where she worked split shifts behind the till in the convenience store, and was about to put the kettle on for a cup of tea, when Ed burst in through the door.

Natasha frowned at him. 'What are you doing back at this hour?' she asked. It was 1pm. 'You haven't been laid off, have you? Tell me, you haven't been laid off.'

'Me? No.'

Natasha breathed relief.

'I quit.'

'What?'

'I've been such a fool, Nat. We both have.'

'Leave London?'

'Yes! We should have left here a long time ago. We should never have come here. Look at what it's done to you. Look at what it nearly did to me.' Ed laughed from sheer relief. He continued to pack and when he had finished packing his own things he began to pack Natasha's things. 'We'll leave first thing tomorrow. We're not trapped, Natasha, and I'm going to prove it to you. Times were good before we came here, well we can have that life again.'

They would leave London. They would take to the road, where homelessness and not belonging did not matter. Such things had no place to the traveller and were not the goal. They would recover their strength. There would be new roads to travel, new horizons. Doors would be flung open to them. Suns would rise and rise. Who knew what would happen? Ed felt the old excitement stir inside of him. There was always that second chance, because there was always tomorrow. Things would be different tomorrow.

'But where will we go? What will we do for money?' asked Natasha.

'I'll carve and you can do your caricatures and street art. We'll busk. We'll buy ourselves a camper van, go and live in the sun! Life will be easier in the sun. Southern France? Spain, even? Why stop at Spain?'

Ed could not work, not to buy things he couldn't. Their acquisition would only imprison him in work. But he would work to buy time, he would work to escape work. It was the only real safeguard against a life spent working that there was. It must be possible even now to survive without full time work. People had existed for millennia without work. Life was all about survival, and survival was easy. All you had to do was to stay alive.

*

Weldon-Veal was clearing out his storeroom. He was taking delivery of a collection of paintings from a new and exciting artist in the morning prior to an exhibition and he needed to make room for them. As Weldon-Veal supervised the shifting of Natasha's canvases he was caused to look at them again. He rested them against the furniture and he hung one or two upon the walls, so as to gauge their effect. He was slowly beginning to understand them, though he still could not bring himself to like them: he would never hang one on his walls, yet he had a feeling about them nevertheless, and, though he disliked the works he could not be certain that others would feel the same way. Weldon-Veal picked up the telephone.

Mister Guggenheim, the wealthy American art collector, had returned to London. On a previous visit to the city, some ten years previously, he had bought a collection of several landscapes by an unknown artist. Ever since that time he had entertained hopes of discovering the artist, and it was with that in mind that he always searched the galleries and exhibitions each time he visited London.

He was in Galleria, being shown a collection of landscapes.

'They are similar, I'll give you that, but look at this,' he pointed. 'No, it's all wrong, completely wrong.' There were problems of angle and perspective. 'It should flow. The sea should become the land, roll inland as hills. No, no, this is forced, forced. And the brushstrokes, wrong, all wrong!' Mister Guggenheim dismissed the canvas. He left the gallery. 'Where next?' he asked Geoffrey Thimblebaum, his secretary.

Mister Guggenheim was determined to make the most of his time in London. There was still a very real chance that he would make a discovery. His last visit to the city had resulted in his purchase of PK's *Shitting Scream*. He had also since then acquired a Sadie Sommer's *Opulent Interiors*.

He spent the remainder of the afternoon visiting the galleries and the numerous exhibitions, as well as poring through the various auction house catalogues on the off chance that he might find something there. He undertook as thorough a search of the city as he was able to make and, though he saw many good works, he did not find any great ones.

Mister Guggenheim grew resigned to leaving London empty handed.

'We haven't tried Weldon-Veal's yet,' said Geoffrey Thimblebaum. He had a map of the city and he had ringed all the galleries and exhibitions that might prove worthwhile.

Mister Guggenheim shook his head. 'I've seen his catalogue. There's nothing there, nothing new or interesting anyhow. Look, why don't we call it a day and head back to the hotel. I'm afraid London's failed us this time, there's not even a stray Enzo to snatch up.' Mister Guggenheim grinned. 'Dissolving paintings? who would have believed it?' He shook his head. 'Do you know what I think? I think London has had it as far as great art is concerned. The artists here, they're just taking the piss.'

Ed and Natasha went to bed early. They had an early start ahead of them in the morning.

'Ed?' said Natasha.

'Yes?'

'What will become of us, do you think?'

'Become of us?' Ed smiled. 'We're going to carry on being us. You can't stop being you, Natasha, can you?'

Natasha sighed, she had her answer.

Mister Guggenheim and Mister Thimblebaum walked back to the car. Mister Guggenheim climbed in to the rear seat. Thimblebaum drove. It was dark and the city was all lit up. They drove fast through the yellowed streets.

'We're wasting our time here, let's head back to the hotel. We've got an early start tomorrow. Maybe we'll strike lucky in Paris tomorrow.'

It was late by the time they returned to the hotel, and it had started snowing. Mister Guggenheim had only just entered his room when the phone rang.

'Mister Guggenheim? Mortimer. Weldon-Veal? The Gallery, Bond Street? Your secretary in New York, she said you were in London. Yes, quite a stroke of luck this, really. I've got something I think that you should see.'

Mister Guggenheim stood in the window of his hotel watching the snow fall gently, silently, on the city. 'I don't know if we got the time, we're flying to Paris in the morning.' Though he wondered whether any planes would be flying with all this snow.

'I really do think it would be worth your while. Really, I do,' said Weldon-Veal.

Someone walked down the street and the snow squeaked. A snowball hit a car with a jolly thump. The noise and the bright white light reflecting off the snow through the threadbare curtain woke Ed. Ed rolled over to wake Natasha.

She was not there.

'Natasha!' He shouted, thinking that she might be in the bathroom. But there was no answer. He yelled again.

Ed sat up in bed. He felt Natasha's side of it. It was cold. Puzzled, he looked around the room.

Natasha's pack was gone, her boots were gone and her coat was missing off the door.

Ed dressed quickly. He flew headlong down the stairs. Pulling open the front door he ran out in to the street where he let out a loud triumphant shout that was almost a laugh.

There, in the snow, were Natasha's footprints.

Ed followed them to the main road. There were other prints now but he had no trouble distinguishing Natasha's prints.

The soles of her boots had been worn treadless and there was a tell tale line where they had split. Laughing and vindictive Ed hurried after them.

Mister Guggenheim stood in Weldon-Veal's gallery, surrounded by Natasha's pictures.

He put down one landscape and he picked up another. He had already spent far more time than he had intended to in the shop.

'We should go,' said Thimblebaum, looking at his watch.

'Go? Goddamit, Thimblebaum, will you forget Paris.' Mister Guggenheim gripped and shook the painting that he was holding. 'It's her, I tell you. Look at this. See, the brush strokes are unmistakable. And there, that rolling hillside. And just look at those suns. Such suns. Suns and suns. Marvellous. Marvellous. After all this time, I've finally found her.' Mister Guggenheim put the painting down. He picked up another painting. 'And look at this, just look at the colour in it, it's so like Van Gogh, only it's better than Van Gogh. And there, that one, it's like Brughel, but it's better than Brughel. She is better than any of them. What a find. These pictures are masterpieces. And you want I should go to Paris?'

'There are more, Mister Guggenheim,' said Weldon Veal.

'More?'

'Yes, perhaps a hundred or so, at least.'

Mister Guggenheim's jaw dropped, rendering him speechless.

'They were meant for an exhibition, only the exhibition never happened, my fault really. And as there was nowhere else to keep them, nowhere safe, I. . . Well, they've just been sitting here, gathering dust.'

'Good God, man, don't stand there explaining yourself, show me, well go on, go and fetch them. Now!'

Weldon-Veal, together with an assistant, disappeared to the back of his storeroom.

'This is incredible, absolutely incredible,' said Mister Guggenheim. 'It is the find of the year, of the whole God-damned century. And there are more!'

When Weldon-Veal and his assistant returned they were carrying a huge canvas between them.

It was so large they could barely manage it through the wide connecting doors.

'Help them with it, Thimblebaum, Christsakes.'

The three men manhandled the picture around so that Mister Guggenheim could see it.

Mister Guggeheim stared.

'My God,' he said.

Mr Guggenheim could not believe what he was looking at. Natasha had given form to ideas that most people wished to express but did not know how. She offered an analysis, yet it was one that the observer could never quite grasp, there was always some new interpretation, some new possibility there:

Screaming skies, screaming traffic. . . . The city roars and races with rage. . . . The world is teeming with furious activity. . . . All this hurrying about, this frenzy for possession. . . . Endless waves of driven people. . . . The mad scrabble city speeds and roars, lives run faster here than in other places. . . . Broken and screaming rocks and bricks, wrecked and burning cars, graffiti scrawled buildings, rubbish tips, wastelands, construction sites, soaring tower blocks. . . . The city spreads. . . . Exit: No Exit. . . . Get away from it all, take a mini break. . . . Exit through the gift shop. . . . There is so much to work for you need never stop. . . . WELCOME TO THE NUTTYPRICE HOUSEPROUD CAR WORLD AND BURGERDOME MEGASTORE SHOPPING COMPLEX. . . . Cars, car parks, pylons, chimney stacks, cooling towers, roads, out of town shopping malls. . . . This Is England. . . . No Fishing. No Access. No Ball Games. . . . Parking £5. . . . No Parking. . . . Private Property. . . . The road cuts through the landscape, tearing us through it. . . . Traffic tearing by, buses, cars, motorbikes. . . . The mad scrabble city speeds and roars. . . . Exit: No Exit.

Colliding worlds, waste grounds and construction sites, and everything twisted, distorted, as though forced in to another dimension. And all life lived on that precarious edge.

This is what Mister Guggenheim had been searching for. That spark of genius, someone with that rare ability to see what was going on in the world and to distil it in to a picture.

Mister Guggenheim let out a great shout of joy.

'Will you just look at this. Look at it. It is so like Picasso, you would think it was by the great man himself. It's like his *Guernica*. No, there is nothing like this! It is unique.'

Mister Guggenheim had spent years, his whole lifetime looking at art, great art - in the Tate, the Louvre, the Prado, but here, before him, was art like he had never before witnessed. It was comparable to the best he had ever seen. And the title, all of the titles – *Strange Buildings, Unusual Shapes. . . . Tall Buildings, Giving Everyone the Finger. . . . Tsunamis of Development. . . . The Relentless Grindstone . . . . The Last Day of the Sales.* They were perfect. Perfect. He detected a definitive narrative to the works. He was overwhelmed by the scope, the depth of feeling and understanding in Natasha's pictures. 'Good God,' he said, 'how could anyone have possibly painted this?' He could have cried with joy at his discovery.

Weldon-Veal made yet another trip to the back of the storeroom. He returned carrying several canvases beneath his arms and two in each hand which he began to arrange around the walls. His assistant likewise.

Mister Guggenheim stood looking at them in awe.

'Masterpieces,' he applauded. 'All of them, masterpieces. What a discovery.' He felt incredibly small before such work. 'More, show me more!' he shouted, following Weldon-Veal in to the storeroom.

Natasha's footprints led Ed down Bishop's gate but then he lost the trail outside Tower Hill Station. There were footprints everywhere. People were streaming out of the station on their way to work, despite the weather.

Ed checked out the station, but she was not there. He asked about her at the ticket sales counters, but without success. Returning to the street Ed picked up her trail on Eastcheap. He followed the prints as far as Cannon Street, where he lost them in the increasingly trampled snow.

Ed wandered the city for hours, searching. But it was hopeless. The snow had been trampled to a grey slush.

Ed walked slowly back the way he had come, his shoulders knocking left and right against the rush of oncoming shoppers and commuters which he did not seem to notice.

The need for her sang deep aches in him. The pit of his stomach wailed the painful emptiness.

It hit Ed like he'd walked in to a wall. The truth behind everything. Behind money, power, work. Behind life itself. Behind love, even. Something so stinking and feral and raw that everyone kept it hidden. It was their greatest fear. Something more important than survival sometimes. Loneliness, emptiness, not belonging.

It had destroyed Natasha.

Suddenly, he no longer had that protection, no secret place nor activity in which to hide.

Over the years, Ed had taught himself to get by on very little, he had preached the gospel of not working, and it had not been enough. He realised that now. What he had needed was a goal, a reason, and Natasha had provided him with that. It was Natasha that had led. It was her ambition, her hopes that they had been following. What would he do now?

Time moved, urged on by the sun and the stars, by time itself, and the crowd, the people and their dreams, were changed, like a kaleidoscope changes and would keep changing.

A front door slammed. Someone else was leaving the street for some new place.

'Nice knowing you,' someone shouted as he left the house.

'You too. Look after yourself.'

'See you around.'

Things were breaking up, were moving on. The whole world was changing, was moving on.

'Bon voyage.'

'If I don't see you again, have a good life.'

Everyone was going their separate, wandering, aimless, hopeful ways as, slowly, surely, they moved apart, upon the roving, never straight, never to cross, wide and dreaming roads which they inhabited.

43

The Beast is Dead.
Long Live the Beast

SUB PRIME MORTGAGE CRISIS. NIGHTMARE ON WALL STREET. LEMMON BROTHERS COLLAPSE CAUSES MARKETS TO IMPLODE. CRISIS SHAKES FINANCIAL WORLD TO ITS VERY FOUNDATIONS. . . .

The papers were full of the news. It was the biggest bankruptcy in history, and it had sent stock markets in to a nosedive. With £5.7 trillion wiped off the world economy it was the largest destruction of capital the world had ever seen. The crisis was now in its third week and it was being reported as though it were the end of the world.

Dawn, and a fierce white sun exploded on the horizon.
   Jigsaw woke in his oceanfront hotel room just outside of LA. He lay there thinking for a moment, a few seconds. There was a sound like breathing that was the sea. He jumped out of bed, crossed to the French windows and pulled back the curtains:
   Clear blue skies, hot sun, bright sunlight blazing off the ocean. It was another great day in paradise.
   Pulling on a pair of red and orange Bermuda shorts and a black and yellow Hawaiian shirt, Jigsaw stepped out on to the balcony in to the warm sun. He rested his hands on the balustrade, turned his face to the sun and closed his eyes. Smiling, he drew in a deep breath. The air smelt of the ocean, of the hot

dry earth, of orange blossom and bougainvillaea.

Palm trees overhung the balcony. Jigsaw spotted a coconut in one of the trees. It would have been no difficult thing for him to climb on to the balustrade and fetch it down. It hung enticingly from the tree like an advert for coconuts. Jigsaw rang room-service and he ordered a coconut, along with breakfast and the day's papers.

OUR MONEY IS DYING, screamed the headlines: BILLIONS WIPED OFF SHARE PRICES AS BUBBLE BURSTS. . . . SHARES TUMBLE AROUND THE GLOBE AS FINANCIAL CRISIS SPREADS TO REAL ECONOMY. . . . TRILLIONS DISAPPEAR IN TO THIN AIR. . . . ZERO GROWTH PREDICTED AS FINANCE EVAPORATES. . . . GOLDEN TOUCH TURNS TO DROSS. . . . MIDAS SHARES PLUMMET FOLLOWING KRYTEN FUND COLLAPSE. . . . COLLAPSE OF MIDAS CORP. . . .

Jigsaw allowed himself a smile.

MidasCorp was no longer his company, and nor was he a partner in Kryten. Max Bringmeen, backed by the other partners of the fund, had taken control of Kryten shortly after joining, ousting Jigsaw as head of MidasCorp in a boardroom power struggle led by the multibillionaire.

Jigsaw returned to his newspaper:

HEDGE FUND MANAGER MAX BRINGMEEN DROWNED . . . DICK FAULT LATEST, FALL NOT SUICIDE, SAY POLICE . . . ATTACKS ON BANKERS INCREASE.

Bankers and fund managers had been assaulted in the streets. Traders on their way to work in the City and on Wall Street had been pelted with coins, with a currency trader losing his eye in one such attack. People were angry. Jobs were being lost. Economies were shrinking. An increasingly angry public were expecting the politicians to put it right. It was disturbing news.

Jigsaw poured himself a cup of coffee, he ate a piece of toast.

It was 10am. before Andy shuffled barefooted out on to the balcony.

The bright sun dazzled Andy. It shone off the white marble patio. He had a vampire's reaction to it. Arm raised, he retreated backwards in to his room to fetch his shades, returning a moment later wearing a pair of Andybans. He crossed to the table, pulled out a chair and sat down.

Jigsaw, resting back in his chair, was dabbing at his mouth with a napkin.

'Ah, breakfast,' said Andy, searching the table.

Two places had been set but there were only empty bowls and plates, the plates smeared with bacon and egg grease, with croissant and toast crumbs. There was an empty toast rack, an empty orange pitcher, and the two empty half shells of a coconut, scraped clean.

'Your breakfast was lovely,' said Jigsaw, putting the now scrunched up napkin on his plate. He reached for the coffee jug.

'Coffee?' he asked Andy.

Andy wanted tea. But there wasn't any. Jigsaw sat drinking his coffee.

Andy stared at Jigsaw. He shook his head. 'I don't understand you,' he said. 'How can you just sit there like that?'

'Like what??'

'Like nothing's happened. Like none of this matters.' He pointed at the pile of newspapers. 'Christ, Jigsaw, when I think of all that money that those bastards cheated you out of. They took it off you, everything, everything you ever worked for. The whole fucken lot. I told you they would. I warned you it'd happen, didn't I?'

'You did, yes.'

'Only you never listened.'

'No. I didn't.'

'They worked one over on you. They shafted you, big style.'

'Did they, really?' Jigsaw smiled. 'But Kryten ended up ruining them, didn't it? It could,' he said, 'have ruined me.'

When the crisis hit, Kryten had capital under management of $200 billion, but the debt financed assets on its balance sheet amounted to $1tr. The fund was over-leveraged and when the crisis hit the money simply disappeared. Bringmeen lost his whole fortune. Most of the partners did.

'Poor Max Bringmeen,' said Jigsaw, 'he just couldn't face living without all that money. He was no one without money.'

Andy scowled. 'No one else is jumping out of any windows though, are thee, eh?'

'Dick Fault?' said Jigsaw.

'He didn't jump, he had to be helped out. He got what was coming to him. Masters of the fucking universe. I hope they all get what's coming to them. They sold us out, those bastards. Years ago. They sold our jobs.'

'True. But just think what might have happened to us if there had been jobs?' cautioned Jigsaw.

The two friends crossed themselves as a protection against work. It was a theatrical gesture, part reflex, though there was a degree of precaution in it.

'It's all right for you,' said Andy. 'You've still got money, you're still a millionaire, you are. Me, I'm absolutely broke. I spent all my money on drink, drugs and women.'

'At least you didn't waste any,' said Jigsaw.

The laughter soon petered out.

They had lost the house in the hills, it had been MidasCorp's. They had lost the yacht. They still had the apartment in London, however, and the fast cars. And the expensive lifestyle to maintain.

Andy sighed. He shook his head. Jigsaw too had regrets.

Certainly, he was still a millionaire, several times over, and, with careful management of his assets, doubtless he always would be, but it wasn't enough. He was no longer a big player. Other people made the decisions now and would hold sway over events. But everything changes: every day people have to rebuild their lives from scratch.

'Don't worry,' Jigsaw told Andy, 'I'll see you right. I wouldn't desert my best mate, now, would I?'

Andy's face showed genuine gratitude and relief. 'I knew I could rely on you, pal. I knew you wouldn't let me down.' He reached over and he shook Jigsaw by the hand, he shook and shook it. 'Thanks,' he said. 'Thanks.' Then, smiling, he relaxed back in to his seat. All the tension had drained from him.

'It's what friends are for,' said Jigsaw.

'We've been through a lot together, haven't we?' said Andy. 'We've had some times together alright,' he grinned. 'Andy and Jigsaw versus the rest of the world,' he laughed.

'I couldn't have done it without you,' said Jigsaw. 'And we can do it again, yes?'

'What?' The smile left Andy's face.

Jigsaw's briefcase lay open on the table. He reached over and he took out some papers which he placed on the table before Andy. He placed a pen on the table.

Andy stared at the papers. 'What the fuck is this?' he asked. But he knew all too well what it was.

Andy's current contract was coming up for renewal and Jigsaw had had his lawyers prepare a new contract for him to sign.

'It's your new contract. I can't secure you any tours without a contract. Just think, this time next year you could be a millionaire.'

Jigsaw was already making plans to refinance himself. He had made mistakes in the past, he knew, but he was determined that it would be much different this next time around.

Leaving Andy struggling to comprehend his new situation he returned to his newspaper:

A PLACE IN THE SUN. GREECE PUTS ITS ISLANDS UP FOR SALE TO SAVE ECONOMY. . . .

There would be plenty of opportunities in the coming months for those shrewd enough and in a position to take advantage of the new realities.

The big players win whatever happens. They can turn anything to their advantage. For them everything is an opportunity. And so they shape the world. It was where the real battle was to be fought, Jigsaw knew.

The kaleidoscope turns and turns. Everything is in flux. But things will soon settle again. They will become rigid until the next time. Meanwhile, the world is being re-ordered according to the new realities.

There was the loud rumble of traffic in the air. It was first thing Monday morning and all over the city people were rushing off to work. Andy and Jigsaw were relaxing by the hotel swimming pool. A white sun blazed fiercely in the gradually yellowing sky. Light blasted off the ocean. It shone off the white walls of the hotel buildings, the white paths. It blasted off the surface of the hotel swimming pool. There was the squeak of footprints on hot dry sand, the sound of a diving board springing back, followed by the splash of water as Andy dived in to the cool waters of the swimming pool. Jigsaw lay propped up on his sun-lounger in the hot sun, his heavy, tanned body glistening in the sun and reeking of sun oil. He was holding up a newspaper, the *New York Times*, watching, from behind the dark refuge of his sunglasses, every female passage along the beach.

A long legged blonde and a busty brunette walked by and his gaze followed them. The couple passed a tall, slim dark haired girl in a white thong and Jigsaw transferred his attention to her. Until a girl with a bodyboard walked by.

Andy climbed up out of the pool and he walked over to where Jigsaw lay sunning himself, he picked his towel up off his sun-lounger, dried himself, then lay down to enjoy the sun.

He was soon bored.

He propped himself upright on his elbows. 'Fancy a wander down the beach, Jigsy, mate?'

'You go. I'm sunbathing, Andy.'

With a sigh, Andy flopped back down on his sun-lounger. He lay looking at the sky for a time. A few minutes. He rolled on to his side and said: 'What about a kick around then, yeh?' Andy's football was under his sun-lounger.

'I'm perfectly happy as I am, thank you,' said Jigsaw, his head turning to watch a woman in a skimpy yellow bikini walk by.

Andy needed a drink. He had put several bottles in an ice-bucket under a towel beneath his sun-lounger to keep cool. He reached beneath his sun-lounger and lifted off the towel but the bucket was empty.

On their sides under Jigsaw's sun-lounger lay several empty bottles of alcohol free Andy-broo.

'You drank all my Andy-broo?' said Andy.

Grinning, Jigsaw raised a half-full bottle of Andy-broo from behind his newspaper. Its sides were still wet with condensation. 'Cheers,' he said.

Disgusted, Andy dropped back on to his sun-lounger.

Jigsaw shrugged. He continued to sip his Andy-broo.

Andy sat and he gazed out to sea for a time.

The sea slid up and down the shore. At the water's edge, a sea potato rolled to and fro on the idle, nothing to do tide. A heat haze obscured the distance, making it shimmer. Distant mountain tops seemed to detach themselves from the land and float idly in the yellowing, white-bluish air. Yet another jet scarred the sky with a white vapour trail.

Jigsaw finished the Andy-broo then he returned to reading his newspaper.

There was an article by Bane Burke in the *New York Times*:

Under the heading, Banking crisis. What crisis? she wrote:

A largely unregulated global financial system developed in the years leading up to the system's recent inevitable near collapse created a wholly new economic phenomenon: capitalism without capital. It was nothing short of chronic recklessness powered by unchecked greed. It created a false sense of money. The money did not exist. Yet here we are still trying to will it in to existence. It is time to push back this rule of money. We have the opportunity to create a radically different world, to cap greed, redistribute wealth, reassess our values. The pursuit of wealth has...

It was the usual Bane Burke, the article just another rehash of her old argument. Jigsaw skim read the article.

Blah blah, he said. He turned the page:

SUPERMARKET WORKER TRAMPLED

A supermarket worker was trampled to death after frenzied shoppers stampeded through a

New York store breaking down the doors in pursuit of bargains. "This crowd was out of control", said police lieutenant Michael Fleming, who described the scene as utter chaos.

Consumer confidence was back on the rise then, Jigsaw smiled. It would be business as usual again soon. He looked up from his paper. 'Vegas in three days,' he told Andy.

Andy was booked to appear at The Happy Crassus for two weeks, with his show, Man And Ball. Then he was off on a gruelling three month tour of the States, 90 venues in as many days, with *Completely Sold Out II*. He was currently performing this show at the LA Laugh Factory.

Andy sighed. He was not looking forward to the tour.

He looked across the pool toward the bar, but fought the urge. Bored, he looked up and down the beach, he gazed languidly along the promenade. He sat upright on his sun-lounger. A long legged and barefooted girl in a pale blue sarong and faded pink T-shirt was walking down the seafront toward the beach carrying a battered surfboard under one arm. She had long blonde hair that flared out sideways as she walked, catching the sun. She walked with her face to the sun, smiling. She passed between Andy, Jigsaw and the sea, continued up the beach for some fifty yards, halted, then jammed her board upright in the sand. She unwrapped her sarong to reveal long slender legs, dropped it on the floor then pulled off her top. Dropped her top on her sarong and then ran toward the ocean, waded in to the sea up to her thighs then dived gracefully beneath the water.

Andy sat watching the water for some time.

The sea was flat calm. Bright sunlight flashed off the unbroken water. A super yacht cruised by on its way north.

It was several minutes before the girl resurfaced, some thirty or so yards out to sea. Andy had the briefest glimpse of her as her back curved up out of the water followed by her legs before she slid beneath the surface again. When she next reappeared it was at the water's edge. She stood, pulling the wet hair off her face and sweeping it back over her shoulders with both hands, then she walked up the beach toward her board. Andy watched her spread her sarong out on the sand and then lie face down on it. She looked over in Andy's direction. Andy looked quickly away. He stared out to sea for time. And when he looked back the girl had turned away from him.

'You want to take off those shades,' he told Andy, 'she'd have been over like a shot.'

'Yeah, along with everybody else. We'd a been mobbed. No thank you.'

Jigsaw returned his attention to his newspaper. He looked over his newspaper toward the beach. There were girls there.

Andy picked up his football. He rotated it in his hands. He span the ball on his finger. He held it in his hands and he sat staring at the ball.

He began to bounce the ball. Dropping it to the floor then catching it.

Two girls, one of them raven haired and wearing a red bikini, the other a brunette in a white one piece bathing suit, came walking along the beach. They saw the bar and they turned toward it. Their lithe bodies, rolling walk and hips, transfixed Jigsaw, causing him to emit a low groan. He raised his beer bottle to them as they passed by, wiggled it, and smiled in their direction.

The girls ignored him. But as they entered the bar the raven haired girl gave a backward glance over her shoulder in his direction.

'I'm in there,' said Jigsaw. And, grabbing up his wallet, pulling on his gaudily patterned black and yellow Hawaiian shirt, his stomach protruding from it, its sides flapping out like wings and trailing behind him, he went hurrying toward the bar with an eagerness born of anticipation.

Jigsaw was balding and overweight, ate too much and did absolutely no exercise, and he thrived on that. He was living the dream.

Andy sat staring at the sea for a time. Then, picking up his football, he walked down on to the beach with it. He kicked the ball. He dribbled the ball between shells, footprints, seaweed, the odd beer bottle and can, an empty Andy-broo bottle, pebbles. . . .

He was soon providing himself with a running commentary: 'Brilliant interception by O'Shea. It's O'Shea with the ball. O'Shea. O'Shea, cuts in from the wing. Here comes O'Shea, powering through the defence toward the box. It's just O'Shea and the goalie now. O'Shea shoots. It's. . . .'

The blonde girl was sitting watching Andy. The ball came at her fast. There was no time to duck. It was the last thing she expected.

Grimacing, half turning away, half crouching, lifting his hands to his head, Andy watched helplessly on as the ball rocketed toward the girl and hit her squarely on the head, fanning out her hair and knocking her flat on to her back.

'Shit!' he cursed. 'Shit, shit,' he repeated. Andy ran up to the girl. 'Sorry,' he said, 'Sorry, sorry. You alright?' he asked her, lifting his shades on to his forehead.

The girl shook her head as she raised herself up on to her elbows, her legs bent, the soles of her feet flat on the sand, her knees not quite together, and she looked up at Andy.

'Yeah, fine. Gee, that was some kick,' she said, rubbing her head where the ball had hit her.

'It was some header,' said Andy, and he pointed to the ball. It was some fifty feet away.

The girl grinned. She stared at Andy, she angled her head at him, frowning. 'You know,' she said. 'You look kinda familiar.'

'Do I?'

'Yes,' she said, and she lifted a hand to her forehead to shield her eyes against the sun.

Andy felt his spirits sink.

'You sort of look like David Beckham,' she said. 'You bent that ball like David Beckham.'

Andy laughed. 'Yeah, sorry about that,' he said.

'That's aright,' she told him. 'Judy,' she said, and she reached out a hand.

Andy took her hand. Her hand was warm, and long fingered. 'Andy,' he said, and he hauled Judy to her feet. She was very tall, a full inch taller than Andy. Her eyes were brown and very large. She had pure white teeth. Her hair was tangled and wild looking. She was very brown. She wore a skimpy pink bikini bottom, and a faded pink T-shirt, both stained with salt. Andy stood holding her hand for some time. She had to tug on it to retrieve it from him. She smiled at Andy. She liked the look of him. She did not know that he was Andy Rant. She had never heard of Andy Rant. Could she play football with him? she asked. 'Please,' she pleaded. She had a wonderful smile.

'Sure,' said Andy.

Andy went off to retrieve the ball.

It was a high pass and it bounced before it reached her. Judy caught the ball, two handed, and she threw it back to Andy. Andy told her to kick it next time. He passed the ball along the ground to her. Judy let the ball roll past her then she ran after it. She ran alongside of the ball, until it had stopped rolling. Then, turning to face Andy, she threw a leg at the ball. Her toe barely connected with the ball. The ball traipsed half-heartedly across the sand toward Andy. It did not reach Andy. Judy laughed at her hopelessness at football. She had a beautiful laugh. Andy passed the ball more gently to her next time. Judy missed with her passes and she could barely kick, not in bare feet. The ball hurt her feet. The day slowed. It stopped somewhere. Andy grew tired of the game. He picked up the ball and he thanked Judy for the game.

'We could go for a drink,' she said.

Just then there was a loud shout of, 'Andy! OY ANDY. ANDEE!'

Jigsaw emerged on to the beach with the girls he had followed in to the bar earlier. He was stood between them, with his arms around their waists. He broke free of the girls and he came running toward Andy, yelling: 'To me, to me!' indicating his head. He was a comical sight, with his round body and thin athletic legs, and the girls began laughing at him.

It was a high dropping cross and Jigsaw caught it on his foot in mid-air and he held it there, shouting out in surprise and then in triumph. The two girls were impressed. Laughing, they applauded Jigsaw.

Jigsaw flicked the ball from his right foot to his left, then to each knee in turn, from shoulder to shoulder and then on to his head. He headed it to Andy. Andy bent and he caught it on the back of his neck. Andy made an aeroplane with his arms and he rolled the ball to and fro along them. Then, standing upright, he shrugged the ball in to the air with his shoulder and he caught it on his foot. Laughing, he passed it back to Jigsaw.

A crowd began to gather having recognised Andy. They formed a circle around Andy that began to close in on him. The crowd began to chant:

'Andee! Andee!' They were holding out pens and pieces of paper, even dollar bills, for him to sign.

Foot to foot, knee to knee . . . Andy repeated Jigsaw's trick with the ball. Then, with everyone's eyes fixed firmly on the ball he kicked it high in to the air in to the sun. Everyone lifted their heads to follow its trajectory. As they stood staring at the rising ball, shading their eyes against the sun, Andy slipped unnoticed through the crowd.

The ball landed outside the crowd.

Andy intercepted it. He dribbled it past Jigsaw, who tried to block him, and then he kicked the ball hard and he chased it down the beach in a southerly direction.

'Andy!' shouted Jigsaw, 'ANDY! ANDEEEE!' he roared, making a megaphone with his hands. But Andy kept on running.

Slowly, the crowd dispersed.

Jigsaw, Judy, and the two girls, their hands shading their eyes against the sun, watched Andy grow smaller and smaller in the distance, until, swallowed by the heat haze, he disappeared.

Andy began to walk. The sun was high in the sky and it was very hot. Andy wondered just how far he could walk before it got dark. Maybe he would carry on walking. He wanted to walk. Tomorrow, he decided, he would hire a car and he would drive up in to the mountains and he would walk there. Jesus, but there was a whole wide world to walk in.

Sod Jigsaw, he said. And his sodding itinerary. Yeh, an comedy too. Sod everything.

Kicking the ball ahead of him Andy broke in to a run.

A woman was walking down the beach toward the ocean. Andy nutmegged her. He chipped the ball over a sunbather. He dribbled the ball around driftwood, between stones, clumps of seaweed, shells. . . . His spirits soared.

He provided himself with a running commentary:

'It's two-all in the dying moments of extra time in this the world cup final. But here come England. It's O'Shea, O'Shea breaking free with a run from deep in his own half. This is a powerful surging run by O'Shea. O'Shea shrugs off a challenge.' Andy swerved around a clump of seaweed. 'He vaults a second challenge.' He jumped over a piece of driftwood. 'It's just O'Shea and the goalie now.'

He looked up.

There was a distant view of mountains on the horizon.

'O'Shea shoots,' he said as he kicked the ball.

'It's there!' he shouted. 'It's a goal!'

'Before enlightenment I chopped wood and carried water. After enlightenment I chopped wood and carried water.'

Ancient Zen proverb.

James Truitt
An Economic Equilibrium: The Theory of Zero Economic Growth in the Modern World.

With an introduction by internationally renowned columnist, Bane Burke.

The purpose of materialism is the consumption of the produce of human labour. The purpose of human labour is the production of material for consumption. The need to consume creates the need to work. The purpose of the promise of wealth is to ensure the desire to work. The purpose of want is to ensure the need to work. The need and desire to work creates wealth. But not everyone can be wealthy. . . .

In this, one of the most remarkable attacks on Capitalism since the publication of Das Kapital, James Truitt, one time CEO of MidasCorp, offers an alternative view on what constitutes wealth and in the process he blows the consumerist fallacy right out of the water.

It is easy to see how this highly acclaimed work earned Truitt an Honorary doctorate from the LSE. On the hardback bestseller list for six months An Economic Equilibrium is the most explosive analysis of growth, capitalism and corporate greed to have been published for thirty years. Truitt chronicles the dawn of a new era and he breathes human sense back in to economics with this spirit of new optimism.

A prophetic book, An Economic Equilibrium warns of what lies ahead unless we act now - the *Economist*.

This book promises to do for economics what Stephen Hawking did for cosmology with a Brief History of Time - the *Sunday Times*.

Friend Ed
E. Larrikin

'They seek it here, they seek it there, they seek it almost everywhere. Is it in Aber? or is it in Mach? Ed's damned elusive haversack.'

A traveller returns home after many years abroad carrying a haversack full of the strangest souvenirs. He loses the pack and he and his friends embark on a journey of discovery.

'Every few decades a book is published that changes the lives of its readers forever. Friend Ed is such a book. With over 27 million copies sold worldwide, Friend Ed has already achieved the status of a modern classic'- *New York Review of Books*.

'This book has had a life-enhancing impact on millions of people' - *the Times*.

The Journeyman
E. Larrikin

A series of short stories on foreign places.

Clemence Tartt
The Outsiders

***The lost masterpiece of the tragic British poet,
now in its seventh reprint.***

Vee and his friends form an artist colony occupying a squat in London's Mayfair. They are going to change the world - by having nothing to do with it. They withdraw their labour and are determined to spend their days on the dole devoted to artistic fulfilment enlivened by the occasional wild party. But the authorities have other plans and the building becomes the battleground between two very different worlds.

A portrait of bitter conflict between the powerful and the powerless for control of their destiny, The Outsiders depicts the lives of ordinary people striving to preserve their humanity in the face of social and economic change.

'A society split apart is on collision course. Tartt not only takes us to the puppet show he also shows us the strings' - *New York Review of Books*.

Natasha Smith's
The Bigger Picture
An Exhibition

On loan from the Guggenheim Collection, an exhibition of the largest painting ever, now on show at the Tate Modern. Comparable to the Bayeaux Tapestry for narrative. More powerful than Picasso's Guernica. This incredible work has generated as many interpretations as it has panels. In the Bigger Picture all the great themes collide.

MAN AND BALL
tomorrow here, 1pm.

Graffiti seen scrawled (in chalk, in poor Spanish) on a wall in a town square in Peru.

Printed in Great Britain
by Amazon